He looked at her. He was overwhelmed by her untutored, uncompromising beauty that managed not only to transcend her ill-fitting pre-war clothes but actually to be enhanced by them . . . He wanted to tell her how utterly beautiful she was, exactly at that moment, that there was no need to do a thing to make herself smarter, or more pleasing, that he wanted to put his face against her untidy hair and breathe it in, and feel her skin with his mouth and her body with his hands. But he stayed silent, eaten up with jealousy of all the men who had seen her since he had last seen her, even those she drove in her ambulance, and those by the fire in this very room who had watched her come in. And he felt himself a cold, closed unlovable being next to her, the sort of creature she could never care for.

Also by Sarah Harrison

A FLOWER THAT'S FREE

SARAH HARRISON

Flowers of the Field

WARNER BOOKS

A *Warner* Book

First published in Great Britain by
Macdonald General Books in 1980
First Futura edition 1980
Reprinted 1981, 1982, 1983
Reprinted by Warner Books 1996
Reprinted 2000 (twice)

ISBN 0 7515 0639 7

Printed and bound in Great Britain by
Clays Ltd, St Ives plc

Warner Books
A Division of
Little, Brown and Company (UK)
Brettenham House
Lancaster Place
London WC2E 7EN

For Jeremy

CHAPTER ONE

'For she's a lady—yuss, and I'm a gentleman,
We're boaf looked up to, and deserves ter be;
For she's a lady—yuss, and I'm a toff—
Me and 'er—'er and me.'

Gus Elen—'Me and 'er'

'Great Heavens! She's astounding!'

Thus, in typical fashion, did Ralph Tennant welcome his second child into the world on 30 September 1892 on the first-floor landing at 20 Ranelagh Road, London SW.

The baby was indeed astounding, being nearly two feet long, weighing ten and a half pounds, and sporting a shock of precociously abundant black hair. Her eyes, which were wide open, were as bright and as steadfast as boot buttons; her long fingered hands waved and clutched like demented sea anemones and her mouth (also wide open) emitted a cry of deafening intensity: her small uvula was clearly to be observed, flickering redly in the black cavern of her throat.

Ralph took her from the nurse and held her up before him, his big hands clasped round her torso just below the armpits. The infant stopped crying. Her large head—whose crest of dark hair made it resemble a rather suffused turnip—sank into her shoulders, but even as it wobbled uncertainly there she returned her father's look with one of sturdy, sightless defiance and her legs pedalled the air energetically beneath the enveloping lacy shawl.

'A wonder,' declared Ralph, smiling seraphically at the nurse, 'a goddamned wonder, what do you say?'

'A beautiful baby girl, sir,' responded the nurse, properly.

'Are you beautiful?' enquired Ralph of his daughter, cradling her on his left arm and gazing down at her scarlet face. 'No, but you may be.' He pushed the baby's head gently to this side and that with his forefinger. There were still little scabs of dried blood and mucus in the convolutions of the ears, and the black hair was partly matted with the same debris of the battle of birth.

'May I look, Father?'

Five-year-old Aubrey Tennant was in his nightshirt, for it was nine o'clock at night. His feet were bare, and as he spoke he lifted one of them and rubbed it up and down the opposite calf, hoping by friction to get some warmth back into it, for he was cold. He had been listening and lurking at his bedroom door for the past two hours, filled with anxiety and foreboding. He could not in his wildest imaginings—and Aubrey's imaginings were never all that wild—picture the process by which a new brother or sister made its entrance into the world. But by the number of attendants and assistants it required, he deduced it must be dramatic.

All that time he had waited, listening, rigid with cold and tension, and then he had heard the squalling—first muffled, then piercing—as his mother's bedroom door had opened and the baby had been handed to his father.

Now he stood, shivering on the ill-lit landing, stoically prepared for whatever shock was about to come his way.

Both the nurse and his father turned to him, both smiled. Ralph Tennant held out his free arm.

'My dear old chap, of course you may. You've got a handsome new sister. Here she is.' Ralph hugged his son to him and bent slightly so that the boy could see the baby's face. Aubrey looked, and looked also at his father. He sighed. He saw at once how it was. He felt, and not for the first time in his young life, that he was old. Not just old by comparison with the baby, but older even than Ralph. It had always been Aubrey's impression that when the so-called qualities of youth were being handed out—gaiety, enthusiasm, insouciance and the like—his share had been given to his father. And now, gazing at the female infant who lay in Ralph's arms, he experienced a kind of weary, but not unexpected, disappointment. It was as he had feared. Another one of Them.

Ralph squeezed his shoulders affectionately. 'What do you think, old chap?'

'She's not very pretty.'

'Nonsense!' The nurse rolled her eyes and pursed her lips. 'She's a beautiful little girl.'

Ralph did not look at the nurse. Instead, he said to Aubrey, 'Quite right. She looks like a bit of scrunched-up red paper at the moment. That's the thing about babies. But she'll blossom, and spread, you'll see, and all those funny wrinkles will smooth out.'

8

'I see.'

'And now you ought to run along back to bed, it's cold and you should be asleep. You can see your sister again in the morning.'

'All right.' Aubrey turned and began to trail back along the passage. Then something occurred to him.

'Is mother all right?'

'Yes. Yes, your mother is quite all right, but very, very tired. I'm just about to go in and see her. Shall I give her your love?'

Aubrey nodded. He would like to have seen his mother himself, but the air was heavy with grown-up secrets. He sighed again, and went back to his room.

Ralph addressed his daughter once more: 'Let's go and see your mother, shall we?' He headed for the bedroom door, but the nurse, a large, strapping woman, barred his way discreetly but solidly.

'Mrs Tennant had a bad time, sir.

'I am aware of that. That is why I wish to see her now.

'I really think it would be better to leave her be for the moment, sir,' said the nurse.

'Madam,' said Ralph, his smile taking on a metallic brightness which, had the nurse been one of his regular employees, would have quelled her utterly, 'I intend to visit my wife.'

'She's very low, sir.' The nurse had no experience of Ralph to draw on, and spoke as she saw fit.

'I am sure she is. And as I believe the estate of matrimony to have something to do with having and holding in sickness and in health, I will now go to her side if I have to shift you bodily to do it.'

The nurse had never in her life before been spoken to in this manner by a gentleman of Mr Tennant's class and position and the shock of the moment caused her to drop both her jaw and her guard, so that Ralph was able to stalk past and into his wife's bedroom without further confrontation.

Venetia's immediate thought in the few seconds after her daughter had burst into the world was: 'I shall never have another.'

'I shall *never* have another.' she said, with such emphasis that the nurse, midwife and doctor were forced to transfer their attentions from the lower part of their patient's anatomy to the upper, which they had all forgotten about in the last few hours.

'You mustn't say that, my dear,' riposted Dr Egerton lamely, although in fact he had no desire to officiate at another lying-in such as this.

When Ralph had finally been ushered from the room at the last possible moment, and under strong protest, Venetia had closed her eyes and clenched her teeth and tried to keep the image of his face in her mind's eye. She remembered someone saying, nervously, 'The shoulders are stuck fast'—it was just about the time she thought her whole body was tearing apart—and even then it had struck her as ludicrous that these people should be commenting on something she could not even see, and yet that all this pain and strife amounted to no more than that. Shoulders stuck fast.

When, with a rush and a slide, the recalcitrant shoulders were at last freed, she made her announcement.

'I shall *never* have another,' she said, and did not listen to Dr Egerton's reply.

The atmosphere in the bedroom had subtly changed. The urgency and tension of a few moments ago had been replaced by a kind of relieved bustle and business. The sheet was whipped out from beneath her and replaced, the midwife vigorously pumped her stomach for the afterbirth, while the nurse and Dr Egerton studied and packaged the baby, whose yells of disapprobation now filled the room.

Venetia observed the tidying-up operation exhaustedly. It seemed to her that the lower part of the bed had become a kind of battlefield while the upper had remained unnaturally chaste and neat. The nurse plumped the pillows and tucked in the clean bedclothes with brisk, jerky movements. They're glad, thought Venetia. They're glad the whole messy business is over. And so am I. A momentous thought struck her.

'What is it? Tell me quick, what is it?'

The nurse came to the side of the bed. 'It's a lovely baby girl, madam.'

'A girl? It can't be!'

'A girl it is, my dear.' It was Bruce Egerton. 'And a fine big one.'

'How big?'

'Over ten pounds, I should say.'

'Oh heavens   ' Venetia rolled her head to one side. She

10

felt completely limp. Limp, and hot, and wet all over with the various effluences of birth.

'Do you want to hold the baby, madam?' The nurse held out the bundle in her arms invitingly.

'I couldn't . . . I haven't the strength. Just let me see, and go and show my husband.'

The nurse bent over and drew back the edge of the shawl where it shielded the infant's face. Two unblinking black eyes glared at Venetia accusingly, and a small red fist lay against the chin as though the baby pondered its fate. Venetia smiled weakly.

'Dorothea.'

'What a pretty name!' The nurse beamed round at the midwife and Dr Egerton. 'I'll go to father.'

A few minutes later Ralph Tennant marched in with his daughter in his arms. The nurse appeared red-faced and flustered in his wake, but Dr Egerton made a soothing gesture.

Ralph went straight to Venetia's side, sat on the edge of the bed and lifted her easily from the pillow with one arm so that she was cradled against his shoulder.

'I love you,' he said. 'And I love her. What can I say?'

'You've said it all. But oh, Ralph . . . never again . . . I feel so tired and sore. I thought I was going to die . . .' She began to cry weakly.

'Well you didn't die. And now you're going to have a rest and get better. Aubrey sent you his love.'

'Aubrey?' Venetia looked up abruptly. 'Poor darling, was he all right?'

'Was *he* all right? Of course he was all right! A little baffled, perhaps, but that's all. I sent him back to bed for now.'

Egerton stepped up to Ralph and touched him on the shoulder. 'Your wife must rest now, too.'

'I know, I know.' Ralph kissed his wife's head and lowered her gently back onto the pillow. He looked up at the doctor, his face bright with proprietary pride. 'How about my daughter, Bruce? Eh? She's astounding, isn't she?'

'She certainly is. A very large baby, and extraordinarily mature.'

'I should say so. Astounding.'

Venetia's last impression before she drifted into blissful

sleep was of her husband and the doctor bent over the baby, their faces full of wonder and admiration.

At that tender age Dorothea Tennant—or Thea, as they called her—had certainly been the object of wonder, and not only from her parents. Venetia Tennant was a beauty and everyone who knew her was curious to see whether her daughter would grow in the same mould. That Thea did grow was certain. She shot up like a weed from the moment she could walk (which she did at eleven months), and became a tall, strong, coltish girl. She had an air of plunging through life precipitously. But a beauty? The waiting world could not honestly say that she was. Nor, most assuredly, did she have her mother's renowned quality of repose. In fact the only characteristic she had inherited from her mother was her height. For the rest she was her father's child, dark-haired, olive-skinned and big-boned. Like him, she had the greatest difficulty in standing still at all and her customary gait was a kind of collected trot, an uneasy compromise between her own desire to charge and Venetia's admonitions about what was ladylike.

When, three years later (and in spite of Venetia's resolution), Thea's sister Dulcimer was born, the onlookers heaved a mental sigh of relief. This little girl was far more what they had hoped for—a peach-skinned, fair-haired, blue-eyed moppet who seemed from the very moment of her birth to have a knowledge of the legacy of beauty and grace that was hers.

Victorian society liked order, and when Venetia D'Acre, beautiful young daughter of a fine old Kent family, had married Ralph Tennant, industrialist, it had lifted its eyes to the heavens and despaired. Venetia, with her breeding and beauty, had long been one of the darlings of the *beau monde*. Her tantalizing air of withdrawn serenity had made her the *princesse lointaine* of most of the young men she encountered. Her remoteness stirred them into believing they loved her whether this were true or not, although to tease was the last thing Venetia intended, for she was shy: her aloofness was simply the distance she put between herself and the world.

When Ralph Tennant, ten years her senior and the owner of a huge South London light engineering factory, had met her at a charity ball, Venetia stood no chance. He pushed aside the barrier, made short work of the distance, and strode into the citadel like the general of an invading army. Within weeks he was calling her 'old thing' and had taken her and her sister to see his factory. He was huge, handsome in a dark and ruffianly fashion, and possessed of a rapacious energy. Any feeble, tactfully raised objections to his union with Venetia he summarily brushed aside. He won her heart by strength of personality and her hand by speed. He persuaded Lord and Lady D'Acre that they had already agreed to the marriage when in fact they were barely accustomed to his presence. Had he made more attempt to conform to the expectations of others they might have worried more about his social standing. As it was they were too thunderstruck by his forthright behaviour to spare a thought for the industrial stains on his pedigree.

In a few short months Venetia D'Acre had become plain Mrs Tennant and the couple had set up house at 20 Ranelagh Road. Ralph was a rich man, and Venetia made the house elegant and comfortable. Though many may have thought the match less than ideal, Ralph made no secret of his opinion.

'I adore her. She has breeding and taste. I have money and brains. How can we fail?' he would ask rhetorically, causing ripples of well-bred shock to eddy in all directions.

As for Venetia herself, she thrived. She grew lovelier by the day; she was tranquil and imperturbable. It mattered not to her that Ralph disrupted her dinner parties, blundered into her At Homes, refused to attend country house parties— much less to shoot, a barbaric pastime—and refused, almost on principle, to agree with a living soul. Venetia rose above it all, and retained her popularity until eventually Ralph was accepted, or at least tolerated, for her sake.

But all the same, friends were pleased to note that the Tennants' third child was the image of her mother and obviously destined for great things. Dulcie, as she was known, was a prettily precocious little thing, and Nanny Dorcas was frequently called upon to present her to visiting friends at teatime. Thea did not take this hard. She was perfectly secure in her parents' love for her, and their love for each other. She was grateful to her mother for recognizing that she would far rather dig for fossils in the back garden with Aubrey than eat small polite cakes on the drawing-room sofa.

At this time, Thea was blissfully unaware that her family was at all different from anyone else's, or that there was anything unusual about her own attitudes, fostered as they were by her father. She admired and took for granted his ferocious intelligence and curiosity. She liked to be told that she resembled him, and never for a moment realized that many of the people who commented on the resemblance thought Ralph a dangerous lunatic and Venetia a little touched for marrying him.

It was only when Thea began to attend the Strathallen School for Girls in Quex Gardens, when she was eight, that the first dawnings of doubt began to appear over her hitherto untroubled horizon. To begin with, she enjoyed school, and lessons, and it was patently obvious that in this she was in a minority of one. She was at an age when the dearest wish of most little girls is to be indistinguishable from their peers. So she dutifully made paper caterpillars numbered with the days of term, and Judas-like dismembered them, a piece each afternoon, as the days went by, hoping not to be found out in her perverted pleasures.

But while she may have succeeded in concealing her thirst for knowledge, she could not alter her nature. And when asked to write an essay entitled 'A Thing of Beauty' she characteristically got the context right, but laid herself open to mockery by sub-heading it 'Joyce Cummings: A Joy For Ever'. Joyce Cummings was head girl of the Strathallen School at the time, a tall, stately young lady who in Thea's fertile imagination had taken root as a kind of hybrid of Ophelia, Isolde and the Snow Queen. The fact that Miss Cummings was also prissy, self-satisfied and narrow-minded had quite escaped her admirer, who saw in her only the ideal of female loveliness to which Thea (she reflected gloomily) could never aspire.

The essay caused a stir. For the first time Thea's guard had slipped, wholly and disastrously. Not that she was by any means the only young lady to have a crush on Joyce Cummings. But she was certainly the first to stand up and be counted in so overt a manner. And the other girls in her class, little traitors every one, whispered and sniggered and congratulated themselves on their hypocrisy.

The headmistress, Miss Violet Strathallen (younger sister to the founder), summoned Thea to her study.

'Sit down, Dorothea,' she said, indicating the spikeylegged, ramrod-backed chair reserved for offenders and petitioners.

Thea did so, tucking her long legs, ankles crossed, beneath the seat. Because there always seemed to be too much of her, and she was anxious to tidy herself away, she pulled her pinafore well over her knees, so that it formed a kind of chute from chin to knee, down which she now stared, resignedly, at her tightly clasped hands.

'I have here your essay entitled "A Thing of Beauty",' observed Miss Strathallen unnecessarily. 'And I should like to have a word with you about it. It seems to me, Dorothea, that you have made an error of taste.'

'Yes, madam.' It was customary at the Strathallen to call the teachers madam.

'As usual, you have written vividly, although your hand-writing lets you down, and I can find no fault with your description of the subject.' There was a pregnant pause during which Miss Strathallen turned the offending pages to the light and perused them in a distinctly theatrical manner. It occurred to Thea that the headmistress was actually enjoying the interview. Miss Strathallen had a large, pale, slightly downy face, like a piece of flannel, and she habitually wore grey—a grey skirt, and a grey blouse with masses of pintucks that travelled down over her formidable bosom in serried ranks, like railway lines. Her hands were also large and pale, like fish, and with a piscean clamminess as well. Thea hated to see them holding the pages of her essay; it was like being kissed by someone who revolted you.

'As I say,' went on Miss Strathallen, 'I feel that your mistake has been in the choice of subject matter. Surely it would have been better to choose something—a little less close to home?'

'I just thought—'

'No, no, let me finish.' Miss Strathallen waved an imperious hand. 'Did you not consider the embarrassment you might cause our head girl? Poor Joyce.'

'But, madam, it was a compliment surely—'

'A compliment? A compliment, to be held up as an object of vulgar scrutiny?'

'I didn't want her to be scrutinized, madam.' A slight emphasis on the first word caused Miss Strathallen to look up sharply.

'I should not like,' she said, in an impressive contralto, 'to

15

have recourse to your parents about this, Dorothea. The incident itself does not merit it, but if you take a defiant attitude . . .' She shook her head forbiddingly. 'Let us leave it there. Write another essay if you please.'

'With the same title, madam?'

'Certainly, we must try to put right what has gone wrong. Choose for your subject this time something less personal—a scene, or building perhaps, or a work of art. I should like to see your faculty for critical appreciation displayed this time, instead of your emotions.' Miss Strathallen was not to know that in Thea the two were inextricably joined. The audience was at an end.

Thea managed to divert the taunts of her classmates with the aid of her bosom friend Andrea Sutton who chose, cleverly, to interpret the essay as a blow for freedom and women's rights. This last claim was potent but baffling, as the only member of the opposite sex to set foot inside the Strathallen was Mr Pardoe, the classics master, and he was so demonstrably downtrodden that he could present no possible threat to anyone. However, by these means Andrea translated Thea's darkest hour, if not into a moment of glory, at least into some kind of presentable regrouping of forces.

'You made it sound quite grand,' said Thea gratefully, as the two girls got dressed to go home at the end of the afternoon. They were invariably last to go down to the hall because they talked and talked, and because Thea almost always lost something or broke the lace on her outdoor shoes.

'What you did *was* grand,' replied Andrea. 'It was a splendid and noble thing. You wrote what was in your heart.'

The difference between the two girls was one which often gave Thea herself pause for thought. She admired Andrea, but was a little wary of her. Andrea was a political creature, even at ten, able to use non-conformity for her own ends. She would take an inbred attitude of Thea's and transform it into an objectively held opinion, or winkle out some hitherto barely noticed feeling and declare it a stance. Sometimes Thea felt herself trapped by her friend's cleverness.

In appearance the two girls were so totally unalike that Ralph Tennant was wont to burst out laughing whenever he saw them together, and advise them to go on the Halls where they would assuredly make their fortunes. Andrea was a small, thin, sandy-haired child with freckles and pale eyelashes and a high, domed forehead. She would have been painfully plain had she not made up in confidence and intelligence what she lacked in looks. She bewitched people with her precocious flow of words, her quickness and her adaptability. She was the only one of Thea's school friends who could easily hold her own at 20 Ranelagh Road. Dulcie, however, could not tolerate Andrea.

'She's boring,' was her most common criticism of Thea's friend, and easily the most unfounded.

'Of course she's not boring, anyone can see that's not true.'

'She bores me.'

'That's different.'

'She's ugly and she talks too much.' Dulcie was quite prepared to resort to outright calumny to relieve her jealousy. To her, Andrea Sutton represented the explosion of the myth that beauty and taste were all that was required of womanhood. Andrea had no looks and little breeding and yet she was popular. She had that special ability to make others feel that if they were not with her they were in some way excluded from a magic circle, where the intellectual elite forever basked in exalted light.

Towards the end of 1902 old Lady D'Acre died, and the Tennants moved to Kent to take up residence at Chilverton House. Thea became a boarder at the Strathallen and as such first tasted the dubious delights of visiting, and began to see why Andrea Sutton was as she was. Up till now Thea's sorties into the homes of friends had been confined to chaste teatime sessions divided dully into 'play', 'food' and 'conversation', only the second of which actually bore any resemblance, and that a faint one, to what she was used to at home. Now she received invitations to spend whole weeks in the homes of other girls.

The strain of those days away was unbearable. There was the jangle of alien conversation, the shock of strange food and habits, the tooth-grinding tension of finding the right moment to tip and thank the servants, and worst of all the growing conviction that her own family were different—that what she saw in other homes was the rule, and hers the exception.

Andrea Sutton's father was a bank manager and the Suttons lived in genteel middle-class comfort in Fulham. Mr Sutton was genial in a forced, artificial way; he patted Thea a lot and bent down to speak to her all the time as if she were deaf, or dumb, or both. Mrs Sutton was pale and sensible and relentlessly proper. Andrea had an older, married sister, Dorelia, whom Thea never met but whom she felt she knew because of Mrs Sutton's constant praising and magnifying of her name. The servants of the Sutton household, though far fewer than in the Tennants', had a washed-out, dreary servility that Thea found oppressive, and when she smiled at the parlourmaid on her first morning the poor girl looked so nonplussed and wretched she wished she hadn't done so.

The atmosphere at meals was such as Thea had never experienced in her life before. There was silence. Wholesome if dull fare was placed upon the table and Mr Sutton served it up. Then there was grace, a different one for each day of the week. From that moment on Thea could never look upon shepherd's pie without blessing it to her use and herself to God's service, nor contemplate boiled mutton without asking the Lord to make her truly grateful for what she was about to receive. During the meal it was customary for Mr Sutton to make remarks and pronouncements, but nothing was expected of the rest of the company but that they receive these like the tablets on Sinai, and be thankful.

'I see South American tin is up,' he would declare inscrutably at breakfast and Mrs Sutton, neat and supportive behind the teapot, would nod and smile thinly and look at the girls to check that this pearl had not been cast before swine. Thea was a sociable child, she would have been more than happy to discuss South American tin with Mr Sutton had she had the least idea what it was, but it was perfectly clear that no response was required. In the Sutton household Arthur Sutton presided like a hearty, thick-skinned, heavy-handed god. The Hippo Deity, Thea dubbed him. She had seen a hippo at Regent's Park Zoo and had been quite struck with the resemblance.

During the day not much attention was paid to the girls, but play in the garden was strictly monitored because of 'mud etcetera' (Mrs Sutton's own phrase). Thea noticed that in her home context Andrea's composure, usually unshakeable, deserted her completely. She whined and complained and caused her mother to hold Thea up as a model of propriety on more than one occasion. Only when they were well away from parental supervision did Andrea become recognizably herself again, and at one moment in particular. This was when Mr Sutton discarded the newspaper and Andrea would choose her moment to purloin it and scamper up the stairs to the safety of her bedroom. Then both girls would spread it on the rug, kneel on the floor and pore over it, their faces suffused and their hair trailing across the page. Thea saw all too clearly now why her friend needed the solace of the printed word and the distraction of current events.

But inevitably the move to the country isolated Thea from her friends. In spite of the visiting she now lived, when at home, in an even more different and separate world. Her first sight of Chilverton House, near Ewhurst, when visiting her grandparents as a little girl, had inspired in her a tumultuous mixture of responses which was never to change. She loved it on sight, but knew instinctively that its powerful magnetic pull would affect her whole life.

It was not a grand country house by the standards of the day. It had but eight bedrooms and presided over a mere seven acres, much of which was thickly wooded. There had been house parties there, of course, and Venetia would tell her daughters about them, but they had been gentle, easy-going affairs, and not the kind where several thousand game birds met a sticky end in the course of a single afternoon. Thea's first glimpse of it, as the carriage trundled precipitously down the steep hill off the Weald, was of its tall red brick chimneys, smoking cosily. Then its roof became more clearly distinguishable, a slate roof patched with moss and lichen. After that the carriage would disappear between tall hedges, and the house remain out of sight until one turned into the circular drive and bowled up to the front door.

Chilverton House was imposing, but never awesome. Despite its size it had been built on an essentially human and domestic scale. Two gables rose at either end, symmetrical and pleasing, like gently-raised eyebrows. The windows, of which there were many, were long and lead-paned, and the front door was approached by two shallow, rounded steps, and overhung by a grey stone porch fancifully etched with pineapples and other exotic fruit. In the summer the whole front of the house rippled and shimmered beneath a cloak of crimson creeper.

At the back of the house nectarines and pears had been trained against the south-facing wall, and their height all but masked the long narrow window which marked the half-landing of the staircase. At one end the kitchen yard was enclosed by a mossy brick wall with an archway througl which might be glimpsed the black iron pump and washing hung out to dry.

Below the staircase window and slightly to the right, a double glass door led from the dining-room out onto the terrace. Like the rest of the house this terrace was pleasant, pretty, but not smart. Moss and various other unassuming country growths sprouted between the paving stones, and along the length of the low stone balustrade that bordered it several of the columns were missing, like a cheerful, gap-toothed grin. One of them had been set up as a bird-table, another as a sundial.

From the centre of the terrace the house's most imposing feature, the Elm Walk, stretched for a quarter of a mile to the gate that marked the Ewhurst boundary of the estate. Magnificent elm trees, like an arboreal guard of honour, flanked the path the whole length of its journey as they had done for several hundred years, since the time when a Tudor manor house had stood on the same site.

The Elm Walk divided the lawn nearest the house into two distinct areas. That to the right, opposite the dining-room entrance, was a place of tranquillity and repose, shaded by lilac and laburnum, fragrant with roses, banked by rhododendrons, the grass as smooth as a carpet. That on the left was recognized as the children's province, a place for games and climbing. Swings, hoops, stumps and nets had wreaked havoc with the turf and the trees were dotted with paraphernalia—ropes, pulleys and platforms—like some eccentric gamekeeper's larder. Further down the walk the grass was allowed to grow and the garden became a rustling wilderness in summer, a mysterious wasteland in winter, occasionally cropped by horses out to grass, otherwise allowed to go its own way.

The whole place was, in short, a children's paradise: not too carefully tended but wayward, warm and welcoming —the very essence, thought Thea, of what a home should be.

It was typical of her father to move out of town just when the whole of the nation, it seemed, was moving into it, but Ralph Tennant was unperturbed. He had become wholly bewitched by motor cars, possessed two fine examples, and declared, in direct contradiction to the generally held view, that the motor car would restore the balance of society and open up the countryside again. It became a common occurrence in the small town of Bromley to see the Tennants chugging and bouncing along the street at fifteen miles per hour, Venetia with her hat tied on by a gauze veil and Ralph resplendent in Prince of Wales checks and deerstalker. When, as was not uncommon, fruit was thrown and cries of 'Stink bomb!' and 'Clear off!' were heard, Ralph would stop the car, clamber down and take issue with the objector, bringing the full force of his personality and undoubted technical knowledge to bear on the subject until his opponent conceded victory out of sheer sheepishness and ignorance.

But on Christmas Eve 1913, when Thea went into the village of Ewhurst to post a letter, she did so on her bicycle. It was a Beeston Humber, a good model- Ralph would never have tolerated anything less than sound in the mechanical line—but even so it was the most uncomfortable form of transport she could have chosen. The track—it would have been hypocrisy to dignify it with the term road, or even lane--leading from the side gate of Chilverton House to the Ewhurst road, was deeply pitted, and to keep any kind of steady course at all one had to stick to a narrow ridge, a sort of hog's back of tussocky grass, down the centre. Thea put up her hand to give her hat a warning pat—the joggling of the cycle was in danger of dislodging hat, hair and all at any moment.

'Afternoon, Miss Thea!'

'Who--oh, good afternoon, William!' Thea's voice, shaken by the progress of the bicycle, came out in a kind of sheeplike vibrato. Laughing at herself, she slowed down and hopped on one foot to stop. William Rowles, the head gardener from Chilverton House, stood in the gloom of a fir spinney, beyond a five-barred gate. With him was his seventeen-year-old son, George. Thea peered over the gate and saw that they had with them her old childhood pony, Joe.

'Hallo Joe!' She held out her hand and George led the pony over to her. He was harnessed between a couple of rough shafts from which thick ropes trailed back into the wood. Thea fondled the pony's whiskery mouth and kissed the white blaze on his forehead. 'What are they doing to you, Joe?'

'Christmas tree, miss,' said George cryptically. It was a special pleasure for him to give this information to Miss Thea, even if it did represent a mere fraction of what he would have said. For George Rowles, pink-faced, tow-haired and six feet tall, was more than a little in love with her. Now the joy of seeing her face brighten was inexpressible, even had he had any hope of expressing it.

'The Christmas tree—of course! Can I come over and see you do it?'

'We'll be a while, miss, we barely started when you come by.'

'Never mind. I'll come and see which one it is, anyway.' Thea propped her bicycle against the bank and climbed over the gate. It was exactly the kind of honest, unladylike action which caused the fires of passion to leap up in George's breast, and he reddened as Thea's long leg described a swishing arc over the top bar of the gate. His father, recognizing with some irritation the symptoms of rigor setting in, grabbed the pony's bridle from him and led the way into the edge of the wood.

'Get the spade,' he ordered curtly over his shoulder. George mouthed something and obeyed.

'This one?' Thea was asking, when he returned. 'It's taller than last year's. It's going to look magnificent.' She grasped the trunk in her gloved hands and peered up between the fragrant dark plumes. Her hat, pulled by the weight of her already loosened hair, slid down her back.

'Oh, wretched thing.' She disentangled the hat, dropped it to the ground, and coiled her hair up again, stabbing it with the pin as though despatching something unpleasant. George watched admiringly. He thought Miss Thea had beautiful hair.

'Don't stand there, you gormless thing,' ordered William. 'Get digging.'

Poor George, fiery with humiliation, began to dig, and so missed the sympathetic smile which Thea gave him. Instead, Thea caught William's eye and reorganized the smile into an expression of dignified interest. William Rowles was a small, determined man with a small, determined outlook on life. For him, the future was entirely contained in the next job that had to be done. He had become more entrenched in this view since old Lord and Lady D'Acre had passed over and he had come into the service of Mr and Mrs Tennant. There had been a time when William had understood the Chain of Being, at least as it affected him. He had known who was above him, and who below, and what the proper order of

22

things was. Now these comforting certainties were a thing of the past. His present employer was quite likely to enquire, abruptly, what he thought of the government, or the new King, or old age pensions, as if it mattered, and drove about the place in that noisome invention of the devil, the horseless carriage. It wasn't that Mr Tennant wasn't a generous employer, but that he didn't seem to know how a country gentleman should behave. And his daughters were no better. This one always looked untidy, and spoke to him as if he were an equal, and the younger one was smart enough and hoity-toity enough for two, but would smile at anything in trousers. Only young Mr Tennant, Mr Aubrey, comported himself correctly, in William's view. He had a bit of sense and dignity. People said he was a dry stick, but then William himself was a dry stick and we like others to resemble ourselves.

To relieve the irritation he felt when confronted with any of the Tennant family, William snapped at his son: 'Don't dab at them roots, hack 'em!'

Thea realized that the venom in William's tone was directed obliquely at her, for interfering, rather than at George for poor digging. 'I must go. I can see it's going to take a long time and I'm no help standing about in your way.'

'Not at all, miss.' William glared at her.

'I'll look forward to seeing the tree when it arrives.'

'That's the way, miss.'

Thea returned to her bicycle and pedalled off in the direction of the village, clutching her hat in one hand, its brim crushed round the handlebars.

The lane began to widen and presently joined the wider road that led down into Ewhurst. The wheels of the bicycle hummed along famously on the tarred surface, and she freewheeled ecstatically down the hill, her green serge skirt flapping like a sail. Sitting ramrod-straight, neck stretched, the wind in her hair, Thea had a wonderful view over the hedges. She was lord of all she surveyed.

The main street of Ewhurst had been metalled and tarred quite recently to make it more suitable for motor traffic, but in fact the expected flood of automobiles had not as yet materialized. Still, the main street was a thoroughfare, and Thea judiciously squeezed the brakes and pedalled more decorously as far as Girdler's Provisions, where a group of capped and booted little boys forgot their game of marbles and watched with interest as she dismounted and propped the bicycle against the wall.

Girdler's Provisions provided almost everything. It was grocer, doctor, post office, newsagent and purveyor of advice to the people of Ewhurst. The proprietors, Gertie and Sam Girdler, took great pride in the variety of commodities and services they offered, and with justification. The shelves were stacked with every conceivable tin, bottle and box that the household could require, some of them a little dusty, since the Girdlers' passion for stock was not always matched by demand.

The wooden counter ran round two sides of the shop and was itself covered in goods, with pills, powders and potions occupying the plum position next to the till. From the roof were suspended pots, pans, sieves, onions, hams, coils of rope, pairs of boots—like a motley gathering of weird bats roosting in the lofty gloom. Across the centre of the room, forming a 'T' with the main counter, was a trestle table, also groaning with goods. On top of the table were papers and periodicals, boxes of apples and dried fruits, jars of jam and honey; beneath it, huge gold-lettered tins of biscuits and crackers, neatly stacked; in front of it, on the floor, sacks of currants, flour and potatoes, along with whatever articles Sam Girdler currently wished to unload from his stock-room—in this case, some kettles and a large tray of toffee apples and sugar mice.

'Ah, good afternoon Miss Tennant.' Sam Girdler rose from the stool behind the counter where he had been reading the paper, and stood with his hands on the edge of the counter, head tilted invitingly to one side. 'And what can I do for you this festive season?'

Sam Girdler must have been sixty, but contrived to look a spry forty by hiding his baldness beneath a cap at all times, and by staining and waxing his neat moustache so that it was so glossy and black it appeared to be painted on his upper lip. He wore a striped shirt, crisply clean but collarless, beneath a black jacket and grey waistcoat. He prided himself on his turn-out.

'I want to post this letter, please,' said Thea, producing her application for a place at Mrs Hoskins's Business and Secretarial College. 'It's urgent.'

'Urgent it may be, Miss Tennant,' said Sam with a sad smile, 'but it's hardly likely to be answered before Christmas now, is it?' He was as usual secretly piqued at being asked for something it was not within his power to provide. 'I'm afraid,' he added.

'Still, it's a very important letter—important to me—and I shouldn't enjoy Christmas unless it was safely in the letter box, do you know the feeling?'

Sam Girdler could not honestly say that he did know the feeling, but he took the letter and produced his stamp ledger from beneath the counter. Miss Tennant put her money on the counter and while he stamped the letter she roamed about the shop, picking things up, and smelling things, and touching things. She was a great one for that, Miss Tennant, and she usually ended up buying nothing.

The letter dealt with, Sam enquired obsequiously: 'Anything else I can oblige you with, miss?'

'I don't know . . .' Thea went to the shelf where the jars of sweets stood in enticing ranks. 'I'd like to buy some sweets, but I've no one to buy them for.' She ran her finger along the sides of the jars: humbugs, toffees, winegums, liquorice whirls, the precious stones of childhood. Sam Girdler gave a little cough and she turned back to him, recalled to the adult world.

'When will the post be collected next?' she asked.

'This evening I should say, miss.'

'Good. I do so want to get things organized.'

'As do we all, miss, as do we all.' Sam Girdler liked to identify with his patrons, no matter how incomprehensible their ways.

'Happy Christmas to you, then, and to Mrs Girdler.'

'Thank you, miss, and the compliments of the season to you as well.'

The bell tinkled, the door closed. The red-nosed marble players looked up at her. As she collected her bicycle, snow began to fall.

Venetia Tennant had summoned Cook with some trepidation, soon after luncheon. She had done so not because she had any worries about the following day's catering, but because it was necessary to show that one gave the matter its proper consideration. Mrs Duckham—'Old Duckie', Ralph called her behind her back—was as temperamental and highly-strung as a racehorse, and required careful handling.

Venetia waited for her in the library, the most-used room

25

at Chilverton House. In the D'Acres' day it had been truly a library, a place of largely unread books and sepulchral hush, heavily curtained; the two drawing-rooms had been inhabited far more. But the Tennants had naturally congregated in the library; Venetia had changed the curtains and furnishings to a warm pink and gold chintz, had seen to it that the fire was lit daily and had contrived to make more shelf space for the family's own books. On a table in the corner were several heaps of periodicals and newspapers: Ralph's passion for cars was matched only by his passion for print.

Venetia glanced into the long mirror that hung over the mantelpiece, and touched her hair. She wanted to get the interview over before Ralph and Aubrey returned from the works. Her husband's witticisms had an unfortunate effect on Mrs Duckham: she was a capable, energetic woman, but humourless and old-fashioned too, and any attempt at levity, especially from her employer, confused her so much that she would go into a kind of speechless, rigid panic until the danger was past.

A knock on the door. 'Come in, Mrs Duckham.' The door slid open just enough for Mrs Duckham, a skeletally thin woman, to slip through. She closed it carefully behind her. The long white apron that usually helped to lend some substance to her whisker-thin figure had been removed in honour of this upstairs audience, and she appeared almost severely narrow and gaunt in her plain blue dress, her hair caught back in a wispy bun on her neck. She carried a large, dog-eared notebook. Venetia dreaded the notebook. Its appearance denoted that some kind of domestic litigation was about to be undertaken.

To lighten the atmosphere a little, Venetia remarked: 'I only want to check the arrangements for tomorrow, Mrs Duckham. I'm sorry to take you away from your kitchen when you must be dreadfully busy.'

'Don't speak of it, ma'am.'

'Tell me, is everything under control? I'm sure it is.'

'As much as it ever will be, ma'am.'

'Dear me, that sounds rather worrying,' said Venetia obligingly, although she recognized this as the opening gambit in a game of words which Mrs Duckham was fond of playing. The game was designed to remind her mistress that she was lucky to have her, Ada Duckham, as cook in this god-forsaken country place. Both parties deliberately overlooked the fact that Ada Duckham had had nowhere else to go when the Tennants moved house, and that her whole life and security rested with them.

'Is there anything in particular?' asked Venetia.

'The geese.'

'Are they not all right?'

'Not big enough. And they looks downright scraggy old birds to me. If you ask me, ma'am—' here she lowered her voice darkly—'I don't think it's the ones I ordered.'

'I shouldn't worry at all about it,' said Venetia. 'I'm sure there will be enough. And we shall all need to make room for your famous plum pudding.' Mrs Duckham sighed heavily; she would not show it, but she was most susceptible to flattery. Venetia knew from experience that she was well on the way to soothing Cook's ruffled feathers. Graciously, she moved on to phase two. 'And what about the Christmas cake? You know Mr Tennant does so enjoy your cake. Is it ready?'

'It is, ma'am. Bar the icing, which I shall see to presently.'

'Wonderful.' It was a fact that as Ralph Tennant got older he enjoyed his tea more and more, and cake in particular. By his decree, the family's main meals were austere by the standard of the day, but when it came to teatime austerity was cast to the winds. He therefore liked to have his first slice of Mrs Duckham's excellent Christmas cake on Christmas Eve. Venetia rationed him strictly on Christmas Day, as the family ate their Christmas dinner in the evening and she could not bear to see him ruin his appetite with the best part of a pound of fruit cake at five o'clock.

'Can you tell me definitely whether the Vicar will be dining tomorrow, ma'am?' enquired Mrs Duckham.

'Yes, Mr Aitcheson will be dining in the evening. Would you like to look over the seating plan while you're here?' Venetia went to her desk and picked up a sheet of paper.

On the seating plan Venetia had placed her shy nephew, Maurice, next to an old family friend, Daphne Kingsley; and Maurice's prickly mother, Sophie, next to the Reverend Aitcheson, on the assumption that he would make the best of a bad job, if not on social then at least on Christian grounds. Aubrey she had placed between Daphne and Dulcie, and Thea beside young Jack Kingsley, for Venetia lived in hope. Jack's father, Robert, was between Dulcie and herself; he always responded well to Dulcie's pretty charm.

Venetia hoped very much that Thea and Jack would get to like each other. Indeed her whole life since her marriage to Ralph had been a triumph of hope over experience, for while she continually expected her family might fall into some socially normal and acceptable pattern, they persistently failed to do so.

Mrs. Duckham cast her eye over the plan and grunted. 'Very well, ma'am. I just hope that you will bear in mind what I said about the goose. If it's not enough, I can't be blamed.'

'No one would dream of blaming you, Mrs Duckham, please don't upset yourself. I have every confidence in you, and in the goose.' Venetia smiled charmingly and turned away to indicate that the interview was at an end. She heard the door close, and went to the window to draw the curtains. The countryside outside was closing in, shutting itself against the snow, which was now falling quite heavily from a slaty sky. It was only half-past three but already the afternoon was bruised and darkened; there was no colour. As she watched, hypnotized by the drifting, spiralling flakes, the cart bearing the Christmas tree turned in at the drive, with William Rowles at the pony's head, and young George walking behind to steady the trunk. Beside the cart, pedalling her bicycle, one hand holding the branches of the tree, the other clutching her hat on the handlebars, was her daughter Thea, the snowflakes resting lightly on her tousled black hair.

Thea saw her mother standing in the library window, and waved. Venetia lifted a hand in reply. Even separated by the window, and the snow, and the gathering dusk, Thea admired her mother's stillness and grace; she stood there like an icon, framed in the long window. For as long as she could remember, Thea had thought of her mother as silver. Her beauty had the pale sheen of silver, her hair was a delicate ash-blonde, her skin luminously white—even her voice, never raised, had a silvery resonance.

Thea admired her mother above all other women. She saw in her the qualities of acceptance, selflessness and stoicism that she herself could never possess. There was about Venetia a grace of spirit as well as of bearing. She was peace. She was order. She was gentleness and strength. As a child Thea had thought that some of the grand ladies who came to the house were like ships—so imposing, cruising about with their towering hats and prow-like figures. Among them, her mother was a graceful galleon, all slender masts and fluttering sails, gliding over a sunlit sea.

As Thea watched, her mother stepped back from the window, raised her arms and lifted her head a little to draw the curtains. For a moment she was like a butterfly, almost transparent, pinned with spread wings against the firelight behind her. Then the curtains closed and Thea realized that it was growing dark, and getting cold. She went in.

Dulcie Tennant had been to see 'Hallo Rag-Time'. Since then she had also been to see 'Hallo Tango' and several of the other fashionable shows, but it was the first that had made the greatest impression. Her only regret was that this cultural treat had not come her way earlier. The show had opened at the London Hippodrome on 13 December last year and had run for several months before Venetia had decided on a few days in London and had booked seats as a treat. Even now, the memory of that magical evening made her heart beat faster. The show had represented all that Dulcie desired out of life: all the fun, the glamour, and—-she smiled to herself —the razzmatazz.

Dulcie stared at herself in the mirror. She spent a lot of her time in rapt inspection of her own face, as though trying to read her fate there. Unlike Thea, she was enamoured of her own appearance. Her only worry concerning it was that she might not be able—or have the chance—to capitalize on its obvious assets. She was bored, terribly bored. It was vital to Dulcie to be more glamorous, smarter and more up-to-date than anybody else—but what competition was there here, buried in rural Kent? Dulcie's need to glitter was frustrated at every turn.

She was tiny and petite. She had not been altogether happy with this state of affairs until now, for she saw all around her the evidence that women should be stately, full-busted and grand. But 'Hallo Rag-Time' had given her fresh hope. Here was a new type of woman—daring, leggy, almost boyish, with extravagant movements and lustrous, come-hither eyes. Dulcie could still recall with heart-stopping clarity the moment when Shirley Kellogg had led the chorus-line along the joy-plank down the centre of the auditorium, banging a drum—every one of the girls dashingly attired as hussars, with trim, tight boots, little flared skirts, and bare knees! Pair upon pair of twinkling legs, high-stepping in time to those rapturous syncopated rhythms. How the gentlemen had roared and clapped and cheered, and the ladies blushed and envied. Dulcie had not blushed, of course. But she had envied.

Suddenly her reverie was interrupted by a pounding of footsteps in the corridor outside. The door opened with a rush and Thea burst in. Dulcie did not turn, but gazed past her own reflection in the mirror. She gave Thea a look she had been perfecting for some time—a little cat-like widening of the eyes and pursing of the lips. She considered the Look pretty, provocative and disdainful. It was, as she had feared, lost on her older sister.

'Dulcie! They've brought the tree—they're just setting it up in the hall now, do come and look!'

Dulcie turned slowly, swivelling on her stool and crossing her legs in front of her. 'I suppose it will be pretty much the same as all the other years.'

'No, it's bigger. It must be twelve feet high. We must all decorate it together after tea, like we always do, we must.'

'I don't see that there's any "must" about it,' said Dulcie. She found her sister's violent enthusiasms trying. She herself was rushing toward womanhood at top speed, but Thea clung to family tradition in a way that she found frankly embarrassing.

Thea saw the tightening of the lips that was the prelude to a display of pigheadedness from her sister. She sat down on the edge of the bed, temporarily deflated by Dulcie's lack of gusto. The decorating of the tree was a family custom which Thea cherished. It enabled her to warm her heart by the love for her family. It also confirmed in her the dark suspicion that she might never find a person or persons to take their place. She spread her large, well-formed hands on her skirt, which was damp with melted snow, and gazed down at them. Dulcie glanced at the small patch of moisture spreading on the carpet round her sister's shoes, and turned back to the mirror.

'Where've you been?' she asked. 'Out in the blizzard?'

'I've been out, yes. It's hardly a blizzard, it's beautiful soft snow, and it wasn't falling when I left.'

'Where did you go?'

'I went to post a letter at Girdler's.'

'Thea! Whatever do you want to post a letter for on Christmas Eve?'

'That's what Mr Girdler said.'

'Good for him.'

'But it was my application for the business college—you know they sent me the form a week ago?' Thea became animated again. 'Well, I simply couldn't bear to have completed the form and have it lying around here. I wanted to get rid of it, to feel I'd done something *positive.* I think I'll go mad if I don't start working soon. I love it here but I do so want to be busy and useful.'

'I know you do, darling, and I do wish you all the best with it. If it's any comfort to you, you're a lot busier than I am—at least you help at the school and write your articles and everything—my ambitions are far harder to achieve.'

'Nonsense!' Thea at once warmed to her sister again, and reached out to pat her shoulder. 'You know very well that you will be a bewitching society beauty, just like Mother.'

'Just like Mother was until she married Father,' added Dulcie. She was old-fashioned insofar as she sided with Victorian society in her view of her parents' marriage. She loved her father— he *was* her father, after all—but secretly resented the fact that her mother, with all her natural advantages, had not made a more conventional choice and married a man in the mainstream of society, who would have launched her, his daughter, with a splash. Having had both his daughters presented at court, Ralph considered his social duty in that direction done. He was a man who genuinely could not see either the pleasure or the advantage in balls, parties, dinners and the like. In this, without realizing it at all, he was actually cruel to his younger daughter. She felt herself held back by his eccentricities. But being held back simply hardened her resolve. She *would* stun society. She would command attention. She would be somebody.

Thea gave the shoulder—noticeably cold—a sisterly little push. 'You're determined to be gloomy. Anyway,' she rose, 'come and see the tree and stop moping up here. It'll do you good.'

'I am not moping.'

'Day-dreaming, then.'

'For goodness sake, Thea, stop being so bossy!' Dulcie's flash of temper quite pleased Thea; it seemed more natural than her assumed veneer of sophistication. She grinned at

Dulcie's cross face in the mirror and went out into the corridor. As she did so, her cousin Maurice Maxwell emerged from his room at the far end.

'Maurice!' Thea was delighted. 'You're back!' She ran to him, hugging him round the neck and planting a hearty kiss on both his cheeks. Maurice smiled shyly, and patted her back. 'As you see.'

Maurice had mixed feelings about being home. It was because of this that he had stayed up at Cambridge for as long as he could.

Mainly, he dreaded seeing his mother. She had been having her usual rest in her room when he arrived, and he was glad that his reunion with her would be swamped by the family en masse at tea. She was, and always had been, the incarnation of the self-fulfilling prophecy whereby if your natural posture is suffering, plenty of reasons will come your way, and Maurice had had to learn to bear this burden of gloom at an age when most small boys are secure in the knowledge that their parents can cope. The premature death of Sophie's impecunious husband, and the consequent removal of herself and Maurice to her brother Ralph's household in Kent, had simply confirmed Sophie in her bitter sense of grievance.

Cambridge had provided Maurice's first real taste of belonging, of contentment. There he was among people who shared his interests and attitudes, who did not expect him to be other than he was—some of them even admired him. Some of his most blissful moments had been with fellow students in his rooms at Clare, with evening gathering and hardening outside the window, the smell of tea and toast, and the exaltation of good conversation.

But then, at the end of the session, there was the return to Chilverton House. He never made that journey from Bromley station without a feeling of sick anxiety in the pit of his stomach, just like the first time. Maurice had been twelve and then, as now, had been a small, pale, thin boy with a shock of unmanageable, straight, brown hair and nervous short-sighted eyes behind round spectacles. He had always been acutely aware of his physical shortcomings. In fact his chief worry on approaching Chilverton House for the first time had been the knowledge that the Tennants were noted for their handsome appearance.

His first view of the house had done nothing to allay his fears. It was not especially large or grand, but it was imposing. It had an air of prosperous confidence, and the pale spring sunshine glinting on its many long windows seemed to give it an inner life of its own. It nestled at the foot of a wooded hill, the grounds spread regally about it, the tall chimneys pointing sternly to the sky.

'Look at me, young Maurice,' it seemed to say, 'and be prepared to subject yourself to my domination.'

And dominated Maurice most certainly had been, though with the greatest kindness. His Aunt Venetia had turned out to be one of the loveliest women he had ever seen, and reduced him to a flushed and stammering jelly whenever she spoke to him. His Uncle Ralph, in spite of his reputation for frankness, seemed sympathetic; Maurice found that he could cope with his brisk interrogations and piercing, perceptive stare once he had grown used to them.

Then there were his two female cousins. Dulcie, then a little minx of six whom he ashamedly feared, was the real terror. She was the sort of child who instinctively recognized a victim, which Maurice indeed felt himself to be. His status as a dependant had nothing to do with this, and he knew it. He was a victim because he was plain and awkward and bookish and because he so obviously cared what people thought. So Dulcie stole his trousers, and drew on his Eton collar, and replaced his knives with spoons at the luncheon table with impunity. But Thea always rescued him.

Sometimes Maurice thought that he would never stop feeling grateful to Thea, not if they both lived to be a hundred. She had, from the very moment of his arrival, been his friend, his champion, his hold on sanity and dignity when all else failed. Even then, though two years younger, she had been as tall as he, with a mane of curly black hair tumbling down her back. Like her father she had a square, downright face with well-shaped black brows, a straight patrician nose and a determined chin. She had looked altogether too tall and too handsome for her calf-length dress and pinny and navy hooped stockings. Dulcie had looked delicious in hers.

But worst of all, then as now, had been Cousin Aubrey. Aubrey was two years older than Maurice and had been away at Marlborough College when he first arrived (whither Maurice was due to join him the next term). Maurice remembered their first meeting with a shudder. He had been watching from an upstairs window as the car chugged up the drive and stopped in front of the door. The chauffeur had opened the door for Aubrey and then hoisted the school trunk out of the back. Maurice, staring fearfully, had seen a big, solid boy step down and embrace his mother rather stiffly. Then they had walked, arm in arm, into the house and Maurice had known he must go down and present himself.

'Hallo Maurice.' Venetia had taken both boys affectionately by the shoulders and stood them face to face. 'Aubrey, dear, this is your cousin Maurice, who's living with us now. I hope you're going to get on famously.'

'How do you do.'

'How do you do.'

The two boys had shaken hands. Maurice had felt his own hand held, but with no pressure and consequently no warmth. He had looked into a face completely devoid of expression—round, stolid, regular, a conformist's face, with rather deep-set grey eyes and brown hair brushed neatly and severely close to the head.

'Do you mind if I go up to my room now?' Aubrey had asked his mother, as though seeking release from some painful but necessary duty.

'Of course, darling, you must be tired, but I do hope you two boys will get together and be friends this holiday. It would be so nice for Maurice to feel he had a friend at college next term.'

But Maurice had never felt he had a friend at Marlborough. During the holidays Aubrey had only that commerce with him that was consistent with politeness and no more, and Maurice, anxious not to appear over-demanding, had spent long hours in his room reading. At school, the two were in the same house but in different forms, and contact was kept to a strict minimum by Aubrey. It would not be true to say that Maurice was unhappy at public school. To be unhappy one must have some experience of happiness, and Maurice had never been truly happy in the whole of his young life. He had simply concentrated on getting by and avoiding drawing attention to his weaknesses. His shield and breastplate at school had been his academic ability, and as long as he was genial, and played up a certain mild battiness, he was not bothered by the other boys. He was labelled a swot, but left alone.

To be fair, Aubrey was no more in the mainstream of college life than his cousin. He was a plodder—dutiful, conscientious, a pillar of the establishment. He did not shine in the classroom or on the playing field, but he exuded a kind of ponderous natural authority which made him an excellent prefect and a force to be reckoned with. He may have been dull, but he was never a figure of fun.

And Maurice had known all through those long, difficult adolescent years that he and Aubrey could never be friends. Despite their differences they shared one characteristic—they found it hard to talk to their fellows. So they went their separate ways, walking as it were along opposite sides of a narrow river, occasionally staring at each other across it, but never making a bridge.

Now, home again for Christmas, Maurice was more glad than he could say to feel Thea's arm tucked tightly through his as they went downstairs. He had a sense, as always, of the Tennant family gathering forces. He frankly dreaded the obligatory togetherness of the festive season. All Maurice wanted of life was to be allowed to go his own way and be no trouble to anyone.

As he and the girls descended the stairs, he heard the roar and crunch of his uncle's car on the gravel drive, and knew that Christmas had begun.

'Mrs Tennant wants tea served in the library,' called Primmy, the Tennants' parlourmaid, as she ran down the back stairs to the kitchen. Because it was almost Christmas, and the master was home, and the tree was up in the hall, she jumped the last three steps and nearly collided with Joan, the hard-pressed kitchen maid who was heading for the larder with a batch of mince pies.

'Mind out! What d'you think you're doing? Nearly dropped the lot!'

'Sorry. I'm sure. But you didn't drop them, did you, so that's all right.'

Sucking her teeth, Joan disappeared into the larder. Primmy skipped through into the kitchen. An ambrosian smell of baking pastry and succulent fruit assailed her nostrils. Mrs Duckham stood at the huge scrubbed wooden table, putting finishing touches to the icing on the Christmas cake with a palette knife. Her skill was astonishing. The knife seemed to have a life of its own as it twirled and jiggled and swooped. The cake was nothing short of a triumph.

'That looks really lovely, Mrs Duckham,' said Primmy, leaning her elbows on the table and her chin on her cupped hands. 'Give us a lick.'

'Get out of it, girl, what are you thinking of?' Mrs Duckham's tone was sharp, but she liked Primmy, a bright, competent girl, and held out the end of the knife. Primmy smacked her lips.

'A real rip-snorter, Mrs Duckham, if you'll allow me to say so!' she barked, in a wicked impersonation of her employer. This time however she did not wait to see the cook's reaction, which she knew would be one of heartfelt disapproval. Instead, she peeped into the servants' hall. Collingwood, the butler, and Edgar, Mr Tennant's chauffeur, were standing by the fire. The latter had spread his hands to the blaze, and his shoulders were dark with melting snow. The Lanchester had a hood, but Mr Tennant would never break a journey to put it up. Primmy found this quirk most amusing but then she, unlike Edgar, did not have to drive to and from Bromley station in all weathers.

Collingwood turned and saw Primmy. He was a stout, balding man whose whole form seemed to have the bland, symmetrical smoothness of an egg, and his voice matched his form perfectly.

'Have you no work to do, Primrose?'

'Not really, Mr Collingwood.'

'Mrs Duckham!' Collingwood strode past Primmy and addressed the cook. 'Surely you can find employment for idle hands?'

'Certainly I can. Come on, girl, and help Joan lay the tea tray.'

Primmy caught Edgar's eye. He pulled his mouth down and bobbed his head in a sympathizing gesture. Primmy began to lay the tray at whirlwind speed. She felt elated.

'They'll be decorating the tree when they've had tea,' she said. 'Can we help?'

'Gracious no, girl,' said Mrs Duckham. 'They've always done it themselves, and that's that.' It was a mystery to Mrs Duckham why her employers liked to wobble on ladders and get scratched and shout their heads off just for the sake of that pagan plant in the front hall, but like it they did and hers not to wonder why.

'I'm going to watch,' announced Primmy.

'You can't!' gasped Joan, deeply conservative.

'Who says?'

'You're not invited.'

'They won't mind.'

'You won't go anywhere while there's work to be done,' cut in Mr Collingwood.

'Is that tray ready?'

'Yes, Mr Collingwood.' Primmy's words were respectful but her manner was bold. 'This one's got the tea things and this one's got the food—which one shall I bring?'

'Can you manage the tea things? It's not so heavy, but you'll have to be careful.'

Primmy cast him a disparaging glance. She prided herself on her ability to do her job well, in all its departments. Her levity was usually just a symptom of boredom with the available tasks. She champed at the bit. Now she picked up the huge tray with ease and watched as Collingwood put on his black jacket and settled it fussily on his shoulders. Then he lifted the second tray—complete with muffins, eccles cakes, chocolate yule log and Christmas cake—and proceeded grandly up the stairs, followed by Primmy.

Primmy had only just entered the Tennant household, at the age of fourteen, when they moved out of London. She was an exceptionally bright and able girl (as her mother had repeatedly said when they had been interviewed by Mrs Tennant), and the eldest of five, so she knew about responsibility. But more even than these excellent qualities, she possessed a calculating nature and burning ambition. She had not wanted to go into service but her mother, a hard-pressed washerwoman, had needed her out of the house and money coming in; and at the time service was the most secure and immediate form of employment for a girl of Primmy's age and qualifications. But Primmy was astute enough to know that, her mother having won the opening skirmish, it was up to her to get what she could out of the experience, and she soon recognized that if she were to be anyone's kitchen maid she had best be the Tennants'. She saw around her, at 20 Ranelagh Road, all the evidence of education, liberal thought and non-conformity which her adventurous nature craved.

Primmy had set out from the first to gain preferment. She had been dutiful, efficient, enterprising. When she had chafed against getting up at half-past five, or cleaning six grates before eight, or mixing silver-cleaning solution until her eyes smarted and her fingers were rough as sandpaper, she had looked inward at her little store of ambition and warmed herself by it.

She was a loner. She discouraged followers and minded her own business. As a child she had been a born leader, always first down the street with 'knock down ginger' and arch-exponent of a wicked game involving the insertion of lighted candles under the rears of patrons of the outside privy. But even though a tomboy she had been sure to get done first whatever was asked of her. Her whole life had been dedicated to the principle of getting on.

Ralph Tennant had been her knight in shining armour. He was the only person whom she unreservedly admired. She relished his eccentricities and was dazzled by his appearance. What was more, he allowed Primmy to borrow books, actually asked her opinion on all sorts of matters, and enquired what she went to see at the Music Hall and bioscope on her days off. In other words he encouraged a freedom of thought in his parlourmaid that would have made other employers blench.

Without doubt, Primmy had hitched her wagon to a star. But now, at twenty-five, she knew the time was fast approaching when she must cast off into the firmament. The winds of change were whispering about the land and Primmy had felt their seductive breath on her cheek as she ran up and down stairs, and opened doors, and observed her betters at work and at play, and this delightful sensation of adventure was partly to blame for her bubbling excitement this Christmas Eve. Next year, thought Primrose Dilkes, will be my year.

The Tennants assembled in the hall to decorate the tree. The fire had been lit in honour of the ritual. All were agreed that the tree was a magnificent specimen, its delicate dark green spire almost brushing the banister of the half-landing, its branches sweeping outwards in a feathery pagoda. Thea had been to the loft and fetched down the boxes of decorations, and the Rowleses had brought in a couple of step-ladders. Thea liked to begin at the top. She started rummaging in one of the boxes for the star of Bethlehem. Dulcie, studiedly unenthusiastic but beginning to warm to the occasion, opened one of the other boxes. Maurice and Aubrey stood awkwardly to one side. Maurice would have preferred to help Thea but felt he should bear Aubrey company out of politeness, having not seen him for two or three months. Aubrey puffed on his pipe.

Venetia and Sophie had drawn up chairs by the fire, Sophie with some needlework in her lap, and Ralph Tennant stood with his back to the blaze, legs apart, eyes bright, bouncing slightly on his toes. He was a man congenitally unable to relax, and the sight of his family gathered together always produced in him a gush of adrenalin, a thrill which he recognized as the atavistic pride of the patriarch. A damn good-looking bunch they were, he reflected, and where they lacked looks (he glanced at Maurice) they made up for it with brains.

'Go on miss!' he suddenly barked at Thea. 'Get up the ladder and put that star on top, we know you're bursting to.'

'All bursting to see me fall off!' laughed Thea. 'But we have to start somewhere, don't we! Aubrey—be a love and hold onto the bottom of this thing, would you?'

'Very well.' Aubrey walked over and grasped the legs of the ladder, his pipe still jutting from between his lips.

'Don't tell me you're nervous,' called Ralph. 'You used to scuttle up and down that thing like a monkey when you were a child.'

'That's just it, I'm not a child now, and please don't put me off!' Thea's face appeared round the side of the ladder, laughing but anxious. 'In those days I didn't wear a long skirt and awkward shoes.'

'Thea, my love . . .' Venetia put in a token admonition, more out of habit than the expectation of gaining any result. She glanced across at Sophie and made a little face, regretful but affectionate. Sophie shook her head.

'They're enjoying themselves,' said Venetia. 'Especially Thea. She loves Christmas.'

'I know,' said Sophie. 'I know you all do.' It was a fact that she did not. 'Do you know,' she added, 'I saw some of those suffragette creatures in Bromley last week when I was buying this embroidery pattern. I meant to tell you at the time.'

Ralph looked down at his sister, struck by the unusual vitality in her tone. 'Good Lord. Did you join them?'

'Ralph.' Venetia frowned at him. 'What were they doing?'

'They were outside Sugden's. They had placards—sandwich boards to be exact—and they were distributing leaflets. One of them was banging a drum, and another was haranguing the passers-by. It was the most fearful din; we could hardly hear ourselves think.'

'Who's we?' enquired Ralph.

'The general public, of course.'

Ralph threw his head back and emitted his huge braying laugh. 'And who, dear sister, is the general public—if not you, me, the suffragettes and the proprietor of Sugden's? You mustn't be so quick to categorize your fellow men.'

'I shall categorize whom I please, Ralph.' Two dangerous little spots of colour appeared on Sophie's cheekbones. 'Some of these women were no more than slips of girls who shouldn't have been parading the streets but at home with their parents, and some of them were elderly ladies who should have known better.'

Ralph leaned down, hands on knees, and peered into his sister's face. 'That's probably what they thought about you. They probably thought "Ah, there's an elderly lady who should know better. Let's bang our drum and discomfort her and then slip her a pamphlet about votes for women, it'll make her day".'

'Don't be facetious. You know that some of the methods these women resort to are nothing short of lunacy, criminal lunacy. You know it as well as I do.'

'I think that shying bricks through Asquith's window and committing suicide on racecourses will not serve their purpose—certainly. That doesn't make the purpose itself invalid.'

The two glared at each other intransigently.

Venetia intervened. 'Thea's very interested, you know. She's been hearing from Andrea Sutton about her group in Fulham. I think it's only being down here in the country that prevents her getting involved. When she goes to this business college of hers, it's only a matter of time.'

'Heaven help His Majesty's Government when she goes,' observed Ralph gleefully. 'I've always maintained that when Thea finally channels all that raw enthusiasm of hers into something worthwhile she'll be unstoppable.'

'She may fall in love,' said Venetia softly, her eyes on the group by the tree, 'and then she won't care whether she has a vote or not.'

'Fiddlesticks to love!' snapped Ralph, whose whole life had been a testament to the power of that emotion. 'Thea has it in her to be one of the Great Women.'

'Great Women,' said Sophie crisply, 'are those who carry out the duties God designed them for, gracefully and without complaint, and who, where possible, lend their strength to great men.'

This was too much for Ralph. He closed his eyes for a moment in an expression of prayer—for patience and tolerance, always unanswered—and then strode over to the tree.

'Dulcie, my dear, you could be more generous with that tinsel.'

'But the tree doesn't want to look vulgar.'

'Who is to say how the tree wants to look? Let it glitter and dazzle like the *outré* ladies in those shows you like so much.' She smiled in spite of herself. 'You're a pretty little thing, aren't you?' he boomed rhetorically. 'Shall we put Dulcie on top of the tree?'

He went round to the ladder. Maurice was now assisting Aubrey to hold it firm, as Thea had come down a few steps and was leaning perilously out to one side to affix an icicle-shaped object to the end of a branch. Both young men looked up at her, Aubrey with brotherly tolerance, Maurice with open admiration and concern. He himself had no head for heights and even looking at Thea up the ladder made him dizzy. Aubrey glanced at his father.

'What possessed Rowles to bring such a huge tree? It takes up the entire hall.'

'Very fine tree.'

'I think it's too big. It's as well Thea doesn't mind risking her neck.'

'Just as well.'

Thea called down: 'Could you pay attention for a moment and pass me some more things while I'm here?'

'I will.' Maurice went to the box. 'Here you are.'

'Thanks. I shall need swivelling round in a minute, I've just about finished this side.'

'You can come down and we'll move the ladder,' said Aubrey. 'It's simply not safe to pull it round a corner while you're on it.'

'Oh very well. All right, all right.'

Ralph grinned, both at his son's fussiness and his daughter's impatience. He glanced at Maurice. 'Good term?' he asked.

'Yes, thank you, Uncle. Most absorbing.'

'Good. I won't ask if you had fun as well, because you and

41

I don't mean the same thing by it. So long as you're happy in your work.'

'I am, thank you.' Maurice thought, and not for the first time, that underneath the prickles his uncle was an astute and sensitive man.

Now Ralph noticed a slight figure in the doorway leading to the back stairs. 'Ah. Primmy. Come to see the tree?'

'It's beautiful, sir.'

'Think it's too big?'

'No sir—very festive.'

'Very festive, hear that? Quite right, my girl, it's damned festive. Want to come and help?'

'Yes, please sir.'

'Come on then, get to it.' Ralph returned to his place in front of the fire.

Primmy caught Venetia's eye. 'Madam?'

'That's all right, Primmy, we'd like your help.'

'Thank you, Madam.'

Primmy knew, as everyone else in the household knew, both above and below stairs, that it was Mr Tennant who made the noise and Mrs Tennant who gave the nod. Primmy adored her master but she respected her mistress for all her gentleness and her soft voice.

Thea called, 'I'm coming down now. Anyone else want a go at the top?'

'I find it quite a resistible offer, thank you,' said Aubrey. 'Dulcie?'

'I wouldn't if you paid me.'

'Sorry, no head for heights,' said Maurice, taking Thea's arm as she came down the last few rungs. 'How about Primmy?'

'Primmy! What a good idea. I'm sure you don't mind ladders.'

'No, miss. But are you sure no one else wants to——?' Primmy herself was perfectly sure, but these motions had to be gone through.

Thea hooted. 'You heard them. Cowards to a man!'

'Very well, miss. I'll have a go.'

The sight of Primmy's back view scaling the ladder, one hand clutching the side, the other holding a handful of her black serge skirt, had a most disturbing effect on Maurice. He had noted it before when watching her back as she went about her business. She had what he supposed was called a

42

trim figure: very spare and almost soldierly. The stark lines of her uniform etched in this trimness. The crisp apron, always impeccably white, was ferociously starched so that it resembled a kind of armour at the front. But at the back, there was something touching about the wide straps crossing her narrow shoulder blades, and the great bow like a snowy butterfly perched on her bobbing seat. Maurice found that Primmy's presence not infrequently brought a lump to his throat and a warmth to his face that he found nothing short of embarrassing. The fact that Primmy was a perceptive girl added another dimension to his unease. What if she knew the effect she had on him? Her pale little cat's face was always impassive when she looked at him, the eyes steady and cool, the lips primly set together, the very model of propriety. But, in her, could not that itself be interpreted as provocation . . . ? He removed his spectacles and began to polish them vigorously.

'Mr Maurice—?' From the tone of her voice Maurice knew it was not the first time Primmy had called him. He looked up, starting violently, but noticing with relief that the other three were at the far side of the tree.

'Sorry, Primmy. What—?'

'Could you pass me some things, please?'

'Oh yes, of course.'

Thea was teasing Aubrey. 'How was your dinner at the works? Did you pull a cracker with the dreadful Mr Burgess?' Ralph Tennant threw a Christmas dinner in the factory canteen on Christmas Eve and Mr Burgess was the foreman, whom Aubrey, unlike his father, gravely mistrusted.

'I did not. I'm happy to say I sat nowhere near him.'

'Did everyone enjoy themselves?'

'I think so—I wouldn't know. It's simply a formality, a gesture, it has to be gone through with. Increasingly so, these days. We have to keep the men sweet.'

'Oh, Aubrey,' Dulcie giggled and widened her china-blue eyes mockingly, 'did *you* keep the men sweet?'

'I do my best. And I don't see what's so damned funny about it.'

'Don't be pompous, we're not laughing at you,' Thea lied cheerfully. 'It's just the thought of Mr Burgess in a paper hat . . . !' She and Dulcie began to giggle and Aubrey smiled, caught Maurice's eye and looked away quickly.

Venetia, watching, thought her family made a pretty picture. On an impulse she put up her hand and felt Ralph's waiting there to enclose it warmly. 'We'll have a lovely Christmas,' she said quietly, as though promising herself, because for some reason that she could not fathom she felt a little sad.

Outside, George Rowles, having bedded down the pony and completed one or two other small jobs delegated by his father, looked in through the hall window at the Tennants and their tree. Miss Thea was like a young tree herself, tall in her green skirt. His heart swelled. He was proud to have made her happy with that tree—the biggest they'd ever had in the hall at Chilverton House. The biggest and the best.

Suddenly, Mrs Tennant rose and walked towards the window to draw the curtains, and George backed off hurriedly. The curtains swished shut. It was dark, but the snow, now drifting and banking against the walls of the house, gave off its queer reflected light. And the air was full of it, twisting and spinning down from God knows where, secret and silent, deadening sound.

George turned up his collar and headed for home.

CHAPTER TWO

'All in a day my 'eart grew sad,
Misfortune came my way,
I 'ad to learn the whole bitter truth
All in a single day!'
                    Vesta Victoria—'All in a Day'

Christmas Day dawned fine and mild, rinsed with watery tentative sunshine, like the first smile after tears. The snow which had seemed so ominous had been routed in the small hours of the morning, and what was left lay patchily in sheltered places, the broken remains of a once-proud army.

Thea looked out of her window with a feeling of disappointment. The thaw had dissipated the delicious excited anticipation of the night before. As she looked, a great dollop of snow slid from the eaves above her window and flopped to the ground, as if to underline the change that had taken place.

But still, it took a lot entirely to dampen Thea's high spirits on Christmas Day. By the time she had dressed, and had a longer-than-usual battle with her hair in honour of the occasion, she had rekindled a sensation of pleasurable expectancy. There were, after all, many things to look forward to.

The family were all present at the breakfast table, except Dulcie. Ralph, always a little crusty without his morning paper, observed Thea's glance at the empty seat.

'Your sister declines breakfast this morning,' he said. 'Happy Christmas!'

'Happy Christmas!' Thea kissed Venetia, helped herself to kidneys and bacon from the sideboard, and went to her place. Sophie was beside her. She wore her grey, reserved for religious feasts of the highest order. Thea thought, not for the first time, what a handsome woman her aunt was, and how well the grey became her.

But the wearing of the grey did not automatically infuse Sophie's bosom with the festive spirit.

'Dulcie should eat a proper breakfast. Especially as we shall be attending matins and luncheon will be late,' she told them.

'She often goes without . . .' Thea smiled placatingly. 'It doesn't seem to bother her. She has a tiny appetite.'

'We don't eat purely to gratify our appetites, Thea. We eat to sustain ourselves. It would be more responsible if Dulcie were to have some breakfast.'

Ralph made an unnecessarily loud clatter with his cup and saucer. 'You seem to be implying that Dulcie will get the vapours in church and embarrass us all,' he said, not looking at his sister, but fixing the dregs of his tea with a basilisk stare. 'If so, let me reassure you. I do not breed the kind of woman who swoons. My daughters are tough. They are known for it. Be comforted.'

Venetia tried to catch her husband's eye, but failed, since he was now biting into his toast with vampire-like ferocity. Instead, with the smooth and graceful change of gear that typified her, she remarked, 'We mustn't be too long, if we're to give the servants their presents in good time before the others arrive. Sophie, the handkerchiefs are exquisite. You're so clever in that way.'

'Thank you. I hope they will be acceptable.'

'I know they will be. Such beautiful work.'

Thea watched for a moment as her mother kindly and expertly soothed Sophie. Poor Maurice; as usual, it was he who suffered in these confrontations. Now he sat rigidly upright, but with downcast eyes, his hands clasping the edge of the table as though it were all that mattered in the world. She put her foot out and gave his shin a little nudge. When he glanced up, she smiled.

'Happy Christmas,' she said.

Later in the morning, Primmy opened her parcel. It contained an embroidered lace handkerchief, worked by Sophie, and a length of cream Honiton lace from the mistress, worked with bees and dog-roses and intricate trellises of bramble. It was beautiful. They had all removed their aprons to go upstairs and she laid the lace round the shoulders of her black dress. It was a lady's present. The lace was the best, the most beautiful, that money could buy. Not much of it, but the very highest quality. She held one of the ends against her cheek and closed her eyes. The lace was like a gift from another world.

After the present-giving the family dispersed once more. Thea went into the library and sat down at Ralph's desk. She took some papers out of the top right-hand drawer and began to read. She had enjoyed some small success with her articles for the *Country Companion*, and this one was within an ace of completion. She felt a little guilty about working on Christmas morning, but there was an hour to kill, and she felt unaccountably edgy.

She glanced at the clock on the mantelpiece. The Kingsleys were to arrive at ten-thirty, in time to walk to church in Ewhurst. She looked back at the article, read a few lines, then discovered she had not read them at all. Instead, she realized with a shock, she was thinking about Jack Kingsley.

If, in Thea's imagination, her mother was silver, then Jack Kingsley was red—red for danger. Reynard the fox. She assumed that the disquieting effect he had on her was because she disliked him, and this assumption caused her further distress, as Thea was not in the habit of disliking people without good reason. So her unease was compounded by guilt.

They had first met when she was fourteen, and he eighteen, on the far side of a hedge where she had parted company with her mare. She had been well to the back of the field, the rest of the hunt had poured over the hedge with apparent ease, and with the pride of extreme youth she had chosen to ignore the little voice inside her which remarked that the obstacle was too high, the drop on the other side too steep, and both horse and rider too inexperienced to cope.

She had set the mare—an altogether more mettlesome mount than Joe—at the hedge too fast, had found herself hopelessly wrong-footed, but committed by speed to a wild leap. The horse had pecked and stumbled on landing, recovering gallantly but not soon enough to prevent Thea sliding down its left shoulder and hitting the ground, leading with her chin. It being January, the ground was icy cold and hard as iron. Thea had momentarily blacked out.

When her eyes opened, the first thing she saw was the face of a horse peering into hers, the long, prehensile lips reaching out, the eyes showing crescents of white at the corners. It was not her mare, whom she could see cropping grass placidly a few feet to the right. This horse was an equine hobgoblin with a hogged mane and a roman-nosed head like a sledge-hammer.

Terrified, she sat up, pushing herself backwards as she did so. At once she felt the blood drain from her face and her stomach churned violently.

'Are you going to be sick?' a voice enquired pleasantly, and another face appeared, above and to one side of the ugly horse.

She shook her head, but kept her lips tightly pressed together for fear of proving denial an empty one. The young man gave the horse's neck a firm push so that it backed off, snapping its head up and down irritably. He crouched down beside her, removing his string riding gloves, and tilted her face back a little.

'Hold on a jiffy,' he said rhetorically, feeling in his breast pocket with his free hand. He brought out a large, clean handkerchief, spat on it and began to dab at a place on the point of her jaw. She winced.

'Hold on. Only a graze.' His face, only a few inches from hers, was intent, concentrating on the task in hand. The feel of the clean hankie, that faint smell of saliva, reminded her of falls as a child, of Nanny Dorcas. She felt too dreadful to object.

He sat back on his heels. 'No further damage. You'll have a terrific lump there tomorrow though.' He tucked the hankie away and squatted there, his forearms resting on his knees, hands dangling, watching her. His face was narrow and clean-shaven, with a long, straight, rather ascetic mouth. His skin was sallow, his hair and eyes a reddish brown. He was not handsome by the standards of the day, but there was a contained, animal elegance about him that one sees in the portraits of Elizabethan favourites. His composure was absolute, Thea's non-existent. Under his calm, steady scrutiny she felt obliged to say something.

'Is Amira all right?' She nodded towards her mare.

'Right as rain. As you see.'

'Did you catch her?'

'I didn't have to. She stopped dead once you decided to get off, a very polite animal. You were lucky to be so far back in the field, though. I nearly came down on top of you myself.'

'I'm sorry . . .' Thea, badly shaken, felt suddenly tearful. 'I should never have jumped that hedge. I feel such a fool.'

'Don't. We all lose our presence of mind from time to time.'

'I suppose so . . .' She glanced at him, trying to deduce from his expression whether he was mocking or sympathizing. But his slightly hooded eyes told her nothing.

Thea braced herself on one arm. 'I must get up.'

'Here.' He held her free arm at the wrist and at the elbow, and supported her as she rose unsteadily. He was half a head taller than she, so she was not obliged to meet his eyes again. Instead she concentrated on his stock-pin—a representation in silver of a grinning fox's mask.

'Do you want to ride?' he asked.

'Yes, I think so. Anyway, I must . . .' She felt the dreaded tears bubbling up once more. 'I can't possibly walk all the way home.'

'To where?'

'Chilverton House.'

'You're one of the Misses Tennant?'

'I'm Thea—' some half-remembered admonition of her mother's nudged her—'Dorothea. How do you do.'

'Jack Kingsley.' He shook her limp hand, which Thea thought oddly formal under the circumstances. 'This is Kingsley land you're making holes in.'

'Oh. I'm sorry.'

For the first time he smiled, apologizing for his little joke, for having taken her in. He led her, still holding her elbow, over to Amira. 'You were fortunate not to catch your foot in the stirrup,' he said, 'or you'd have a broken leg to go with your lumpy jaw.'

'I'm suitably grateful.' She smiled too, feeling a little less awkward. He gave her a leg up, and she settled in the saddle and took up the reins. Her head ached a little, but her stomach had subsided.

'How are you?' He stood at the mare's head, looking up at her.

'Much better, thank you.'

'No need for that. I'll ride back with you.'

'Oh, but really it's not necessary, I shall be perfectly all right. You'll miss all the rest of the hunt if you do that.'

He shrugged. 'I'm coming back with you.'

Thea was not in the least sure that she wanted Jack Kingsley's company the whole way home, but he was obviously not to be deflected. He rescued her hat from beneath the hedge, brushed it off with his sleeve and gave it to her. Then he replaced his own and remounted the ugly horse which at once sidestepped and laid its ears back mulishly.

'Will you lead the way?' he asked.

They had ridden back in silence along the lanes. Their only company had been, briefly, that of the fox, who appeared suddenly from the left-hand hedgerow, looked at them for a moment with ferocious fear, panting, then trotted across the lane and through the hedge at the far side. This private view of the creature that only minutes before they had been pursuing so murderously shocked Thea.

'Poor thing,' she said, vowing never to hunt again.

'He's clever. Look how far he's backtracked already. They probably won't catch him.'

'I hope not.'

'There are too many of them, you know. They have to be culled.'

Thea felt reproved. They rode the rest of the way in silence.

As Thea sat in the library, engrossed in her uneasy memories, the object of her anxiety set out from the Kingsley home in his new Vauxhall. Jack never drove a car but that his spirits soared and his heart lifted. The experience gave him the kind of exalted thrill that he hoped to gain one day from some less material source. So far, his life had signally failed to come up with such a source.

He had been through the public school and university mill, had travelled, and done all the appropriate, upper-class things that had been expected of him. He had been through the London season, Cowes, Henley, shooting in Scotland and gambling in Biarritz. But the mill had spat him out still more dispirited and dull than before. He had joined the army, *faute de mieux*. He believed in his own as yet untested ability to make a good officer. Sometimes he felt so restless, so full of unused energy, that it was almost a physical pain.

He smiled wryly to think that a few years back he had been the catch of the season, the chosen prey of every debutante's mother, the sacrificial lamb at many a ball and house party. But now those same predatory parents would hardly spare him a glance. He had had his hour, and chosen to ignore his opportunity. Now, for all society cared, he could fend for himself.

The Vauxhall reached the steep upward slope of the Weald. The sound of its powerful engine roaring into a higher register was music to Jack's ears. He looked forward to showing the car to Ralph Tennant, to demonstrating its

50

finer points, its niceties of design and engineering. His own father was simply not interested in cars. Jack could also picture, with the utmost clarity, himself taking Thea for a drive. He could see in his mind's eye the way in which her black hair would escape from beneath her hat, how her eyes would shine with the thrill of it, and her cheeks be whipped pink by the wind . . . But he also knew that the picture would probably remain locked in his imagination. For Thea, who loved all the world, whose friendship was so freely given, even to the most undeserving—Thea could not like him.

He used the word 'could' to himself, for he had always had the impression that she tried, that she did her best, but repeatedly failed; and this was even harder to bear. He was aware that he must seem stiff and reserved—he could not help that—but it seemed that even his attempts to flatter and please her advanced his cause not at all. There was something in him, something he could not help, some inherent flaw of mind or character, that prevented Thea from warming to him.

The road emerged from the wooded crest of the Weald and began to wind down into the Ewhurst valley. The chimneys of Chilverton House became visible, rising above their cloak of elms, smoking comfortably. The car gathered speed down the hill and Jack savoured the feel of the cool, clean air rushing past him, like water, and the hedgerows flashing by.

Round a left-hand bend . . . and now he could see the whole house, standing solidly behind its apron of gravel and lawn. Since he had first accompanied Thea back to Chilverton House seven years before Jack had regarded it with affection. It was the place where, magically, his life seemed to take on some meaning; the place where his introspective nature would unfurl and bask in a warm reflected light. As an only child, the experience of the Tennants' family life was something wonderful to him. The mere fact of seven people living together under one roof was a source of fascination. He himself had never known the easy, rough relationship of brothers and sisters, their honest and casual love. Even the trials of Maurice, the sparring of Ralph and Sophie—even these he observed with delight and admiration. And, at the centre of it all, Thea.

He turned into the drive, revving the engine to announce himself, and as the tyres sucked and crunched on the gravel Dulcie opened the front door and ran down the steps.

Jack liked Dulcie, but rather against his better judgement. She was incorrigible but amusing; irretrievably worldly but touchingly innocent; often bored but never dull. What was more, she actually admired and envied him for those aspects of his life of which he was rather ashamed—that period of house parties and balls and society flirtations. It seemed unjust that the whole thing had been squandered on him, and would have meant everything to Dulcie. She needed so little to make her happy, just frivolities which many girls took for granted, and yet for her they were worlds away.

This morning she appeared smart as paint and pretty as a picture in a cream high-necked blouse with a pearl choker, and a soft blue wool skirt, belted, with two large pearl buttons at the waist. Her whole demeanour was so sunny that Jack was relieved—Dulcie was like a child, doted on but capricious, upon whose changeable moods an anxious adult world was dependent for its tranquillity.

Now she ran over to the car, blowing him a kiss in passing. 'Jack! You've bought a new car! Or was it a Christmas present from some rich, beautiful lady?'

Jack smiled. 'Certainly not. You know very well I don't keep company with that kind of lady. At least, I beg your pardon—' he inclined his head in a little bow—'not that rich.'

'Too kind, sir, you're too, *too* kind.' She walked round the car, running her hand over its shining bodywork. 'Does it go fast?'

'It can go up to thirty miles an hour.'

'Goodness! And are you going to take me for a spin?'

'We'll see. Where is everybody?'

'Oh—about the place. Come on in. Where are your parents?'

'Horsedrawn, somewhere on the Weald. They'll be here in time for church.'

'Church!' Dulcie made a face, and linking her arm through his led him towards the house. She lowered her voice to a stage whisper. 'What a bore.'

'Christmas is not simply a bunfight, you know.'

'Don't be old-fashioned, it doesn't suit you.'

'I'll be flattering instead. You're looking especially pretty today. How will that do?'

'Perfect!'

The hall was empty, except for Ralph's Alsatian, Homer,

who lay at the foot of the stairs. A few pine needles from the tree had fallen on his back; he had been lying there for some time. He wore the utterly baffled and melancholy expression of a dog who senses a disruption of routine. He lifted his head and grumbled as Jack and Dulcie entered.

'Stop that at once!' Dulcie went over to him and tapped his nose. 'You know Jack, so stop being cantankerous.'

A breathless Primmy scuttled into the hall. 'Captain Kingsley—I'm sorry, sir. Mr Collingwood was in the cellar with Mr Tennant and he can't have heard the bell.'

'That's all right, Primmy. I didn't ring it. Miss Dulcie heard the car.'

'Very good, sir.' Primmy took Jack's coat. 'Shall I tell anyone you're here?'

'No need to raise a hue and cry. Is anyone in the library?'

'Only Miss Thea, I think.'

'We'll go and keep her company for a while.'

Thea was sitting at the desk, writing. When Dulcie and Jack entered she turned, her pen still in her hand. Dulcie put her wrist to her brow in a gesture of mock horror.

'Thea, whatever are you doing?'

'Just trying to finish my latest offering for the *Country Companion*. I realize it's not very festive of me . . . but I have finished with it, as of this second! Hallo, Jack.'

'Happy Christmas, Thea.' Jack went over to her and kissed her cheek as she rose, but she was making a business of pushing the chair back and gathering her skirt, and did not reciprocate.

Thea felt sheepish at having been caught. She supposed that Jack must perceive her articles as trivial—merely an idle woman's way of filling time.

'What are you writing about?' he asked.

But at that moment the door opened and Venetia appeared. She wore an oyster-coloured suit with a brown fur trim, a big ivory brooch at the neck. She smiled when she saw Jack and went over to him, her hands outstretched.

'Jack! I'm so sorry I wasn't here to greet you, there were one or two things—' She kissed his cheek, still holding both his hands in hers. Venetia liked Jack, for one very good reason. He was like her. She understood him. Many people found him cold and distant, but she recognized in him the warmth of a slow-burning fire that needed only the fanning of a more extrovert nature to make it leap into life. She had been like that, aloof and defensive, always keeping her emotions safely locked away. But when Ralph had come along, he had allowed no such shilly-shallying. He had simply announced his own love and then set about the task of teaching her to accept it. Jack, Venetia thought, needed someone like that; and in her opinion Thea was the person most fitted for the task.

But now, as ever, it was Dulcie who hovered at Jack's shoulder, and Thea who stood apart. And she looked so handsome today . . . Venetia gave a little sigh. Thea was wearing a plum-coloured costume which, although a few years old, had always suited her. It had a little waistcoat underneath the jacket, picked out in black frogging, and she wore it with a white blouse which had a frilled jabot at the throat. The slight mannishness of the outfit became Thea very well, and her black hair was more disciplined than usual, piled up high, accentuating her fine neck and jaw.

'Don't look so pensive, darling!' It was Dulcie, running past to open the front door. 'Everyone's here!'

Venetia realized she had fallen into a reverie, Jack followed Dulcie and Thea said, *sotto voce*: 'And Aunt Sophie is already by the front door, hatted and gloved and champing at the bit!'

Primmy, taking a short cut down the front staircase, stopped on the hall landing and looked out of the tall, mullioned window. She could see the returning church party moving up the Elm Walk. They looked peaceful and leisurely, figures in a winter landscape.

She ran on down the stairs, across the hall and down to the kitchen. 'They're on their way. They're coming up the Elm Walk, Mrs Duckham.'

'Right, girl. Would you pop upstairs and check the plates and the silver?'

Primmy went up to the morning-room. The table had been moved to one side, against the far window, and the buffet was laid out upon it. Homer, who had been lying by the front door, chin on paws, like a dog on a tomb, rose and followed her in. He recognized her quick step as a sign that the others were due to return.

Primmy did not like dogs. In her view, animals should be

outside, or in a zoo, not cluttering up the house and spreading hairs which she had to sweep up. The dog, however, knew that her authority was supreme only when the house was empty. He stood just inside the door of the morning-room, his tail swinging placatingly, watching her check over the buffet table. She ignored him. He took a few paces further into the room and sank down with a bored little sound, something between a whine and a yawn. Primmy glanced over her shoulder.

'Get out! Homer—out!' She did not like that dog anywhere near food. She knew he would certainly be allowed in when the family got back, but she was not having him anywhere near the buffet till then. There was chicken in aspic, salmon, fruit salad, cheeses—heaven knows what depredations he might wreak.

Homer laid his ears down and thumped his tail, but did not move. Primmy would not be bested. The fact that it was Mr Tennant's dog added a certain piquancy to the confrontation. She marched over and pointed, arm extended rigidly, to the door.

'Homer! Out!' The dog rose slowly and paced towards the door, his whole body expressing gloom and resentment. He looked over his shoulder. The black-sleeved arm still pointed inexorably towards the hall. He retired once more to the doormat.

Primmy dusted off her palms in triumph and returned to the buffet. It looked delectable, a shining, colourful display of gleaming textures and rich hues. The sheer beauty of food in an upper-class household took Primmy's breath away. In her own home special treats like a joint, a pudding or a cake were tasty and sustaining, but never so voluptuously seductive to the eye. Food was brown or beige, occasionally green. It smelt good but it looked drab. Here food was not simply fuel but a lavish pageant.

Voices in the hall disturbed her daydreaming. She quickly ran her thumb down the sides of the piles of plates and dishes, counting under her breath, and performed the same operation with the silver cutlery, laid out in gleaming fanshapes on the damask cloth.

Then she slipped across the hall as Collingwood smoothly welcomed family and guests back to the house, and relieved them of coats and hats, warm rich cloth, fragrant feathers and fur. Homer, in an ecstasy of delight, wagged his tail and brushed among the skirts and trousers as Primmy went downstairs to the servants' hall.

Thea sat in the window-seat, her glass of wine beside her, relishing the sensation of being between the warmth and conviviality of the room and the pale, washed-out chill of the midwinter afternoon. In that odd way that December days have, there seemed to have been nothing between the promise of early morning and the gathering gloom of evening. The sun had tricked them, had seemed to be ascending the heavens with a friendly smile, only to slip away over the horizon like a thief and leave them cheated, in the dark.

Before lunch, everyone had placed their presents by the fireside and Dulcie had distributed them. She had not been able to lift Ralph's present to Thea—it was a typewriter, the very latest model. Thea had been speechless with delight and gratitude, touched by his understanding, thrilled by his extravagance. He had merely adjured her to 'make good use of it' and issued one or two brisk instructions as to its operation. Both Aubrey and Maurice had given her books. Aubrey's was useful—a large volume of natural history which, as he pointed out, should assist her in her journalistic ventures. Maurice's book was poetry—Gerard Manley Hopkins. Only Ralph and Jack, among the others present, had even heard of him, and when Dulcie tried to read some she cast it aside in great disgust, dismissing it as tedious and incomprehensible. But Thea thought it a wonderful present and told Maurice so, in a whisper, as she kissed him.

Now the presents had been given, received, unwrapped and exclaimed over. Paper lay about on the floor and Homer nosed among it like a looter on a battlefield.

Jack walked over, fishing in his jacket pocket. He stood in front of Thea, his back to the rest of the room. 'I hadn't forgotten you,' he said.

Thea looked up. 'I hadn't given it a thought,' she said, not entirely truthfully.

'Here. I hope you like it.' He produced a small package and held it out in his fist, palm down, as in a child's guessing game. Thea held out her hand and he dropped the package into it. He stood and waited as she began to undo it, then abruptly walked away as though impatient with her fumblings and tearings.

Thea came first to tissue paper, and then to a necklace. It

was a silver choker, consisting of a series of flat, shield-shaped pieces, linked by fine chain. Each piece had an enamelled flower, perfect in every detail, in the centre, in brilliant jewel colours. The necklace was beautiful and strikingly unusual. It was exactly what she would have chosen for herself. Yet again it was as if Jack could read her mind. She replaced the gift in its tissue and walked over to him. He was replenishing Dulcie's glass at the table.

'Thank you. It's lovely.'

He turned, with a smile. A polite smile, thought Thea. He had intimated closeness with his gift, and had now retreated behind company manners, leaving her exposed and vulnerable.

'It's so unusual.' She knew she was blushing; her cheeks burned.

'Yes, I thought so. It's very old, as a matter of fact. It was my grandmother's.'

'Oh . . .' Thea was taken aback. 'Are you sure you should have . . . ?'

'I did ask,' he said.

Dulcie giggled. She had had several glasses of mulled wine. 'What did you think, Thea—that he stole it?'

'Of course not!' Thea was sharp. 'It's just that I feel so honoured.'

'It's exactly right for you,' he said. 'Will you wear it this evening?'

'Of course.'

'Have you seen what he gave *me*?' asked Dulcie childishly, holding out her wrist. On it was a bracelet in the shape of a snake, its tail in its mouth. Its garnet eyes glowed redly. It was very modern, the epitome of the current trend for all things oriental. It was also a fine piece, cleverly worked and heavy, solid silver.

'Isn't that gorgeous,' said Thea admiringly, relieved to have attention drawn away from herself. 'It's so up to date as well. Jack, you are clever.'

'I'm fussy about presents.' He turned and cut himself a piece of Stilton, closing the topic.

'I was just asking Jack to take me for a drive before it gets dark,' said Dulcie. 'Wouldn't that be fun? Everyone else will go to their rooms and *rest*—imagine? I couldn't possibly rest!'

'I'm quite happy to stay in,' replied Thea. 'I shall sit by the fire and look at my new books.'

Dulcie was hanging on Jack's arm. She looked as appetizing as a ripe fruit, shiny and ready for plucking. Jack patted her hand. The gesture was a little too slow to be entirely avuncular.

'I'll certainly take you for a drive if you'd like to. But you'll need to wrap up warmly.'

'I will—I will, this minute!' She flew from the room.

Jack leaned back on the table edge, set down his glass and took his cigarette case from his breast pocket. 'Do you mind?' he asked.

'Not at all.'

Jack used time in lighting the cigarette. Then he folded his arms and exhaled the smoke, peering through it at some point on the opposite wall. He thought: how ironic that it is Dulcie I am taking for a drive, just to gratify her whim. Dulcie, not Thea. 'Are you quite sure you won't come with us?' he asked.

She shook her head. 'Quite sure. I shall be cosy by the library fire. I shan't be alone.'

It struck Jack as odd that she should reassure him about that.

Dulcie reappeared. She looked ravishing. Jack found himself smiling, reflecting the brightness of her delight. She wore a blue coat trimmed with steel-grey fur, and a grey fur pillbox hat.

'I'm ready!' she cried. 'Ready to go!'

'So I see.' Jack went over to her. 'And if I may say so, that is a most becoming hat.'

Jack took Dulcie up onto the Weald and then turned right, where the road wound along the crest, with the bare woods like a silent army on one side and the soft Kentish fields rolling away to the other. The afternoon air was crisp and sharp as spring water, making Dulcie's cheeks bloom and her eyes sparkle. Jack relaxed. It was pleasant to give Dulcie a treat. It induced a cosy feeling of self-gratification, like spoiling a little girl and being told how terribly nice one is. It was easy. With Dulcie Jack knew that he was not himself, but the man she saw him to be, the man she told him he was.

She sat a little forward in her seat, her lips parted, her smoky breath whipped back from her face by the wind. At the end of the road, where it curved to the right to encircle the spur of the hill and return to the valley, there was a bare, pine-needle-carpeted patch at the edge of the wood, the estuary of a much-used footpath. On an impulse, Jack turned into this space, swinging the car round so that it faced across the road and over the fields. The cathedral hush of the pine woods hung about them after the roar of the engine had died away. Dulcie clapped her hands.

'Isn't it lovely? And your car—it goes faster than Father's.'

'Ah well, it's a coupé. It should.'

'I see.' Clearly she didn't.

'A sports car. Nippier. More zip.'

'Yes. I *do* see.'

She leaned back in her seat for the first time. The fur beneath her chin and framing her face enhanced the kittenish quality of her prettiness. She widened her blue eyes. Her lashes were spiky, like stars in the dusk. 'Why did you stop?' She had lowered her voice so much that only the consonants gave it form, like drops of water in a well. Its sudden quietness was a shock, almost an invitation to intimacy.

Jack lit a cigarette, leaning his elbows on the steering wheel, not looking at her. 'It's a splendid view.'

'We shall have to drive home in the dark.'

'It isn't far. We have headlamps.'

He smoked for a moment. He could smell Dulcie's scent. Somewhere down in the fields an answering skein of smoke wandered into the air. Suddenly he felt Dulcie's hand on his arm. He turned to look at her.

'Come here,' she said.

He leaned back, still holding the lighted cigarette, a defence against sensuousness.

'No, not that,' she said teasingly but still softly. 'I mean this.' She took the cigarette and dropped it over the side of the car. Her hand slipped to the back of his neck and exerted a firm, light pressure, drawing his head down to hers.

Because of her smallness, the delicacy of her touch and the softness of her voice, Jack was disarmed. He could do nothing so rough as to refuse her. He allowed his lips to be drawn to hers, where they rested with almost polite gentleness, passively, kindly. But then her other hand slid round to his back, quick and firm, gripping him. He could feel the small fingers spread between his shoulder blades. At the same time her body arched against his. Her excitement was infectious, arousing him, demanding more urgency. There was a wild, passionate, childish hug, and yet her kiss was not childish and neither was the voice in which she whispered: 'Please Jack. I want to know what it is. I want to *know*.'

He drew back from her, startled. Her face, tilted back against the car seat, had a heaviness, a puffiness, as after sleep or tears, the eyelids drooping. Her lips were full, parted, almost round—Jack was forcibly reminded of the expression 'a rosebud mouth': it had meant nothing until then. Her hands slithered from him and fell to her lap, like dead leaves from a tree. There was an intense, electric languor about her. She offered herself.

'Dulcie.' He put a hand to her cheek, cupping her face gently, but she batted his arm aside.

'Don't. Don't be brotherly. I couldn't bear it.'

'What would you have me be?' He was irritated by her petulance.

'You know . . .' She looked away for a moment; he thought she was going to cry, but then she turned back and her face burned bright and fierce.

'You *know*.'

'You want me to make love to you.' He was coolly frank, rubbing salt in her self-inflicted wound.

'Yes.'

'I couldn't,' he said firmly, but inexplicably feeling that the cock had crowed for the first time on some grim, pre-ordained treachery. 'You *must* understand why.' She must be either obtuse or thick-skinned.

'You don't want to.' She pouted, but she was hurt. Her honesty touched him, increasing his frustration.

'I could want to—very easily. But that's not all there is to it.'

'Then what?'

'You're very young.'

'Old enough.'

'Dulcie, listen. You *are* young. And pretty. You will have men at your feet, believe me. No need to be desperate.' He looked intently into her face, angry but anxious, willing her to understand, not to seek more punishment. Her lip trembled, but he had never known her cry and she did not give in to tears now.

'You don't have a very high opinion of yourself if you think I'm so desperate,' she said, with a touch of wry humour.

He stroked her averted head with the back of his hand and this time she did not brush him off. He curled the hand into a fist and gave her cheek a push, not entirely gentle. 'Dulcie. Come *on*.'

They sat for a moment in silence. Then Jack turned and impatiently switched on the headlamps. The gush of light helped to quench the little guttering flame of desire inside him. It restored normality.

Dulcie seemed to have reached some conclusion of her own. 'Yes, let's go back,' she said, quite brightly. But as they pulled away she added, 'Don't think I've given up.'

He pretended not to hear.

Thea was sitting on the library sofa with Maurice. They had lighted one lamp and this, with the flickering glow from the fire, was the only light in the room. They had been reading the Manley Hopkins book together. For Maurice, it had been two hours of complete serenity and contentment; for Thea, only partly so. Outside the womb-like warmth and serenity, the gentle half-light of this room, was the cold and dark—and Jack and Dulcie driving through it, laughing, talking. Talking of her? But why should they? She could not prevent one small, anxious part of her mind from wandering away, asking these troublesome questions . . . When at last they heard the front door burst open, the sound of their steps in the hall, and their voices, loud and fresh from out of doors, Thea started guiltily.

Maurice closed the book. The end of peace. 'Here they are,' he said.

Dulcie came into the room, her coat still on, her fur hat swinging from one hand. Her face glowed healthily. She perched on the arm of the sofa. 'We had a marvellous drive. Right up to the woods, and along the top—you could see for miles.'

'Wasn't it dark?' asked Maurice.

'Not when we were there.' Thea thought she detected a defensive note in Dulcie's voice. 'Anyway, what have you been up to?'

'Reading.' Thea smiled at Maurice to include him, to show that she had been content. 'Reading and talking.'

'Stuffy things,' said Dulcie, but she bent and kissed Thea's cheek as she said it. Thea, whose attitude to her sister was one of 'beware the Greeks', looked up at her in surprise.

'What was that for?'

'Christmas.'

'What about Maurice?' Thea teased.

Maurice's head jerked up in consternation. 'I . . .I—' he stuttered. Dulcie stopped his words with another kiss. Her lips felt cold and firm, the kiss was quick and light as a snowflake. Maurice blushed.

Dulcie laughed gaily and began to unbutton her coat. Thea sensed something febrile about her, even the removal of the coat had a wantonness about it. Jack appeared at the door. As usual, his mood was less easy to gauge.

'We hear you had a good drive,' said Thea.

'Yes.' He came over and squatted down by the fire, holding his long-fingered hands to the blaze. 'Yes, we did.'

'I suppose we shall have to think about changing soon,' she went on, trying to make a group of them once more, to paper over the cracks she saw spreading like a spider's web across their harmonious peace.

'Yes,' said Maurice, eager to escape now that Jack and Dulcie had returned. 'Actually I think I'll go up now, if you'll excuse me.' He stood, awkwardly pulled at his jacket, made a little bowing movement of self-excuse, and fled.

Thea sighed. 'It's so cosy. I can hardly be bothered.'

'Oh, I'm longing for this evening!' said Dulcie, standing behind the sofa, knees slightly bent, surveying her reflection in the mirror over the fireplace. 'Heaven knows, we get little enough fun down here, and I intend to make the most of it.'

Thea tilted her head back and looked up at her sister. 'You're right, it will be fun. I just feel lazy.'

'Come on.' Dulcie took Thea's hand and gave her a tug. 'Let's go up together and then we can do each other up, and choose jewellery and things like we used to.'

Her good humour was infectious. Thea rose and allowed herself to be led from the room. Jack placed the guard in front of the fire and followed.

'Don't forget the necklace,' he said. But when Thea looked back to assure him that she wouldn't he was already intent on some book of Ralph's on the desk, his brow furrowed in concentration. The door had been opened, but closed in her face.

Christmas dinner. The candles were lit, their soft, caressing light flattered the faces of the people round the table. Talk ebbed and flowed, heads turned this way and that, nodded, assented, agreed; the clink of glass and cutlery provided a gentle counterpoint. Thea thought: tonight we are *all* friends; it should always be like this.

She was wearing the necklace. Jack had not commented on it beyond a brief nod when she had first appeared. She was not altogether certain whether it went with her dress. She had changed into a green taffeta dress with a deep cross-over bodice and the fashionable narrower skirt. The skirt felt as though it was catching at her ankles all the time but Dulcie—whose choice it had been—had said it looked quite the thing and insisted she wear it. Dulcie had also assisted most painstakingly in the arrangement of her hair, which was centre-parted, curving back from her temples in two smooth wings. The whole effect was rather Grecian, and was not particularly complimented by the addition of the necklace, but Dulcie had assured her . . . She glanced at her sister suspiciously for a moment. It was most unlike Dulcie to take such an interest in anyone's appearance but her own.

Thea was not the only one observing Dulcie. Jack had been talking to Venetia, but now he sat back, turning the stem of his glass between his fingers, disposed to look on.

Dulcie was immediately opposite Jack and Thea. The existence of an odd number, the dreaded 'spare man', had taxed all Venetia's ingenuity in arranging the seating plan. However, her scheme had apparently not worked, for whereas her younger daughter was on her most sparkling form, Thea remained unusually withdrawn. So far she and Jack Kingsley had not addressed a word to each other, beyond what was dictated by politeness.

Dulcie was flirting outrageously with Robert Kingsley, whosm already ruddy complexion had taken on an apoplectic shade of crimson. The feather on her headband bobbed animatedly as if in some exotic courtship dance. Thea looked from her to Jack, who was watching Dulcie intently, his head a little on one side as one who observes with interest, and admiration. Abruptly he turned to Thea.

'Penny for them?'

'Oh . . . I was just thinking how agreeable it is when everyone is as cheerful and friendly and well-disposed towards each other as they are at Christmas. But I suppose it's as Mr Aitcheson said in his sermon—too easy at Christmas. What a pity we can't sustain it.'

'And you were hoping to find the solution inscribed on my left cheek.'

'I'm sorry. I was miles away, I didn't mean to stare.'

'The necklace looks fine.'

'Do you think so? Thank you. I wasn't sure about it—with this particular dress, I mean, but Dulcie thought . . .' She floundered, fingering the necklace with one hand, smoothing her skirt with the other.

Jack held up a hand to stop her. 'You look lovely. I like it all.'

The obvious sincerity of the compliment took her aback. But before she had time to respond he had leaned forward to address Dulcie, who was laughing at some remark of his father's, her eyes round, fingers spread in a fan across her nose and mouth in affected shock.

'I hope,' he said, 'my father isn't saying something improper.'

'Of course!' Dulcie clasped her hands at her breast and looked wide-eyed from one man to the other. 'I should be bitterly disappointed if he wasn't!'

Venetia smiled indulgently. But the smile on Thea's lips had died.

'Games!' cried Dulcie.

It was a quarter past midnight. The others of the party had retired in dribs and drabs over the past half hour, starting with Sophie and ending not two minutes since with Ralph. Dulcie, Thea, Aubrey, Maurice and Jack were in the library. They had not left the dinner table until nearly eleven o'clock, having played snap-dragon until their eyes and fingers smarted from snatching the raisins out of the blue haze of flaming brandy.

Thea sat on the floor by the fire, her knees bunched under her chin, her arms clasped round them, staring into the flames. While she sat there the fire was her talisman and friend, keeping her in its spell, saving her from conversation. She felt melancholy, and disappointed because of it. Christmas was tarnished, for the first time ever, and she could not quite say why.

But Dulcie was on the crest of a wave of high spirits. 'Who's for games?' she repeated, twirling round in the middle of the room, her arms flung out theatrically, her skirt ballooning.

Aubrey walked over to the hearth and tapped his pipe on the edge of the fireplace. 'You've had too much wine,' he observed drily.

'Nonsense! Don't be dreary. Everyone's had too much.'

'It doesn't go to everyone's heads to quite the same extent.' Aubrey began to light the pipe, puffing and sucking, pushing the tobacco down with his index finger.

Jack, who was sitting on one end of the sofa, legs stretched out, said: 'I'll play.'

'And me,' said Maurice, wretched at the prospect but knowing that Dulcie could make him more wretched for not playing.

'Good for both of you!' cried Dulcie. 'Thea?'

'I don't think . . . It depends . . .'

'Spoilsport. Somebody persuade her.'

Maurice said, 'Do play, Thea. Please.'

Thea smiled up at him and held out her hand to be pulled up. 'Oh, all right.' She knew Maurice needed her support. 'What shall we play, then?'

'Murder,' said Aubrey with feeling.

'There aren't enough of us,' said Jack. 'You need plenty of suspects.'

'Charades,' said Dulcie. 'No—I know! I'll be someone and you ask me questions to find out who I am.'

'What about the rest of us?' asked Thea. 'It sounds a bit one-sided.'

'Anyone who wants to can have a go after me—it's just that I've thought of someone good.' She ran out of the room.

'It's all a plot to satisfy her vanity,' said Aubrey.

'She's certainly in good form.' Jack shook his head. 'It lets the rest of us out quite nicely, though, doesn't it?'

Maurice agreed. 'Indeed it does.'

'Have another whisky,' Aubrey addressed Jack. 'We may need it before this is over.'

The whisky was duly poured and still Dulcie did not return. The four of them sat still and in silence. It was as though they had depended on Dulcie for energy and now that she had withdrawn they were frozen in a state of suspended animation. The only sound was the shuddering and flapping of the flames, and the occasional rustle as a log slipped.

The door swung open, and Dulcie entered. She had removed her shoes and stockings, and carried a large tray or plate, covered by a cloth. She had applied kohl, or something like it, to her eyelids, sweeping the line out to one side in an oriental effect. Her face was set, her eyes staring. She closed the door behind her back, and advanced unsmilingly into the

65

centre of the room, and began to hum. The sound was tuneless and atonal, a kind of high-pitched plainsong. In the middle of the rug she began to dance, undulating and posturing, passing the plate from hand to hand, twisting her free arm in snake-like movements. The bracelet on her arm shone, her feet stamped and pranced soundlessly on the carpet, her hips swinging lasciviously. The diaphanous stuff of her skirt swished to and fro and as she swayed more vigorously it was possible to see the pale skin of her thighs, gilded a little by the firelight gleaming as she moved.

She faced the fire and began to bend backwards, holding the plate perilously above her, at arm's length. As she bent over her face with the great black eyes became eerie and mask-like, upside down; the marabou feather almost brushed the ground. Her body was almost completely arched; the material, pulled as smooth as blue water, poured over her small breasts, her stomach, her braced, wide-apart legs. The fire, shining through her skirt, lit up the lower part of her body in a flickering silhouette.

'She looks like a dervish,' whispered Thea.

Dulcie's weird, inverted face now hung a mere three feet from Jack's knees. He did not move. She began to straighten up again, still keeping the covered plate above her head. When she was upright she stood for a moment, rocking from foot to foot in time to some inner rhythm, her lips parted in a small, secretive smile. She faced Maurice and Thea, but it was obvious she did not see them.

Then suddenly she swung round, sweeping her skirt to one side with her free hand. She sank onto one knee and held out the plate to Jack, inclining her neck and body towards him in a way that was at once suppliant and slightly reptilian. Jack, nonplussed, spread his hands in a gesture of helplessness. Dulcie, in answer, raised her free hand slowly and whipped off the cloth that covered the plate.

On the plate lay a sheep's head, cooked and partly denuded. The flesh had a leprous, shredded appearance, the bones showing through patchily like those of a corpse that has decomposed in water.

A sheep's head was a common sight in the kitchen at Chilverton House. Mrs Duckham bought them for Homer; she stewed them, gave the meat to the dog and preserved the skull to make stock. But the sight of the head here in the library, among velvet, chintz and leather, was obscene.

Thea put her hand to her mouth and looked away.

Maurice stared, fascinated, murmuring, 'Very good . . .'

Aubrey was deflating. 'How perfectly revolting.'

Dulcie ignored them, holding her position in front of Jack, staring unblinking into his face.

He sat still for a moment, as if in deep thought, studying the head, then leaned forward and remarked imperturbably, 'John the Baptist, I presume?'

The spell was broken. Dulcie sat back on the floor with a bump, put the plate down and grimaced. 'You guessed. It was too easy.'

'A tribute to your acting ability. You make a good Salome.'

'Too kind.' Dulcie put her hands to her face. 'Can I borrow a hankie?'

Maurice produced one, large, clean and crumpled, from his trouser pocket and Dulcie began to scrub at the black round her eyes. There was a scratch and the door swung open to admit Homer, tail waving, excited by the smell of the head.

Aubrey picked up the plate and placed it precariously on the mantelpiece. 'We must get that wretched thing back where it belongs before the dog gets it.'

'Did it give you all a shock?' asked Dulcie, staring round at her audience. 'I thought it was rather a brilliant idea.'

'It certainly gave me a fright,' said Thea. She felt that some message had been passed, that they had all watched a rite which they might view but not comprehend. She could still see, with hallucinogenic clarity, the mask-face, the swaying body, the sinister, cloth-covered plate . . .

'I'll take this back,' she said and left the room, carrying the sheep's head at arm's length. It was slightly rancid. It was odd, she thought as she walked swiftly across the cold, dark hall to the back stairs, how this ordinary household object had been imbued with an almost occult presence by Dulcie's charade. She found herself walking more and more quickly, fear nipping at her heels, until she practically ran down the back stairs, past the open-mouthed Mrs Duckham, last of the servants to retire, and into the larder. Once there she placed the plate on the slab and covered it with a wire-gauze meat safe quickly and firmly, as if trapping a rat.

Back in the library it was obvious that a discussion had been taking place.

Dulcie was saying, 'Let's have one round of sardines before we go to bed.'

'I thought,' said Aubrey, 'that other people were going to have a turn at this acting thing.'

'Well—does anyone want to?' She looked round.

Jack shook his head. 'How could we hope to follow that?'

'Sardines it is,' said Maurice, and then, deciding that honesty was the best policy, 'I certainly don't want to act.'

'How about you?' Dulcie asked Thea. 'Will you play sardines?'

"All right, just once. Who's going to hide?'

' *You*—go on, *you* hide. You know the best places.'

'So do we all, except Jack.'

'That's true.' Dulcie went to Jack and slipped her arm through his, smiling up into his face. 'I'll help Jack.'

'How long will you give me?'

'Fifty!'

'Right.' Aubrey looked down at his watch. 'Starting now. And don't make it too difficult.'

Thea ran from the room. She knew exactly where she would hide. She was thoroughly spooked. She wanted a snug dark corner where she could see and not be seen, a wall behind her back so that no one could creep up on her. She ran up the stairs quickly and lightly, two at a time, her skirt clutched up in one hand, and turned along the corridor, past her mother's room. She could hear her parents' voices, lowered, her mother's soft laugh. Secrets. She broke into a run, to escape the quiet voices and whatever else she might hear. There were tears in her eyes. She felt like a child that has been ostracized, left out of some important and prestigious scheme.

She opened the door of the nursery. The curtains were open and the room was full of pale, dusty moonlight. There was no furniture in the room except for the tall fitted corner cupboard, the bed covered with a sprigged bedspread, and a flaky white-painted washstand with a bowl and pitcher. Such toys as had been kept out of sentimental affection were stowed in the cupboard, except for two. Dasher, the dappled rocking horse, stood by the window, his nostrils dilated crimson, his hooves forever prancing in a wild, arrested gallop. Dasher's neck and head reminded her of something that she could not at once place.

The other childhood relic was the shop. Ralph had built it

for Dulcie on her eighth birthday. It was a simple wooden structure across the far right-hand corner of the room. There was a door at one side and an open hatch in the front, with a counter on both sides of the lower ledge. Around the two walls that formed the back of the shop were ranged shelves. Venetia and the children had stuck labels on all kinds of old household jars and packets and filled them with shells, dried peas and beans, beads, little scrunched-up balls of silver paper—these formed the shop's 'merchandise'. There was a pair of scales and a stack of paper for wrapping on the counter.

Thea opened the door and stooped to enter the shop. With a sigh of relief she huddled down, ducking her head to below the level of the counter. She was safe.

After a minute or so she caught a distant cry of 'Co-ming!' and heard the library door open. There was a murmured discussion as to who should take which direction, and then footsteps trickled away on various courses. Someone was coming up the stairs, accompanied by Homer. She could hear the rhythmic click of the dog's paws on the polished wood. At the top of the stairs the footsteps halted, making decisions, then set off in the opposite direction. Thea smiled to herself, hugging her knees beneath her chin.

Just then, with a shock, she saw a face peering in at her through the hatch—a long muzzle, great bat ears pricked, a tail wagging in greeting.

'Homer! Go away! Good dog—off you go!'

Homer's tail wagged faster and he cocked his head on one side, fascinated by this crouching, half-hidden figure. But eventually, having resisted several pushes, he wandered out again and Thea heard him flop down with a sigh outside Ralph's door.

Minutes passed. She heard Mrs Duckham's tired, old woman's tread, plodding up the back stairs to bed. Then, almost at once, the door of the shop opened and Aubrey sat down beside her. She jumped, then silently laughed. He still held his pipe.

'You'll have to put that out, they'll smell it,' she whispered, taking it from him and putting it on one of the lower shelves. Aubrey shifted uncomfortably on the hard floor.

'It's going to be a shocking crush when the next person turns up,' he complained, trying to find a rest for his back against the wall.

'That's half the fun.'

'Mm.'

They sat for a moment in silence. The rough tweed of her brother's trousers abraded Thea's bare arm. It was comforting, dependable.

'Is anyone else close?' she asked.

'Maurice. I kept on meeting him. I guessed where you were right away, but I had to shake him off.'

'And the others?'

'Looking downstairs.'

'Sh!'

Maurice appeared in the doorway. He looked tentative, even nervous. With her neck agonizingly bent Thea could still just see his face as he looked round the room, his glasses glinting in the moonlight. For a moment she thought he would not come in at all and then something seemed to catch his attention, for he walked into the middle of the room and looked around again, a little self-consciously, bending this way and that as though his feet were nailed to the ground. Finally he went to the far corner and opened the corner cupboard. Thea began to giggle, her shoulders shaking. The cupboard was divided into shelves, and could not have housed a cat, let alone a person.

Realizing his mistake, he shut the door quickly and lifted the coverlet of the bed, peering under it. Then, with sudden decision, he approached the shop and looked in through the hatch. Thea at once put her finger to her lips and motioned him to come in.

Aubrey pressed up closer to her, squeezing his legs into the space between her back and the wall and leaning against them, thus conveniently presenting Maurice with the broad expanse of his back. Maurice crouched awkwardly, holding the door shut behind him.

A silence that was almost palpable fell around them. The house seemed to be falling deeper and deeper into an abyss of unconsciousness, as if they were the only people still alive. Their breathing sounded unnaturally loud, scratching the glassy surface of the still night.

After what seemed like hours, but was in fact about ten minutes, Aubrey said, 'They're never going to find us. Let's give them a clue.'

'I think it's a trick,' said Thea. 'Dulcie knows all the old hiding places. She's just not trying. She intends leaving us here all night.'

'In that case, I'm going to bed.' Aubrey heaved himself stiffly into a kneeling position, grazing his head on the corner of a shelf. 'Damn!'

'Sh!'

'What?' Maurice, his arm throbbing with the effort of holding the door behind his back, released it, and it swung softly open.

Thea shook her head, listening intently. The silence flowed round them like a rising flood, filling the dark rooms and passages. But she had heard something. A laugh. A light, small laugh, no more substantial than the drip of a tap, somewhere in the distances of the house. 'I thought I heard Dulcie.'

All three listened again. Nothing.

Aubrey said, 'I'm off to bed. If Dulcie's up to her tricks, I've had enough.'

'Me too.' With relief, Maurice crawled out backwards and stood up, flexing his aching arm. Aubrey followed.

'Thea? You're not going to stay there all night?'

'I don't know. No, I suppose not. What about Jack?'

'What about him? In collusion with Dulcie, obviously. Leave them to it.'

'I'm sure you're right.' Thea came out. She had snagged her dress on the rough wood of the shop. The necklace felt suddenly tight, choking her. The three walked back along the corridor. At the head of the stairs, Thea said: 'I'm going down to get a drink, or an orange or something—I'm dreadfully thirsty, it's all the wine. Can I fetch either of you anything?'

'No thanks.'

'Goodnight, then.'

'Goodnight.'

She watched Aubrey stride purposefully to his room and Maurice hover, as though he would have said more, and then follow hesitantly. She went downstairs, and into the morning-room. The table had been laid up for breakfast. On the sideboard stood a tall-stemmed silver dish containing fruit. She went over and selected an orange.

Carrying the orange like a charm she came back into the hall. The library door stood open; she could see the red and grey rubble of the dying fire behind the black bars of the

71

fireguard. Someone—Mrs Duckham presumably—had been in and removed the ashtrays and whisky glasses and drawn back the curtains. She opened the dining-room door. The dinner table was cleared but she could still smell the brandy, the smoke, the odours of conviviality like ghosts in the dark air. She closed the door.

The only remaining rooms on the ground floor were her father's study and the seldom-used drawing-room. She went to the drawing-room and opened the door stealthily, like a spy.

The room was sepulchrally cold, for no fire had been lit in it for weeks. The exquisite furniture—most of it French, and priceless—stood about foppishly: elegant, polished, impractical. In the two tall cabinets valuable porcelain and glass shone, spotlessly imprisoned. Paintings, mostly large and gloomy, slumbered darkly in great heavy gilt frames. In the centre of the room, facing the tall marble fireplace, with its back to the door, stood a Louis XV *chaise-longue*, elegantly striped in red and cream. The sweeping, languorous curve of its back was presented like the turned shoulder of a courtesan to prying eyes.

As Thea entered, her first impression was that the room was empty. But as she turned to leave, something arrested her, some ripple in the air, some sound so tiny that she caught it with her mind more than her ear. She froze, listening, every sense alert, every hair pricking. And then, as she watched, a leg appeared, draped over the arm of the *chaise-longue*. The leg was Dulcie's, neat, small-boned, with a well-turned ankle and high-arched foot. It wore a pale oyster-silk stocking, ending above the knee. It dangled flaccidly, voluptuously, the flesh of the thigh slightly spread where it rested on the wooden arm.

A rhythmic, sibilant sound which Thea now recognized as breathing became stronger. It grew quicker and more urgent. Thea took a few steps forward. The room seemed bigger than she remembered, the *chaise-longue* further from the door, its back higher and more solid. She quickened her pace and reached it, grabbing the back with one hand as if to stop herself from falling.

She was looking down directly into Dulcie's upturned face. The face was unseeing, the eyes veiled, her breath sighing between parted lips. Her whole face had a bruised, softened appearance, like an overripe fruit.

Jack lay on top of Dulcie. His left arm was beneath her, encircling her waist, while his free hand grasped the arm of the *chaise-longue* behind her head, the arm braced. His face was pressed into the curve of her neck and shoulder. It was his breathing that Thea had heard, short and quick, like a dog panting.

Dulcie's peacock-blue skirt was drawn up into a crumpled swathe at the hip. Her hands rested lightly on the back of Jack's neck. Like some beautiful insect-eating flower she seemed passive, voluptuous, deadly. The inevitability of her conquest hung about her in a kind of aura. As Jack's thrusts became sharper, quicker, her neck arched and her face turned into the back of the *chaise-longue* in a movement that contained both pain and pleasure, her jaw drooping a little so that Thea could see her tongue, pink and shining. Suddenly her hands slid sharply down his back, pressing him into her, imperious, the fingers like claws. Jack's back humped. His face slid down onto Dulcie's breast.

The pattern which had been asserting itself all evening, all day, was now crystal-clear to Thea. She stepped back abruptly, horrified at her own voyeurism.

'No!'

Her voice sounded crabbed and accusing, an old woman's voice. As if in response Jack slid from Dulcie and knelt at the foot of the *chaise-longue* like a praying child, his face in his hands. Thea thought he spoke her name but the loathing in her was too strong to allow her to answer.

Dulcie lay there, gazing up at her. She lay in the same position, legs splayed, arms now thrown back above her head. The insides of her thighs gleamed with moisture. She was smiling.

Jack buttoned his trousers, combed his fingers through his hair and rose, a little shakily. He looked straight into Thea's eyes. In his expression there was neither guilt nor defiance, but a kind of desperate sadness. For a long moment he held her with that look. She felt that her horror and disgust were pinned on the end of it, that he challenged her to give them free rein. Now, of all times, he was demanding something of her, and she was incapable of giving it.

Dulcie sat up, and leaned her forearms on the back of the couch, her chin on her crossed wrists, surveying them. She exuded an air of complacency, like a satisfied cat. She bloomed. In contrast Jack looked stiff and gaunt. Thea's earlier impression was reinforced. She was in the presence of an immutable force, of which she herself had no experience but which she was just beginning to understand.

She glanced at Jack and he made the smallest move towards her, scarcely more than a quizzical tilt of the head.

'Keep away!'

One hand flashed out in self-defence. She began to back from the room, shuffling like a sleepwalker or a cripple, slightly bent, keeping her eyes on Jack, feeling behind her with her free hand. By the door she stumbled against a chair and dropped the orange, which thudded and rumbled on the polished wooden floor.

Then she was gone, running up the stairs, blind to the second watcher who stood in the dark corner by the library door, small and still.

On the floor the orange lay round and bright, like a staring cyclopean eye.

CHAPTER THREE

*'Playmates were we: Little we thought it then
How we should change, when we should all be men!'*
Bessie Bonehill—'Playmates'

Thea ran into her room and sat on the edge of her bed, pressing her fingers against her eyes. She sat rigidly upright. Perhaps if she herself kept very stiff and still she could reduce everything to a pinprick of stillness—simply wipe out the quick breathing, the jerking bodies, the clutching hands, the gasps . . .

The door opened with a little rush, and closed again quickly. Thea's eyeballs ached with the pressure of her fingers. A slight tilting of the mattress beneath her told her that someone had sat down on the bed. She lowered her hands and saw Dulcie, leaning against the barred wooden bed-end, arms folded. Her face now was completely composed, the eyes steady, even accusing. But Thea noticed a stain on her skirt, and a feral, tainted odour which emanated from her.

'Go away,' she said dully. 'Please go away.'

'Why?' Dulcie's tone was truculent, matching the folded arms, the defiant stare. She was spoiling for a fight.

'Because this is my room and I want it to myself,' replied Thea, determined not to let her have it.

'Just so you can sit and sulk self-righteously,' said Dulcie. She had been carrying the feathered headband, and now she placed it fancifully over the knob on the bed-end, and began stroking the feather with the back of her forefinger.

Thea clenched her fists, tighter and tighter until the finger-joints throbbed and shook with the pressure. Anger and disgust boiled up in her. She had made no accusations, apportioned no blame, had wanted nothing but to escape, to be swallowed up in darkness and silence and solitude. And yet Dulcie had followed, still strutting and posing, still seeking acclamation. And she had the gall to sit there and tell Thea she was sulking. Thea glanced at her. Her eyes

75

were smudgy from the Salome make-up and there were two small reddened patches on her bare breast, just below the left collar bone. Thea remembered Jack's face sliding down, the skin of his cheek dragging slightly . . . Dulcie must have noticed her look, for she raised her hand and touched the patches, lightly, with the ends of her fingers, as though they were raw or burnt. The gesture was deliberately sensuous.

Suddenly Thea stood, towering over Dulcie. She reached out stiffly, like an automaton, and grasped her sister's upper arm, squeezing it viciously, her fingers making white bars on the flesh.

'*Get out!*' They were instinctively speaking in lowered voices because of the sleeping house, but Thea spat the words into her sister's face. 'Get out! I can't bear the sight of you or the smell of you sitting on my bed.' She picked up the headband and threw it on the floor; she did so with all her strength but because it was light it floated, and skittered across the floor like a dead leaf. 'You are *not wanted* here, do you understand?' She pinched the arm more tightly, gave it a shake. 'Or are you so vain that you can't?'

There were tears of pain in Dulcie's eyes but she wrenched away from Thea's clutching hand. She tried to get up but Thea was standing too close, pinning her to the edge of the bed, and she fell back again. She curled her legs up beside her and edged backwards into the centre of the bed.

Thea felt that she was being deliberately provoked, and was frightened by the violence of her own anger. It shook her to the very core, her whole frame quivered with it.

'How could you?' she asked, her voice trembling. 'How could you—in this house?'

Dulcie laughed derisively. Her overweening vanity filled the room like cheap scent. 'So that's it. I might have known. What's so sacred about this house? It *is* just a house, I suppose, not a temple of chastity?'. She spread her skirt, revealing the stain. She licked her finger and began rubbing the patch with studied indifference.

'It's our *home!*' Thea said with vehemence. But she felt that she was defining her own anger rather than reaching Dulcie. She saw now that was impossible.

'Oh, our *home!*' Dulcie copied her, then shrugged. 'And I've defiled it, of course. Just by doing what everyone does, by enjoying myself? What do you think Mother and Father do when—'

'Stop it!' Thea leaned forward and aimed a slap at her sister's face. But Dulcie evaded the blow, swinging her feet off the other side of the bed, putting its width between them. She stood up, smoothing her skirt.

'You know what it is, don't you?' she asked casually, but the smile that curved her lips was irrepressibly gleeful. 'You wish it had been you.'

Thea was struck dumb. She turned her back on Dulcie to escape the smile, but it seemed to hang before her eyes like the Cheshire Cat's, a great, smug grin of self-satisfaction, mocking her, out of reach.

'The thing is,' went on Dulcie, pleased that the shaft had gone home, 'that now *I* know about men. I know what it is they want, I know how to give it to them. Jack has shown me.' Her voice taunted Thea as she approached her. 'And you don't.'

Thea stared at her.

'Oh yes.' Dulcie walked past her to the mirror and prinked, rubbing her lips with her middle finger. 'I know how to please men.'

'What?' Thea was aghast at her sister's conceit.

'I've always known, Jack just proved it. I have an effect on men, just as mother always has. You've said so yourself, before now. It's a gift.'

The fact that she had indeed said so herself, often, made Thea even angrier. Her affectionate compliments were being thrown back at her as excuses for the inexcusable. 'You're a silly little girl,' she said, coldly and deliberately. 'And the more you brag about your pathetic conquest the more childish you appear. You bore me. Go away.'

She had wanted to hurt, and she had succeeded. Dulcie swung round, enraged, her eyes blazing. 'How *dare* you say that? How *dare* you? I am a woman now—more of a woman than you'll ever be, with your stupid typewriters and articles and business courses. I've left you behind and you're jealous. That's all there is to it. Don't ever call me a child again, you don't have the *right*! And I—I spit on you!' She spat on the carpet between them.

But Thea no longer had the energy to argue. She felt drained and exhausted. She slumped down on the bed again. 'I am not jealous,' she said quietly, flatly, as if intoning a mantra. 'I am not at all jealous. But I'm tired. And I want you to go.'

'I will. Don't worry.' Dulcie retrieved the headband from where it lay on the floor, flounced to the door, opened it and paused histrionically, her hand on the knob. 'I hope you think about us—all night,' she said, and went.

Thea did.

After about an hour's fitful sleep she awoke. Her whole body seemed to throb, it was clamorous with sensations she did not recognize, it had awoken her to pay heed to its demands. Trying to ignore it she drew up her knees tightly, almost to her chest, hugging herself, and lay there, curled like a foetus in the dark. But it was no good. There was no comfort, no gentle maternal heartbeat, no hammock of tepid fluid in which to be rocked and soothed. Handfuls of rain spattered like stones on the window; she felt as though her room were hurtling through black space, pitching and whirling. She turned on her back. As a child she used to stare at the ceiling when she couldn't sleep and 'paint' pictures on it. But now the only picture she saw was Dulcie and Jack, tightly joined, rhythmically coupled, the movements that were both violent and tender . . . Involuntarily her hand strayed down to her breasts, as though feeling them for the first time. The nipples started rigidly through the cotton of her nightgown. She slid her hand down over her stomach until it gripped her at the very core of her being. She moved it gently, tentatively, her legs parting in an instant response, her body melting. Irresistibly, desperately, she quickened the movements of her hand; it was as though she had started a pulse that sent out its ripples wider and wider, until her legs jerked up and her head tilted back in a spasm of shameful pleasure.

As soon as it was over she began to cry, the first tears she had shed in years. She staggered from the bed and went over to the washstand to pour herself some water from the carafe. On the way back she caught sight of her reflection in the long mirror on the wardrobe door and was suddenly filled with self-loathing and disgust. She sank back onto the bed, sobbing convulsively. It was Dulcie's final triumph.

'Oh my God,' she beseeched the darkness. 'What have I done? What am I?'

George Rowles was in the stableyard at six o'clock on the morning of Boxing Day. It was part of his duties to look after the horses, assisting the ostler, Meredith. Apart from the old pony, Joe, there were only four horses left in the stables at Chilverton House, a stables built to house twelve. A whole section of the mews had been converted into garage space for the Tennants' two motor cars. Meredith was understandably bitter about this; his truce with Edgar the chauffeur was a guarded one, and he resented George insofar as he was a manifestation of the changes that had taken place. Time was when Meredith had had two grooms under him, lads he'd trained himself, who knew horses inside out. George could not be trained in that way, even had he not been slow, for he had other jobs to do, helping his father in the garden.

This morning George had been set to mucking out. Generally he and Meredith would do it together, at about nine o'clock, but Meredith had the day off today and the job had to be done early as one or two of the horses were usually taken to the big meet at Conningham. Miss Thea liked to go, she was a good horsewoman, and sometimes Mr Aubrey and Captain Kingsley went along too.

It was the sensation of performing a task especially for Miss Thea that ennobled the dawn mucking-out for George. It lent a kind of sacred purpose to the shovelling of horse-dung and acrid, steaming hay and the carting about of heavy feed-boxes and buckets of water. Since the coach horses had been sold there was not so much tack to clean, but Meredith had become fanatical about the turn-out of the remaining horses and their quarters, as if to vie with the gleaming brass and glossy leather upholstery of Edgar's automobiles.

George went out into the yard, a bucket in either hand. The pump was in the far corner. From the pump you could just see nicely through the tall stone arch to the front of the house. He set the buckets down and began to pump. The lever squealed and grated and the water rattled into the iron buckets.

Suddenly the front door opened and a figure appeared. George guiltily and hastily lowered his eyes to the bucket, pumping more vigorously. The water reached the rim and in the quiet moment of changing the buckets round he heard the crunch of approaching footsteps across the gravel. He glanced up. It was Captain Kingsley.

'Morning, George.'

'Good morning, sir.'

George gawped. He simply could not take in the fact of Captain Kingsley, complete with great coat, cap and case, standing in the stableyard in the thin, chilly dawn—as spruce as you please. The strangeness of the situation threw him completely.

'I'm leaving now,' said Captain Kingsley, very quiet and polite as usual. 'Will it disturb your work if I get my car out?'

George stepped aside and flapped his arm stiffly. 'Only mucking out, sir.'

'Thanks.'

George placed the other bucket beneath the spout and began working the arm of the pump, his eyes on Captain Kingsley's retreating figure. A moment later the growl of the Vauxhall's engine broke the silence, first muffled and then sharp and penetrating as the car backed out into the yard. Captain Kingsley drove slowly forward and stopped by George. He leaned over from the driving seat, one hand on the opposite door. George thought he looked uncommonly tired. Hangover, most likely.

'Had to get back early. I'm feeling a bit rough, as a matter of fact, so I shan't be attending the meet I'm afraid.'

George was flabbergasted to be the recipient of excuses. He blushed furiously and hefted the buckets, the muscles bulging on his thick, bare forearms. ''Sall right, sir. Sorry to hear that. Thank you, sir.'

Captain Kingsley kept him pinned and squirming with one of his funny looks, and then straightened up, giving the door of the car a little pat as he did so, as if putting a full stop to the exchange. Then he drove off, and the yard settled back into its early morning quiet. George could hear one of the horses stamping and banging about, disturbed by the noise of the car. He returned to his duties, shaking his head in bafflement.

Jack had gone no more than a hundred yards along the road when he saw Thea up ahead, walking in the same direction, her cape huddled round her, head bent. He drew level with her and stopped. She quickened her stride slightly and moved on. He switched off the engine, climbed down and called her. 'Thea! Where are you going?'

She did not reply. He ran after her and fell in beside her, matching his stride to hers.

'Where are you going?' he asked again.

'Nowhere.' Her voice was small, muffled, almost inaudible.

'What are you doing?' He laid his hand lightly on her sleeve and she stopped dead, though still staring ahead and not at him. Her face was white, the eyes circled by great bluish shadows.

'You look terrible,' he said.

She shot a small, bitter look at him. 'And you,' she replied, 'look fine.'

He deserved that. There was nothing he could say, nothing he could do, to soothe her pain. He felt wretched. 'I'm going,' he said, pushing his hands into his pockets and gazing down at the ground between his feet.

'Very well.'

'Obviously I wouldn't dream of . . .'

'No.'

'So I suppose I want to say goodbye.' It was funny the way that came out when actually goodbye was the very last thing he wanted to say.

'Right you are. Goodbye then.' She had adopted a kind of icy hauteur that was quite out of character. He hated to see her so changed, and through his doing.

'Thea—'

'Goodbye.' She began to walk rapidly away from him, her cape wrapped tightly round her.

Defeated, he turned and began to walk, then to run, back to his car. He got in, and drove past her, without looking back or taking his eyes off the road. When he was well out of earshot he threw his head back and yelled at the flat, grey sky: 'God damn it to hell!'

But he felt no better.

At breakfast, Venetia remarked pleasantly to Daphne Kingsley: 'Poor Jack. I'm so sorry he couldn't stay, that he's not well. You must give him our love when you get back. He wrote me the sweetest letter.'

Daphne sighed. 'It's so inconvenient for you . . .'

'For *me*? Not at all.'

'Just the same . . .' Daphne was discomforted. Knowing her son as she did, it was patently obvious that he had made an excuse, and gone for reasons of his own. It was not like him; he was usually so scrupulous in his day to day dealings with other people. She felt cross with him and embarrassed for her friends.

'The young don't think,' said Sophie, as if making the definitive statement on the matter. 'They don't think and they don't care.'

Sophie was not the ally Daphne would have sought. What did she know about it?

Venetia shook her head. 'He wrote me the sweetest letter, so apologetic. He obviously feels far from well. I think he's done the best thing.'

'But a dawn flit? I don't know . . .' Daphne sighed again and smiled at Venetia, knowing she understood, but regretful just the same.

'You mustn't give it another thought,' said Venetia, who had thought of little else for the past three hours. 'We all know each other quite well enough, I think. . . .' She looked to Ralph for support. He was making some point to Robert Kingsley, leaning forward and stabbing his forefinger into the tablecloth for emphasis. He looked up, feeling her gaze on him.

'I beg your pardon?'

'Jack—we understand, don't we?'

'But of course! If the poor chap feels a bit below par, let him escape and hide his head for a bit. It was my daughters, I suspect, keeping him up till all hours. I don't grudge him a bit of peace—Lord, no.'

My daughters . . . Venetia looked at Thea. Dulcie's place was empty, as usual. 'Will you be going to the meet, dear?' she asked. Thea looked up from her barely touched toast; it was unlike her not to eat a good breakfast.

'No, I don't think I will. Not this time.'

'I heard George out there very early. Are you sure?'

'I said so,' Thea snapped, then closed her eyes momentarily as if taking a grip on herself. 'I'm sorry.'

'Whatever's the matter with everyone this morning?' asked Sophie. Maurice removed his spectacles and began to massage his eyeballs. Venetia looked more closely at Thea. The girl looked exhausted. She was pale, and her eyes were sunk into their sockets, with great bruised shadows beneath them.

'Do you feel all right, dear?' she asked gently. 'You look worn out—you don't suppose you're going down with something too . . .?'

'I'm all right.' Thea added a smile to take the edge off her words. 'Thank you, but I am all right. Truly.'

'At least you staggered to the breakfast table,' said Aubrey, the voice of practicality. 'Dulcie's still festering in bed.'

'That's right,' said Sophie. She looked as though she would have continued the homily, but Ralph's eyes were fixed on her with such a threatening intensity that she fell silent, pursing her lips a little to indicate that there was more she might have said, at a different time and place.

Robert Kingsley leaned across and gripped Thea's wrist, giving it a little teasing shake. 'High jinks last night, eh? After the old fogies had gone to bed?'

'We played a couple of games.' His hand was hot and heavy. The normally pleasant jolliness of his face seemed crude and intrusive. She felt trapped. 'I wouldn't call it high jinks.'

'But would *we*?' he riposted. He and Ralph laughed.

Aubrey pushed his chair back, slapping his leg with a loud sound. 'Since Jack's not here and Thea doesn't feel like it, I think I shall forgo the hunt as well—' He looked up as Dulcie came in. She looked fresh and groomed.

'Good morning,' she said, with a little mock-curtsey, announcing herself, enjoying their surprise.

'Good heavens!' Ralph stared at her. 'What did we do to deserve this unexpected honour?'

'Why not? I was hungry. I decided I wanted some breakfast.'

'You're a sight for sore eyes,' said Robert Kingsley, as Dulcie went to the sideboard and helped herself to bacon. She sat down next to him, flashing him a brilliant smile as she did so.

'And how is everyone today?' she asked. Her manner was buoyant and bright; it was as though she fed off the lethargy of the others.

'We are without Jack this morning,' said Venetia. 'He wasn't feeling too well, so he's gone home.'

'Oh?' Dulcie buttered her toast and picked up a piece of crisp bacon in her fingers. 'What a shame. He seemed all right yesterday.'

'It's our contention you girls wore him out,' chuckled Robert.

Dulcie nibbled her toast like a squirrel. 'Us? Never! *Did* we, Thea?'

'I don't suppose so . . .' Thea could have died of shame.

Aubrey rose from his chair. 'Well, if you'll excuse me . . .'

Suddenly and quite unexpectedly, Maurice remarked: 'Dulcie acted Salome last night. She presented Jack with a sheep's head.'

Dulcie looked at him sharply. It was most unlike Maurice to volunteer information of this sort. He had taken the game out of her court and it annoyed her. Thea also looked at him. He seemed his usual self. He was obviously trying to please, to show Sophie that he had been part of the alleged 'high jinks'.

'She was excellent,' he went on. 'Quite an inspired performance.'

'Shut up, Maurice.' There was no mistaking the asperity in Dulcie's voice.

'A bit saucy, was it?' enquired Robert. 'Make a spectacle of yourself, did you?'

Dulcie shrugged pettishly. 'How silly,' she said. 'It was nothing at all, only a game.'

'You were awfully good.' Maurice seemed intent on walking the rim of the volcano, unaware of the sparks and rumblings so close beneath his feet.

'Nonsense.'

'Yes you were. Jack thought so. He guessed right away.'

'Of *course* he did!' It was Sophie who had spoken, and her tone was so unusually animated that she instantly had the attention of the whole room. 'It was a particularly well-rounded performance.'

'What on earth do you mean, Aunt Sophie?' asked Dulcie, her voice high and brittle. 'You weren't there.'

'Not for the opening act, perhaps . . .' Sophie smiled secretively. 'But I was there for the finale.'

'Really . . .!' Dulcie laughed and glanced round the table, eliciting the support of the others against this rubbish.

Sophie clasped her hands together beneath her chin in the manner of an *ingénue,* the gesture slightly obscene beneath her sour, elderly face. 'You sustained the character admirably,' she said. 'I can vouch for that.'

At this Ralph fixed his sister with a profoundly threatening look. 'Sophie!' he commanded. 'Perhaps you would be good enough to explain what you mean by all these veiled hints.'

'She doesn't mean anything,' said Dulcie. 'How could she?'

'You be quiet.' Ralph did not look at his daughter, but kept his eyes on Sophie. 'Come on, out with it.'

'If you want—'

'I do want.'

'Very well. As you know, I went to bed early last night.' She paused and gazed round at her audience. She could not remember the last time she had held the attention of so many people at one time; it was a heady and exhilarating experience. She relished the anticipatory silence. You could have heard a pin drop.

'We know, we know.' Ralph was impatient.

'Well then, in spite of retiring early I did not sleep well. For one thing there was a great deal of noise, and for another I find more and more these days that a lot of rich food does not agree with me. At about one o'clock the discomfort was so great that I decided to come down and fetch myself a glass of mineral water, and perhaps walk around a little . . .' She paused again. She could see the dawn of realization on the faces of her nieces. They knew now what was coming, but they would have to squirm while she finished the account in her own time. 'I encountered Mrs Duckham, on her way up to bed, who was good enough to fetch me a drink, and then I went to the library to find a book. As I came out I heard noises.' She waited, lips tightly closed.

'Noises?' It was Venetia.

'Yes. From the drawing-room.'

Another silence.

'What sort of noises?' asked Robert. 'Rats? Burglars?' He laughed hopefully, but no one paid him any attention.

'At the time I didn't know what the cause was. But at that moment Thea came down the stairs.'

Thea! Everyone looked at her. Another character comes onto the stage: how would she be implicated? The atmosphere quickened.

'She came down and fetched an orange from the dining-room,' continued Sophie. 'Then she wandered about as if looking for someone. She didn't see me. Finally she opened the drawing-room door, and there they were.'

'Who?' asked Maurice innocently. Thea's heart leapt, her cheeks burned with shame.

But Dulcie pushed her chair back violently, and threw her hands into the air. 'Oh what's the use? There *we* were, Jack and I!'

'Yes?' Daphne Kingsley was anxious. 'And—?'

Sophie rose majestically. 'Dulcie will tell you,' she announced. 'I saw it all—she dare not lie now.' And with that she left the room, leaving a vapour-trail of unease in her wake.

Ralph turned to Dulcie. 'Do you intend finishing this scenario?'

'By all means.' Dulcie was truculent. She was trapped, but she wouldn't give in. 'Thea caught Jack and me in flagrant —whatever you call it.'

'*Flagrante delicto . . .*' supplied Maurice in a hushed tone, mesmerized.

Someone let out a little gasp. The sheer awfulness of Dulcie's behaviour almost overshadowed the substance of her admission. Homer pushed the door open and ambled in, nosing round the table for crumbs. But the deathliness of the hush impinged even on him and he sat down beside Ralph's chair, gazing about him expectantly.

Ralph spoke first. He addressed Thea. 'Is this true?'

She nodded.

'*Look at me!*' She did so. 'Is it true?'

'Yes.'

'Dulcie?'

'Of course! You heard Aunt Sophie.' She stood up, with a flounce. 'I suppose I'm not welcome any more, so I'll run along.'

'Sit down!'

Dulcie plumped down again. Her cheeks were red, but her lips were firm, her chin tilted up. She was not yet ready to be castigated. Venetia leaned her elbow on the arm of the chair and covered her eyes with her hand. Daphne Kingsley rose and left the room. As she closed the door they all heard a little sob.

'Tell me one thing,' said Ralph. 'Who, in your estimation, was responsible for this—affair?'

'It takes two, you know—'

'I am aware of that!' Ralph's huge hand struck the table so that the cutlery leapt and rattled. 'I repeat,' he said, very quietly. 'Who?'

'I seduced him.'

That word! Thea could not look at Dulcie. How *could* she? How could she be so vain, so foolhardy, so cruel?

'Right.' Ralph was suddenly businesslike. 'Finish your

breakfast. I should like to see you and Thea in my study in one hour's time.'

'That's all right. I'll come now.'

'You will not. I could not be responsible for my actions. One hour.' He turned to Robert. 'Bob—a walk, perhaps?'

Robert Kingsley followed Ralph from the room. He suddenly looked like an old man.

Aubrey went over to the grate and riddled the fire loudly and vigorously. In the ensuing silence Maurice rasped the toast crumbs on his plate. Round and round; round and round. Dulcie picked up a piece of crisp bacon in her fingers and snapped a piece off. Munching, she looked round.

'He told me to finish my breakfast,' she said, in mock apology for her healthy appetite. 'So I am.'

The door stood open. After a few seconds there were brisk steps in the hall and Sophie reappeared.

'Did I leave my spectacles here?'

'I don't know,' said Thea automatically. She could not believe her aunt had actually walked back into the room.

'Why do you need them, anyway? It seems to me you see very well without them, and in the dark, too.' Dulcie's voice shook with fury.

Sophie ignored this remark. Indeed, she appeared not even to have heard it, fussing round her place at the table searching for the missing spectacles. 'Well, they're not here,' she said finally. 'So. What's everyone going to do today?'

Aubrey snorted with impatience. 'You may as well know, Aunt, that thanks to your good offices, and Dulcie's lack of discretion, the day is effectively ruined. But I for one have no intention of dancing attendance on the culprit. I shall go riding. Good day.' He stumped from the room. Thea felt a rush of pride and affection for him. His downrightness, his ruthless attention to the truth, that was what was needed. They were all too ready to participate in Dulcie's little drama, to play supporting roles to her self-appointed Grande Dame. Maurice sat as still as a statue.

Suddenly Sophie leaned across the table, beaming, and wagged her finger in Dulcie's face. 'What a naughty girl you are, Dulcimer,' she said, with revolting coyness. 'You always were a naughty little girl.'

At ten o'clock precisely Dulcie and Thea stood outside Ralph's study. The Kingsleys had left half an hour ago.

Aubrey was out riding. Venetia and Maurice were in their rooms; Sophie was in the library, doing her tatting. The house was quiet. Behind them, in the hall, Primmy was kneeling, sweeping the rug with short, even strokes, gradually working from side to side and backwards, very thorough. She knew that something had happened.

Thea knocked.

'Come.'

The study was a shambles. A shambles on a grand scale, a Wagnerian chaos. The servants were not allowed in there, so the stupendous untidiness was overlaid with dust and dirt. It was a small room, swamped beneath the darker side of Ralph's nature. It was as though here, in his private place, the violence in him let rip. Things lay about where he had dropped them. The wastebin overflowed with paper—letters to the newspapers, unpublished treatises, periodicals fallen from grace. The bookshelves were a pageant of disarray, with the books lying back to front, on their sides, some spread-eagled, open. One could imagine their owner furiously leafing through them in search of a particular reference and then, on finding it, leaving them like wounded on the battlefront, their pages limply hanging, spines broken, covers bruised and torn. The desk was invisible beneath more paper, some clean, some written on in Ralph's jagged, widely-spaced hand. In one corner lay an old jacket of Ralph's for the dog to lie on, and a couple of bowls, one full of fly-blown water. Dust was thick everywhere, and the wooden surround beyond the matted carpet was dotted with balls of fluff and dog hairs that drifted, like tumbleweed in a ghost town, when the door opened and closed.

On entering the study, Thea was always reminded of a picture she had seen as a child. It depicted Beethoven, old and deaf, his hair wild, his eyes staring, pounding the keys of his piano so hard that the strings started up from beneath the lid like affronted nerve ends. The picture had frightened her, with its image of a powerful personality raging against despair. And her father's study frightened her too.

He stood at the window, with his back to the door. She was sharply aware of his enormous size, his height, the width of his shoulders, almost blotting out the light. His arms were folded, his head drooping a little, as though deep in thought. But she knew that it was an act, that he would turn on them and be merciless.

Dulcie was determined to carry the fight to the enemy. 'Well,' she said, moving some old newspapers from a chair and sitting down, crossing her legs elegantly. 'Here we are.'

Ralph did not reply. He stood in silence for a full minute longer and then turned ponderously. His was a cold and slow-burning rage. Peppery and volatile in small matters, he could nurse a deadly and deliberate anger for days over something he considered important. It occurred to Thea that never in her whole life had her father struck her, or any of them, in anger. But the fact that he was huge and strong and fiery had been a warning in itself; they had always recognized that he could strike them, that perhaps there were times when he would have done, and only Venetia's presence had prevented him. And now she was not here. All these years they had been living on borrowed time, on credit. And now the reckoning had come. Thea felt physically sick with fear. He towered behind the desk, leaning his knuckles on the edge. Thea saw the huge veins, like ropes, pulsing on the back of his hands; the thick black hairs on the wrists; the sweeping moustache and broad, leonine brow. 'Do you know,' he asked, his voice tense and quiet, 'do you know what hurts me most about this squalid business?'

Thea shook her head. Dulcie drummed her fingers on her knee, surveyed her nails.

'It is the discovery that my daughters are *stupid*!' He spat out the last word with disgust. It ranked among the most potent in his arsenal of invective. 'I thought that whatever else they might be—headstrong, gauche,' he looked at Thea; 'venial and vain,' Dulcie's turn. 'That whatever their faults might be I had succeeded in inculcating the notion of civilized behaviour.' He paused. 'But now,' he went on, his voice cutting across introspection like a razor, 'I find that you are like a pair of children. Brainless, self-indulgent, inept. . . .' He waved his arm to indicate his scorn for them, the wealth of calumny he would pour on them if he had the time. Some pieces of paper that had been precariously piled on the edge of the desk slipped, and fluttered to the ground, spreading as they did so. Nobody picked them up.

'Dulcie.' His voice was sweetly conversational now, the surgeon's knife closing in on them to dismember them with ghastly accuracy. 'Dulcie, you disappoint me. You say you—' he paused, knitting his brow as if battling with disbelief, '"seduced" Jack Kingsley.'

'Yes.' She looked back at him, impertinent and direct.

'And how many men friends do you have, my dear?' She pouted. 'Very few.'

'And how many of the few have you known—in the Biblical sense, you understand?' He tilted his head, looking quizzically into her face.

'None.' She addressed her lap.

'I beg your pardon?'

'None!' she shouted, squirming with humiliation.

'Precisely. So we may look upon this episode as an exercise in self-gratification. You are bored. You believe yourself to be languishing in obscurity. So you cast about, and pick on Kingsley, a frequent guest, a friend since childhood.'

'You're talking as if he had nothing to do with it. Why should I take all the blame?' Dulcie was close to tears.

'My dear,' said Ralph, 'I am quite sure that the wretched Kingsley is even at this moment regretting every second of this unattractive liaison. Indeed he will probably regret it for the rest of his life. He was indulging you, Dulcie, as we have all indulged you from the moment you were born.'

'You'd never have known a thing about it if Aunt Sophie hadn't—'

'That will do! Your aunt is a bitter, unhappy woman. I make no excuses for her behaviour in the matter. What's done is done. And yet you displayed no delicacy, no tact, no shame when she betrayed you. Not even a little dignity. You speak aggrievedly of blame, but you went out of the way to call down blame upon yourself, you wanted your guilt. So. You have it. I blame you.'

Dulcie shrugged, her lips trembling, and began to pick at the frayed tapestry cover of the chair seat.

'I am ashamed of you, Dulcie,' went on Ralph inflexibly, 'not for what you did—it is one of the more enjoyable activities available to us—but because of your attitude to it.'

He transferred his attention to Thea. 'And you, Thea. How could you bring yourself to connive at this business?'

'I hardly connived at it. I don't even know what you mean by "connive".'

'Oh but you do, dear girl, you do. In your heart of hearts you were an accessory to this little crime as surely as if you had been in Dulcie's place.'

'What should I have done, then? Come and told you?'

'Just that,' he said. 'Until now you have been a valuable

90

corrective influence on Dulcie,' he went on levelly, as though the latter were not in the room. 'I have relied upon you to temper her excesses and flatter her good points, to criticize her with affection when she oversteps the mark. It is a responsibility you have discharged admirably. But last night, and this morning, you abdicated it.'

Thea took a deep breath. 'But whose fault is it that we are stupid?' she asked passionately. 'Whose fault is it that we are such a bitter disappointment, that we are immature and—uncivilized? Whose fault is it that we're eaten up with prurient curiosity? Whose *fault*?' She glared at him, hating him for the first time in her life. Hating him for his enormous male confidence and conceit, his intelligence, his selfishness, his blindness. 'It's your fault! It's all because of *you*! Oh yes, you wanted us to be well-educated and ambitious and original, and independent. But when did you teach us how to mix in company? When did you have a party for us, or ask people to the house? Never. You buried mother and now you're burying us, turning us into a couple of eccentric old maids before we've even started to live! Why can't we be like other girls and enjoy ourselves, why do we have to be so different? We live here like hothouse plants, dreaming our little dreams, whiling away our days, content to be your girls, persuaded by you that that is enough. Well it's not! And I, for one, am not content any more. The sooner I can escape and live my own life the better!' She stumbled and halted.

Ralph raised his eyebrows.

'And then we shall see who's independent,' she added, played out. She was trembling all over. Roused by the violence of Thea's speech, Dulcie stood up beside her. Ralph looked steadily at them for a moment, then threw his head back and laughed, long and loud, the noise of it filling the small room. With that laugh, he threw Thea's pride and anger and pain back in her face as if it were so much empty prattle. Outside in the hall Primmy, polishing the banisters, wondered what had occasioned so much mirth when the object of the meeting had so obviously been a gloomy one. When his laughter had subsided Ralph shook his head incredulously.

'Well spoken, daughter! A very fine speech. And now I will tell you what I have in mind for these two hothouse plants. Your prayers have been answered. I intend to send you to Vienna for an indefinite stay.'

He surveyed their faces with immense glee, as though

expecting them to crumble and form two small piles of dust on the worn carpet.

'I beg your pardon?' asked Dulcie.

'I am going to write to your mother's sister, Jessica von Crieff. She has continually over the past couple of years been asking you to visit her family there, and I have continually refused. I felt that you, Dulcie, were too young and you, Thea, had other and more absorbing matters in which to involve yourself. But now I see that this trip is exactly what you crave. There you will live as they live—very grandly, I believe. You will attend balls, parties and soirées without number, you will be taken here and there to operas and theatres, you will enjoy every kind of cultural and social delight. *And,*' he gave them a meaningful look, 'you will be expected to behave. It will be both salutary and entertaining for you. I am halfway through my letter to Jessica and it will be posted today.' He sat down and held out his arms before dropping his hands to his knees, as if to say: 'There you are. What do you make of that?'

'I see,' said Thea.

'May we go now?' Dulcie asked. Ralph nodded. She turned to leave, but as she slipped past Thea there was a wicked brightness in her face. When the door closed after her they could hear her footsteps, light as a feather, running up the stairs.

Thea confronted Ralph. 'It's not fair, you know it isn't. What about the business college?'

'What about it? You have the rest of your life. You said you wanted to escape.'

'Yes, but to live my life in my own way, not to fritter away my time in endless dancing and polite conversation!'

Ralph chuckled, but more gently this time. 'Still, my dear, you need a taste of society and frivolity, if only to make you realize fully how vacuous it is. You will go to Vienna. When you come back, we'll see about the college.'

'You gave me a typewriter.' Thea was close to tears. That had been the final betrayal, the kiss of Judas. But then, of course, that had been a thousand years ago, before The Fall. Since then her world had burst, fragmented, blown away, and left her rootless on a howling lonely plain.

Ralph picked up a pencil that lay on the desk and began to tap it, first one end, then the other, on the blotter.

'Does Mother know?' It was a forlorn hope, but Venetia

might rescue her, might see the injustice of this draconian punishment and stay Ralph's hand.

'No. But she will be delighted. She has always felt that I did not give enough time to your social advancement.'

'I don't want to go.' She meant it to sound strong and emphatic, but it came out like a plea.

'It will do you good. Besides, someone has to keep an eye on Dulcie.'

'Oh, it isn't fair! Why should I be her watchdog? Do you realize that this isn't a punishment for her at all? You're giving her exactly what she wants.'

'Not exactly. She is going to have to learn to curb her appetites and behave in a socially acceptable manner.'

'I see. In other words you are getting rid of both of us the very second we are any trouble to you, and leaving me to carry the responsibility. And it wasn't me who—'

'I know that.' Ralph's face was suddenly forbidding. Perhaps she had gone too far. He continued to play with the pencil. Tap and turn; tap and turn. She had the sensation that she was the pencil, being idly manipulated, that if she overstepped the mark she would be snapped in two. She went to the door. As she turned to close it after her she saw her father's face. The fierceness had gone, and was replaced by a look of sad understanding that was unbearable. She shut the door quickly, shame washing over her in a sour flood.

As she crossed the hall Dulcie appeared on the landing, bright-eyed and excited. 'It was all right in the end!' she exclaimed in delighted amazement.

'Yes.'

Dulcie ran off on some secret ploy, well-pleased with the outcome. Ralph's look, Dulcie's demeanour, something half-hidden in her own mind, were beginning to come together. When she saw her own face in the hall mirror, she knew what it was. She paused, staring at her own haggard reflection, and made herself say it, like an exorcism.

'I *am* jealous,' she said, through stiff, dry lips. 'I am jealous. And I *do* wish it had been me.'

Thea trailed along the corridor to her room. She was in the grip of a dreadful apathy. She was conscious of the broken shell of her life lying about her: the articles she would like to write; the horses in the stable, waiting to be ridden; the new typewriter, not yet tried. Where was the point in it all now that she was banished? At the door of her room she changed her mind. She did not want her own company now; she wanted comfort and sympathy. She knocked on the door of Maurice's room.

'Who is it?' Maurice was always cautious.

'Me. Thea.'

'Oh! Come in.' As she entered he was already halfway across the room to meet her, hesitated, turned and finally remained where he was.

'Am I disturbing you?' She glanced at the books on his dressing table.

Maurice waved his hand airily. 'I wasn't really concentrating.' He went to the table and shuffled his books into a neat pile. He had learned early in life that neatness and order were a good defence; it was possible to set up a barrier of tidiness between oneself and the world. If all one's possessions were safely put away in drawers and cupboards they could not be scrutinized by prying eyes. During Dulcie's reign of terror it had been possible to make things harder for her by placing everything out of reach. In those days his room had resembled a prison cell in its clinical sparseness. Now he looked at Thea sympathetically. 'I'm sorry. About this morning.'

'Why are you sorry, silly? You didn't do anything.'

'You know what I mean. I was sorry for you. What did Ralph say?'

'Oh . . .' She wrapped her arms tightly about her as if chilled, and walked over to the window. 'He's sending us to Vienna for an indefinite stay. It will do us good, you see. Teach us to behave like ladies, show us society at play —that sort of thing.' The bitterness in her voice shocked him.

'But I didn't think he cared for all that?'

'He doesn't. But he has decided, in his wisdom, that it's just what we need. It will give Dulcie a much-needed lesson in etiquette.'

'And you?'

'I go along to keep an eye on her.'

'Good Lord, that's a bit steep. I mean, she's the guilty party, and as far as I can make out she gets a holiday while you act *in loco parentis*.'

'It's not only that.' Thea stared at the skeletal elms that clustered round the curve in the drive. It was raining again;

George Rowles was raking the tyre marks from the gravel drive: a separate and uncaring world.

'Then what?' Maurice came and stood beside her.

She felt for his hand, found it, and folded it in hers. 'A lesson for me, too. There are things I need to learn. He may be right.'

'Oh.' It was obvious to Maurice that she would not enlarge on this other reason. She sat down on the window seat, giving his hand a little tug to draw him down beside her. She still gazed out, apparently absorbed in her own thoughts. Not wanting to disturb her he looked out also. It was from this window that he had watched the Tennants come and go, heard their voices raised in greeting and farewell, watched with fear and envy as they went about their business with long, purposeful strides. From here he had seen the motor cars roar round the drive like dragons, and clattering, bobbing groups of returning riders. Here he had seen a white-faced Thea returning from the hunt with Jack Kingsley at her side. She looked now as she had that frozen January morning: pale, lost, young, shaken.

'Dulcie behaved abominably,' he said, with sudden vehemence. 'It was unforgivable.'

She shrugged. 'Anything's forgivable.'

'I can't agree.' For once he would speak his mind. In all the years that Dulcie had made his life a misery he had soaked up the punishment and never complained, not wanting to be thought a whiner. But now that Dulcie had hurt Thea he could, and would, say what he thought with complete justification. 'What she did with Jack—it was no better than a prostitute.'

'Maurice!' Thea gave him a little smile of affectionate amazement.

'It's true. And the fact that she made that scene at breakfast, upsetting everyone, deliberately setting out to be shocking—it only proves my point. She will do anything for attention. Anything.'

'I know, I know.' Thea squeezed his hand. 'I know she's impossible. But she might not be like that if she had more fun. That's all she wants really—fun and gaiety and flirtation and all those things. But because she doesn't get them she goes wild and behaves badly.'

'You're very magnanimous.'

'Not really. Last night I could have killed her. Now I'm

just tired. I feel as though someone's been battering me all over. I just want to rest. Did you know,' she went on, almost dreamily, as though talking to herself, 'when Mother was a girl everybody did it at the big houseparties. I don't mean husbands and wives, I mean that people were specially invited who were having affairs with each other, and they used to look at the name cards on the doors and after they'd gone to bed it was all change. The done thing, in fact.'

'Surely Venetia—'

'Oh no, never Mother.' Thea shook her head. 'She loved Father, you see.'

Maurice did see. Thea set great store by her parents' love for each other; part of Dulcie's crime had been to spoil her picture of that love.

'Even the King—King Edward—had Mrs Keppel,' said Thea.

'Yes.'

'I saw her once. Did I ever tell you? She looked nice, but not as nice as Queen Alexandra. She was a very handsome woman, and serene, and strong. Strong enough to bear all those burdens, in a foreign country, and with a husband who couldn't resist a pretty woman. She never lost her dignity, and he always loved her, you know.' She looked at Maurice earnestly.

He was touched. It was as though she were in the confessional, testing the validity of her creed, seeing whether it still held good.

'What upset me about Dulcie,' she went on, staring anxiously into his face, eliciting his absolute understanding, 'was that she did it for herself. Not for love, or even friendship, or even—' she searched for words, 'for common human *warmth*. She didn't give anything, she didn't care, she *took*.'

Maurice nodded. He could imagine.

'I actually saw them,' she said quietly. 'And it wasn't making love, it was fornication—what the Bible inveighs against.'

'What a pity you discovered them,' said Maurice gently. 'If you hadn't, you might never have known.'

'What difference does that make?' Her voice broke. 'It's happened, and now everything is out of joint.' She covered her eyes. Her mouth shook a little; she looked very vulnerable.

'This Vienna thing,' Maurice said with distaste, 'when will you go?'

She shook her head, her hands still to her face, afraid to speak, afraid of crying.

'I was wondering,' he went on, although in fact the idea had only just occurred to him in a blinding flash, 'if you'd like to come to Cambridge for a few days. A little holiday—you know, away from it all. Before going to Vienna . . .' He floundered and stopped. He needed to have a surer idea of her reaction.

'Really? Are you sure I wouldn't interfere with your work?'

The sun broke through. She wanted to come. Maurice, gratified by his success, drew strength from it and pressed on. 'I shall go back tomorrow or the day after. There's nothing for me to stay for.' He paused, not wanting to appear plaintive but wishing to be frank. 'It's much better if I go back soon. I could find somewhere for you to stay—say early February. We could do all sorts of things. I could show you around, take you into college, you could meet some of my friends. Ralph won't want you to go before the end of February, I shouldn't think. The weather . . . the crossing . . . these things have to be arranged. I'm sure there will be time.'

Thea put her arms round his neck and kissed him, though he could feel tears on her cheek.

'Dear Maurice! I'd like to come. What would I do without you?'

Jack parked the car in the garage, leaving his case on the back seat, thrust his hands deep into his coat pockets and began to walk away from the house, down the hill to the long lake after which it was named.

It was eight o'clock. The early morning mist had almost cleared, but some still lay, like a great curling feather on the surface of the water. To the left of the lake the beechwood stood in a dark clump, its spiky crown dotted with old rooks' nests. On the far side, beyond the mist, the hill appeared more impressive than it actually was—mysterious and remote, the glass mountain of the fairytale. That was what it had been to Jack when he was a boy, not a real, muddy hill but a mythical place, full of promise. Although it was on Kingsley land he had not been allowed to play on it then; the far side of the lake was out of calling distance, and there was dangerous swampy ground in the valley in which Daphne had been convinced he would meet a sticky end. But on his first holiday home from Winchester he had set aside childish prohibitions and set out to climb the hill and explore the folly that stood at the top. The folly was the whim of a long-gone Kingsley ancestor. It had been built as a tall stone tower, but subsidence had rendered it treacherously unstable, and the top had crumbled away so that it now resembled a broken tooth jutting from the hillside. But once Jack had discovered it, it became his place, whatever he wanted it to be. He had spent hours there simply savouring his independence. Even the fact that it was dangerous, liable to fall down and crush him to pulp, merely added to its charm. He had no brothers and sisters, no one to share it with. The only other person he had ever wanted to take there had been Thea, and he had not known how to phrase the invitation. 'Come and see my secret hideout'—? Too childish; it was so much more than that. Besides, when she visited, it was always *en famille* and Dulcie would most certainly have pestered to be taken as well. So it had remained a secret, a bolthole.

Now he reached the lakeside and began to walk round it, through the woods. The cawing of the rooks splintered the still air. It was clammy down here, and he turned his wide collar up to meet the rim of his cap. He walked quickly between the silent regiment of trees, the sound of his footsteps deadened by the carpet of damp leafmould. A squirrel rippled across the path in front of him and ran in fits and starts up a tree, its sharp rat's face peering round the trunk at him. He emerged from the wood and began to climb the steep hill to the folly. The hillside was ill-drained and not much used as grazing land. It was pitted with rabbit burrows and here and there a chain of molehills erupted on its thistly, unkempt surface.

The folly stood on the brow of the hill like a drunk, just about keeping its balance, the fallen stones at the near side of its base acting as a kind of wedge to keep it upright. Jack toiled up and round to the back of the tower. Originally there had been a neat, arched doorway here, but now there was simply a gaping, jagged hole with dead, wintry tatters of weeds sprouting from between the stones. Jack ducked his head and went in. There was a smell. It was so strong and acrid that he gagged and clapped his hand to his mouth to stop the bile that gushed up his throat. At first he could see nothing in the semi-darkness, but he could picture the flat, earth floor, cracked by a few giant thistles, the walls scabrous with lichen and moss, and on the far side the now-rotten wooden box that he had carted up here as a boy. It had contained candles, matches, some sweets, string, bits of wire, a few copies of *Boy's Own Paper,* and an old tea caddy with his special treasures: penknife, marbles and fossils. Everything, in fact, that a resourceful boy needed to survive in the wild. Most of these things had long since crumbled and mouldered, but he had not had the heart to clear them out. No one came here, they were doing no harm. The mere fact that they had survived so long prevented him from moving them. Let them stay here, relics of childhood, until the folly finally fell.

Leaning his back against the stone wall he slid to the ground and sat there, his hands linked between his bent-up knees, looking out of the crooked doorway. A flat orange sun like a coin stood in the sky beyond the hill top. He felt as though he had at last reached sanctuary. He thought that Venetia would probably have read the note by now, and either accepted it or known at once that it was lies. Dulcie and Thea would have confronted each other and said —what? He could not forget Thea's face as she had backed towards the door, the essence of misery. He still could not believe that he had done what for all the world he had never intended.

He shook his head, defeated. The smell in the enclosed space suddenly assailed him again, and his curiosity was pricked. He glanced over at the dark mass of the wooden chest. The rising sun illuminated another, longer shape next to the box. He rose and went over, putting out a foot to nudge it.

It was the corpse of a man. Due to the degree of putrefaction and the generally unkempt appearance of the body it was hard to tell of what age, but it was clearly that of a vagrant. When Jack pushed it with his foot it shuffled into a different position like a pile of sand, shifting without moving. Some piece of tattered cloth fell away to reveal the face, or what was left of it, grinning wildly up at Jack. Small flies scurried over the cheeks, in and out of the eye sockets; the grizzled hair lay lankly on the earth floor like sheep's wool.

Jack stared for a moment, then glanced at the chest. It had

been rifled. The tea caddy was open, and the contents removed and scattered. One small object was unfamiliar, and he picked it up. It was a small oval medallion or perhaps a picture, presumably the tramp's property, but too filthy and chipped to be clearly identified. He put it in his pocket. In the corner behind the body the last of the candles had been embedded in the ground, and had burnt almost to the earth before going out.

Jack stooped and laid his cap delicately over the face. Then walked quickly from the folly and began to run, stumbling down the hillside. The bolthole was no longer his.

CHAPTER FOUR

'Sweet Saturday night,
When your week's work is over,
That's the evening you make a throng,
Take your dear little girls along.
Sweet Saturday night   .'
  Victoria Monks –'Sweet Saturday Night'

On the Saturday after Christmas Primmy had a day and a night off. She could leave Chilverton House mid-morning, or whenever the cleaning was done, and was not expected back until Sunday evening.

She looked forward to this break with mixed feelings, since she would be going home. On her regular days off she didn't make the trip up to London, but generally went into Bromley, shopping with Joan or on her own—she was not afraid of her own company. But a weekend meant home.

Primmy had no illusions about her family. She was certainly not ashamed of them, nor was she especially proud. When her youngest brother, Sam, had been killed on the railways two years ago her mother had not even let her know until she had visited three months later. This was at least in part because Mrs Dilkes's writing skills couldn't stretch to it, but also because she knew it wasn't that important to pass on the news. Primmy had hardly seen Sam since she had gone into service, when he had been a snotty-nosed six-year-old, and there had been little enough love lost between them then. When Primmy did find out about his death, she was philosophical. She had experienced no sense of loss, for she had lost nothing. Lots of people told her again and again that it was a 'crying shame' and a 'shocking waste', but she herself had neither cried nor been shocked. It had happened, and there was an end to it.

As regards her mother, Primmy did not love her, nor did she feel she owed her anything. If there was anything to owe she had done her bit, and more, both as a child and since entering service. Of the seven shillings a week she received from Mr Tennant—good wages for a parlourmaid—she passed on three shillings to her mother, and she visited as often as she could. The only feeling she had for her was a grudging respect for simply having survived the rigours of life in the East End, almost always without financial support and, since Mr Dilkes' flight, without adult company either.

But Primmy could never quite forgive Mrs Dilkes for having sold her into service. She could still remember, with a twinge of humiliation, the way her mother had talked about her when they went to be interviewed at 20 Ranelagh Road. 'She's a good, clean girl! . . . she'll do as she's told . . . used to helping me around the place with four brothers and sisters . . . I'm sure she'll give satisfaction, ma'am.' She had spoken of Primmy as though she were a commodity, which in her eyes she was: a commodity to be bartered, a good strong, capable girl, well able to bring in a few shillings a week.

They had fought about the decision the night before. Primmy had stubbornly refused to go, and her mother had taken her by the shoulders and shaken her like a rag doll, while the other children sat round, watching with pop-eyed interest. Primmy had retaliated with a push that had sent Mrs Dilkes staggering across the kitchen, careering into a clothes-horse laden with washing and sending it flying. The children, half-thrilled and half-terrified, had scattered like chickens to roost round the edges of the small room. The washing was spoilt, and that had really got Mrs Dilkes' dander up. She didn't slave away over other people's dirty linen just so her stuck-up little cow of a daughter could tip it all on the floor. She set about demonstrating her skills in the field of unarmed combat. She was no taller than Primmy, but she was tough and wiry and she had bested her husband most Saturday nights for many years; a fourteen-year-old girl presented no serious problem. She had sprung forward, grabbed Primmy tightly and expertly by the hair at her temples and wrenched her head from side to side till the girl's eyes watered with pain. She had bawled at her that she *would* go to Ranelagh Road and she *would* get the job, adding for good measure that if this were not the case she, Lily Dilkes, would personally see to it that Primmy's life was made a misery. Further protest had obliged her to box Primmy's ears with all the force at her disposal, while holding her bent back across the table. Primmy had neither agreed nor begged for mercy, but she had stopped arguing because she was physically unable to continue. This had been enough to signify her capitulation to Mrs Dilkes, and the matter was closed.

These events had added extra irony to the next day's interview. Primmy had set out doggedly silent. Not sullen, but absolutely mute. Mrs Dilkes was anxious (and Primmy knew it) to effect a rapprochement with her daughter so that a united front might be presented to Mrs Tennant. It was downright awkward to have to take along a silent, staring great girl with nothing to say for herself. Besides, Primmy had a large plum-coloured contusion on her left cheek-bone and Mrs Dilkes wanted to be sure that its true origins would not be disclosed. But Primmy had not spoken. She had quite ignored her mother's wheedlings and cajolings, and her attempts to catch her out by asking sudden questions of an unconnected nature. She had been up early, made herself neat and clean and prepared tea and porridge. The rest Mrs Dilkes could manage on her own.

She had stood like a statue while her mother grovelled to Mrs Tennant, her eyes fixed on the window. Outside she could see two little girls playing in the garden, one dark and one fair. They ran and jumped and twirled, but she could not hear them, only her mother's voice droning on. At last Mrs Tennant had turned to her and said, in her gentle, refined voice: 'Miss Dilkes—or may I call you Primrose?'

It had been a sweet moment indeed, one to relish and savour. Here she was, dragged along against her will, and blow me down if that wasn't the politest anyone had ever spoken to her. Her mother had looked aghast. But she had got the job.

As they left, Mrs Tennant had come over to her and asked: 'Whatever have you done to your face, my dear?'

But before she had been able to blurt out some appropriate lie, her mother had said: 'It's my husband. 'E's a bit free with 'is fists I'm afraid. It's the drink, you see . . .' She nodded darkly, woman to woman. Mrs Tennant had looked confused, then understanding.

'Oh, of course . . . I'm so sorry. Poor child.'

This blatant treachery had shocked Primmy, not least because it could almost have been true. It seemed too much to add to poor Mr Dilkes' catalogue of crimes, long enough already. As soon as they left the house she had resumed her mantle of silence.

Soon after that Mr Dilkes had gone, and the already

threadbare fabric of Primmy's relationship with her mother had finally torn. They no longer warred, they simply kept their distance.

On this Saturday, after the chores were done, Primmy went to her room on the top floor and got ready. She took off her black dress and discarded her apron and cap; she would need clean ones on Monday, anyway. She had already, the night before, packed a small bag with a few things, and laid out her day clothes on the chair. She put on a blue suit with a tight-fitting jacket, and a pale blue blouse with insets of open work at the collar and cuffs. She knew she would be cold, so she decided grudgingly to take her old black coat, rusty and worn though it was. In addition she had wrapped a piece of flannel round her middle, beneath her bodice, as a precaution. She kept her thick black stockings on—she had packed her one fine pair—and she had also packed the piece of Honiton lace, just in case; she had no plans to go out, but one never knew . . . finally she put on her best black shoes and her hat. The hat was Primmy's pride and joy; she only owned two, and this one was one of her few extravagances. She had saved up and purchased it at Sugden's on her last day off. It was black fine straw, in the shape of a large inverted rose bowl; the brim was wide and straight, shading the eyes, and around it was draped a long, spiky feather, a very dark blue shot with turquoise. Primmy felt very dressed up in the hat, particularly as it added a good four inches to her overall height. When the crowning glory had been duly speared with a hat pin, she put on her gloves, picked up her case, glanced critically round her impeccable room for the umpteenth time, and went down.

At the foot of the back stairs she put her head round the kitchen door. "Bye, Mrs D.'

'Primmy! You startled the life out of me!' Mrs Duckham was pouring strong tea from an enormous willow-pattern pot into a collection of cups and saucers. Primmy could hear the others in the servants' hall. The cook put the pot down and stared at Primmy's hat.

'You're wearing it then,' she remarked cryptically.

'Like it?'

'Very grand, I'm sure.' It was clear that Mrs Duckham did *not* like it. Primmy had known she wouldn't. The hat was a little too grand for a parlourmaid on her day off; it showed that Primmy was committing that most heinous of crimes in

Mrs Duckham's book: putting on airs and aping her betters.

Primmy knew better than to protract the exchange. 'I'll be off then. I did that mending, it's in the cupboard on the first landing.'

'Thank you. We'll see you back tomorrow then.'

'That's right.'

'In time for your tea?' Mrs Duckham called after Primmy's receding back view.

'Don't bother about that. But don't worry, I shan't be late.'

Mrs Duckham sucked her teeth. That hat!

Primmy went through the yard and round past the stables to the side gate. She waved to Meredith who was saddling up one of the horses. He smiled and began to say something, eager to gossip, but she walked on, pretending that she hadn't heard. She was afraid of horses. There were only a few things she feared, and her policy was simply to avoid them. She marched briskly on her way. The carrier's van was to meet her on the corner of the Ewhurst Road.

It was a frosty morning. It occurred to her that she had not been out of doors for any length of time more than four times in the past six months. She covered miles each day but all of them on stairs, along corridors, in and out of rooms. She gazed at the outside world through windows. Now its freshness and abundance were almost too much for her; she felt like a nun emerging from years in a convent.

The biting cold attacked her. Her toes began to ache and her nose and cheeks were numb. Of course, she was cold for most of her working day, her hands were usually mauve and her skin goose-pimply beneath her dress, but that was a condition of work in a big house. One laid endless fires but did not sit by them. The greatest luxury was to huddle round the fire in the servants' hall, though Collingwood and Mrs Duckham had their chairs in the plum positions next to the fender. You could always stand by the stove and lift your skirt so that the warm air breathed up your drawers, but Mrs Duckham understandably forbade this practice when she was trying to cook. In spite of all this Primmy had not been prepared for the icy air outside. She walked faster and faster, stumbling on the rough, frozen ground. She hoped Tim Warren would be on time.

He was. As she reached the road he appeared, puttering up the hill from the village in his green van with the curly red and white writing on the side. It rasped to a halt beside her and she ran round in front and climbed up into the passenger seat with relief. Tim Warren eyed her as they moved off.

'Going up to London then, are you?' he asked unnecessarily.

'That's right.'

'You look real fine.'

Primmy glanced at him sharply to ascertain whether or not this was a compliment, and found that it was. 'Thank you,' she said accordingly.

Tim Warren fancied his chances with the ladies. Driving about between Bromley and the surrounding villages as he did, delivering goods to the shops and the big houses, he considered that he had a wealth of experience. Like a sailor who boasts of a girl in every port, Tim reckoned he set hearts a-fluttering in at least half a dozen different places. But his self-important grinning and winking merely set Primmy's teeth on edge. He was doing it now, so she folded her hands on her lap and resolved to watch the countryside go by and pay him no attention. But one of Tim's most useful attributes was a remarkably thick skin. After a few minutes, during which his eyes were only intermittently on the road, he asked roguishly: 'Someone waiting for you up in London?'

'No,' replied Primmy emphatically.

'I don't believe it,' said Tim, changing gear with a grind and a flourish. 'I bet the lads flock round you up there in the Big Smoke. That's it, isn't it, there's a whole crowd of them waiting to see you? Go on, admit it.'

'I shall do no such thing.'

'Going out tonight?' he went on, unperturbed, relentlessly pursuing his highly individual picture of Primmy's activities. 'Sweet Saturday night,' he yodelled lasciviously, 'when your week's work is over . . .' He peeked at her again. 'Eh?'

Primmy turned her head, intending to quell him with yet another crisp retort. He had black curly hair beneath his cap, and a spotted kerchief knotted at his throat. His lips displayed a grin of such gigantic proportions and unshakeable good humour that she found herself smiling back.

'That's it!' he cried, delighted at yet another conquest notched up to the infallible Warren charm. 'That's my girl—"That's the evening you make a throng, Take your dear little girls along . . ."'

Primmy cursed herself for having involuntarily opened the

flood-gates of his genial self-esteem. She would be given the full treatment now, all the way to Bromley.

When Tim stopped to let her alight at the station, he asked, 'Want a lift tomorrow evening, then?'

'Only if you're going that way.'

'I'm going that way for you, princess.'

'Please don't put yourself out. I can easily take the bus and walk. I've done it before.'

'What, all that way in the dark?' He made saucer-eyes of affected shock. 'And in that hat? I'll be going. See you tomorrow.'

'Thank you. I should be on the five o'clock.' Primmy smiled at him again, safe now that she was out of the van. He treated her to a final face-folding wink and slammed the door.

There were a number of people on the London train, it being Saturday. When she had bought her one-and-sixpenny return ticket she walked up and down the waiting carriages for a minute or two before selecting herself a corner seat in a compartment with a woman and her small daughter. She detected a certain timidity in herself these days; she simply wasn't used to free and easy mixed company, her life had been ordered and confined for too long. She had been braver in that way as a child. When she was thirteen a boy called Tony, who lived in their street, had treated her to a show of his privates in the schoolyard. They had miraculously changed shape and size under her fascinated scrutiny, and she had cautiously touched them, which had reduced Tony to a state of panic-stricken excitement. He had at once suggested that they take the experiment a step further, but this had not been such a success: on both sides the spirit had been willing but the flesh proved hard to handle. The net result had been uncomfortable—Primmy could still feel the cold, gritty bricks rasping her back—and singularly lacking in transcendent passion. They had finished up sticky, bewildered, but still friends, and Tony had bought her a saucer of cockles with cash purloined from his father's beer tin.

This was the sum total of Primmy's sexual experience. She was not only a naturally moral girl but an intensely single-minded one. A childhood spent watching her mother swimming against the tide had instilled in her such a savage determination to better herself that she closed her mind to everything else. A boy called Dick had come closest to

107

winning her over but that had come to nothing in the end, she reflected a little sadly.

The train pulled in at New Cross and she got together her things and lit out briskly on the walk to Deptford. Her initial sensation of being a recluse recently returned to the world was here increased a hundredfold. The harsh, noisy vitality of the streets buffeted her. There seemed to be throngs of people on the pavements, all shouting at the tops of their voices, and the road was crammed with traffic, most of it horse-drawn. Because it was Saturday, a feeling of incipient holiday pervaded everything. There were stalls in the sidestreets, and on one corner a Punch and Judy show was playing to a large and vociferous crowd. Above the general hubbub she could distinguish the familiar nasal cry of a totter. The area was full of them, and during the summer they kept their horses hobbled down on the flats by the river. As children she and her friends used to go down there and feed them titbits and, if they were lucky, got a ride, all of them in a bouncing joggling row on the broad slippery back.

She passed a pub. Its window shutters were open on to the street and there were as many as twenty-five men standing outside in the cold, drinking their beer. As she walked by, head held high, a child approached the window with a large, chipped enamel jug. She could remember doing that herself, going along with the jug to buy porter at twopence a pint for her exhausted parents. But those had been in the good days, when Dad had been at work. Later he'd done his boozing alone, and instead of making him genial and demonstrative he'd wasted its good effects on his cronies and then staggered home to wreak havoc on his family. On these occasions he had been, quite literally, 'not himself'. An amiable, easygoing man, he drank to deaden his disappointment with himself, but as the effect wore on the disappointment was exacerbated by guilt over another day and another few bob wasted, and he'd light into whoever was nearest. The next day he would be first sullen and silent, then grudgingly apologetic, finally crazily optimistic—and this was the mood in which he'd go to the pub again, always half-expecting to meet a man who knew a man who knew of a job to be had.

Primmy felt very conspicuous as she passed the pub. She was sure the men were staring after her, making remarks . . . After about half an hour's walk she turned into Grove Road.

It looked the same as always. It had a certain grimy cosiness; even in this weather some women were sitting or standing on their front door steps, aprons on, watching the world go by, and children clattered and squawked in the street. Nobody recognized her, and she didn't look for faces she knew but marched on to Number 15. For the first time since starting out she felt faintly uneasy about the hat, but to stop and remove it now would simply draw more attention to it.

At the door of Number 15 she stopped, raised her hand to knock, then thought better of it and walked in. Her mother was by the stove, giving Eddie a bath. It seemed incredible to Primmy that after all the months away she should walk in at this precise moment, an unusual enough event at the best of times.

'Hallo, Ma,' she said.

Mrs Dilkes straightened up, surveyed her for a moment, than gave a curt nod and returned to the job in hand. ''Allo, Prim.'

Primmy walked over to the tin bath and bent over. Eddie, now twenty-one, sat with his knees bunched up, staring down into the scummy, tepid water, dabbling it idly with his finger.

'Hallo, Eddie. Eddie? It's me, Primmy, come to see you.'

He looked up phlegmatically. Something like recognition slipped across behind his slightly unfocused eyes, and Primmy smiled encouragingly, but he only returned to his dabbling of the water between his legs.

'He's no better then,' said Primmy, setting down her coat and case on the table and reaching to remove her hat pin.

'What d'you expect?' asked her mother. 'There's no miracle healers in Deptford as I know of.'

Primmy watched her mother systematically scrub Eddie's back. As children they had all been habitually dirty; it took real elbow-grease to remove the grime from their skins, which partly accounted for the infrequency of their baths. Now that Eddie was a full-grown man the task was still more arduous. The scrubbing completed, Mrs Dilkes slooshed some of the murky water over him, and hauled on his arm to encourage him to stand. This he did, like a leviathan rising from the ocean bed, the water streaming off him in torrents. Mrs Dilkes whipped a small towel off the stove rail and laid it on the ground, and handed him another, not much bigger, with which to dry himself. She pointed to the towel on the ground.

'Come on then. Out with you,' she said testily. Eddie obeyed, and began to dry himself with slow, apathetic movements. Primmy gazed sadly at his large frame. He had always been big, the biggest in the family, but his body lacked tension and maturity. He was like a great overgrown baby, soft and clumsy and somehow unfinished.

'How are you managing?' she asked her mother.

'What? Him?' Primmy nodded. 'It's not so bad. It'll be the workhouse or the asylum for him when I'm gone, but he's not much trouble to me now.'

'How about the others?'

'I don't see much of Frank,' she said, referring to Primmy's third brother, on the railways like Sam. 'He's got others to think of now—Sarah's expecting again.'

'How many's that?'

'It's her third, but he makes good wages. Lisbeth brings in a bit here though, and Eddie helps me at the shop Thursdays.'

'Shop?'

'Tailor's shop.' Mrs Dilkes avoided her daughter's eye. She knew Primmy's views on sweated labour. Primmy had even offered to give her more of her wages, but she wasn't having any of that. It was her life, after all.

Primmy knew better than to comment. 'What can he do to help?' she asked.

'He does as he's told,' said Mrs Dilkes threateningly. 'He sweeps up the bits, makes tea—sews buttons on sometimes, but Mr Steen don't like that.'

Primmy could imagine. She had been to a sweatshop with her mother once before, just after Dad had left home: a dark, damp basement packed with exhausted-looking women, like prisoners, working with a dreadful manic concentration for a measly few pence. Their skins had been pallid, their eyes dull and incurious like those of dead fish on the fishmonger's slab. Some women simply fell asleep at the table, and no one took any notice, except to wake them up if their employer was on his way. A lot of them were severely bronchitic and the sound of their wheezy breathing and hacking coughs had filled the fetid air. Primmy had been frightened. It was an aspect of her own way of life, her own people, that she did not care to accept. Her life till then had been rough poor, frequently squalid and sometimes violent, but the air in that room reeked of a more terrible and deadly affliction—despair.

Eddie finished drying himself and dropped the towel on the ground. Mrs Dilkes slapped him sharply on the buttocks.

'Pick that up!'

He stared at her bovinely.

'Go on! Pick it up!' She smacked him again, her hand making a loud report on his damp skin. Primmy watched curiously. Eddie was huge, her mother tiny. But Eddie stooped, picked up the towel and handed it over. Mrs Dilkes fetched a bundle of clothes off the chair.

'Here.' She put them down next to her son. 'Get those on.' She looked at Primmy. 'I'll make a cup of tea.'

'Thanks, I could do with one.' Primmy watched her mother perform the familiar ritual. The brown, chipped teapot stood on the shelf above the stove; her mother had to reach on tiptoe to get it down, but she hated being helped. The tea caddy, black with a red and gold picture of a well-heeled Indian couple on it, stood next to the pot. The gold had largely rubbed off now, giving the smug Indians a patchy, part-worn appearance. Mrs Dilkes put four large spoonfuls in the pot and shifted the black kettle into the centre of the hob to speed up the boiling of the water.

Eddie was in a fix with his trousers. He had got one leg in, and was vainly treading the air with the other, unaware that he was standing on his braces. Primmy went over to him; she had always been able to 'manage' Eddie.

'Come on, let's get you sorted out.' She stood next to him, with one arm round his waist. With a sharp, competent tug she whipped the braces out from beneath his right foot with a snap, and spread the left trouser leg on the floor, holding the waistband at a convenient height for his pawing foot. Leaning on her heavily, he plunged his foot into the hole. Primmy slipped from beneath his heavy arm and went round to the front, pulling his braces up over his shoulders with an affectionate pat. As she went to button his trousers she started back in surprise.

'Eddie!'

His impressive erection peeped at her between the 'V' of his open trousers. She looked up at his face. It was benign, a serene smile of immense affability spread all over it.

'Primmy . . .' he mumbled.

She smiled at him. Her mother's back was turned, making the tea. Primmy put her finger to her lips, and glanced in that direction. Eddie nodded and grinned and began to struggle with his buttons over the mercifully subsiding bulge.

Mrs Dilkes poured tea, and handed Primmy a cup, and half a large mugful for Eddie. They sat down at the table. Eddie stirred his tea vigorously and continuously, chink, chink, chink, until the dark brown liquid spiralled into a whirlpool in the centre of the mug. He was still smiling to himself.

'He's very cheerful all of a sudden,' observed Mrs Dilkes suspiciously. 'Eddie, what you been up to?' She leaned forward, trying to catch his eye. He was bent over the mug and a fringe of his lank, straight hair shielded his face.

'It's all right,' said Primmy, 'he just recognized me, that's all.'

'Well, that's something I suppose,' said Mrs Dilkes. 'What you going to do with yourself then, Prim?'

'I don't know . . .' Primmy picked up her cup and sipped the strong, sweet tea. 'Tell you what, though. I've got some money for you.'

'Oh.' Mrs Dilkes never liked to appear too eager. She needed the money all right, but she would never ask for it, or be too thankful when it appeared. She wouldn't give Primmy the satisfaction. Primmy opened her bag and fished out the cash, in a brown envelope.

'Shall I put it on the shelf?'

'That's best.' Primmy slipped the envelope behind the wooden clock on the mantelpiece and returned to the table. 'So what's Lisbeth doing these days?' she asked, not really interested but knowing she should enquire.

'Working up the corset factory. Twelve bob a week, not bad.'

'No, not bad at all,' said Primmy dutifully.

'Getting wed soon, you know,' said Mrs Dilkes reprovingly. Despite her own demonstrable failure in this department she still regarded marriage as the ultimate triumph in any girl's life. In her eyes, Primmy was an old maid already. And there was no need for it, either. She was just too blooming stuck up.

'Oh? No, I didn't know. Anyone I know?'

'Jim Saunders. Him that works round the grocer's.'

'I remember.' Jim Saunders. He had always been a highly

respectable boy. At school he had been stodgy, and a sneak to boot, and in later years he had worn a brown overall at work, and a brown suit at home, and conducted his life generally in shades of brown. But then, thought Primmy, who am I to criticize anyone for dullness, still single and in service. 'When's the great day, then?' she asked.

'In the spring, most likely,' replied her mother. 'They're going to live near his people up the road.'

'Very nice.' That was typical, of course, reflected Primmy. Lisbeth had always been ashamed of her own family, what with their poverty and Eddie being simple and Mr Dilkes having done a bunk. Primmy despised her for her lack of backbone. As a child, everything had reduced Lisbeth to tears and wails of 'It's not fair!' as if she, poor little Lisbeth Dilkes, were the victim of some grand diabolical plot. It had made Primmy's blood boil then, and it was clear things were no different now. Lisbeth had latched onto the most respectable boy in the neighbourhood and, having got him, was making damn sure she kept her distasteful origins at arm's length.

'She'll be home at six,' said Mrs Dilkes. 'I've got a bit of bacon for tea.'

'Fine. Ma . . .' Primmy approached the subject cautiously. 'Would you like to go out tonight? I mean, we could go to the variety. I've got the money, it could be my treat. Must be ages since you went out.'

'I don't know about that.' Mrs Dilkes was clearly completely thrown by the suggestion. The fact that she had always enjoyed a good show, and hadn't been to one for she didn't know how long, didn't prevent the conflict that raged in her breast. For against that fact was set her ingrained determination not to appear pathetic, nor to accept favours too readily. Something occurred to her, a useful aid to martyrdom.

'It's him, you see.' She nodded at Eddie.

'I thought we could ask Lisbeth to stay with him.'

'She won't like it.' Mrs Dilkes shook her head lugubriously.

'So what?' Primmy felt irritation rising. 'I bet she doesn't help much as a rule.'

'She's a good girl,' said Mrs Dilkes doubtfully. 'She works hard and she's got a lot on her mind recently, what with getting married.'

'Well, as to that, I work hard too and I don't get to see a

113

show very often these days. I bet Lisbeth and Jim go all the time.'

'I wouldn't say that.'

'More often than us, anyway.'

'Yes . . .'

'Well, then.' Primmy was becoming more determined by the second. She wanted to go to the music hall, and taking her mother would save her going on her own and also fulfil her vague sense of obligation. She watched her mother's small, lined face, the cramped battleground for several warring urges. The sharp cheekbones were red with broken veins, the thin mouth set in a tight, straight line.

'*If* Lisbeth stays,' she said eventually, her voice leaden with pessimism.

'She will.' Primmy realized she sounded almost threatening, and added: 'She could have Jim round. They could have a nice quiet evening together and pretend they're married.'

'Hm.' Mrs Dilkes was pretty sure Primmy was making some kind of joke but as she was not accustomed to either the detection or appreciation of jokes she let it pass.

'That's settled then.' Primmy picked up her things and started for the stairs. 'Usual place?'

'There's nowhere else that I know of,' responded her mother acidly.

Primmy went up the narrow staircase. Number 15 Grove Road had one room downstairs with a small scullery off it. Upstairs, there were two rooms. When the whole family had lived there, Lisbeth, Primmy, Sam and Frank had shared the one room, boys in one bed, girls in the other, and their parents and Eddie had had the other room. Now that only Lisbeth and Eddie remained, the arrangements stayed the same, so that Lisbeth had the second room to herself. She had made the most of this, Primmy noted. Lisbeth had laid down a veneer of niceness and respectability over the shabby utility furniture—china animals, a cloth on the chest of drawers, a highly coloured alpine landscape on the damp-patterned wall over the black grate. The second bed had gone: that meant end to end in Lisbeth's, but Primmy was used to that. It was her sister who wouldn't like it, after all this time.

She put her case in the corner next the narrow wardrobe. She wouldn't unpack it, there was not enough there. She went over to the mottled window and looked down into the back yard, and beyond that into the back yard of the house opposite. To right and left, the same view, all the yards small and gritty and hemmed in by blackened brick walls. But you could tell, she reflected, which houses were still proper homes, where there was a man about and a modicum of domestic harmony. Those were the yards with little flower-beds, empty now but still neat and tended. Others had tubs, or climbers to conceal the walls. The Dilkeses' yard was a weed patch, with giant thistles forcing their way through the broken concrete and rubbish. When Mr Dilkes had been around the yard had sported some cabbages and potatoes, and a handsome show of geraniums in a sawn-off barrel.

Ruefully, Primmy thought to herself that she had actually loved her feckless, hopeless father, just a little. There had not been much room in her life for the luxury of finer feelings, but Albert Dilkes on a good day had inspired a few. He had been a gentle, genial man, who badly needed to be liked. It had not been entirely his fault that he couldn't hold a job down: part-time dock workers were the chaff of the work force —only a handful got work each day and the rest were discarded to the winds. It was no wonder they became demoralized. Her father's had been a sunny, pliant nature, but soft. At least he hadn't turned to petty crime, like so many; he had simply become more and more harassed and downcast, his gloomy lethargy only broken by the bouts of drinking and subsequent violence. Two little incidents in particular stood out in Primmy's memory. On one occasion, after he had received a notably savage tongue-lashing from his wife, Primmy had sat down by him on the front step, and he had showed her a photograph: a small oval picture of a young woman.

'Guess who?' he had asked, holding the photograph under her nose.

'Don't know.'

'Go on, guess.' There had been something half humorous, half desperate in his voice. Primmy was no fool, his tone gave him away.

'Must be Ma,' she said.

He had nodded, replacing the picture slowly and dreamily in his pocket. 'That's right. Your mother.'

'She was very pretty.'

'Ho, yes. She was a catch, Lily Masters was. I always liked flower names—that's why we called you Primrose.'

'Oh.' Primmy felt embarrassed, but very conscious of her responsibility. He needed her to stay and listen.

But after a long, sad-eyed silence his only other remark had been: 'Primmy girl, don't you ever forget how pretty your Ma was.'

'No.' She had shaken her head energetically, and he had patted her knee and wandered off to the pub, whistling 'Lily of Laguna', always one of his favourites.

Now Primmy thought: they didn't give Lisbeth a flower name; she had come too late.

The other incident had been the matter of the dog. Mrs Dilkes had come upon her husband feeding butcher's scraps to a stray in the back yard. The animal had been a canine down-and-out, rickety, mangy, old through neglect if not in years, and a practised sponger. The sight of the dog wolfing down fat and lights right outside her back door was too much for Mrs Dilkes, who had flown at them, sending the animal scuttling agitatedly into the house where the children had treacherously released it, and raining blows on her husband's averted head and shoulders.

'You realize you've given that good-for-nothing dog more meat than we see in a week, do you?' she had screamed, pummelling him with her small, hard fists. This was a point which Mr Dilkes appreciated all too readily. The shame of being a bad provider was daily brought home to him. But feeding the dog had made him feel a bit better about it. Here was a creature who was actually lowly enough to accept something from him, and with obvious gratitude, too. Why, even the small sum Mr Dilkes took to the pub was provided by his wife, and that not out of kindness but because she wanted to put on a good front. The cupboard love in the mongrel's rheumy eyes had been balm to Albert's wounded pride.

Primmy sighed and turned away from the window. She supposed that all these things, these distant, disconnected happenings, had made her what she was today. And yet they seemed so separate from her, belonging not simply to another place and time, but to another world.

She went downstairs and spent the next hour or so playing dominoes with Eddie at the table, while her mother ironed, and drank tea. At six o'clock as predicted, Lisbeth returned. Primmy at once rose, and went over to kiss her dutifully. 'Hallo, Lisbeth.'

'Hallo, Prim. Had a good journey?'

'Yes thanks.'

'Hallo, Mother.' *Mother!* Trust Lisbeth. Primmy watched as her sister kissed Mrs Dilkes, but not Eddie. He did not look up, but continued to pore over the dominoes, breathing heavily, his face only inches from the table top. Lisbeth took off her coat, hat and gloves, and laid them fussily over the back of a chair.

'What about you, then?' said Primmy, as Lisbeth poured herself a cup of tea. 'Getting married. Congratulations.'

'Thank you. Yes, we're very happy.'

'And got a place, too, Ma tells me.'

'That's right. We got a nice little flat, not far from Jim's folks.'

'Lovely.'

Mrs Dilkes slapped a folded tablecloth down on the table so that the dominoes scattered. Stoically, Eddie began to put them away in their box, one by one. Primmy rose to help lay up: Lisbeth stood by the window, sipping her tea. She was a plump, pale girl with frizzy dark hair pulled back into a bun. Her rather pudding face might have been jolly, had not its bulges been set in an expression of stolid self-righteousness. Her walk, even her stance, was dumpy, smug, prematurely middle-aged. A clutch of vicious juvenile resentments stirred and growled in Primmy as she distributed knives and forks.

'I thought I'd give Ma a treat,' she said casually. 'Take her to the variety at the Empire. You could stop here for this evening, couldn't you?' She carried on with her task, not looking at Lisbeth, but the pause after her question told her it had come as a shock. Do her good.

'Mm? What do you say?' she repeated, straightening up, hands on hips. Mrs Dilkes was busy, shaking the rashers about in the pan murderously, refusing to take any part in the affair.

Lisbeth gestured uneasily at Eddie's hunched back. 'What, mind him?'

'Just the once. Ma does it all the time, after all.'

'Jim was going to come round after tea . . .'

'Just the job! The two of you can spend a cosy evening here, then. You won't be on your own, I mean.'

'I don't—'

'Thanks ever so much. Lis.' Primmy went over to her mother and peered over her shoulder. 'That smells good.'

In the event, they had left Lisbeth on her own, the unfortunate Jim having been subjected to a fiercely whispered diatribe on the freezing doorstep and packed off home; obviously minding Eddie did not constitute a properly romantic activity. Primmy felt no pangs of conscience. Eddie was no trouble; she had set him to some knitting, with big needles and string, and he was perfectly quiet and content.

They left at seven. Second house at the Empire was at eight, and they had a bus ride and a bit of a walk to get there. On arrival, Primmy had bought two seats in the fourpenny balcony; the rough and tumble of the threepenny gallery, she reckoned, might prove too much for a woman of her mother's age and uncertain temper, and she didn't want the evening marred by a scene that could be avoided. Their seats were rather round to one side, but they had a good view of the stage. The theatre was packed. The bobbing rows of heads in the grandly-named 'fauteuils' down below wavered beneath a pall of smoke. The noise was a warm, enveloping roar.

Primmy glanced speculatively at her mother. She had got quite smartened up, in a long black double-breasted coat, and a hat like a big plant pot with a once-bright artificial tea-rose on the front. Her pinched face looked out like a monkey's from beneath the brim. She had worn the very same hat on the occasion of the old Queen's diamond jubilee, when there had been a street party in Grove Road. There had been a man with an organ out on the pavement, and a little mongrel dog in a red jacket that had danced to the music with everyone else. You could go into any house in the street and eat and drink, and Mrs Dilkes had laid on ham sandwiches and fruit cake and tea. It had been a very happy day, and the hat with the rose had looked very becoming with a pink blouse and striped blue and pink skirt. Albert Dilkes had been in work, then; life had been briefly and treacherously imbued with a lustre of well-being.

The show began. Primmy glanced at her programme sheet. There was the usual assortment of turns—jugglers, acrobats, contortionists, comedians—and at the top of the bill a singer described as 'The Nightingale of the Thames', one Victoria Hubbard. Primmy sat back and prepared to be swept along by the entertainment. It was not hard; the music was lusty and tuneful, the audience noisy in its participation, and even the bad acts had a robust vitality that precluded criticism. The Flying Fortunatis, resplendent with waxed handlebar moustaches and costumes encrusted with artificial gems, flew with varying degrees of agility through hoops, over tables and each other, and finally into a teetering, mind-boggling human pyramid that lasted just long enough to gain applause before collapsing like a pack of cards. Drayton Doubleday—'the Biggest Laugh you've ever had'—was an enormously fat man whose speciality lay in appearing to be clumsy but always saving himself from disaster at the last moment. His vast bulk hurtled, pirouetted, cannon-balled from one side of the stage to the other to the accompaniment of delighted 'oohs' from the audience, never quite culminating in the cataclysmic crash they expected and half hoped for. A young man with a fine tenor voice serenaded them with among others, 'Lily of Laguna', during which Primmy did not look at her mother, and he was followed by a strident, aging actress, Mabel Hyde, who delivered two dramatic monologues, both long and unremittingly gloomy.

By the time Victoria Hubbard tripped on the audience was hot and volatile. But the Nightingale of the Thames was a match for them. She bore a resemblance to Marie Lloyd upon which she had capitalized nicely. She was pert, busty and would run to fat in middle age. But for now, in white organdy and pink roses, with a twinkle in her eye and a thin, true cockney-sparrow's voice, she was everyone's sweetheart or favourite daughter. Suggestive, but never threatening; seductive, but jolly; outrageously lewd and touchingly sentimental. She had them in the palm of her plump white-gloved hand. To end with, she sang 'The Boy In the Gallery' and up there in the close-packed warmth the faces shone like lanterns, and handkerchiefs, answering the song, fluttered like snowdrops. Mrs Dilkes sat very straight and upright, but Primmy thought she detected a dampness on her gaunt cheekbones.

In common with most of the audience Primmy and her mother did not stay for the bioscope show. The jerky, flickering black and white pictures were dull after the noise and colour of the variety, and they had a bus to catch. Outside, it was freezing. An icy wind hurtled down the street and the two women buttoned their coats tight and walked fast. Suddenly, Primmy felt a touch on her arm.

A voice said: 'Primmy? Is it—?' The words were snatched back into the darkness by the wind.

She stopped and looked up, her eyes watering with the cold. Two people stood there, a young man and a girl. Both were smiling, the man confidently, the girl with a sort of excited anticipation.

'I'm sorry . . .' Primmy was confused; she didn't recognize either of them. Her mind was still running on the show. People were barging past, fighting the cold, anxious to get home.

Behind her, her mother said brusquely, 'See you at the stop.'

'Ma—oh all right.' Mrs Dilkes hurried on, and Primmy looked back at the young man. He was about her own age and height, fair, and smartly turned out in a checked suit, red waistcoat and curly-brimmed hat. But in spite of the dandyish clothes and the neatly trimmed and curled moustache his face was likeable, young and carefree with clear summery blue eyes. He stood there, smiling broadly, presenting himself to her with such evident pride and pleasure that in the end Primmy could not help but remember.

'Dick?' she murmured. 'Dick?'

'The very same! I told you she'd remember,' he added to the girl at his side, who nodded energetically, her eyes on Primmy's face.

'She should do,' said the girl without rancour. 'You talk about *her* enough.'

Primmy smiled nervously. 'Does he?'

'If he's told me about you once it must be a dozen times. You made quite an impression on him.'

Dick laughed delightedly. 'Primmy, I'm sorry. This is my wife, Alice.'

'How do you do.' Primmy put out her hand but Alice stepped forward and kissed her cheek. It was a gesture of genuine friendship but it made her feel old.

'I feel I know you, anyway,' Alice was saying, Dick's arm about her shoulders.

Primmy stared. He had hardly changed, for all that he looked such a toff. He'd always taken a pride in his appearance, even in those days, the sort of lad who could impress a would-be employer. But apart from the natty suit and hat it might have been yesterday that he'd sauntered up and announced: 'I'm Dick. What's your name?' The evening had been hot and dusty and languorous, the grey of Deptford gilded with a stale, sweet yellow light, the end of an afternoon at the end of summer. It had been on a day off from Ranelagh Road. She'd worn a blue dress with white daisies printed on it and a wide collar trimmed with white ric-rac. She'd already grown out of it, really, and it was faded, but it had been a pretty dress just the same. They had gone for a walk and watched the boats on the oily river and shared a sticky bun. Afterwards as he walked her back to Grove Road there had been an air of celebration about the mean little streets, with people meandering just for once, milling about, soaking up the sunshine and smiling at one another. They had met again a few times on her days off, but then the Tennants had moved to the country and nothing had come of it.

And now there he stood, as smart and handsome and smiling as ever, quite good enough to eat in fact. Certainly Alice thought so, for she hung on his arm like a limpet.

'Where are you living now?' asked Primmy, anxious to emphasize her unfamiliarity with Dick's circumstances.

'We've got a little place in Southwark, over the garage.'

'The garage?'

'We have to move with the times, you know,' he said with a grin.

'His own little business, it's ever such a success,' added Alice, gazing up adoringly into his face.

Primmy, watching them, saw clearly how it was, and how it would be in ten years' time. Dick would be stouter, slightly self-important, but so jolly that no one would mind, and Alice would beam benignly in the background, with a baby in her arms and three or four children grouped round her skirts. They'd be comfortably off, hard-working and god-fearing, the very paragons of domestic virtue. And it could all have been hers.

'How wonderful!' she said. 'I should have known you'd do something clever with your life.' She looked at Alice. 'You're a lucky girl.'

'Oh I know,' said Alice. She was pretty, Primmy noticed, in the way that the Nightingale of the Thames had been pretty: a likeable, workaday beauty with a curvaceous figure and a cheerful smile. Ideal for Dick.

'I must be getting along,' she said. 'My mother's waiting at the bus stop and if we miss the last one we'll have to walk.'

'Do give my regards to her, won't you?' said Dick. He'd

always had a knack with Mrs Dilkes, treating her far better than she deserved.

'I will. Sorry she dashed off. I don't think she recognized you.'

'No offence taken. But remember me to her, just the same.'

Primmy turned to go, but Dick caught her sleeve. 'How long have you got? Couldn't you come and visit us?'

'Oh do,' echoed Alice. 'That would be nice.'

Primmy floundered. 'I'm only home for one night, I go back tomorrow afternoon. I really don't think . . .'

'For old times' sake?' He gave her a frankly flirtatious smile, teasing and tempting her. But it was the smile that decided Primmy. She could not go.

'I'm sorry, Dick. It's so kind of you both, but I really haven't time. Perhaps another day . . .' She began to walk away. ''Bye. It was so lovely to bump into you.' She started to run, to show them that she must catch the bus, but also to escape. Tears, not just from the cold, slipped down her cheeks and were dried by the bitter wind.

The bus was drawing up, and her mother was about halfway down the queue. She did not acknowledge Primmy's breathless arrival. They just made it; Mrs Dilkes got the last seat and Primmy stood in front of her, uncomfortably pressed against her bony knees. She hoped her reddened eyes and nose looked like products of the cold. But when eventually some people got off and she was able to sit down by her mother, Mrs Dilkes said: 'I told you you should've encouraged him when you got the chance.'

'You knew who it was then?'

''Course I did. He was the only lad with a bit of style in our area and you were too posh for him.'

'That's not true. I went down to the country.'

'You could have made sure of him by then, if you'd wanted to. And now he's found someone else, and doing very nicely by the looks of him.'

'He runs his own garage in Southwark.'

'There you are. I knew he'd do all right for himself. Well, I hope it teaches you a lesson.'

'You don't understand.' It was true though. She had never really wanted Dick; her eyes had always been fixed on some point over his head. Her tears had been not for Dick, but for the old days, for the gentle flirtation in the tarnished London sunshine, for the sticky bun and the daisy-printed dress. For belonging. Now, she belonged nowhere. Not at Chilverton House, for all the Tennants' liberal thinking, and certainly not here. She was on her own.

'You've never known what was best for you,' Mrs Dilkes was muttering. The incident had given her an opportunity not to be too grateful for her evening out.

'Shut up, Ma,' said Primmy, suddenly tired of her mother's carping. 'Mind your own business, can't you.'

'Oh very well. That's the way it is. Very well, then, I'll be quiet, don't you worry.' They completed the bus-ride and the walk, locked in their separate silences.

When they got back to Grove Road the house was dark, both Lisbeth and Eddie were in bed. Mrs Dilkes took an oil lamp and Primmy lit a candle and they went up directly, by mutual consent.

Lisbeth was curled snugly in the brass bed, her frizzy hair spread about the pillow, her mouth slightly open. Shivering, Primmy changed into her cotton nightdress and slipped into the bed from the other end. As she did so she heard her mother bumping about in her room, sucking her teeth and generally making a performance. Wearily she climbed out of bed again, hugging herself against the cold, and peeped round the door.

'Anything the matter?'

'Eddie—he's wet the bed.'

'I'll give you a hand.' She relit the candle and took it in, placing it on the greasy little wood and wicker table next the bed. The pale, fluttering light showed Eddie half-sitting, half-lying on his bed. The acrid smell of urine filled the room, but years of sharing beds with younger brothers and sisters had made Primmy unsqueamish—she was quite used to this type of nocturnal activity. It was plain her mother was angry. Eddie looked bleary and confused. She went over to help him off the bed but paused, shocked.

'What's this?'

He was tied to the bedstead. Not very tightly tied, but enough to restrain him from getting out. A piece of none-too-clean washing line went across his middle, crossed beneath the bed and tied again on top. His natural lack of physical co-ordination had seen to the rest. Primmy began to struggle with the knot. She could not remember when she had been so angry.

'Did Lisbeth do this?' she asked in a ferocious whisper.

123

'She must've. Here, sit him on my bed. I've got one spare sheet.' Mrs Dilkes seemed more put out about the bedding than the rope.

'Does she often do this? Do you?'

'I never done it in my life.' Mrs Dilkes was quick to deflect the censure in her daughter's voice, but she could not honestly say she felt that strongly about the matter. It was as good a way as any of keeping Eddie out of harm's way but unfortunately it had led to bed-wetting, which was inconvenient. She had gone to great pains to teach Eddie to use the chamber pot at night, and here were all her lessons gone to waste.

Primmy discarded the rope and helped Eddie up. His expression, looking at her, was pitiful. He was confused, and felt guilty and ashamed without quite knowing why. Primmy sat him on the edge of her mother's bed and kissed his face.

'That's all right, Eddie,' she said quietly, stroking his hair back off his forehead. 'That's all right.'

Mrs Dilkes fetched a sheet out of the battered wooden ottoman in the corner and Primmy helped her remake the bed with swift, practised movements. Then they tucked Eddie up again and Primmy fetched her candle and went to the door.

'No one should *ever* do that, you know,' she said, with absolute conviction, knowing that she was right.

'I've never done it in my life,' replied her mother again, crossly. Primmy believed her. Whatever her faults, Mrs Dilkes was not lacking in common sense: she would be able to see the drawbacks of such a measure. But it was obvious that she had condoned it, or at least turned a blind eye to its being perpetrated by others from time to time. However, there was no point in going on at her; she had stood by Eddie in her grim, impatient way; she was not the culprit.

'Night, Ma,' said Primmy, and went back to her room.

As she got into bed she let fly a hard, jabbing kick at Lisbeth's plump backside.

'Ow! Steady, Prim, look out!' The voice was sleepy but aggrieved. Primmy lay down on her side, rigid, holding the bedclothes in a bunch under her chin. The bed joggled as Lisbeth resettled.

'Lisbeth.'

'Mm?'

'That was cruel, what you did to Eddie.'

'Oh, that . . . he doesn't even notice.'

'But he wet his bed. He was miserable. If you tie him up you're not even letting him do the things he can do for himself. It's so selfish.'

'He's all right . . .' It was clear Lisbeth was dropping off again.

'Oh hell!' Primmy's face contorted with rage and frustration, she pulled the blanket up over her head. 'Damn stupid little cow!'

The next day she rose early, leaving her sister still asleep and breathing stertorously, and packed her things. The Honiton lace lay, neatly folded, unworn. That was the trouble, there was nowhere she could wear it. There was one thing she wanted to look for, before she went, a sort of memento. It was the picture of her mother as a girl. Mrs Dilkes and Eddie were down in the kichen, so she hunted swiftly and silently through the upstairs cupboards, but it was not to be found. It was as though her father had never existed; there was not the slightest trace of him anywhere. Disappointed, she gathered up her things and went downstairs. Mrs Dilkes displayed neither surprise nor sadness at her early departure. Eddie sat at the table eating a slice of bread and dripping. Primmy went over to him and put her arm round his shoulders. He continued to munch, his eyes vacant. He was 'low' this morning, she could expect no gestures of affection from him. She gave his shoulders a squeeze.

'Look after him, Ma.'

'I do, don't I?' Mrs Dilkes was affronted.

Primmy went to her and kissed her gaunt cheek. It was true, after all. 'Yes, you do.'

'See you next time, then, shall we?'

'Yes, probably . . .'

Primmy paused. There were a million things she had not said, just about everything, in fact. There was no more time now, so she stuck to salient matters: 'If I don't see you soon I'll send the money as usual.'

'Right.'

Primmy left. Outside it was still cold, the wind of last night screeching down Grove Road, tearing at the dusty little privet hedges and sending the rubbish bouncing and dancing in the gutters. Primmy made a silent salutation as she went, for she knew that she would not be back. She could no longer pretend, even to herself, that her past had a hold on her. She would have to be her own woman now, but it would have been nice to have found the picture.

'Whose party are we going to this evening?' Thea asked Maurice. They were sitting in a small café in Trinity Street, having had lunch, and were now sipping coffee. It was Thea's second day in Cambridge. Maurice had found her a bed in digs in Jesus Lane under the auspices of a cheerful, energetic widow, one Mrs (Don't-Have-Any) Moore, for which the rent was fifteen shillings a week all found. For Thea, the accommodation might have been the Ritz for the pleasure it afforded her.

Maurice, when he answered her question, was studiously non-committal. 'Chap by the name of Louis Avery. He lives on my staircase.'

'What's he like?'

'I thought I told you.'

'No, I meant what's he *really* like? What do *you* think of him?'

'He's all right.' Maurice idly drew a face on the steamy window. When he got to the mouth he turned it down in a kind of disapproving grimace. 'Actually, I don't care for him all that much.'

'I knew it!' Thea laughed. She had been pleasantly surprised to see how much more confident her cousin was away from Chilverton House. He had been decisive, demonstrative, masterful in his care of her. He even looked different, taller and more erect; his clothes appeared to fit him better, and he wore them with a slightly wry, professorial air that suited him. Now, in the snug and humid atmosphere of the café, he resembled an amiable and perspicacious bird, his eyes sparkling behind his glasses.

'So why are we going?' she asked, still laughing, shaking her head at his perversity.

'No reason not to. One doesn't refuse a perfectly genuine invitation simply because of a vague feeling. We're not at daggers drawn or anything. Besides, I think you might enjoy it.'

'Don't go just because of me.'

'I should have to go anyway, I've run out of excuses. Anyway, there's nothing radically wrong with the fellow, he's just not my cup of tea.'

'Why?'

'He's pushy. Very bright, very able, very ambitious. Wants to go into politics.'

'And you mistrust him.'

'In a way. I expect it's just that I anticipate being trodden on by people like him as they race up the ladder of life.' He looked at Thea teasingly. 'You'll like him.'

'After all you've said about him, that's hardly flattering.'

'Women do like him.'

'I'm not "women".'

Maurice shrugged. 'We'll see. In any event his ladykilling activities will be somewhat curtailed tomorrow. I understand he has a lady friend from London staying in Cambridge for the weekend.'

'It sounds as though the place will be cluttered with imported females.'

'Among whom,' said Maurice with an old-fashioned air, 'you will be the handsomest.'

Thea heard him take a little breath as though he were about to say something else, but instead he cleared his throat and there was silence. Maurice was thinking of Primmy. Primmy, who so often bustled uninvited into his idle imagination to torture him with all the fires of hell. If he had ever needed evidence of the intrinsic sexuality of his nature, Primmy provided it. He had exchanged no more than a handful of words with her in his entire lifetime; she was separated from him utterly, by class, by rank, by her own inclination or indifference. And yet her physical proximity, in that house where he was always tense, made him so wretched he could hardly bear it. All day he would avoid looking at her, only to lie awake in the dark and picture her in her top-floor room, removing her black dress, her cap, letting her hair down and brushing it. And then he was bitterly ashamed of himself, because she was a servant and he could not even intimate his feelings without appearing crass and ludicrous.

'Cheer up,' Thea was saying. 'It won't be that bad, and think of the post-mortem we'll be able to have.'

He stared at her absently.

'Maurice?' She smiled, puzzled.

'Oh, quite,' he said. 'Finished?'

Later Thea went into Maurice's bedroom and changed. She had brought her things with her, for it had not seemed worth returning to Jesus Lane on a cold, dark evening. She put on the green Christmas dress and the necklace Jack had given her. When she was ready, Maurice put the guard before the fire, turned down the lamps, and led her up the staircase two floors. The stairs were cold and draughty. Maurice knocked on a door and it opened wide, emitting a warm wave of light and conversation.

The young man who had opened the door held out his arms in greeting. 'Maurice! Excellent fellow, it's good to see you. And this must be Thea.' He took her hand and led her forward into the room, surveying her at arm's length like a painting.

Maurice said: 'Yes, this is my cousin, Thea Tennant. Thea, this is our host, Louis Avery.'

'How do you do.'

'Hallo, Thea.' He stepped forward and kissed her cheek. 'Welcome.'

'Thank you.' She glanced at Maurice, but his face was owlishly impassive.

Louis took her arm. 'Come on, Thea, let us find you a glass of something.'

'Yes—how lovely.' She was propelled expertly to a table in the corner. Champagne was duly poured, with a flourish, and handed to her with a little bow. Louis picked up his own glass and clinked it against hers.

'Here's to better acquaintance.'

'Certainly.' She took a gulp of champagne and felt suddenly awkward; he was just staring at her, smiling. To break the silence, she added: 'It was very kind of you to include me in your invitation.'

'Hardly. Your cousin is a splendid chap but not, shall we say, an ornament to society?' Thea smiled. 'Whereas you . . .' He made a courtly gesture taking in her hair, dress, shoes, everything. 'Delightful!'

Thea looked round for Maurice. Ornament to society or not, she needed his comforting presence. Louis followed the direction of her eyes.

'Don't worry about him,' he said. 'He'll be deep in blamelessly academic intercourse by now. Your cousin is a fellow who doesn't like to be rushed, and I have a tendency to rush people.' He wagged his finger. 'I have learned my lesson.'

He turned to greet someone at his side, and Thea studied

him. He was short, trim and dapper. His hair and moustache were dark, his eyes quick and brown. All his movements were spare and accurate, as though he never suffered from indecision, but there was an archness in his manner that aggravated her.

'Do I annoy you?' he asked pleasantly, his neat hemispherical eyebrows shooting towards his hairline. Heavens, had she been *that* transparent?

'No!' Her voice was quite shrill with guilty protest. 'Of course not. What an extraordinary question.'

'Not really. I do expect frankness, you know. I am frank myself.'

'I am being frank, and you do not annoy me.'

'Ah!' He detected the testiness in her tone. 'Now you *are* annoyed.'

'No. Disconcerted, perhaps . . .'

'Disconcerted?' He pondered this for a moment. 'Yes, a very sound, polite, upper-class word covering a seething multitude of sins.'

'You're determined to misinterpret me.'

'I? A seeker after truth, no more. Tell me,' he put a confidential hand on her shoulder, 'what does Maurice say about me?'

'Nothing.'

'Rubbish! People always prepare the way in these matters.'

With relief, Thea remembered something both true and unincriminating. 'There was one thing. He said I should like you.'

Louis hooted with laughter. 'Good old Maurice! Clearly meaning that he doesn't. Good God . . . !'

He was still laughing when a voice broke in: 'Louis. Stop playing games with the poor girl.'

Thea turned to acknowledge her saviour. 'Andrea!'

Louis glanced from one to the other. 'You know each other?'

'We were at school together.'

'Say no more.' Louis rolled his eyes heavenward. 'I shall leave you to your enthralling memories. Andrea darling, don't monopolize Thea. A waiting world, you know . . .' With a sweep of his arm he indicated the rest of the room. 'And,' he added, putting his arm around Andrea but leaning towards Thea, 'there is smoked salmon, there is York ham, there is Stilton cheese, on the other side of the room.'

'Go away, Louis.' Andrea pushed his encircling arm away, smiling at Thea, not really annoyed. 'Go and corner someone else.'

'I am already gone.'

Despite a sporadic correspondence, the last time Thea had met Andrea Sutton had been at a meeting of the Strathallen School Association, three years ago. Then, their relationship had still been intact. Now, she sensed, there was ground to make up. Andrea had certainly changed. For one thing, she looked astonishingly smart, in a brown velvet suit and cream shirt with a tobacco silk artist's bow at the neck. Her sandy hair was pulled back into a chignon, but teased into curls around her face. She would never be pretty, but as always she had got the very best out of herself. She was in command.

Andrea spoke first. 'So. What brings you to this seat of learning?'

'I'm here visiting Maurice, actually—you remember Maurice?' She pointed him out.

Andrea peered, thoughtfully. 'Hmm . . . yes, of course. Maurice.'

'He's in his final year now. His rooms are down below, on this staircase. I'm really a complete interloper here. Are you—?' She tried desperately to recollect Andrea's last letter, but failed. The letters always seemed more taken up with ideology than news.

'If you're about to ask whether I'm studying here, the answer is no. The dreaming spires hold no allure for me. I'm still in Town.'

'Wait a minute. You're not Louis's lady from London, are you?'

'Heavens, I suppose I must be, though not entirely Louis's.'

Thea felt awkward. Andrea reached past her and helped herself to a small cigar from a box on the table. She lit it, drew on it expertly, and stood with it cocked in her right hand, surveying Thea through the smoke.

'And what have you been doing this many a day, Thea?'

Thea was suddenly seized by the conviction that Andrea would not want to know, once she began telling . . . 'Oh, nothing much. I taught at the local school for a while, and I still help there from time to time. And I've been writing a bit.'

'Really?' Andrea's voice brightened with interest. 'What, if one may ask?'

'Just some pieces for the *Country Companion*—you know, rural subjects, nothing earth-shattering.'

'You mustn't run yourself down. Getting into print is nine-tenths of the battle. Once you've had a few things published you're in the running, they take notice of you.'

'They?'

'Editors. I speak from experience, I've been working on the *Herald* for the past eighteen months.'

'Andrea, how marvellous! *The Herald?*'

'As ever is. I got a job as secretary to the features editor, and I'm now a junior—very junior—reporter on the women's page.'

'You didn't tell me.'

'I've been more involved with other things.'

'The WSPU?'

'M-hm.' Andrea drew on her cigar.

'Have you . . . Are you very militant?' Thea trod carefully.

'I have been to prison, if that's what you mean, but only for four days, and no forcible feeding.'

Her matter-of-factness shocked Thea. 'It must have been terrible.'

'Not as terrible, in a way, as I should have liked.' She smiled and was, for a moment, the old aspiring Andrea, more recognizable. 'I was cheated of my martyrdom.'

'But what happened?'

'I went to a conference at Caxton Hall to protest against the Cat and Mouse Act—you know what I mean?' Thea nodded. Under the act, suffragette prisoners on hunger strike were released when they reached a critical stage, only to be re-arrested as soon as their friends and relations had nursed them back to health. Andrea went on: 'I attended as a representative of the Women Writers' Suffrage League. Anyway, at the end of the meeting a dozen or so of us were nominated by the chairman as delegates to take our resolution to the Home Secretary. He refused to see any of us, and when Mrs Pethick Lawrence tried to put our case to some MPs nearby the police seemed to appear out of nowhere. A few of us refused to budge . . .' She shrugged. 'We were arrested.'

'You were very brave.'

'Very determined, and very stubborn, I should say. The constable who put me in the Black Maria kept on asking if he was hurting me . . .' She shook her head, as if baffled by human behaviour. 'Anyway! You *must* come to Town, you've been buried in the country far too long.'

'Perhaps.' Thea suspected that the implied criticism of her family might be a retaliatory move. The only time Andrea had been to stay at Chilverton House, it had not been a success. She had been intensely argumentative, and Thea, as her patron, had been exhausted by the burden of responsibility she herself had to carry. Alone, Andrea had been sweet reason itself, but as soon as the family congregated for any purpose Thea found herself caught in a constant verbal crossfire. Her loyalties on both sides had been strained to breaking point.

She changed the subject. 'I may come in the autumn, I do have plans. But Dulcie and I are going abroad for the summer.'

'Oh? The Grand Tour?' Andrea was sarcastic.

'We're going to visit family in Vienna.'

'Fancy *having* family in Vienna!' Andrea leaned over and stubbed out her cheroot. Thea would have liked very much to pull her hair but instead she gazed politely about, seeking rescue. It came, in the form of Maurice.

'Andrea, I had no idea you knew Louis.'

'Well, there you are—it's surprises all round. How are you, Maurice?'

'Fine. But peckish. Shall we drift over there, Thea? Louis must have spent a fortune.'

Thea was delighted by Maurice's calm; he was neither dazzled by Andrea nor curious about her. He was indifferent.

As they made their way across the room, Louis called out: 'Ragtime everybody!' He wound up the phonograph. Above the hissing and crackling the stealthy lilting strains of a piano rag tinkled seductively. He bounded over and swept Andrea into his arms. 'Let's show them how it's done.'

Amid cheers and whoops they took to what there was of the floor when the other guests had pressed back to the sides. Andrea was a little too stiff to be a natural dancer, but there was no doubt she and Louis knew all the latest steps. As she watched, Thea thought that she would never be able to fathom her friend—if Andrea was still her friend. She was a sufficiently ardent suffragette to spend four nights in Holloway gaol, but enough of a socialite to demonstrate ragtime with someone like Louis Avery. And on top of all that still

132

secretly resentful of what she saw as the Tennants' privileged existence.

The music was delightfully syncopated, slyly tuneful. Thea tapped her foot and glanced hopefully at Maurice, but he looked glum.

'Let's get some food,' he said, and though she would have liked to watch the dancing, Thea followed him to the table.

Later, as they were taking their leave of Louis, Andrea pressed a newspaper onto Thea. 'Don't look so taken aback. It's a copy of *Votes for Women*, our official organ. Read it properly, now, buy it again when you can, and when you come to London get in touch.'

'Thank you. I will.'

'Here's my card.' It said: *WSPU, Hampstead Group. Local organizer: Miss Andrea Sutton, 10 White Bear Hill, NW3 (evenings only).*

'I'm impressed,' Thea said, putting the card in her bag.

'Don't be. It's a common task, I'm just one of the bossy ones.' Her sudden flash of honesty commended itself to Thea. She took Andrea's outstretched hand and smiled to show there were no hard feelings.

'I'll be in touch.'

Louis saw them to the door. Apart from their odd exchange at the start of the evening, Thea had not spoken to him, but he was effusive. 'You have a beautiful cousin, Maurice. You must produce her more often.'

'She is not mine to produce,' said Maurice drily, but Louis ignored him.

Instead he took Thea's hand in both of his and clasped it warmly, gazing intently into her eyes. She felt a strong desire to shake him off, tell him not to be silly.

'I shall see you again,' he said.

'I'm in Cambridge for another five days.' She deliberately misinterpreted his forecast.

'No. We shall meet in the future. Our paths will cross.'

Maurice went out onto the landing and stood there, hands in pockets, waiting. Thea tried to disengage her hand but to her astonishment found it imprisoned still more firmly.

'Goodbye,' she said brightly. 'Thank you for a lovely evening.'

He removed his hands, spreading them in the air as though completing a conjuring trick. '*Au revoir*, Thea Tennant,' he said, as they hurried down the stairs. '*Au revoir. À bientôt.*'

CHAPTER FIVE

'First time I'd been in foreign parts,
Did I like it? Bless your hearts!'
Marie Lloyd—'The Coster Girl in Paris'

Thea put her gloved hand to the steamy train window and rubbed, making a little spy hole. 'I think we're here,' she said. 'Dulcie?'

Dulcie opened her eyes and rolled her head on the red plush seat. 'I beg your pardon?'

'We're arriving. Come and look.'

'I don't have the strength. What time is it?'

'Late afternoon.'

'I thought it must be next year at *least.*' She closed her eyes again.

Thea returned her attention to the window. The train was crashing and thundering over an iron bridge; beneath them, and stretching away into the distance, was a vast expanse of water. The Danube, so far from being blue or in any way picturesque, was grey with silt and choppy with spring waves, and the Waltz City itself was not clustered along its banks, but simply an uneven line of buildings up ahead.

The middle-aged couple in the corner, who had boarded the Vienna Express at Linz, rose and began fussing with their bags and coats. They looked fresh and at ease. Thea blinked. Her eyes were puffy and hard-edged with tiredness; her clothes felt stale and sticky. A wave of panic swept over her. They were almost there, the clattering rhythm of the train was labouring, and she and Dulcie were still sitting in their seats like a pair of graven images. With a sudden burst of energy she got up and hauled one of the bags down from the overhead luggage rack. They had a trunk in the guard's van, which would have to be dealt with on arrival, but their hand luggage was here, and would have to be got onto the platform by their own efforts. She gave Dulcie's shoulder a shake.

'Dulcie! Get a move on for heaven's sake, we'll be there in a minute.'

'All right, all right. Don't fuss.'

'Just lend a hand, that's all.'

Dulcie stood up stiffly. The journey had not been to her taste. In fact she had decided that the adage 'It is better to travel than to arrive' was nothing short of heresy. Travelling was not consistent with her careful toilette, and its opportunities for sparkling social intercourse were few. She was not someone who found scenery, even foreign scenery, fascinating *per se*, and she had the greatest difficulty concentrating on a book for more than half an hour at a time. Consequently, discomfort was made still harder to bear by boredom. And it had been long, so interminably long. The boat-train had deposited them at the Gare du Nord in Paris early the previous evening. She trailed about in her sister's energetic wake until the Express had been located, and since then the tedium had been alleviated only by stops, which afforded them a short breath of air but little entertainment, as one station (she pointed out, often) looked much like another. They had taken a couple of meals in the dining-car, but she had not been hungry, and though half the journey had taken place at night this had afforded no relief as she had not been able to sleep. She wondered at Thea's capacity for enthusiasm. With cries of delight she would point out the place-names on the various platforms—Geneva, Zurich, Munich, Salzburg—and refer voraciously to her guide book. From Linz onwards she had even tried out her German on the middle-aged couple and Dulcie had leaned her head back and closed her eyes with a martyred air. Not only did she have no interest in the couple, solid teutonic burghers of the most dreary kind, but she did not wish to air her ignorance of their guttural and unlovely language. Her troubles had started the moment they boarded the cross-channel ferry, for the sea had been huge, and the boat's pitching and rolling had reduced her stomach to soup, obliging her to spend the whole voyage, moaning and whey-faced, on a seat in the first-class saloon, while Thea explored.

Now she bent, unsteadily, and surveyed herself in the long mirror above the opposite seat. Horrible. Her face was peaky and pinched, her eyes reddened, and her hair a mess. She pulled on her hat, furiously tucking in the worst ends.

The Austrian gentleman, who had been helping Thea with the cases, addressed himself to them. 'May I assist further?' His phrase-book English was softened by a Viennese accent.

135

He and his wife had been visiting their married daughter and her family outside Linz, he had told Thea.

'*Nein, danke*. Someone is meeting us. You've been a great help already.' Thea nodded and beamed like a mandarin to underline her good intentions, her gratitude. She felt British-ness, like a conspicuous rash, breaking out all over her.

The man—he had gentle eyes and a little grey moustache —lifted his homburg in farewell. 'Then we leave you. Happy holiday,' he said, and ushered his plump, motherly wife out of the door.

'Thank you,' said Thea with feeling. She would dearly have liked to grab them, implore them to bear her and her sister company for a few more minutes, to provide an element of continuity as they stepped from the sanctuary of the train into a different world. But of course one couldn't do that.

With a rattle, a roar and a shriek the Express drew into the Bahnhof Franz Josef. The figures on the platform flashed by jerkily, liké images in a magic lantern show, gradually slowing as the engine puffed to the end and stopped with a sigh. Thea and Dulcie gathered up their belongings and moved to join the shuffling queue in the corridor. As they stepped down onto the platform they were engulfed by the shock of foreignness. The language that rang around them was not quite German but something softer and stranger; the clothes and manner of the people imperceptibly different; even the light filtering through the sooty glass vault of the station seemed clearer and more brilliant than at home.

They stood there, two English girls abroad, their bags about their knees, gazing round anxiously. Aunt Jessica's most recent letter had said that her son Josef would be there to meet them, but Thea had never seen him before and consequently had no idea what manner of man she was looking for. Suddenly she remembered something.

'The trunk! I'd better find a porter. You stay there and keep an eye out for Josef.' She hurried up the platform in the direction of the guard's van. Dulcie, watching her dully, saw her accost a porter, with much pointing and gesturing. The porter in his turn nodded, shrugged, looked up and down the platform. Dulcie's heart sank. My God, the trunk had been mislaid and all her decent clothes were in it. Her view of the scene wavered and melted in tears.

Just then a voice to one side of her enquired 'Miss Tennant?'

She brushed her eyes hastily and turned. To say that the appearance of Josef von Crieff was a pleasant surprise would have been gross understatement.

'It *is* Miss Tennant, I hope?' he asked again, with charming diffidence.

'Yes, yes it is.' Dulcie pulled herself together. This was territory she recognized. 'I'm Dulcimer—Dulcie. How do you do.'

'I am delighted to find you at last.'

Dulcie's own delight was enhanced by the fact that she had half-expected a plump, stolid youth, possibly bespectacled and wearing a Tyrolean hat. Instead of which, here was Lieutenant Josef von Crieff of the 1st Kaiser Franz Cavalry Regiment, bowing over her hand and expressing his joy at finding her at last. His uniform—complete with jauntily cockaded cap (now held respectfully in the crook of his arm), high-collared jacket, narrow trousers fitting as smoothly as the skin of a cat, gleaming boots and glittering spurs and sabre—was altogether ravishing. Gazing back into his grey eyes and leaving her hand in his for a telling extra second, Dulcie felt that life might yet improve. With one proviso.

'My sister's gone in search of our trunk,' she said.

'But I already have the trunk,' he responded, right on cue, indicating a porter just behind him with the offending baggage loaded on a trolley.

'Goodness, what a relief!' Dulcie treated both men to her most melting *coup d'œil*.

'But which one is your sister?' Josef peered.

'That's her.' Dulcie pointed out Thea's tall back view in the green and brown checked cloak, dwindling rapidly against the tide of departing passengers, the diminutive porter scuttling beside her.

'I must go and tell her all is well,' said Josef, and hurried off. Dulcie saw him touch Thea's arm, bow once again, smile, introduce, point back towards the trunk; Thea laughing out loud, always so direct.

Thea, in her turn, felt that she had momentarily been transported to the stage of some romantic Ruritanian operetta, that at any moment her saviour would clap his hand to his breast, burst into song, and declare to the astonished patrons of the railway station that he must go to war, but leave his heart behind. Now he replaced his cap, took her arm, and steered her solicitously back to Dulcie.

'The carriage is waiting,' he informed them.

They followed like lambs, across the station concourse. There were uniforms on every side; dragoons from Bohemia and Moravia, hussars from Hungary, infantry from Vienna, sappers, pioneers and jaegers—the 'emperor's coat', in all its dazzling variations, ravished the eye. Plumes and cockades bobbed and bowed like the crests of exotic birds, spurs clinked, sabres swung against the glistening leather boots. Thea's first and most vivid impression of the Austrians was that they were a nation of soldiers.

Outside on the forecourt Josef saw them into the carriage, supervised the loading of the trunk and cases on to the roof and issued some instructions, in German, to the driver. Then he climbed in and sat down opposite them, removing his cap and placing it neatly beside him on the seat. He studied his fellow-passengers.

He noted with pleasure that both were good-looking. One was blonde and dainty, like a doll, a type he recognized instantly and instinctively steered clear of. She looked as delicate as Dresden china but was almost certainly as tough and calculating as an alligator. The other, older girl was something different. Her beauty was more unusual, more uncompromising, and the light of humour and intelligence positively shone from her face. There was a kind of directness, an essential altruism in her look, her smile, her manner, that caused Josef's cautious, sensitive spirit to unfurl a little.

'Did you have a good journey?' he asked, with every appearance of genuine interest, crossing his long legs with a jingle of spurs.

'Dreadful!'

'Excellent!' They both spoke at once, and all laughed.

'But you must be tired?'

'Not really,' Thea replied. 'A little dazed, perhaps, with so many new impressions.'

'Of course.' He nodded sympathetically.

Thea thought him one of the best-looking men she had seen. All her life, male acquaintances had suffered by being held up for scrutiny against the exacting criterion of her father. Except for Jack Kingsley, who for some reason had set himself outside comparison. But here was a man who, despite his youth, had a majestic physical presence, a burnished and heroic beauty.

He was tall, slim and elegant, wearing his uniform with exactly the right degree of insouciant dash. His hair and moustache were corn-yellow, his eyes a frosty grey. But overriding these physical attributes, and exalting them, was an air of strength mildly contained, like that worn by the face of a young Roman emperor on a coin. One tiny blemish, a small white scar on the corner of his lower lip, lent his calm features a vulnerability. Now he cleared his throat and Thea looked away hastily, sharply aware that she had been staring.

'Actually,' he had only a slight accent, but still the Englishness of the word sounded odd, 'I have asked the driver to take one turn round the Ringstrasse before returning home. Will that be too much, on top of your travels? It will not take long.'

'No, no, that would be marvellous,' said Thea. 'In a way it will help to get us used to Vienna before meeting . . .' She floundered, not wanting to appear rude, or loth to meet his family. But he put up a hand to banish her embarrassment.

'I understand.' Thea had the impression that he did, and was grateful.

Dulcie was peering out of the window. It was the first time she had expressed an interest in her surroundings since leaving home. 'We're going over another bridge,' she exclaimed. 'Are we crossing the Danube again?'

'No, not the Danube, but the Danube canal this time,' he said. 'And on the other side we come into the Stubenring, the first part of the Ringstrasse. The Ring was the perimeter of the old city, you see; we are in effect circling ancient Vienna.'

They clopped along for a few minutes, all eyes politely fixed on the moving picture framed by the carriage window.

'Parkring,' Josef murmured, dutifully but unnecessarily as they drove past beautifully laid out gardens. The road along which they travelled was very wide. On either side a double row of trees, frilly with the first green of spring, divided the boulevard into areas for pedestrians, trams, horsedrawn and motor vehicles. Beyond the trees, a seemingly endless display of dignified baroque architecture processed like imposing ladies at a levée. Thea, feeling Josef's gaze upon her, felt constrained to acknowledge the magnificence of his city.

'It's splendid,' she said. 'Very grand.'

'Grand, yes, certainly,' he agreed, as though about to add some qualification. He spoke excellent idiomatic English but with a slight formality that betrayed it as his second language.

'Tell us what the buildings are,' said Thea. She suggested this not purely out of interest but because she sensed that he would be more at ease if he felt himself to be of use. They leaned forward together. His boots creaked, she could smell the polished leather and also observed that the golden hairs of his moustache had a natural tendency to curl. Every so often he would put his hand to his upper lip and smooth it with thumb and fingers.

'What about me?' It was Dulcie, prettily aggrieved.

'I am so sorry.' He leapt to his feet and indicated that she should take his place opposite Thea. 'I will sit next to you,' he added, as though guaranteeing her safety from dragons.

In fact, when Dulcie had taken his seat, it was Thea he sat by, occasionally pointing to the Palladian edifices that passed before them, or drawing their attention to some sight of greater interest on the other side of the Ringstrasse. There seemed to Thea to be a quite extraordinary concentration of grand and important buildings along the length of their route. The Court Opera House (not the largest, but the most beautiful opera house in the world, Josef opined) . . . Pallas Athene, goddess of wisdom, optimistically guarding the parliament building . . . the Imperial Royal Theatre . . . the Natural History Museum and Art Gallery, facing each other across the monument of the Empress Maria Theresa . . . the new Hofburg, standing out like a great white grin against the fine, well-proportioned features of its old counterpart, its half-columns and serried ranks of windows criss-crossed with scaffolding, evidence of faith in the future of the Habsburg dynasty . . . a little further on, the Heldenplatz . . .

'Heroes' Square,' Josef translated. They looked: a pleasant, airy space, sporting two handsome equestrian statues. 'We do have more heroes,' he added, smiling, 'but statues of heroes are so dull. As it is, the square is very pretty in May, with all the lilac in bloom. A charming place to walk.'

In May. The two small words brought home to Thea and Dulcie the enormity of the step they had taken. May was weeks away; it was only just April, now, the lilac was nowhere near in bloom and yet they would see it and still have months to spare, away from the familiar idiosyncrasies of home. In Kent it would still be cold, the spring would not be so advanced as it was here. Venetia would be having her

140

cup of tea in the library; Edgar would be reading the evening paper in the front seat of the Lanchester outside Bromley station; the daffodils beside the Elm Walk would be bending and tossing in a sharp wind.

Here, the air was balmy. As they turned into the far stretch of the Ringstrasse a soft rain scattered down in the sunshine and a rainbow appeared, irreverently pretty, over the ornate rooftops. From the arched window of a massive building on their left a column of cavalry swept forth and moved past them round the Ringstrasse, the traffic, including their own fiacre, stopping respectfully to allow the horsemen room. Thea saw faces, haughty in profile beneath high peaked caps; horses with necks arched like book-ends, and streaming tails; firm gauntleted hands on taut reins; and all other sounds were blotted beneath the clatter of trotting hooves.

When they had passed, the fiacre moved gently on its way, and Josef indicated the large building. 'Rossau Barracks,' he announced. 'My place of work, you could say.'

'Are you on leave?' enquired Dulcie.

'Off duty, but not on leave, not yet,' he replied, with tremendous fervour, as though glad to be asked something concerning himself. 'But soon I shall be, in your honour.' He inclined his head in a way that made Dulcie think that if he had been standing he would have clicked his heels also. She felt the great yawning gulf of foreignness between herself and this Viennese cousin. Her high hopes on first seeing him were subsiding by the second. He was courteous, kind, undoubtedly handsome—but distant. He made her feel young. She sensed in him a built-in disapproval of some aspect of her character that she was powerless to change. Looking at him now, sitting by Thea, his golden head close to her dark one, Dulcie felt resentful, irritable and left out.

They passed along the Schottenring and then turned sharp right into the old Inner Town, along Neutor Gasse, into Salzgries and then right again into a quieter, residential street. Thea saw that they were in an area of solid opulence, that the great baroque houses on either side were nothing short of palaces. She moistened her lips and swallowed. Her father's voice rang in her ears: 'There you will live as they live, very grandly I believe . . . and you will be expected to behave . . .'

'We are here,' said Josef.

As Josef and his charges left the station, Baron Thomas von Crieff, returning from his regular appointment with the doctor, turned into Helenastrasse and began covering the two hundred yards or so to the family mansion. He remembered that his wife's nieces would be arriving at any moment, if indeed they had not already done so. The thought made his pale, aquiline features assume a more than usually melancholy expression. He hoped the girls would not prove too much of a trial. His wife had not seen them for years and the extraordinary volley of letters they had received from the girls' father had not served to alleviate the Baron's misgivings. There had been dark references to domestic problems, to the girls' having led too sheltered a life. The elder, so far as he could deduce, was a blue-stocking, and the younger a flirt. His spirits plummeted. They would be there for months, demanding his attention and politeness, denying him the solitude he craved. He swished his cane ferociously. The others would have to take care of them.

He opened the small door in the wrought-iron gates and walked, laggardly, up the drive to the imposing entrance of his house. There had been a spring shower, and the nymphs and cherubs that adorned the guttering high above dribbled like so many senile old men. He went up the steps and let himself in at the door. Minna scuttled across the hall to meet him and take his things.

'Thank you, Minna.' He avoided catching her eye. The girl annoyed him; she seemed always to be fighting a losing battle with a hysterical giggle, her plump Slav face was perpetually bulging and dimpled with stifled, idiotic mirth. The girl was a fool. But Jessica liked her; she set great store by good humour, and whatever her faults Minna was certainly good-humoured. In the drawing-room he was relieved to find only his wife and two younger children. Jessica, sitting on the rose and gold brocade sofa by the fire, looked up from her perpetual embroidery.

'Hallo, dear. How was it?'

'Satisfactory, thank you.' Annelise and Dieter did not acknowledge his arrival. They were playing taroc at the card table in the far corner of the room. Sometimes he wished he had never taught them the game; the lower half of their faces seemed to be permanently masked by a hand of cards.

'Hallo, children.'

'Hallo.' Only Dieter spoke, his brow furrowed in thought. Jessica smiled indulgently—boys will be boys—and patted the plump sofa next to her.

'Come and sit down,' she suggested to her husband.

He did so. 'Where are they?'

'They'll be heré any moment. Josef's gone to meet them at the Bahnhof.'

'You're very calm. The preparations are all complete?'

'Why shouldn't I be calm?' Jessica chuckled, snapping off a strand of silk and picking up her work basket off the floor. 'They are my nieces, not a couple of trolls.'

'Yes, yes, of course. Annelise!'

'Mm?'

'Dulcimer is about your age, I believe.'

'So Mama keeps telling me.'

'You and she could be friends, do things together. You will look after her, won't you, like a good hostess?' Anything, he thought privately, anything at all as long as they are kept away from me.

Annelise leaned back in her chair, legs stretched before her, surveying her fanned cards. The position accentuated her chubbiness. She would be enormously fat in middle age, thought Thomas; why couldn't Jessica put her on a diet? He was frequently irritated by evidence of *Schlamperei*, the demon sloppiness, in his womenfolk, which he put down to their English blood. It was to be hoped that the arrival of the English girls would not make things worse.

'Annelise, did you hear me?'

'Yes! Of course I shall look after her, but presumably she is capable of managing without me. I'm not her nursemaid or anything.'

'Certainly not, but politeness dictates—'

'I know, I know.' Annelise slapped down her cards and flopped forward, chin in hands, face averted to the window. 'I'm sick to death of being told how I must behave with these cousins.'

'Now why don't you run along and get ready, they'll be here in a moment,' said Jessica imperturbably, setting her sewing aside.

'I *am* ready,' was her daughter's response.

'Well Dieter is not.' Dieter groaned, pushed his chair back and left the room with poor grace. 'And perhaps you'd tidy

143

those cards up and go and make sure that Minna and Cook have tea prepared.'

Annelise began shuffling the cards together. 'Whatever do they want to drink tea for?'

'Tea,' said her mother, smiling, 'is the British drink, or hadn't you heard?'

'I thought they were coming here to live like us.'

'They are our guests, and we shall make them completely welcome. We shall speak English, and drink tea if necessary, so be a good girl and do as I ask.'

Annelise put the cards in the desk and walked from the room with a sauntering, time-wasting gait.

'Where is de Laszlo?' asked the Baron, referring to his younger son's tutor.

'In his room, I believe.'

'What is Dieter doing loafing about playing cards at this hour?'

'Lessons are finished for today.'

'But his work is poor, has he been set no studying to do in his own time?'

'I don't know, dear. I suppose not.'

'But why not?' The Baron struck the arm of the sofa in a fit of annoyance. His wife widened her eyes; there was no point in losing his temper with her. 'I shall have to have a word with de Laszlo. Dieter will not improve unless he is pushed.'

'Peter came with excellent references,' said Jessica, picking threads of silk from her skirt with finger and thumb.

'I am aware of that, I employ the man. But whatever his talents he is not using them to the full in the case of my son.'

'You speak to him then, Thomas,' said his wife, with a satisfied inflexion, as one who has suddenly seen the light at the end of the tunnel.

'I will.'

Jessica sighed, to signify her empathy with her husband's overriding problems, and rose to stand before him. Other people's capacity for gloom and despondency never failed to astound her; she simply did not know what they found to worry about.

'And how,' she enquired brightly, to take his mind off things, 'was Doctor Freud?'

When Thea had been shown to her room by Annelise she found her things already unpacked, the dresses hanging in the wardrobe, smaller items neatly disseminated in drawers and interspersed with small sachets of lavender and lemon verbena. Her nightdress looked small and childish where it lay on the pillow of the vast ornately canopied bed; her own tortoiseshell brush and comb had been placed next to the porcelain set on the dressing-table. There was a rank of exquisite cut-glass jars and bottles with silver stoppers, and a mirror with so many cunningly angled facets that no matter where she was in the room she could see an image of herself. The room itself was by far the grandest that Thea had ever slept in. The ceiling seemed a million miles away, and was painted with a florid, rustic scene peopled with muscular shepherds and dimpled, submissive maidens in diaphanous dresses. As well as the palatial and richly curtained bed there was a beautifully inlaid desk, complete with writing materials, and two wing-backed chairs with their own footstools, all covered in the same rose and gold brocade that she had admired in the drawing-room. She noticed that the room seemed to be on the corner of a wing or projection of some kind, for it had two immense windows, reaching almost from ceiling to floor, one looking straight out over the garden and the other giving onto a kind of courtyard on the far side of which she could make out a stable block. Another part of the house ran at right-angles to this window and beneath the row of windows she saw the graceful arch through which the carriage had departed after depositing Dulcie, Josef and herself at the front door.

She went over to the other window and saw that it had doors which opened onto a small balcony, complete with a scrolled iron seat and table. The garden below was large for a town house, surrounded by a high brick wall and apparently laid out in an L-shape, for away to the right she could see a small white summer-house or gazebo, still within the circling arm of the wall. Even the garden had a formal richness, with paths and pools and statues. The velvet lawn did not look as though it had ever suffered the indignities of croquet hoops or cricket stumps, nor the weedless borders as though they had been the repository of balls and dogs' bones.

To the right of the bed was another door and on the far side of this she discovered to her delight a little bathroom. The bath had gold griffon's feet and gleaming taps, there were three pink towels on a rail, and a large jar, similar to those on the dressing-table, full of bath salts. Tired and travel-stained as she was, the bathroom was altogether too potent a temptation for Thea. After all, what else was there to do between now and dinner, which would be at half-past seven? If she lay down on the bed she would never wake up, it was too soon to change and she didn't feel able to concentrate on reading a book or writing a letter. She turned on the taps.

Just as she had discarded her clothes, let down her hair and slipped into her dressing-gown, there was a knock on the door. At once, Thea felt guilty. Supposing they wanted her downstairs? Supposing she should not have run a bath without asking someone? Or perhaps it would have been correct to summon the maid to do it for her? She stood in the centre of the room and cleared her throat. 'Come in.'

It was the little Austrian maid, her straw-coloured plait making a halo about her pink face. She looked at Thea, then to the bathroom door from which steam drifted invitingly.

'Is everything all right?' she enquired, in a thick accent. 'You have found everything, Fräulein Thea?'

'Yes thank you, everything. Thank you very much.' Thea was sure that so many thanks were not called for, but she felt absurdly embarrassed. 'By the way,' she added, 'I hope it is all right for me to have a bath?' She waved a hand in the direction of the bathroom.

Minna grinned. 'But of course. That is your bathroom.'

At once Thea felt doubly foolish. 'Yes. Well, thank you.'

'Ring please if you need anything.'

'I will.'

Minna trotted out and Thea sank gratefully into the hot water adding, before she did so, a liberal handful of the bath crystals as evidence of her independent spirit.

As she lay, relaxed in the fragrantly steaming tub, she reflected that for the first time she had experienced what others experienced upon being introduced to the Tennants. For once she and Dulcie had been the strangers, the outsiders, the objects of scrutiny and, most probably, criticism. She was conscious of the fact that they had been foisted upon this family by Ralph; they had not necessarily even been welcome, it was impossible to tell. But Thea, who more than most liked to be liked, was determined that they should be. Provided Dulcie comported herself reasonably, and could resist the temptation to show off, all would be well.

Her Aunt Jessica had hardly changed in the fifteen years since they had last met. Thea could remember Venetia bringing her up to say goodnight to them all as children at Ranelagh Road. She was not as beautiful as Venetia, but she had been pretty and smiling, with a soft cheek and a nice smell, and she had given them all some Turkish delight with instructions that it was to be eaten that very instant, in the dark, no matter how much icing sugar got on the bed-covers. Evidence of such anarchism in an adult was enough to endear her to the three children at a stroke, though Aubrey had kept his portion till the morning anyway.

Now Jessica was still smiling and fond, but her hair was greyer and she had become rather fat. She, at least, had fallen upon the sisters with every evidence of real pleasure, kissing and hugging them, and asking for news of home without waiting for the answer.

Of her husband, their Uncle Thomas, Thea was not so sure. His thin, dry hand had taken hers; his pale, hooded eyes had surveyed her from behind gold-rimmed spectacles; his voice had uttered the formalities of welcome—and yet he might as well not have touched, surveyed, or spoken, for all the contact there had been between them. He had looked at her as though to consign her features to memory, and never look again. He displayed neither curiosity nor warmth, but only a courtly indifference.

The daughter, Annelise, was not of a type that Thea instinctively liked, but she recognized this as a prejudice of her own and not due to any real fault on the girl's part. She was eighteen, a few months older than Dulcie, plump, pretty and creamy-skinned with hair just dark enough not to be carrotty, and a scattering of freckles over her nose and cheeks. She had kissed and hallo-ed nicely enough but, Thea recalled, she had not been above reminding them that in Austria tea was drunk only as a therapeutic beverage and not for pleasure. When Minna had brought the tray she had refused a cup, and they had found themselves sipping theirs in front of an audience, like creatures from another planet. There was about Annelise a craftiness which precluded easy acquaintance. She was a minx; they would have to win her friendship by out-facing her. But then, she was not the only minx in the house now. . . .

The little boy, Dieter, was ten. Having shaken hands sullenly he had pointed out that it was his birthday in two weeks' time. There had been something threatening in his tone, as if he wished to make clear to the English girls that their presence in the house would make no difference to whatever atrocities were due to take place on that day. Jessica had smiled indulgently at him and expressed the hope that they wouldn't object to attending a birthday party for the family and assorted friends. Thea did not object, though the corners of Dulcie's mouth had turned down in distaste. At least a child's birthday party was an occasion with some common factors which must surely cut across the bounds of nationality.

And then there was Josef. She closed her eyes and laid her head back, luxuriating in her thoughts. Her pleasure was increased by the knowledge that the attraction was mutual. Thea had had few men friends, and those she had were simply that—friends who happened to be men. They were people she liked, whose company and conversation she enjoyed, or whom she had simply known for years, like Jack Kingsley, though her relationship with him, even before the events of Christmas, had never been easy . . . She had never before met a man who so directly reminded her of her femininity, who called to it and played upon it so that she was aware of herself only as a woman.

She thought, for the first time in many months, of Dulcie and Jack, and then of Josef. She looked down at her body in the softly clouded, steaming water, its pale, curving length mysterious beneath the surface, making silky white islands where her breasts and knees broke it. Closing her eyes again she laid one hand thoughtfully on her neck and let it rest there for a moment before letting it slide down over the rest of her body, gliding into the delightful warmth of the water. She thought of it as Josef's hand, and her body answered the thought with disturbing directness.

Her eyes snapped open and she sat up and leaned forward to let the water out. As she did so the taut buds of her nipples brushed her thighs and she was aware of the melting openness that her daydreams had aroused. She climbed out and dried herself vigorously on the largest of the pink towels, routing desire with energetic movements. But she still could not prevent herself from planning, with voluptuous care, what she would wear for dinner.

Half an hour later she sat at the dressing-table, dressed in a white satin and lace blouse and a black velvet skirt. She brushed her thick hair and piled it up thoughtfully. She quite liked her neck.

The door opened a chink and her aunt's face appeared round it.

'May I come in?'

'Of course, Aunt. I was just changing, I hope I haven't been too long?'

'Not at all, my dear, not at all. I hope you are comfortable?' Jessica drifted across the room touching things, twitching the quilt, straightening the curtains.

'Yes, perfectly, thank you. This really is a magnificent room, I feel like royalty.'

'Good, good . . .' Jessica went to one of the chairs and perched on the arm, brushing the seat with the back of her hand. 'Personally I don't care for the magnificence so very much. It's not what you'd call homely, is it?'

Thea was surprised by this admission; her aunt seemed ill at ease. She busied herself by twisting her hair into a thick coil and pinning it at the nape of her neck. Jessica watched her.

'My maid will help you with that, if you like,' she offered diffidently.

Thea laughed through a mouthful of pins. 'Heavens, I wouldn't dream of it, my hair is a perfect nightmare! I couldn't possibly ask anyone else to battle with it.'

'You don't have a lady's maid at home?'

'No.' Thea grimaced. 'Quite honestly, it would make me nervous. We don't have many staff anyway.' She anchored the heavy loop of hair and turned her head this way and that to see the effect. Conscious of her aunt's eyes still resting on her, a little wistfully, she turned and said warmly: 'It really is kind of you to have us, you know. We do appreciate it.'

Jessica beamed. 'You have no idea of the pleasure it gives me.'

'Mother and Father send their love. I think Mother was quite jealous of us!'

'I'm sure she was, poor lamb, they really must come when your father can tear himself away from his work. Tell me, Thea . . .' Thea sensed that Jessica had at last come to the point of her visit, 'there isn't anything it would help me to know, is there? I mean, I had the impression from Ralph, in his letters, that something had happened.'

'Not really. Nothing important,' Thea lied gamely.

'Please don't misunderstand me. I hate to pry, it's just that . . .'

149

'Only a family tiff. Really.'

'Dulcie—she's always been a handful, hasn't she?'

'I suppose so. I think the trouble is that she gets easily bored. There isn't much to do in the country and Father's never really understood why anyone should want a social life. So—' she shrugged, 'this trip will do her all the good in the world.'

Seeing that her aunt still looked dubious, she added, on the premise that a small helping of the truth now can save a giant portion later: 'The fact is she had an unfortunate affair. Nothing much, but she's very young, and the man was quite wrong for her, and she handled it badly. You understand I'm sure. It seemed like the end of the world to Dulcie—' God forgive her—'but she'll get over it. She needed a change and some fun and I'm sure she'll have both here.' She smiled disarmingly.

Jessica rose, apparently satisfied. 'I'm so glad you confided in me, dear. It's just that I feel I've been entrusted with you both, so to speak, and I wouldn't want to do anything wrong, you see. Your father wasn't terribly *clear* in his letters . . .'

'That's all it was.'

'Good, good.' She went to the door and then paused, adding, 'By the way, don't let my husband's manner worry you. He is always a little taciturn. He has such a lot on his mind; his father died recently, you know, and it was a dreadful blow. He has been looking forward to your coming every bit as much as the rest of us, I promise you.'

Peter de Laszlo smoothed his hair with one hand, adjusted his tie, and left his bedroom to go down to dinner, closing the door carefully behind him. He dawdled down the stairs, idly inspecting the parade of haughty von Crieff ancestors which hung along his route. They were a fishy-eyed bunch, and no mistake; you could see where the old man got it from.

Peter had been Dieter von Crieff's tutor since the New Year, but he was not entirely happy with his position. He was well-paid and lived in comfort but he felt his status to be ill-defined. The Frau Baronin treated him like a son, the Baron like a lackey and Annelise and Dieter watched him as though it were only a matter of time before he blotted his copy-book. As for the other son, Josef, he was like a man from another age. You couldn't dislike the fellow, but neither

150

was there much chance of striking up an intimate friendship. That uniform of his said it all.

Dinner was the only meal of the day when the whole family ate together. Peter breakfasted early, with his pupil, the Baron usually arriving as they left the table and the Frau Baronin taking coffee in her room. The breaking of Anne-lise's fast was dependent on her plans for the morning; if there was no riding, visiting or music lesson she would stay in bed. Luncheon was informal, and if he were lucky Peter could have a tray in his room; otherwise he ate with whoever was in, but as a general rule this number did not include the Baron.

Dinner, however, was both formal and communal, and tonight was important because of the presence of the two English girls, whose arrival he had heard a couple of hours earlier. About them he was curious, but on the whole not optimistic. English girls were notorious, were they not, for their loud voices, their big feet, and for having the kind of *derrières* that looked better in the saddle than in a skirt.

To add to his misgivings he sensed that for the last few days the Baron had been spoiling for some kind of confrontation. He was always distant, but recently his whole manner had reeked of disapproval. Peter knew what it was: Dieter's work was not good. But he was a lazy little devil; what did the old man expect, miracles? The fact was he simply could not accept that his son was mediocre. Never mind, perhaps the Frau Baronin would stick up for him as she had done in the past. She was hopelessly susceptible to flattery; Peter would rag her mildly about the fact that they both had English blood in their veins, even though his was tempered with some Hungarian. They had a lot in common, he would say, holding her chair for her, smiling nicely, and the old dear would fall for it hook, line and sinker, making it awkward for her husband to be too harsh.

Peter paused in the hall. The black and white marble tiles stretched away on all sides, making him feel like a pawn on a chessboard. A polite, muted burble of voices issued sporadically from behind the door. It didn't sound terribly lively. A light footstep pattered behind him: it was Minna, done up in her evening outfit of black, with white frills fluttering cheekily in all the right places. She was taking some silver cutlery into the dining-room. Peter winked at her and she snorted hysterically and clapped a hand to her mouth. It was astounding that, no matter how often he winked at her, she always found it equally outrageous. He squared his shoulders and entered the drawing-room.

The Frau Baronin bustled over at once, took him by the arm, effected introductions in her breathless, disorganized way and offered him an aperitif, which he refused. It amused him to give the impression that he rarely drank. With an air of genteel self-effacement he went to stand by his charge, who was slumped in an easy chair, nursing a glass of mineral water and looking sulky in a brown suit and stiff collar. The Baron stood in the centre of the room, apparently distilling the secrets of the universe from the pattern on the carpet.

Quietly, but just distinctly enough for his employer to hear, Peter enquired: 'Dieter, did you finish the mathematics I set you?'

'I got stuck.'

'So you did not finish?'

'I couldn't.'

'But if you have a problem, Dieter, you must come and consult me. Just because lessons are over does not mean I am inaccessible. I am always ready to help.'

'Yes.'

'So we had better begin twenty minutes earlier in the morning and tackle the difficulty.'

'All right.'

That should do it, thought Peter. The Baron showed no signs of having heard, but then he rarely did, even when addressed directly. Satisfied that his point had been made Peter transferred his attention to the others, who were talking in a group near the fireplace. The English girls were a pleasant surprise. The dark one Peter discounted because, although handsome, she was taller than he and it put one at such a disadvantage. Besides, the son and heir appeared to have earmarked her for preferment already. But the younger one—so petite, so exquisitely pretty, and with those naughty, naughty eyes . . . She looked across at him now and smiled dazzlingly. He returned the smile, with a slight incline of his head. Enchanting.

Dinner that first night had been painstakingly devised by Jessica to consist entirely of Austrian dishes. It opened with Fischbeuschlsuppe, a thick, piquant broth made from the lungs of freshwater fish, with a dash of lemon. She did not actually care for it herself, but her husband was fond of it and it was both unusual and indigenous. The soup was followed by the famous Tafelspitz, a special cut of boiled beef served with a chive sauce, entirely delicious. To conclude, she had felt honour-bound to serve Sachertorte, in the hierarchy of which her own cook's did not rank high, but she would not have dared send out for one from the *Konditorei* for fear of losing an otherwise excellent worker.

All this she had ordered to be washed down with what she thought to be a very pleasant local white wine, a Grinzinger. The Baron pursed his lips when it was brought to the table.

'I apologize,' he said, addressing Thea and Dulcie, 'for drinking white wine with beef. We could have had an excellent French claret, but my wife was determined that you should partake only of local fare.'

'I think it's a splendid idea,' replied Thea.

'And it's not so bad,' said Josef on her left. 'Father, you are too particular. You'll spoil our cousins' enjoyment if you criticize it so much.' He smiled at Thea and raised his glass in a toast. Sitting thus close she could see that his hair curled over the edge of his upright collar at the back. She experienced a strong desire to touch it. She thought she knew how it would feel—springy and glossy, like the fur of some fit and vital animal.

'I prefer white anyway,' vouchsafed Dulcie, taking a mouthful to prove it.

The Baron appeared not to hear. He was peering into his glass as though expecting to see an octopus lurking on the bottom. 'We could not serve a native red wine because it is undrinkable,' he murmured gloomily.

'What nonsense, Thomas!' Jessica looked round the table: wasn't it absolute nonsense?

'It's no more than the locals say,' affirmed her husband, attacking his beef. The matter seemed to have had a disproportionately adverse effect on his humour. Thea glanced at the others. They seemed quite untroubled. All were stolidly tucking in to their food. The only sound was the chink of knives and forks. She did not like to look round at Josef again because the silence made her nervous.

Peter de Laszlo was seated between Dulcie and Dieter. He eyed the latter's plate with distaste. He had made a kind of trough between his potatoes and turnips, through which he was channelling a turgid stream of sauce. The child was one of the nastiest eaters he had ever come across. He tapped the boy's arm and, when he looked up, made a reproving face at his plate. For one thing, there was never any harm in appearing custodial of the boy's manners, and for another he wished publicly to dissociate himself from all *Schlamperei*. Annelise, however, was more direct.

'Ugh! Look at Dieter's plate, Mutti. He is revolting!'

'Eat nicely, Dieter.'

'What did I do wrong?'

'You made a disgusting mess of your food!' shrilled his sister. 'You may not care, but why should the rest of us have to look at it? It quite puts me off.'

'Eat nicely, dear,' Jessica reiterated. Dieter complied by consuming what was left at such speed that it was a wonder it stayed down at all. Thea looked on in admiration, but when she glanced at Josef she noticed that his mouth was set and tight: he was embarrassed by the exchange.

Peter turned to Dulcie. 'Have you had a very wearing journey, Miss Tennant?' he asked quietly.

'Dulcie will do. Yes, it was fearful. I think I must be a very poor traveller, I was exhausted.'

'It is a long way,' offered Peter. It had been his intention to strike up a conversation with Dulcie alone, but such was the dearth of small talk generally that he felt compelled now to address the entire table. 'It's a shame you've missed the Heuriger,' he said, 'since you like our local wine.'

'What is that?' asked Thea, including Josef in the question.

But it was Peter who answered. 'It's a splendid occasion, isn't it, Frau Baronin? Everyone goes out to the villages —perhaps Dornbach or Grinzing—and the wine-growers hang a wreath outside their homes to invite passersby to come in and sample the new wine.'

'It sounds fun,' said Thea.

'We take our own food, and sit on wooden benches in the garden, and listen to music under the stars, and sing—'

'How charming!' cried Dulcie, quite carried away, but also intent on keeping de Laszlo's attention to herself. 'When is this?'

'In October,' said Josef, quite curtly. Thea saw that he was looking at de Laszlo with cold dislike.

'Perhaps we shall be here then!' carolled Dulcie.

There was something in her manner that reminded Thea forcibly of the reason for their visit. She observed Peter de Laszlo, still extolling the delights of the Heuriger. He was svelte, sallow and dark, with large speaking eyes and wavy hair, worn rather long. Like gypsy violins in a sophisticated restaurant he was sweet to the ear, charming and seductive, and yet distinctly bogus. It appeared that Josef was not alone in mistrusting him, for all the time he talked the Baron's head sank between hunched shoulders like a tortoise's into its shell, and his heavy, veined eyelids drooped with boredom and distaste. No love lost there either, she surmised. She felt a light touch on her wrist.

'I am sure you will love Vienna,' said Josef. 'Tomorrow, perhaps you would like to see more of the city?'

'Indeed I would.'

'We could take the carriage and ride around, have some coffee in one of the old coffee-houses. I should like to show you. Do you like opera?'

'I've never been to one.' She blushed, but he seemed pleased.

'Then I can introduce you to it, it will be my honour.'

Annelise leaned across. 'Don't let him bully you into too much opera, Thea; it's so boring, and all of it's far too long.'

'Thea will be the judge of that,' he reproved gently. 'In my opinion opera is the highest art form. At its best it is an almost spiritual experience.'

Annelise laughed, but without malice. 'Watch out, Thea.'

'I am sure I shall love it,' said Thea, truthfully, and was repaid by a look of such tender admiration and confidentiality that she knew instantly that hours of opera would be a small price to pay for the joy of this serious man's company.

The meal relapsed into silence with the arrival of the Sachertorte. Thea and Dulcie were subsequently to learn that the long silences during that first dinner were not on account of their presence, but characteristic of all dinners in the von Crieff household. The Baron exemplified the Austrian attitude to food, which was one of almost ceremonial single-mindedness: one sat down at the table to eat, and social intercourse of all kinds was entirely secondary to this purpose. Consequently, conversation was limited to the intervals between courses and for the rest of the time one cleared one's plate at a steady pace—not fast enough to

155

affront the digestion, nor slowly enough for the food to turn cold.

After three glasses of Grinzinger, however, Dulcie was not inclined to do as the Romans did. On the contrary, she was becoming more animated by the second, enjoining her hosts to take her 'everywhere, absolutely everywhere!' because she was 'simply dying to see everything!' Though she might have been rushing in where angels feared to tread as far as the Baron was concerned, it was clear that she had disarmed the rest of the family. Jessica beamed upon her like a beneficent sun; Annelise suggested that they go shopping together at the earliest opportunity; and even Dieter, dismissed from the table after the dessert, suggested sheepishly that she might enjoy the Big Wheel at the Prater, whereupon she placed a kiss on his fiery cheek and vowed she should ride upon it with none but him. As for Peter de Laszlo, his expression was one of rapt delight as though, on peeling off the layers of an unpromising parcel, he had discovered its contents to be, after all, exactly what he had wished for. Josef, Thea noticed, seemed to reserve judgement on her sister, watching her display of bubbling vivacity in thoughtful silence, smoothing his moustache.

When they had withdrawn from the dining-room for coffee, Dulcie was whisked to the card table by Peter and Annelise to be initiated into the mysteries of taroc, while Thea and Josef sat down with the Baron and his wife. With the coffee poured, Jessica placidly returned to her embroidery and Thea, partly to prevent herself staring at Josef and partly from a sense of duty, addressed her host.

'This is a beautiful city, Uncle,' she began tentatively. 'Josef took us round the Ringstrasse before we came here this afternoon. It's very fine.'

'You think so?' He looked at her over the rim of his cup. Surely he was not going to disagree?

'Yes, I do. It's so symmetrical and elegant—built to a plan, not like most of our towns in England.'

'Mhm. Good,' was his cryptic reply.

Thea soldiered on. 'The Hofburg is magnificent. Is the Emperor in residence there?'

Her question hung in a dead silence; the Baron appeared not to have heard. Jessica stitched away tranquilly.

Josef rescued her, saying quietly: 'The Emperor is at the palace of Schönbrunn, to the south, beyond the Ring.

It's a beautiful place, and more peaceful; he prefers it there.'

She listened gratefully. Even his tone of voice was a gentle reassurance, almost a caress. But the Baron's voice, cold and sharp, cut across it peremptorily.

'The fact is, our noble Emperor is fast becoming a recluse. In Schönbrunn his rooms are like a caretaker's—an iron bedstead, no running water, no personal comforts whatever. He remains dignified but aloof. Each day the editor of one of the moderate newspapers appears before him to apprise him of the political situation. In the summer he will retreat still further to the Kaiser Villa at Bad Ischl in the Alps, with only a few other old gentlemen for company.'

'You make it sound so sad.'

'It *is* sad,' said Josef.

'Those are the facts.' His father was curt. Thea sensed tension between them.

'The Emperor,' said Josef, 'whatever his faults, is still the anchor of this nation.'

'We are *not* a nation!' The Baron's voice rose angrily. His wife glanced up for the first time. 'A child can see that the days of the imperial house are numbered. We are hopelessly, fruitlessly divided. Do you realize that we have had twenty-one cabinets in forty-three years? That there are no fewer than two dozen political parties, opposed not only to the government but to each other? And the Emperor? He is opposed to all of them—opposed to parliament, opposed to democracy, opposed to franchise.'

'If that is the case—' began Thea.

'I have just told you that it is.'

She drew breath. 'If that is the case, then he is the last emperor. He must be.'

She saw the Baron look at her, surprise dawning on his face, but when she looked at Josef she saw that he was shocked.

'I'm sure Thea isn't interested in all this,' said Jessica, holding the coffee pot aloft interrogatively.

'Oh but I am,' said Thea truthfully.

The Baron picked up his newspaper. 'Anyway, enough of it,' he said. 'It is a depressing topic.'

Josef rose. 'If you will excuse me, Mother.'

'Must you go dear?' Jessica caught his hand, and he stooped to kiss her cheek in reply.

'Father.'

The Baron looked round his paper. 'Goodnight, Josef.'

'Goodnight, sir.'

Thea went with him to the door. The others waved their goodnights from the card table.

In the doorway he turned and took her hand. 'I shall see you tomorrow afternoon, then. Shall I call for you at three?'

'That would be delightful.'

He lifted her hand to his lips. There was something devout in his bent head, his lowered eyes, his hand beneath hers as if receiving the host. She again wanted to touch that curling yellow hair.

He straightened, but retained her hand for a moment, holding it fast. 'Thea,' he said intensely, anxiously, his voice lowered, 'Thea, the Emperor is a noble man, a stoic. He believes the Habsburg Crown to be a divine right. He has endured great personal suffering in his lifetime. His brother, his son, his wife—all met violent deaths.' He stared into her face, assessing her reaction.

She was astonished. 'I am sure that is true, but—'

'We owe him loyalty, Thea.'

'Well,' she smiled; she did not care what she said, 'perhaps you do.'

He released her hand with a sigh. She was glad she had agreed with him.

'Till tomorrow then.'

'Till tomorrow.' She watched him walk away across the great hall, a solitary, dignified figure.

The following day was to set the pattern for many others. In the morning, Josef would be on duty, either at the barracks or at the Hofburg, and Peter was ensconced with Dieter in the austere schoolroom at the top of the house. The Baron would breakfast early, never forgetting to enquire of de Laszlo what special educational forays he had planned for the day. He would then take a turn round the garden, head bowed and hands behind back, and retire to his study for an hour or two. At twelve he would leave for his club by car, from where he would not return until mid-afternoon. Jessica rarely broke her fast until ten and this she did by taking coffee and rolls in her room. At eleven she would emerge pink, powdered and refreshed and lead Thea, Dulcie and Annelise forth on an expedition. She seemed to have no other aim in life than to keep her nieces amused, and clearly welcomed the opportunity to indulge in her favourite pastime, shopping.

On the very first morning she ordered the carriage to convey them to the Kärntnerstrasse and insisted on buying each of them a dress, in a shop the interior of which resembled a potentate's palace. Out of an ingrained habit of thriftiness in matters of dress, Thea was inhibited by the price of everything, though Dulcie entertained no such scruples, and in the end under her aunt's enthusiastic urging she gave in and chose a gown of caramel lace and moiré with a broad brown velvet sash, trying not to think of the money so lightly charged to Jessica's account.

As her aunt supervised the packing up of the purchases, Thea remarked to Annelise: 'I can't help feeling guilty. Aunt Jessica must have spent a fortune on us in here.'

Annelise, covetously fingering a rose satin peignoir, waved a hand dismissively. 'Don't give it a thought. We're not short of money, you know, and besides, if she wasn't spending it on you she'd be spending it on herself—she has accounts in half the shops in the city. It's her hobby, it keeps her happy.'

Thea, obliged to accept this explanation, nonetheless considered it an odd, even a cold-blooded one. But a few days in the company of her aunt dispelled her reservations. There was no stopping Jessica. She showered them with presents. Never a day passed but that she pressed upon them some 'little something' that she 'simply couldn't resist': fans, jewellery, scarves, perfume, chocolates, they flowed from her in an endless stream which no amount of well-bred protest could stem. It was abundantly obvious that the giving of gifts and the spending of money did indeed keep Jessica von Crieff happy. For the most part her life was lonely, barren and dull. She was a lively, kindly woman trapped in a tomb of soulless wealth. The Baron was seldom with her except in the evenings and even then he seemed more to tolerate than to welcome her company. She had few friends, for he did not care for entertaining, and they went out but rarely. Clearly it salved his none-too-severely troubled conscience to allow his wife to spend his money as she would.

After further surveying, admiring and deliberating in the Kärntnerstrasse they repaired to Demel's. Among *Konditorei*, of which there were hundreds in Vienna, Demel's held an unchallenged position of supremacy. It was far more than a pastry shop: it was a hallowed temple to the confectioner's art. There was an air of near-religious solemnity about the front room, *das Gewolbe*, with its dark panelling and vast white-draped tables, like altars, laden with torten, brioches, pastries and gateaux. The waitresses who served them with an air of lordly detachment were, Jessica informed them in an undertone, recruited straight from school, wore long black buttoned boots beneath their black serge skirts, and marched to church on Sundays in tight formation, like crack troops or novices in a closed order. Haste was the hallmark of a plebeian upbringing.

'It is an unwritten house rule,' Jessica whispered, 'that *Herrschaften haben Zeit*. Ladies and gentlemen *never* hurry. And these waitresses are all ladies!'

As with the service, so with the food. It would have been an insensitive customer indeed who did not feel that he was not simply filling his belly and thickening his waistline, but engaging in a holy rite. Everything consumed on the premises was made there also, and every chef employed in its making a specialist. Chocolate-makers, cake-bakers, marzipan-moulders and candy-decorators: each had had their own guild and their own strict code of practice. It was said that every sugar-baker was a trained sculptor, and this Thea and Dulcie could well believe. For the window of Demel's, now that Easter was approaching, was a mouthwatering *tour de force* of culinary skill. Marzipan trains, gingerbread houses, peppermint lakes, sugar waterfalls, nougat castles and chocolate mountains capped with snowy cream—a complete edible landscape of sweet perfection.

'Heavens! Can you wonder the women run to fat?' whispered Dulcie as they left. For not only had they all four partaken of a huge slice of fruit torte swathed in whipped cream, and coffee topped with the same, but Jessica was leaving the shop bearing a large beribboned white carton packed with further delights for teatime.

Of course, there were days when Jessica set aside her own predilection for the frivolous and the fattening and dutifully did the right thing by her nieces. Stalwartly, she accompanied them to the Natural History Museum, where they stared respectfully at the remains of the oldest inhabitants of the Danube Basin, mammoth tusks and bones found in the subsoil of Vienna. As Dulcie said, 'Surely one prehistoric skeleton looks just like another? It's boring!' But Jessica was so obviously well-intentioned that they went along with her without complaint. Doggedly, she took them to St Stephen's Cathedral, to the dwellings of numerous composers in the far-flung suburbs of the city, to galleries, churches and palaces without number. But she could never quite keep the note of relief out of her voice when the witching hour of one o'clock was reached, and she would announce: 'Luncheon-time!'

It was left to Josef to show Thea the special character and magic of the city his mother had never truly felt at home in.

On the first afternoon he called for her punctually at three. When she came to the top of the stairs she saw him there below her, standing with his back to her, his cap held at his waist.

'Josef.'

'Thea!' He turned to greet her, a smile of great sweetness illuminating his usually rather serious face. He came to the foot of the stairs and stood there, one hand outstretched to receive hers. She ran down to him, her feet barely skimming the steps, her hand slipping into his like a bird returning to its nest. This time he did not raise it to his lips but held her at arm's length, admiring her.

'You look lovely. Are you ready?'

'Thank you, and yes I am.'

'Is your sister coming?'

Thea was taken aback. She had not yet learned that for Josef von Crieff propriety was part of a firmly held personal creed. It had simply not occurred to her that Dulcie had been included in the invitation. But before she could fumble for a reply, Dulcie supplied it by appearing on the landing with Annelise.

'Thea! We are going to take Dieter to the Prater—hello, Josef—and Peter is coming, and we are going to see if Annelise's Lieutenant Eggars can, too!'

Thea beamed. 'That's all right, we are going for a drive.'

'But, Josef!' wailed Annelise. 'The carriage—'

'You take it.' Josef waved an indulgent hand. 'I think we shall take a fiacre.'

'You're a lamb!'

Annelise and Dulcie ran back to their rooms to prepare for the outing and Josef and Thea left. It was a fine fresh afternoon, not as warm as the day before but with that anticipatory golden glow in the light which reminds one of long summer days to come. She took Josef's arm and they walked from the house at Helenastrasse to the Graben, hub of the old inner town, to pick up a fiacre from the rank by St Stephen's. As they approached the row of smart hansom cabs she saw that many of the gleaming pairs of horses had sprays of early blossom tucked into their brow-bands, and strands of coloured ribbon twisted in their manes and tails.

She pointed delightedly. 'Aren't they lovely?'

Josef nodded. 'The Viennese cab-driver is very conscious of appearances. Now look—' he touched her hand, 'see the first fellow in the line there? Watch him light his cigar. It's part of his uniform, he won't attend to us until it's ready.'

They drew level with the foremost fiacre and Thea looked up. The driver was a handsome, stocky fellow, turned out in a sporting brown and yellow check suit and brown bowler; his weather-reddened face was framed by an impressive spread of mutton-chop whiskers, and from the centre of it jutted a thin, ten-inch 'Virginia', one of the better inventions of the state tobacco monopoly. This he commenced to light by removing from its centre a long straw which he lit, and then replaced with a colossal concentration. Not until the operation was completed to his satisfaction, and the cigar smouldering comfortably, was he ready to give them his undivided attention. Josef directed him to the Volksgarten and they set off. Thea, less nervous than she had been during the drive from the station, looked out, enchanted by the huddled baroque and romanesque houses, with towers and casements overhanging the street like a picture from a book of fairytales. Sometimes, between the houses, a flurry of crooked stone steps or a narrow cobbled footpath would dart steeply away, the secret passage to some maze of smaller streets.

Josef, watching her rapt face, said: 'Remember, Thea, when you look at this city, that you are in a theatre and watching a performance.'

'Should I!' She tore her gaze away from the scene outside and he leaned forward, elbows on knees, like a storyteller.

'Indeed you should. The Viennese are a race of actors *manqués*. They perform their roles flawlessly against their exquisite scenery.'

'They? You exclude yourself from this troupe of actors?' she teased him.

'Oh no.' He was emphatic. 'Far from it. I have never trod

162

the boards in my life but I too am part of the play. Look—'
He indicated, with a long, expressive hand, his uniform,
from top to toe. 'This is a costume for the stage rather than a
battle, isn't it? I think so. I need do nothing, this costume
marks me out for a particular role.'

'And that is?'

'The Emperor's man.' He seemed to consider this enough,
deflecting the course of the conversation from himself with
the ease of one accustomed to do so often. 'But don't think we
are calculating or cold. It is not all vanity or artifice. We are a
passionate people buffeted by a harsh history. Vienna has
survived plague, siege and war by shrugging them off as acts
in a drama.'

He sat back, his fingers touching the tiny scar on his
mouth. As if to reinforce his words they passed the massive
and imposing Plague Memorial, an awesome monument to
death executed in lush baroque style. 'I dare say my mother
will take you to a great many churches,' he said, as the fiacre
began the descent to the Ring, and the road widened, leaving
the secret closeness of the old town. 'When she does, see how
different they all are, each with its special character. This is
because the Viennese goes into his church as he does into his
favourite coffee-house or pastry-shop, quite casually, and he
likes to feel he belongs. So he selects his church to suit his
own character. He has his tailor, his barber, his *Konditorei*—and his church.'

She laughed, delighted with the idea. 'I'll bear it in mind.'

They were in the Ring now, part of the broad river of
trams, buses, cabs, carriages and riders which somehow
contrived to appear leisurely in spite of its volume. They had
been this way with Jessica only a few hours previously and
yet already she saw it with different eyes. Of course it was a
stage, she could see that now. People strolled, turned,
paraded like mannequins; horses stepped high, with arched
necks and flaring tails; even the buildings emanated a sense
of occasion as though conscious of their contribution to the
show. The very air hummed with a kind of soft, melodious
murmur which reminded her of the thrill of a theatre
orchestra tuning up, and which she came later to recognize as
the distinctive sound of Vienna: the half-heard melodies of a
thousand different musicians, a tune that never ended and
which pervaded the life of the city.

Yet continually she observed how this gentle mist of sound

would be broken, by the passing of soldiers along one or other of the wide highways, the crunch of marching boots, the jingle and clatter of cavalry, or the piercing clarion shout of a bugle from Rossau Barracks. The city, she thought, was like a still summer lake whose peaceful surface belied the swift and treacherous currents beneath. There was indeed the music. But, everywhere and at all times, there were also the soldiers.

They alighted at the Volksgarten and began to walk. On either side of the park, rising from the sea of treetops like great ships, stood the Hofburg and the Burgtheater, solid, elegant, harmonious, the afternoon sun glinting and glancing off a myriad windows. Beneath the trees the green spaces of the garden were quite unlike the great city parks of London which Thea could remember. The Volksgarten was neither so grand nor so spacious as Hyde Park, its dimensions were more domestic; and yet the care lavished on its appearance was evident in everything from the lawns like emerald carpets to the cupola, filigreed as a wedding cake, wherein played a band in dazzling uniforms of kingfisher-blue and gold. Paths of white gravel curved and swung among the trees as though following the figures of a swirling waltz. And the roses! To Thea's enchanted astonishment some were already in bloom and there were untold thousands yet to come—enough roses and more to fill a long summer with their ravishing colour and fragrance. Josef picked one long-stemmed bud, its petals ripening from creamy coral to deep flame, and tucked it in the lapel of her brown jacket.

'Should you?' She touched it gently. Whether it was allowed or no, she could not now bear to be parted from it.

'What is one, amongst all these?' He made an expansive gesture. 'They bloom from March to October. Besides, you deserve one, even if it were to defy the whole might of the Imperial Royal Guard!'

They walked on, the music ebbing and flowing on the light breeze. The same breeze riffled the silver-green leaves of the linden trees so that they gave off a delicate frou-frou as soft and urbane as the rustle of a lady's ballgown. Borders bursting with spring flowers were scattered over the lawns like cushions, and the brilliance of the ubiquitous uniforms studded the scene like jewels. Thea felt her heart leap for happiness, for she too was pàrt of the show, with Josef at her side, his favour in her buttonhole, and one of her most fetching hats—she was glad she had worn it—with a masse of creamy tulle swathing its broad, shady brim.

So heady was the sensation, like a draught of champagne, that she who abhorred coyness could not resist asking flirtatiously: 'Tell me, Captain—what part do I play?'

He stopped, and looked down at her contemplatively, his eyes moving over her face like the sensitive, searching hands of a blind person, absorbing every detail.

'You are . . . you are the lovely English lady with the gay free spirit and the light in her eyes.'

'Thank you.' A little embarrassed at having called forth such precise and high praise she looked away, hoping her hat-brim would hide her red cheeks. But he calmly tucked her arm through his and led her on.

'There is always music in our theatre. It is part of the air, we breathe it, it is life to us. They say that in the Wienerwald even the birds sing in tune.'

'How romantic. How does anyone do any work in such a place?' She shook her head in disbelief. 'I'm perfectly certain that if I lived here I should become the complete hedonist, fit for nothing but strolling in lovely parks, and dancing and generally having a good time. All my good intentions and my high ideals and ambitions would fly out of the window—and the worst of it would be I shouldn't care!'

'That's it!' he laughed aloud, and then wagged an admonitory finger. 'But don't let yourself be tricked. We call our city "das Wien" and pretend it is neuter but in our hearts we know her to be feminine. She is capricious and challenging, a lady with the heart of a wanton. Be warned!'

They circled the park and re-emerged onto the Ring, where Josef hailed another fiacre to take them the half-mile or so to the Café Heinrichshof opposite the opera house. Josef selected a table near the window and placed the order.

Thea looked about. It was certainly quite unlike what in England was understood by a café. They looked out onto the elegant façade of the opera house across the street, but the decor of the coffee-house was hardly less opulent. Long windows at the front reached almost from floor to ceiling, and were framed by heavy tobacco-brown velvet curtains, faded in vertical streaks by the sun. The tables were either of dark polished wood with immense carved pediments or great spheres of veined marble, like Stilton cheese. Overhead, from a ceiling of cathedral height, were suspended huge branching chandeliers of brass and silver. But it was the atmosphere more than the appearance of the place which intrigued Thea. It seemed to have more in common with a select but informal club than a high-street dispenser of light refreshment. Not everyone, by any means, seemed to be drinking coffee, though most had cups before them, and very few were eating. Instead they talked, played chess, wrote letters, or browsed contentedly through some of the vast assortment of papers and periodicals, in all languages, which lay spread over a long table in the centre of the room.

Curious about this leisurely manner of the café's patrons, she asked Josef, 'Won't they be asked to leave if they've finished their coffee and they're not going to buy anything else?'

'Ah!' he laughed, 'you have observed the special character of the Vienna coffee-house. It is a second home to the people who come here, it would be unthinkable for them to be turned out. We could sit here all day, as some do, drinking no more than two or three cups of coffee and a few glasses of water, and no one would disturb us. This is a meeting-place, a market, a forum, a library, a fashion show—and last of all a coffee-shop.'

Their order arrived, coffee whose ambrosian scent hung like incense in the air above the pavements of Vienna, and Josef's special choice, Sicilienne, fresh raspberry and vanilla icecream soaked in Malaga wine and decorated with dried grapes. Even this confection, served in an elegant cut-glass dish, had a sort of self-conscious beauty, so that it seemed desecration to attack it with a spoon.

After a brief exchange with the waiter in German, Josef introduced her. Her hand was clasped warmly, and the words 'Fräulein Thea' repeated over and over again with much bowing and beaming, as though they were to be consigned to memory once and for all.

'I can see they know you here,' she laughed when the waiter at last bustled off and she addressed herself to the pink and white slopes of her Sicilienne.

Josef lowered his voice conspiratorially. 'The fact is, even if they didn't, they would pretend to, otherwise there would be dreadful loss of face. Here, a face without a name, or better still a title, is almost no person at all. I've heard it said that humanity begins at "Baron".'

'But I have no title!'

'No, but they will assign you one before long, I promise you. Tell me, do you like it?' He pointed at her dish.

'It's delicious, one of the nicest things I've ever eaten.' She was blissfully happy. The icecream was the most delectable she had tasted since her first-ever icecream at the age of four. Outside, a squad of the Imperial-Royal guard marched in heart-stopping splendour to the Hofburg, and as someone opened the door of the café the sound of a silver band gushed into the room like spring water.

It was an hour before they left, during which time Josef talked about his city with all the affection and enthusiasm that his mother could not muster, and promised Thea so many outings and experiences that her head span. Only on the way home did he relapse into silence, abruptly and totally, surveying her thoughtfully, his hand over his mouth. Because his silence seemed not inimical, but merely pensive, she remained quiet herself and concentrated on the new and enchanting landscape outside the cab window.

At Helenastrasse he asked the fiacre to wait, and came to the door with her. He still appeared preoccupied. 'Tomorrow I cannot see you,' he said. 'The next day is Dieter's birthday, I shall come round then.'

'I'll look forward to it.'

'And I.' He kissed her hand. 'So until then.' He turned to leave.

'Josef—' He looked back at her. 'Josef, thank you. Thank you so much.' She could not convey to him adequately the pleasure she had taken from this tranquil, sunny afternoon spent in his company. And yet to thank him enough would be to tell too much.

He smiled and made a dismissive gesture with his hand. 'It's Vienna you should thank. She delights in a fresh audience.'

She watched him go, and then rushed in and up to her room, there to pick over in delicious, miserly secrecy the gems of the last two hours. Not even the news that Dulcie's afternoon had not gone so well could tarnish her happiness. Dulcie entered, without knocking, at six o'clock, and plumped down on the bed with evident ill-humour.

Thea, feeling inclined to tease rather than to indulge her, enquired carelessly: 'Did you have a good time?'

'It was all right. How about you?'

'Marvellous!'

'Well . . .' Dulcie lay back on the pillows and surveyed Thea, who was standing in her shift selecting a dress for the evening. 'It was all right for you going off on your own like that. We had to put up with that whiny boy all afternoon.'

'You were very keen to take him.'

'Yes, but I didn't know he'd be such a pest, did I? He wants attention all the time—' Thea smiled, 'and he went on and on at me to go on the Big Wheel with him.'

'You promised you would.'

'I dare say, but it was huge, and you know I can't stand heights. They put you in these horrid little cabins, and it made me feel sick.'

'Oh poor Dulcie!' Thea stepped into the caramel lace dress and went over to her. 'Do me up, would you?' When she had done so she sat down by Dulcie on the bed and put her arm about her shoulders, but she couldn't help laughing. 'My poor little sister, what a terrible time you've had!'

Something of Thea's golden good humour must have infected Dulcie, for she smiled grudgingly in spite of herself and glanced at Thea from beneath her lashes. 'It wasn't all bad. Peter is so charming. I won a honey-cake heart at the shooting-range, you know!'

Thea clapped her hand to her brow. 'I hope no one was standing too close at the time.'

'Don't be rude. Lieutenant Eggars said I was a very good shot, and Peter told me to eat it at once and make a wish on the first mouthful.'

'And did you?'

'Yes, but it had masses of cinnamon which I've never liked . . .'

'That's probably what made you sick!' Thea collapsed in helpless laughter.

'I hate you,' said Dulcie without venom, 'I really do.'

'What did you wish?'

'Never you mind.' Dulcie rose and swirled her skirt about her. She had on a blue dress, the colour of harebells. She looked like a well-coiffed dryad. 'I like Peter. He sat with his arm round me all the way home. To stop the carriage shaking me about too much.'

Something knocked at Thea's conscience. 'Dulcie . . .'

'Don't say it!' Dulcie covered her ears with her hands. 'I don't want to hear it. And people in glass houses, remember . . .'

Thea had to acknowledge that. It was a case of 'physician, heal thyself'. 'Just be careful,' she said. 'We are guests, after all.'

'Never fear, I shall be the model guest!' announced Dulcie. She went to the door. 'I am going down to make eyes at the Baron.'

'Dulcie!' Thea reproved, but felt the laughter bubbling inside her like champagne.

Dulcie swished out and closed the door, then opened it again. 'By the way,' she enquired, her eyes round and innocent. 'Does the brave Lieutenant really wear a poker inside his jacket, or haven't you had a chance to find out yet?'

She just shut the door in time before the pillow struck it with a thud.

So the first days passed. And both Thea and Dulcie found it far easier to forget the reason for their visit than they had ever imagined possible. As the weeks slipped by the events of Christmas took on the insubstantial quality of a half remembered bad dream, fading with every minute, its misery dwindling to a pinprick down the corridor of time. And between them and its rapidly disappearing shadow, a brilliant colourful throng of happy occasions jostled for supremacy, elbowing guilt, anxiety and caution aside until they were lost entirely to view.

To be sure Thea's indolent conscience did occasionally rouse itself, but only in the most half-hearted manner. Peter de Laszlo was emphatically not the escort she would have chosen for her sister, had she had any hand in the matter; in fact she would far rather have seen Dulcie encouraging a bevy of admirers, which she could quite easily have done, instead of this one smooth, sweet-talking and, Thea thought, saturnine young man with his opaque black eyes that seemed to mock all they saw.

Occasionally it did look as if Dulcie might abandon him. She had ample opportunity, for his position in the household precluded his accompanying them on many occasions. At one rather tedious *Hauskonzert* which he was unable to attend, Dulcie actually brought the proceedings to a halt with her covert nods and speaking glances to the clutch of subalterns in the front row. Given the choice between the stout, bejewelled matron delivering Schubert on the pianoforte, and Dulcie, bright and beautiful as a kingfisher in her blue dress, there was no doubt who claimed their attention. The pedestrian thump of the instrument was all but drowned by the scrape of boots and chairlegs as they strained to catch her eye. Thea, sitting between Josef and Dulcie, had been torn between mirth and embarrassment, the former finally conquering as one of the young blades, more ardent than the rest, fell completely off his chair with a tremendous clatter. This disruption, and the ensuing gales of laughter from the nearest onlookers, caused the mortified pianist to retire in a huff while the wretched hostess, ignorant of the real cause of the disturbance, tried vainly to restore the serene and cultured tenor of the evening.

The whole episode was so full of natural farce, the young man so genial and charming, and Dulcie so admirably innocent and wide-eyed, that Thea was convulsed. But Josef had not been amused.

'These are kind people,' he muttered reproachfully to Thea over supper, 'and friends of my parents. Your sister should exert more self-control.'

'And so should your officers!' she retorted, beginning once again to laugh. But she stopped when she saw he was genuinely put out. 'Please don't be cross, she doesn't mean to offend.'

'You think me stuffy.' He stabbed a mouthful of salmon with his fork, cast down over his perfectly proper response to the incident.

Thea was overcome by remorse. 'Oh no, of course not. You're absolutely right. But look at it this way: it's only because she's so happy and enjoying herself so much that she gets carried away. And that's good, isn't it?'

He shook his head, doubtful about the validity of this argument.

She touched his hand. 'Isn't it?'

He could not remain cross with her for long. The sun broke through. 'If you say so!'

The remainder of the evening passed off smoothly enough, with the hostess cleverly enrolling the offenders in her cause, and persuading them to render choruses from the more popular operettas, which they did with verve and feeling.

But on this, as on many other occasions, Peter de Laszlo would be waiting at Helenastrasse, his spell over Dulcie still apparently unbroken by the intervening flirtations, his manner now as casually proprietary as the owner of some wild and beautiful bird who looses it to fly free, but knows it will return.

One warm May night Thea had heard a sound on the landing in the small hours, and thinking it might be Dieter, who sometimes walked in his sleep, opened her bedroom door to take a look. To her astonishment it was Dulcie, in her nightdress, her hair over her shoulders and her small white feet bare.

'Dulcie? What on earth are you doing?'

'Oh!' Dulcie's hand flew to her mouth, then her eyes closed in an expression of relief. 'Thea, you made me jump. I'm just going to get a drink.'

'But don't you have water in your room?'

'Yes, but no glass. The maid took the carafe and glass to be washed and she's forgotten to put them back. I'm hot, I want a glass of water by my bed.'

'Oh I see . . . Goodnight then.' Thea had closed the door, her heart, for some reason, pumping wildly. As she got into bed she told herself that all she had to do was to give Dulcie a glass of water from her own room. But she had not wanted to test her, to call her bluff. It might spoil everything. And as she lay awake, straining her ears in vain for the sound of Dulcie's return, she felt a gnawing mite of envy.

But for the most part she was either oblivious to, or simply did not care, what Dulcie did. All her feelings, all her energies, were concentrated in the time she spent with Josef. She was aware that in his company she was not quite herself but, as he had predicted, adopted the role that had been assigned her. This did not disturb her. On the contrary there was a delightful sense of freedom in playing this 'lovely English lady with the gay free spirit'. It was wonderful to start, as it were, with a clean slate, to have assumed overnight a nearly perfect persona and with it a man who worshipped her. For worship her he did, there could be no doubt of it. If she could sometimes have wished for more positive proof, for the feeling of his arm about her instead of linked through hers, for his lips against her own instead of brushing her hand, she dismissed the wish as sheer impatience. He was hers, she knew it, and he would show her in his own time. And meanwhile she taught herself to savour the anticipation and the agonies of longing, so that when the moment came, it would be all the sweeter. She learned to

171

stifle that part of her nature that she knew instinctively would alienate him, and to be the very epitome of what he admired in a woman. And she was rewarded by the look that turned her legs to water, the voice that spoke direct to her heart, the glancing, solicitous touch that set her skin alight beneath her clothes.

He took her everywhere, as he had promised, expending enormous care and energy to ensure her enjoyment. She saw, with him, and partly through his eyes, the quiet, symmetrical majesty of the palace of Schönbrunn, and tried to picture 'the Old Man' as the Emperor was affectionately known, living his dignified but lonely existence within. She went to the Prater where they joined the joyful parade along the Hauptallee, and ate and drank in the outdoor cafés, in a giant fairground so full of music that when one moved away from one band, another was up ahead, leading you on and on, inviting you to forget care and have fun. With a sure sense of what she would appreciate he took her to the Spanish Riding School and she sat entranced by the Lippizaner horses. Under their skilful riders they became not mere animals of flesh and blood but creatures of almost ethereal beauty and grace, their caressing hooves attached to the ground by no more than a silken thread. Afterwards, Josef took her round to the stables and she stroked one of the horses and fed it sugar lumps, marvelling at its great black melting eyes, fringed by frosty lashes.

To prove to her that the birds did indeed sing in tune in the Vienna woods, he took her riding there and she found that they were not simply woods but hills in which one could journey all day and see no one, with the fresh lacy green of summer forming a filigree canopy overhead and the city lying like an indulgent sleepy friend, in no hurry for them to return, far below in a trembling haze.

They listened to a superb rendering of Beethoven's Fifth and Pastoral Symphonies—those written in the Heiligenstadt —at an alfresco concert in the church square of St John's Nepomuk, where the façades of the old houses all round not only seemed like the faces of other listeners but to provide acoustics as perfect as those in any concert hall. The very air was in tune, not simply with the music but with her mood, so that she knew she could do no wrong.

He took her—with a charming display of diffidence, as though he had taken seriously Annelise's warning about boredom—to the opera, to see a performance of *Die Meister-singer* with the magnificent tenor Leo Slezak. But he need not have worried. To Thea in her present mood the whole evening, not simply the music but the setting and the atmosphere, was nothing short of magical. From the moment of their arrival, and the long procession up the sweeping staircase, like the faithful ascending to heaven, she accepted Josef's description of opera as a spiritual experience. Certainly no pains and expense had been spared to ensure that it was. The Court Opera was the Emperor's own, he took a keen personal interest in it, and the Hof-Loge or Court Box was always occupied by some member of the arch-house even though the Old Man himself was no longer a theatre-goer. If there were any deficit—a state of affairs which everyone, including the Emperor, was at pains to avoid—it was made up out of his private purse, and not the taxpayer's. To the relief of the highly discerning, but conservative, Viennese audience the unpopular Gustav Mahler (or 'Malheur' as he had become known) had been replaced as Hofopern Direktor by the elegant and aristocratic Felix von Weingartner, chief conductor of the orchestra. Mahler had been a dour, tetchy perfectionist whose motto was 'Tradition is negligence'; what a relief to have a debonair, civilized man at the helm, who knew how to please people instead of antagonizing them! Gazing about her during the orchestra's tuning-up, Thea thought the audience every bit as impressive as anything that might appear on stage, the men resplendent in full dress uniforms or glistening white waistcoats and tails, the ladies gorgeously pampered, faultlessly assured. Even the ushers, in discreet brown, gold-braided uniforms, were as dignified as dukes. When the light went down, the hum of voices died away, and the great curtain rose on the opening act, Thea was transported.

All evening Josef watched her. There was something childlike in her capacity for wonder. Her expression was rapt, the lips slightly parted, two small creases of concentration between the bird's-wing black brows, as if she were determined not to miss a thing. If Josef could have captured and crystallized her excitement and pleasure he would gladly have done so, and made her a gift of it. He was a man who admired, above all things, sincerity. All forms of double-dealing were anathema to him: it was what made him a good soldier. In his cousin he perceived, he thought, that most remarkable of qualities in a woman: the inability to dissemble. Ever cautious about displaying his most private feelings, he thought that here was someone to whom those feelings would not appear laughable or foolish but would accept them with dignity and understanding. And she was beautiful. He was proud to be seen with her and to glimpse the heads turn as they walked together. Every so often as she listened to the music a strand of her long black hair would fall on her shoulder and she would put up a hand to tuck it back in place. Once, she forgot to do so and he did it for her, feeling with a little shock how the pale ivory skin of her neck was warm and vibrant where his hand brushed it. She wore a green dress and a strange, pagan-looking necklace that struck a discordant note; he imagined that the small shield-shaped pieces of which the necklace was composed must also be warm from her skin, and he envied them their smooth, intimate proximity. She turned to look at him and mouthed 'Thank you', putting her own hand to her hair as if in apology for its waywardness. He looked back at the stage, suddenly racked by violent, unfamiliar feelings.

At eleven o'clock they emerged to find that a soft rain was falling. He left her side for a moment to hail a fiacre and she waited for him, still slightly dazzled and overwhelmed by the grandeur of the opera. The audience flowed round her and out into the night like a bright river, some of the ladies remaining behind while transport was fetched, others hurrying beneath hastily opened umbrellas. Beneath a streetlamp a little to the right of the main entrance she caught sight of a short, bearded man, conspicuous for his air of watchful stillness. He was dressed in a long, dark coat, the collar turned up, and a wide black hat, from the brim of which the rain drops pattered onto his shoulders. As she watched, two young women came from behind her and ran over to him. At once he became animated, holding out his arms to embrace them in the soft pool of drifting, rain-filled light. He questioned them eagerly as they all three hurried off arm in arm to join the queue for the Last Blue—last tram of the night. Amid the theatrical throng of opera-lovers they seemed a strangely unselfconscious group, aware only of each other, heedless of the rain.

Josef returned and they ran to the cab. As they drove past the tram queue she pointed to the bearded man, the two girls still clinging to either arm, talking animatedly.

'Who's that?'

He followed her pointing finger, peering out into the gleaming rain-filled street. He saw at once who she meant and sat back again. 'It's the Jewish doctor, Freud.'

'Freud?' She was astonished. 'Sigmund Freud?'

'Those were his daughters with him. They go to the opera a good deal.'

She craned over her shoulder to catch another glimpse of the man, but they were too far away now. 'Do you know him?' she asked.

'No.'

She was too excited to notice that he was being short to the point of rudeness. 'Then how did you know it was him?'

'My father knows him.'

'Really?'

He did not reply. His face was turned away from her, gazing out of the opposite window. Suddenly realizing that she was treading on delicate ground she abandoned the next question she had been about to ask. But after a short pause he cleared his throat and said: 'My father is a patient of his.'

'I see.' She was careful not to allow her surprise to creep into her voice. It was clearly a matter which embarrassed Josef and would be better left unexplored, if she were not to spoil their time together.

They went on to Sacher's for supper. By the time they arrived they had managed, mainly by Thea's efforts, to cast off the small shadow that had fallen across the otherwise sparkling happiness of their evening. But on arrival at the restaurant Thea quickly forgot the incident. Once past the door she entered another world, timeless, luxurious, almost womblike in its separateness. Wine-coloured velvet and thick pile carpet deadened sound so that one had the sensation of walking on air. Tables were spread with glistening white damask cloths that fell to the floor, and were laid with immaculate silver and cut glass, each with its own centre-piece of roses at exactly the right stage of bloom. Above, chandeliers like clouds of scintillating crystal shed their light on a clientele of unsurpassed breeding and beauty. As they sat down at their table the strains of a discreetly positioned string orchestra stole across the room, and Thea observed their fellow diners and tried to pinpoint what it was that distinguished them from the wealthy and fashionable in any great city, reaching the inevitable conclusion that it was their inherent theatricality. Here, rich and lovely women were not simply fashionable but ostentatiously exotic and eye-catching, their heads crowned with flowers and feathers, their necks, arms and hands entwined with necklaces, bracelets and rings. Many of them sported long cigarette holders of jade, ivory or ebony, from which protruded the elegant and slightly raffish cylinder of a black sobrani.

Josef misinterpreted her stare. 'You need not worry. You are the loveliest.'

'Oh, I should never be so smart. It's not in me.'

'You are worth twenty of them. Fashionable women!' He spat out the words as if they disgusted him.

She felt slightly guilty for having so obviously admired the women he despised. Determined to keep him from sliding further into the black mood whose brink he seemed to be pacing, she asked cheerfully, 'Tell me about opera. I adored this evening, every bit of it, but I'm so ignorant. I want to learn.'

As usual, he responded quickly to her directness, and proved an interesting and passionate talker on the subject, as on any that appealed to him. Throughout the meal she questioned and he talked, and she in turn admired not just his encyclopaedic knowledge of opera but his mouth, his hands, his eyes which turned from stern grey to summer blue when he became enthused. The waiter came and served coffee, and Josef ordered a brandy. Thea would have liked one herself, but something deterred her. Once he put his hands over his eyes as if suddenly tired, and his mouth, with the white streak of the scar, looked so inexpressibly sad that she longed to place her own upon it there and then, to swiftly and simply banish whatever personal ghost haunted him.

'Josef?'

He brought his hands down and cupped them round his brandy glass. 'I'm sorry.'

'Someone walked over your grave,' she offered.

He laughed. 'What an odd thing to say!'

'It's just an expression.'

The restaurant was beginning to empty, to show its bones. The orchestra played a lilting, inconsequential refrain, pretty and light and somehow touching in its delicacy. Among the glittering lights, wraiths of smoke curled and hovered like the ghosts of the brilliant evening now ending. The waiters

176

moved among the tables, silent, dark and expressionless, the faint clink of plates and glasses accompanying their progress.

'We shall be the last,' said Josef, and there was something in the cadence of his voice, a dying fall which made her shiver. Impulsively she put out her hand and placed it on his where it lay on the table.

'You're sad,' she said. 'Don't be sad.'

'Perhaps I am a sad person.' He smiled as he said it, but she sensed it was no more than the truth.

'Why? Why should you be?'

'It's not necessary to have a reason. Some of us are born sad.'

'And some have sadness thrust upon them.' He nodded, acknowledging the reference. He looked down at her hand where it still rested on his. Then slowly, as if watching himself, he turned his own palm upwards and folded it around hers.

'I have never been accustomed to love, you know,' he said rather stiffly. 'I don't believe I have ever in my life either given or received it.'

'I'm sure that's not true. You must have received love—as a child, for instance.' And now, she thought, and now, if you would only take it. But he brushed aside her remark almost scornfully.

'No, no. Ours is a strange family, Thea. My father is a fine man in many ways, a responsible husband and parent, but cold. Besides, he is fighting a battle with himself.' Thea recalled the association with 'the Jewish Doctor'. 'And Mother,' he went on, 'has never been happy in Austria, and she sees her children as Austrians, with the result that we are almost strangers. She has showed more affection to you and your sister over the past weeks than she ever showed us as children.' He glanced up at her, saw her pity and held up his hand. 'Say nothing, it's not necessary. These are facts, not grievances. I mention them only to explain my ignorance of love.'

He released her hand which, in his vehemence, his eagerness to be understood, he had held fast, almost too tightly. 'I do not even have many friends,' he went on. She could see what it was costing him to confess these things, longed to tell him that it did not matter, that she did not want to hear. But she knew also that she was privileged to hear them; he was sacrificing, for her, his pride and his self-esteem and it would be wrong of her to reject them.

'Neither at the Gymnasium, as a boy, nor now, in the army. I do my job, but I do not inspire friendship. Possibly,' he looked up at her anxiously, for the first time deliberately engaging her sympathies, inviting her opinion, 'possibly this is because I have no experience in affection.'

'Or just as possibly there are not many with whom you have much in common,' she teased him gently, wanting to prevent him from castigating himself further.

'That would be a generous analysis,' he said, but she could see it had been the right thing to say.

'Tell me about yourself,' she went on. 'I want to know. I want to know what it's been like to be you all these years when I didn't even know you existed.'

'You see me before you. I don't hide anything. You have formed your own opinion by now.'

'But I'm interested.'

'Well then, I am a cavalry officer, twenty-seven years old, and I expect to remain in the army until such time as I inherit the family estates.'

She made a face, reproving him for giving her such a paltry answer. 'What estates?'

'The house at Helenastrasse. And Wolzhof, Father's country estate in Styria.'

'Your father must be a very rich man.'

'Yes he is. But he is born to it, so it hardly matters. He does not enjoy his wealth, he simply administers it.'

'But perhaps you will enjoy it, when it's yours.'

'No.' He frowned. 'I don't care to think about it. It's a duty, that's all.'

'I suppose it must be like a family business,' she ventured. 'We have one, you know, in London. My brother Aubrey will take it over when my father . . . retires.' She realized she could not bring herself to speak of Ralph and death in the same sentence; the two concepts were utterly at variance. 'I think he looks forward to it.'

'It's not the same thing. You couldn't understand.'

She was cut to the quick, and had to look away so that he shouldn't see the tears that welled with awful readiness into her eyes. It was that 'couldn't'; with one word he had set the seal on their differences, the chasm that yawned, dark and empty, between them.

But almost at once she felt his hand on her cheek, turning her face to his, and his eyes, when she met them, were contrite.

'Thea . . . Thea, I'm so sorry. I meant nothing, nothing.' He brushed with his finger her lower lashes, feeling for the tears he suspected were there. 'Forgive me.'

That was something Thea could do, and with ease. She realized almost at once that she had not been angry with him, but with herself for falling short.

Somewhere on the far side of the room a light was turned off, the music ended and was replaced by the muted scrape of chairs, the rustle of music being gathered up for the night. The Herr Ober, a respectfully unobtrusive but eloquent figure, took up a position by the door, offering the most discreet of hints.

In the street outside the rain had stopped, but not before it had called forth from every park and garden in Vienna their distinctive scent of lilac, roses and laburnum. And as they walked, more closely now than ever before, they heard the wistful pure sound of a clarinet in some neighbouring attic room, played by the last musician left awake in the city of music.

On his way back to the barracks Josef encountered a brother officer, one Dietrich Clement. He half-hoped to pass him by but Clement, also returning after an evening spent playing cards at the Heinrichscafé, was in an expansive mood.

'Von Crieff! Hey, Josef von Crieff!'

'Oh. Good evening.' Josef paused to allow Clement to catch up with him.

'Going back?'

'Yes.'

'Mind if I walk with you?'

'Not at all.'

Josef did mind, but it couldn't be helped. Dietrich Clement was a nice enough fellow, one of a crowd who regarded the army as a kind of exclusive club, and went out on the town every night.

'What have you been up to?' he enquired of Josef as they walked along.

'Accompanying my cousin to the opera.'

'Doing your duty. That's right!' Clement laughed genially. 'Tell me, what are they like, the English females?'

'Charming young ladies, both of them.' Josef wished he had never mentioned them. It was slighting to Thea to be spoken of in that way.

'And that's all?' Clement hooted. 'You're a sober devil, and no mistake. When do the rest of us get a peep at them?'

'I couldn't say.'

'As you please . . .' Clement chuckled to himself.

They walked in silence for a while, Clement humming softly. On the corner they encountered a woman coming from the opposite direction. Clement stopped abruptly, doffing his cap and clicking his heels.

'Fräulein Bauer, good evening.'

The woman stopped and smiled. She was tall and elegant, with a long, pale, swan-like neck and slanting eyes. Her clothes were fine. She seemed a lady of quality but Josef knew well what she was; he had met her before. She cast him an amused look, smiling, inviting.

'Do you know my friend and brother officer, Josef von Crieff?' enquired Clement, introducing Josef with a flourish.

'I think so.' Fräulein Bauer extended her hand and Josef bowed over it. Her glove was scented, her wrist narrow. Her fingers in his exerted a light pressure.

'Fräulein.'

She withdrew her hand and clapped it lightly against the other one. 'Well now! Would you gentlemen care for a glass of wine?' Her voice was full of laughter. 'My apartment is close by.'

'I don't know. What do you say, von Crieff?'

'It's late.'

'Oh, just one glass!' She made a teasing face and stepped in between them, linking her arms through theirs. 'Come, only a nightcap.'

She was a dark, beautiful woman, not unlike his cousin. Josef allowed himself to be led.

An hour and a half later he returned to the barracks. He ran up the stone staircase to his room and closed the door behind him, leaning back against it as if the hounds of hell were snapping at his heels. He was shaking from head to foot.

As he undressed he could smell Fräulein Bauer's scent on his clothes and taste the winy flavour of her tongue in his mouth. He felt, as always, a flat, anti-climactic self-hatred.

The woman had met his desperation with professional skill and practised charm, caressing and flattering him, telling him he was the best . . . God! He sat down on the edge of the bed and pressed his brow onto his knees. He tried not to think of Thea but her face hung before him like a reproach.

He had left the Fräulein lying in bed. She had lit a cigarette, poured more wine, been ready to talk and laugh. But he had abandoned her, not once looking back at her surprised face, half-amused, half-aggrieved. He had pulled on his clothes and fled. Always the same.

But now, because of Thea, it was a thousand times worse.

Baron von Crieff sat in the drawing-room sipping his customary tall glass of hock and seltzer before retiring. The room was mercifully quiet. Dulcimer, de Laszlo, Annelise and her witless lieutenant were in the music room at the other side of the house. He could hear the Tennant girl's gay, silvery laugh, but only faintly, over the broken sounds of the piano as someone tried, unsuccessfully, to play. That girl's laugh always gave the impression that it had been provoked by some remark of exceptional ribaldry.

He sighed. He wished they would go to bed. It was very late, and he cherished the nocturnal silence of his home, the feeling of being the last one awake. At least Jessica, whatever her shortcomings, knew his habits and had gone up some time ago. He twirled the stem of the glass before his face and watched the bubbles shoot to the surface and burst. He felt tolerably content. The bad dreams had all but gone, the Doctor was pleased with him. He had, quite fortuitously, encountered Freud at the Tabak Trafik that afternoon, both of them purchasing their favourite cigars. The Doctor had informed him that he would be going on holiday soon, but it had turned out that his absence would coincide with the von Crieffs' stay at Wolzhof, so things could not have turned out better.

At last: the footsteps in the hall, the whispering and giggling; they were going up. The front door opened, presumably for the departure of young Eggars, but someone came in as well. He heard the familiar voice, louder than the others, not so conspiratorial, the older sister back from the opera.

He waited until silence had once again settled over the house and then retired himself. He went up the stairs slowly, his arms at his sides, head erect. He knew exactly how many steps in each flight.

As he passed Dulcimer's room he could not help but notice that the door was ajar, and that she was sitting at the dressing-table in her shift, brushing her hair. He paused, listening to the sibilant strokes of the brush. She stood up, quite unselfconsciously preening, piling her hair on top of her head with one hand. Beneath the thin shift he saw her breasts lift, and the hem of the garment rose to reveal her neat, white ankles. When she released her hair it tumbled down her back, as fine and abundant as a child's. Thomas hurried on, and as he did so the girl began to hum tunelessly, the thin sound like cigarette smoke on the night air, drifting and wandering, following him along the dark gallery to his room.

Everyone at Helenastrasse, with the possible exception of the oldest and the youngest members of the family, looked forward to the Eggars' summer ball. This was partly because it would be the last big social event they would attend before departing to the isolation of Wolzhof, and partly because they knew it would be a lavish and enjoyable evening.

Herr Fabrikant Heinrich Eggars was the wealthy and influential owner of a factory which produced components for railway engines. It did so in great volume and to a high standard of workmanship; he had nothing to be ashamed of. With his hard-earned cash he had bought for himself, his dear wife and beloved only son a palace in the approved baroque style in the fashionable Ulrichsplatz, where he employed an army of servants to attend his needs and uphold his status, and where he entertained all the best people in the earnest hope that they would entertain him back.

Yet in spite of all this Heinrich Eggars was an anxious man. He knew, and the knowledge gave him many a sleepless night, that no amount of material success and expensive entertaining could admit him to the top rank of Viennese society. Since the days when the Emperor Leopold I had issued a special police decree dividing his subjects into five distinct categories, the highest of these categories had been reserved for the aristocracy. Nothing achieved by an ordinary mortal, no matter how praiseworthy nor how rich the reward, could put him on a par with these exalted beings with their inherited supremacy.

It had therefore been one of Heinrich's most sacred wishes

to encourage the liaison between his son Erlich (for whom he had purchased a commission in one of the very best cavalry regiments) and the only daughter of one of the most blue-blooded families in Vienna, Annelise von Crieff. This relationship, if crowned with marriage, would bring him the status he craved. And a summer ball on his home ground might give the bashful Erlich just the required boost to his confidence . . .

Herr Eggars spared no expense. When the Frau Baronin von Crieff asked if her younger son's tutor might attend the ball—he had been so good to her English nieces, apparently —he was only too happy to oblige. He was sure the tutor was an excellent fellow, and it was characteristic of true aristocracy, of course, that they were not snobbish. Besides, the Frau Baronin, such a nice women in spite of being English, had actually persuaded her husband to come along, a quite unexpected feather in the host's cap.

His efforts were certainly not wasted on Thea. She had never in her life seen such opulence displayed at a private party. The Eggars' residence—it was half as large again as the von Crieffs'—sported its own ballroom, the décor of which was nothing short of palatial. Giving free rein to his delusions of grandeur, Herr Eggars had seen to it that the ceiling was embellished with a Grecian bacchanal, the walls with crossed swords, rows of lances and magnificent tapestries, and the minstrels' gallery with its own suite of chairs and music-stands all in gilt. But all these trappings could not disguise the essential grandeur of the room's proportions, the slender white columns spreading into elegant fans, the exquisite carving on the gallery balustrade, and the row of tall graceful arches that ran the length of one wall, with glass doors leading to the garden. Through these Thea could glimpse a great circular sweep of terrace, bathed in golden light from the ballroom and dotted with stone vases spilling over with flowers. Beyond the terrace an avenue of poplars led the eye away to the glimmer of a lake, in the centre of which two leaping white horses breathed fiery fountains into the still night air.

Along the opposite side of the ballroom stood a dozen massive candelabra in the form of lifesize stags in polished carved oak, the many branches of the antlers supporting the tall white candles. Between the calm-eyed stags stood footmen in livery of mulberry, white and gold, their faces puce with the weight of their uniforms and the combined heat of the blazing candles, bearing silver salvers laden with frosty glasses of champagne. Music, the spirit of Vienna, spilled joyously from the gallery onto the gathering throng beneath, telling them that only this moment mattered, that the past was best forgotten and the future left to itself.

When the von Crieff party had helped themselves to champagne Frau Eggars led away Jessica, smiling benignly, and her husband, grim and resigned, to the drawing-room to join the other older guests. Almost at once, and to their complete astonishment, Thea and Dulcie found themselves besieged by would-be partners. Both sisters had inevitably become sought-after during their weeks in Vienna, both because they were attractive and by virtue of a certain novelty value. Until now, and especially in Thea's case, admirers had kept their distance because of her association with Josef von Crieff, but no such inhibitions were in evidence tonight. It was generally known that both girls were to be whisked off to Styria in a few days' time and every young buck in the city worth his salt intended to have a last fling with *'die englische Fräulein'* before they left.

Dulcie, as usual, entered into the spirit of the occasion with a will, making a performance of selecting a partner, closing her eyes and pointing a capricious finger which caused a good deal of jostling and pushing. Thea glanced back at Peter de Laszlo. He appeared, as usual, not to be in the least put out but to quite enjoy the role of owner-spectator which he had allotted himself. He helped himself to a second glass of champagne, lit a cigarette and leaned indolently in the doorway, watching Dulcie and the scene as a whole with his customary detached and slightly scornful air.

As a group of enthusiastic blades hemmed her in, pressing their various suits, she looked round wildly for Josef. But he appeared to have accepted her popularity on this night and smiled at her, standing back and letting the others take precedence. His smile, and the little nod which accompanied it, went straight to her heart; he was telling her without doubt that she was his, that he trusted her, that the last dance and the last word would be his. As she at last accepted the invitation of a long-haired young man with soulful eyes and damp palms, she saw Josef cross the floor and address two shy girls of no more than seventeen who stood by the window looking anxious. She saw their faces light up at the approach of this handsome officer and she was glad of it.

Her partner whirled her energetically round the room, clasping her a little too tight and telling her in husky broken English that he was in the second violins of the Hofkapelle. At this stage in the evening Thea was prepared to attempt conversation, even to try out her ever-improving German, but as little as an hour later she had long since given up. There was no need and no point. She rarely danced with the same person twice, and all that was required of her was to dance well, to smile, to nod and enjoy herself, all of which came easily to her. And she was conscious of her desire to look beautiful and vivacious, not to these eager young men but to Josef, who she knew was watching her.

She danced and danced until she was dizzy and her feet ached, though she hardly noticed. The Viennese were in their element. Here was the glittering setting that they most enjoyed: men like peacocks, ladies like birds of paradise, music as sweet as spun sugar all making up a confection of carefree beauty as delectable as anything in Demel's window. Eyelashes drooped and fluttered, hands met, cheeks brushed and arms encircled waist after waist with cavalier fickleness. And Dulcie and Thea were part of it.

After supper many of the older guests left. Jessica approached Josef and Thea and the others where they sat at a table near the stupendous buffet.

'My dears, the Baron and I are leaving.'

'Oh Aunt, must you?' Thea loved all the world. 'It's such a gorgeous party and you haven't danced yet.'

'I know.' Jessica sounded a little wistful. 'Still, our dancing days are over and Thomas is tired. We shall take the car so you come in the carriage, when this is over.'

Josef rose. 'Goodnight, Mother.'

'Goodnight, my dear.' Jessica kissed him. Thea, watching them, reflected that whatever Josef might imagine to the contrary he had his mother's love. But something, a sort of shyness, prevented her from showing it as she would like. Thea felt for her aunt.

'Be good, won't you?' Jessica exhorted with a little fluttering wave and then she was gone, to gush and compliment the portly Frau Eggars on the magnificence of her hospitality while the Baron stood bored and lugubrious in the background, hands behind back, like a stork on a mud-flat.

An inevitable relaxing of protocol accompanied the departure of the older guests. The Eggars parents, foreseeing such a development (and not wanting to appear bourgeois and narrow-minded), fatalistically incarcerated themselves in the drawing-room.

Erlich, flushed and exhilarated escort to the indifferent Annelise, was among the initiators of the horse play. Under the phlegmatic gaze of the musicians, who were taking a break and addressing themselves to white wine and cold meats, the subalterns played 'hunting'. A large brocade cushion stood in for the prey, the object of the game being to spear the cushion and carry it through the 'enemy' camp of the opposing team. The predictable result was that the cushion, unmercifully savaged by swords, lay in tatters on the polished floor while the air swirled with tiny feathers like a snowstorm and the high-spirited huntsmen careered round the perimeter of the dance floor, whooping victoriously.

This was followed by a near-suicidal form of leapfrog in which the number of backs to be jumped over was increased by one at the end of each circuit, so that the last man to go might have as many as a dozen backs to clear. This being impossible, the result was total collapse. With a tremendous roar, the whole row fell to the ground like a pack of cards. Some of the participants were hurt. One young man with red hair and white skin cut his head, and the blood trickled down his cheek to stain the crisp collar of his dress jacket. This, however, seemed merely to add to the enjoyment. Pretty girls clustered about him, dabbing at the blood with silk hankies, clinging to his arm, and he smiled down at them, a hero, his eyes wide and staring with a kind of lunatic gallantry.

Thea laughed and cheered with the rest, but when she glanced at Josef he looked serious and drawn, his hand to his mouth. He caught her eye and appeared to recall himself abruptly to the present.

'Shall we dance, now?'

She nodded. The ragged, deflated cushion was kicked from the centre of the floor and retrieved by an impassive footman but a few feathers still fluttered over the boards like confetti as the orchestra began to play once more.

It was the first time she had danced with him all evening, but he was grave and silent. She had done something wrong and she didn't know what it was. As the dance ended she saw Dulcie appear, like Juliet, in the gallery, talking to the musicians, gesturing, begging them some favour. There appeared to be some dissent and discussion but after a few moments agreement was reached. Thea watched dully: what was Dulcie up to now? It was made plain in a few minutes. Tentatively, but with increasing gusto as they warmed to their theme, they struck up a tango. Peter accompanied Dulcie onto the floor, to loud cheers from the onlookers. Dulcie was in her element.

Josef took Thea's arm and led her out to the terrace. At once the tranquil loveliness of the early summer night enveloped them, distancing the feverish gaiety of the ballroom.

'What's the matter?' she asked. She could not bear not to know.

'It's nothing.'

'Don't treat me like a child!' For the first time she was impatient with him. She had been on the crest of a wave, entirely his, and he had let something come between them.

'Very well.' He turned to face her. 'You were laughing at those foolish games.'

'Everybody was. I know they were foolish, but . . .' Thea spread her hands, powerless to explain.

'Those young men. I cannot understand why you find that kind of thing funny. Why do you laugh at them?'

'I don't know . . . I suppose they were being silly, but everyone has to be silly sometimes. Don't they?' She remembered his annoyance after the fiasco at the Hauskonzert, but almost at once she sensed his sternness become more tentative. Wanting desperately to say what he would like to hear, she added, 'Anyway, this is the most wonderful evening of my life. Magical.' It was true. She looked at him anxiously.

'Of course, you're right,' he said, suddenly smiling again, and held his arm for her to take. 'It was only foolishness. Shall we take a walk, Fräulein Thea?'

'A pleasure, sir.'

She bobbed a curtsey and he led her along the terrace in the warm, silvered darkness. As they did so the tango ended, amid cheers, and a waltz began. Thea hummed. Josef's arm slid about her and they danced, lilting and turning to the music. He held her only lightly but he danced well and they moved as one, carried on the tide of melody. For Thea, the moment was bathed in the extraordinary unsullied happiness of certain childhood memories, or of indulgent daydreams of the future. She could scarcely believe that such happiness was here, and now, and hers.

The waltz ended, but he kept his arm about her. Looking up into his face she was reminded of a line in Chaucer that she had read in school.

'He was a verray parfit gentil knight . . .' she murmured.

'What is that?' He smiled.

'Part of an English poem.'

'Ah . . .' His face came down and his lips closed on hers, softly. His arms encircled her gently. And she thought, with apocalyptic delight: at last, I am in love!

CHAPTER SIX

'He took me out for walks and oh! he was so nice!
He always used to kiss me in the same place twice.'
                                    Vesta Victoria—'Poor John'

Josef pushed open the tall glass door and walked slowly out
onto the terrace. The garden lay still, soft and damp in the
early morning, the grass grey with dew, every leaf picked out
with drops of moisture. Away to the east, behind the spire of
St Stephen's, a big bronze sun swam up through the mist,
drawing in its train a hot summer's day.

It was the middle of June. Today they departed for Styria,
to Wolzhof, the day would be busy with preparation and
travel. But for now it was cool and quiet. A sparrow fluttered
down and perched on the drooping head of one of the white
stone dryads that flanked the steps from terrace to lawn. It
sat there, cheeky and common, tilting its head this way and
that, its bright beady eye appraising Josef. The bird's
mundane vitality accentuated the calm, resigned beauty of
the statue. Josef thought that Thea's face was like that of the
dryad. She had that quality of nobility, of natural dignity. He
was deeply impressed with the similarity. It satisfied his sense
of order; it helped to crystallize his image of Thea and blot
out those few aspects of her character which he did not fully
comprehend, and which he put down to her English upbringing.

He went down the steps and across the lawn, his footprints
leaving dark patches on the wet grass. He wore civilian
clothes for the first time in months, and it made him feel
unprotected and soft, like a snail prised from its shell. When
he was not a soldier he was not quite sure what he was. He
turned the corner and passed through the rose arbour. The
trellises were quite hidden in roses at this time of year, mostly
pink and red, his mother's favourite flowers. Later, when the
sun was full on them, the scent would be drawn out of them
like incense, but now they were cool and wet. He walked
right to the end of the garden, to the summer house. The door

was locked—the gardener was fussy about his tools—but Josef did not want to go in. Instead he sat down on the steps, looking back towards the house. Its windows were curtained, impassive. Behind them, people would be beginning to wake, to dress, to pack. He himself had been awake for hours, it was an army-instilled habit that was hard to break. He leaned his elbows back on the verandah step behind him and closed his eyes. He thought of Thea.

For the next month he would be able to see as much of her as he wanted; they could be in each other's company constantly if they so wished. It was a prospect at once delightful and unnerving. He did not want to offend, to go too far, but at the same time he wished to behave in a manner that would commend itself to her as honourable and sincere. After the holiday she would be returning to England, and she would be lost to him. She would go back to her other life, of which he knew nothing, to her ambitions and her writing and her other friends. He had never liked to ask outright if she had a special admirer in England, though the possibility caused him agonies of anxiety. She had never mentioned anybody, but she would be too well-bred to do that, anyway.

The other factor which inhibited Josef was his father. He was plagued by the notion that the Baron was watching all of them, that he disapproved of Thea and Dulcie and would set his face against any real attachment between them and his own children. Josef would have preferred it otherwise. For some reason, although they had little contact with each other and were far from close, his father had a profound influence on him, like a heavy chain or collar, the whole time he was at home. In his own room at the barracks he became the person he wanted to be. He was good at his job, decisive, efficient, respected by the men and highly thought of by his senior officers. He found the strict forms and patterns of military life soothing and secure, and he was physically brave. When he thought about death, which was not often, he hoped passionately to die in battle, though at present the likelihoood was remote. Talk of war was so commonplace as to be ignored.

'Good morning.'

He opened his eyes with a start. Thea stood at the foot of the wooden steps. She wore a green and white striped skirt and a white blouse and her hair was down, pulled back into a bunch at the nape of her neck. Josef stood up.

190

'Good morning. I didn't hear you coming.'

'I didn't mean to make you jump.'

She sat down on the step and indicated that he should do the same. 'I hope you don't mind my joining you. I saw you come out, and it's such a lovely morning.'

'I am glad you came.'

'That's all right then.' She closed her eyes, smiling to herself. She had picked a daisy on her way across the lawn, and was twiddling it between her fingers. She looked serene and happy. Still with her eyes closed, she remarked: 'You look different out of uniform.'

'Do I?' Josef looked down at himself. 'Yes, I feel different.'

'It's nice. You seem more approachable.' She turned to look at him now as if to confirm herself in her opinion.

'Am I usually so remote?'

'Well, not remote exactly—but very soldierly.'

'I *am* a soldier.'

'Yes.' She nodded seriously. 'Of course.'

It occurred to him that she might be teasing him. On an impulse he reached out and stroked her hair. She did not move, but continued to stare down at the daisy head, spinning like a small white top between her fingers. He let his hand slip down over her hair, down her back to her waist. Her stillness moved him. She seemed to understand so perfectly what he wanted in a woman. When he pulled her towards him she bent as lightly as a sapling, the daisy falling from her hands, her face tilting upwards to meet his lips. Her arms hung at her sides in an attitude of submissiveness. He slipped one hand beneath her trailing hair, where her neck was warm and secret, and felt that her head too was heavy, her lashes lying still on her cheeks, her lips slightly parted. She was at once passively acquiescent and enormously sensuous. He curled his fingers in her hair and twisted her head a little to one side, kissing her neck in the little hollow between her jaw and her ear.

She made a small sound, hardly more than a sigh, but it was enough. He withdrew, ashamed of his excitement, ashamed of her uncanny skill in arousing it. He could not look at her. She rested the side of her face against his shoulder but he could not touch her either.

'Josef.' Her voice was sad. He tried to say something in reply, but his throat was dry. He coughed nervously.

'We should go back to the house,' she said, rising and

beginning to walk slowly across the lawn. The hem of her skirt was dark where it brushed the wet grass. She swung her arms slightly like a child idling on its way to an unpleasant destination.

Josef followed her. The house was beginning to wake up. At one of the upstairs windows a figure stood, looking out, watching them. A white face above black clothes. The Baron.

Thomas moved away from the window. So Josef was out in the garden with Thea Tennant at this hour in the morning, and the girl's hair was flopping all over her shoulders. Everyone would be in a light-hearted, holiday mood, he supposed. Everyone but him. For them, the annual trip to Wolzhof was a holiday; for him it was torture. There would be no distractions, no escape either from his family or from his memories, and worst of all, no appointments with the Doctor.

The Doctor went to the Tyrol for his holiday, accompanied by his wife and children, and he thoroughly enjoyed it. He had made a point of telling the Baron what an excellent thing a holiday was, refreshing for both body and soul. It was all very fine for him, he could choose where he wanted to go. He was a great walker, he said: he liked to put on lederhosen and walk for miles over the slopes, collecting flowers and mushrooms, which he would put in his hat. He liked nothing better, he said, than to be with his family under these conditions. The whole conversation had depressed Thomas immeasurably. It seemed treacherous of the Doctor to admit he enjoyed his holiday, when Thomas needed his undivided attention.

Dulcie met Annelise on the landing. The latter gave her a sly look from under sandy lashes.

'Well, you'll see it today.'

'What?'

'The castle. Wolzhof.'

'You keep saying that as if I shall faint dead away the moment I clap eyes on it.' Dulcie was infuriated by the continual hints that she would be astounded by the Baron's mouldering old castle. The more they hinted, the more determined she was to remain unimpressed.

Annelise shrugged. 'I should eat a decent breakfast for a change. It's a long journey.'

'What, with *nothing* to eat?'

'It's just that it's difficult to eat. You'll see ' Annelise took considerable pleasure in needling Dulcie about the impending holiday. She herself did not look forward to it with much enthusiasm. It was not that she would especially miss the attentions of Lieutenant Eggars, but that she did not relish the prospect of playing gooseberry to Dulcie and Peter de Laszlo for a solid four weeks. God knows, Dulcie had had enough young men to choose from since she arrived; Jessica had arranged theatre parties, dances and dinners, but Dulcie and Peter had struck up an unholy alliance. It had been tedious for it meant that there was very little respite to be had from their affairs. They were both there, all the time, in the house, making eyes at each other and fooling about. Annelise didn't know what Dulcie saw in him; he was frightfully pleased with himself and not all that handsome, but Dulcie claimed to have some kind of special gift with men, so perhaps that was it. Whatever the explanation, it would do no harm to rag her a little about the holiday.

Now Dulcie looked wary. 'How long does it take to get there?' she asked.

'Ages. We go on the train because Papa doesn't like driving that far.'

'When do we get there?'

'This evening. The cars come to meet us at Graz, and the drive takes an hour and a half. Dieter will feel sick.'

'Why?'

'Because the road's like a switchback, that's why.' Annelise did not need to mention the incident of the Big Wheel. She had fed Dulcie the cue, it would be enough. 'So he will have to get out and jump about and Papa will get crosser and crosser because he hates going to the castle anyway.'

'Then why ever does he go?'

'It's the family home, Dulcikins, he has to put in an appearance sometimes.'

They began to meander down the stairs. 'What will we do all day?' enquired Dulcie.

'That's a good question . . .' Annelise was enjoying herself. 'We can walk, talk, eat and drink, play cards . . ummm '

'Good grief!'

Annelise burst out laughing. 'Don't worry, it's not as bad as all that. We can take the car out sometimes provided we don't use too much petrol. And there's a lake, we could swim, but it's freezing—' She relapsed into helpless mirth again at Dulcie's horrified expression. 'And there's a tennis court!' she shrieked, delighted with her success. 'Anyone for tennis?'

'You're being foul to me,' Dulcie pouted. 'Now I know why your father hates it.'

'Oh, it's got nothing to do with that, he *loves* tennis, my dear.'

'Then what?'

'Unhappy childhood, dear.' Annelise made a face and put her fingertips together in what she took to be the manner of a medical man.

'I'm not surprised!' Both girls fell about again at this witticism.

On the half-landing Dieter was swinging on the newel post, waiting for them. Dulcie ran to him and gave his bottom a pat. He blushed mightily. He was at that awkward age when cousinly bottom-patting aroused in him a confused reaction somewhere between embarrassment and ecstasy, and Dulcie knew it.

'How's my boy?' she asked.

'Very well, thank you.'

'That's the way. Are you looking forward to the holiday?'

'Yes,' he responded automatically and slid down the banisters, his plump legs squeaking on the polished wood.

'We'll all have a lovely time!' declared Dulcie.

As Dieter squirmed round the dining-room door he observed his tutor pouring himself coffee at the sideboard. Blast. Blast and damn. He himself had already eaten, he had only come in here to escape the girls, who still stood chatting on the stairs behind him. Now he was between the devil and the deep blue sea.

He could only take so much of his cousin Dulcie. Her presence, her voice, her scent and—gosh!—her touch, brought on such a confused plethora of sensations that it took his breath away. His face burned crimson and his legs turned to jelly; and somewhere in between there was an awful tension, an embarrassing swelling and stiffness. It was best when she was there, within sight and earshot, but paying him no attention.

He turned to leave, to find a bit of peace, but it was too late. De Laszlo had seen him.

'Good morning, Dieter.'

'Morning.'

'Hands,' came the automatic remonstrance.

Dieter removed his hands from his pockets. The girls were crossing the hall now, coming closer

'Have you had breakfast?' asked de Laszlo.

'Yes Ages ago.'

'Then run along and make sure you've got those books together '

'I thought it was supposed to be a holiday,' muttered Dieter

'What's that?'

'Nothing.' Shoving his hands back in his pockets, he slouched out. The girls, coming in, brushed past him, greeting Peter and laughing. Dulcie touched Dieter's head lightly as she passed, her soft sleeve brushed his ear.

Out in the hall he glanced back. Dulcie was being playful with his tutor, they were teasing each other. Their demeanour put Dieter on the rack. He knew there was something going on; he had seen things, only little things, but the part of him that was rapidly growing up understood their implication He was insanely jealous. Dulcie knew that he knew, and her every remark, every glance and gesture, invited his complicity and his co-operation. She knew only too well that he was hers to command. So he watched, understood, suffered. And was silent.

The journey to Wolzhof was in fact every bit as tedious as Annelise had predicted. Every year Jessica forgot, or made herself forget, what an effort the whole expedition was, and every year it was brought home to her afresh.

The exigencies of the journey itself were exacerbated by the fact that for the preceding few days the entire family had to live on short commons and in relative discomfort. Minna, the cook, the butler and the chauffeur went on in advance, with the bulk of the luggage, the latter driving the Baron's black Bentley, the rest going by train. Jessica was never entirely happy with this arrangement; she was not sure what they all got up to in the intervening period, but it was very necessary, and the only way for the rest of them to arrive in any kind of comfort. Wolzhof was as cold as a morgue; even in summer, it was essential to keep at least half a dozen vast fires burning and to light the great stove in the kitchen well in advance to ensure hot food, for it was notoriously temperamental and the logs were usually damp. The beds had to be aired and the family's rooms cleaned. The only people generally in residence there were Thomas's agent, Kessler, and an elderly living-in couple who saw to the most rudimentary of caretaking and housekeeping tasks. Privately Jessica thought the old couple not worth their keep, but they were too stricken in years now to be simply turned out, one had a responsibility to these people.

Because the family spent so little time at the Schloss they had to transport vast quantities of essentials from the house at Helenastrasse. Cutlery, linen, kitchen supplies, all had to go, as shopping in Styria necessitated an eight-mile run in the automobile over inordinately tortuous roads to the nearest town, and once there the shops were hardly what she was used to. Even the chauffeur had to take several large cans of petrol with him to ensure they were not all completely stranded. Thomas left an old car at Wolzhof permanently for Kessler's use, but he liked to take the Bentley as well to ensure his own independence during their stay.

Jessica had to admit that, once there, she herself unreservedly enjoyed being at the castle. It was good to get away from the bustle and routine of Vienna, but she dreaded the fuss contingent upon their going. Also, there was Thomas's humour to contend with. He hated Wolzhof; it was a duty and a burden to him and it reminded him, poor man, of his father, so recently passed away. She could understand all this, of course, but it was hard to put up with his grim face and black looks. She had tried to persuade him for his own sake to sell the castle on his father's death, but he would not listen.

As to the journey, the species of soft cheap coal used by the Imperial royal railway meant that, no matter how carefully the carriage windows were closed, clouds of soot permeated the compartment. It was therefore essential, so as not to arrive looking like a nigger minstrel, to retain one's hat and gloves, and in the case of the ladies, veils too. The notice on the window which advised in three languages 'Leaning out of the window is prohibited' was scarcely necessary.

Annelise's dark hints as to the difficulty of eating proved to be nothing less than the truth. There was no dining car on the Graz train but it was possible to include in the price of the ticket a three-course meal, to be consumed on the station at the halfway stage, where the train paused for about twenty minutes As the train drew in, the waiters would be ready with huge trays bearing the food, each dish covered with a clean cloth The entire party alighted from the train, found a seat on the platform and the meal was served. But the first course, a rather greasy chicken broth with noodles suspended pallidly in its depths, was so hot that no one could make headway with it, and when the whistle blew for departure most of the party were barely halfway through their veal, and still hungry.

What with soot, hunger and tiredness it was a somewhat jaded party which eventually alighted at Graz to be met by the two von Crieff cars. Both the black Bentley and the large plum-coloured Daimler Benz sported the Baron's crest on their radiator. a yellow shield with a black ram's head, reminding Thea uncomfortably of a representation of Old Nick she had seen in a book as a child.

They had been on the train for five hours; it was late afternoon as the cars left Graz and began to climb into the fastnesses of the Styrian countryside. As they went, the first relieved burble of conversation faltered and died as one by one they fell prey to the stern and awesome magnificence of their surroundings. Thea, travelling in the first car with Dulcie, Annelise and Josef, thought she had never seen such majestic countryside outside the pages of a book of fairytales. Great hanging palls of dark pine forest draped the flanks of jagged grey mountains that soared above the winding road like a coven of giant witches. The hum of the car engines was like the impertinent buzz of flies around some gigantic sleeping animal. High among the crags, in the rocky ridges, deep gorges plummetted into darkness, occasionally split by the glitter of a plunging waterfall. Sometimes they rounded a bend and were treated to a surprising picture of lushness—the almost too-green brilliance of the lower slopes, studded with flowers, bright between the massed trees, soon lost again to view as the road zig-zagged on its tortuous way.

But not even the splendour of the country along their route could have prepared Thea for the castle of Wolzhof. It was eight miles from Graz, but the journey had taken almost three-quarters of an hour due to the winding road and steep gradients. At half-past six the road levelled out on the crest of a ridge and Josef put his hand on her shoulder.

'There!'

She followed his pointing finger. There, far below them, even below the point where the frail meandering ribbon of road seemed to drown in a sea of black trees, a lake lay like a mirror in the slanting sunlight. On its surface the surrounding woods and mountains were reflected in perfect detail, base to base like the picture on a playing card. And from some hidden point on the shore beneath them a stone causeway reached out like an arm into the water and at the end of it, Wolzhof, its four towers gleaming as if it had newly risen from the depths of the lake, the sun glinting on its many-paned windows.

Josef caught her expression and understood it. 'It is not what you expected?'

She shook her head. 'I don't know what I expected, but certainly not this.'

The car plunged down into the wood. The light filtered prismatically through the treetops so that they passed through shafts of gold and patches of dappled darkness, with the darkness getting deeper all the time. Thea looked at Dulcie, who sat in the corner of the seat, rather huddled, her head leaning on the window, gazing out. She looked pale and dejected. The road wound down through the trees for what seemed an age, until suddenly they caught the glint of the lake; then they were out of the darkness and driving along level ground, with the trees like a black curtain to one side and on the other a low stone parapet between them and the lake shore. Where it lapped on the narrow stony beach the water was crystal-clear and friendly but out beyond the castle it appeared almost black.

'It must be very deep,' said Thea, almost to herself.

'Not this side,' Josef reassured her. 'The Schloss is built on a natural peninsula, but in the centre and over there,' he indicated the enormous mountain directly opposite, 'it is deep. There is no beach, just . . .' he made a diving motion with his hand.

Thea was silent, looking out towards that still, black water. She half-expected to see some weird thing break the surface, a spiny long-necked dragon or perhaps a hand holding a sword, the loose sleeve trailing back from the pale arm. But there was nothing.

The car turned onto the cobbled causeway and slowed down. Ahead of them the great arched entrance to the castle was like the gaping jaws of a marine monster waiting to engulf them. As they drew nearer Thea could see the dark patches of damp on the stone walls, and the undulating pattern of green slime where the lake had lapped and licked for centuries. The cars drew into the courtyard and pulled round to the main doorway. A smaller door, like a mousehole, opened at the bottom right-hand corner of the expanse of rough wood and Minna appeared, mouse-like herself, smiling and coy, comfortingly the same, uncowed by her surroundings.

They alighted from the cars stiffly, a little travel-dazed, as the Baron stalked ahead into his castle; Kessler, who had been driving the first car, followed him anxiously. The doors, slamming shut behind them, made a sound like pistol shots that echoed and reverberated round the high towers and walls. Minna stood back, dimpling, and they went into a hall which seemed to rise to a dizzy height, with great stone flags on the floor as much as four feet across. Some of them had archaic writing, smudged by the footfalls of countless generations. As the luggage was brought in and Jessica conferred with Minna, Thea went over to the wall on their left, the whole of which was covered by an enormous tapestry, a hunting scene with gentlemen and ladies, dogs and horses in a forest glade. The men wore Styrian green hunting tunics, jaunty hats and short, flaring capes; they were handsome, bearded and hard-eyed. The ladies were deathly pale, with fine arched brows and waxen complexions, all their clothes encrusted with gold and silver thread. Horses and dogs had a knowing, an almost sexual, physical presence, their lips drawn back to reveal ranks of teeth, scarlet tongues lolling, muscles bunched and knotted beneath glossy hides. The whole group seemed to have arrived unexpectedly at the very eye of the forest, to have lost their way and be in a state of frozen anxiety bordering on fear. The fine rich clothes of the people stood out sharply against the lowering dark of the tree trunks massing behind them, door after door closing, shutting them in.

'Ancestors.' Thea started, her hair pricking. It was Josef, standing beside her.

'You have a great many.'

He shrugged. 'Too many. Father's is a very old family. Come, I'll show you to your room.'

The Baron had disappeared with Kessler Jessica and

Annelise were already halfway up the stairs while Dulcie and Peter comforted the ailing Dieter who had arrived distinctly green and was sitting in an enormous throne-like wooden chair with his head on his knees. Josef called to them.

'He should go out in the fresh air for a while.'

'Poor little thing . . .' For once Dulcie was wholly sincere, as she herself had been feeling quite dreadful for the past twenty minutes. 'Come on Peter, let's take him out for a walk.'

'Very well, but where?'

'If you go back into the courtyard,' advised Josef, 'and through the gate opposite the main entrance, you will come into the garden.'

The notion of the castle having a garden had not occurred to Thea. As they made their way up the first flight of stairs, which were made of solid stone, as cold as a tomb, she said: 'I didn't think there was a garden.'

'But certainly. It's very pretty, and we have a tennis court as well. Do you play?'

'Yes. I used to, quite a lot, but I'm very out of practice.'

'Never mind, we shall have a game; there are plenty of racquets. My Father is very good, he has to be disadvantaged.'

'Handicapped.' She smiled at him.

'That's right. He was a junior champion in his youth.'

It was all so odd, so surprising, so utterly unlike any place she had been to before. Thea felt suddenly tired, stabbed by a pang of unbearable homesickness. There had been a letter from Venetia just before they left Vienna, wishing them a happy time on holiday, telling them to buy any clothes they needed, saying how marvellous the rhododendrons were this year, and that Homer had a septic foot. Apparently Ralph had taken him to the vet in Bromley and nursed him back to health with positively maternal care. And Aubrey had sent his love and promised to write, and the Kingsleys had been over on Sunday, but she hadn't mentioned Jack . . .

Halfway up, the staircase divided into two branches to right and left, wooden now, and Josef took her arm and guided her to the right. They came out onto a wide landing, with many more paintings and tapestries and two suits of armour, eerily small, on either side. Opposite the stair head was a row of arched windows reminiscent of a cloister. Through these Thea could see the lake spreading apparently for miles in all directions. She went over and looked down. The surface of the water bobbed and rocked thirty feet below, eroding the stones with gentle insistence; surely one day it would simply burst in and wash the contents of the castle away? She felt cold. The whole place was rather dank, chilled by the lake and its own emptiness.

'You're shivering.' Josef put his arm round her shoulders. He felt astonishingly warm; it was a great comfort.

'I expect I'm just tired.'

Her room, when they reached it, was oddly small, certainly not as large as the boudoir at Helenastrasse, and half-moon shaped, for it was in the east tower. There was one window, with a broad sill, through which you could look back at the causeway and the shore, with the dense pine woods blotting out the road. The room was sparsely furnished. Thea guessed, correctly, that it was generally locked and out of use and had been hastily prepared for the extra guest with what bits and pieces could be taken from other apartments. Its bleak, makeshift appearance increased her sense of alienation. For the first time in many years she would have liked to share a room with her sister. Her cases had been brought up but not, this time, unpacked. Wearily she wondered if this were her task, or someone else's.

Josef read her thoughts. 'Minna will be up, while we're having dinner. Don't bother with those unless there's something you need. Everything takes longer, you see, because of the size.' He waved a hand, a little proud of the place, but apologizing also, for he saw that she was overcome.

'Where is Dulcie's room?' she asked, going to the window seat and sitting down heavily.

'In the other tower, on the other side. It is no distance.'

She felt that he only half-understood her trouble. How could he begin to appreciate the outlandishness of this place to her? It was part of his life. To give herself time to compose herself she looked over her shoulder at the causeway.

'I shall feel like Rapunzel.'

'Rapunzel?'

'She let down her hair,' she explained, her face still averted, her voice shaking a little. 'She let down her hair in a long rope and the handsome prince climbed up to rescue her from the tower where she was imprisoned.'

'I see.' She felt his hand touch her hair as it had done this morning, back in that other, more civilized world from which they had come. She longed to turn and hold him but knew instinctively that she mustn't, that to do so would drive him away. Instead she closed her eyes and allowed herself to feel the light touch through her whole body, so that when he had gone she would remember it not just with her mind, but with her skin and her most secret self.

That night after dinner, when the others had gone to bed, Thomas von Crieff set out on a tour of his domain. He undertook the tour as a form of exorcism. The ghosts that lurked at Wolzhof had to be outfaced. If he went straight to bed, and to sleep, they would come creeping and whining from their dark corners to plague him and invade his dreams. They might do that anyway, but at least he could steal a march on them, alarm them before they alarmed him.

He stalked, erect and determined, through the great rooms with their grim wooden furniture and dark panelling, watched by the glassy dead eyes of stuffed animals—moufflon and chamois, their magnificent ringed horns sweeping back from timid, sheep-like faces. The huge fireplace in the big hall contained the remnants of the log fire that had burned all afternoon, now reduced to a rustling, stirring pile of leprous grey ash. He passed the pale, stiff faces on the hunting tapestry without a second glance. He patrolled the dank, almost empty wine cellar and the game larder where Kessler's most recent kills hung from the ceiling. The larder smelt sickly sweet of putrefaction. The corpses—hare, pheasant and partridge—swung slowly on their wires, their limp heads dangling from pulpy, shot-filled bodies, their small eyes like pearl buttons, milky in death.

He walked round the courtyard, and through the double iron gate onto the terrace. The lake was black taffeta in the moonlight; the glossy leaves of the bushes by the parapet glistened; the water sucked and surged round the struts of the wooden landing-stage. The mountains loomed, opaque black against the star-pricked grey of the sky, watching him impassively. Somewhere out in the centre of the lake something moved, there was a tiny gulping splash that only accentuated the silence around it. He peered, but could make out nothing. He returned to the courtyard, closing and securing the gates behind him; entered the castle, throwing the three heavy bolts across on the main door; and went up the staircase to bed, pausing only to pay homage to the portrait of his mother, who looked down on him with her wry, cold smile.

The following afternoon Josef and Thea stood leaning on the parapet, looking out over the lake. It was hot, but a little whispering wind from the mountains joggled the rowboat on its moorings and rattled the glossy leaves of the rhododendrons.

The garden at Wolzhof was not large, in fact the tennis court represented the only difference in size between it and the garden at Helenastrasse. It was laid out in a wide apron, spanning the north side of the castle. Nearest the walls of the Schloss was a pleasant gravel terrace, where the others now sat, sipping cold lemonade. From this, the lawn sloped, at first steeply, then gently, to where the lichen-covered parapet divided it from the marshy border of the lake. The grass here, Thea noted, was less well-kept than that at the city house. It was starred with small flowers and patchy with moss and plantains. Down by the landing-stage near the beach, it was a brilliant, treacherous green with spiky rushes, like bayonets, thrusting through it.

The tennis court, with net in place and white lines etched in by Kessler, was to the left, placed in such a way that the screening trees and shrubs would prevent wild balls from plunging into the lake. It looked extraordinarily out of place, utterly at variance with its surroundings.

As Thea watched, a large silver fish suddenly broke the surface of the water, described a clear, fluid arc in the air and re-entered the lake as cleanly as a knife blade. It happened so swiftly she had barely begun to lift her hand to point.

'Did you see the fish?'

'The lake is full of them. We shall catch some.'

'It's just that it looks so dark and secretive . . .'

They turned and began to stroll back to the terrace. The sun shone warmly on the stones of the castle and dazzled on the tall lead-paned windows, giving the place a more friendly, an almost domestic prettiness. The people relaxing in front of it added to this impression. Jessica sat on a tall basket chair before a white wrought-iron table on which rested the tray bearing the lemonade jug and long-handled spoon. She sat still, apparently staring out over the lake; only on closer inspection could one see that she was sound asleep, her face tilted to the sun, lips smiling placidly. Slightly behind and to the left of her sat the Baron, alone on a hard garden bench, legs crossed, reading the day-old paper he had purchased on Graz station the day before. He wore a suit of cream linen and a crisp white panama hat.

Opposite Jessica on the other side of the table stood the rickety swing-seat where Dulcie and Annelise lounged, rocking gently, nursing their glasses of lemonade. On the grass at the foot of the slope Dieter and Peter de Laszlo sat perusing a book of elementary Latin grammar, but not apparently with much determination. Everyone was at ease. The journey was accomplished, the weather sublime, a whole spectrum of choices was theirs. No hurry to decide, no pressure to plan. Today could well be wasted, for there was a whole month of tomorrows.

Happy, Thea lay down on the bank, her hands linked behind her head, her eyes squinting into the sun. The soaring height of the surrounding mountains made the sky here seem more lofty and infinite, as though they held it up like tentpoles. In soft, low-lying England the heavens met the land comfortably at a visible, not-so-distant horizon; they embraced the earth and cushioned it with plump clouds. Here you were trapped way beneath the sky, like an ant under a glass bell jar.

As she gazed, she saw a black speck, like a particle of dust hanging against the blue. It was so high up she could not tell whether it moved or not. She put out one hand to touch Josef's arm, and raised the other to point. 'What's that?'

'An eagle.' It appeared he had no difficulty in seeing it.

'It looks tiny, like a lark.'

'Oh yes, it's a dot to us, but to him we are perfectly clear. He already has his eye on a mouse, or a rabbit. He is watching it now.'

They remained still, their eyes on the distant bird, Thea with her hands cupped round her eyes to shield them from the penetrating light. After about a minute the eagle plummetted, falling like a stone through the air and disappearing below the craggy wooded skyline two miles away on the far side of the Wolzsee.

Thea let her hands close like shutters over her eyes, which were watering. Something had died, a brutal and violent death. At this moment the eagle would be pinning down the still convulsing body with hard, hooked talons, mantling his wings over his kill, reaching down to tear at the soft fur and gouge the flesh. He would be looking around, challenging all-comers with fierce yellow eyes, his scimitar beak glistening dark with warm blood, his cape of tawny feathers fluttering in the mountain wind. It was happening, they had seen it happen, and yet there had been no more evidence than a speck in the sky.

Josef turned to his father. 'Shall we play tennis?' he asked.

The Baron looked up, somewhat distractedly, from his paper. 'What's that? Yes, yes . . . by all means.'

'But you will play too?'

'I think not.'

'I hear you're a first-class player, Uncle,' put in Thea, rolling onto her stomach and resting her elbows on the top of the bank.

'Nonsense.' He was curt; what did she know about it? 'You play, you play and enjoy yourselves.'

'Can't *I* play?' Dieter's face screwed up threateningly.

'Don't cringe, sir! You may ballboy and make yourself useful, and take a turn when your betters say you may.'

'Oh, all right.'

The Baron returned to his paper. He did not really know why he went to such lengths to keep himself abreast of the news, for most of it merely confirmed him in his gloomy opinions concerning his country, and yet he needed to feel prepared, to know the worst. Here in the isolation of Wolzhof, where he was habitually melancholy, the squabbles and anomalies of Austrian political life seemed doubly ludicrous. He was certain of one thing. The nation was in decline. Signs of the rot were everywhere, from the near-senile Old Gentleman shuffling around Schönbrunn (and, it was said, using a secret exit to enable him to dine with his common theatrical mistress), right down to the sentimental vulgarity of the contemporary operettas, so accurately aimed at the new lower-middle classes. The man who had headed the government since November 1911, a Styrian aristocrat named Karl Count Sturgkh, had finally seen fit to suspend the Austrian parliament only three months ago, so that a nation which in the Baron's opinion already teetered on the brink of anarchy was left with no democratic representation. And this at a time when the threat of war with the turbulent Balkan states hung over them all like the sword of Damocles.

It was the Baron's opinion that the Old Man and his pack of toadies did not see that war, and the winning of it, might be the saving of Austria. They had held back two years ago when the Albanian conflict had seemed to make war in the Balkans inevitable; it was said that the Emperor feared to lose provinces. But insurrection was lying in ambush in Dalmatia, Croatia and Bosnia, and a firm hand must be shown.

He sighed heavily and covered his eyes with his hand. Nemesis was at hand, and those who had seen it coming would not be thanked. Last year the industrial depression had reached a new low. Unemployment and bankruptcies rose steeply, and financial equilibrium had been further endangered by new loans and by the increase of military preparations. And the army itself was in poor shape; this organization, which was supposed to be the strong link that bound the dilapidated monarchy together, was as tainted as any other part of the political organism. A year ago one of its colonels was found to have betrayed plans, albeit not vital ones, to the Russians, under threat of blackmail on account of his homosexual private life. The Baron grimaced; the wretched fellow had been virtually ordered to commit suicide. Typical of the streak of vulgar hysteria that ran right through society.

'Typical,' he said aloud.

'What's that, dear?' enquired his wife, not opening her eyes, nor really interested.

There again the Emperor, approaching his dotage more rapidly every day, was beginning to adhere more and more rigidly to old forms learnt in his youth. He refused point-blank to speak to any minister on a subject outside his special jurisdiction, and this enforced departmentalization caused chaos and encouraged the small intrigues and storms in tea-cups which had blotted the escutcheon of Austrian politics for so long. Thomas von Crieff could see it all.

Racked with irritation and foreboding he watched his son and the English girl wander up to the castle to change for tennis. There was some sort of altercation among the others and then they too followed, Dieter clinging to the younger sister's hand, swinging on it like a baby. What hope was there?

The tennis proved enjoyable. Thea was frankly glad that the Baron had declined to play; she was not in the mood for the hard-fought match. As it was, Peter partnered her, and Josef partnered Dulcie and Annelise by turns.

The chances of orderly play were from the outset slim, since only Josef and Annelise had anything approaching the right dress and footwear, and the assortment of racquets dug out of the games room suffered from a variety of ills ranging from warped frames to missing strings. But the lack of the right equipment proved a good leveller; everyone missed and muffed to the same extent, and after half an hour everyone on the court, including the initially sulky Dieter, was helpless with mirth.

Then suddenly Thea, chasing a sharply angled drive from Josef, stumbled and only stopped herself from measuring her length on the ground by snatching at the wire rope that supported the net. Her palm was already red and blistered from the oversize grip of the borrowed racquet, but when she stood up and examined it she found to her shock that she had removed a strip of skin two inches long from the base of her thumb to her little finger, and it was bleeding copiously. The sight of the blood and the shock of the fall temporarily unmanned her. To her shame she could hardly see the wound for tears.

Josef was by her side at once, full of self-reproach. 'Thea, I'm so sorry.'

'It wasn't your fault, it was a good shot . . .'

Dulcie came up in time to hear this last. 'Don't be so *British!* Let me see.' She looked. 'It must jolly well hurt.'

'Come, you should wash it and cover it,' said Josef. 'Will you excuse us? Do carry on.'

He put his arm about her shoulders and walked her slowly up to the castle. The Baron had gone in, but Jessica looked up.

'Everything all right?'

'Thea cut herself. Nothing too serious, but it needs a dressing.'

'There are things in the bathroom.'

'Very well, I'll see to it.'

Thea's legs shook. When they'd passed through the iron gate into the cool gloom of the courtyard he kissed her brow and brushed the wisps of clinging hair back off her hot face. She knew, with the sixth sense she had recently developed, that her debility excited him.

Upstairs in the large sunny bathroom he washed her hand

with almost feminine tenderness and care, and she saw that his own hand shook a little as he applied ointment and a length of cotton bandage. She submitted passively to his ministrations. When he had finished he kept her hand in his and bowed his head to kiss the inside of her wrist, his mouth hot on the thin skin. In the mirror behind him she could see reflected his back, with two dark patches of sweat, like maps on the white shirt, the collar pulled back off his neck where his head bent to kiss her arm. She raised her eyes and saw, staring back at her nakedly, her own desire.

She touched his hair. 'We had better go back,' she said, and her voice trembled. 'Or they'll wonder what we're doing.'

It was about a fortnight later that somebody suggested swimming. It was exceptionally hot, day after day of cloudless blue skies and a shimmering haze over the surface of the Wolzsee. Life had slowed down, almost to a standstill. The party rose late and dawdled through the day. Josef had been shooting with Kessler, and had taken them all boating on the lake, but they had caught no fish. They had walked, lazed, played cards and a little more tennis—though only Josef had taken on his father. But now lassitude had taken a hold. There was an air of indolence over Wolzhof, but also an air of suspense. Surely one could not go for so long without some kind of excitement?

In this atmosphere it was only natural that when the Baron decided to take the Bentley and return to Vienna for a few days, everyone experienced a considerable release of tension. The relief occasioned by his absence was most evident at mealtimes, which were more animated and protracted, with loud laughter and noisy conversation.

It was at lunch on the third day after the Baron's departure that Peter suggested: 'Why don't we swim in the lake?'

'Yes!'

'What a brilliant idea!'

'Oh yes, do let's!' The enthusiasm was universal.

'It's very cold and quite deep,' warned Jessica. 'You shouldn't go out too far and you should wait at least an hour after luncheon.'

Dulcie and Thea had brought bathing costumes because Ralph had felt they were a necessary adjunct to any holiday, especially one abroad. The notion of mixed bathing, which would have been risqué, if not taboo, on the chaste beaches of south-east England, seemed hardly to merit a second thought here. Dulcie and Thea had occasionally been bathing at Folkestone and Broadstairs, though Dulcie's costume rarely got wet above the hips. Ralph was a keen swimmer, who believed it not only to be an enjoyable recreation, but an essential skill in the natives of a maritime nation. He and Aubrey would do a majestic breaststroke up and down their part of the shore while the girls immersed in the ladies' section. Their bathing costumes were designed more for modesty than action, consisting of a long, full-skirted over-dress with puff sleeves, matching knickers, and a voluminous type of tam o'shanter. All this clothing soon became water-logged and consequently heavy, and a severe impediment to movement. This did not bother Dulcie, who found the water cold and the waves threatening and the sum total of whose aquatic activity was a little light paddling.

After lunch Jessica retired to a seat in the shade, with a few soft cushions and a big hat. Her warnings duly delivered, she wished only for the young people to enjoy themselves and indulge their natural high spirits. She herself would pick up a book, scan it desultorily, nod off and finally snooze conten-tedly for an hour or so.

Away from the castle walls it was cooler, with a slight breeze off the water; the girls' bare arms started into goose pimples and Dieter jumped up and down hugging himself. Peter de Laszlo sat on the end of the landing-stage, his legs dangling in the water, his skin very white against his black swimsuit. Dulcie crept up behind him and gave him a playful push; he turned and caught her by the waist, dragging her down beside him. Thea saw that their movements with each other were relaxed and intimate, they seemed to understand each other's bodies to an alarming degree. Dulcie was carrying her bathing hat, her hair was in a knot on top of her head, but several wisps trailed on her neck and temples, as light as thistledown.

Josef waded out into the water with big strides, his arms held high, waving like the sails of a windmill. Abruptly, he turned to face the shore and plunged in backwards, thrashing his legs and feet, spraying those on the shore with icy drops. Dulcie shrieked and stood up, backing away. Peter pushed himself off the end of the jetty and dropped into the water with a tremendous splash. A skein of ducks rose from the rushes a few hundred yards away and clattered into the air in consternation, a broken black chevron against the grey of the mountain wall. The sound of their flight and the shouts of the bathers echoed around, bouncing from peak to peak like fragments of splintering glass.

Thea, with Dieter, tried the water tentatively. It was icy, so cold that it numbed her foot almost at once, and so clear that she could see every one of the tiny gravelly stones on the bottom. Dieter clutched her hand, giggling and gasping in a mixture of anxiety and delight. For the first time Thea warmed to him, and squeezed his hand. He didn't have much of a life, always being either chastised or ignored, nothing was ever arranged for his benefit. Even the birthday party, she recalled, had been a soulless affair. He had no close, rough and ready friendships and no brothers or sisters of the age or inclination to play with him.

They advanced together into the still, cold water. The sun burned fiercely on Thea's bare back, between her dress and her cap, but her legs from the knee down were numb. She turned to look at Dieter. His face was pinched with cold.

'Can you swim?' she asked.

He shook his head, his eyes popping, shoulders shuddering and hunching. All the soft ginger hairs on his forearms were standing out in shock.

She gave his hand a friendly shake. 'I think I'll plunge,' she said. 'It's the only way I shall get in. But don't you come in too far, stay at the edge.'

'All right.' He seemed relieved to receive this advice from an adult, thereby absolving him from further effort without loss of dignity.

Thea took a few more steps. She was now waist-deep. She looked down and saw the pale columns of her legs, wavering beneath the floating canopy of her skirt. For a moment she wondered again if the lake harboured some watery troll who would slither from his pit out in the deep, dark water to grab her and haul her down into the depths. She saw the bobbing heads of the two men, one dark, one fair, about twenty yards in front of her, their strokes leaving soft, radiating vees on the surface. Behind her, still perched on the end of the landing stage with Annelise, Dulcie called: 'Go on Thea, be brave!'

Be brave . . . be brave . . . be brave . . . the echo flashed and faded round the lake. Josef lifted an arm, beckoning her in.

In a sudden upsurge of do-or-die bravery she flung herself forward. The shock of the freezing water took her breath away for a moment; she felt herself floundering, fighting for air. But she kept doggedly moving towards Josef, and in a moment her breathing became more regular. Josef began to swim towards her, and Peter moved away to the right, round towards Dulcie. Annelise came down the steps to join Dieter, who was running about in the shallows, beginning to enjoy himself.

Josef came level with her. His hair was plastered to his brow, dark with water; the stripes of his blue and white costume rippled and merged beneath the surface as he trod water and shook his head like a dog to clear his eyes. She smiled at him, still breathless.

'It's so cold!'

'If you keep moving you will be warmer. Let's swim to the side, then we shall be in our depth, too.'

He struck out towards the corner of the L-shape formed by the parapet and the criss-cross legs of the jetty. She followed him, already failing; her clothes seemed leaden. He looked over his shoulder.

'Are you all right?'

'I don't think I can get there.'

He swam back to her. 'Hold onto my shoulders.'

She did so, and he pulled her with him. She could feel the flexing and releasing of his shoulder muscles as he swam; his head bobbed so that her cheek was rhythmically brushed by his wet hair. His legs, beneath hers, bent and stretched, forcing them forward; the cloth of his costume billowed and flattened as the water moved past him. They reached the edge and he tilted her backwards. To her great relief she could just touch the gravelly bottom. She held onto one of the wooden struts for support.

'I'm sorry,' she gasped, 'to be so helpless. I think it was the cold.'

'I don't see the other girls swimming,' he commented. They stood in shadow, the steps of the landing-stage concealing them from Annelise and Dieter. The others were along at the end, they could hear them laughing. But they themselves could not be seen, or heard.

When he put his arms about her waist it was as natural as breathing. The water rocked them together as lightly and gently as two lily pads. She no longer felt the cold, but her skin started to meet his—every hair, every pore, already erect in the freezing water, was sensitive to his touch. The skin of his face, beneath its veil of water, was smooth as an apple. With a shock she realized that as he held her she could feel every part of him with a piercing distinctness. In the lilting water she let her hands drift down, over his shoulders and beneath his arms. With her fingers she traced the rippled column of his spine, felt him move in response still closer. A small tuft of golden hair glistened above the neck of his costume. His hips met hers and she felt herself quicken and melt at their strange, root-like, urgent pressure. His thighs leaned, causing her own to part slightly beneath them.

The water gave their every moment a languid grace; it seemed to participate and assist in their caresses, they could not help but touch. His arm, encircling her, turned her slightly, and his other hand he laid on her throat, fingers spread, almost as though he would choke her. But instead he let it rest there as he kissed her. Her head tilted back. The cap, dislodged, floated away, and her hair spread and waved like waterweed about her face. He moved his hand down, tracing the shallow valley between her collar bones, passing with feather-lightness over her breasts so that his palm did no more than greet her nipples, and then moved on to rest, like a star, on her stomach. She felt that her whole life began and ended with his hand, it was all that mattered. She was suspended in pleasure, losing herself, and yet so acutely aware that his touch was almost a pain. He slipped his hand round her waist, then beneath her buttocks. With ease, because of her weightlessness, he lifted the lower part of her body to meet his. Her head fell back; the water lapped in her ears, deadening sound. She would gladly, willingly, have drowned at that moment. He sank below the surface, still holding her waist, his face against her stomach, then down, kissing her legs, holding her so that his mouth was a warm rosette on her frozen skin. She looked down and saw him there in the water, a merman, his yellow hair flowering about his head like a sea anemone, his movements slow and heavy and graceful. When he rose again the water streamed from him; she envied it its all-enveloping closeness, its intimate, pervasive touch. But his eyes were closed, and when he opened them she saw the look she most dreaded. Shame.

They were in deep shadow. A few yards away the shadow

ended abruptly, the lake dazzled in the afternoon sun. Above them and away to the right they could hear the bumping of the others' footsteps as they clowned about on the wooden jetty. They stood very still in the shadow, and very close, but no longer touching.

'Thea!' A piercing shriek shattered the stillness, pounding footsteps thundered on the boards up above, others followed, there was laughing and a resounding crash. Suddenly Dulcie's inverted face appeared over the edge. Against the light she looked dark and wanton, her hair had come untied and the strands hung down about her face. A crash, and a rasping sound: someone was dragging her back. Her face, laughing hysterically, disappeared; her fingers gripped the edge for another moment, white with pressure, then they too slipped. There was a good deal of shouting and screaming, Dulcie's yells predominating.

'No! No, you beast! Someone help me!'

Suddenly Thea was bitterly cold. Her teeth were chattering, her skin blotched blue, she was shuddering seismically, chilled to the marrow. Without looking again at Josef she waded to retrieve her cap, and then back to the steps. The boards of the landing-stage were warm and dry; the sun beat down with comforting directness. Dieter was jumping up and down, shrieking with mirth, pointing.

'Thea! Peter is going to throw Dulcie in the water!'

At the end of the landing-stage a vigorous struggle was in progress. Dulcie had her back to the water, Peter was trying to catch her up beneath the legs. He already had one arm firmly locked about her back.

'He shouldn't, really . . .' Thea felt oddly removed from the tussle, but something knocked at her conscience; there was something wrong. 'He shouldn't.'

Peter suddenly snatched up Dulcie beneath the knees. He had her. Her head tossed, her feet paddled the air furiously, comic but desperate. She swung her free hand to smack his face and at this moment, whether motivated by surprise, revenge or mere playfulness, Peter launched her over the edge. He watched, hands on hips, as she hit the water with a smack, her scream cut short by the crash of the water.

Heavily, in her wet bathing dress, Thea began to walk forward. Suddenly, reality returned. 'Peter! For goodness sake, she can't swim!'

213

She ran, the water dripping from her, her footprints showing dark on the dry boards, quickly fading in the sun. She could hear Dulcie thrashing about, but Josef was still down there. Surely Dulcie couldn't be far out of her depth? She was suddenly afraid. As she drew up with Peter she caught his surprised and slightly sarcastic expression and it enraged her.

'For God's sake, what a stupid thing to do!'

'She could have told me.'

'Yes, but she *wouldn't*, would she?' She had the impression that he understood that, that it had something to do with his actions.

To her relief, Dulcie appeared to be within her depth. Josef was with her; she was floundering towards the steps, clinging to his arm, her face chalk-white. She climbed the steps heavily, her breath coming in gasps, her lips grey. Peter walked over and held out his hand to pull her up.

'I'm sorry. I didn't know you couldn't swim. Are you all right?'

She did not reply, but slapped his hand away, accepting a towel from Annelise and hugging it round her. Everyone was suddenly serious, concerned, hoping for the best. Thea noticed that, just as at home, they were all hoping that Dulcie would be lenient with them. But it appeared her fury was reserved for Peter.

'You idiot! You great bullying idiot, I might have drowned!'

'It's not that deep just there. I knew that.' He was calm.

'You thought it was funny, I suppose?'

He waited, looked at her, smiled. His eyes were cold. 'Yes.'

'God, I hate you! I hate you! You've spoilt everything!' She stood there quivering with fury and frustration, her small hands bunched into fists at her sides, her head thrust forward in that belligerent way that Thea recognized so well. She stepped forward and touched her younger sister's shoulder.

'Come on, Dulcie. You've had a fright, that's all.'

'Go away!' Dulcie did not even look at her, but shook her hand off like a dog with a fly.

'You're making a fuss over nothing,' said Peter. Thea was astonished at his insensitivity. He was being deliberately brutal, and what gave him the right? Now he picked up his towel and began to rub his hair with fast, jerky movements, leaning forward so that the drops spattered on the ground.

'What are we standing around for?' asked Annelise. 'Let's go and get dressed and lie in the sun.'

They began to straggle back across the grass. Jessica looked up and waved benignly, still half asleep.

But Thea, as she turned to go, caught Dulcie's expression as she looked at Peter. She was still angry, but there was something else. He put his towel over his shoulder and walked straight past her, breaking into a run to catch up with the others, not sparing her a glance. And, Thea noted with a shock, she loved it.

The boy retreated into a side road. The sound of the crowd surging and growling in the nearby main street was like a hungry lion on his scent.

The late June day was fine and hot. The sky between the rooftops was a stinging blue, the shadows stencil-clear on the chalky walls. He was aware for the first time that he was sweating profusely. His collar felt tight and his shirt and thick jacket tugged and sucked at his sticky skin. His mouth was dry. The gun, tucked into his clammy waistband beneath his jacket, dug into his ribs and stomach. His heart pattered and jumped, his breath came fast and shallow. He was terrified, and ashamed of being terrified. All he wanted at that moment was to go home and forget the whole thing.

Two of the others had failed. The bomb had missed, and the other lad hadn't even succeeded in drawing his revolver. The target had been within reach and clearly visible, but still they had failed. The grand scheme seemed to have a jinx on it, so why should he have to bear the full load of responsibility? He wasn't even convinced of the rightness of the cause.

Soft, quick footsteps sounded behind him and he turned to see the fourth boy. His face was pale and his upper lip, covered with a downy pubescent moustache, was damp.

'I couldn't do it,' he said, his voice whiny and childish. 'I looked at her, and I just couldn't.'

'Why not?' He felt the more aggressive because it was his own fear he questioned.

'I felt sorry for her. She looked nice, a bit like my mother.'

'You're soft.'

'I can't help that . . . What will you do? They've got the others.'

215

'I know that.' He was quite proud of the scorn in his voice. 'I shall wait here.'

'But they're not coming this way.'

'I have to think.' He could smell the other boy's fear. He'd wet his pants, quite probably. Pathetic. 'Run on home then, if you're going to. Don't stand by me looking like that or we'll both get caught, it's written all over you.'

'You're going to stay, then?'

'I told you. Now *go*.'

The other boy turned and ran away down the side street, his shadow flittering like a moth over the sun-baked walls, his feet in soft-soled shoes making no sound. A fat old woman looked out of her doorway, peered up and down the street without interest, disappeared again. Nothing much doing. Everyone was out today, watching the important people go by.

Now that he was alone again, the boy wondered if he had done right. He had burned his boats now, that was for sure. If he ever saw the other members of the Society again they would want to know why he had failed, when he had been so ready to boast. But it would be difficult. He was no longer quite sure where the target was. He had been approaching the town hall when the other two had muffed their chances.

Mind you, the man might be an impatient, undemocratic tyrant, but you had to admire his nerve. His reaction to the attempts had been one of clear irritation. He had looked about him, his face scarlet with rage, had shouted at his escort, his chauffeur, the crowd, had half raised himself from the car seat to see whence the atrocities had originated. Far from hurrying on he had shown every desire to slow down and sort the matter out there and then. But his wife was with him—it was their wedding anniversary after all—and he clearly did not want to expose her to more danger than was necessary; he had pressed on, towards the town hall . . .

Quite suddenly, its approach muffled by the noise of the crowd, the car swung round the corner into the side street. The four people sat in it, staring straight at the boy, as the chauffeur braked, and looked over his shoulder, preparing to reverse and turn. The sun shone in their eyes and the woman, who was plump and middle-aged and not bad looking, put her hand up to shield her face. Next to her the man sat, his red face glowing fiercely beneath his burnished helmet. His gloved hand, resting on the side of the car door, tapped up and down impatiently. His eyes were cross and vacant.

The boy could hardly believe it. They did not even appear to see him. He had all the time he wanted to step forward, and up onto the scorching running-board of the car. They barely even looked surprised when he drew his revolver and levelled it at the target. He felt at once calm and wildly elated. His chance of greatness, handed to him on a plate

He squeezed the trigger. The revolver bucked in his sweat-slippery palm. The chauffeur's eyes widened in astonishment, his mouth gaped. The target grunted and sagged forward, the blood seeping and spreading through the thick cloth of his field-marshal's uniform. The escort, sitting next to the chauffeur in the front, made a move to rise. Ecstatically the boy aimed at him and fired. He missed, but the woman gave a little sound as though she had suddenly met someone she recognized, and slipped down a little next to her husband, her head tilting to one side.

Like a dream, it had been seconds and felt like hours.

At once they were all there. People clamoured and ran and pointed and the police were tight around him, gripping his arms, twisting them, hurting him because they had failed and he had won. He had carried out the plan. Total success.

They were shouting at him in loud, angry voices.

'You! What's your name?'

'A murderer and still wet behind the ears . . .'

'Bloody little killer! One of those damned secret societies . . .!'

'Who are you? What's your name? Speak up!'

The boy felt as though the outside of his body were made of iron, deflecting the blows and the buffeting and the insults. Inside the iron shell he was calm and happy. And when he spoke, he spoke from this inner tranquillity.

'Gavrilo Princip is my name,' he said sweetly. 'I killed the Archduke, and his wife. I am Gavrilo Princip.'

On 28 June they went for a picnic. The Baron had agreed to their having the use of the Daimler Benz for the day, provided only Josef drove it. Lieutenant Eggars had joined the house party on a few days' leave and Dieter had been left at home with his parents, under strong protest.

Their mood was carefree as Josef drove round the east end

of the Wolzsee and began to climb the slopes on the far side. Dulcie sang, in a shrill, piping voice, *'He'd have to get under, get out and get under . . .'* And everyone smiled indulgently. They had cold pheasant and white wine in the hamper, and all day ahead of them; why shouldn't she enjoy herself?

The site Josef had selected was about a third of the way up the Wolzberg, where the woods began to give way to the rock face, and where a stream became a foaming waterfall. They parked the car at the roadside, unloaded the hamper and a couple of rugs and began to walk. It was only about a quarter of a mile, but they seemed almost at once to be quite cut off, the trees closing in behind them. They fell silent, listening to the sound of the water up ahead and the solitary, resonant call of a bird, high above the treetops.

They came out on a narrow stretch of green, studded with rocks. Above the stream a small rainbow glistened in the spray. Beyond it the mountain climbed steeply. To their right, below the waterfall, lay another stretch of greensward, following the river on its winding route to the Wolzsee.

They laid out the rugs at the edge of the wood, not too close to the water because of the fine, pervasive spray. Peter poured some wine and they sat sipping it, a little overawed by their surroundings, like people in a cathedral.

A chamois appeared on the very edge of the opposite slope, perched like a great insect on the rock face, his feet planted on some impossibly tiny ledge, his great horns sweeping regally on either side of his wary face.

'Look!' said Thea. 'Isn't he handsome?'

People and animal watched each other with mutual respect. Suddenly Dulcie leapt to her feet, flinging her arms in the air. She wore a long chiffon scarf of rose pink, and she tossed the ends in the air like butterfly wings.

'Shoo!' she cried. 'Go on, shoo!'

The animal started back, his head snapping as though awakened from a dream. Then he turned on his hind legs and appeared to leap into space, his legs poised like a rocking horse's. He made no sound, it was hard to believe he had been there at all.

'Why on earth did you do that?' asked Thea angrily.

Dulcie sat down, flinging the ends of the pink scarf about her shoulders. She looked immeasurably pleased with herself. Ever since the swimming incident she seemed to Thea to have been in a perpetual state of high excitement; her behaviour had been incomprehensible.

'Why not?' Dulcie said.

'Because it was unnecessary,' volunteered Peter.

'Does everything have to be necessary? I wanted to see what he'd do.'

'So did we all,' said Peter, 'and now he's gone.'

'They frighten me,' said Annelise coyly. 'What if one attacked us?'

'You know very well they wouldn't do that,' her brother reproved her. 'They are very shy, they come to see what our intentions are.'

'And now they know,' put in Peter caustically.

'They've got huge horns,' wavered Annelise, shrinking affectedly against Lieutenant Eggars.

Erlich Eggars, though extremely rich, was a plain and shy young man, with a stolid, beefy appearance and anxious eyes. He knew the summer ball had advanced his cause not one whit, and was henceforward prepared to be no more than a convenient accessory to Annelise. Now he blushed as she leaned against him.

'There's nothing to be afraid of,' he muttered lamely, wishing everyone were not listening to him.

'Isn't there?' persisted Annelise, smiling treacherously at Dulcie from her position beneath the bold Lieutenant's chin.

'Of course not,' was his stalwart reply. Dulcie spluttered. Josef frowned. There were times when he disapproved most strongly of his sister and his cousin. 'Let us eat,' he suggested.

They were hungry, and the food was good. When they were finished they lay back, disinclined to move. It was Peter who rose first, stretching his fists high above his head. 'No good lying here all day. Who's coming for a walk?'

Dulcie groaned, but smiled up at him, screwing up her eyes against the sun. 'Why are you being so hearty?' she enquired, crossing her arms over her face.

'I don't want to go to sleep.'

'Oh very well . . .' She held out a hand and allowed herself to be pulled up, stumbling slightly so that she fell against Peter and he had to put an arm round her. Annelise and Eggars followed suit, and the four of them wandered upstream. The small sound of their voices drifted back for a while, but was soon lost beyond the insistent rushing of the water.

Josef rolled on his side, his head propped on his hand.

Where his cheek rested on his palm it was pulled slightly, giving him a quizzical, somewhat oriental air. His hair pushed between his fingers like young summer grass. He watched Thea. She could feel him watching her. She lay on her back with her hands at her sides, her head inclined a little in his direction. Her hair was tied back loosely in a green scarf, but she had lifted it off her neck so that it fanned out behind her head in a dark halo. Despite her efforts, her skin had tanned slightly in the sunshine.

'You look like a Red Indian,' he remarked, still watching.

'Does it look awful?'

In reply, he leaned over and kissed her. She felt the sudden coolness as his face came between her and the sun. She put up her arm but he withdrew. She could not see his face against the light.

'What's the matter?'

'I have to apologize.'

'For what?'

'You know very well. I have behaved very badly. The other day—the swimming and so on . . . I am sorry.'

'I wasn't aware there was anything to be sorry about.' She smiled at his shadowed face. His seriousness weighed heavily on her; she could not understand him.

'I lost my control.'

'So did I.'

'You? You are always so generous.' He sounded agonized.

'Generous? But Josef,' she sat up, pushing him back a little so that she could see him properly, 'I wasn't being generous. I wanted to, I really wanted to.'

He shook his head, lowering his eyes. 'I went too far,' he repeated. 'Please believe me when I say I realize that.'

'I believe you *think* so,' she said. 'But it isn't true.' She bent her head, trying to look into his eyes, but he seemed to be locked away in some private place of guilt. Suddenly he rose, thrusting his hands into his pockets and walking a little towards the river. He looked wretched. Thea got up and went over to him; she put her hand in his and stood close to him. On an impulse she slipped her arm about his waist and kissed his temple, and the corner of his mouth. She willed him to understand her, her feelings, her need of him. But he was stiff, his eyes averted, his hands still in his pockets. She realized with a jolt that her advances were distasteful to him. Her face was hot.

'I'm sorry,' she whispered. She could have wept for humiliation. She walked back to the rug and lay face down, completely still, her lips pressed tight together to stop their shaking.

About an hour later, the others returned. Dulcie looked from Thea to Josef. 'Hallo, you two!' she said. 'Have you had fun?' She was only mildly curious; she didn't really care.

Thea rolled over, rubbing her eyes as if she had been asleep. 'Hallo, how far did you go?'

'Oh, we wandered about . . .' Dulcie flopped down on her stomach, her feet in the air, ankles crossed. The pink scarf lay across her shoulders, and she had a small white star-shaped flower tucked in her hair above the left ear. The back of her dress was criss-crossed with the imprint of grass. It seemed that nothing, at present, could alter her good humour.

The afternoon became cool and they packed up the things and began to wander back to the car. Annelise had an angry red patch on her shoulders between her hair and the collar of her dress. Her pale redhead's skin could not take the sun. Dulcie, on the other hand, had acquired no more than a sprinkling of freckles; she complained about them, but knew very well that they suited her.

When they reached the car, Peter asked: 'Josef, may I drive back?'

'Out of the question, I'm afraid. The Baron prefers that I should.'

'Don't be dreary,' said Annelise. 'Papa's not even here to see! Let Peter drive the first part.' She looked round for support. Eggars, hating to be aligned against authority, even by implication, moved a little away from her and gazed out over the lake.

'I'd rather he didn't,' persisted Josef. 'It has nothing to do with me.'

'It's all right, old chap,' said Peter with a charming smile, 'not if it pricks your conscience.'

They began to stow the hamper in the back, to fold up the rugs and put on coats for the journey home. Josef appeared depressed and preoccupied.

As they were about to get in, he said rather brusquely, 'You may drive for a while, Peter, but I beg of you to go carefully.'

'Of course. Trust me.'

Thea thought that if ever there was an empty exhortation, it was that. By tacit mutual consent she and Josef did not sit together; he sat in the back with Annelise and the wretched Eggars, and she squeezed into the front passenger seat next to Dulcie.

The whole time that Peter drove Dulcie whooped and shouted like a child. The pink scarf, now tied round her hair, streamed back in the wind, sometimes flapping across Thea's face so that she could hardly breathe. Dulcie begged Peter to drive faster, but he ignored her. His driving seemed uncharacteristically cautious and circumspect, even allowing for Josef's admonitions. She did not seem to care; unusually, she appeared not to expect her challenges to be taken up but simply to be listening to her own voice, indulging in a private revel.

When Josef at last drove into the courtyard at Wolzhof, it was in deep shadow, the sun having fallen away behind the towers to the west. After the rush and roar of the car journey, and Dulcie's excited shouting, the silence was deep and dead.

Minna opened the door and Dieter ran out to meet them. Dulcie hugged and kissed him. Thea could not understand her apparent affection for the boy; it was not as if normally she even liked children, and he was not an especially pre-possessing example of the species, yet she was all over him.

They went in, and upstairs to change. On the way up the stairs Thea saw a screw of paper on the step in front of her, obviously fallen from someone's pocket. Automatically and uncuriously she picked it up. In her room she put it on the dressing-table and proceeded to change. It was not until she sat down to brush her hair that she idly opened it. It was a piece of exercise book paper; on one side, on ruled lines, were the vestiges of what appeared to be a French vocabulary list; on the other, one word, in Dulcie's handwriting: 'Yes.' It meant nothing to her. She threw it away.

That night she awoke shortly after two. There was no sound except the small shift and slap of the water against the wall. Her curtains, wide open, hung lifeless in the still June night. The moon was a pale mottled disc like an honesty pod in the sky.

Something had wakened her. She had not been dreaming, nor too hot, nor thirsty, nor had she consciously heard anything—and yet her mind had registered something, right through the blanket of sleep, and she had woken up.

She got out of bed and opened her door. Without a doubt there was someone down in the big hall. She was frightened. Frightened of the castle, of going out into the gallery and looking down at what? Or whom? Perhaps the haughty hunters and staring, pale-skinned ladies had stepped from the tapestry and were processing up the stairs, their slinking hounds sniffing a trail that might lead to—she shut the door abruptly and leaned against it, standing quite still for a moment or two so that the horrors her imagination had conjured up would not be disturbed and come after her.

When her panic had subsided she crossed to the window and sat down on the sill. The black lake, the mountains, they were familiar and friendly beside the terrors in her head. She could see the causeway, an opaque black line from the castle wall to the mainland, the escape route . . . As she watched, the car glided smoothly into the picture, moving along the causeway like a stalking cat, its headlamps sending a soft triangular beam in front of it. She watched it dreamily, distanced by a sense of unreality. It moved slowly; there was hardly any sound, no rude shock or blinding realization. When it turned into the road and began to move upwards into the trees she saw a flicker of pink, Dulcie's scarf caught for a second in the moonlight. Then as the trees encroached the headlamps flickered, dimmed, vanished and reappeared before being swallowed up completely in the night. Gone.

'Yes,' whispered Thea to herself, aghast at herself for not having known before. 'Yes.'

CHAPTER SEVEN

'*And I'd like to go again*
To Paris on the Seine,
For Paris is a proper pantomime . . .'
    Marie Lloyd—'The Coster Girl in Paris'

Thea awoke the next morning plagued by the absurd idea that she would have to be the bearer of bad tidings, that everyone else would be in a state of blissful ignorance which it would be her unenviable task to shatter.

This was far from the case. Kessler was in the habit of rising at dawn and had discovered almost at once that the Daimler Benz was missing. Dieter, like most small boys, was up with the lark and at the same moment that Kessler found the garage empty he observed, peeping into Dulcie's room, that her bed had not been slept in. She was a notoriously heavy sleeper, and as her bed was empty, Dieter instantly deduced that it had not been used at all. He experienced the first stirrings of unease.

Something prompted him to go and knock on Peter's door. No reply. He pushed it open a little and peered round. The bed lay virgin neat and smooth in the soft first light.

Dieter felt suddenly sick. His face was cold, his stomach bubbling, his palms clammy. His mind raced ahead . . . So this was what it had all been leading up to. The enormity of his own, albeit passive, implication in the crime was borne down upon him. He sank beneath its weight, sliding down the wall to sit in a heap on the floor, weak with terror. He could not bear to contemplate the reaction of his father to such an outrage.

Footsteps down the big hall, quick urgent strides in heavy boots: Kessler. The rhythm and tenor of the steps altered as Kessler started up the stairs. At the junction he paused. He had seen Dieter slumped in Peter's doorway.

'Mr Dieter!'

Dieter shrank against the wall. Kessler came up the next flight quickly, trot, trot, trot. He was a big, tall man with a ruddy complexion and opulently curling whiskers. His appearance contrasted oddly with his worried expression.

Dieter struggled to his feet, wiping his eyes and nose frantically with his sleeve.

'Mr Dieter.' Kessler came up to him. He carried his jaunty felt hat in front of him, turning its brim between big hands. Dieter could see drops of early morning moisture clinging to the fibres of his hairy jacket. He was breathing fast.

'I'm sorry to come charging up like this at this hour, but would you happen to know if the Baron is awake yet?'

Dieter shook his head dumbly. Why wouldn't Kessler just go away, give them all more time, stop rushing trouble into their lives with such an air of importance?

'I wonder what would be best . . .' Kessler looked around him nervously. He seemed to be in an agony of indecision.

'What's the matter?' asked Dieter in a small, choked voice.

'The car's gone,' Kessler replied, almost absently; he had all but forgotten Dieter's presence. 'The Benz. I'm damned if I know what's up.'

'Dulcie and Peter have taken it,' said Dieter.

'What's that?'

'Never mind.' Dieter could not summon the courage to repeat himself. 'Do you want me to tell Papa?'

'Sorry?' Kessler looked at him as though seeing him for the first time.

'Shall I tell Papa about the car?'

'Oh . . . no. No, I'll tell him when he comes down.'

Kessler plodded dejectedly away down the stairs. Dieter suddenly knew whom he would go and see.

Thea lay on her side, stiff with anxiety, rehearsing what she would say. It never crossed her mind not to tell, to wait until the matter came to light of its own accord. The terrible secret weighed on her like a millstone. After all, she had been sent on this trip to chaperone Dulcie, and what had happened? All their hosts' kindness, their hospitality, their tact, had been thrown back in their faces. And the worst of it was she had known what was going on. But she had honestly believed that Peter would respect his position of trust, that Dulcie would too, that there were certain natural curbs. Instead of which, this . . . She buried her face in the pillow, clenching her teeth with misery.

A hand touched her shoulder, gave it a light shake. She

rolled her head and saw Dieter. He was fully dressed, but his face was haggard.

'Dieter? What are you doing here?'

'They've gone! Dulcie and Peter have gone, and they've stolen Papa's car!'

Poor little thing. She sat up and held out her arms to him, and he crept into them like a stray dog. Thea remembered the reverse side of the note, the French vocabulary list, Dulcie's untoward fawning over Dieter. There was no doubt now what was bothering the child. When he pulled away he glanced at her nervously, trying to assess her reaction.

'I know about it,' she said. It might comfort him to know that she, too, carried the burden of knowledge.

'But how?'

'I heard them last night. I wasn't sleeping well, and something woke me. When I looked out of the window, I saw the car driving away.' She saw in his eyes a question which he was too incoherent to voice, but which she answered. 'There seemed no point in waking everyone. It was too late, we couldn't have stopped them.' She shrugged. Her protests sounded lame. The fact was, when she had seen the car moving out along the causeway, it had all suddenly seemed inevitable, the result of some demonic but irrefutable logic against which it was futile to struggle.

'Don't worry,' she said helplessly, taking Dieter's cold hand in hers. 'Don't worry. What can happen, after all?'

He shook his head, pulling his hand away and wringing his fingers together in his lap. 'It was my fault.'

'Silly! Of course it wasn't. It can't have been. They were two grown-ups, they knew perfectly well what they were doing.'

'But I should have *said*! I knew what they were doing,' he moaned in an agony of confession, wanting her understanding and her absolution.

'So did I,' she said. 'I found a note; Peter or somebody must have dropped it on the stairs. It was torn out of your French book.'

He put his head in his hands, tears oozing out from beneath his pale, sandy lashes. Thea desperately cast around for a glimmer of hope. 'Dulcie and Peter would have run away anyway.' She pulled his hands down, and tilted his chin to make him look at her. 'I shan't tell.'

The first tentative rays of relief showed in his reddened eyes. 'Promise?'

'Promise. Cut my throat.'

'Oh thanks, thanks *ever* so much!' The relief became a veritable sunrise, lighting his whole face. 'Papa is going to be furious!' Now that he was less frightened he made this observation with some relish.

Thea nodded. 'I know.'

'He didn't like Peter anyway. I could tell.'

'Or Dulcie.'

'No.'

They sat looking at each other, barriers of age, sex and background temporarily breached in their contemplation of the situation. Finally, Thea said ruefully: 'I'll tell you one thing: *my* father isn't going to be very pleased about all this, either . . .'

They managed to exchange an anxious, conspiratorial smile.

By nine o'clock the news had already burst upon all the inhabitants of Wolzhof. Thea was struck by the difference in the response of the von Crieffs to a crisis from that of her own family. Here there was no shouting or arguing, no high drama and taking of sides. Instead a cold, vengeful silence pervaded the castle; everyone crept about, avoiding the Baron and hoping not to be implicated. Both Josef and Kessler were summoned to the presence for as much as an hour apiece and emerged looking serious, and somehow older. Dieter kept to his room; Annelise sat in the drawing-room staring at a novel; Jessica fluttered about like a moth caught in a net, frantic but ineffectual.

She and Thea encountered each other on the terrace. Both had come out in order to escape the claustrophobic air of the castle. It was not much better out here; the atmosphere was heavy and humid, breathlessly still.

She came over and took Thea's arm. Her face seemed incapable of coping with the dreadfulness of what had happened. And her opening remark underlined her unfailing grasp of the inessentials.

'My dear . . . whatever will your parents think of us?'

'They're not going to blame you, Aunt Jessica. On the contrary, I should think they will feel thoroughly ashamed of

Dulcie, and sorry that you had all this to cope with. I still don't know how my sister could . . .'

'She was led astray, my dear, led astray.' Jessica sounded quite uncharacteristically definite. 'My husband never trusted Peter de Laszlo, though I must say I always rather liked him. And my husband has been proved right. I was thoroughly taken in by the man, and now he has been shown in his true colours. And your poor little sister, after that unhappy business in England . . .' She shook her head sadly. Thea felt a pang of conscience. Why should this nice, well-meaning, middle-aged woman assume all the guilt which rightfully belonged to Dulcie?

'Aunt Jessica, I wasn't completely frank with you about Dulcie.'

'Weren't you, dear?'

'No. I'm afraid the "unhappy business", as you call it, was largely her fault.'

'Oh.' Jessica did not seem to know how to respond to this. In a way it was easier for her to accept her own story, to see Dulcie as a guileless young thing abducted by a cad, than to apportion blame so close to home.

'You must understand,' Thea went on, 'that they are both guilty. They hatched the plan together.' She paused for a fraction of a second, then went on: 'And they both did it knowing quite well what they were letting themselves in for, and the effect it would have on everyone else.'

'They stole the car.' Jessica made this announcement as though she had at last found something worth complaining about. 'They actually stole a valuable motor car!'

At this moment the others came through the iron gates onto the terrace. It was clear the Baron had been rounding up his family preparatory to making a statement. Josef looked serious and gaunt; Thea's heart went out to him but he did not come over to her, standing instead just behind his father, as though deliberately aligning himself with his own family in time of trouble, and against her. His eyes looked towards but through her. It was as though he had hit her, in front of everyone.

Dieter ran to Jessica and stood close to her, hanging on her arm like a child half his age. Now that he felt himself safe from direct accusation he was quite enjoying this adult drama being played out over his head. The sky above was a dense, opaque grey, patterned with the faint smudges of gathering clouds. The lake was dead calm. There was going to be a storm.

The Baron addressed them in a clipped, incisive tone. He appeared business-like, but a small pulse beat in his left temple. 'Obviously, we must return to Vienna at once, and every effort must be made to find out where these people are. May I ask first if anyone knows anything—*anything*—that might assist us in this?' His cold gaze swept over them, and Thea felt it incumbent upon her to say something, even if only to relieve the others of doing so.

'I'm afraid it came as a complete surprise to me, I had no idea they were planning such a thing. I do know that Dulcie hates travelling, so perhaps they won't get far . . .' Her voice tailed away; she could hear for herself how lame it sounded. The Baron stared at her in disgust.

Jessica said: 'The best thing we can do is to go home, send a telegram to Thea's parents, and then notify the police.' It was odd, Thea thought, that they treated Dulcie as though she were dead; she and Peter had become 'these people'; Ralph and Venetia were 'Thea's parents'. They could not bear to speak Dulcie's name.

'The police, most certainly,' the Baron snapped. 'Apart from anything else, they have stolen an automobile. I intend to have legal and financial redress for everything. Everything!' The pulse flickered like a flame beneath his pale skin.

Josef said quietly, 'I shall go and tell the servants to begin packing.'

'Do that, yes.'

Josef walked away. He seemed already to be a soldier again, an officer with unpleasant duties to perform and no time to spare for the luxury of feelings. Thea was an outsider. There were influences at work here to which she was not subject and her claims, if she had any, on Josef's attention had been swept aside. She could almost have felt sorry for Dulcie, for being the object of such calculating anger. But she was at that moment sorrier for herself, dragged yet again into the churning wake of Dulcie's excesses.

The Baron was talking again. 'So we know nothing. Not where they have gone, nor how, though we may readily surmise *why*.' It was not a joke. He appeared to be working himself into an even greater rage; his face was white, his voice thin and sour.

Suddenly Annelise said: 'Dieter, don't you know anything?'

Thea caught her breath. Dieter glanced up at his mother as though hoping for protection. But how could she protect him? She knew nothing.

'No,' he said, with little conviction.

'Why should he?' asked Jessica.

'He was with them nearly all the time,' said Annelise.

'Dieter?' The Baron transferred his attention to his youngest child as if seeing him for the first time. 'What do you say to this?'

Dieter squirmed. Thea took a deep breath, appalled at Annelise's stupidity. She herself would intervene, gloss things over; it was the least she could do.

But before she could say anything, Dieter was blurting it out: 'I never thought they'd do something like that!' His face was crumpled, sagging, his voice a long wail of misery. Thea put her hand to her eyes.

'So you knew what was going on?' The Baron took a step forward, his arms very straight at his sides. He reminded Thea of some fierce, sharp-faced predator picking up the scent of a cornered prey.

'They were always messing about . . .' Dieter was in tears now, noisy and wet, wiping his sleeve across his nose. 'Anyone could see that.'

'Apparently not.' The Baron used sarcasm like a knife. 'It would appear you were the privileged one.'

Thea could stand by no longer. 'I knew they were fond of each other,' she said softly. 'But we were all thrown together so much—'

'Dieter, you will have no luncheon!' the Baron cut in, ignoring her, not even glancing at her. 'Come to my study when we have had ours.' He turned and strode away towards the iron gates. The rest of them stood like statues, Dieter snuffling against his mother's arm.

At the gates the Baron stopped. 'And no supper either.'

When he had gone, Thea turned to Annelise. 'Why on earth did you do that?' she asked. She could not believe anyone could be so thick-skinned.

Annelise shrugged. 'I was trying to help.'

'You must be mad!'

Dieter had begun to sob, burying his face in Jessica's dress. All the bravado that had boosted him earlier had gone. The violence of his distress was quite shocking.

'There, there,' murmured Jessica, stroking his head distractedly. 'But you must remember how important it is to own up.'

The astounding irrelevance of this piece of advice seemed to merit no response. A few large, tepid drops of rain spattered down. Almost at once, after the days of sun, the strong peaty smell of wet grass and foliage rose from the garden. The oily surface of the lake was stippled with the shower. The sulky, uncertain sky of earlier was now lowering, and it was suddenly cooler.

'We must go in,' announced Jessica, as though glad of an excuse for practical activity. 'And we should begin to pack if we're to go home tomorrow.'

Dieter pulled away from her, sniffing loudly, and thrust his hands deep in his pockets.

'Come on, Dieter, it's going to rain.'

'I don't want to come in.'

'You'll be soaked,' remarked Annelise conversationally.

'I don't care,' Dieter shouted at her. 'And you shut your mouth—sneak! Tell-tale!'

'Dieter, that will do,' reproved his mother. 'Stay out a little while if you must, but be sensible and come in when the storm starts or you'll catch cold. There is no point in sulking.' She and Annelise began to walk towards the castle.

Thea felt terribly afraid, but helpless. 'I'm sorry, Dieter,' she said.

'It's not *your* fault.'

'I know, but I'm sorry it's worked out like this.'

'Hm.' She realized that he was not trying to be rude, but to hold back further tears.

'What are you going to do?' she asked. 'I don't like to think of you out here all on your own, feeling miserable. Won't you come in? You could come to my room, help me pack.'

He shook his head. '. . . by myself,' he mumbled.

'All right. But not for too long.'

He did not, or could not, reply to this admonition, but ran away down the grassy slope towards the lake. As she went through the iron gate Thea saw him sitting on the parapet, his hands tucked beneath him, shoulders hunched, like some wretched roosting bird, with the rain spattering down on him.

She went up to her room in the tower and began to assemble her belongings in a state of dream-like dissociation. She felt exhausted, yet she was not entirely numb. At the back of her mind there was a dull, black ache. Because of Josef.

There was a knock at the door.

'Come in.'

He opened the door and entered, turning to close it meticulously after him. She sensed at once that he was using every second to gain time, to compose himself. He put his hands behind his back, like his father, and walked to the window.

'I'm sorry about Dulcie,' she said dully. 'She's spoilt everything.'

He cleared his throat. 'You shouldn't take her misdemeanours so much upon yourself.'

'I was responsible for her.'

'Be that as it may,' he turned and faced her, 'the deed is done, we shall have to make the best of it. Besides, there is other news. Grave news.'

'What?'

'The Archduke Franz Ferdinand and his wife have been assassinated at Sarajevo. It happened yesterday.' Thea remembered the picnic. 'It will almost certainly mean war with Serbia. Of course I shall have to rejoin my regiment at once.'

'War?' She was dazed. 'Surely there must be . . .'

'There is no alternative. There may be some time-wasting, but it will be war in the end, and soon.'

'I see.' She sank down on the bed. She felt icy cold. The room was dark as the storm gathered.

Josef walked over and stood before her. 'So this is farewell.'

'I don't see why . . .' She struggled feebly like a trapped animal, protesting against the inevitable. He put his hands on her shoulders and guided her to her feet. She felt that she was being set aside, not heartlessly but with a kind of relief.

'I know you will be brave,' he was saying gently. 'And I must be, too.'

She stared back at him, speechless. Was he really saying she would not see him again? Somewhere deep inside she boiled with rage that he should so readily allow these other claims to take priority over hers. War? He must surely be exaggerating. The cataclysmic events of the past two days here were all she could cope with or believe in.

He let his hands fall from her shoulders and took a step back. 'Goodbye Thea.'

She stood motionless, nerveless. The fact of his imminent departure knocked at her brain like the half-heard rumblings of a distant avalanche. Her lips formed 'goodbye' but there was no sound.

He lowered his head in a slow, dignified little bow, almost as though she had dismissed him; took one further step back, and then went to the door with the restrained, careful tread of a man in church. He opened the door silently, stepped through, and closed it behind him with infinite care and downcast eyes.

Josef could remember his mother reading him the story of the Little Mermaid. She was given legs, on which she would be able to dance as lightly as thistledown for her prince, but every step would cause her unspeakable agony. Now, walking away from Thea's closed door, he felt as if each footfall were physical pain. But he had to go. There was going to be war. There was no question but that he had done the right thing. So why, in the face of all these real and urgent pressures, did he still feel that he had just now wilfully turned his back on life? At the head of the stairs he paused. All he had to do was go back, take her in his arms, say that although he must leave it was not for ever, because life without her would be no life at all. If, at that moment, Thea had opened the door and called him, he would have gone to her. But the door remained closed and the room silent.

He went down the stairs and out through the iron gates into the garden. The sky was a rushing, frowning purple, but the rain still only light. Dieter was sitting on the wall and Josef went over to him.

'Dieter, you had better go in.' The boy's arms below the short sleeves of his shirt were already rough with goose pimples and his teeth were chattering. Josef pulled off his own pullover and huddled it round Dieter's shoulders. 'Run along.'

Dieter slipped off the wall. His lips were mauve with cold, and he held the pullover round him with clenched white fingers. His face, when he looked up at his brother, was pitiful. 'What about Father?'

'What about him?' Josef was surprised at the fierceness in his own voice. 'He is not angry with *you*, especially. Just keep your head down and let the storm blow over.'

233

'Yes, Josef . . .' Dieter trailed off across the lawn, but then stopped for a moment. 'Aren't you coming?'

'In a while.'

Josef stood by the wall where Dieter had been sitting, staring across the choppy, fretful lake. He thought: if only things had been different, if Dulcie had not behaved as she did, if I had not been recalled, if we had more time, I could have . . .

But he knew it wasn't true. Force of circumstance had saved him from his inadequacies; he had had his chances and failed to take them. He had retreated time and again, and had now done so for the last time. He let out a sound that was part anger and part misery, that blended with the sobbing wind and the pattering rain, and brought his fist down with such force on the wall that he broke the skin. He stared at the row of oozing blood spots, and as he did so the rain grew suddenly harder, and washed them away before his eyes.

The storm rumbled and flashed round the Wolzsee; the water grew choppy and the trees stirred and sighed in the gathering wind. Having done what packing she could, Thea made her way to Dulcie's room. She wondered how much her sister had taken with her. No elopement could possibly run its course under the burden of the luggage that Dulcie normally carried.

The room was neat. The small things had been taken from the dressing table—brushes, combs, bottles of scent—but the wardrobe revealed most of Dulcie's clothes still hanging there, like ghosts. Thea gathered them up and laid them on the bed. She had better pack them. No one else would.

The empire through which Peter de Laszlo shepherded an irritable and apprehensive young English lady was one in the grip of war fever. The assassination of the Archduke Franz Ferdinand and the Countess Sophie was simply the final straw that broke the back of the monarchy's patience. The crime of Gavrilo Princip and his handful of grammar-school braves was just a symptom, an eruption on the already disfigured skin of Austria-Hungary's political life.

The assassination at Sarajevo, it was universally agreed, must be seen as a challenge not only to the Empire's position as ruler of Bosnia but to her declining prestige as a great power. Touchily, Austria-Hungary's statesmen demanded overt and immediate vindication. Her huge army, accumulated during peacetime in order to preserve peace, unbalanced her so that the slightest movement could cause a military landslide.

Dulcie did not believe in war. But, though she could ignore the war-clouds, she could not prevent them gathering, and as she and Peter made their way west to Paris her nerves were torn to shreds by their continued threatening presence. She became plaintive and belligerent by turns. Peter noticed that the spirited cavalier air she affected with such style in the drawing-room and on the dance floor deserted her with alarming rapidity when she was obliged to spend an hour or two on a train. And her looks, dependent as they were on her humour, fluctuated proportionately.

However, the die had been cast, and on 2 July they reached Paris and found a couple of rented rooms in the Place d'Agnette in Montmartre. The bohemian flavour of their new address resuscitated Dulcie's flagging spirits like a whiff of salts. She at once began to recover. Here she was further away from all the tedious war-talk, and Paris had long held sway in her imagination as the capital of taste and fashion. She still had some of her holiday allowance, and Peter had his private income; they could live like kings. Borne on a wave of optimism she went out and purchased two smart dresses and then sat down in high good humour to write to her relations, exhorting them not to worry about her. It did not for one second occur to her that the inconvenience to themselves might be greater than any imagined harm to her person, or that they might have greater and more pressing worries than for her safety. She was a creature of the moment. She had run away to Paris, for what she supposed was love. The horrors of the journey behind her, she allowed herself to bask in the fulfilment of this long-cherished dream.

'. . .*As merry as a robin, that sings on a tree,*' she hummed to herself as she lay in bed at eleven o'clock in the morning, a week after their arrival. They had not been in the rooms long enough for much dirt to have accumulated, they ate out or not at all, and they had paid the concierge a month's rent in advance. Geraniums flowered on the little iron balcony and the smell of strong coffee floated through from the other room: the perfect love nest.

Peter put his head round the door. 'I'm going out.'

'Darling Peter . . .' She stretched out her arms to him but he did not come in. 'Why?'

'I have things to do. And you should be up.'

'Why?'

'Stop saying "why" like a spoilt little girl, and get up. You could clean this place for a start.'

'It's perfectly all right. Come over here and kiss me.'

'No. And don't say why. I don't want to, is why. You look a slut, lying there.'

'Do I?'

'Yes, and it doesn't suit you. Stir yourself.'

'What will you do if I don't?'

'I shall make you.'

'Go on then.' She smiled at him flirtatiously. It was what they both liked, she wasn't afraid of him. He stood there in the doorway. She continued to beam, settling back on the pillows and throwing her arms back over her head, wrists crossed, in an attitude she knew he found appealing.

When he did come over to her, she was caught quite unawares both by his speed and his strength. He was at the bed in two strides, had caught her wrists in one hand, so tight that she gasped, and dragged her onto the floor with a crash. She landed on her back; it knocked all the breath out of her, the game was moving too fast. He straddled her, on all fours like a dog, panting slightly from the exertion. She sensed his excitement but also, for the first time, his intention to hurt her.

'Peter . . . ?'

He took her hands, one in each of his, and laid them back on either side of her head, leaning heavily on them so that her fingers began to go numb. He released one hand and fumbled with his trousers, at the same time elbowing her legs apart roughly. She resisted, because she was not ready, but that made him still more impatient. He came into her at once, hard and fast, and it was painful because she was dry, like rough bark grating inside her, and he was forcing his whole weight down upon her each time as though he wanted her to split in two. His hands he kept planted on the floor on either side of her, and his eyes watched her all the time so that she could not hide. Even when she closed her eyes she could feel him looking at her, using her. And when the dreadful hard stabbing was over he kneeled and stood up so quickly that she was left lying there, discarded, disgraced, her nightgown up around her waist, on the grubby carpet.

'Now perhaps,' he said, 'you will get up and dress yourself.'

It did not take her long to recover. She had a selective memory. Within minutes of his departure, she was dressed, and her hand shook only a little as she combed her hair.

Ralph had received a telegram from Thea, the substance of which took him a full minute to digest. When he had finally done so he emitted a roar like that of a wounded tiger. His enormous fist descending into the litter of paper on his desk sent sheets scudding in all directions and pencils raining to the ground. Homer, who lay on his blanket in the corner, started violently and then shambled over to his master, cringing in apology in case it had been he who had caused the outburst.

Ralph let out another roar, this time ending in a moan of disbelief. 'How could she? What's the matter with the girl?'

He snatched up the telegram again and peered at it, as though mistrusting the evidence of his eyes. But there it was, its enormity somehow emphasized by the small, inoffensive grey print: *Dulcie eloped to Paris with von Crieff tutor. Letter follows. Thea.'*

'"Eloped to Paris?"' he muttered. '"*Eloped?*" Damn her!'

A soft knock on the door heralded Primmy, standing there with a look of polite, and slightly reproving, enquiry.

'Everything all right, sir? Did you call?'

'Primmy.' Ralph fixed her with a smouldering look and held up the telegram between finger and thumb. 'Primmy, do you see this?'

'Yes sir.'

'Know what it is?'

'No sir. It looks like a telegram.'

He ignored her reply. 'It is a knife in my bowels.'

'I see, sir.' He glanced up at her but she was poker-faced.

'Where is Mrs Tennant?' he asked.

'Resting, I believe sir, in her room. She's not been feeling too good.'

'Thank you, Primmy.'

Dismissed, she turned to leave. As she closed the door behind her she heard the sound of paper being sharply torn in half.

Ralph waited for about ten minutes—as long as his rage

and impatience would allow—and then went upstairs to visit his wife. As it happened, she had woken up and was sitting by the window, writing a letter. She looked up as Ralph entered and smiled.

'What is that you're doing?' he asked brusquely.

'I'm writing to Thea.'

'Don't.'

'Why ever not?'

'I have just had a telegram from her. Dulcie has run off with the von Crieffs' tutor.'

Venetia rose and came over to him. The smile was still half-there; she didn't believe him. 'She can't have.'

'What makes you think that? She can and has.'

'The telegram . . .' She held out her hand, asking for concrete proof.

'I tore it up. Thea said a letter was on its way, but that will be all excuse and explanation. The fact is, Dulcie has run away. Eloped. *Eloped!*' He foundered again on great rocks of incomprehension.

'But where?'

'To Paris. With this . . . *tutor.*' He pronounced the word as if it were the worst kind of insult. Venetia went back to her chair in the window and sat down unsteadily. The colour had seeped from her face, her stomach churned. She was losing a battle with unconsciousness, was only dimly aware of her husband working himself up to new heights of fury.

'I shan't understand the girl if I live to be a hundred. She's anti-social, untrustworthy, immature—God knows I have tried!' He stamped over to the window, looming over her, leaning his hands up on either side of the frame, his head sunk between his shoulders. His outline against the light swam and flickered before Venetia's eyes. She could not form words, or even make a sound. She wished that he would look down and see her plight. Instead, he suddenly threw his hands up.

'There's nothing else for it. I shall go to Paris, find her, and bring her back if I have to drag her by the hair. There's God knows what going on in Europe since that Sarajevo business, it's not safe apart from anything else.' He slammed both palms against the glass with a boom.

Venetia's last sight of him as she slipped forward was of his face, at last turned towards her, first wrathful, then astonished

When she came to her senses a few minutes later the first thing she saw was the same face, this time uncharacteristically contrite. She was lying on the bed and she felt her hand, which was cold, clasped like a small stone between Ralph's two large, warm ones. The moment her eyes opened he snatched her up, squeezing her so that she could hardly breathe.

'Thank heavens! What did you do that for? You looked like a corpse.' He laid her back against the pillow.

Weak as she was she had to laugh. 'Thank you so much!'

'What's the matter? Are you ill?' His staccato interrogation brought her round like a whiff of salts, as no soft words could have done. She was ill and she knew it. At the beginning it was nothing, a malaise. But recently there had been a worsening. She had pains. She did not mention them to Ralph. He was not good at coping with illness, and besides there had been nothing definite. But now the knowledge that all was not well with her made her fearful. What if something happened, and he was not here?

'Yes, I am.' She gripped his hands. 'I am.'

'But what the devil is it?' Anxiety made him bluster. Instantly, in an automatic desire to soothe him, she retracted.

'Oh, nothing much. I'm just a little under the weather.'

'I must say, you look frightful.' Suspiciously he scanned her face.

'Truly, it's nothing. I was shocked over Dulcie.'

'Now, now.' He became masterful, more confident on this familiar territory. 'Don't upset yourself over that young lady. I'll go over and bring her back in no time.'

'But I don't want you to go!' She felt so horribly vulnerable.

'Nonsense!' He patted her hand. 'I can be there and back in three or four days, with the baggage in tow. And Thea, too. We'll all be together again.'

'We'll never all be together again . . .' she murmured. She knew it.

'What's that? Now come on, old thing, be a stoic. I have to go, you must see that, and as soon as possible. Aubrey will be here . . .'

'Send *him*!'

'No.' There was a quizzical note in his voice, as if he couldn't believe it was her talking. 'He's too valuable at the works, he virtually runs it these days. Besides, it's my place to go.'

'It's *not* your place to go!' Her voice rose in panic she was too weak to suppress. 'Your place is here with me!' She began to shiver violently. She felt sick and her head reverberated like a gong. She clung to his hand. Beyond the spots of light that dazzled and jumped before her eyes she saw his expression soften.

'Very well,' he said quietly, separating their hands and standing up. 'Very well. For you, I'll stay.' He went to the door. 'I'll send for some tea—make you feel better.'

As the door began to close after him she whispered, 'Ralph, who *will* go?' Her conscience pained her terribly.

'I don't know.' His voice was flat. 'I'll think of something. Perhaps Thea, I don't know.'

When he had gone she turned her face into the pillow and wept luxurious tears of selfish relief. She heard his voice, loud, imperative and angry on the stairs, summoning Primmy.

'Take some tea up to Mrs Tennant, would you.'

'Yes, sir. How is she feeling?'

'A bit off colour.'

Ralph stumped past Primmy into the library and stood indecisively in the middle of the room, his arms folded. Now that he was no longer with his wife he experienced a fearful pang of anxiety for her. Primmy had said Venetia hadn't been feeling too good. Could it be that everyone knew something he didn't? She had looked dashed peculiar. What kind of heartless swine would he be if she was really ill and he was away? Perhaps, after all, he would stay, and write to Thea as he had only half-heartedly suggested, and get a doctor in to his wife to confirm that there was nothing much the matter . . .

In a black mood he called Homer and left the house for a long walk.

The family had been back at Helenastrasse for two weeks when Thea received letters from her father and from Dulcie. They had been a wretched two weeks. The house had been a morgue, and they like zombies moving aimlessly about in it. Dieter had had terrible flu, and been confined to bed for several days. Nothing had been done about the runaways. The car had been found outside the station at Graz, with a letter for the Baron from Peter de Laszlo lying on the driver's seat. No one knew whether he had read it.

Talk of war was everywhere in Vienna, the Austrians

bristled with aggression after the assassination. The great powers of Europe which had faced each other across the frail frontiers of unbridled national sovereignty were poised in a balance so delicate that at any moment it could be fatally and irrevocably tipped. Thea felt herself to be an outsider, looking on at some private, heated argument. Who knew when the combatants might turn on her and use her as their scapegoat?

Josef had rejoined his regiment at once. The army was alerted for mobilization at a moment's notice. The great ponderous machine of war snatched him away and swallowed him up with terrible efficiency.

She had written to her father as soon as they were back. She was desperate to regain her own identity. These, after all, were other people's problems, another country's war. She craved the normality of England, the soft variety of an English summer, the familiar foibles of her own family, friends she loved and enemies she recognized.

So when Ralph's letter arrived she fell upon it greedily. Even his tall, furious black handwriting, racing imperiously across the envelope, barely leaving room for a stamp, was like the handshake of a long-lost friend, firm and reassuring.

'Dearest girl,' he wrote. 'Don't blame yourself. It was my mistake, and I curse myself hourly on account of it. I wrongly supposed that Dulcie was susceptible to improvement, but plainly this is not so. Whereas you, my dear Thea, have been a tower of strength, putting up with me and with her, and to what end? It is all a mess.' Thea smiled to herself. She could almost hear him speaking in that tone which was a blend of anger and embarrassment, admitting fault but always with a bad grace. His glowing portrait of herself was partly due to his own guilt. She had not been so very virtuous; on the contrary, she had thought of little else but herself and the gratification of her own wishes since arriving in Vienna. She had even regarded Dulcie's liaison with Peter as a useful decoy, something to keep Dulcie out of trouble while she concentrated on her own affairs. The only time she had criticized it was when she had intended quite deliberately to hurt her sister, and she had succeeded. Certainly, she was no plaster saint, but there was no harm in letting Ralph think so for a while. She badly needed sympathy and affection, and she would glut herself on it while she could.

The letter went on: 'I realize it is a lot to ask, but could you *chase after the prodigal daughter and try to persuade her to return? I have no intention of killing the fatted calf but neither am I quite ready to let her go to the dogs. And who is this young man, in God's name? You characterize him as the young von Crieff's tutor, but that tells me nothing. Is he the villain of this piece, or is she? It is perfectly maddening not to know. I have written to Baron von Crieff with my profound apologies and so on, it is most chastening when I specifically courted an invitation. I would come myself now, and put Dulcie over my knee, but your mother is somewhat below par (as who should wonder?) and I don't like to leave her, although Aubrey insists all would be well. In any event, if you could act* in loco parentis *this one more time, darling girl, you will bask for ever in the gratitude of your loving but harassed parent.*

'I salute you. Father.

'(P.S. When you see her, be as blunt as you like. I authorize it.)'

Thea read and re-read the letter. It had brought her father into the room with her and, which was more important, had reinstated him in his rightful place in her affections. They were friends once more, and allies.

The other letter, received the following day, was from Dulcie. It was written on dainty powder-blue notepaper, with a tiny embossed rose in the top right-hand corner, but the writing was hectic and barely legible. There was no address.

'Darling Thea, Wasn't I awful? I don't suppose for one moment that you or anyone else is ever going to forgive me, but I thought I'd write anyway to let you know that I'm quite all right. I am writing to Father and Mother too. We had a vile journey, I nearly died, but now we're in Paris in our own little apartment (Montmartre, no less!) and as happy as birds on a twig. We are right by a dear little market. Peter had some money, as you know, but he is looking for another teaching post to help out. I have bought two lovely Paris gowns, so much more elegant than anything you'd find in stuffy old London!

'You won't come chasing after me, will you, because it won't do any good. We shall most likely get married soon, and then there will be nothing you can do, anyway. I suppose the deadly old Baron found his car all right. I bet he was more cross about that than anything!' Cross! Even Dulcie's lan-

guage reflected the petty dramas of infancy. *I'm sorry if we caused a stir, but it seemed the only thing—to make a clean break and live our own lives, I know you're in favour of that. One day I shall come back to Chilverton House as Madame de Laszlo, fearfully à la mode, and then we'll all be friends again. Till then I dare say you're better off without me. Lots of love, don't cry for me. Dulcie.'*

The strange little note of candour in the last lines of the letter touched Thea. So there was some sense of guilt, however small, beneath all the chatter.

But what was this talk about marriage? For some reason, it had never crossed Thea's mind that marriage might be part of her sister's plans. What had Dulcie to do with honouring and obeying, with having and holding in sickness and in health? Far from making everything right, Thea was quite convinced it was entirely wrong. Peter had probably mentioned it to Dulcie in the way that one quiets a screaming child with promises of a sweet. It could not be right. She would go and see for herself.

The prospect of the journey before her did not intimidate her. Bludgeoned by so much in the last few weeks, she felt utterly fearless. A kind of reckless courage took hold of her. She, who a few short months ago had never travelled beyond her native shores, now viewed with fatalistic calm the trip west to Paris, with war threatening and closing on all sides. She knew now that she would rather do it alone. Her solitariness was simple and clean. The worst that could happen was that she might die. And for the first time in her life Thea actually considered death and found it an acceptable, if not a desirable, alternative.

She left the house at Helenastrasse almost unnoticed, early on the morning of 31 July. She had despatched her trunk and Dulcie's to England, never expecting to see either again. She had said her farewells to the family the night before. Her last act before leaving was to walk down to the rose garden, where she picked one long-stemmed yellow rosebud and put it in her buttonhole. Then she looked across at the summerhouse. It had been a morning like that that she and Josef had sat there. She could almost see their ghosts, in each other's arms, lips together, one fair head and one dark one beyond the screen of roses.

After a gruelling journey from Vienna she arrived in Paris

at midday on 1 August. As she emerged from the station into the suffocating heat and crush of the street, the first thing she saw was a news-stand, with the headline emblazoned on its front:

'GERMANY DECLARES WAR ON RUSSIA! FRANCE ISSUES ORDERS TO MOBILIZE!'

She stared at it, trying to take in its implications. It was noisy, the panicky torrent of a foreign language flowed round her, the scorching sun beat on her head. So the war that had snapped at her heels all the way across Europe had finally overtaken her and reached this city first.

Gazing wildly about her she considered her position. She had made no preparations, she did not know Dulcie's precise whereabouts and now it appeared that she might be too late. She had rather naïvely assumed that she would walk from the station, hire a cab and go straight to Montmartre where a few judicious enquiries would lead her to her sister. All of a sudden, that seemed a forlorn hope.

The crowds on the pavement were voluble and excited, on the borderline between hilarity and hysteria. Wishing to align herself with them, to be less marked out as a foreigner, she went over to the news-stand and took a copy of *Le Matin*, which she tucked beneath her arm. As she stood fumbling in her bag for money, her case held between her straddled feet, she was nearly bowled over by a big man who was reeling around clutching a half-empty wine bottle. He wore a suit but his stiff collar had come adrift and his tie was missing. His eyes were rheumy in a scarlet, puffed-up face. Thea staggered, caught at the edge of the news-stand, and turned on him angrily.

'Look out, can't you?'

Her voice had a startling effect on him. He stopped in his tracks, teetering slightly, peering at her. For a moment, she thought he was going to do her some violence. She turned away, scared stiff and trying to discourage him with a show of indifference, but to her surprise he laughed out loud. Suddenly he was close to her, pressing up against her so that she could feel his large body in a state of importunate arousal.

Other people were jostling around them, staring at them in goggle-eyed excitement. The newsboy stood grinning at the two of them, saying something in French which she could not catch. To her horror, the drunk's arm went round her and he planted a moist kiss on her neck. The onlookers burst out laughing.

'Get off! Let go, for God's sake!' Thea struggled and jabbed her elbow into the man's solar plexus. He grunted, jack-knifed, and dropped his bottle with a crash. The crowd jumped out of the way of the spraying splinters.

Thea turned, stumbling over her case, to confront her assailant and watched in astonishment as he straightened up smiling, his arms spread wide, his features wreathed in an expression of mawkish apology. Everyone else was still grinning stupidly.

Someone behind the drunk waved a cap and shouted: '*Vive l'Angleterre!*' The cry was taken up, hats bounced in the air, arms waved. '*Vive l'Angleterre!*' '*Vive la belle Anglaise!*'

Thea smiled weakly, her heart still racing. So her Englishness was some kind of protection. That was good for her immediate safety, but the implications, only half-realized, bothered her. She had not understood that she was part of the fever; she sensed the fickleness, the potential nastiness of the crowd. That wet kiss had been intended as some kind of salute, but it might as easily have been an assault. No one had cared about her evident distress. It was safer not to be singled out in any way.

'*Merci . . .*' she murmured, and resolutely transferred her attention back to the newsboy, producing a French note from her purse and offering it to him. He put up a hand as if to halt traffic, and shook his head. She gave the note a little shake, nodding at the newspaper under her arm.

'*Non,*' he said, shaking his head again with annoying slowness, closing his eyes at the same time. '*Absolument pas.*'

'*Pourquoi?*' she asked.

He took the note and, holding it under her nose, tore it delicately into tiny pieces.

She was aghast. 'What ever did you do that for?' she exclaimed in English.

A lively discussion broke out on all sides. Thea's French was moderate but she could not follow the argument. The newsboy was vociferous in his own defence. Some were apparently on her side, others on his. Finally a woman poked Thea in the shoulder with her finger. She was elderly, with a kindly face, wispy grey hair in an untidy bun.

'*Mam'selle,* the paper money—it is almost worthless.'

'What . . . ?' Thea heard her, but could not comprehend.

'Vous devez . . .' the woman looked round for assistance with her English. Others gave advice. Everyone had an opinion.

'Monnaie!' someone shouted. *'La monnaie!'*

'Coins,' said someone else, and was cheered for his linguistic prowess.

So that was it. It was a contingency that had never occurred to Thea. She gazed down at her virtually valueless bunch of notes, her eyes blurred with tears of frustration. She had come thus far, only to be blocked by something she should have had the sense to foresee. When a hand took her elbow and guided her to one side she allowed herself to be led. Away from the knot of people at the news-stand Thea saw that her friend was the same elderly woman who had advised her about the money.

'Ne pleurez pas,' she said, patting Thea's arm. And added, in the quaint, archaic English of the schoolroom: 'I pity you.'

'Thank you,' Thea smiled at her. 'You're very kind.'

'Maintenant, venez avec moi.' The woman led her gently across the road and down a sidestreet. Thea had no idea where she was being taken, but her guide was so purposeful that she went willingly. They stopped outside a small *pâtisserie.* It was locked, and the shelf display in the window was empty, scattered with a few crumbs, currants and flakes of pastry. Like most of the other small shops they'd passed, it was closed. The woman produced a key and gave it a conspiratorial shake under Thea's nose.

'Voilà!'

She unlocked the door and Thea followed her into the shop. The sun had been streaming through the glass frontage all morning and inside it was hot, the air full of the fragrance of baking. The woman raised a finger.

'Attendez!' She walked round behind the counter and went to the till. Suddenly Thea realized what she intended doing.

'Oh no—you mustn't!'

The woman sprang the till open and began to count out money. *'Mais oui, certainement!'* She scooped up a handful of coins and brought them round to Thea in cupped hands, indicating with a nod of her head that she should open her bag. Thea was overwhelmed.

'You can't possibly do this. What about yourself? *Que ferez vous?'* With a jerk of her laden hands the woman again

246

encouraged her to open her bag. Reluctantly, Thea took the money, about a hundred francs in usable cash.

'Merci, Madame, merci mille fois, vous êtes tres gentille.'

'Oh . . .' The woman spread her hands expressively. *'Pour les Anglais . . .'* Nothing, apparently, was too good for them at present. She chuckled at Thea's bafflement. *'Lisez les nouvelles.'* She took the newspaper from Thea's other hand, unfolded it and passed it back to her. Thea read slowly, translating. Von Emmich, the German general commanding the Army of the Meuse, had demanded a free passage across Belgium, and declared that destruction of bridges, tunnels and railways would be considered as hostile acts. And last night's bulletin from London had declared categorically: 'We desire peace and shall do our utmost to preserve it . . . In this vital issue we shall only be guided by two considerations, the duty we owe to our friends and the instinct of self-preservation.' Two irreconcilable statements of intent.

She did not read on, but made a rueful face at the woman. The two of them stood there for a moment in silence, in the closed shop. A gang of youths ran up the road outside, yelling and holding aloft some kind of home-made banner.

An older man appeared outside the glass door, carrying an armful of planks and plywood, giving the door a light kick to gain admittance.

'Mon mari,' the woman explained, opening the door. The man gave Thea a curt nod and said something in rapid French to his wife, waving an arm at the window. The distant clamour and shouts from the streets washed through the door from behind him.

'I must go.' Thea made for the door.

'Au revoir.'

These people had their own lives to manage, and the woman had been kind enough already. The man stood aside, giving her a more sympathetic look as she passed.

'Au revoir.'

She went into the street. Directly opposite a white-plastered wall glittered in full sunlight. In the centre of it, a large pink poster stared at Thea. It was the mobilization order. Although criss-crossed with a grid of fold marks, even from where she stood Thea could easily read the recently filled-in date in neat, fresh type: *'Dimanche 2 Août, 1914'.* The shock of seeing that date was instantly eclipsed by another, sharper one.

'My case!' She remembered with horror that she must have left it by the news-stand. The loss of it, as she set off doggedly in the direction of the main road, seemed to have stripped away still more of her sadly eroded sense of identity. She grimly clutched her handbag with its precious *'monnaie'*. She now faced the horrendous problem of finding Dulcie, and soon. In order to stand any chance of leaving the city in the next twenty-four hours she must be back at the station that night: the forecourt and ticket hall had been jammed with foreigners trying to get out of Paris, and reservists en route to rejoin their regiments.

She started to walk, hoping that she was going in the right direction for Montmartre. There was scarcely any traffic about. The motor buses had been requisitioned, and what few cabs and private vehicles were on the streets were hopelessly overloaded and travelling at a snail's pace through the crowds.

The air was full of a fine, powdery dust and within minutes of reaching the main road Thea was covered in it, her suit grey and the skin of her face like sandpaper. She repeatedly tried to work up a mouthful of saliva to ease her parched throat. High above, a huge dirigible like a tricoloured tethered whale floated against the blue of the sky. It looked festive, but its presence there was ominous. On every side she saw the blank, closed faces of shuttered and boarded-up shops, often with the pink splash of the mobilization order adorning the bare wood.

The mood of the people on the street was turning sour, curdling in the intense heat. Violence was beginning to erupt. She turned one corner and almost fell over two well-dressed middle-aged men wrestling on the pavement like schoolboys. A growing audience of passers-by egged them on. The men were bad fighters, unfit and untutored, and there was much eye-gouging and hair pulling. Everyone roared: it was excellent sport. Further on, outside a branch of the *Banque Nationale,* a queue several hundred yards long had formed in the broiling heat for the sole purpose of exchanging paper money into coins. The queue was kept in line, and in some kind of order, by a detachment of the *Garde Républicaine,* but tempers were running short on all sides; exhausted women lashed out at grizzling, sweaty children, the elderly wilted, and as Thea passed she was almost pushed over by the heated jostlings of some of the queuers nearer the main door. She dropped her bag, the clasp flew open, and several of the coins spilled out onto the road. Her face burning with shame, she knelt in the gutter to gather them up.

As she rose, unsteadily, she caught the expression of one of the waiting women. She was already turning away, addressing some remark *sotto voce* to her neighbour, eyes slanting accusingly towards Thea. In this situation her Englishness was no guarantee against hostility. Thea stumbled away, hoping desperately to find a cab. Her feet and ankles, aching after the long journey, were now swollen and sore, and the front rim of her left shoe had cut right through her stocking and was digging into her instep. Walking was becoming agony. At last she saw a car, but it was an open touring car full of French officers on their way out of the city. The car slowed down at a junction and was instantly swarmed over by dozens of people wanting to pat, kiss or even just touch these new heroes of the moment. Thea fought her way out of the crush, fiercely clutching her bag.

She turned and was met by a huge steel wagon, drawn by six horses, traversing the length of the street and discharging quantities of sand and gravel onto the road surface. It was this gravel, crushed under foot and by the wheels of vehicles, that was causing the fine, sharp dust in the air. Thea understood from the conversation of two women at a nearby window that the grit was to provide a surface on which the horses of the *cuirassiers* would not slip if they had to charge to enforce law and order. The gravel, newly laid, got into her shoes and she could feel her stockings worn through under the balls of her feet. The grit wagon rolled past like a great dragon, the wheels thundering and jouncing, the team of huge horses at full stretch, eyes frantic, heaving flanks streaked with foam, mouths gaping and yawing on the bit.

She clung to the walls on the inside of the pavement, edging round corners like a fugitive. A pleasant looking young man with a small child perched on his shoulders stopped and stared at her. He said something, but the noise of the wagon drowned his words.

'Montmartre?' she mouthed back, and then shouted at the top of her voice: 'Montmartre?'

'Ah.' Glad to be of service, he pointed.

She pointed the same way, anxious to confirm the directions. 'That way?'

'Oui, oui, c'est ça.'
'Merci.'

She started off again. Exhaustion was beginning to toughen her, to make her dogged and single-minded.

She finally reached the city centre. There she found that a mob had gathered outside a large German art shop, 'Cristallerie de Karlsbad'. Exhibited behind huge plate glass windows were porcelain, glass and bronze, everything from tea services to statuettes. A man seized a wooden chair from a nearby newsvendor's stall, swung it about his head, and let it fly with a tremendous crash into the shop front. Glass flew, people near him screamed and ducked, hands flew to faces. Thea saw one smartly dressed woman with blood trickling from beneath the rim of her chic hat, but she was shouting and laughing, quite hysterical. More missiles were thrown, stones, books, even shoes, and then the door at the side was forced and the mob surged into the shop and began to hurl the contents out into the street. About a ton of Teutonic art, furniture and bric-à-brac hurtled onto the paving stones and was wantonly destroyed. Porcelain was hurled to the ground and stamped on, glass thrown against the walls, chairs and tables reduced to matchwood.

Thea was horrified. She shouted at the man next to her: 'The shopkeeper has done nothing!' but he didn't seem to hear her. His mouth grinned, his eyes goggled; he was transfixed by the antics of his countrymen, and loving every moment of it.

After about ten minutes of unbridled destruction a detachment of the *Garde Républicaine* came on the scene and succeeded in clearing the mob. The street was littered with debris, scintillating with a million fragments of shattered glass and china. When the *Garde* had moved on a man appeared from the shop, carrying in one hand the twisted remains of a bronze figure. It looked terrible, like the mutilated, burned-out body of a child. He caught Thea staring at him and swung the statue aloft.

'Filous!' He yelled. 'They only sell this trash to tourists!' And he smashed the figure to the ground so that it bent convulsively yet again. Thea did not speak, she was terrified of giving herself away as one of the gullible tourists who put cash in the pockets of the *'filous'*, the 'thieving' German shopkeepers. When the man turned away to look for more loot, she ran, until her side hurt and she could barely breathe.

But violence was everywhere. Near the Place de L'Opéra, a crowd was wrecking a German restaurant. A youth was busily engaged in smashing the front of the premises with a wooden hatstand taken from inside. Delighted onlookers cheered with each blow of the hatstand and the lad's face was puce with effort and pride; it was his finest hour. A few blocks away the showrooms of the Benz Automobile Agency were coming in for the same treatment. At the front of the showrooms stood a Daimler Benz of precisely the same model and colour as that in which Dulcie and Peter had made their getaway. A group of people swarmed over it, dismembering it, scraping the paintwork with shards of glass, tearing off the windscreen wipers, slashing the seats and smashing the mirrors and headlamps. Sickened and shaking, Thea hurried by. If they could do that to a car, what might they do to a person?

She sheltered for a moment in a shop doorway to catch her breath and collect her thoughts. The ground all round her feet was littered with broken glass, and on the door some patriotic wit, referring to the Kaiser, had daubed in white paint: *'A bas Guillaume le Bandit!'*

Closing her eyes she combed her damp hair back off her face with shaking fingers, and mopped her brow with her sleeve. She scarcely noticed that a car had drawn up beside her until a plummy, unmistakably British voice enquired: 'You all right? Can we take you anywhere?'

She opened her eyes. She must have imagined it. But no, a huge Bentley stood at the kerb, overflowing with people, like a celestial chariot bearing the faithful to the gates of heaven. At the helm, but now leaning across in her direction, sat a middle-aged lady of majestic build, clad in a fawn tweed suit and voluminous felt beret. Thea walked forward and put her hand on the side of the car to steady herself.

'Are you English?' she asked, disbelievingly.

'Absolutely.'

'Oh, how wonderful! I'm trying to get to Montmartre to find my sister. There doesn't seem to be any transport . . .'

'Our hotel's in Montmartre, my dear. Hop aboard.'

Thea hopped. So there *was* a God, and this conveyance was indeed a celestial chariot. The day once more shone with hope, her feet felt better and her head stopped aching.

There were four people already in the car, apart from the driver· two dazed elderly ladies and a young woman with a stern-faced little boy of about Dieter's age. All of them looked whey-faced with tiredness. Thea sensed that they had been in the city a long time. The young woman gave her a faint, washed-out smile.

'Where are you all going?' asked Thea.

'Back to the hotel,' replied the other. 'We've been to the station to get order numbers. We're hoping to leave tonight.'

'Order numbers?'

'Yes, they're handing them out, one to a family. My husband stayed behind to keep our places in the queue.' She caught Thea's baffled expression. 'You need one to get a ticket, you see.'

'Oh.' Thea sank back, her new-born hope already tarnished. Then a thought occurred to her. 'Did you say you'd be going back to the station tonight?'

'Yes. Why?'

'What's the driver's name?'

'Mrs Dancy.'

Thea leaned over and tapped the big woman on the shoulder. 'Excuse me . . .'

'What can I do for you?' She changed gear with noisy *élan*.

'I gather you'll be leaving tonight . . .'

'*I* shan't, my dear, but I shall be driving back to the station, if that's what you mean. Why, want a lift?'

'It would be simply marvellous if—'

'No problem, no problem at all.' She waved one big, leather-gloved hand airily. 'Mind you, I shouldn't think you'll go tonight—haven't got an order number.'

'No.'

'Never mind. We British are good at queueing. Important thing is to get there.'

'Yes. Thanks awfully.'

'Don't mention it.'

Thea sat back. One of the old ladies, and the little boy, had fallen asleep. The boy's mother sat with her head resolutely turned to one side, staring at the crowded pavement. Her hand, where it clasped the boy's shoulder, was white. She was close to tears.

They began to climb the hill to Montmartre, above the dust to a point where they could look down on the rest of Paris; it still looked peaceful, spread in the summer sunshine.

'Tell you what,' said Mrs Dancy over her shoulder to Thea.

'I'll drop you at our place, the Hotel Beauvoir, and then you'll know where to come this evening.'

'Thank you.'

'Any idea where your sister lives?'

'No . . .' Suddenly she remembered. 'She said she was next to a little market, I think.'

'I should think that would be the Marché d'Agnette. The Place d'Agnette's not too far from us, about ten minutes' walk. You can manage that?'

'Oh yes.'

Soon the Bentley drew up outside the Hotel Beauvoir and Mrs Dancy issued instructions to Thea as to how to get to the Place d'Agnette, and warnings to be back 'for wheels to roll' at five.

'Dare not hang about after that, d'you see, so get here if you can.'

'I will, and thank you so much, I can't tell you how—'

'Don't mention it. Run along and find your sister.'

Thea set off resolutely, much encouraged by this stroke of luck. It was an omen. Things would work out. She would find Dulcie frightened by the situation in Paris, and only too glad to come back with her. It was just after two, and the sun was high, a patch of intense whiteness in the pale blue and cloudless sky. She found the Place d'Agnette quite easily, and began to knock on doors. At several she got no reply; at others, people looked out of upstairs windows but did not come down. Those who did answer seemed unable to pay proper heed to her enquiries, or even to understand her. She learned that there had been some kind of atrocity in the area the night before. Monsieur Jaurès, the socialist leader, had been murdered, shot through the head in the front room where he had been sitting talking. The guards were out on the streets. By a quarter to three she had got nowhere, and her legs were like lead. Her underclothes were soaked through with perspiration and her face and hair caked with dust. Failure once more stared her in the face.

She tried the bell of the corner house, Number 45. It was a tall, narrow, once-white building with a peeling green door and a small iron balcony on the second floor on which stood a sawn-off barrel containing leggy geraniums. The basement door was opened by the concierge, a thin, tired-looking middle-aged woman. Behind her, clustered round her faded print skirt in the semi-darkness, hovered a handful of big-eyed, shock-headed children. There was a warm, aromatic smell of onion and garlic. When Thea asked, the woman replied laconically: yes, she knew the young English lady and the dark gentleman, they had two rooms *'au deuxième étage'* and kept themselves to themselves. Thea thought there was something hostile, more than mere sullenness, behind the woman's eyes, but she thanked her politely and the woman trudged up the area steps and admitted her at the front door, watching her for a moment as she made her way upstairs.

The hall was narrow and dark, with greasy wallpaper patterned with grapes and vines, and a strip of matted carpet down the centre. But here the attempt at gentility ended. The stairs were bare, the paint on the wall beside them flaking and densely printed with dirty fingermarks, like leopard spots. The seediness was alleviated by a succession of small watercolours on the wall, scenes of Paris, perhaps donated by some hard-up artistic tenant in lieu of rent.

She reached the second floor and found herself facing a brown-painted door. It was scratched and scored all over with hundreds of initials, among which she searched in vain for Dulcie's and Peter's. It would have been a comfort to find them. She knocked. Silence. She knocked again. After another long silence, footsteps approached the door, and it opened.

It was Dulcie. She had obviously just stepped out of bed. She wore her white cotton nightdress and a large fringed shawl swathed round her shoulders. She appeared slightly thinner than before and unusually pale, even for her. These factors did not detract from her prettiness, but lent another dimension to it which Thea found saddening. The bright new slate had been written on, it would never be quite unmarked again.

'Hallo,' said Thea. 'I had to come.'

Dulcie clapped her hands to her face in a melodramatic gesture and walked away from her sister into the room. Thea followed, closing the door behind her.

The room was of average size, poorly furnished, with a small stove in one corner. The sunlight, pouring in through the open balcony door, cheered it somewhat, but there was no denying its basic seediness or the fact that it had not been cared for. Motes of swirling dust swam in the sunbeams, and gleaming patches of grease patterned the wall by the stove. There was no evidence of habitation, no books, flowers or possessions to be seen, except a carton of coffee grounds on a side table and a couple of out-of-date newspapers on the floor next to a chair. Of course, they had brought nothing with them, but even so the place was soulless; it had all the marks of a transit camp rather than a home, even for a pair of undomesticated love-birds.

Thea stood in the middle of the room. Now that she was here, she felt full of energy and initiative, confident of her ability to win Dulcie over.

'Where's Peter?' she asked.

'Out.'

'Doing what?'

'It's none of your business, is it?' Dulcie sat down a creaking, cream-painted wicker chair and began running the backs of her nails up and down the arm with a rattle. 'Looking for a job,' she added.

'How are you? Both of you?'

'Perfectly all right. I told you not to come.' She rounded on Thea, but did not quite meet her eyes. 'I was having a lie-in,' she muttered.

'I don't suppose there's much else to do.' Thea intended the remark to be sympathetic, but realized at once that it was a mistake.

'Your ideas of things to do aren't necessarily ours, so there's no need to be superior.'

'I didn't mean to be.'

'Oh *no!*' Dulcie flapped an impatient hand. 'Of course you didn't mean to, you just can't help it! She folded her arms tightly, so that the shawl creased around her narrow shoulders. She looked taut as a coiled spring. 'I suppose Father told you to come.'

'He suggested it. I'd have left you alone, but there was one thing that worried me in your letter.'

'Well?'

'You talked about getting married.'

'What of it? We probably shall.'

'Does Peter want to?'

'I don't see it's any of your business.'

'Has he asked you?'

'We've talked about it.'

'Recently?'

'Fairly recently.' Dulcie stood up, arms still folded, and walked out to the balcony, remembered she was still in her

nightdress and walked back again, glaring at Thea. 'Stop
interrogating me! I'm not coming back, I don't want your
advice, and Peter will be here in a minute. Go away and
leave us in peace.'

'Is there any coffee?'

'There might be.'

'May I have some?'

Dulcie went to the stove and peered into the chipped
enamel jug that stood on it. Thea sat down in the only other
chair, a faded upholstered wreck, the entrails of which
sagged dismally on the floor beneath the seat. It creaked and
swayed ominously as she lowered herself into it. Dulcie
poured water from the enamel jug into the tin kettle, and
bent to light the gas, turning it up too high so that it almost
singed her eyelashes and made her jump back. Thea looked
away. She wondered how many times a day Dulcie burned
her lashes, and what they ate. Dulcie had never been near the
kitchen in her life, she had not even been interested in
hanging round Mrs Duckham as a child, except when there
was a cake-bowl to be scraped. She hated the mess of
cooking. After a long, awkward silence during which the gas
purred sullenly and a faint odour of charring pervaded the
room, Dulcie produced two mugs of coffee, very black and
not a little gritty.

'Sorry, no milk. We have to go out for it.'

'That's all right.'

Dulcie sat down once again in the basket chair, nursing her
mug in both hands. Her hair needed washing, it hung in limp
strands about her face.

Trying a different approach, Thea said: 'Young Dieter got
into the most awful hot water.'

'Did he?'

'Yes, because he knew about you and Peter and didn't say
anything. The Baron put him on short commons and he
caught a dreadful cold. He was quite ill after we got back to
Vienna.'

'You don't blame me for that, surely?'

'You could have been a bit more sensitive about his
position. You kept it from everyone else, why not from
him?'

'He was always *there*, the wretched child. What could we
do?'

'I don't know.' Thea sipped her coffee. Dulcie continued to

stare down into her untouched cupful, scraping one draggled lock behind her ear with her fingers.

'Do come back, Dulcie. You don't look happy.'

'How would you know?' Dulcie challenged her. 'We're *very* happy as a matter of fact.'

'You look thin.'

'I needed to lose weight.'

'Rubbish. I can't think what made you do it.'

'Can't you?' Dulcie darted her head forward. 'Can't you really? Have you never heard of *love?*' she taunted. 'You were always so stuck on it!' Everything about Dulcie at that moment suggested that love did not at present figure in her life. She looked peaky, embattled and defiant. Now she swilled the cold coffee round in her mug and muttered, as if it were what she had really intended to say: 'I can't face them at home.'

'Oh, Dulcie!' Thea flew to her side, all remorse, knelt by the chair, tried to look into her downcast face. 'Don't be such an idiot! We just want you back. We're frightened for you, the news is so bad and we're all worried sick. No one's going to read the riot act, I promise you.'

'Anyway, I want to be with Peter,' added Dulcie without conviction.

'But do you *really?*' Thea took the bull by the horns. 'Are you sure it's not a game, that you weren't just flattered?'

'*Flattered?*' Dulcie rounded on her. 'How dare you patronize me like that? I'm not so hard up for admirers that I'd have to run off with the first one who asked me!' It was as if she'd been waiting for this opportunity to attack her sister.

Thea tried to keep calm, not to rise to the bait. 'He seems to have some kind of hold over you, something evil—'

'He is strongly attracted to me,' Dulcie snapped, haughtily. 'And I to him!'

'All right, all right . . . But you're not allowing yourself any choices, and you're so young.' Thea paused, letting all that sink in, and then added, 'And what about the war? Paris is not a good place to be at the moment.' She pointed towards the street. 'Have you been out there? At all?'

Dulcie leaned back, twisting the fringe of her shawl in her fingers. 'Of course I have.'

'Then you must know what it's like. It's very ugly, there's a bad feeling in the air. And Britain will be in it too, you know.' Dulcie shot a glance at her. 'Honestly. We shall have to come to Belgium's defence, everyone can see that.'

'Well I can't! I don't believe the leaders will let it happen. Nobody wants a war, so they'll find a way round it.'

'But they haven't and they won't. Grow up, Dulcie!'

The two sat in silence, Thea still on the floor by Dulcie's chair. The silence was punctuated by the sound of footsteps coming up the stairs. The door opened to admit Peter. Unlike Dulcie, he looked exactly as he always had, *soigné*, conscious of his own handsomeness. He carried his hat, and a rolled-up newspaper. On seeing Thea he paused only for a fraction of a second before coming in and placing hat and paper on the table.

'Hallo, Thea.'

'Peter.'

'Is there any coffee left?'

Dulcie did not answer, but he went to the stove and went about the business of heating the brew quite composedly, his back to them, not bothering to hurry. When he was ready he turned and walked onto the balcony, leaning back against the iron railing with the sunlight behind him. He balanced the mug precariously on the edge of the geranium tub and pulled a packet of cigarettes from his breast pocket, lighting one and dropping the match into the street below.

'So. What brings you here?' His tone was light, civil, cool.

'What would you say?'

'Giving chase?'

'If you like to put it that way. Trying to make Dulcie see sense. In her letter she mentioned—'

Dulcie squirmed. 'Don't for God's sake start on *that.*'

'Dulcie!' Peter's voice was sharp. 'Be quiet! Why aren't you dressed yet? *Va t'en.*'

Thea watched, amazed, as Dulcie rose and left the room submissively, without a second glance at either of them. The room crackled with the electricity his command had generated. Small hairs rose on the back of her neck. She looked at Peter, a dark, expressionless figure against the sunlight, his cigarette smoke curling about his head.

'Tell me,' she said when the bedroom door had closed. 'Are you going to marry Dulcie?'

His shoulders lifted almost imperceptibly.

'I should say that I think it would be quite wrong for her to marry you. I am not here to encourage it, quite the opposite. I want to take her home.'

'You can try.' He tapped the cigarette on the rail, dislodging the ash.

Thea was maddened by his calm. 'There is going to be a war,' she said. 'France is going to war with Russia against Germany and Austria.'

'So they tell me.'

'What will you do?'

'Do? I shall do everything in my power to avoid taking part in it.'

'But Dulcie—she could be in danger. She has no idea what war would mean.'

'She wanted to come.'

'My God, do you care for her at all?' Thea put her hand to her eyes. He seemed unreachable.

He considered his reply carefully. 'Yes . . . In my own way.'

'I don't understand you.'

'Don't you really?' He turned to look at her, affecting surprise. 'But I'm such a straightforward fellow. More so than most. I will not pretend to feelings I don't have.'

His cold frankness chilled Thea. They stared at each other, openly inimical. The babel of the street rose from below, the piercing repetitive cry of a newsboy. War! Dulcie came back from the bedroom. She wore a dress that Thea had not seen before, she supposed it to be one of those bought in Paris. It had narrow blue and white stripes, with crisp white piqué collar and cuffs. Her hair was up, her face washed.

Peter held out his hand to her. 'That's better.'

She went to him, and he pulled her against him and kissed her hard on her mouth, as if imprinting his authority on her and demonstrating it to Thea. When he lifted his head there was a red halo round her lips where his had pressed. He turned her to face Thea, but kept one arm about her. He looked at Thea over her head.

'You had best go back to England and leave us alone,' he said.

'And what shall I tell them?'

'The truth.'

She looked at them, at Dulcie's small white face above the childish piqué collar; and Peter's, challenging, implacable. She noticed for the first time, now that her hair was up, a bruise on Dulcie's jaw just in front of the left ear. It was yellowing, an old bruise. Something about the picture they made together disturbed her immeasurably.

'Dulcie,' she said, stepping forward and placing her hand on her sister's shoulders. 'Dulcie, I'm so worried. Won't you please, please come with me now? Just leave everything and come. I sent your trunk home, all your things will be waiting for you. I'm going now, and I want you to come too.' She kept her hands on her sister's shoulders for a moment, exerting a slight pressure, willing her to comply. She could not tell what Dulcie was thinking; her eyes were vacant.

Thea stepped back. She went to the chair and picked up her bag. She looked back at Dulcie. Peter's arm was still about her, she could see the knuckles of his fingers showing white. Dulcie looked small and frail, pinned against him like a medieval child-saint martyred at the stake.

Thea moved towards the door. 'Come on,' she said evenly. 'Follow me. I want you to, more than anything else in the world. We all do. Think of Mother. Think of how dull we shall all be without you to brighten us up, Dulcie.'

Just for a second she thought that Dulcie gave a tiny, convulsive movement. It showed in the tightening of Peter's arm. She reached the door and placed her hand on the handle.

'I'm going now.' She tried to keep the panic out of her voice. 'Come on.' She opened the door. The bleak little wooden staircase fell away before her, a one-way street. She tried once more. 'Dulcie! Come on.'

Peter moved his arm. Thank God! He had finally seen sense, he was going to let her go. But Dulcie, released, stood stock still. He let her stand there for a moment, as though taunting Thea, and then took her shoulders and turned her to face him. He put both hands to her neck, encircling it easily, and kissed her. Thea saw Dulcie's head shake under the ferocity of the kiss; only Peter's hands prevented it from snapping back. Her arms were at her side, rigid fists clenched. Thea closed the door and ran down the stairs. As she burst into the street a great dry sob broke from her, but the passers-by were discussing war, and did not notice.

Thea ran all the way to the Hotel Beauvoir. When she got there, Mrs Dancy presented her with an order number. One of the old ladies had been taken ill during the afternoon and admitted to hospital; the other one was her older sister, and they would both be taken care of until such time as they could get out of Paris. It was an ill wind, averred Mrs Dancy. She would run Thea and the woman with the young son to the Gare du Nord, and return herself to the Beauvoir, since she was one of the few with a car who could be of service.

Thea took the order number, but without relief. Dulcie was not with her, she had failed, and now things were conspiring to hurry her from the city with indecent haste.

At the station they found a gigantic queue stretching back from the ticket office. Mercifully the young woman's husband had kept places, and they joined it half way up. Better still, he had bought some chocolate and fruit and a bottle of Vichy water, now quite flat and tepid, but still refreshing. Others round about had pieces of cheese, bread, sponge cake, boiled sweets, and all were conscientiously shared and rationed, for no one knew how long they would have to last.

They got tickets at eight, and learned that the next train would not be till three-thirty the following morning. The ticket holders, as they filtered through to the station concourse, set up makeshift camps with baggage and coats, huddling together on the hard and rubbish-strewn ground, preparing to sit the night out and sleep when they could.

When the train arrived, a little early, there was no rush. They were all too tired. They simply filed into the waiting carriages like sheep, dragging their forlorn possessions with them, and sank down thankfully on the hard seats.

In the still-dark early morning of 2 August the train pulled out from beneath the black canopy of the station, away from Paris, with its dark sky scythed by the white arcs of searchlights, towards Dieppe, Dover, and home. As the train rattled through the still countryside towards the Channel coast complete strangers sagged on one another's shoulders, holding each other up, mouths hanging open, heads jolting with the rhythm of the wheels on the track.

After dawn, when they wakened, they saw the soldiers. They were at every station, hundreds of them, the ranks of uniforms lining the platforms. The sight of them stirred the tired passengers, who leaned out of the windows and waved and wished them luck.

At Rouen they changed trains and were engulfed by crowds of reservists. Many of them were bidding farewell to their own families; most were mere boys, swamped by their blue army greatcoats, their backs straight but their eyes anxious, eager but unprepared for the great adventure.

One of them approached Thea and asked, in French, what her name was.

'Je m'appelle Thea,' she said. *'Je suis anglaise.'*

'Tu rassembles à ma soeur,' he said. The use of *'tu'* seemed perfectly appropriate. He was so young. He had a moustache, but it was soft and fluffy and there was a spot on his chin. *'Que je t'embrasse?'* He blushed furiously and made a little gesture with his cap at the families all around. *'Il n'y a personne pour moi.'*

In answer she put her hands on his shoulders and he kissed her lightly and awkwardly on each cheek, a kind of gentle bump. Then he stood back, to attention.

'Merci, mam'selle.'

'Bonne chance.'

He was gone before she realized she had not asked his name. She pushed her way to the edge of the platform as the troop train pulled out, the windows piled high with faces. Suddenly she spotted him, wide-eyed and solemn, in a corner seat. She waved frantically, barging up the platform, trying to catch his eye. But he did not see her and the train bore him relentlessly away, its receding image shrouded in a pall of smoke; its whistle shrieking triumphantly far down the track.

Thea spent the rest of the journey in a black depression. If that young man were not first killed himself, it would be his duty and his intention and that of Aubrey and of Jack to kill the Hun. And Josef was the Hun.

They reached Dieppe at two in the afternoon and found a throng of several hundreds on the quayside, watching for the flag that would herald a boat. The word was that if no boat arrived by three-thirty, none would be coming. There was nothing to eat or drink. People delved in their bags and shared what they had. 'The feeding of the five thousand,' someone commented drily.

Three-thirty came, and went. The flag lay in a sullen heap at the base of the flagpole. There would be no ship. The realization crept through the crowd like a grey shadow. Someone burst into tears; others sat down, head in hands.

Thea thought: it's like Paris, it's happening to us too. None of us is going to escape. She had developed an angry heat-rash all over her body and her feet were raw She longed for a wash and a change of clothing. She was perfectly certain she looked dreadful and smelt worse, the only consolation being that everyone did. She sat down on the ground amidst the forest of legs and leaned her brow on her bent-up knees.

Then suddenly a small, incredulous voice on the edge of the crowd piped up: 'The flag! Look at the flag!'

Heads lifted and turned, eyes squinting into the bright afternoon sun. The small scrap of material jerked up the pole and hung there flaccidly in the still air.

'The flag's gone up!'

All eyes were on the glittering horizon. There it was. No more than a dancing speck on the hazy line between the sea and sky, but definitely there. A boat, and it would take them home.

CHAPTER EIGHT

'Why should I follow your fighting line
For a matter that's no concern of mine?
I shall be asked to a general scrap
All over the European map,
Dragged into someone else's war,
For that's what a double entente is for.'
    Verse from 'Punch', August, 1914

It was Tuesday 4 August. Hot, still, listless, dog-day weather. The garden of England dozed under a shivering haze of heat, dust and pollen. Fragile English skins reddened, peeled and freckled by a scorching bank holiday weekend returned sadder but no wiser to work. The English Channel lapped lethargically at the baking, but now empty, beaches. And despite the heat, the sense of winter waiting in the wings, of summer having lasted too long and at too high a temperature pervaded people and places. The humour of the British was tinder-brittle, ready for the flint.

At 9 am Ralph met Primmy on the stairs. He knew that in some way over the past few weeks their relationship had subtly altered, and he accepted this alteration. Primmy was about to fly the nest. And as she prepared to try her wings he had to stand back a little, allow her the freedom she needed. He noted that her naturally sallow London complexion was as pale as ever, despite the blazing sunshine over the weekend. She had had the Monday off, but he knew she had not gone up to Town.

'Good day, Primmy.'

'Morning, sir.'

'If that's for my wife, I'll take it.'

'It's no trouble, sir.'

'I didn't suggest it was. I said I'd take it.'

'Very good, sir.' She passed him the tray with Venetia's pitifully light breakfast on it.

'Fetch me one of those, would you, Primmy.'

Poker-faced she went to the white bowl that stood on the

table in the hall and removed one of the half-open roses, long-stemmed and languid, the colour of buttermilk.

'Just lay it on there.'

She placed it on the lace cloth next the milk jug. She wondered if anyone would be putting roses on her breakfast tray when she was fifty-odd, and decided it was unlikely. She allowed herself the luxury of looking directly at her employer's face as he scrutinized the tray. She admired a man who was not ashamed to show his parlourmaid that he loved his wife.

'Thank you, Primmy.'

'Thank you, sir.'

She went down the back stairs, where it was cool and dark, like a dungeon. She realized that Mr Tennant knew she was looking round for a new position. There was an air of farewell about all that she did at the moment. Yesterday Edgar had taken her to the fair out on the other side of Ewhurst and she had felt that it was a game, the very last time she would be able to act so gay and carefree and young and silly, and she had made the most of it. There had been one of those travelling preachers, gaunt and wild-eyed and hectoring, telling them all the end was nigh, and funnily enough she'd been inclined to believe him. The end of something was certainly nigh. She'd had to drag Edgar off to the coconut shy, and laugh and shriek a lot to disguise her fear and sadness. And it had been ever so hot. When they got back she had gone to her room and lain on her back on the bed, and just stared at the ceiling, motionless as a corpse, trying to make her mind as blank and calm as the cream paint up above.

Now, down in the kitchen, it was stifling and Mrs Duckham was in a carping, unreasonable mood because things were going off before they were eaten, and the pastry was sticking, and no one's mind was properly on their work. Primmy allowed herself a last breathing space on the corner of the stairs, listening to the cook abusing poor perspiring little Joan, before taking the plunge and joining in the fray.

Ralph went up the stairs slowly, carrying the tray as if it were a holy vessel. When he reached Venetia's door he laid the tray on the table that stood just outside, and knocked.

The table in question had been moved to its present position since he had begun taking Venetia her tray from time to time. He had quickly discovered that it was well nigh impossible to knock on the door while carrying a large and cumbersome burden, and that if he placed the tray on the floor it was extremely difficult to lift it again—even for a man of his size—without slopping milk, or tea, or both, or sending the toast careering to the ground. He wondered how on earth Primmy had managed, and took to watching her. He noticed not only that she was amazingly strong but that she had developed certain skills to a fine art. As she approached the door she would slide one arm beneath the tray, fingers curled round the edge, leaning well back to balance its weight. She would give the lightest of knocks with her free hand, keeping perfect balance as she did so, and when the response came she would flick open the door with a single deft movement, pushing it so that it swung wide enough to admit her, but not so wide that it crashed back violently. If for any reason it did not open far enough she would administer a discreet shunt with her hips in passing. She made the whole operation look damned easy.

Now he heard his wife answer. He opened the door, picked up the tray and entered, closing the door after him with his foot as he did so. Venetia was sitting up in bed, the pillows banked behind her. Her long ash-blonde hair—increasingly more silver than gold—lay in a thick plait over one shoulder. She wore an oyster-coloured satin nightdress and a beige lace bedjacket. The fineness of the materials and their neutral colours emphasized the ethereal delicacy of her skin. As usual, Ralph was moved by this first sight of his wife. He would wake up with a feeling of optimism and normality. There was nothing much the matter with her, the doctor had said so; she just needed feeding up, jollying along, not to be allowed to brood and mope. But then, when he went into her room, there she was, looking so goddamned other-worldly, as though she were living on borrowed time.

He could not come to terms with it. He could not understand the process which had taken place in his wife's mind and which had changed her from a calm, contented, fleshly woman to a wraith. Whatever that process was it was utterly foreign to his nature. To him, adversity was an electric charge, an enabling force; it aroused in him the fiery determination to fight and to win. But the events of the past month had defeated Venetia. They had quenched the light and doused the fire and, worst of all, they had stifled hope.

He went over to the bed and placed the tray on the bedside table. Then he bent to kiss her, taking her hand in both of his as he did so. It felt limp and unresponsive, the skin of her cheek beneath his lips was tissue-fine. He half expected to see a bruise where he had kissed her.

'How are you?' he asked, sitting on the edge of the bed, still clasping her hand. 'You look beautiful.'

She smiled. He hated that smile of hers. There was something patronizing in its sweetness as though she were protecting him, holding back some vital secret so that he could blunder on in blissful ignorance.

'I'm not hungry, Ralph,' she said, glancing wanly at the tray.

'Never mind, you should eat something. We can't have you wasting away. Who would be diplomatic with the servants if you starved to death? And look, old Ducky's boiled you a fresh egg, and there's some of her home-made marmalade. For God's sake don't turn up your nose at them or there'll be hell to pay.'

She smiled again, this time more reassuringly. 'I think I'd choke.'

'Nonsense! I will not have defeatist sentiments aired in this room.' He pumped her hand up and down on the quilt. 'Eat! Thea will be home soon and what will she think of me if I've let you starve in her absence?'

'Very well. I'll try.'

'That's better.' He shifted the tray onto her knees and began tapping the top of the egg, his vast spatulate hands fumbling with the tiny spoon and the fragile fragments of shell.

Venetia watched. She adored him. She could not imagine life without him. Indeed he *was* life: the force, the power, the energy, the light. But it took all his exuberance and strength to sustain her just now. Her health was deteriorating. Her family, her *raison d'être*, was breaking up. And now war loomed. Everyone talked about it, seemed almost to want it; had they gone mad? Why should noble little England join in that far-off foreign quarrel? And then there was Dulcie, run off to France with some young man she did not even know. They had not heard from Thea; perhaps she would bring her back with her when she came. But knowing Dulcie, Venetia feared the worst. Of course, Ralph had been wrong to send the girls away like that, but she knew him well enough not to remind him of the fact. He knew, too. And the knowledge festered in his conscience like a much-picked scab.

Nothing would be the same. She would lose everything. She could feel even Ralph slipping from her. He was concerned, loving, attentive, but larger issues claimed his attention. The internecine squabbling of the great European powers, which depressed and terrified her, stimulated and fascinated him. He was a man of the world, and she was losing him to the world. If war came, as it must, everyone would go: Aubrey, Maurice, the young men on the estate, the servants; the grass would grow all round her, and she would fall asleep for a hundred years . . .

'Soldiers?' enquired Ralph, knife poised over the buttered toast.

'If you like.'

'Do *you* like?'

'I don't mind.'

He sliced the toast inexpertly, and stuck the first section in the top of the egg. 'There you are.'

With an effort she began to eat, taking a tiny mouthful and chewing for as long as possible to put off the moment when she must take the next. It was not that she was revolted by the food, she had no pain this morning, but she simply could not be bothered with it: the effort required was too great.

'Has Aubrey gone to work?' she asked, partly to take Ralph's mind off the business of watching her eat.

'He has. I wanted to be here in case we hear from Thea, or she gets back. Anyway, he offered to hold the fort today.'

'Dear Aubrey.'

'He's astonishingly dutiful. I shall miss him.'

'Yes.' Oh dear, it always came back to the same thing. 'He will be a great loss at the works.'

'If he goes.'

'He must go. He's special reserve.'

"Yes, but I mean war has not even been declared . . .'

'Simply a matter of time. Tomorrow, the next day—no later. Grey was cheered in the House yesterday for his speech in favour of Britain's supporting France and Belgium. He even read aloud the Belgian telegram appealing for our help.'

'Don't . . . don't.'

'We have to face facts.'

'I shall face them when I have to, and not before.'

268

'I doubt it.' Ralph beamed at his wife. At least her antipathy to the very idea of war animated her. Wickedly, he added: 'Anyway, Asquith has given the Germans till midnight to provide assurances that they'll respect Belgian neutrality. It's a mere formality, a foregone conclusion.'

'Oh God.'

'*He* is not likely to intervene. Now eat up.'

Wearily she picked up another finger of toast. She could see the familiar look of ebullient defiance informing her husband's features. He was not a man made for dancing attendance in sick rooms; it was like seeing a huge express engine steaming and snorting in a quiet country siding. Purely to win back his attention and his approval, she said: 'I'll get up this morning.'

'Good! Splendid!' His joy was like a firework display. 'Thea will be pleased.' He kissed her warmly, nearly reducing the breakfast tray to a ruin. 'I must go and see Collingwood. Eat as much as you can, I'll tell Primmy you'll ring.'

He left, waving to her from the door as if going on a long journey. He was so eager for encouragement, so ready to be optimistic. She felt sad that she could not supply more of what he wanted to hear. Now he had gone she was once again utterly dejected. She leaned back, pushing the tray away from her, but not before she had picked up the rose and buried her nose in its soft, waxy petals. Its fragrance was overpowering. She closed her eyes and tried to think of happier times.

Later that morning Ralph flung open his study window and shouted at Venetia, where she sat in a basket chair on the lawn. 'Thea will be home this afternoon! She sent a telegram from London!'

Venetia lifted a hand in acknowledgement. He could not see whether she smiled or not.

'Good news, eh?' he yelled. 'A tonic!'

She lifted her hand again, not quite so high this time, a little gracious wave, like a queen.

'That's right!' Ralph closed the window and looked down at the scrap of yellow paper. 'First-rate news,' he said again to himself, shaking his head. He was baffled.

At one o'clock Thea boarded the Bromley train at Charing Cross. She had no idea whether she would be expected or not. She had battled with the crowds at the post office first thing that morning to send a telegram to Ralph announcing her arrival but in the present frenetic atmosphere she was not confident of the message getting through.

All the passengers had been found beds in the hotels in the Victoria area. Thea had shared a room with two other women at the Burma House Hotel in Pimlico. But after all her good intentions she'd only been able to discard her filthy outer garments, torn stockings and split shoes before falling into a death-like sleep. This morning she had bought more stockings, and had a skimpy wash, but that was all. Confronted with a mirror for the first time in several days she had found her appearance a shock. She had lost pounds in weight, her eyes were sunken, her hair tacky and stiff with dirt. She also had the unmistakable symptoms of a heavy cold; her neck ached, she was shivery, and her throat hurt when she swallowed. This was the result of the crossing, during which most of the batch of refugees had been obliged to remain on deck in heavy rain. She fully expected to fall asleep on the train, but once ensconced in a corner seat she found she couldn't. Her exhaustion had moved on to a different plane, she was tense and febrile, her brain racing hither and thither trying to marshal the confused impressions of the last few days. Coming to her home capital from Paris had been like reading a story backwards: here there prevailed the mood of exhilarated anticipation that she had found in Paris on her arrival there. She could not help but view it with mild scepticism: she had watched that mood turn sour in France, and the same would doubtless happen here. A man in the crowded post office had been regaling a spellbound audience with tales of Russian soldiers passing through the great London railway termini 'with the snow still on their boots'. No one seemed inclined to question the likelihood of snow remaining on boots while the temperature teetered in the eighties. They wanted to believe it. They were romanticizing the war before it had even, for them, begun. Sitting in her corner seat in the train, gazing out at the green and gold August countryside, she could not picture an England at war. The drifting shreds of smoke lent the scene beyond a distant, theatrical air, the intense heat gave it a stillness. Because of the exceptional summer there would be an early harvest, there were reapers out already in some of the fields, little figurines waist-high in the sea of yellow corn, arms uplifted against the sun, watching the train go by. The wooded distances shimmered in the heat. Who, she asked herself, would have the energy to fight in such weather? Perhaps it would never happen. . . Her fellow-travellers in the compartment were two young couples, the girls pretty in cool blue and pink dresses and shady hats, the young men crisp and dashing in blazers and boaters. Their faces shone with heat and the enjoyment of safe flirtation. They made Thea feel old, although she could have been no more than a year older than the eldest of them. Their giggling, rustling presence was comforting; they simply did not look like people entering upon war.

She made a conscious effort to project her thoughts ahead, to picture her home and how it would be. She knew how the garden would look, suspended in late summer, nothing much to do except eat the fruit and vegetables so lovingly tended earlier in the year, mow the grass occasionally and let things descend the arc toward autumn.

The train drew into Bromley station and she alighted in the wake of the courting couples. The platform felt small, and she very conspicuous on it in her reduced state.

Edgar was waiting for her at the barrier. 'Welcome back, miss,' he said, warmly enough, but she felt the curious glance he gave her.

'Thank you, Edgar, it's lovely to be back.'

She followed his slim, spruce figure to the car. She had forgotten how much time and care was lavished on the turn-out of her father's automobile and its driver. They both positively scintillated, she almost burst out laughing at the odd figure she must cut—a scruffy, down-at-heel, haggard young woman being driven away in this gleaming chariot.

'So it's war, miss,' Edgar observed, as they pulled away from the station forecourt.

'Yes, I suppose so. I'm afraid it's inevitable.'

'What's going on, then—over there, I mean?'

'Everyone was excited at first—as they are here—but by the time I left it was getting frightening. There were mobs on the street, destroying everything German.'

'Serve 'em right, miss.'

'Well . . . perhaps.' She did not have the energy to take issue with him. It depressed her unutterably to think that Edgar would be just like those people, wreaking havoc, wild for revenge, hellbent on mindless destruction.

He must have sensed her mood, for the only other remark he had was to enquire: 'No Miss Dulcie this time?'

'No, not this time.'

Both of them kept their eyes on the road.

They arrived at Chilverton House at five o'clock. The rasp of the tyres on the gravel sent up a fine powder into the air. William Rowles was hoeing the edges of the circular rose border at the front of the house. He looked up at their arrival and gave a severely attenuated, but distinct, nod of greeting. He looked precisely as Thea had pictured him as she had sat on the train: deliberate, dour and timeless. He accepted the comings and goings of his employer's daughters without demur.

The virginia creeper round the door hung flat, overlapping endlessly like red dragon scales in the breathless heat. As Thea climbed down from the car she could feel the very air vibrating on her skin, droning with bees, twittering with larks, a rich soup of English summer sounds.

Edgar went up the steps ahead of her, but she held out her hand.

'It's all right, Edgar, I'll see myself in.'

'Sure miss?'

'Of course. You put the car away.'

'Very good.'

As the Lanchester swung round the drive towards the stable archway the front door opened. In the cool gloom beyond Thea saw the small, white figure of Primmy, like a moth, but Ralph overtook her with a wave of dismissal and came down the steps, arms outstretched.

She willingly and relievedly abandoned herself to his crushing embrace.

'Thea, darling girl! Welcome home!'

'Father.'

He pushed her away from him, holding her face between his hands. 'My God! You look frightful. What have we done to you?'

'Nothing.' She smiled at him, amused at his frankness. 'I simply haven't had much time to spend on my appearance.' It was so good to see him. After the rigours of the last few weeks he appeared hugely genial, she could not imagine how he had ever inspired fear in her. But perhaps because of this he seemed smaller, too, as if her picture of him before had been rather larger than life and now her experiences abroad had

reduced him to his proper size. The impression was underlined by the fact that he had discarded his usual dark suit and
striped waistcoat in favour of a light shirt, and cream flannels
suspended from powder-blue braces. This seasonal adjustment to his dress lent his large figure a youthful, almost
vulnerable appearance.

She kissed him again, feeling, perversely, that it was her
place to reassure him, to be strong in spite of her unutterable
weariness.

'Where is everyone? I didn't expect to find you here.'

He slipped his arm through hers and began to walk her
round the side of the house. 'Didn't you? You thought I'd be
cracking the whip at the works when my daughter returned
from the theatre of war? What a charming picture you have
of me!'

She squeezed his arm. 'You know what I mean.'

'Of course. I decided to remain at home today on the off-
chance we might hear from you, and in the event I'm glad I
did. Aubrey kindly offered to oversee things at Southwark. I
am a figurehead merely, these days; my presence is not
essential. In fact, your brother handles the men rather better
than I.'

'They adore you!'

'*Adore* me? Do they? That's a thought. I shall take it as a
compliment. I also stayed at home because Venetia has not
been well, as you know.'

'Yes. Where is she?'

'In the garden waiting for us. I rely on you to promote
instant recovery. I'm damned if I know what's the matter
with her, it worries me.' They walked round towards the
garden. As they walked, Ralph enquired, 'No Dulcie?'

'No Dulcie.'

He nodded.

They could neither of them quite bring themselves to take
the matter further, so soon after the fragile joy of reunion, for
fear of spoiling that joy.

Venetia sat in a patch of shade next some rhododendron
bushes. She did not see Thea and Ralph at once, and Thea
noticed that she looked listless, her hands resting idly in her
lap, her head leaning back as though she had been propped
up in the basket chair. Homer lay by her, and as they
rounded the corner he staggered up and began to make his
way towards them, ears laid back in greeting, tail thrashing,

but walking slowly and with a slight limp. Thea remembered the septic foot.

The dog's agitation caused Venetia to look up and she rose and came to meet them. Her slow, graceful walk was the same as ever but as she drew closer Thea observed a fine tracery of lines, like a veil, over her face, lines that had not been there before. And her eyes were sad.

'Mother! Oh, it's good to see you!'

They embraced. Venetia scanned her face. 'But my dear, you look so tired.'

'I am, rather. Or I ought to be. At the moment it's just lovely to be home, but I expect everything will catch up with me tonight.'

'Has it been terrible?'

The grand scale of this question left Thea speechless. In wanting to say everything, she could say nothing. Ralph sensed this, and saved her from having to try.

'Thea will tell us all there is to tell in her own good time,' he said. 'Now she needs to unwind, and rest.'

They went over to the group of chairs and sat down. The shade was cool and green, like water. Thea was overwhelmed by love for her home. Its beauty, its special essence, the product of all the feelings it had nurtured for so many years, it wrapped and soothed her the moment she was back. The sweet and sensuous relaxation taking place in her transcended, for that moment, all her cares.

Primmy emerged from the side door of the kitchen courtyard and came over the grass in her quick, competent way, her black-shoed feet tripping along like little hooves. She wore her pale blue summer dress, with starched white collar and cuffs, and a white apron; her frilled cap rested like blossom on her neat brown hair. She looked almost pretty. But the dress and collar reminded Thea of Dulcie, held prisoner in Peter's arms, and she looked away for a moment. How could she so soon have put that picture out of her mind?

Primmy came up to them. 'Would you like some tea now, madam?' she asked Venetia.

Venetia glanced at Thea. 'You'd like some tea, darling?'

'Yes please. Hallo, Primmy.'

'Hallo, miss. It's nice to have you back.'

'Thank you. It's lovely to be back.'

'Mrs Duckham's made gingerbread.'

'She's an angel.'

Primmy smiled her small, brisk smile and marched back over the lawn; very erect, every hair in place. Ralph watched her go.

'That girl is not long for this job,' he murmured. But since this was a regular observation of his neither Thea nor Venetia responded to it.

Instead, Thea said: 'So we shall be in the war.'

Ralph nodded emphatically. 'Tonight. When the ultimatum runs out.'

Venetia turned her head away as though she had spotted something of consuming interest at the end of the Elm Walk.

'How long is it going to last?' Thea asked.

'Years.'

'Years?' She was genuinely shocked, not least by the emphasis with which he said it.

'I'm sure of it. And if the politicians have any sense they will see that it will take more than a few months to stop the Prussians over-running Europe—'

'What about Dulcie?' Venetia turned back to them sharply, as though she hadn't heard their conversation. 'What is she doing?'

'She's living in Paris, with Peter de Laszlo. She wouldn't come back, though I did my best.'

'I'm sure you did . . . but how will she manage? How do they live?'

'He has a private income, I believe.'

'Not for long!' interjected Ralph drily.

'Probably not, but when I was there he was looking for a post. They have quite a nice small flat in Montmartre.'

'But Dulcie can't cook . . .' Venetia's eyes suddenly brimmed with tears, and she looked away again, her fingers clutching at the thin material of her dress. 'She can't do anything for herself.'

'Not at the moment, but she can learn.' Thea felt the forced confidence in her voice beginning to ebb away. 'She seems to lead a charmed life, I'm sure they'll cope somehow.'

'Does this fellow *love* her?' enquired Ralph incredulously.

Thea thought quickly. Her father would welcome and accept the truth. Her mother could not bear it. 'He never had eyes for anyone else,' she replied, not meeting his gaze.

They sat there for a second, both parents looking at their daughter, Ralph searchingly, Venetia with a sad, weary understanding. Primmy, the *deus ex machina*, brought the tea. She opened the legs of the tray, made to set it in front of Venetia, changed her mind and placed it instead, perceptively, before Thea. She looked none of them in the face. She was the soul of efficiency and discretion. She knew, they knew she knew, but her integrity and tact were absolute. She skimmed back over the lawn.

Thea poured tea and handed gingerbread, searching her mind desperately for something to cheer Venetia. 'She might still change her mind and come back,' she said, aware that she was clutching at straws, and that they must know it.

'On her own?' Venetia sighed. 'She'd never do it. She's never been anywhere on her own.'

'No, I know. Well, at least it's some consolation that she's *not* on her own at the moment. She does have Peter.' She looked miserably down at her plate.

Ralph sat back, as if disappointed in her performance. Venetia turned away again. There was something poignant in her averted head, the straw hat shielding her face. Her hands lay in her lap, the fingers of the right endlessly twiddling the wedding ring on her left. Thea noticed that the ring was loose.

Almost as if he had been watching the same thing and thinking the same thoughts as Thea, Ralph moved his chair, placing it beside his wife's. He took her left hand in his, linking his fingers through hers, and clasped it tight. Leaning his elbow on the arm of his chair he rested his cheek on their joined hands. The two of them sat like a single statue of two people, not looking at one another but straight ahead, mutely inseparable.

Thea felt a sudden overwhelming need to bend and pat Homer rather than continue looking at them while they sat there.

'If you'll excuse me . . .' she muttered. 'I don't feel too well.' And she walked to the house without looking back, barely able to see where she was going.

Sophie closed the library door and sat down at the desk to write to Maurice. She wrote to her son once a week, without fail, and whether or not she had anything of moment to report. She wrote to a set pattern and in a formal style, and always covered the same amount of paper, though she had

had to reduce the length somewhat recently because her already tiny handwriting had shrunk.

It was a point of honour with her never to chivvy her son about not communicating with her. He did so, in fact, about once a month, but it would have been nice if he could have responded to each of her own letters. As it was he frequently forgot to reply to specific enquiries about his health and activities; she felt herself to be palmed off with superficial items of news. It also rankled with her that he sometimes wrote to Ralph and Venetia under separate cover. What could he possibly have to say to them that she could not quite properly pass on herself? It was no easier to bear when Venetia went out of her way to acknowledge these letters: 'We had such a sweet letter from Maurice . . . it's so good of him to write when he's working hard, you're very fortunate in your son.' Sophie simply felt that she was being forced to share this, her only positive proof of individual identity.

To add to her discomfort, she disliked summer, and this one had been inordinately long and hot. If she was busy she nearly expired, if she was idle she was racked by guilt. The bright, glaring light pouring in through the windows day after day seemed an intrusion on her orderly life. And she could not go along with Ralph and Venetia's habit of eating out of doors; she could not imagine what prompted them to indulge in this outlandish practice. How could one hope to have a civilized meal sitting on uncomfortable, wobbly chairs, and under the constant threat of swallowing an insect? She had been pleased to note that Aubrey did not care for it either, but went along with them out of what she could only suppose was filial politeness.

Clamping her lips together in a spasm of irritation, she wrote the date neatly in the top right-hand corner: Wednesday, 5 August 1914. With a heavy sigh she glanced at the copy of *The Times* that lay on the stool next to the desk. The words 'BRITAIN AT WAR' were spread over the entire front page in huge red capital letters. Sophie accepted the news as inevitable; Britain must do her duty, and the women of Britain must send their men off willingly and stoically. She would not falter; she would wave goodbye to her only son with a straight back and dry eyes, the sacrifice was her privilege.

'*Dear Maurice,*' she began, in her minuscule hand, '*I trust you are well and that the heat and today's sad news are not oppressing you.'* She paused. She always gave her letters a lot of thought. *'What exactly is keeping you at Cambridge? It would be pleasant to have your company and support in these trying times, I feel so much alone.*

'Thea arrived home yesterday afternoon—without Dulcie. Everything has, of course, been disrupted on her account. Yesterday Ralph stayed at home and Venetia came down before luncheon for the first time in weeks. No one knows precisely what ails your aunt, but she is certainly allowing it to get the better of her, and this at a time when we should all be summoning up our reserves of fortitude and resolution, not giving up the ghost. My own opinion is that it is a disease not of the body, but of the mind. My brother is behaving like a silly youth over the whole business, it is most tiresome.

'I suppose you know that Aubrey will have to join up at once, as a member of the Special Reserve. I shall miss him sorely, he is so often the voice of sanity in this household.

'Jack Kingsley actually came round to pay his respects the other day. I do not know how he has the effrontery, but Ralph and Venetia seemed actually pleased to see him. I do not understand their values.

'I suppose that you, too, will be joining up? It is clear now that men of intelligence and patriotism have no alternative but to enter the service of His Majesty. The speedy conclusion of the war must depend on the immediacy and efficacy of Britain's entry.'

Pleased with the sonorous ring of this last sentence, she paused again. As she did so she heard footsteps in the hall and the door opened. Thea stood there. The girl looked like a cadaver, deathly pale and skinny.

'Oh, Aunt Sophie . . .' she murmured, vaguely. 'I'm sorry, I didn't mean to disturb you.'

'That's perfectly all right.' Sophie sat upright in her chair, pen in hand. 'I was merely writing to Maurice.'

'Please give him my love.'

'I shall of course pass on the good offices of everyone.'

'Um . . .' Thea wandered across the room to the bookshelves by the window. There were goose-pimples on her bare arms, in spite of the heat, and she was shivering.

'Are you feverish?' enquired Sophie sharply. God knows what complaints the girl might have contracted abroad.

'Yes. I'm afraid I probably am. A chill I think. We got soaked on the boat on the way back.'

'Did you.'

'Yes.' She suddenly saw the book she wanted and reached it down. 'Anyway I'm going to bed now, out of everyone's way.'

'A very good idea.' Sophie watched her niece walk stiffly back to the door.

When she reached it Thea turned and asked: 'Will Maurice be coming back? I mean, sometime soon?'

Sophie thought quickly. She did not want to admit to Thea that she did not know. She opted for a half-truth. 'He's so busy,' she sighed. 'But he intends to make a visit in the near future.'

'Oh good.' Thea nodded. 'I'll be off then.'

'Right you are.'

The door closed, and Sophie resumed her letter. *'As for myself I am well, but I find this intense and persistent heat enervating. We all worry about Dulcimer, though God knows why we should when she brought all this upon herself. Jack Kingsley seemed distressed to hear of the goings-on in Austria, I only hope he comprehends the full weight of his own responsibility in all this.*

I shall close now, and take a short rest before changing for dinner. I keep to my room a good deal at present. Would it be too much to ask you to come down here soon and see your mother? You know how much I depend on you, and now that we are at war there is not long left.' She stopped, re-read the last few words, crossed them out and wrote: *'And we do not have long to be together.'* Then she signed and sealed the letter and placed it in her bag for posting the following morning.

Primmy went into the kitchen yard and sat down on the narrow stone surround of the pump, her back against the shaft. Until the Tennants had moved to the country she had never really taken account of the sun. Sunshine in Deptford was not something to be basked, revelled and luxuriated in. In fact it showed up the essential squalor and shoddiness of the area in uncomfortably sharp relief. Apart from the outing with Dick, Primmy's memories of summer in Grove Road were of fighting the heat, escaping from the bright light, feeling the grit sticking to your sweaty skin, wishing you had the proper cool, pretty clothes for the weather, and knowing the wish was sheer sentimentality. Ranelagh Road had been better; at least there the sunshine was reckoned as a bonus, she had a cooler uniform for hot weather, and there was less work to do in summer But here in Kent she had become aware of the reality of changing seasons. Little courageous green spikes really *did* push their way through the frozen ground in January, flowers bloomed and birds sang in summer, grass grew so abundantly that it had to be cut, bees hummed over the herbaceous borders. It was a revelation to her. And like a flower herself she turned her face to the sun and drank it in, though she was very careful not to get burned, for she was prone to freckles.

A butterfly twirled and dipped in front of her face and then alighted on her lap, spreading its tortoiseshell wings, attracted by the gleaming white of her apron. She looked down at it, feeling privileged; her hands, resting on her knees on either side of the butterfly, looked very hard and cracked and coarse beside the insect's soft, delicate perfection. She curled them into fists, and the butterfly flew away.

She heard Edgar in the kitchen, talking to Mrs Duckham. He must be back from collecting Mr Aubrey from the station. Mr Tennant had stayed at home again today, and now Miss Thea had taken to her bed. It seemed that everyone was at sixes and sevens these days, *and* it was war. Edgar came out into the yard carrying a cup of tea. He placed the cup on the stone ledge by Primmy while he removed his jacket and undid his collar studs and tie. Then he retrieved the cup and leaned against the brick wall by the garden door. She glanced up at him. She liked Edgar; he was a realist, like her.

'All right?'

'Hallo, Prim. Blimey, it's a purler.'

'It is hot.'

Edgar sipped his tea with noisy relish, the condensation from the steam joining the beads of sweat on his forehead and nose.

'Are you going to join up?' asked Primmy curiously.

'You bet your life I am. Catch me staying at home. I'm going to see Mr Tennant before the end of the week.'

'He'll miss you.'

'He'll live. He can drive himself. I want to be at Shorncliffe with the rest of them next week.'

Primmy nodded. She understood Edgar wanting to go to war, she felt rather that way herself. There was a buzzing thread of excitement in the air.

As if reading her thoughts, he said: 'What about you? Will you be staying on?'

'I don't know . . .' She closed her eyes, smiling enigmatically up at the sun. 'No, I think I'll move on. If the men go to war there'll be jobs going all over the place, proper jobs and no one left here to do them. It's time I went.'

'Well, well.' Edgar sat down, back against the wall and looked at her in amused admiration. 'You're a dark horse. What you got in mind?'

'Nothing special. I'll look around.'

'What if there's nothing?'

'There'll be something, don't you worry.'

'Poor old Mr Tennant,' Edgar chuckled. 'He'll have no one left.'

'I shan't leave him in the lurch. I've got a replacement.' Until that moment the idea had not occurred to Primmy, but now it seemed the most natural thing in the world. 'There's someone who could step right into my shoes.'

'Blow me, you *are* organized! Can a chap ask who?'

'You can ask, but I'm not telling. Not till I've got it properly worked out. It wouldn't be fair.'

'Have it your own way.' Edgar addressed himself once more to his tea, giving his head a little shake as he did so, laughing at her independence. Gazing into the red mist of her eyelids against the sun she began to formulate the letter she would write to her mother that evening.

It was nine o'clock when Ralph tiptoed into Thea's room: she had been sleeping fitfully for two hours. The curtains were drawn and the room was cool and gloomy. As he pushed the door he could hear her breathing, regular, but rather shallow. He presumed she was still asleep but as he crossed the floor she turned onto her back, one arm across her brow, and smiled at him.

'Hallo, Father.'

'I brought you some of Mrs Duckham's lemonade.'

'That's kind, thank you.'

He put the tray on the bedside table and poured her a glass. Then he held the pillows against the bedhead while she pulled herself up.

'You make a lovely nurse,' she teased him.

'I'm sorry you're ill. What a homecoming.'

'I'm sorry too, but it can't be helped. Anyway it's nothing, just a chill and overtiredness. I shall be all right tomorrow'

'I hope so. But you mustn't rush it.'

'How is Mother?'

'Not too good. Worried about you.'

'But what is really the matter?'

'Deuced if I know. No one knows. I got old Bruce Egerton down from town to try and crack it, but he was stumped as well. He diagnosed a mild form of anaemia, not nearly enough to debilitate her as much as this. It has to be more than just a deficiency of red corpuscles; she seems to have lost interest in life.'

'Poor Mother, everything has been too much for her. It's up to us to bring her round.'

'Up to *you*, dear girl. I have failed.'

He looked so cast down that Thea laughed. 'Don't be silly, you're her whole life, and you know it.'

'Hmm' He looked at her from under his eyebrows, grudgingly flattered.

Thea sipped the lemonade. 'That's good,' she sighed appreciatively.

'By the way, I have some good news for you,' he said.

'Oh?'

'I contacted that secretarial establishment of yours. They will take you next month, for a twelve-week course.'

'That's wonderful!'

'I'm glad you're pleased. I was worried unless you had given up the idea.'

'I had, almost. But not because I didn't want to.'

'I should say my motives are not entirely altruistic. With Aubrey joining up and the consequent inevitable shake-up at the works, I am going to need an efficient and compatible assistant.'

'You mean me? But I shall be a complete beginner!'

'Under my tutelage you will soon learn. You've been longing to get your teeth into a proper job for years. This is your chance.'

'I don't know what to say. Thank you.'

'Don't thank me. I'm not doing you a favour, I am providing myself with the best possible help. I predict that I shall have a factory full of women by this time next year, and if the war goes forward as I think it will I may well hand the plant and the workforce over to munitions production'

'Munitions? Surely that won't be necessary, there are existing sources to cope with that.'

'Nothing like enough. I have a feeling about this war, Thea, and I am not alone. Lord Kitchener has said that we shall need an army of millions to defeat the Germans and I share his view. I try not to voice it in front of your mother because she is not able to think rationally just now. She refuses to believe the war will happen at all. But nonetheless it is my opinion. And if the war lasts years, our existing supplies of weapons and ammunitions will barely see us through till Christmas. We could be left with millions of men in Europe virtually unarmed and defenceless.'

Thea put her glass down She leaned her head back on the pillows and covered her eyes with her fingers. Munitions? Guns to shoot the Hun.

'Father,' she said quietly.

'Yes?'

'I have to tell you—but not Mother, not just yet. When I was with the von Crieffs, their son, Josef—'

'You need say no more, unless you want to.'

'Thank you.' She looked into his eyes and saw there the extraordinary strength of affection and understanding that had been her source of happiness for as long as she could remember. He leaned forward and kissed her brow.

'That's hard for you, Thea, very hard. And I can't make it any easier.'

'You do. Just by not blaming me.'

'How could I blame you? For what? Falling in love?'

'I don't know that I did fall in love . . .' She tried desperately to recall the precise nature of those confused, ecstatic, far-off feelings, and failed. 'I simply don't know.'

'An ignorance you share with most of the human race, I assure you.' His voice was gentle.

'All I do know is that now I am at home, in England, I see that we must fight, and what we are fighting for. And yet I can't bear to think of him as the enemy—to think that other people that I love and trust are going to want to kill him. Am I supposed suddenly to hate him after—' She broke off, unable to continue.

'I know. I know.' Ralph rose and went to the window, drawing the curtain a little. The gentle evening light filtered in. 'I think, Thea,' he said slowly, looking out over the garden, 'I think that we, you and I, must see the war itself as

283

the enemy. When I say I shall make munitions it is because I wish to end the war as speedily as may be. I am a fatalist. The war is upon us. You may be sure that if extra weapons are not supplied the carnage, the suffering and the consequences will be far more dire than any we can imagine now. We may as well grasp the nettle. And if—I say *if*—your Josef were to be killed by Aubrey, you should remember that it was war that killed him. No recriminations.'

He looked back at his daughter to perceive the effect his words had had on her. She lay back on the pillow, her head averted. Her black hair trailed down over her shoulders like a widow's veil.

On Friday 7 August two occurrences marked the day for Maurice. He received a letter from his mother, and he made his decision. Increasingly over the past week he had felt the decision forming, at first tentatively, then resolving itself so that now it was precise and clear in his mind. Now that it was fully-fledged, he felt solitary, but oddly confident. As the sunny days dragged on and on, he saw himself as a man apart, calm and rational, while the rest indulged their hitherto hidden streak of xenophobic lunacy. He was tranquil.

When Sophie's letter arrived he took it to his room and read it. So she, too, had war-fever. On reflection, it was not so strange; he should have expected it. The mention of Aubrey caused him a moment of the old anxiety, but no more than a moment. As for Jack—he must have had his reasons for visiting the Tennants. He wondered what Thea made of it all, and what had passed between her and Dulcie. He experienced a shaming sense of relief that Dulcie had finally burned her boats. She was out of the way. He did not really care what happened to her, she was bound to survive.

It was clear that he could not postpone much longer the moment when he would have to return to Chilverton House and face up to them all. His mother was plaintive; he owed her the truth, no matter how unpalatable that might be. He suddenly wanted to be brutally frank, to make them all see that he had a will of his own, and would exercise it. He sat down to write to Sophie.

'Dear Mother,' he wrote. *'Thank you for your letter, and the news contained therein I shall keep this brief, as you will doubtless be glad to learn that I shall be coming down to*

Chilverton House at the end of this week, though only for a short while.

'With regard to your questions, I have decided not to join up—even supposing they would have me, poor figure of a man that I am! I am against this war as I think I should be against any war, and I have no intention of fuelling its flames by even such an insignificant amount. Do not bother to write back, I shall not revise this opinion.*

'Please give the rest my love, and especially Thea. You may tell them of my decision or not, as you wish. For myself, I have no intention of making an issue of it, and shall not mention it unless asked.

'I look forward to seeing you soon. Take care of yourself. Your ever-loving son, Maurice.'

He folded the letter neatly, placed it in the envelope and left his room to post it. He walked along King's Parade with a measured tread. On one corner a recruiting sergeant had set up a booth on a small dais and there was a queue of sixty-odd bright-eyed, red-faced men of all ages, lined up and waiting to take the King's shilling.

Maurice walked the length of the queue, his head held high and his eyes steady. When he reached the letter box he slipped the envelope into its red and grinning maw.

It was done.

It was only then that he gasped, for he realized he had been holding his breath.

CHAPTER NINE

'For old times' sake, don't let our enmity live,
For old times' sake, say you'll forget and forgive;
Life's too short to quarrel,
Hearts too precious to break—
Shake hands and let us be friends, for old times' sake.'
Millie Lindon—'For Old Times' Sake'

If Maurice had had the foresight to postpone his visit to Chilverton House for a couple of weeks, all might have been well. But some perverse compulsion to grasp the nettle, to get it over with, drove him down to Kent on Tuesday 11 August. Insofar as he had made any assumptions about his meeting with his family he had set store in there being safety in numbers. Whatever small spark of hostility was kindled by his decision was unlikely to flare into a mighty conflagration if the rest of the Tennants were there to draw the fire. But in this case his instinct for self-preservation, an instrument finely tuned by experience, played him false.

Of course, had he been privy to the fluctuating moods of his family over the past two months, he might have known better; but as it was he had been hiding at Cambridge, furtively guarding his guilty secret until it was ready to hatch.

He knew that his aunt had been unwell, but he did not appreciate to what extent her illness was the product of her state of mind. And in the days before his return her morale had struck a new low due to the inevitable resignations of her staff; Edgar was gone, young Joan was hinting at it (according to Mrs Duckham, who maintained that no one but the Tennants would be soft enough to employ the girl) and now, hardest to bear, Primmy had come to her at the weekend, looking wary but determined.

'I'd like to hand in my notice, ma'am,' she said.

It was Sunday morning. Ralph and Venetia were in the library; Sophie, Thea and Aubrey had gone to church Ralph looked over his paper at Primmy; in the distance the bells of St Catherine's Ewhurst pealed and cascaded, summoning the faithful.

'*Et tu*, Primmy?' murmured Ralph.

Primmy knew she was being quoted at, she could tell it from the tone of voice. She kept her eyes on Mrs Tennant, it was her habit to ignore quotations. Ill-educated she might be, but she would not allow herself to be intimidated by this evidence of sophistication in others.

Venetia had been going through menus at the desk. Now she had turned in the chair, and her long, thin fingers gripped the arms tightly. She looked gaunt and sad. Primmy hardened her heart.

'We shall be sorry to lose you, Primmy,' said Venetia. 'You've helped us for so many years. You're like one of the family.'

'Yes, well, I'll be sorry to go, ma'am.' Primmy lifted her gaze to the vase of copper beech that stood on top of the desk. It was safer.

Venetia sighed tremulously. 'Where are you going?'

'I haven't decided yet, ma'am. I've got a few ideas though.' Her ideas: how she treasured them. They were not lightly to be shared.

'I'm sure you have,' said Ralph, rising from the wing-chair and slapping the paper against his leg. He yawned and stretched like an animal.

For once, Primmy could have wished Mr Tennant elsewhere. His restless, meddling presence was not assisting the passage of this interview. From a deliberate desire to shock him she played her trump card.

'I wondered if you'd be looking for someone, ma'am? To fill the position?'

'I suppose we shall.' Venetia sounded exhausted. 'I can't think about it at present, this is all such a shock. Perhaps a girl from the village . . .'

'I'd like to make a suggestion, ma'am,' said Primmy to the copper beech. From the corner of her eye she saw Ralph's black eyebrows shoot up in curiosity. Venetia's reaction was more one of bewilderment.

'Oh? Who would that be?'

'My mother.'

'Your *mother?*' This was Ralph, who dropped his paper on to the chair as one who had found far more enthralling matters than the progress of the war to engage him. 'You did say your mother?'

'Yes sir.'

'Wouldn't she be a little old for the work?'

'Not really, sir. She's younger than Mrs Duckham, and she's ever so strong.'

'That I can believe,' said Ralph. 'And may one ask whether you have mentioned this proposed arrangement to her?'

'I've written to her, sir. I've not heard back yet.'

'Primmy,' said Venetia very gently, 'I can't imagine that your mother would want to come all this way out into the country when she's a townswoman, born and bred. It's a kind thought of yours, but just the same . . I think she would be lonely.'

'She's lonely now, ma'am,' said Primmy staunchly. 'There's only Eddie there now that Lisbeth's married, and he's a worry.'

'Eddie?' Ralph thrust his head forward quizzically, eyes narrowed. With a keen appreciation of other people's motives, he sensed a plot of major proportions.

'That would be your brother,' obliged Venetia, 'the one that's not well.'

'He's slow, ma'am, that's all, like a big child. The way things are my mother can't mind him much longer. She's got her living to make, she'll have to put him in an asylum and he's not going to like that.'

'So what do you foresee happening to Eddie if your mother comes down here?' asked Ralph.

'He could come too, sir.'

'Of course!' Ralph waved his arms in the air in an expansive gesture of magnanimity. 'Of course, let them all come—your mother, your brother, your married sister, perhaps. Do they have children, by the way? We mustn't forget the children. And what about any pets—parrots, puppies, that kind of thing? My God, girl, what do you think this place is, a charitable institution?'

'Ralph!' Venetia reprimanded.

'No, sir,' replied Primmy, colouring slightly. 'I was trying to help.'

'Trying to help.' Ralph began to patrol to and fro between his wife and Primmy, hands behind his back. 'Let me get this straight. You are asking us to employ your mother—whose opinion, incidentally, we do not yet know—and to take in your retarded brother as part of the bargain. Am I right or am I wrong?'

'Right, sir.'

'You are a phenomenon, but I suppose you know that.' Ralph stopped before her and looked her up and down like a peppery general addressing a promising but wayward private. 'Why should we take responsibility for your brother? And apart from selfish considerations, what about him? We have no specialist knowledge or training, what can we possibly do for him?'

This was a question Primmy could not answer without appearing to grovel unacceptably. How could she tell Mr Tennant he was the most admirable, the most liberal, the most cultured being she had ever met, that no one however underprivileged could come into contact with him and not be enriched and improved? Instead, she said: 'He could work, sir. And you wouldn't have to pay him.' As soon as she'd said it she could have bitten her tongue off.

Ralph roared with laughter.

'Aha! How fortunate! Slave labour . . .' He shook his head, gasping in an access of mirth.

The two women looked at him, Primmy with tight-lipped resentment at his flippancy, Venetia with raised eyebrows and a faint smile: she liked to see her husband laugh, but increasingly could not laugh with him.

'What could he do, your Eddie?' asked Ralph.

'All simple jobs, sir, the kind of thing George Rowles does. Some days he's better than others, but he can fetch and carry and wash the car and clean out the horses and do a bit of weeding. All sorts.'

'What of the days that are . . . not so good?' enquired Venetia tactfully. 'You must be quite frank with us, Primmy, otherwise it wouldn't be fair to your brother.'

'I *am* being, ma'am.' Primmy was a little aggrieved. 'He'd give you no trouble, and he'd earn his keep. You wouldn't have to mind him, Ma knows how to handle him, she's done it for years. He's as gentle as a lamb and biddable, I'm sure he'd like to work for you—and he'd be happier in the country.' Primmy was being entirely sincere, but she was also aware that sincerity was her most powerful weapon in winning over the Tennants. The sheer audacity of her request, its direct appeal to their better natures, was its strength.

'We shall have to think about this,' said Venetia, glancing at her husband, who was still staring at Primmy, 'shan't we, dear?'

'Certainly. And so will Primmy's mother.' Ralph returned to his chair and shook open the paper again with a brisk snap.

'Are you in a great hurry to go?' asked Venetia.

'The end of the month will be quite all right, ma'am.'

'I'd be happier if I had some idea where you were off to.'

'I want to do nursing.' She'd said it. It was out. Mercifully, Mr Tennant did not appear to be listening.

'Nursing? Really?' Venetia was utterly taken aback. 'That's very commendable, Primmy. Let us know if you need any help from us, won't you?'

'Yes, ma'am. You've already been a great help.'

'I hope so.' Venetia drifted with practised tact and grace in the direction of the door. 'Mr Tennant and I will discuss your proposal and in the meantime you must let us know—honestly, mind—what your mother feels about it.'

'Yes, ma'am.'

'Off you go then.'

Primmy bobbed and left the room. Venetia sat down in the chair facing her husband, who lowered his paper to his lap with a gusty and expressive exhalation of breath.

'What's the mother like, for heaven's sake?' He sounded both exasperated and amused.

'I only met her when she first brought Primmy. A ferocious, wiry little person—'

'So that's where Primmy gets it from.'

'Primmy had a bruise on her temple,' Venetia murmured, almost to herself, 'and Mrs Dilkes said her husband had done it, but I remember thinking it was she.'

'A liar and a beater of little girls. What do you think?'

'I think it would be wrong of us to judge her on those grounds. It was a difficult interview, the poor woman was bound to come out of it in a bad light. Obviously she wanted Primmy to get the job, she needed the money.'

'And what of this secondary clause—the brother?'

Venetia knew Ralph did not really seek her opinion on the matter. He was in the process of making up his own mind, weighing the pros and cons, asking himself the questions that had to be asked and reaching his inevitably humanitarian conclusion. Although he appeared to attack the idea she knew that ultimately he would come down in favour of it. He sat there tapping the ends of his fingers together, savouring the intricacies of the situation, his eyes bright with interest.

Venetia rested her cheek on her hand, her wrist pale and willow-thin beneath the weight of her head. Her lids drooped over her eyes, the tiny veins like leaf-markings on the translucent skin.

'I can't decide. I can't think about it any more,' she said. 'Tomorrow will do, surely . . .'

Ralph glanced at her, comprehended, and clasped his hands together in a gesture of finality. 'Tomorrow!' he cried, with an air of jovial anticipation.

When Primmy's letter, whose careful phrasing had taken some days to compose, eventually arrived at 15 Grove Road it coincided with that rare thing, a visit from Lisbeth and Jim. It was only their second since getting married at the beginning of May. Lisbeth had no desire to bear her mother company over and above what was dictated by common politeness, but she did quite enjoy vaunting her secure, respectable married state before such a receptive audience. In addition to this, she had a second ulterior motive for the visit in August. The war had led to an outbreak of rampant patriotism in the East End, as everywhere else; wherever you looked the men were flocking to the recruiting stations to join the New Army. Lisbeth had been as susceptible as the next woman to this epidemic, and it pained her a little that Jim had been declared unfit to serve due to his bad chest; he had suffered from asthma since childhood. This fact in itself might not have been enough to upset her, had her husband not displayed a quite indecent complacency about it, telling everyone that 'someone had to mind the shop' and making obscure, sniggering references to an army marching on its stomach. She felt upstaged by acquaintances who were bravely bidding farewell to their spouses and sweethearts, and tried to salvage what prestige she could from the situation by telling people that poor Jim was heartbroken to be left behind, and that the extra work load at the shop would most likely carry him off, as he was 'not a well man'. It was particularly important that Mrs Dilkes should be made to see the pathos of Jim's rejection, before she got going with her sharp tongue. Hence the visit.

Normally Lily Dilkes would have spent hours painfully

deciphering Primmy's letter—her reading was rudimentary and she was too proud to ask for help—only to lay it aside, worn out by the unwonted intellectual exercise, and entirely forget the contents. It was usually stuff about the Tennants and the country, very dull; all she was interested in was the enclosed cash. But on this occasion she had barely got through the first sentence when there was a knock at the door and there were Lisbeth and Jim. So she left the letter lying on the table while she ushered them in and made tea.

'Hallo, Mother,' said Lisbeth. 'How are you?'

'How d'you think?' rejoined Mrs Dilkes acidly, banging the kettle down on the hob.

'Good, good,' said Jim, who didn't know how to take his mother-in-law. Lisbeth kept her hat and coat on, and sat down gingerly at the table as if expecting to disturb vermin. The fact that she had lived her entire life at 15 Grove Road until three months ago, and must know it to be clean, did not prevent her from going through this little ritual. She had moved up in the world now, and took every opportunity to broadcast her social elevation.

They both ignored Eddie though Jim, to give credit where it was due, had some pangs of conscience about the large, hunched figure in the corner and would occasionally cast a tight, timid smile over his shoulder only to look away again hurriedly on meeting Eddie's blank, impenetrable gaze.

Poor Jim Saunders, he was not popular. None of them really liked him—not Eddie, not Primmy, not Mrs Dilkes, not even Lisbeth, really. In the first two, he recognized an instinctive antipathy, but in the second two there was an ambivalence that he could not for the life of him comprehend. He could see that Lisbeth was pleased with her new lifestyle, and that her mother was suitably impressed, and yet he sensed that, in spite of it, they looked down on him. He was at a loss to know how to win their favour.

Mrs Dilkes sawed bread savagely. Lisbeth cleared her throat and said: 'Poor Jim has been turned down by the army.'

'Has he really?' Mrs Dilkes did not look up.

'Mm. His bad chest, you know.'

'Dearie me.'

Jim coughed noisily to reinforce his wife's point. 'Still, as I say,' he began in a tone of cheerful resignation—but stopped abruptly on receiving a sharp blow on the ankle that brought tears to his eyes. He looked aggrievedly at Lisbeth Was he just supposed to sit there and listen to her?

'He's not a well man,' said Lisbeth darkly. 'Are you dear?'

'I'll live,' responded Jim, but saw from his wife's face that yet again he'd said the wrong thing. He coughed once more to rectify the matter.

'There'll be a big work load in the shop with the other man gone, let's hope it won't be too much,' went on Lisbeth with a sigh.

Mrs Dilkes crashed a plate of bread and jam down on the table with such force that the slices jumped. 'You don't get anything for nothing,' she remarked, silencing them.

Jim was right to be wary of her. In spite of her goading of Primmy, Mrs Dilkes did not like him, and she was actually quite glad to be rid of Lisbeth. What rankled was that Lisbeth had achieved those goals that she had earmarked for Primmy. Her hostility towards her eldest daughter sprang from her close identification with her. After all, Primmy was the product of that far-off time when Mr Dilkes's inexpert attentions on Saturday nights had not been wholly repulsive and had even, on occasions, caused her to forget herself and succumb to the thumping, throbbing energy of the moment. She saw in Primmy the better points of both herself and her husband and the similarity both pleased and infuriated her. She had wanted Primmy to cancel out her own failure, to be looked up to as a respectable married woman, instead of scorned as a deserted one. It would have given her intense pleasure to see Primmy installed as Mrs This or That, giving orders to the grocer (a role filled in Mrs Dilkes's imagination by Jim Saunders), and possibly employing a maid of her own. Now, through her own stupid fault, it looked as though she were destined to be that even lowlier form of life, an old maid. Lowlier because for her there would be no man to blame, nor hard-luck story to tell.

Now there were Lisbeth and Jim sat at her table like Lord and Lady Muck, sipping their tea with genteelly puckered lips and ignoring the plate of bread and jam. That was another thing. They knew perfectly well—or Lisbeth did, anyway—that the jam was a luxury, only opened because of them, and yet they declined it with polite smiles. Jim would give his stomach a little rueful pat to indicate that he was too full of good things already, and Lisbeth would take a piece, only to leave it after one mouthful, as though unaccustomed to such coarse and solid fare. It drove Mrs Dilkes wild. She had to provide the stuff, and then she and Eddie were left with a mound of it that they could not eat fast enough, so it all got stale. At times such as these Mrs Dilkes could cheerfully have throttled her younger daughter.

'I predict we shall be making a handsome profit by this time next year,' Jim was saying in his shopkeeper's voice, referring to some new line stocked by the emporium. Mrs Dilkes watched his small mouth forming the words and nodded automatically. In the corner Eddie was attacking a slab of the neglected bread and jam. He was a noisy eater, and the churning, squelching sound of mastication punctuated the frequent pauses in the conversation, causing a look of pain to cross Lisbeth's features. Mrs Dilkes took special delight in not breaking these silences so that the rhythmic mashing of Eddie's jaws eventually drove Lisbeth or Jim to start up again.

'We bought a lovely sideboard,' said Lisbeth, pointedly raising her voice, 'from Cready's, you know, the one on the corner of—'

'I know the one,' Mrs Dilkes reassured her.

'It has an antique finish,' added Jim.

'Very nice.'

'Mind you,' Lisbeth giggled, 'it'll take a bit of polishing. It'd nearly fill this room, wouldn't you say, Jim?'

Jim glanced up and down, assessing the dimensions of 15 Grove Road. 'Oh yes, easy I'd say. The thing is, as soon as we can, to get a girl in to help.'

'That's right, I could do with help in a place that size.' They both looked at Mrs Dilkes to make sure the point had gone home. Mrs Dilkes's heart, an organ used but infrequently, ached for Primmy.

'What'll you do with yourself all day if someone else does the housework?' she asked gruffly.

'Be a lady of leisure I suppose!' Lisbeth's voice rose to a squeal at this witticism.

'After all,' Jim leaned forward, eyes bulging, to denote the risqué nature of his next pronouncement, 'we may not be just two for very much longer.'

Amid the gales of mirth that this provoked, Mrs Dilkes sat in amazement. 'You mean that you're . . . You're never . . .?'

'Oh no—not yet!' Lisbeth shrieked again.

As they recovered themselves, mopping their eyes, sniffing and gasping, Lisbeth spotted the letter. 'You heard from Primmy then?' she cried, picking up the letter and starting to read it. Clearly she assumed her mother had already read it, but Mrs Dilkes wasn't bothered: there was never anything personal in Primmy's letters. She and Jim watched Lisbeth as her eyes flicked to and fro down the pages. She turned it, finished it, and put it down.

'Well, well,' she said, making big round eyes, her voice arch and artificial. 'Are you going then?'

'Going?' Mrs Dilkes realized she might have let herself in for more than she bargained for. 'Going where?'

'Down there. To the country.' Lisbeth flicked the letter with the back of her hand, and turned to her husband. 'Primmy's leaving service. She's suggesting Mother takes her place—*and* takes Eddie.' She gave Jim a meaningful look.

Mrs Dilkes was stunned. But her desire to keep her end up and not to lose face was greater than her surprise. 'I'm thinking about it,' she said, rising to fetch the kettle.

'Oh!' Lisbeth pulled her mouth down and her eyebrows up. '*I* see! We're going to keep them waiting, are we?'

'It's a big decision,' said Mrs Dilkes, secretly delighted with her own sang-froid. 'I need a bit of time.'

'Fancy . . .' There was barely concealed amazement in Lisbeth's voice. She was in two minds about the idea. On the one hand it would be convenient to have her mother out of the way, but at the same time she had a sense of being by-passed and having her thunder stolen. What was Primmy going to do? She didn't say. Just like her to be so close. 'Why would they want you?' she asked. 'And *him.*' She jerked her head in Eddie's direction. That really stuck in her throat, Eddie going to live in a big posh house in the country. She picked up the letter again.

'You could bring Eddie,' Primmy wrote. *'He'd like it down here in the country and you won't have to mind him on your own all the time. He can do a few jobs, now they are short of staff. I'm sure it would be for the best.'*

Mrs Dilkes poured a stream of boiling water into the pot. She was beginning to enjoy herself, if only because of Lisbeth's obvious discomfort. 'Of course,' she said, 'I'm not sure it would suit me. I'm my own woman here.'

'It sounds a wonderful idea to me,' said Jim, whose

motives were clear: it would be the perfect way to get rid of the old termagant. 'The country air'd do both of you a power of good, you'd be looked after—'

'I wouldn't have this house,' said Mrs Dilkes.

'That's true, but what's so good about it?' asked Jim.

'It's mine.'

'Hm.' Jim grunted in a way that thoroughly disparaged the ownership of such a dump.

'Besides, I've lived in London all me life,' went on Mrs Dilkes. 'What would I do in the country?'

'You'd have a job, you'd be busy,' Lisbeth assured her, realizing, as her mother appeared to retract, how much she wanted her to go. 'Someone else to do the cooking, nice meals—think of it!'

Mrs Dilkes thought of it. 'Maybe,' she said. She looked about her. The room was small and damp and cramped, and while never dirty—she saw to that—its untidiness was colossal. Other people's washing was everywhere in varying stages of readiness: in piles on the floor, depending damply from the rickety clothes horse, airing on a line over the stove. She had to take in more and more, for she could no longer rely on the tailor's shop as a source of extra income; even at this early stage in the war ladies had patriotically cut back on clothes and hats, and orders had dropped by a third. She was undernourished and she ached in every limb; she went to bed exhausted and awoke unrefreshed.

Outside the small window grey city rain, greasy with industrial dirt, coal dust and petrol fumes, fell in gloomy stair-rods. Lisbeth and Jim sat there, fat and smug, not eating her good bread and jam. Eddie was very low, pasty and apathetic, hugging himself and rocking on his chair in the corner. She knew he should have more to do, that he was better when he was occupied, but so often it was easier to perform simple tasks herself than to waste time assisting and encouraging him. So he sat there, dull-eyed and hopeless.

'Maybe,' she said again, more thoughtfully.

That evening, when Eddie was in bed, she sat down with a stub of pencil and a piece of lined paper and wrote her reply. It was to the point. *Dear Prim, Eddie and me will come you say when. Ma.*

The evening of 11 August was Aubrey's last before leaving for France. He had joined his battalion at Maidstone the previous week but had returned that afternoon to make his farewells. Thanks to his own unsentimental, businesslike nature the atmosphere was not emotionally charged. Everyone was tired and quiet. Nothing had been heard from Dulcie or, as far as they knew, from Maurice.

The evening might have passed off peacefully enough had not the pre-dinner drinks been disturbed by the rush of wheels and crunch of hooves of a pony and trap on the drive. Ralph went to the window to see who it was. In the hall, on the edge of the patch of sunlight admitted by the open door, Primmy welcomed the new arrival.

'Why, Mr Maurice! We weren't expecting you.'

'Maurice!' Thea flew from her chair. Maurice stood just inside the door in a crumpled cream linen suit, spectacles at half-mast, bag in hand. He was smiling, pleased but diffident, as Thea kissed and hugged him. Primmy trotted upstairs with his bag, and Collingwood took his soft felt hat, brushing it off and hanging it on the hatstand.

Thea drew Maurice into the library, hugging his arm. 'It's Maurice!' she announced unnecessarily, smiling at everyone. She watched, beaming, as he greeted the family, kissed Venetia, shook hands with Ralph and Aubrey.

Sophie, in the corner, sat rigid with discomfort. She had only received Maurice's appalling letter the day before, she had not had time to prepare herself, and she had certainly not expected him back so soon. The end of the week, he'd said. She had the impression that in his perverse, mild-mannered way he had deliberately tried to catch her out: telling her those dreadful things and then just turning up, when he must know that his very presence in the house was a threat to her happiness. She clasped her hands together on her lap in a tight, hard knot, trying to feel strong. It was ironic that she generally went through this little ritual from choice: the waiting until he had greeted everyone else, the modest hanging back until she was noticed—she, the person most deserving of his attention. This time all she wanted was for Maurice not to see her.

She watched, paralysed with anxiety, as he spoke to her brother and sister-in-law, and smiled in his thoughtful way into Thea's face as she talked. How could he be so calm. when he was about to ruin everything?

As if hearing her thoughts he turned suddenly and came directly over to her He must have been conscious of her from the moment he'd entered the room in spite of the fact that she'd been masked by the others. He bent over and kissed her awkwardly, his tie flapping down on her lap.

'Hallo, Mother, how are you?'

Sophie tilted her cheek, eyes closed to receive his greeting: the kiss of Judas. 'You didn't say you would be coming so soon,' she said coldly.

'Didn't I? I can't remember.' Maurice straightened up. 'I thought from your letter you were anxious to see me as soon as possible.'

She stared straight in front of her. Now he was insulting her! It was truly unforgivable. He stood by her for a moment, his hand on the back of the chair, a token attendance; but she would not speak to him, the words would have choked her. After a minute or so, during which he hovered at her shoulder and the others tactfully drew in on themselves, he went back to Thea and accepted a glass of sherry from her. Now that he had left her she watched him again, fascinated by his composure. There was something different about him, a self-reliance and a separateness which had not been there before. She was cut to the quick. Had he no shame? She hoped against hope that he would not broadcast the dreadful truth. She realized it could not remain secret for ever, but just for tonight, with Aubrey still here . . . Surely he wouldn't be so tactless? Staring across the room, she caught the eye of Venetia, who was sitting on the other side of the fireplace. But years of grim restraint precluded the sharing of anxiety, and she looked away again with a little jerk of her head.

It wasn't until the end of dinner that Aubrey, provoked by some fateful twinge of curiosity, or perhaps by mere politeness, leaned back in his chair and asked: 'What will you be doing now, Maurice?'

'Doing?' Maurice peered disingenuously through his glasses.

'I mean, in the war,' said Aubrey deliberately.

'Oh . . . continuing with my thesis, I dare say. Lingering in the groves of academe.' Maurice smiled a gentle, placating smile.

'There will be a job for everyone,' said Aubrey sternly. Thea looked from one to the other, detecting the current that passed between them, the old mistrust crackling again.

Maurice said: 'I'm not really looking for a job.'

Sophie sniffed loudly. Ralph rose and fetched port from the sideboard. When he had sat down he poured himself a glass and pushed the decanter, in its silver coaster, to Maurice. Maurice passed it on.

'I'm quite sure,' he added, folding his napkin and pressing it smooth, 'that there will be enough patriots to fill the jobs without me.'

He meant, Thea knew, to be self-deprecating, to defuse the situation, but his choice of words had been unfortunate. Aubrey heard what he took to be sarcasm, the abhorred manifestation of intellectual snobbery.

'You're not a patriot? Is that what you're telling us?'

'He didn't say that,' said Ralph.

'It's what I understood from his remark,' retorted Aubrey, not looking at his father.

Maurice shook his head. 'I love England, of course—'

'But you're not prepared to fight for her?'

'Well, to be precise, it's not England we're fighting for.' Maurice's voice was getting quieter and quieter, almost deferential, as if he wished to bleach from the substance of his words any taint of personal acrimony.

Sophie turned her head away and fixed her gaze on some distant point in the garden. Aubrey pushed his chair back and crossed his legs. The crisp lines of his uniform accentuated the squareness of his shoulders, the belligerent jutting of his cleft chin, and lent a kind of official authority to his icy, scrutinizing gaze.

Ralph leaned forward and interposed mildly: 'Sophie, if you don't want port would you please pass it on.'

It was evidence of his sister's distress that she did not take the opportunity to upbraid him for his uncouth habit of passing the port while the ladies were present. Instead, she slid the decanter on its way without a murmur. It moved past Venetia to Aubrey, who helped himself.

Maurice said: 'Ah . . . as I see it, we are stepping in on behalf of others.'

'Yes. That is our duty and our privilege as a responsible power.'

Sophie twitched. It was hard indeed to hear these noble sentiments, with which she so heartily agreed, voiced by her nephew and not her son.

Maurice rolled his napkin and slotted it meticulously through its silver ring. Then he laid it neatly by his mat.

'Let me just say that I think our involvement in the war can only add to the misery and loss of life. And I am against that.'

'But our entry into the war is expressly designed to curtail these things!' Aubrey sounded affronted.

'How can it?' asked Maurice, and then repeated, rather sadly, 'How can it?'

'We shall stand by our allies and defend them, and prevent the German war machine destroying Europe.'

'But you will assist it. You will fuel it.' Maurice's voice had dropped almost to a whisper. The others sitting round the table were a captive audience. You could have heard a pin drop. 'We must agree to differ,' added Maurice, looking directly at Aubrey for the first time.

'Is that all you can say? Is that all there is to it?' Aubrey's blustering would have been ridiculous if his anger had not been so obviously real. 'I confess myself astounded!'

'It's only my opinion, Aubrey, no offence was intended.'

'But offence may be *taken*!' replied Aubrey with an uncharacteristic verbal flourish. 'And not just by me. I sincerely hope you realize that, Maurice old chap, or you are in for some nasty shocks.'

'Perhaps. I hope not.'

'I'm sure you do! I'm sure you hope this war would simply go away and leave you in peace with your books and your sensitive social conscience, but it won't, you know.'

'I didn't say that.'

'The day is fast approaching when you will have to account for this conviction of yours.'

'Obviously, if I have to, I will.'

'Hm.' Aubrey got up. Thea could see the muscle bunched in his jaw; he was furious. 'If you'll excuse me.'

He left the room. Ralph helped himself to a second glass of port and glanced round the table. He was obliged to acknowledge a sneaking machiavellian pleasure in the goings-on. Watching the confrontation between his son and his nephew was like having an argument with himself: his own views fell somewhere in between. He certainly could not condemn Maurice. Indeed, the chap had displayed a certain dignity and forbearance that had swung the argument a little in his favour.

'What was all that about?' asked Venetia, almost sleepily. 'Why must people argue all the time?'

'I'm sorry, Aunt,' said Maurice, smiling at her. 'It was rude of us.'

'I don't know what got into Aubrey, attacking you like that,' she went on. 'Shall we have coffee in the library?'

They rose. Sophie muttered something and stalked from the room.

For the first time that evening Thea caught a glimpse of the old Maurice, blushing and awkward, as his mother passed him, holding her skirt in to her side as though avoiding the contamination of his touch. She went over to him.

'You had to say it, didn't you?' she said, both admiring and reproving. 'You simply had to.'

'Lord. How I hate scenes.'

'It'll blow over. He leaves tomorrow.'

'It'll blow over for now, that's all.'

'Well, that'll do.'

'I suppose so, I honestly didn't come down here to—'

'We know that.'

Maurice looked at her, and she returned his look steadily. She had always been there, at his side, with that trusting, confident look, always. He smiled ruefully. 'I don't deserve you,' he said. But for some reason the remark struck a wrong note, or reminded her of something, and she followed the others out into the hall.

'Where's he gone?' asked Ralph of the world at large, standing in the middle of the hall. Homer, lying at the foot of the stairs, thumped his tail in acknowledgement of the beloved presence.

'It's not like him to sulk,' said Venetia.

They went into the library. Aubrey stood by the window hands in pockets, staring out into the thickening dusk. Venetia went over to him and put her hand on his shoulder.

'Aubrey? Aubrey, do come and shake hands with Maurice.' She sounded just as she had all those years ago, addressing the two mutely incompatible schoolboys. 'I can't bear this, it's so silly just when you're going away. Please, for me.'

Aubrey turned. Maurice stood just inside the door, hands behind his back, brushing the carpet with the toecap of his shoe. To Thea, beside him, it appeared that Maurice was in control, held the cards, waited for Aubrey to make his move.

'Please,' said Venetia again, giving her son's sleeve a little tug.

Thea was embarrassed. This was not right, it could only make things worse. A year ago Venetia would not have behaved thus, she would have had more sense. She was only doing it now to preserve her private illusion—for illusion it was—of peace and harmony and family unity. And in doing it she denied Maurice and Aubrey their right to independence and maturity, reducing their differences to the level of a petty childish squabble.

Aubrey removed his hands from his pockets. Ralph made a noisy business of looking for something in the desk, pulling the drawers in and out with a clatter.

Abruptly Aubrey walked over to Maurice and held out his hand. 'I am doing this for my mother,' he said harshly. His outstretched arm was poker-stiff, the hand rigid as the blade of an axe.

Maurice looked down at it as if pondering a complex mathematical problem. Then he shook his head. 'Better not. What, after all, is the point?' So reasonable and conciliatory was his tone that at first all present thought they had misheard him. Venetia continued to smile encouragingly. Aubrey's hand remained extended, shaking slightly.

'I beg your pardon?' he asked.

'I'm sorry,' Maurice cleared his throat, 'I said I thought it pointless to shake hands and mean nothing by it. Let's just agree to differ and no hard feelings.'

Aubrey lowered his arm sharply as if snapping to attention. 'I see.'

'I'm sure it's best.' Maurice stepped aside to admit Primmy with the coffee tray.

Sensing the atmosphere she paused for a moment, looking around expectantly. Ralph cleared a space on the desk and beckoned her over. She put the tray down and turned to leave. As she crossed the room she sensed instinctively that Mr Maurice was the centre of attention and that, unusually for him, he appeared not to mind. She caught his eye and he gave her a little smile, with something sad and secret in it. For the first time Primmy was impressed by Maurice as a man and not merely a shy, short-sighted, impoverished cousin of the high-powered Tennants.

As she closed the door on the almost palpable silence in the library she felt a biting pang of curiosity. Usually she understood, if not specifically then at least instinctively, what the situation was at Chilverton House at any given time;

there was a pattern of characteristic reactions which she could read like a book. But this time she sensed a drastic change in the order. Roles had been swapped and speeches rewritten. It was all she could do not to crouch down by the door with her ear to the keyhole, but she had never yet spied on her employers and she resisted the temptation to do so now. As she walked across to the morning-room she heard that ominous silence broken by a low voice.

'I'm glad the whole family is here,' said Aubrey, 'to see this.'

'My sister is not,' observed Ralph, 'and just as well, given her propensity for overreaction.'

'Well, it's not a very edifying scene,' agreed Maurice, removing his glasses and polishing them on his tie. 'I just think it's such a mistake to paper over cracks.'

'What an odd way you have of expressing yourself.' Aubrey stared at his cousin with the accumulated scorn and mistrust of more than a decade.

But Maurice might still have escaped, had he not murmured, with the very best of intentions: 'I try to be truthful.'

The next moment there was a roar from Aubrey: 'By God, you cowardly little runt!'

Amid a flurry of movement, violent and yet muffled by carpets and armchairs, there was an unpleasant cracking sound, a pair of spectacles flew towards Thea, and Maurice was sprawled with his back against the door, his face sickly white and his upper lip cleft by a glutinous trickle of dark blood. Nobody moved. Aubrey stood there, a lock of hair hanging over his left eye, his fists clenched by his sides, shuddering.

No one moved. Even Thea suppressed her instinct to go to Maurice; the best help she could give him now was to let him be. She picked up his glasses and folded them carefully: they were not broken. Maurice began to get up, gingerly placing hands and feet as precarious props and using the door to assist him. His thin frame looked like a marionette being hoisted from the horizontal to the vertical by a series of randomly pulled strings, all weird angles and loose joints. When he was finally upright Thea stepped forward and handed him his glasses. He put them on with great care—his nose was pink and sore—combed his fingers through his hair, and then delved in his breast pocket for a large white handkerchief, with which he attempted to staunch the flow from his nostrils. Seeing that it was hopeless he folded the handkerchief into a kind of pad, pressed it to his upper lip and said, rather in the manner of the Elephant's Child: 'I thick I'll go to by roob, if that's all right.'

'I'll come.' Thea opened the door and followed him into the hall. He turned, swayed a little, but brushed off the solicitous hand she placed beneath his elbow.

Primmy, who was in the morning-room laying up for breakfast, heard the door open. She was so alert that the small sound made her skin flinch. Even on this side of the closed door she had felt the current of uneasiness reach out and touch her.

She stood on the far side of the table by the sideboard, rubbing a fork on her apron. She could see part of the hall and the foot of the stairs. Homer curled like a pressed tongue on his blanket. Maurice appeared, with Thea just behind him He tottered a little and she put out a hand, which he brushed away. Back in the library there was a thick silence like London smog. Thea went back in and it swallowed her up, the door closing once more behind her.

Primmy stared, holding her breath. Maurice walked slowly to the bottom of the stairs, one hand to his face, head bowed; with the other hand he reached out and grasped the newel post, leaning heavily. His knees appeared to be sagging dangerously.

Primmy went to the morning-room door. All through her life she had coped and cleaned and mopped up messes; it was not just force of circumstance but something in her character, a compulsion almost.

'Mr Maurice? Are you all right?'

He looked at her over his shoulder. The top part of his face was white, the bottom part obscured by a large bloodstained handkerchief which he held to his nose.

'Dear, dear.' She put down the fork and went over to him. He said nothing. Without being able to put a name to it, Primmy recognized a state of shock when she saw one; she also recognized a kind of dignity in his silence, his rejection of Thea's helping hand. Her earlier impression, of his being the focus of attention, was reinforced. Something in her was plucked by his aloneness. When she put her hand on his arm she hoped he would not brush it away like Thea's, and he did not.

'Come on,' she said, 'let's get you upstairs.' His arm was nothing, skin and bone, under the crumpled sleeve of his jacket. When he let go the newel post he swayed for a second, but she was steady as a rock. She'd manhandled her dad up the stairs at Grove Road many a time when he'd been legless, and he was twice the size of Maurice. Together they toiled up, a stair at a time.

They stopped for a breather on the half-landing, while Maurice folded the sodden handkerchief inside out. 'That's the way,' she said.

They went along the corridor to his room. She pushed the door open, still supporting him with her other arm, and led him over to the bed. Because of his absence the room was unnaturally neat and bare; his still unopened case stood by the bedside table. What a homecoming, thought Primmy. With her free hand she whipped the towel from the rail on the washstand and deftly spread it over the clean pillowcase.

'You lie down,' she said, helping him to do so. 'There we are.' She removed his shoes, one at a time, undoing the laces with quick, sharp tugs. His feet were as cold as stones, she could feel them right through his socks, and she chafed them briskly between her hands.

'Now,' she said, standing up, 'don't budge and I'll fetch something for that nose.' His eyes stared back at her over the ever-reddening handkerchief. Clicking her tongue she went along to the big bathroom and fetched a bottle of witch-hazel from the cabinet. Then she returned to the bedroom and poured some water out of the ewer into the washbowl and placed it on the floor beside the bed. Without asking, she opened his case and rummaged until she found his face flannel, which she dropped into the water. Firmly, she pulled away the hand holding the handkerchief from his face. His nose was a mess, and he seemed to have bitten his lip, too, but experience told her that it looked worse than it was.

'You'll live,' she said. 'You'll have a couple of lovely shiners in the morning.' She squeezed out the flannel in the cold water and mopped the bloodstained areas with quick, gentle dabs. The water in the flowered bowl turned a swirling pink. When his face was clean she applied witch-hazel to his nose and sponged his hand. It was a familiar routine, she was at home with it. The fact that the object of her ministrations was her employer's nephew made little difference. Her final act before going to pour away the dirty water was to fold the cold, wet flannel into a neat square and place it on his forehead.

She rinsed out the bowl, dried her hands and came back. He was gazing expectantly at the door as she entered, and she went over to him.

'How is it?'

He nodded, managing a crooked smile. There was nothing else she could do; she ought to be going, but she didn't want to.

She was standing so close that he scarcely had to move to take her hand and she would have had to take two steps back to prevent him doing so. She did not step back, even a little, but allowed her hand to be held. It did not feel all that extra-ordinary.

They stared at each other and he spoke for the first time: 'Primmy, do you think I'm a coward?'

She did not know why Maurice should ask her, of all people, such an odd thing, but knew that the question must have its roots in whatever strange events had taken place in the library a few minutes ago. It was obviously important that she answer truthfully.

'No,' she replied. 'I don't.'

'Good.' She made to leave, but at once he gripped her hand more tightly. 'Don't go.'

'I ought.'

'Sit down, just for a moment.'

She perched, straight-backed, on the edge of the bed. In a few minutes he was asleep. She was able to bring up the overhanging sides of the counterpane to cover him, and remove his spectacles, which were being pushed all skew-wiff. As she did so, she studied his face. It was a type of face quite outside her normal experience, not cast in the mould of what she would generally think of as handsomeness. And yet beside it other faces, even those of men she had admired such as Dick and Mr Tennant, seemed coarse. The pallor of the skin, the sunken cheeks and sensitive mouth, and in the middle of it his poor old nose—she was deeply touched, there was a lump in her throat. He hadn't uttered one word of complaint, not one. A coward? Not likely. Her face was only inches from his. She wanted to kiss his cheek, it seemed the natural thing after tucking someone up. She leaned forward, a phalanx of powerful foreign emotions bearing down on her out of nowhere—

Suddenly a door opened downstairs and there was a brisk, heavy thunder of feet on the staircase. She shot to her feet, shaken to the core. Her heart pattered behind the crisp bib of her apron, the gleaming whiteness of which was now adorned with a rust-coloured bloodstain. Oh lor—what had she been thinking of? She scarcely recognized herself she was so flustered. She walked swiftly from the room, closing the door behind her, but nothing could prevent her from encountering Mr Aubrey at the top of the stairs. He didn't appear to have seen her, but when he did he stopped dead. Apparently it was not only she who felt awkward.

'Oh, Primmy . . .' Mr Aubrey rubbed his hands together and cracked his knuckles. She stood sideways on to him, hoping he wouldn't notice the stain. 'Is he all right? Mr Maurice?'

So he knew anyway, or had guessed, where she'd been. 'Yes, sir.'

'Nothing serious, then?'

'No, sir. He's asleep.'

'Mm. Good, I won't disturb him, then.' There was, unmistakably, a note of relief in his voice. She passed him and began to descend the stairs.

'Primmy.'

'Sir?' She paused, one hand on the banister.

'Thank you . . . for helping.'

'That's all right.' She didn't bother with any more 'sir's' but dashed back to the morning-room and laid the table like a whirlwind.

When, a few weeks later, Thea told Andrea Sutton about Aubrey punching Maurice on the nose, she threw back her head and laughed.

'Oh, priceless! How I wish I'd been there!'

Thea was partly hurt, partly infected by her hilarity. 'It wasn't in the least funny, I assure you,' she protested with a smile. 'Poor Maurice, he was so dignified, and Aubrey absolutely puffed up and scarlet with fury like a turkey cock. I suppose it did have its comical side,' she admitted. 'But the fact is, Maurice will be very lucky if the worst he gets is a punch on the nose.'

'I know, I know, what a heartless creature I am.' Andrea

composed her mirth-shattered features, blinking wet eyes at her friend. 'It's just that your whole family is so outrageous. There's dear papa, so radical, so *outré*; your darling mother, all blue blood and sensibility; Aubrey, the very model of filial propriety; Maurice the intellectual, Dulcie the would-be society beauty, Thea—' she paused reflectively, 'the new woman. And now look at you, in total disarray! Unspeakable goings-on in Montmartre, fisticuffs in the library—whatever next?'

They were sitting in a crowded tea-room in Heath Street, NW3, no more than ten minutes' walk from Mrs Hoskins's college. It was their first meeting since Thea's arrival in London and the past hour had been taken up with telling Andrea of events at Chilverton House. Outside, it was a nostalgic early autumn Saturday afternoon, bright but cool, the ever-lengthening shadows barring the brave sunshine, the first few handfuls of yellow leaves floating down from the handsome trees in Church Row. People were going about their business with the slightly increased energy and purpose that autumn brings.

Thea and Andrea sat in a corner, their pot of tea on a flowered enamel tray, and some fingers of buttered toast on a white china plate on the lacquered wooden table between them. Andrea's appearance was, as usual, smart and *soignée*. She wore a brown dress and jacket, with a coral scarf knotted undergraduate style at the neck, and on her well-groomed head a brown and green tam o'shanter. On her arrival she had been carrying a brown umbrella with a knobbly amber handle in the shape of a goose's head. This odd accessory in Andrea's hands looked stylish and unusual.

'How are things at college?' she enquired when she had finished laughing.

'Not too bad,' Thea smiled wryly. The fact was, she found it rather tedious. 'Some of it's dull, but it's all in a good cause, and not for long, anyway.'

'I don't know how you can contemplate going to work for your father,' said Andrea, shaking her head incredulously.

'Why ever not?'

'I'd have thought you'd want to spread your wings, escape! Get away from them all!'

'Not at the moment . . .' Thea felt disinclined to tell her friend that at the moment she was only too glad to seek the shelter of her family, whose foibles and faults she knew and understood, and who understood her. She thought of Austria, and Paris, and closed her eyes for a second.

'What's the matter?'

'Oh—nothing. I've had enough adventures for the present.'

'You must have more!' declared Andrea. 'Will you come to our meeting?'

'When is that?'

'Next Tuesday, at my flat. We meet on the first Tuesday of every month, so it's a pretty routine affair, but I'd like you to be there. We have a male speaker.'

'Oh? Who's that?'

'You'll see.' Andrea gave a secretive smile. 'Will you come?'

'Yes.' Thea hesitated. 'But Andrea—let me make up my own mind, won't you?'

'Of course!' Andrea widened her eyes innocently. 'Have I ever done otherwise?'

'Perhaps not intentionally. But sometimes you make assumptions.'

'Do I? Yes, well, I do assume you are for universal suffrage. If that assumption is wrong we may as well go our separate ways.'

Thea avoided meeting Andrea's eyes. She was so quick, so clever, so compromising; her peculiar energy sucked your individuality away. 'Of course I support votes for women. But there have been times that I felt the methods of the WSPU have been improper—'

'*Improper!*' Andrea laughed scornfully. 'If propriety were all we cared about we'd be sitting at home with our embroidery.'

'I meant inappropriate,' said Thea patiently. 'I can't believe that crimes of violence advance the cause. For instance, the NUWSS—'

'Oh, Mrs Henry Fawcett's brigade.' Andrea waved her hand disdainfully. 'They may be admirable, dignified women, but it is the Pankhursts who have made female suffrage into a burning issue. The NUWSS was just part of existing society, the politicians probably welcomed it as a way to keep intelligent middle-class women occupied. The WSPU is not to be fobbed off.'

'But Christabel went to Paris,' said Thea. 'Was that brave?'

'She was with us in spirit,' retorted Andrea. 'Christabel is a rare being, a great orator, an inspirer of people. Someone like that is not subject to the same rules and ethics as the rest of us.'

'Perhaps not.' Thea felt. nonetheless, that she had made her point. 'Shall we go?'

They buttoned their coats, and edged between the crowded tables to pay their bill. Outside in Heath Street there was a crisp breeze; the passengers on the top of a passing bus had rosy cheeks. One or two couples, the men in uniform, walked pressed together for the last time.

Andrea and Thea walked to the crossroads. 'So you'll come, anyway,' said Andrea. tapping her brolly smartly as she walked.

'All right. What time?'

'Seven. Do you know where I am?'

'I can find it.'

They stopped on the corner. Andrea said: 'By the way, in all this talk of Maurice and Aubrey and Dulcie you haven't told me what you thought of Vienna.'

'I will, some time.'

'Yes. please. Did you dance the nights away in the arms of a debonair officer with twirling moustaches?'

'Not exactly.' Thea looked at her friend and saw to her relief that she was joking. 'The business with Dulcie seems to have overshadowed everything else at the moment, but there were happy times

'I should hope so.' Andrea's mind had already drifted on to other matters. 'See you on Tuesday, then.'

'I'll be there.'

They parted, Andrea to march down High Street and turn off along Flask Walk towards White Bear Hill, Thea to toil up Hollybush Road, thence to Mrs Hoskins's in Arkwright Road.

The college consisted of two houses, one for teaching and administrative purposes, the other for accommodation. Of the forty or so young women attending the college, all were residential except for a handful whose homes were near enough to facilitate the daily journey to and fro. Rules for the residential students were strict. Supper was at six-thirty and attendance at this solemn rite was compulsory for all; evening outings were limited to two a week, and students had to be back by ten, and leave a note of their whereabouts in a large tome in the front hall, presided over by whichever member of staff was on duty Thea chafed against this regime; it precluded so much of what she wanted to do while in London. Even to go to an art gallery or museum after classes finished at three in the afternoon was difficult, with the long bus journey back up to Hampstead in order to get ready for supper. She made light of the regulations in her letters home, not wanting to appear ungrateful, but she chafed against them nonetheless.

She opened the front door of the dormitory house and crossed the hall, under the watchful stare of Miss Doherty (Business Studies).

'Good evening, Miss Tennant. Supper in half an hour.'

'Yes. Thank you, Miss Doherty.'

Thea made a face to herself as she ran up the stairs. As one of the older students, she had been allotted a room to herself on the top floor whose dormer window afforded a view over the rooftops of London—the busy Finchley Road, the quiet leafy avenues of St John's Wood, and in the distance the West End and the City, so near and yet so far. She was glad of the view. On clear afternoons she fancied she could see right over London to Kent.

In her room she removed her hat and coat and stood before the mirror on the chest of drawers to do her hair. On the stairs and in the rooms on either side she could hear the muted talking and giggling and whispering that permeated the air of Mrs Hoskins's students' hostel. She knew that some of the other girls thought her stand-offish, but she couldn't help it. Here she had the old sensation of being different, an oddity, and it was not pleasant. It reminded her of the Strathallen.

The supper gong sounded and she joined the rest of the girls on the stairs. They all talked about the war, it was so exciting. Everyone had a brother, or an uncle, or a cousin who had joined up; and some, like Thea, were going straight from college into jobs vacated by men. They all had the sweet taste of freedom on their lips, the music of independence in their ears.

Mrs Hoskins herself, an admirable woman who had long ago perceived the typewriter as a liberator of females, shook her head over the modern young women. They were mercenary, ambitious and slapdash. She noted with distaste their propensity for giggling and the relative speed with which they learned the words and music of popular songs when they laboured and stumbled interminably over their work. They groaned and sighed over accountancy and filing and yet they expected to walk into good jobs with high salaries. They were sadly interested in rewards, instead of in a job well done for its own sake.

As for the war, Mrs Hoskins could see that the effects at home would be great and far-reaching no matter what the eventual outcome in Europe. She was a staunch patriot. Mr Hoskins had been killed by the Zulus in South Africa and she had been proud that he died for his country. The union had had no issue and, secretly, despite her bluff and businesslike exterior, Mrs Hoskins saw her students as surrogate daughters. Many of them were with her for several months, and had never been in London before; she took her responsibilities seriously. But regrettably the war brought out the worst in most of them. They revelled in its opportunities for sentimentality, fell in love with any man in uniform, and handed out flowers to those queueing at recruiting stations, like women of easy virtue instead of properly brought-up middle-class girls who should have known better. It was her earnest hope that if these were the women who were to be the custodians of hearth and home while the men were at the front, they would pull themselves together and fulfil their roles properly.

Supper was always presided over by Mrs Hoskins herself and one other member of staff. There was a roster for the serving of food, for Mrs Hoskins believed that girls from comfortable backgrounds should be taught a proper spirit of service. Grace would be said together, and silence observed until the plates had been handed round and Mrs Hoskins lifted her own knife and fork.

Thea found that she was usually quite unable to get a word in edgeways at the table; and this state of affairs suited her perfectly. She was able to eat, listen and smile when required; she was quite happy to be an observer.

However, on this occasion she found herself sitting next to Amy Broadhurst, a jolly girl from Sussex who thought she had a special talent for drawing people out. No one was too reserved, no topic too sacred, to win exemption from her amiable interrogation.

'What will you be doing, Thea?' she asked, in a tone of breathless interest. 'I mean, when you leave here?'

'I'm going to work in my father's factory.'

'How exciting!' Amy looked round at the others to

make sure they realized how exciting it was 'What sort of factory?'

'Light engineering.'

'Goodness! Whereabouts?'

'In Southwark.' Thea wondered if Amy would cry 'Southwark!'

Instead she announced importantly: 'They say a lot of factories may be turned over to munitions before long. A friend of mine has got a job in munitions production. It's quite dangerous, she has to wear special clothes.' A ripple of serious approval ran round the table.

Thea said: 'I think our factory may go into munitions next year.' And at once wished she hadn't.

'No! How wonderful!' There seemed no end to Amy's capacity for wonder. 'And you will be there!'

'Yes,' said Thea. What else was there to say? She felt an insane desire to giggle. To change the subject, she added: 'I must make the most of the weeks here, though.'

'Yes, of course,' replied Amy solemnly and then, addressing the company at large: 'Thea works frightfully hard. She puts the rest of us to shame.'

'That's because I only have a short time.' It was never comfortable to be picked out as a paragon of virtue.

'Something tells me you're a suffragette, too,' said Amy. There was a sly, teasing note in her voice.

Thea looked at her in surprise. 'Merely a sympathizer, I've not been involved in the campaign.'

'Ah, but you will be soon, won't you?' asked Amy roguishly, giving Thea a confidential smile. 'I saw you with Andrea Sutton.'

So that was it. Thea shook her head. 'She's just an old friend, we were at school together. She lives near here.'

'I know. She's the area organizer for the WSPU.' Amy was triumphant. 'I saw her one Sunday making a speech up by the Round Pond. She's a wonderful person.'

Thea felt obliged to dispel a little of this dewy-eyed hero worship. 'She's very astute,' she responded guardedly, 'but she is the suffragette, not I, although I do support their cause.'

'Naturally.' Amy nodded, the sharer of Thea's secret. It was most trying; the girl was a born busybody, a spier on other people's affairs. Fortunately the conversation was terminated by the advent of chocolate blancmange, the igloo-shaped portions slithering in their china bowls like jellyfish.

Thea addressed herself to hers and Amy began to draw out some unfortunate on the other side of the table.

On Tuesday evening Thea set out for White Bear Hill immediately after supper. She hurried down the stairs and signed the book in the front hall as quickly as possible, hoping not to meet Amy or any of her hangers-on. Next to her name, and beneath the date, she wrote 'Visiting friend locally'—the truth but not the whole truth.

She toiled up the hill to Fitzjohn's Avenue, then up to the village and along Heath Street as far as the tall red brick hospital. Here she turned right down a steep cobbled hill and forked left into White Bear Hill. This was a road with tall terraced houses on one side, and a scattering of more opulent detached residences on the other. During the day you could glimpse the Heath beyond the end of the road, the lovely friendly Heath with its quiet walks and hills and gently shady trees, whence Thea fled on Sunday afternoons, pretending it was the Weald.

She walked up the street on the terraced side, peering at the black leaded numbers on the stained-glass fanlight of each door, until she reached Andrea's. She went up the flight of stone steps and peered again at the small list of names in their metal slots by the bell. But while she was still looking she heard footsteps on the other side of the door and it rattled and opened to reveal Andrea. She pulled back the door with a flourish and stood aside.

'Come in, come in! We saw you walking down the hill from the window.' She closed the door after Thea and instructed: 'Up one flight, the door on the left.'

As they went up the stairs Thea wondered what they had said about her when they had spotted her solitary figure coming down the hill. She felt suddenly self-conscious.

The door stood open and she entered, conspicuously the last to arrive, while Andrea closed it after her and helped to relieve her of her hat and coat. There were eight other women in the room, sitting in a circle, and a man—the speaker whom Andrea had mentioned, no doubt—sitting at a table in the corner, sorting through some notes. Andrea laid her things on a chair and motioned her to sit down. The other women nodded, murmured, accepted her. They were serious, high-minded people, not for them the frivolity of small talk.

The man at the table turned and came over, leaning over behind her chair and saying in her ear, 'Thea Tennant! I told you it wouldn't be long.'

Louis Avery's lips were curved in a smug smile that seemed to indicate that the whole affair was of his own arranging.

'Hallo,' said Thea. She could not inject any enthusiasm into her greeting.

'I'm so glad you came.'

'Andrea invited me.'

'Andrea is a good organizer.'

He pulled up a chair next to her and sat down. He kept looking at her complacently as though he had conjured her out of a hat, as if she had no free will of her own.

Andrea stepped into the centre of the circle of chairs and clapped her hands. The soft talk faded into silence.

'Good evening, and thank you all for coming. Now you will have noticed that we have a new friend and supporter here this evening, someone I have known for many years and whose dedication to the cause I can vouch for.' Thea felt her cheeks colouring; really Andrea presumed too much. Andrea went on: 'Her name is Thea.'

Thea looked up and nodded. One or two of the women smiled encouragingly.

'We don't bother much with surnames or titles here, Thea,' said Andrea. 'We deem it unnecessary. We prefer to know each other as individuals, as comrades in arms. So, we have—' she swept her arm round the circle of women, 'Chloe, Dora, Louise, Charlotte, Ruth and Esme.' She looked over her shoulder. 'And our speaker for tonight you have already met. Louis.'

'Indeed we have,' said Louis, in an exaggeratedly gallant tone which seemed to Thea quite inappropriate.

The meeting began. Thea confined herself to listening and making mental notes. The secretary, Chloe, read out the minutes of the previous meeting, apologies from non-attenders, and the dates of various public meetings over the next few weeks. It was noted with favour that thanks to the Home Secretary's sensible decision since the last meeting, trade unionists and suffragettes who had been convicted of taking part in violent strikes had been unconditionally released. Fears that the new ruling might not be enforceable had been momentarily whipped up by the re-arrest of a former suffragette prisoner, Mrs Crowe, on the twenty-first of August, but the Home Secretary had intervened at once and it appeared that a new era of tolerance had dawned, ironically, with the outbreak of war.

At this point, copies of *Suffragette* and *Votes for Women* were distributed, along with copies, made by Andrea, of Emmeline Pankhurst's 'Circular Letter' of 13 August, setting out the official WSPU reaction to the war emergency. Amid the general rustle and talk, Thea cast her eye over this document. It was clear that Mrs Pankhurst was more preoccupied with the impact of the crisis on the WSPU than with the predicament of the nation as a whole. Shrewd leader and egocentric that she was, she had made use of a God-given opportunity for placing her organization in the spotlight.

'. . . *We believe that under the joint rule of enfranchised women and men, the nations of the world will, owing to women's influence and authority, find a way of reconciling the claims of peace and honour and of regulating international relations without bloodshed. We nonetheless believe also that, matters having come to the present pass, it was inevitable that Great Britain should take part in the war, and with that patriotism which has nerved women to endure torture in prison cells for the national good, we ardently desire that our Country shall be victorious—this because we hold that the existence of small nationalities is at stake, and that the status of France and Great Britain is involved.'*

Something about the tone of the letter disturbed Thea: it was too strident. But she kept her views to herself.

It appeared that the assembled women were present for a variety of reasons, ranging from a need for intelligent company to a desire for status and a genuine concern in women's suffrage. Esme, a handsome, aristocratic older woman, appeared to be the elder statesman of the group, loved and respected, and Thea could see why. She had been involved with the campaign since its inception, in spite of the fact that she obviously had much to lose by her association with it. Her voice was quiet, her smile warm, and her grey eyes deep-set and heavily shadowed, as though the flesh had been worn from her face by suffering and experience. Around her mouth were some small whitish marks, scar-tissue from grazes inflicted by forcible feeding. She did not talk much, but listened attentively, always stroking the back of one hand with the fingers of the other. When she caught Thea's eye, she smiled.

Andrea supported Mrs Pankhurst's letter by speaking well and fluently of the need for the WSPU to aid recruitment and for every woman to play her part in the war effort. Then it was Louis's turn. He had now been adopted for a safe Liberal seat in Hertfordshire. It appeared that Maurice's predictions about his future were coming true; he was on the way up. He spoke well and with touches of humour which would have been welcome if they had not, Thea considered, been somehow facile. He was *too* good a speaker. His manner was sincere and yet he lacked sincerity. He affected an air of youthful idealism and yet she knew he was no idealist but an opportunist, and this just one more opportunity. His short speech was specifically designed to place himself in these women's favour, and yet she suspected that he patronized them. His last words, delivered with intense emphasis and a burning look that raked round the room, omitting no one, were the very ones that adorned a recruiting poster, to be seen on every fence and wall: 'Women of Britain—' pregnant pause; 'say *Go!*' He looked down for a moment, as if moved. His timing was excellent. 'Thank you for listening.'

Thea joined in the murmur of approval, impressed in spite of herself by his smooth professionalism.

Andrea retired to the small kitchen with a couple of the others to make tea and set out biscuits. There was a general release of tension; people turned in their seats and talked animatedly, several of the group changed places, laughed, touched their hair and clothes as though they had not liked to while the serious business of the meeting was in progress. Louis Avery went to the table in the corner and began to buckle his briefcase; he had spoken without notes.

Esme approached Thea. 'How do you do.' She held out her hand. Its grasp was warm and firm, her eyes direct and humorous. 'You are not as committed as Andrea would have us believe, I think.'

'I'm committed to the idea.'

'But some of our methods repel you.'

'They seem counterproductive.'

'Let's sit down.' Esme did so herself, and patted the seat next to her. 'I think,' she went on, 'that history will show that the end justified the means, and that the means used by the WSPU were largely instrumental in achieving that end.'

'And you speak from experience,' Thea admitted. 'Really I have no right—'

'You have every right, my dear! Every right in the world. But don't be dissuaded from joining us because you feel Andrea is pushing you, that would be uncharitable.'

'I like to make my own decisions.'

'Quite so. And we need people like you, Thea. We need people with minds of their own. Don't make your decision a reaction to Andrea, make it because you feel it the right thing to do.'

'I'll try.'

'How long have you known our area organizer?' There was something pleasantly teasing in Esme's voice.

'We were at school together.'

'Ah . . . and old rivalries die hard. I know.' She patted Thea's knee. 'Just be yourself, Thea, that's my advice.'

As Esme adjured Thea to be herself, Louis, surveying the scene from the corner of the room, reflected that Thea was nothing short of perfect, just as she was. His attentions to her, which she so clearly found annoying, were not wholly insincere. He found her admirable in every way: handsome, forthright, intelligent, and yet with an air of untarnished innocence which was most refreshing.

For some time now Andrea had been his escort, and very creditably she had filled the rôle. Her smartness and quick-witted conversation, not to mention her political awareness, had all been tremendous assets, and for that he was grateful. But he was on his way now, it was time for a change. Andrea and the WSPU, still desperate for publicity, hopelessly upstaged by war, were a little *passé*. Thea Tennant, at this crucial moment, seemed the embodiment of all that was fine in British womanhood. How delightful—not to say reward-ing—it would be to have such a woman at his side during the coming months. But flattery and social tricks were not the way to win her. She was less susceptible to those than even Andrea, they seemed actually to repel her. No, Thea Tennant must be won over by deeds. For now, he would let her go on her way.

Thea reached the gate of the hostel at nine-thirty. There was a light burning in the hall, and a few more on the first and second floors. She paused for a moment, catching her breath, for she had been hurrying and the night was quite cold. Also, she wished to compose herself, for she half felt that her activities over the past couple of hours must be plain to read from her face, that her half-truth in the book would be detected by the gimlet-eyed Miss Doherty.

As she stood, hand on the gate, she heard a step behind her, and turned sharply. She had not known there was anyone there.

A voice said: 'Thea?' A tall figure stood on the edge of the pool of light shed by the street-lamp.

'Who is that?'

'Come on, Thea.' Whoever it was, he smiled; she could hear it in his voice.

'I'm sorry,' she snapped nervously. 'Who *is* that?'

Jack Kingsley came towards her, removing his officer's cap. 'Know me now?'

'What on earth are you doing here?' She felt flustered. His presence seemed a threat and an intrusion. He had grown a moustache, it made him look older.

'I came to see you,' he said. And then, teasing her: 'Not, as you seem to think, to peer in at the young ladies' windows.'

'Of course I didn't, but I thought . . .'

'Don't worry, I leave for the Front tomorrow. I was held back to help at training camp. We catch the boat train first thing in the morning.'

'I see. Well . . .' She put her hand on the gate to show that she must go, that her time was limited. 'I have to be in soon.'

'By ten, the lady told me,' he said, and laughed at her aghast expression. 'So you have about twenty-five minutes.'

'You went in?'

'Of course. She was more than helpful, told me you were visiting a friend locally, but that you'd have to be back in an hour or so. "Rules are rules,"' he mimicked, 'and being a military man I could readily appreciate the point. So I came out here and waited.'

'How did you know I was here—I mean at the college?'

'I asked. Contrary to general expectation, I have not severed all contacts with your family. I called on your parents, they may have told you.'

'I think someone mentioned it.'

'They're civilized people, your parents. A quality I know you value. They didn't turn me away.' There was a slight but appreciable emphasis on the first word of the last sentence. Thea was glad it was dark so he couldn't see her face redden with annoyance and embarrassment.

'I can't see that we have a thing to say to each other,' she said, lifting the latch, but he caught her sleeve.

'Alternatively, we have everything to say.'

She looked down at his hand, and he removed it. 'But I don't have much time, I told you,' she said, 'and I can't ask you in.'

'I know that. And I don't have much time either.'

She was not immune to the poignancy of this last remark, though she knew it to be unintended. She closed the gate, relenting a little. 'What shall we do then? We can't stand here.'

'Shall we walk for a bit?'

'Very well.' It would certainly be better to move from here, where she felt sure curious eyes watched from behind half-drawn curtains, and that at any moment the mistress on duty might appear in the porch to investigate the voices at the gate.

They walked slowly up the hill, their strides matched. Behind them, on the Finchley Road, the lights of cars and motorbuses ebbed and flowed and the occasional clop of hooves rang in the crisp air. It would be the first frost of the autumn.

Typically, Jack zas silent. Having told her there was everything to say, he was leaving her to say it. She felt the old unease in his presence, was very conscious of his shoulder nudging hers, his feet moving in time with her own. He always seemed to know something that she did not.

To break the silence, she said: 'Maurice is a pacifist.'

'Yes.'

'Oh. You knew?'

'Everyone must have known. To say "Maurice is a pacifist" like that is a statement of the obvious. I suspect what you mean is that he has declared himself opposed to military service.'

'You can imagine the scene between him and Aubrey. Poor Maurice.'

'I don't know so much about that. At least he has the courage of real conviction to see him through, whereas poor old Aubrey, like the rest of us, has only some rather confused instincts. Now tell me, what of Dulcie?'

The abruptness of this question startled her. Here was the hallowed, sensitive ground being not merely trodden but jumped upon, with caution thrown to the winds.

'All right, I suppose. We've none of us heard from her for weeks.'

'But you saw her in Paris? How was she?'

'You're very concerned.' She could not keep the note of sarcasm out of her voice, but he was matter-of-fact.

'Of course. I feel responsible.'

'She's in a muddle, you know Dulcie. It's all fairy tales and games with her. I couldn't say how she is, and neither could she.'

'I see.' He added nothing. No comment, no apology. He seemed to be reflecting on her remarks, drawing his own conclusions.

'And did you enjoy Austria?' He sounded rather formal, distancing her. He had always been good at that.

'What a question!'

'That heart of yours—still intact, is it?'

She could not fathom him. He exasperated her. His words seemed to hide, rather than convey, what he actually wished to say.

'That,' she retorted crisply, 'is none of your business.'

'I'm sorry about poor Dulcie, though . . .' he muttered.

They reached the top of the hill and stood for a moment. A constable walked slowly round the opposite corner and began on his stately way down towards the Finchley Road, hands behind his back.

'We might as well do the same,' said Jack. They turned and began to go back down, rather more quickly. He put his hand on her arm and it made her feel stiff and awkward, but it would have seemed petulant to shake it off. When they reached the gate again he enquired: 'Tell me, do you ever wear that necklace I gave you?'

'Yes.' She almost wished she could have denied it. She wanted him to go away, to stop reminding her and upsetting her.

'Good.' He sounded genuinely pleased. 'Do go on wearing it.'

'I imagine I shall. It's a very nice necklace.' She hated herself for being so cold and dull, she could have cried for frustration.

'Think of me when you wear it,' he added. And she knew that she would, and resented it. 'I don't have all that many people to think of me, you know I need all the support I can get.'

321

'Your parents . . .'

'Ah, but parents act on instinct and we love them for it. I should value the remembrance of someone who had to make a positive effort of will to do so. And if that person were you, so much the better.'

'Very well,' she said stiffly.

'Splendid.' He replaced his cap. 'A promise is a promise, mind.' She almost reminded him that she had not actually promised, but something told her that in effect she had.

'I must go,' he said. She realized, and was chagrined that she had even thought of it, that he was not going to kiss her. A kiss had been the casual, friendly greeting between them for all the years she had known him. Not that she wanted to be kissed by him, and yet the omission marked some change in their relationship which she did not understand.

'Goodbye,' she said, suddenly panicky and distressed, tangled in a net of confused feelings that choked and restricted her.

'Goodbye, Thea. Let's hope it won't be long.'

'Yes.'

He took a step back in a military way and then turned and began briskly walking down the hill, turning his coat collar up as he went. The fat constable on the far side of the road began to cross to her, watching Jack's departing back view.

'Good luck, sir!' he called after him. And then, opening the gate for Thea: 'Brave lads, miss. A brave lad, your sweetheart.'

Jack was not the only one to receive a token of his compatriots' fine feelings while visiting Thea. Maurice, who called to see her on his way back to Cambridge, was also singled out for attention.

His arrival coincided with the end of afternoon classes, so he and Thea walked up to the Heath. For once, they had not had much to say to each other, but their silences were companionable; each respected the other's need to look inwards and ponder.

It was fresh but sunny and they sat on the side of the hill above the Vale of Health for a while—Maurice frail and donnish, his nose still rather blue from Aubrey's punch, his shirtcuffs frayed, tie askew. He looked so ill-equipped, Thea thought, to withstand life's shocks, and yet here he was positively courting them. He talked a little, and Thea

322

listened. She herself felt disinclined to talk, she let him have his say.

'I'm afraid,' he said at one point, fixing his gaze on the flame-coloured trees below, 'that Aubrey was right. I mean about having to stand and be counted.'

'Probably he was. But only about that.'

'Thank you,' he smiled wryly. 'The thing is,' he went on earnestly, 'that this war will last longer and be more dreadful than most of us imagine now. And as it gets worse people who hold my views will be called on to account for them. We shall be . . . immensely unpopular. You may find it's not easy to be my friend.'

'I dare say not. But I'd be a poor sort of friend if it was always easy for me.'

'Yes, but just the same . . .'

'Just the same.'

He turned to look at her. Three girls were sitting a few yards behind them on a bench; they talked in soft voices, intermittently.

'Come on,' said Thea. 'I'm getting cold, let's find a cup of tea.'

They rose, brushing themselves off. As they trudged up the hill Thea noticed that one of the girls on the bench was Amy Broadhurst. She waved to her, and Amy smiled back. Thea wondered if she had been listening.

She and Maurice had some tea in the village, and then he walked back with her to college. At the gate stood Amy and her friends, also apparently just returned from their walk. They almost appeared to be waiting for them.

'Hallo, Amy,' said Thea. 'It was nice up there today, wasn't it?'

'Yes. Hallo.' Amy looked curiously at Maurice. Thea thought one of the other girls stifled a smirk.

'I'm sorry, let me introduce my cousin Maurice.'

'How do you do.' Amy held out her hand. Maurice took it and gave it a small shake, closing his eyes and nodding his head like a secretary bird. Thea was surprised to see Amy place her other hand on Maurice's with unwarranted warmth. Then she and the other girls hurried in to supper, not looking at each other.

'So. At least I shan't lose *you*,' she said cheerfully, turning back to Maurice. But he was not looking at her. Instead he was staring intently at some tiny object in the cupped palm of his right hand. 'What's that?' She smiled and bent over to see.

'A present from your patriotic lady friends,' he said. His voice was thoughtful. He opened his hand flat. The object was a small white downy feather, probably from a pillow or quilt. It trembled for a second, soft as a snowflake, before the treacherous autumn wind slid between them and whipped it into instant obscurity.

CHAPTER TEN

'*Now, lads, for France, the enterprise whereof*
Shall be to you as us like glorious,
We doubt not of a fair and lucky war . . .
For who is he, whose chin is but enriched
With one appearing hair, that will not follow
These culled and choice-drawn cavaliers to France?'
William Shakespeare—*Henry V*

Aubrey lay on the floor of the cattle truck, his neck painfully cricked against the wooden slats of the side, the rest of his person pressed and pinched by the crush of bodies all round. The rhythmic joggling of the truck reminded him with regrettable regularity that he had a strong desire to pass water, and also that the whole of his right arm had gone to sleep. The rivulet of blood from the graze on his head had run as far as the corner of his left eye before drying into a brittle scab, so that whenever he blinked his eyelashes caught on it. His mouth felt gluey and stale. In the various hollows and recesses of his body perspiration had gathered and was beginning to irritate his skin beneath the coarse, unyielding stuff of his uniform. But overriding all these ignominious physical discomforts was bleak disappointment: the dour, inescapable fact of failure.

It was the afternoon of 27 August. Two weeks since the diabolical business with his cousin. Twelve days since sailing from Dover for Boulogne. Two days since being taken prisoner.

He gave vent to a gusty sigh, with just enough emphasis to convey anger as well as fatigue. He wondered sourly what the warriors of the fatherland themselves thought of this unlovely means of transport, provided as it was by a paternalistic German government for their removal to the front line of battle. Manifestly no consideration had been given to such niceties as cubic area per man. Officers and troops lay packed on the floor like moribund sardines, gasping for air.

Of course, he reflected, the Channel crossing had not been

a lot better. The men of the British Expeditionary Force, the flower of the British army, had travelled in appalling discomfort, jam-packed onto boats without even the most basic amenities. But somehow that had been different. They had been carried along on a flood-tide of optimism. The British, alone among the great powers involved, had entered the war with a 'cause'—the neutrality and independence of Belgium. Safe from invasion behind the mighty guns of the Grand Fleet they sallied forth, talking idealistically (and in many cases uncomprehendingly) of 'the war to end wars', 'the war that would make the world safe for democracy'. He himself had used these phrases, and all in good faith. Thousands of reservists, many of them rudely startled out of the cosy expectation of a civilian future, were called back to their regiments, there to don the rough khaki uniforms that were stiff as sandpaper after years in mobilization stores, heavy, putty-coloured ammunition boots, vein-restricting long puttees and newly issued webbing equipment, a bewildering maze of straps and buckles. Thus attired and in high good humour they left Dover harbour in an average of thirteen ships a day. Fifty thousand tons of shipping, loaded to the gunwales with soldiers whose response to the repeated rhetorical question 'Are we downhearted?' was a full-throated *'NO!'*

There had been a great deal of singing, Aubrey recalled. The troops had heard that the Germans had a General von Kluck and it had taken no time at all for some bright spark to compose, and thousands more to memorize, a new set of words to the tune of 'The Girl I Left Behind Me':

> 'Oh we don't give a fuck
> For old von Kluck
> And all 'is bloody army . . . !'

They had chanted with irrepressible vulgarity and at the tops of their voices. The BEF had resembled a monster stag party on a day trip to France rather than a disciplined fighting force en route for the front line. It had been the same story at Boulogne. The BEF was accorded a welcome that was rapturous even by the standards of the demonstrative French. Not to be outdone by the Argyll and Sutherland Highlanders, whose piped rendition of the Marseillaise had almost caused a riot, the men of the 1st Battalion Kentish

Light Infantry had removed their caps and treated the mesmerized crowd to a sonorous version of 'Hold Your Hand Out, You Naughty Boy'. So completely did they convince the onlookers that this ditty was some kind of patriotic hymn that women were seen to weep openly, and old men spring shakily to attention.

While a French brass band responded with a semi-ragtime 'Auld Lang Syne' the citizens of Boulogne got down in earnest to the business of fêting the new arrivals. Females from eight to eighty fought for the opportunity to kiss a cheek. Gruff sergeants were garlanded with flowers, the hauteur of high-ranking officers was softened by the persistent onslaught of female embraces. Even Aubrey's embarrassed scowl availed him nothing. Two big fat *'bonnes'* descended on him, patting his cheeks and ruffling his hair with repeated cries of *'Comme il est beau . . .!'* until he was practically crushed by the combined pressure of their mountainous starched bosoms.

One could only suffer it graciously in the knowledge that others were in the same boat as oneself. Aubrey spotted a Grenadier Guards sergeant-major, a renowned disciplinarian, the present scarlet of whose cheeks was matched only by that of the rose behind each ear. Giggling, chattering children swarmed over bemused young troopers like locusts, leaving them denuded of cap badges, buttons and shoulder numbers, while local girls made it up to them with showers of *'petits cadeaux'*—sweets, posies, brooches, anything that would convey their affection and good wishes to the English soldiers.

Reactions to this welcome varied from the nervous to the frankly exploitive. Aubrey felt for the young cavalryman who sat puce-faced on his horse, paralysed with discomfiture, as three hooting young women unwound one of his puttees and bore it away over their heads in triumph, like a banner.

But at the other end of the scale were those, notably the cockneys of whom there were a fair number in the Kents, who had already mentally supplied a footnote of 'Some 'ope!' at the end of Lord Kitchener's stern warning pasted on page one of their paybooks: *'In this new experience you may find temptations, both in wine and women. You must entirely resist both temptations, and while treating all women with perfect courtesy you should avoid any intimacy.'* The avoidance of intimacy with the gentle sex, especially when it was pressed upon them, was something the average red-blooded Londoner was not cut out for.

Someone in the corner of the truck interrupted Aubrey's reminiscences with a volley of hacking coughs. The German guard, who stood opposite the door, was puffing and sucking on a long pipe filled with (in Aubrey's estimation) a particularly noxious species of cheap tobacco. Because the guard was standing up he was not subject to quite the same paucity of oxygen as his charges. The current of air from the door, which seemed to slip over the rest of them, must breathe on his face quite pleasantly. It seemed therefore that he added insult to injury by smoking the pipe. That Aubrey missed his own pipe severely merely increased his annoyance over what he saw to be a quite gratuitous piling-on of discomfort. Clearing his throat noisily he strained his head this way and that and reached the conclusion, based on a few facts and a good deal of the most superficial judgement of appearances, that he was the most senior man in the truck. He hauled himself into a sitting position.

'Excuse me,' he said, in a tone which did anything but beg excuse.

The guard, a man of about thirty with square shoulders and a cleft chin very much like Aubrey's, removed the pipe and stared at him phlegmatically.

Aubrey lifted the arm that had not gone to sleep and waggled a stiff finger. 'Please,' he said loudly. 'The pipe.'

A few heads turned to watch. They were all weary. Where did this chap find the energy to complain over such a small matter?

The German surveyed the pipe ruminatively, turning it this way and that as he exhaled a gentle stream of smoke that wavered and broke with the rattle of the train. Finally he replaced it between even teeth, bared in a grin.

Aubrey said: 'It is extremely hot. Hot.'

'*Sehr warm*,' volunteered a linguist to the right of Aubrey.

'Thank you.' Aubrey nodded. 'The pipe is offensive. We should be most grateful if you would put it out. *Aus.*' He paused. '*Bitte*,' he added, without warmth.

The rudimentary German was not necessary, since it was plain from Aubrey's gesture and demeanour what it was he required. The guard folded his arms and returned his gaze to the door. His complacency infuriated Aubrey. He opened his mouth to remonstrate once more but quite unexpectedly the

328

guard barked: '*Halt's Maul!*' And then again, still without looking at him, shouted with unexpected venom, and such a wealth of implied threat that the few prisoners who had roused themselves to take an interest in the exchange fell back resignedly into their previous attitudes. Aubrey, though not himself intimidated, saw that he was outnumbered, and let his head drop back with a bang on the side of the truck.

The journey seemed to be lasting an unconscionably long time. A true islander, Aubrey was not accustomed to the idea of large adjacent land-locked nations. It seemed incredible that a train could carry on and on like this, through the same monotonous arable countryside for hour after interminable hour.

The clacketty-clack of the truck began to slow and slur. The guard made his way to the door, picking his way over the recumbent bodies, and peered up the line ahead. He then knocked the pipe out on the outside of the truck and stuck the stem into his breast pocket. They were coming into a station.

Uncomfortable and tedious though the journey was, it was still preferable to the breaks in monotony afforded by stops. A tightening, a perceptible winching-up of exhausted nerves, went round the prisoners. As the train drew in at the platform they could hear the shouting and yelling. Aubrey could see the rows of women, many of them shaking their fists above their heads, hurling imprecations and abuse at the prisoners. It had been the same all along the line. Huge crowds were assembled on the platforms, bridges and embankments for the purpose of cheering their own men bound for the front, and howling derision at the French and English captives going the other way.

This particular stop was going to be especially unpleasant, Aubrey noted, because a German troop train was just about to pull out from the platform opposite. The coaches were wreathed with garlands and swags of cloth in patriotic colours. The grinning soldiers, on the crest of a wave of nationalistic ardour, put out their hands, like messiahs, to touch those of the women that fluttered below, and blew kisses over the heads of the mob. As they drew out their departure was accompanied by the frenzied chanting of chauvinistic songs, and flowers and favours were cast onto the line to be crushed by the hastening wheels.

But, as the prisoners had come to expect, the hostility directed at them was in direct proportion to the adoration engendered by the troop train. The guard braced his arms against the sides of the door, legs apart, to withstand the onslaught. Its ferocity when it came was horrifying, and especially so to Aubrey because the perpetrators were women. Arms and hands reached into the truck to scratch and push and tear, fingers hooked like claws or bunched into fists, or clutching like the ravening mouths of small blood-thirsty animals. The men nearest the door edged away but there was so little room it was impossible to go far. One did not have to know much German to appreciate that the insults hurled were of the grossest kind, and that not even the most severely wounded were exempt. A young private with a broken arm had his sling ripped from shoulder to elbow so that he yelped in agony, and another with a bandaged head was repeatedly pushed with such violence that he eventually keeled over, mercifully unconscious. To give credit where it was due, the stocky guard did his utmost to keep the mob from his charges, but he would have had to be superhuman to succeed.

A lad of about eighteen behind Aubrey began to cry. Aubrey peered over at him.

'Don't do that, soldier. Pull yourself together.'

'I can't . . . I can't . . .'

'You must. You'll make them worse.' But it was hopeless, the boy continued to weep and Aubrey sat up to block the taunting women's view of him.

A nurse elbowed her way through the crowd and the guard let her through. The women outside fell back a little. Far from bringing succour and relief Aubrey knew precisely what to expect from the nurse. Her attentions to the prisoners were cursory to the point of brutality. She cast an eye over a few dressings, her hand prodding and tweaking roughly, and replaced the torn sling without care. She then circulated some water in a large metal can, which was overfull and cumbersome to hold so that many of the more debilitated prisoners had barely wetted their lips before she had passed it brusquely on to the next. For the guard there was a slab of chocolate, an apple and a large mug of strong, steaming coffee. He took the offerings without demur and asked also if he might retain the water can.

When the ordeal was over and the train began to heave ponderously out of the station the guard set out, expression-lessly, to compensate for the behaviour of his countrywomen.

The chocolate was broken up with meticulous care into small pieces, and circulated in his helmet. And in its wake he carried the water can, going down on his knees to assist every man to take a proper drink. There had been nothing for the prisoners but an occasional bowl of watery broth and a lump of black bread since the journey began. But the guard was only human too. The round completed, he went back to his place and savoured his hot coffee, accompanied by another pipe of the pungent tobacco. His mute and grim apology had been made, his soul was refreshed. Aubrey allowed himself once again to slip back into reminiscence, like a child picking a favourite scab, knowing it will not heal but still getting a ghoulish pleasure out of seeing the blood.

Mons. A nightmare. Small smoky villages, lowering slag-heaps, a flat, grimy landscape pitted with coal mines and criss-crossed with barbed wire. Digging in near Nimy Bridge, the uncertainty, everyone jumpy, the feeling almost of relief when the shells began whining and plunging in and around the Mons-Condé canal. Sudden, bubbling silence, smoke in the background. Waiting, the cold bony elbow of the Lee-Enfield hard against his cheek, the lion's tread of his secret heart on his eardrums. And then the silent explosion of shock at their first sight of the enemy, a solid wall of grey, coming over the skyline in columns of four, shoulder to shoulder, moving unhurriedly through a field of mustard, the yellow flowers parting, falling, disappearing, beneath their boots . . . and then the whistle! His own screeched order—'Rapid independent fire!' The wall of grey collapsing in wave after wave, the tangle of bodies reminding him of the writhing lugworms he had used as fish-bait as a child. He alone must have killed more than thirty men, but with less sense of rage and pain than he had felt at the moment when his fist had struck Maurice's nose. Too many dead for one's emotions to cope with. And after the stuttering roar of the rifles, silence again, as they watched the not-quite-dead turning and rolling and twitching. And then crazy shouts: 'We've done it!' 'Victory!' Men jumping up and down like monkeys, waving their arms in the air, thinking the war was won, just like that.

That hadn't lasted long. The shells had started once more, and this time in earnest, with the bite of vengeance; on and on, whine and howl, until the mustard field was a khaki sludge. He'd felt a dull, painless impact as something struck his temple a glancing blow, the smooth rivulet of blood combing through his hair and slithering over the scorched, gritty skin of his face. A man had reeled towards him, his face screaming, though Aubrey couldn't hear the words above the din, the hands reaching out to grasp his lapels like a drunk cadging for money. The man caught him, he was a dead weight, and they both began to fall backwards. Then he'd seen that the top of the man's head was sliced off, like a boiled egg with the cap removed, the soft and glistening contents revealed. Aubrey passed out with the dying man on top of him.

Remembering this, Aubrey shuddered. And as he did so his protesting bladder gave up the unequal struggle and emitted a hot, stinging flood that, with the heat and the uniform, would certainly give him a rash.

On returning to Cambridge in the autumn of 1914 Maurice felt it necessary to make contact with others of like mind to himself. It wasn't hard. The men still up were now either medics, theologians or pacifists; the rest had gone. For this reason the Fabian Society, of which Maurice was a member, consisted almost entirely of these three categories, and women. Maurice found the spirited ladies of Girton a great comfort; there was not quite the strain put on the resolve of these women, especially out here in Cambridge, that there was on that of the men, and their cheerful determination was heartening. For Maurice especially it was hard to be constantly in a minority, to have one's smallest opinion challenged and harried. He would state his case if pressed, but he intended no provocation by doing so; the last thing he wanted was to attract heated and violent argument. After years of agnosticism he found himself drawn to the Quakers, not for religious reasons but simply because their quiet, contemplative meetings represented exactly the peaceful ideal he aspired to.

There was widespread talk of conscription and when it might come; there was never the slightest doubt that come it would, and that when it did the pacifists would have to club together and organize. They sought each other out more and more, honed their opinions on each other, trying in some small way to prepare themselves for the shocks they knew lay ahead. For Maurice, the fear was crystallized by an incident that took place about a week after his return, at a time when he still dared to hope that a pacifist might not automatically be a pariah.

He and one or two friends were invited to the home of a respected don for sherry one early evening. It turned out to be a pleasant occasion, mercifully free of war talk, and he returned to his rooms soon after eight in good spirits, full of jubilant optimism that there were still enough sane people left in Cambridge to fill two hours with civilized conversation.

He walked in to find Dawson, his scout, standing in the middle of a scene of utter chaos. His rooms had been ransacked. Drawers and cupboards had been pulled open, books and papers examined and thrown aside, pockets turned inside out. Even the bed had been stripped, and the waste-paper basket emptied so that the contents were scattered all over the floor.

Dawson spread his hands helplessly. 'I'm sorry, Mr Maxwell, really I am, there wasn't a thing I could do.'

'But who . . . ?' Maurice picked up a favourite book and began smoothing the pages. He could feel the hatred still swirling in the air like poison gas, and deep in his gut a cold fear of physical violence, and a revulsion at the way his things had been treated, his private place defiled.

Dawson went to the mantelpiece. 'They left this.'

It was a postcard. Maurice took it and read the one word, written in black ink in swift, dashing capitals: 'SCUM!'

'Who was it?' he asked again.

'I couldn't say precisely who,' said Dawson cautiously, 'but I could say this. I got the impression you'd been invited out specially.'

'You mean . . . it was all arranged?' Maurice could not believe it.

''Fraid so. I'm sorry Mr Maxwell, you know that.'

'I know Dawson, and thank you.' He looked round the room. 'Well, I suppose we'd better clear up.'

They did so, Maurice going at the task with ferocious energy. Long after Dawson had gone he went on, putting every least thing in its place, remaking the bed and dusting every surface, to eradicate the stains of hate left by the strangers. When at last he lay down to sleep he felt calm, empty, fatalistic. It had begun. The daggers were drawn.

Meanwhile, daggers of a no less lethal kind were drawn at Chilverton House. It took only the briefest of encounters between Mrs Dilkes and Sophie to prove that the Almighty had not intended them for friends. Lily Dilkes arrived with her dander well and truly up, absolutely determined not to be intimidated, confident in the notion that she was doing the Tennants a favour. They were desperately short of staff, what with Primmy off to join the VADs at the end of the week, Edgar gone already, Joan left to become a munitionette, and George Rowles champing at the bit to join up as soon as he was eighteen. There was no doubt in Lily's mind that *they* needed *her* and not vice versa. Besides, the house in Grove Road had been hers—her father had given it them when they got married—and the sale of it had given her a small nest-egg which she sat on with miserly pride. She told herself, not quite truthfully, that with the aid of the nest-egg she could just up and leave if the post didn't suit her.

So it was with head held high that Lily Dilkes alighted from the train at Bromley, with Eddie in tow. She accepted a kiss from Primmy who was there to meet her and boarded the trap, driven by Meredith, which Mr Tennant had laid on for their journey to Chilverton House. She didn't much like the look of the trap, which seemed flimsy, or of the horse, which was leggy and skittish, and she would not part with her hand-case though she allowed Meredith to strap the larger box to the back. She liked even less the look of the countryside. She had never in her life seen so much green, nor so much emptiness. The furthest she had ever been from the East End was a day trip to the seaside, and that had been full of people too. Her life had been confined, cramped and crowded for too many years to allow her to accept these wastes of grass and mud, ramparts of hedge and vast tracts of trees. She glared suspiciously around her, giving vent to the occasional long sniff as evidence of her disapproval. She also boosted her failing confidence by nagging Eddie, who was slumped in rapt silence, his chin resting on the side of the trap, his staring round eyes taking in the scene. Unlike his mother he was delighted with what he saw. There seemed to be no bustle, no challenge and no threat for miles around.

Mrs Dilkes prodded him sharply with her finger. 'Sit up!' she snapped. 'Pull yourself together, do, you look a fright.'

'Don't go on at him, Ma, he's enjoying himself.'

'Hm. What does he know?'

'Nice isn't it Eddie?' asked Primmy.

He looked up at her and nodded beatifically. 'Lotsa trees,' he affirmed.

'You wait till you see the garden,' she said, 'and the stables, and everything.' She stopped abruptly, aware of her mother's sharp, perceptive gaze resting upon her. She had been talking as if the house were hers, and after this week she would not have even the most tenuous claim on it.

They arrived, the trap bowling into the drive with a flourish, carried by the impetus of the hill and the horse's recognition of the home straight. Lily clutched the side convulsively.

'Oh Lor . . . !'

'It's all right, Ma, it's safe as houses.'

Meredith deposited them at the side of the house near the back entrance, placed the Dilkeses' small trunk just inside the arch, and took the trap to the stable yard. Primmy led the way into the kitchen.

It could have been worse. There was only Mrs Duckham there and the new kitchen maid, Faith, who wouldn't say boo to a goose. After a certain amount of initial sniffing round the two women found common ground in their condemnation of the war and the inconvenience it caused, and Primmy was able to relax and drink her cup of tea while they talked. Eddie addressed himself enthusiastically to an enormous slab of Mrs Duckham's madeira sponge.

When they'd all finished, Primmy said: 'I'll take you up to your room Ma, if you're ready.'

'I'm as ready as I'll ever be. Eddie!' Her voice made Eddie jump. He had been picking up the crumbs off his plate with a spit-moistened finger. 'Stop that, and come on now.'

'By the way,' said Mrs Duckham, 'Mrs Tennant came down earlier. She said she'd see you in the library about five, when you've had time for settling in.'

'Very well.'

It was just their bad luck to be spotted by Sophie as they went up the back stairs.

'Ah, Primmy,' she said, coming across the hall. 'Is this your mother?'

Primmy's heart sank. If there was one person she would rather her mother had not met as the first representative of the Tennant household, it was Mrs Maxwell. Resignedly she came forward. Mrs Dilkes stood behind her, her heels together, her small, red, calloused hands clutching the handle of her big bag. Eddie came forward with Primmy. dwarfing all three women.

'Good afternoon, Mrs Maxwell,' said Primmy. 'Can I introduce my mother, Mrs Dilkes.'

Sophie peered round Primmy's shoulder. 'How do you do,' she murmured, and looked away again just in time not to see Lily step forward, hand stiffly outstretched. 'And . . . ?' she enquired, fixing Eddie with a wide-eyed, quizzical stare.

'My brother Eddie.' Primmy put her hand on his arm. 'Say hallo, Eddie.'

He beamed. 'Hallo.'

'Hallo, Eddie.' Sophie's voice was ingratiating. 'You're going to help us too, are you?'

''Sright.'

'That's splendid, simply splendid. I think it is a wonderful idea. I do hope you're going to like it out here in the country, Mrs Dilkes.'

'Beggars can't be choosers,' intoned Lily. She had a plentiful stock of withering clichés.

'Oh, but *you* are not a beggar, Mrs Dilkes,' cried Sophie. Primmy held her breath and prayed for deliverance. Her mother would stand for a very limited amount of this type of patronage, and she'd only been in the house half an hour. 'You and Eddie are doing absolutely the right thing,' went on Sophie relentlessly. 'And rest assured that all of us here are only too glad to help out in these troubled times. Only too glad,' she added with a pious intonation, accompanied by a facial expression of pained virtue.

Primmy took the initiative. 'If you'll excuse us, Mrs Maxwell, I have to get Ma and Eddie settled in before they see Mrs Tennant.'

'Of course, you run along!' Primmy and her mother turned to go, but Sophie caught Eddie's sleeve, feeling in the pocket of her skirt for something as she did so. 'Eddie . . . do you like chocolate?' She produced two squares wrapped in silver paper. Eddie at once put out a vast paw and took it. 'That's a good boy. I'll give you some more tomorrow. You and I could be good friends.'

'Eddie!' Mrs Dilkes's voice was sharp. 'Come along, we haven't all day.'

'Bye-bye, Eddie,' said Sophie, giving a girlish wave.

'Bye.' He went, munching on the chocolate.

Sophie bustled away to the library. Suddenly she was aware of a whole new range of possibilities, limitless in their potential.

Dulcie sat on the balcony, waiting for Peter to come back. It was the middle of September but the weather was dull and warm, very unseasonal she thought. She sipped her wine and wished it was chilled. Below her the streets had their now-familiar dead, deserted look, with many shops completely closed and others functioning in only the most desultory fashion. The cafés were severely undermanned and had lost their gay, convivial atmosphere. The great art treasures were being systematically removed from the Louvre and Luxembourg Galleries and buried in a great bomb-proof vault. Gold and other *Banque de France* securities were being loaded onto huge trucks and hauled out of Paris. The fine hotels had been turned into hospitals, and the clerical staff of the big department stores were largely employed in rolling bandages and producing supplies for these hospitals. Nothing was as she had hoped.

The first excitement of the war had been shattered by the disappointment of Mons. The valiant French and the heroic British had been unable to withstand the German advance and had been forced into inglorious retreat. The BEF had been practically wiped out. There had been awful casualties, and many prisoners taken, and now Paris was a grim, watchful place, starved of news and fearing the worst. There were no lights at night except the ghost-like beams of the huge military projectors as they ceaselessly swept the sky. The gay hubbub of the city had been stifled; the newsboys were even forbidden to shout out the name of the papers they sold. It was all dark, and hush, and gloom.

And during the day it was not a lot better. Roads into the city were jammed with a steady, shuffling procession of Belgian refugees. All the *joie de vivre* had gone, to be replaced by what Dulcie thought was a very dreary business-like rushing about, as though everyone had suddenly decided it was a crime to look cheerful. After four o'clock each afternoon people crowded to the gates and walls of the city to scan the skies for German aeroplanes. French aviators were under orders to leave the skies over Paris clear for the anti-aircraft artillery.

One afternoon about ten days ago she had joined the line of

watchers on the fifty-foot ramparts to the south-east of the city. Smart gentlemen with binoculars rubbed shoulders with anxious, aproned women, and children who played about perilously near the edge.

Fortunately, after a few initial fluctuations, the price of food had remained fairly stable, and people were passing around cold meat and cheese that they had brought with them; it was almost like a picnic. Dulcie munched on a slice of garlic sausage, stared at the comfortingly empty sky and began to enjoy herself. Even when the plane appeared, humming and whirring like a gnat above the sullen horizon, it didn't impress her much. She had seen the riflemen down in the streets, and the great anti-aircraft machine guns pointing menacingly upward: they would blow *that* little thing to kingdom come! The plane drew nearer with alarming speed, another appearing behind it and to the right. As it zoomed past Dulcie could see the peculiar insect-like head of the pilot with great flat goggle-eyes and smooth, leather-covered skull.

From their grandstand position, Dulcie and the others watched as both planes circled over the city at a disdainful few hundred feet, with the rifle fire from the furious French soldiers rattling around them. They seemed to be actually taunting the groundlings, displaying their invincibility, pouring salt into the wound inflicted by the disaster at Mons. Dulcie was frightened but also, secretly, thrilled by their daring and their arrogance. The first pilot began to circle higher, then veered off towards the Eiffel Tower, where he dropped several bombs, like a cheeky boy shying stones at a neighbour's favourite shrub. The whole of Paris vibrated and blazed with enraged rifle and machine-gun fire. One bomb struck the Tower and, as it exploded, tore off several minor struts, which spun away like matchsticks. Then he began to circle again, higher and higher to a height of two or three thousand feet, dropping more bombs as he went, until finally he sheered steeply away, whined over the heads of the crowd on the ramparts, and off into the open sky.

The air over Paris was stained by the grotesque, grey patterns left by exploding picric shells, and the smoke rising from the bombed buildings. Out over the open country an air skirmish was now in progress; once the Germans were away from the city the French planes, hitherto kept in check, were loosed like eager hounds on their scent. They far outnumbered the two Germans and the latter, recognizing that in this case at least discretion was the better part of valour, and having made their point most satisfactorily, disappeared with alacrity.

Dulcie had been rather impressed with the whole thing. Standing up here on the lofty vantage-point, oohing and aahing and munching sausage, it was almost like a circus. No dreadful damage had been done, as far as she could see, and the confrontation had been rather dashing and gentlemanly. She set off on the long walk home with a renewed sense of excitement.

But her route back to Montmartre took her past one of the bombed areas. A couple of small shops had been hit and were now a smoking wreck. The crackle of burning was punctuated by shouts and the high, hysterical note of a woman crying. On the other side of the street a fiacre had been struck by flying debris and shrapnel. The cab had collapsed on its side, and the driver lay half-beneath it. He lay still, and was apparently quite unmarked except for a swelling gout of blood at the corner of his mouth. The horse, stretched on its side, had a gaping hole in its flank through which its purplish intestines bulged, silky and convoluted. To Dulcie's horror the animal was not dead, but kept trying to lift its head from the tangle of heavy tack that weighed it down, and stare about it with wild, white-edged eyes. From the side window of the cab a hand protruded, the thumb hooked beneath the handle as though the owner had been in the act of alighting. Between the wheels sat a little girl. She was crying, her mouth gaped and her face was contorted, but such was the bedlam all around that her small screams were inaudible. She wore a pretty white blouse and black and white check skirt. A few yards away from her lay a little felt hat with a ribbon round it. Both her legs had been encased in long white socks. The lower half of one of them was now not there, nor anywhere to be seen. The leg ended in a torn, shredded stump.

Dulcie stood transfixed with horror. People were busy with the fire opposite; they paid no attention to the stricken fiacre or the little girl. What now? Was she supposed to do something? How could she? She had no idea how to help. To her relief a black limousine bearing the Red Cross flag drew up and two efficient-looking women alighted, one in nurse's uniform and the other, obviously the owner of the car, quite smartly dressed. Terrified and sickened at the thought of being pressed to assist these ladies in their errand of mercy she ran away, her heart pounding with shame and relief.

Since then she had not gone out in search of the war again. Let it continue without her; she was not cut out for a heroine. Just the same, the time hung heavy, she had a sense of waste about her own inactivity. She saw very little of Peter. His teaching post had collapsed with the outbreak of war, and she knew him to be restless and edgy. He was out for the most part of each day, though doing what she had no idea, just walking the streets probably. Spy fever was rampant, it was uncomfortable to be an alien in Paris at the moment, especially a Hungarian. On his instructions she had trailed along to the nearest registration office, set up as an auxiliary to the police station in a local library, and had stood in a queue for three hours to obtain her *'Permis de Sejour'*. When she had got into the office she and the rest of her group had had to wait for a further hour and a half while more registration blanks were brought from some far-off corner of the city. By the time her turn came she was so exhausted and irritable that it had cost her nothing to lie flagrantly. She had said with a calm voice and a steady eye that she was employed as a nanny-cum-English teacher by a French family and her papers had been given her without further demur, accompanied by cursory advice as to the advisability of leaving the city as soon as possible. The ease with which she had carried out this deception quite restored her good humour and she had boasted about it to Peter.

She refilled her glass and glanced across at the peeling church campanile opposite. Even allowing for the clock's erratic behaviour another hour had gone. Boredom buzzed and droned over her like a fat bluebottle. She wasn't even sure whether she expected Peter back. Every day when he went she subconsciously prepared herself for the fact that he might not return.

She rose, stretched, and went into the apartment to fetch a cigarette. She had taken to smoking lately, both as an antidote to boredom and as a kind of defence. While her hands and lips were occupied with a lighted cigarette it was more difficult for Peter to grasp her. Besides, she actually quite enjoyed it: it made her seem more of a woman of the world in her own eyes.

When she had lit the cigarette she took it out onto the

balcony and leaned her folded arms on the iron balustrade, staring down into the street below. The rash of posters and proclamations spawned by the war were beginning to flake and peel away; tatters of pink and yellow paper drifted along the gutters. There weren't many people about. A couple of cyclists pedalled steadily past, their faces set. In front of the shuttered church two cab-drivers were watering their horses at a stone trough. As she watched, one of them looked up and caught her eye. She smiled. He removed his hat and returned her smile with a broad, lascivious grin. Still with his eyes on her he put out a hand and touched his friend's arm, drawing his attention to Dulcie. He, too, looked up, gave a little bow and a distinct wink. They looked immensely knowing, and yet genial. She took a sip of her wine and raised her glass a little. The first man passed the reins of his horse over to his companion, saying something *sotto voce* which made them both laugh.

Galvanized by a sudden dreadful thought she turned, leaving the bottle on the balcony, and went into the apartment, closing the glass door behind her, her heart tripping and stumbling. She was elated and astonished and not a little fearful. She parted the net curtain and glimpsed the man, standing in the middle of the street, looking up expectantly. How long would he stand there? Might he try to come up? She could not remember whether or not the main door was bolted. Sometimes it yawned wide open all day.

As she stood there suspended between excitement and foreboding there was the staccato sound of someone coming rapidly up the stairs, two at a time. Convulsively she clutched the iron handle of the balcony door behind her back. Surely it couldn't be the cab-driver? She was between the devil and the deep blue sea.

'What in hell's name's the matter with you?'

It was Peter, in evident ill-humour. His mouth looked thin and tight, his eyes cold. He was like a hard black stick after the warmly blooming smiles of the drivers. The difference was sharply apparent. She recognized her disappointment, and why she was disappointed. It was a revelation that had taken only a few seconds.

He threw his case and coat down on one of the creaking chairs and stared at her, openly hostile and accusing. 'Well? You look as if you've seen a ghost.'

'Do I? No. No, I . . .'

'Oh for God's sake!' He pressed his fingers to his closed eyes and took a deep, rasping breath. 'Don't dither, don't take me so literally.' He pulled off his jacket and threw it down in an access of irritation. 'Do we have any wine?'

'Yes.'

'Well? Where is it then?'

She stood aside and made an ineffectual flapping gesture in the direction of the balcony.

'I'd like a glass if it's not too much trouble,' he said with heavy sarcasm.

'Oh, of course . . .' She turned and opened the door, stiff with anxiety. As she went out she saw the cab drivers, both back on the far side of the road, smoking and talking unconcernedly, having apparently forgotten about her. She picked up the wine bottle and her own half-empty glass and slid back in as swiftly as possible. Peter was not in the room. She drained her glass, wiped it perfunctorily on a tea towel, and refilled it.

Peter reappeared from the bedroom. He had removed his collar and undone the top two buttons of his shirt. He took the glass without thanks and swallowed the contents in one go.

'I'll have another,' he said. 'I see you've been swigging the stuff in my absence.'

'Hardly swigging.'

'Don't be disingenuous, Dulcie, I wasn't born yesterday. We had two bottles yesterday, each with a different label, and this is not the one we started last night.'

It was true, she could not deny it. Recently, and for the first time in her life, Dulcie had actually wanted a drink. Not simply to alleviate boredom, nor to be sociable, for there had been no one to drink with. But for the fortifying effect it had upon her.

'What if I have had a few glasses?' she retorted huffily. 'It isn't a crime. I haven't had much fun, you know, while you've been out.'

'Fun . . . ?' He sounded incredulous. He sat down, and held his glass against his forehead. Dulcie irritated him more and more. Her childishness, which had so captivated him initially, drove him to distraction. Her perfectly genuine helplessness in practical matters was rapidly becoming a trial: she was a dead weight. And yet these very qualities were the ones that so spiced their activities in the bedroom. The faint look of real fear that flitted behind her eyes of late

342

excited him immeasurably. And, he had grudgingly to admit, she had spirit. In spite of everything—their poverty since his allowance had been cut off, the exigencies of the war, their mutual disillusionment and his treatment of her, which he would have been the first to concede was less than loving—in spite of all this there was a plucky indomitability about her. Like a frail buttercup in a patch of choking thistles she survived, her bright head high, her slim figure erect, her eyes wary but defiant. He wished she were not so infernally pretty; it was going to make what he had to say all the harder.

He glanced at her and caught her with her hand to the yellowed net curtain, peering down into the street. 'What the devil's wrong? You're so damn jumpy this afternoon.'

She snatched back her hand as if scalded, and her cheeks coloured. But as usual she defended herself by attacking him. 'I have been on my own a lot lately, or hadn't you noticed? I'm entitled to be jumpy.'

'You are entitled, *ma chère*, to nothing,' he said, with cruel precision. She turned her head aside, lips set, presenting him with her particularly fetching profile, with its rounded chin and short, straight nose, the thick lashes, darker than her hair, now cast down, throwing a butterfly shadow on her cheek. 'Who's out there anyway?' he asked suddenly, striding over to the window and pulling back the curtain.

'Nobody!' She walked quickly back into the room, as if trying to distract his attention.

'A queue of frustrated lovers surprised by my return?' He let the curtain go and turned to look at her.

'Of course not!' She laughed brightly. It was quite true, there had been no one in the street. But something in her manner provoked him. She began to wander away.

'Where are you going?'

'Nowhere. Do I ever go anywhere?'

'I wouldn't know. As you pointed out, I'm not often around to find out.'

She gave a little sigh, and went over to him. This was territory she recognized. 'Here I am.'

He encircled her with his arms, pinning her own to her sides, and planted his mouth on hers. She felt willow-thin and vibrant, but she had lost weight since coming to Paris and was getting a little bony for his taste. Her eyes were closed as he kissed her, and he saw a tear ooze from beneath her left eyelid and slide down over her temple and into her hair. It was the first and only tear he was ever to see her shed. By the time he released her there was no sign of it; she looked back at him levelly.

Without further ado he went to the bedroom and she followed. The bed was still rumpled from last night: after all this time she still had not the least idea how to keep house nor, apparently, was she willing to learn. She had no aptitude whatever for homemaking. All her efforts went into her appearance; her milieu was unimportant to her. The bed, with its air of wanton sluttishness, both annoyed and titillated him. He could picture her lying in it alone when he had gone, missing him, perhaps dreaming of him, tossing her head, rolling from side to side, her slithering legs pushing and tangling the messy bedclothes.

'Oh, I never made the bed . . .' she murmured, observing rather than apologizing. She perched on the edge of it and put up her hands to release her hair. He stood on the other side, undressing methodically. He admired, with detachment, her narrow, tapering back, her sensitive fingers feeling and fiddling for the pins, then combing through the unfurling yellow strands as they fell to her shoulders.

He finished undressing, and lay down on his side behind her. He liked watching a woman undressing for bed; there was something ritual, almost sacrificial in it. She knew that he liked it. Her hands moved to the front, out of sight, unbuttoning her blouse with little neat movements of her wrists. When she had undone the bottom button she pulled the blouse out of the waistband of her skirt and shrugged it off over her shoulders onto the bed; it was made of some silky stuff, it slid down her arms with a whisper. When it reached her wrists he caught it and twisted it, imprisoning her.

She leaned forward to counteract the pressure. Her skin was very fine, and the stippled curve of her spine stood out. She rested her forehead on her knees, her hair falling round her legs: she looked utterly submissive. He slipped the blouse off over her wrists but she left her arms lying there, the hands palm upwards and softly curled, like ferns. He got up and walked round in front of her, bending to wind his fingers in the curtain of hair that fell on either side of her knees. Grasping her thus he pulled her upright and then back onto the bed where she lay, staring up at him with wide eyes, her hands still behind her back Outside in the street a group of children screamed shrilly: *'A bas les sales Boches! Coupez les gorges!'* and one of them supplied a disgusting guttural sound to illustrate the suggestion.

Dulcie caught her breath sharply as he began to remove her skirt and remaining underclothes without ceremony. When he had done so she tucked her legs beneath her and hitched away from him up to the end of the bed where she lay curled like an ammonite.

He grabbed her and began roughly and systematically to force her limbs apart, to turn her from ammonite to starfish. She resisted mutely, her eyes staring all the time. She was strong, in spite of that transparent pale skin, with the bones showing through. Her small frame was locked in a kind of rigor from which it was surprisingly hard to shake it. But the more difficult it proved, the more he wanted it, and in the end he won. She simply burst apart, opened herself to him when she knew she could resist no longer. Both of them were slippery with sweat, and her arms were already colouring where he had wrenched at them. He would not let her look away: when she rolled her head to one side he gripped her jaw in his hand and forced her to face him; he would teach her to drink, and smoke, and stare out of windows . . .

And yet when he slid from her and lay across the bed, panting and hot, he was conscious of her continued composure. She said nothing; he heard only the slight rustle of her clothes as she picked them up from the floor, the click of her hairpins on the bedside table. Then he saw her legs move past the end of the bed. She put the hairpins on the dressing table, the clothes on the stool, and began to dress.

He watched, impressed once again by her toughness. Her gamine figure, even more so now that she was so thin, had none of the voluptuous secrecy of most female bodies. There were no rolling curves and dark, hidden places, no bitch-scented moist hollows and sliding mounds of flesh. But she had the frank sensuality of a small girl. She was the only woman he had come across who could walk about naked without the slightest *pudeur* or self-consciousness. She had very little body-hair and what there was was no more than a golden down like the bloom on a peach. But this naturalness, while he found it most appealing, was also unnerving; in some odd way her body seemed to say, 'Admire me, take me, but you can't own me.' He had the uneasy feeling that it would be the same—spare, trim, and debonair—no matter whose bedroom it disported itself in.

To dispel his unease he said brusquely: 'I'm going. I'll be off tomorrow.'

'Oh?' The word was devoid of expression, politely enquiring.

'It's hopeless here,' he said, pulling the counterpane over himself. 'I want to get back to Hungary while the going's good.'

'*Is* the going good?' He detected a definite note of irony in this remark and was taken aback by it. It was quite unlike Dulcie to bandy words.

'No, it's not,' he said, 'but it's clear to me I can't make a living here in Paris. I'm a danger to us both.'

'Oh! So you're leaving me for my own good?' There it was again.

'Partly.'

She tucked her blouse into her skirt with brisk, business-like movements, brushed out her hair, twisted it into a coil on top of her head and secured it with some pins. 'So,' she said, turning to face him, giving a little glance over her shoulder at her back view in the mirror. 'What am I supposed to do when you've gone? Knit socks for the troops?'

'Go home. Go back to your nice family and your domineering sister . . .'

'But I don't want to. I've finished with all that.' Peter made a face of utter cynicism. 'I *have*. I've started a new life.'

'We tried a new life. It didn't work.'

'Speak for yourself.' He couldn't believe it was Dulcie talking. 'I don't give up so easily.'

'Dulcie!' Feeling suddenly disadvantaged by his nakedness he reached over for his clothes and began to pull them on. 'Don't be a fool. You won't have me to depend on. I'm going. Tomorrow.'

'So you said.'

He tried a different tack. 'How do you think I'll feel about going if I know you're hanging about here in Paris on your own?'

She laughed, and began to button his shirt in a manner that was almost motherly. 'Now don't pretend that what I do is going to have the least effect on your actions, because we

346

both know that isn't so. Just be yourself. Go, and forget all about me.'

'I could never—'

'Of course you could.' She went over to the window and stared down into the square. He found himself wondering again whether her arm, raised to hold aside the curtain, was a signal. He padded over to her in his stockinged feet and looked down. Nobody to speak of. He put his arm round her.

'What will you do?' he asked almost gently. 'You can't even keep this place tidy, let alone earn a living. How will you pay the rent?'

'I'll think of something. But it would be nice,' she slid sweet blue eyes in his direction, 'if you could give the woman some rent before you go.'

'I'll give her what I can afford.'

'You're a dear. And in the meantime I shall write to Father and ask him for a loan.'

He was staggered. 'On what pretext?'

'I shall say I want to start a small business.'

'A lie.'

'How do you know? And that I need a bit of capital, isn't that what people do? He'll be amazed.'

'Of that I haven't the least doubt.'

He stared at her. Her wrist, where it protruded from the cuff of her blouse, was reddened, and there were two purplish blood-blisters near the corner of her mouth. Far from detracting from her prettiness they lent it a touching piquancy. She looked heroic, and for a moment he wondered if he did want to leave her. But the next second his eyes took in the untidy room, the grubby net curtains and the worn carpet, and his nostrils were assailed by the fusty smell of the air, much-used and seldom changed. No, it wasn't worth it, and there were plenty more fish in the sea. It was time to jettison pretty Dulcie Tennant. But he couldn't help being stung by her readiness to let him go.

'I'll be gone tomorrow then. I'll leave some cash with the concierge.'

'That would be kind.' She walked past him and into the living room and he sat down to put on his shoes. When he followed he was amazed to find her tidying up purposefully. He stood transfixed as she plumped cushions, threw open the balcony door, picked up newspapers and collected smeary wine glasses. Perhaps it was just a last-minute ploy

'What's all this in aid of?' he asked.

'If I'm going to be on my own, I have to get organized,' replied Dulcie, picking up the hooked rug and taking it out to hang over the balcony railing. Somewhere on the other side of the city the clatter of rifle-fire punctuated her movements. It was just turned four o'clock.

'Mm.' He thrust his hands into his pockets and leaned against the door jamb. 'Perhaps we should go somewhere tonight, what do you say? A sort of farewell thing.'

She was smoothing a chair cover, a lock of hair hanging over her brow. Her movements had the unconscious neat grace with which small practical tasks endow the doer. When she straightened up she brushed aside the lock of hair with the back of her wrist, a gesture clearly copied from some past housemaid. He had to admire her gall.

'If you like,' she said.

'I was asking if *you* would like.'

'All right, yes.'

'*Le Chat Noir* is still open, I passed it today.'

'Then I can have mussels.'

'Whatever you like, if they have it.'

That night she was at her most sparkling. Peter rekindled with ease his first desire for her. Other people in the restaurant—English and Americans, a few French sailors—stared at her admiringly; she was so pretty and vivacious she lit up the room. She got slightly tiddly, something she did less often now that she was more accustomed to drink, and her high, clear laugh rang out. Her eyes were bright and teasing, her cheeks pink.

When they got back he made love to her for the first time with regretful tenderness. Afterwards she had fallen at once into a deep, childlike sleep, her lips parted, one leg flung over him in trusting abandon. He was touched. He did not sleep well, and very early, just before dawn, he extricated himself from the leg and the warm turmoil of the bedclothes, packed his few things, and left.

When she awoke and found herself alone in the bed Dulcie felt a great sense of release, like a balloon that has bobbed taut on the string held by its owner and then is suddenly let go to soar above the housetops. This freedom might cause a little vertigo to begin with, but she would conquer that with her scheme.

She got up early, made herself some coffee and then began her schedule. First, she wrote to Ralph. She knew that mail was subject to long delays but it would reach him some time. She explained that she was safe and well, there was no cause for alarm, but that she could put to good use any small financial donation he saw fit to send her. She would repay him she said audaciously, with interest, by this time next year. She was going to set up a kind of shop, with the help of others, better qualified than herself, to help with the wartime shortages. She hoped this sounded both plausible and deserving. It could even be very loosely regarded as the truth.

Next she compiled a shopping list. She had no grasp of economics, but she did have a clear idea of the kind of things she wanted. Checking her finances and finding them sadly lacking she went down and bearded the grumpy concierge in her den. Had she received the rent from Monsieur de Laszlo and if so might she have one week's worth back for shopping she must do today? She'd be eternally grateful, it was so inconvenient . . . Something in her manner had won over the usually surly woman, and she got the money on the understanding it would be repaid as soon as possible, as the landlord would be round next week. Then she put on a jacket and boater and went shopping. The local market was a sadly depleted affair, but she enjoyed the novel experience of choosing and bargaining, and came away pretty well satisfied.

Back at Place d'Agnette she set to work to complete the smartening-up operation begun the previous afternoon. She placed some apples in a bowl, a bottle of wine on the shelf next to the stove where the glasses stood, and her nicest fringed shawl, the one she had worn the day Thea called, over the appalling wicker chair. Flowers in a cracked vase were the final touch before she turned her attention to the bedroom. Here she changed the sheets (a clean pack was placed outside the door fortnightly but she had not used them that frequently), and flounced the pillows. She removed the gloomy old painting of a field that hung over the bed, and replaced it with her flowered boater which sat quite nicely on the rusty nail and certainly looked jollier. She opened the window and looped back the net curtains to let the sunshine in. Then, on second thoughts, she unhooked the net curtains altogether and bundled them into a drawer for washing at some later date. She wished she had a gramophone but that was a refinement that would have to come later.

With the stage set she turned her attention to the leading lady. She went first to the communal bathroom, overcoming her revulsion at the ancient chipped bathtub with the great black scar along the bottom, and with its plimsoll line of greyish scum and occasional wiry hairs. She cleaned it out, washed quickly but thoroughly, and fled back to her room. Here she teased and twirled her hair into the full, fluffy style that suited her best, and put on her smartest suit. She didn't want to look common. Then, after a last look round, she went out.

She had already decided that her best setting would be a café. Many were closed but there was one near the Basilica Sacré Coeur which was well enough patronized by artists, shopkeepers and French servicemen to have remained in business. She sat down at a table on the pavement, ordered an anisette from the hard-pressed elderly *'garçon'*, and began her wait. It was not long. And despite her careful plans she felt a thrill of surprise when someone came and sat down at her table. Not just someone in need of a seat, she knew that, for he took the chair next to hers rather than the one opposite, and he leaned forward on the small metal table: she·felt it rock slightly on uneven legs as his weight pressed upon it.

It was even more of a surprise when the voice, which she had for some reason assumed would be French, turned out to be cockney.

'Can I get you another of those?'

She looked round, widening her eyes slightly. It was the look she had first tried last Christmas and had since perfected.

'Eh? Come on, I'll get you one.' The sergeant took her almost-empty glass, but she retrieved it and drained the last dregs, looking at him over the rim.

'Attagirl!' He grinned at her and then swivelled round on his chair, looking for the waiter. 'Oy! Over 'ere!' He turned back to her, still grinning, and she rewarded him with a small, self-possessed smile. He was rather· older than her scenario had allowed for, and his abrasive English-ness was a shock. She decided instinctively not to let him know she was his countrywoman. His attitude to her depended,·she sensed, on his being intrigued by a French mam'selle·

350

He ordered another anisette for her and a beer for himself. She saw that he was not bad-looking, being large and well set-up, with brown hair and moustache and hazel eyes. Perhaps it was better, after all, that it should start with an older man, there was something comforting about that. She felt absolutely no anxiety or trepidation.

'You've had about a bellyful of us lads, I'll be bound!' he declared roguishly. 'I'll be off myself tomorrow, only got the one night here, so make hay while the sun shines!'

She smiled and shook her head. *'Pardon?'* Her French vocabulary was minimal but her accent was good.

'Never mind . . .' He laughed at her genially, taking a long swig of his beer and wiping the foam from his upper lip with his sleeve. 'You only live once, that's what I say,' he declared incontrovertibly, and she nodded.

'Parly-vous English?' he asked, with aplomb.

She lifted her hand, finger and thumb close together. *'Un peu.* A . . . liddle . . . bit.' She was beginning to enjoy herself.

He patted her arm. 'That's the way. Another?'

'Merci.' This time she pushed the glass over to him, and then took a packet of cigarettes from her bag, a move that he watched with obvious admiration. When the drinks were brought she indicated that she needed a light, and when a Frenchman at the next table leant forward with a match cupped in his palm she made use of it expressionlessly, her hand resting on his. She was determined not to appear amateurish.

As they drank the sergeant relapsed into silence, though he did, on catching her eye, treat her to his enormous grin. He contented himself with downing his beer and humming to himself, drumming his fingers on the table. He was simply waiting. Either she was a better actress than she had thought, or she had not needed to act at all. The latter possibility both excited and frightened her.

She savoured the last drops of her own drink and then stood, putting her hand up to her hair and looking round unhurriedly in a way that she hoped displayed both her poise and her figure to advantage. Right on cue the sergeant rose too, placing some cash on the table.

'Can I walk you home?' he asked, lifting his eyebrows to dizzy heights to show that he was asking a question.

'Mais oui,' replied Dulcie. She sauntered leisurely up the street. He seemed to hesitate for a moment, but then he came

abreast of her and gave her his arm. It was an exhilarating moment. That so little effort could achieve so much!

At the steps of the apartment she paused. She had mentally rehearsed this moment until she had it off pat. First she scanned the area and the windows for peeping toms. The coast being clear, she went to the top of the steps, opened the door and glanced over her shoulder. For the first time she treated the sergeant to a frankly come-hither look. Gleefully he bounded up after her and the door closed behind them.

When, in later years, Dulcie looked back on her first patron (she never thought of them as customers) it was with affection and a little sorrow, for he was almost certainly dead. He had turned out to be a surprisingly gentle lover, considerate to a degree, a little overcome by his luck in finding such a lovely, classy girl. His large calloused hands had moved wonderingly over her skin, his moustache had tickled her in all manner of unexpected places and she had felt curiously safe in his warm, anonymous embrace, lifted by the ecstatic pumping of his well-muscled buttocks. She had enjoyed it, and when he was over and he lay there damp and dishevelled and spent, she had treated him to several small attentions which he had never hoped for in his wildest dreams and which in no time at all caused him to groan and exclaim 'Steady girl' until he was obliged to begin all over again.

Afterwards she fetched the wine and they both had a glass, while she sat up in bed, and he got dressed and talked.

'Used to have a stall in Berwick market, years ago, my family were all market people, but I got itchy feet so I joined the regular army. It's not a bad life in peacetime—not so bad in war either, eh?' He winked at her to show what he meant. 'But I don't know what this show'll be like, and that's a fact. They say it'll be all over for Christmas, wouldn't say no to that, I'd like to be back with the wife and kids for Christmas.'

He pulled up his braces with a snap over his khaki shirt, running his thumb up and down a couple of times. He seemed to feel no awkwardness in mentioning his wife in front of Dulcie, sitting there with no clothes on, and Dulcie liked him for it. She wished wives no ill, she was just a businesswoman.

As his clothes went back on so did a certain stiffness of manner, as if the resumption of His Majesty's uniform restored a sense of guilt. But he remained civil, and slightly paternal.

'Will this do?' He took fifty francs from his pocket and laid it on the bedside table, looking at her anxiously, clearly having no idea of the value of the foreign currency. Dulcie did not want to cheat him, but at the same time she was determined not to undervalue her services. She had surprised herself, so it was certain she had surprised him. She stretched out her hand, making a little rubbing motion with her fingers and thumb, indicating that he should give her what he had. It wasn't much, and most of the rest of it was English. She took the remaining francs and returned the rest.

'*Merci beaucoup,*' she said. '*Tu es très aimable.*' She had heard people in shops say this and was sure it would serve quite well.

He put on his cap, and pulled on his jacket. 'Cheerio then.'

She lay down, leaning on her elbow, her cheek on her hand. '*Au revoir.*'

'Oyrevor.' He opened the door and paused for a moment. 'Take care, won't you, love, there's a war on.'

She closed her eyes and opened them again in recognition of this advice. As he left, she blew him a kiss. That night she repaid the concierge, drank several glasses of wine, locked her door and went to sleep early.

CHAPTER ELEVEN

Major Jack Kingsley, officer commanding 'B' Company, the 1st Battalion Kentish Light Infantry, led his men into the communication trench at 1900 hours the night before Christmas Eve, 1914. He was followed by his second in command, Captain William Massie, and the four platoons with their respective commanders following at twenty-minute intervals.

The whole of the 1st Battalion had been in rest camp at Wieseghelm, near the Ypres salient, for a week. It was galling to have to return to the front line trenches just before the festive season, but somebody had to mind the shop, and anyway no one entertained very high hopes of Christmas this year. 'B' and 'D' Companies were to go right 'up', while 'A' and 'C' stayed back in the reserve trenches. Of the two alternatives the former was generally considered preferable. If you had to be at the front you might as well be right in there swinging, instead of hanging about in the background, suffering boredom on top of all the other hardships of trench life. You could as easily be caught by a shell or mortar in reserve as in the front line; you were just a sitting duck.

Jack not only understood perfectly the mood of his men, but shared it. They felt a weary fatalism which had been if anything deepened by a few days in rest camp, where the routine was designed to prevent any easing-up of military discipline. Too much freedom, it was firmly believed, would undermine the automatic acceptance of this discipline. So the term 'rest' meant merely not being in danger of one's life. Every day they followed the same routine. Each morning there was roll call; inspection of arms, equipment and quarters; baths, delousing and head inspection; lengthy and rigorous drill; and in the afternoon organized games, rugby and cricket for the officers, football for the men. Even the supposedly 'free' evenings were frequently taken up with divisional concerts, attendance at which was more or less obligatory. One did at least get more sleep, but in the case of the men even this benefit was heavily qualified, since the rates paid to civilians for a private's billet was a mere 21 centimes: this provided at best a hard, narrow pallet, at worst a place in the hay in some barn or loft, and both were usually shared.

Still, when they had set out from Wieseghelm five miles and one hour ago they had been relatively both refreshed and purged, with shorn heads and skin and garments free from pests. Already they were soaked, and their boots caked with mud, and it was only a matter of time before their body-heat hatched the louse eggs which had tenaciously survived both baking and brushing, and they'd all be scratching like monkeys again.

Squelch, squelch, squelch. The bottom of the trench was a morass, the surface like sump oil, thickening to something like glue a few inches down. The darkness was absolute.

'Shocking in here sir,' said Bill Massie.

'It is. Shocking.'

'We should put some of our fellows on to it.'

Jack smiled to himself in the dark, glancing over his shoulder at Massie. He was twenty-one years old, a young man possessed of unshakeable public-school sang-froid, the very epitome of the ruling-class ethic, the natural foe of sloppiness, degeneracy, and untidy mud. Even in the blackness Jack could see the smooth gleam of his cheeks and the glint of his shiny fair hair beneath his cap.

'This kind of thing is so bad for morale,' went on Massie. 'How can one expect the men to evince a proper fighting spirit when they have this to contend with?'

The question did not need an answer. Bill Massie believed that a 'proper fighting spirit' would win the war: Jack thought it tantamount to suicide. To send tired, loyal, baffled men over the top simply to maintain an 'offensive posture'— how he loathed the phrase—was to provide enemy artillery with a vast, unmissable target. The much-vaunted élan of the charge, whether by infantry or cavalry, was nothing but a cruel sham in this war, a vain, naïve anachronism paid for with carnage on an unprecedented scale.

'Christ.'

'What's that, sir?'

'Nothing.'

There was over a mile of the communication trench still to negotiate and the going was appalling. Since the middle of October, Jack had kept a masochistic record: there had been only eight dry days, and half of those had been below freezing. The area around Wieseghelm displayed all the classic properties of the Flanders countryside: it was below sea-level, with above average rainfall. You only had to dig down a few feet to strike water, and that which glooped up from the earth was instantly swelled by that which pattered down from above. Sometimes Jack felt that the war was being fought on a slippery, floating wad of mud, tenuously suspended between endless water.

As it was, this was the only trench currently in use leading to this part of the sector. The rest were flooded out, and the troops were forced to follow the rim of the trench, and risk the numerous hazards contingent upon such a course of action. There was a very real danger of drowning, either in the trench itself or in one of the shell craters that bordered it. It was unbelievably difficult to drag a man out of the slough once it had taken a grip on him. Only a few weeks ago they had been obliged to abandon a soldier from No. 3 Platoon who had stumbled into a shell-hole. They had done all they could without jeopardizing the lives of more men, but when the bobbing green slime reached his mouth and choked his cries they had given up. His horrified, bulging eyes had screamed at them and one hand had pawed at the viscous surface before he went under and the water closed over him.

The memory had haunted Jack for no more than an hour In that time they had passed another twenty-odd (visible) corpses in various stages of disintegration; the soldier from No. 3 Platoon simply took his place in their ranks. He was lucky in a way. The seventy-seven pounds of equipment, the greatcoat leaden with liquid mud, the ten-pound pair of boots that had pulled him down had now been exchanged for a regulation harp, standard issue. The steady hiss of the rain was punctuated by the suck and squelch of the men's boots and the occasional pithily worded complaint.

There was a slither and a loud splash a little way back, and Jack halted. It could mean one of two things· either part of the side of the trench had collapsed, or someone had fallen. He peered back into the gloom.

'Shall I go and take a look, sir?'

'If you would, Captain Massie.'

Massie trudged away, his legs straddled to get some purchase in the mud. The man behind him leaned against the side of the trench. Every respite was a bonus. Jack reflected that the men of 'B' Company already looked less like soldiers than mutations risen from the primeval swamp. He shifted his feet a little to prevent them sinking.

Massie returned. 'All right sir. Fellow fell asleep on his feet.'

'On the go again now, is he?'

'Yes sir.'

'And not hurt?'

'No sir, just wet.'

They moved off again. A Very flare from the German lines a mile and a half away shot into the sky and momentarily illuminated the scene, like sheet lightning, so that they felt vulnerable although they were below ground level. It exposed the oily, heterogeneous nature of the liquid through which they waded.

At shortly after 2100 hours—it had taken a full hour to walk the last half mile—'B' Company waded into the front line trench and began to distribute themselves along the length of the traverses and firebays, while the 3rd Lancasters moved out. There was little exchange between the two. The men leaving were exhausted, soaked, punch-drunk. It was someone else's turn to suffer.

Jack and Bill Massie set up Company HQ in a large dugout in the support trench. There were about half a dozen such dug-outs in the area allotted to one company. Company HQ and the MO's quarters were top priority, another two were for the use of officers, the last two for men. This one, Jack reflected, was fairly typical, and rather better than some. Three-quarters of an inch of sagging candle on a saucer revealed a small room, not much bigger than the average larder in a country house, equipped with a small table and folding chair. A shelf had been scraped out of one side, and shored up with planks, and here he laid his coat and groundsheet for bedding. His batman, Harman, was addressing himself to a brazier in one corner.

'Sodding beggar's gone out,' he observed truthfully.

'They left plenty of matches.' Jack passed them over.

'Sir.' Harman reached out and took the matches, his gaze still resting intently on the recalcitrant brazier. As the commanding officer's servant Harman waged his own, private war—against cold, dirt, hunger and thirst—and he waged it with a fighting spirit of which General Smith-Dorrien himself would have been proud. He would tease, titillate and bully the brazier into life as one might a frigid woman.

Jack understood Harman's determination to kindle the damp rubble in the brazier but he wasn't over-anxious for him to succeed. The atmosphere was already rank and foetid enough without overlaying it with a pall of fumes. The only ventilation in the dug-out was the door aperture, and it was not unknown for sleeping men to die of asphyxiation in these conditions, a high price to pay for warmth.

But sleep now was out of the question. As relieving officer there was the inventory of trench stores to be checked, sentries to be posted and an endless procession of fatigues to organize. The eternal rain had been preceded in this instance by a couple of days of arctic cold, with the result that the fabric of both parapet and parados was cracked and unstable. He also noted that the existing supply of duckboards would be nowhere near enough to replace those that had sunk, or simply floated away, over the past week.

First things first. 'Captain Massie.'

'Sir?' Bill Massie's handsome, cool-eyed young face shone with alert interrogation like a well-trained gun dog. He had been the pride of the Malvern cricket team.

'Dish out the rum ration would you?' He indicated the earthenware gallon jar in one corner. 'Take some with you. I believe Captain Snathe has the other bottle.'

'Will it be quite—'

'Quite.'

'I just thought that . . . er . . .'

'It's cold, wet and late, Captain Massie, and in a few hours it will be Christmas Eve. Just dish it out, there's a good chap.'

'Yes sir.'

Jack watched as Massie was swallowed up by the hissing darkness outside. When he looked round he caught Harman staring at him with a mixture of sympathy and admiration and averted his eyes hastily.

There was a rat in the far corner by the door. Its expression, unlike Harman's, was one of dispassionate assessment. He took a step towards it and it was gone with a flip of its plump, sleek body, to observe him from some more covert position in company with its thousands of friends and relations. It was not the attentions of individual rats that disturbed Jack, loathsome though they were, but the fact of their multiplying and flourishing on the substratum of decaying humanity that lay beneath this part of Belgium. Sometimes he had a nightmare in which he saw a huge moribund body, as big as a town, being swarmed over by rats like Gulliver among the Lilliputians, pitted and eroded by their sharp feet and nibbling yellow teeth.

The rain battered down with renewed ferocity on the sheets of corrugated iron that formed the roof of the dug-out. It sounded as though a cavalry charge were taking place overhead. He opened the folding chair and sat down at the table to check over the roster for sentry duty. Certain men were exempt—stretcher bearers, expert snipers, machine gunners and other such valuable specialists—but for the rest it was three hours on, three hours off, and twice as many were needed at night. The platoon commanders would have seen to it that men were posted as soon as they entered the trench, but it was his responsibility to see that there were enough, and that the rest of the men were fully occupied. He huddled his cape around him and went out. The rain hissed and sizzled on his head and shoulders.

The smell had got no better. Jack had made a particular study of the odour of the trenches, breaking it down with almost scientific care into its component factors. This deliberate analysis helped him to be rational about it when it first slithered up his nostrils after a spell away, and the bile swamped his mouth. It was a sort of cocktail: two parts excreta and urine, not just the contents of the latrines, but of almost every available pit and puddle; two parts acrid smoke from the sullenly spluttering braziers; two parts filthy men in filthy clothes; two parts the chloride of lime liberally scattered to prevent risk of infection; and ten parts putrefaction: rotting cloth, rotting vegetation, rotting people. In warmer weather one had to add to this list the creosol sprayed to get rid of the clouds of flies.

He hauled his feet in and out of the mud. Every so often he would half-step on a pair of legs protruding from the parados where some soldier had scooped out his own 'funk-hole' rather than risk the noxious atmosphere of the dug-out. Once he stepped on one of the few remaining duckboards, laid end to end for reasons of economy, and it snapped up and delivered him a painful crack on the knees. It was dark as a bag. During rest periods Jack made an effort to remember the day-to-day discomfort of trench life, so that it would not shock him on his return, but this rarely worked.

He almost bumped into another hulking, dripping figure. It was Captain Hallett, officer commanding No. 2 Platoon. He was a stout man with a sense of humour and Jack liked him.

'That you, sir?'

'Captain Hallett. Everything in order along there?'

'As much as it'll ever be, I imagine. I've got six posted on the parapet, about a dozen shoring up the bits that have collapsed, and most of the rest on sumps. It'll do damn all good, every hole they dig will be full again in half an hour, but it's employment for idle hands.'

'Exactly so.' Jack smiled. 'Rum been round?'

'Much appreciated, sir.'

'Much needed. Get a couple to check the wire in an hour or two, would you?'

'Will do.'

'Thank you. Carry on, Captain Hallett.'

Jack squelched on up the trench. A few yards further on he passed Massie and the rum-orderly on their way back. There existed an air of resolute activity that he knew would be only short-lived. By this time tomorrow night, in spite of all their efforts, the malaise of the trenches would have begun to take a hold. By Christmas Day they would all have reverted, to a greater or lesser degree, to the level of animal existence dictated by their surroundings. Some would be dead anyway, and others screaming their heads off at the Advance Aid Post.

He paused to examine a section of the parados that was bulging ominously. The water captured in the cracks was beginning to swell the fabric, it was only a question of time till it burst. A group of soldiers were doing their best.

'We'll have to replace most of these bags, Corporal,' said Jack. 'Get some men on to filling more first thing tomorrow after stand-to. Just do what you can for now.'

'Yes sir.'

What the soldiers could do for now was to trawl the bottom of the trench for debris—any debris—that would serve plug holes and cracks. It was perfectly common to see the bloated, cushiony forms of severed limbs, and even whole cadavers, used as auxiliary ballast.

Satisfied that at least three-quarters of 'B' Company were busily engaged in some purposeful activity, Jack returned to HQ. At least on this first night there was not the pile of 'Comic Cuts'—the stack of memoranda and directives from GHQ—nor harrowing lists of dead and wounded to be made out. But by tomorrow the paper work would have swelled to its usual proportions. It was part of the policy of keeping you on your toes. Sometimes Jack hated all Staff Officers as he had never hated the enemy, and when his men said 'stuff the Staff!' he vehemently and silently seconded them.

Harman had made a superhuman effort to make the dug-out look both homely and businesslike. He had laid out Jack's and Massie's bedding on the shelf and disseminated their kit as neatly as he could. He had also coaxed a grudging glow from the brazier and brewed some tea. Massie sat on his greatcoat on the floor, his long, booted legs stretched out before him, a mug of the precious liquid clasped in both hands.

Harman held aloft the dixie-can. 'Cuppa, sir?'

'Thank you.'

The tea tasted of chloride of lime, and of the various other substances that Harman had heated in the dixie-can since the beginning of the war, but it was warm and wet. Harman watched Jack take a sip, like a fond parent watching a child sample its birthday cake.

'All right, sir?'

'Excellent, Harman. I don't know how you do it.'

'Practice, sir. Practice and bloody-mindedness.'

Jack was aware of the esteem in which he was held by Harman. The esteem was both welcome and reciprocated, and yet he was shamed by it. The more terrible the war became, and the more appalling the conditions in which it had to be fought, the more moved he was by the decency of his men. Their loyalty and tolerance and their almost phlegmatic courage were rock-solid. There were times when he frankly loathed having to call upon them, despised the authority to which they so readily deferred and the accident of birth which allowed him to order self-sacrifice as if it were routine.

'What would you be doing at home, sir?' enquired Massie.

'You mean for Christmas?' Jack sat down heavily. Massie was fond of the if-you-were-at-home game, which he found both fruitless and painful. 'I don't know, really. We're pretty quiet. We generally go to some old friends on Christmas Day.' He thought of Thea, and fell silent.

'. . . it's tradition for us to hold a dance at the house the night before Christmas Eve,' Massie was saying. 'My mother says annually that she's going to cut the numbers down, but it always seems to be half the county. You don't know the Dalkeiths, do you? Sherbrooke? Mean anything to you?'

Jack admitted that it didn't.

'Different part of Kent from you, of course,' conceded Massie. 'They have two of the most delectable daughters. If I get leave in the new year I fully intend to pay a call on Sherbrooke Hall. My golly, we've had some times at the Christmas dance. . . !' He laughed happily, shaking his head. 'Still, we can do our best, can't we? There'll be a big post tomorrow, and I fully expect a hamper.'

Bill Massie's hampers bothered Jack. Judging by past experience it would probably be from Fortnum's and would contain a number of luxurious items including Stilton cheese, chicken breasts in aspic, goose liver pâté and at least a couple of bottles of excellent wine. Massie would not be the only one to receive such a hamper; they were perfectly commonplace among the officers, and it was even known for whole cases of hock or burgundy to arrive, while the men were brewing tea with water taken from shell-holes. The men did not resent it, it was part of the scheme of things. What would they do with such a hamper? Everything they received they had to carry on their backs; you couldn't lug around pounds of sugar and dozens of pairs of socks and mittens, much as you might like to. All you could do was share your haul with a group of friends, in the expectation that they, in their turn, would share with you.

But the crass inappropriateness of the hampers bothered Jack. He had specifically written to his mother to dissuade her from over-spending, although he knew it went against the grain with her. For him there would be, with luck, some marmalade, bars of chocolate, digestive biscuits, the inevitable but welcome socks, cigarettes and a book. Any additional foodstuffs he would pass on to Harman, who had no family.

He rubbed his eyes. The inventory must be checked.

Massie stood up in a single athletic movement. 'Shall I get some men out to check the wire, sir?'

'Yes. I have already told Captain Hallett.'

'Rightie-ho.'

Jack located the inventory and began to read through it. It was difficult to equate the neat lists of words and figures with the saturated rubbish that lined the trench. You just fed the stuff into the mud, and the mud swallowed it up.

He was disturbed by a scrabbling in the corner. A large grey rat had climbed onto the shelf where Harman had placed the rations, and was addressing itself to the tin containing bully beef. It was almost certainly not the same rat that he had seen earlier, but he felt that it must be, that it was his particular and personal enemy.

He went to the doorway. 'Harman!' He kept looking over his shoulder at the foraging rat.

Harman appeared, carrying a spade with which he had been digging the officers' latrine. His low-browed face seemed concertina-ed almost to nothing between cap-muffler and greatcoat collar.

'Can I borrow that spade a second?'

'Certainly, sir.' Harman handed over the implement.

The handle was cold and gritty in Jack's hands. He advanced on the rat, which continued to nibble at the tin, one paw holding the top firmly. With swift accuracy Jack thrust the spade between rat and tin and flicked the animal onto the ground. Then before it could scuttle away he lifted the spade and brought it down on the creature's back with a force that made him grunt. Harman joined him as he peered down at the flattened corpse, neatly bisected, the eyes still bright and officious, the toes flexing.

'Don't know why you bother, sir,' said Harman. 'There's 'undreds of 'is pals just waiting to take over.'

'I'm aware of that,' replied Jack, 'but it makes me feel better.'

'Right you are, sir.'

Jack handed the spade back to Harman and picked up the two halves of the rat, examining them closely. The enemy. He then went out of the dug-out and hurled the chunks over the lip of the trench with a straight-armed lob.

Harman, sparing a proprietary glance for the rations, saw

another two bustling grey shapes in the shadows beneath the shelf, attracted by the blood.

Dawn stand-to on Christmas Eve saw a marginal improvement in the weather insofar as the rain no longer hammered down in stair-rods but was diffused into a soft, pervasive Scotch mist. It was less vicious, but just as wetting.

The officers and men of 'B' Company, standing tense and stiff on the fire step with rifles at the ready, peered over the parapet as the creeping dawn light illuminated the all-too-familiar characteristics of no man's land. The name was apt. The war had created a whole new country, set apart from space and time and from all recognizable geographical features; a country of eruptions and craters, strewn with refuse, bounded by hedges of barbed wire and peopled by the dead.

At this point the German line was about two hundred yards away. When Jack had visited the two men in the forward observation sap at midnight they had been able to hear, quite distinctly, the voices of their German counterparts a mere stone's throw away. One of them had sneezed and they had heard the automatic, whispered '*Gesundheit*' to his companion.

The various rudimentary periscopes and mirrors rigged up in the firebays showed the enemy wire with unnerving clarity. It was a widely known fact that the Fritzes did not have to move about as much as the British. This was the third sector that the 1st Kents had served in since September, and 'B' Company had been shuttled back and forth continually since their arrival at Wieseghelm four weeks ago, from rest camp to front line to reserve trench and back again. All this movement and activity had its advantages; you only had to tolerate the rigours of the front line in short bursts, and it alleviated the stultifying boredom of life in rest camp, but nonetheless it was unnerving to move into a new position under the watchful eye of a static, well-dug-in enemy.

Stand-to lasted an hour. A long, damp, chill hour in which every trickle and drip of the settling mud sounded like the prelude to an attack, and every tree stump looming through the mist beyond the wire looked like the first of an advancing horde of Boche. There was something both eerie and ludicrous about stand-to, knowing that the enemy, just over

364

there, were doing precisely the same thing, eyes straining and ears pricked, water creeping down the backs of their necks. The quiet was unearthly.

Nothing happened. At seven everyone stood down, apart from sentries, to prepare and eat breakfast. A tacit truce was observed at this time for an hour or so while the needs of the inner man were attended to by means of strong, tepid tea, army biscuit and whatever extras had been purchased in rest camp.

In the dug-out Jack ate some oatmeal biscuits and St Martin's marmalade. Massie was in high spirits.

'Too quiet I'd say, sir, wouldn't you? It makes my fingers itch. I'd like to charge over there and blast them to kingdom come right away.'

'Don't give in to the temptation, Captain Massie,' said Jack drily.

Bill Massie laughed his ringing laugh. 'Good Lord sir! Wouldn't dream of it.'

Jack watched him sceptically. He was sure Massie did dream of it. He envied him his placid, smiling sleep and those dreams of derring-do which certainly enhanced it. Beside Massie's golden, privileged confidence he felt himself to be a twisted, ignoble creature, stained by doubt and cynicism.

'Orders are to sit tight for the moment,' he said. 'Nobody wants a bloodbath on Christmas Day.'

'Heaven forbid.'

Jack glanced sharply at Massie. He had the firm impression that the younger man regarded him as a mild eccentric, to be humoured and agreed with but not necessarily to be taken too seriously.

'Rifle inspection,' he announced curtly.

The day dragged on its damp, tedious, uncomfortable way. After rifle inspection, more fatigues. The daylight had revealed the full extent of the damage to the trench walls, and a large number of men was delegated to fill sandbags and rebuild those sections that were worst affected. The remaining duckboards were disinterred from trench stores and laid down, and a party organized to go back along the communication trench soon after dark to fetch fresh supplies.

Lunch at twelve consisted of the inevitable biscuits yet again, plus bully beef. Rumour had it that there were moves afoot to advance company field kitchens closer to the front line so that hot food could be provided, but so far nothing had happened. The bully beef had all the delicate flavour of boiled webbing, and the biscuits were so infamously hard that all kinds of bizarre methods were used to render them edible. Today Harman and one or two other adventurous souls had soaked theirs in water, drained off the excess liquid and mashed the ensuing unappetizing pulp with evaporated milk. The verdict was "orrible' but most of the mess was eaten, swallowed rapidly as children take cod liver oil.

Shortly after lunch the post came up, almost twice as much as usual. Special care had to be taken at this time, because the excitement generated by the arrival of the post could cause fatal carelessness, and the German snipers were both quick and efficient, pampered crack marksmen, with no responsibilities other than to look out for the momentarily visible head or arm that might appear above the parapet. On one memorable occasion an officer who had failed to keep his head down when visiting a sentry had been hit simultaneously by two snipers, several hundred yards apart.

Apart from looking at the envelopes to ascertain the identity of the sender, most put their letters and parcels aside to savour in some darker, quieter moment. It was the supreme pleasure, the link with sanity and home; you didn't want to waste it.

For Jack there was the expected parcel from his mother, which he knew would contain letters from both parents, and two other letters. One was from Venetia Tennant, the other from Thea. He had written to the latter a few weeks ago, being very careful to keep the tone of his letter general, with plenty of news and nothing that might frighten her off. And it appeared he had succeeded. He had wanted a letter from her more than anything, and here it was, perhaps the first of many . . . He put it with the rest of his post on his makeshift bed. There was generally a quiet period in the small hours of the morning. He felt what he knew, rationally, to be a quite unjustifiable elation.

In the middle of the afternoon as he pored over a stack of paper from GHQ he received a visit from the Roman Catholic padre, David Morrish. He was a handsome, ruddy-faced man in his thirties, with a thatch of curly black hair.

'Afternoon Father.'

'Jack. How's it going?'

'Very quiet so far. Too quiet, almost.'

'Let's hope they're not planning a Christmas surprise,' said

Morrish, fishing some cigarettes out from beneath his cape and offering one to Jack.

'Thank you. Let's hope so indeed. One can't help feeling it would be doubly hard, not to say ironical, to be shot to pieces on Christmas Day.'

'No difference. No difference at all.'

'Not actually. But in effect.'

'Mm.' Morrish smiled, and drew deep on his cigarette. He was astonishingly calm, it was one of the qualities that made him universally popular. It was unlikely that many of the men of the 1st Kents had been regular church-goers in peace time, but they accepted, and even welcomed, the presence of a man of the cloth when death was a fellow-traveller. There had to be something else, some higher authority who knew something that they didn't, who knew why it was all happening. There had to be, otherwise one might as well give up. And men who, if they'd been asked a year ago, might have dismissed Catholicism as a lot of incense-swinging mumbo-jumbo, were prepared to concede that at the front the Catholic priests won hands-down over their Anglican counterparts. To be fair, the Anglicans were under orders to stay away from the fighting. But the Catholics positively sought it out, in order to be on hand to deliver extreme unction to the dying. And it was natural enough to have a greater affection and respect for the man who shared your burdens and risked his neck with you. On top of that, Morrish's manner and appearance were more those of a sportsman than a man of God.

Jack felt a great liking for him as he sat there in his streaming cape, his black hair plastered to his brow, the cigarette held in one blunt, dirty hand. It was good that there was someone like that, whose raffish brand of godliness was acceptable, even in conditions designed to breed the fiercest atheism. They were all in it together, saint and sinner, and they would never forget. He remembered something he had been forced to learn by rote at school, which ran through his mind with perfect aptness: 'For he today that sheds his blood with me shall be my brother; be he ne'er so vile, this day shall gentle his condition.' Unintentionally he spoke the last six words aloud.

Morrish laughed. '"And gentlemen in England now a-bed,"' he supplied, 'will never be able to conceive of what it was like. We're on our own, Jack.'

367

They sat for a brief second in understanding silence, Morrish studying Jack's face, smiling. He liked Jack, and he worried about him. The man's conscience was tearing his loyalties into little pieces. Outside, a man was carolling 'We three kings of orient are' in a nasal baritone.

'So what can I do for you, padre?' asked Jack.

'No, no. It's a question of what I can do for you,' replied Morrish, dropping his cigarette stub with a fizz on the damp floor, and grinding it beneath his heel. 'If it's going to be the least help to anyone—anyone—I'll come round either tonight or tomorrow.'

'Whenever it suits you.'

'Very well then. I'll bring mass to anyone who wants it.' He rose. 'I see you've had the post.'

'Yes. I hope they'll all live to enjoy it. Most of them believed they'd be home for Christmas.'

'If they believed that then there's hope for me yet.' Morrish grinned.

The barrage began only half an hour after he'd left, in the late afternoon. It was just before dusk stand-to, when they had almost decided it was to be another quiet day. It lasted for an hour and a half, and was unusually savage, as if the Germans were trying to stun them. The usual pattern for an isolated barrage would have been about half a dozen shells every ten minutes in the area occupied by one company. Now there were a dozen or more falling every minute. Every five minutes or so there would be a short pause, and then the shelling would begin once more so that nerves were constantly being winched up to another notch of tension. The noise ceased to be something heard with the ear, and became an almost palpable entity, a screaming, roaring, shuddering wave of sound that buffeted the whole body and bludgeoned the senses into shrinking submission. For the gunners it wasn't quite so bad; they at least had the satisfaction of retaliating in kind. For the ordinary rifleman it was the torture by blunt instrument that he had come to expect.

For every four howitzer shells there would be a shrapnel to ensure that the men kept their heads down. The air buzzed and whined with lethal debris and each new shell that landed in no man's land sent up a further burst of mud and fragmented refuse.

The most likely reason for a sustained barrage of such ferocity was that it heralded an infantry charge. The only other possible alternative was that it was a 'box barrage', the prelude or softener to a trench raid later that night. But this seemed less likely for the shells were falling the length of the trench, and not laying waste an area on either side of the target. But when at last, around 1800 hours, the silence lengthened, at first patchily, and then remained unbroken, nothing else happened. Those still in their positions held their breath and strained every sense to perceive the enemy onslaught that might be advancing through the dark, but there was nothing. The only sounds were those of the aftermath: sounds as familiar as they were unpleasant. The groans and screams of the wounded, the soft sighs and sobs of the almost dead, and the toneless, repetitive crying of the shell-shocked.

There was, apparently, nothing left to do but clear up. The stretcher-bearers set about the soul-destroying task of retrieving the dead and dying; soul-destroying not just by its very nature, but because it was impossible to do thoroughly. Some men had been blown right out beyond the wire, or onto the wire itself. Others had dragged themselves into the relative cover of a shell-hole only to die a lingering death by drowning in the stagnant liquid, often joining others, of both sides, who had met the same fate before them. Priority had to be given to the wounded who were accessible, who could be collected without endangering other lives. Some of them, spitting blood, or literally holding the contents of their stomachs in place with clasped hands, praised their Maker for sending them 'a blighty one'. Jack had seen men die in extreme agony on the table at the Advance Dressing Station, men upon whom war had visited the supreme treachery, and who even in their pain could only rail against the cruel fate that was to send them, instead of home, into oblivion.

Christmas morning dawned bitterly cold. All through the night the temperature had dropped and the sky cleared so that for the first time in weeks they had been able to see the stars, and the mild, benign, yellow eye of the distant moon. Perfect Christmas Eve weather in which to watch your friend die with his parcel still unopened.

A sort of brittle brown rime had formed over everything. The 1st Kents, their faces grey and blotched with fatigue, went about their tasks dressed in an extraordinary motley assortment of clothing—army issue fur jerkins, cap-mufflers, scarves, mittens, coats and groundsheets. The metamorphosis was complete; they were no longer men but trench-creatures. The sodden clothes of the night sentries had stiffened like board in the freezing temperatures. Many were beginning to experience the first symptoms of trench foot, the chronic numbness that came from standing for days in icy water in the same pair of boots and socks. The kit bags of the dead had already been rifled for extra pairs; it was something a pal would be glad to pass on to you.

All through the long, cold misery of stand-to they had to listen to a boy who was dying in voluble agony a few yards out between the parapet and the wire. His high-pitched babbling sawed the grey stillness like razor blades on glass. When he sank into brief periods of unconsciousness you could hear birds singing. Another man had crawled to within a few feet of the parapet before expiring. He lay on his back, his neck arched, the face already stiffened and frozen like a grotesque upside-down mask, glaring back at his comrades in the trench.

With the assistance of the platoon commanders and company MO, Jack made out the casualty returns and lists of the missing and dead. Having watched the wounded lurching on stretchers carried shoulder-high along the communication trench, he felt only relief on behalf of the dead. Shrapnel in particular caused injuries of appalling brutality, tearing through flesh and bone, ripping off whole sections of face and body, and leaving jagged holes through which brains, sinews and intestines could be seen with nightmare clarity. Every such wound inflicted on one of 'B' Company was a bitter reproach to Jack. He himself had been nearly four months in Flanders and had suffered no more than a septic louse-bite and a mild kidney infection. He felt that in some way his wholeness was being paid for by these men, some of whom would never walk or sing or make love again.

After stand-to someone remembered it was Christmas Day. Parcels and letters were opened, and the mail of those no longer present was collected up. After breakfast Morrish appeared, holding a dog-eared prayer book and looking haggard.

'You haven't opened your mail,' he observed. 'Though I see Captain Massie has.' He glanced meaningfully at the hamper in the corner. Something occurred to him. 'Where is he by the way?'

'In the pink. He's out there somewhere, boosting morale ' Jack's face was grim.

'He's an astonishing young man. Immune to pessimism, it seems.'

'He believes in the rightness of our cause, it's as simple as that.'

'Lucky chap.' Morrish peered out of the door. 'Many out there?'

'Quite a few. One poor little devil's been yelling all night. I think it's Private Daniels, he's got ginger hair. He's gone a bit quieter now, though.'

'Show me.'

Jack took Morrish up into the nearest firebay and on to the firestep. The boy lay very still now, and silent, but he had thrown both arms over his face. One of his hands was very white, the other was caked with rusty blood.

'There he is,' said Jack, pointing. 'It is Daniels.'

'How old?'

'Eighteen—I don't know. Too bloody young! And on Christmas Day . . .'

'I'll go over.'

'Be careful. Wait a minute.' Jack rummaged in his pocket and brought forth a handkerchief which, by virtue of relativity, might pass for white, and elicited the rifle of the sentry on the left. Fixing the bayonet he tied the handkerchief to the end and lifted it above his head, waving it from side to side. It was impossible to predict whether or not such a signal would be respected. On this occasion the snipers appeared to be in a mellow frame of mind, the Christmas spirit kindled by last night's barrage. The small flag remained intact.

Morrish scrambled over the top and began to wriggle towards Daniels, arm over arm. When he reached his side he laid the boy's arms by his side, felt his brow, and listened to his heart with a frown of concentration. He might have been in a quiet sunlit English bedroom. At last he opened the prayer book, stretched full-length in the mud next to Daniels, and began to whisper in his ear. It was a theory of his that a man too far gone to see or hear normally could absorb a voice that was physically very close with some inner ear or sixth sense, and derive some comfort from it. It was common to see Morrish prostrate next to a dying man, one arm flung over him, muttering to him like a cajoling husband to a sleeping wife.

Jack focused his eyes beyond the wire, still holding the grubby truce flag above his head. He could sense the anxiety of the sentries on either side. Suddenly Massie appeared beside him. When he spoke his voice, always bubbling with his natural optimism, contained a new note of baffled delight.

'Sir—can you see?' He placed one hand on Jack's shoulder, and pointed with the other. 'See it?'

A small answering white flag had appeared above the German trench. Jack waved his own in acknowledgement. The German flag rose higher, there was something beneath it.

'Stone me . . . !' The sentry to the left of them, the one whose bayonet Jack held, stretched out a mud-caked boot and nudged a friend who was dozing with his legs braced across the trench. ''Ere, Spider, take a look at this!'

Spider roused himself and hauled his bulk onto the firestep. He looked, gawped, rubbed his eyes with a filthy hand. 'It's never a ruddy Christmas tree . . . ?'

'It bloody is!'

'It is too sir,' affirmed Massie.

The tree wavered for a second as if testing the atmosphere and then, gaining in confidence, revealed its full height above the parapet. The men of 'B' Company, their curiosity thoroughly aroused, dragged themselves up to take a look. Heads appeared above the line opposite.

Morrish, his task completed, knelt up beside the dead private, crossing himself. He remained there for a moment, his hands resting on his knees, and then looked, with the others, at the bobbing Christmas tree.

'Someone's coming over,' he said. 'Will you look at that?'

They did. The man holding the Christmas tree scrambled right out of the trench and stood there, waving the tree above his head. He shouted something, his voice small and distant in the bitter cold.

'Fröhliche Weihnachten,' repeated Morrish. He placed his hand for a moment on Private Daniels' head, in an unmawkish gesture full of natural affection. 'Merry Christmas.'

'Come on,' said Massie. 'Why not?'

In twos and threes, at first heavy and clumsy with caution, they climbed out of the trench and headed for the gaps in the wire. Opposite, the Germans were doing the same, they took courage from the fact and began to run. Subterranean beings that they were, they felt light-headed and vertiginous to be walking upright in no man's land instead of crawling on their bellies or charging, bent double and blinded by fear. They could see a hill, a road, the remains of a farm to the south. They were after all in the Belgian countryside, and it was Christmas. They saw the invisible enemy become human —tall, fat, thin, young and old with pallid, unshaven faces, and sodden greyish clothes, and feet heavy and ungainly with clotted mud.

Jack looked along the trench. Nearly everyone had gone. Massie was already there, Hallett was scrambling out.

Morrish stood up. He was plastered in mud, above which his red face and black hair appeared more than usually bright.

'Two wrongs don't make a right, Jack,' he said gently. 'The cliché will serve. We might as well wish them a happy Christmas.'

Jack tried to speak, found he could not, and cleared his throat. Slowly he laid down the bayonet with its scrap of white material. He pointed at Private Daniels. 'They killed him—among others.'

'The dead won't mind. The wounded don't care. And the rest are there already.' He walked away towards the gap in the wire. Jack waited for a moment, staring at the body of Private Daniels which was taking on all the characteristics of a discarded object, losing identity and becoming part of its surroundings. It had already sunk a little into the surrounding slime. Then he stood up stiffly and followed. He walked out at a tangent to the rest of the men, still not ready to extend the hand of friendship to Daniels's killers. The cold bit into his face, the sky was lowering with snow. He stood aloof and a little to one side as the men of 'B' Company swapped cigarettes, attempted conversation, shared bars of chocolates, showed photographs. Massie was in the thick of it, he heard him laugh. At this distance one could hardly tell the two sides apart, the scattered groups of men had the dejected, innocent camaraderie of cattle herded together for sale or slaughter. No individuals now, and no enemy: just a crowd of cold, filthy, homesick men trying to make the best of a bad job.

He unbuttoned his breast pocket and felt for the packet of Players. His fingers were numb.

373

'One of mine?' A pleasant voice with only a slight German accent addressed him from behind. He swung round with a start. A group of three German officers stood there. By the look of their uniform he did not think they belonged to the same regiment that had emerged from the opposite trench. The shock of their sudden, unexpected arrival unnerved him.

'Thank you.' He took one of the proffered cigarettes and accepted a light from one of the others. He noticed angrily that his hands were shaking. 'God it's cold,' he said by way of explanation, turning his coat collar up and stamping his feet.

'We shall have snow,' agreed the first officer, clearly the only one with any English. The others smiled warily. 'This is a strange Christmas,' he added.

'Yes.' Jack drew long on the cigarette. The silence was awkward, but what the hell could you say? Like a prayer answered, Bill Massie disengaged himself from the group and came striding over towards them. When he was close enough, Jack performed introductions.

'My second in command, Captain Massie.'

'How do you do.' Massie grinned.

'Happy Christmas. A cigarette?'

'Ah! I've a better idea. Try one of these.' Massie produced a slim box of cigars like a conjurer taking a rabbit from a hat. 'Christmas present.' The Germans each took a cigar, and lit them with murmurs of appreciation.

Jack was aware of a great chasm of disastrous incomprehension on the edge of which they all teetered nervously. The situation was so bizarre as to be surreal. He latched onto a practical point that bothered him. 'You're not from over there—' he pointed with his cigarette in the direction of the German trench, 'are you?'

The first officer shook his head. 'No, that's right. We are with the Austrian cavalry division. We are resting our horses at that farm.'

'This really is extraordinary!' exclaimed Massie. Jack thought he would have been at home on a New Guinea headhunt. 'Where were you chaps heading for?'

Jack frowned at him. It was tantamount to asking for military information.

The man evaded the question pleasantly enough. 'This is not a war for the cavalry,' he said. 'We do very little fighting, it's chiefly reconnaissance.'

'Bad luck!' Massie was sympathetic. He walked round to fulfil his social obligations with the other two; he had a smattering of fourth-year German.

'Do you have a family?' Jack asked. It seemed suddenly terribly important to know.

'Parents, a sister and a younger brother. I'm not married, if that's what you mean. You?'

'The same. Only parents. I sometimes think if I were killed tomorrow what a lot I should have missed.'

'But if there is a wife and children there is more sadness.'

'That's true.' Jack warmed to the Austrian. He had a tactful dignity which was salvaging some sense from the situation. Abruptly he held out his hand and the other man shook it. He felt very conscious of his filthy, unkempt appearance beside the cavalry officer, who was smart and clean by the standards of the trenches. He was a little taller than Jack, a strikingly good-looking man.

'Look,' said Jack. 'The men all seem to be exchanging some kind of memento. Perhaps you'd take this.' He lifted the flap of his breastpocket and unpinned the fox's mask tie-pin that he'd had from boyhood. He didn't really know why he'd kept the thing so long, or why he still wore it, except that it was a kind of emblem of continuity. 'It may seem a little odd, but I don't have anything else. Perhaps you could show your grand-children and tell them we weren't all monsters. I'm Jack Kingsley.'

'Thank you. It's a good idea.' The Austrian took out a battered wallet and riffled through the contents. 'What could I give you . . .? I know. Not so valuable, but of some historical interest perhaps. A photograph of my family.'

Jack took the picture. It showed a group of people sitting in carefully posed attitudes on a terrace: a thin, distinguished-looking elderly man; a plump, smiling woman; a sulky adolescent girl; a small boy, and his new acquaintance, in full dress uniform.

'It's . . . er . . . not completely up to date.' The man put his hand to his face and smoothed his moustache. 'My name is on the back.'

Jack glanced at the immaculate copper-plate writing. 'Thank you.' He was touched. 'Thank you very much. I shall keep it. You never know, after the war . . .'

'They're playing football, sir!' It was Massie. Jack looked

over at the men, who were indeed lumbering and slithering about in pursuit of a ball.

'Do you play?' asked the cavalry officer.

'No.'

'We play rugby,' explained Massie. 'He's a first-class fly-half.'

'Rugby .?'

'Rugger, you know? You throw it.' Massie removed his cap, took a couple of crab-like steps sideways and slung it, two-handed, towards the Austrian who caught it and passed it back with a polite smile.

'I see—throwing, not kicking.'

'That's right.' Massie replaced his cap. They all watched the game for a moment. None of the men, on either side, was really fit enough to keep it up for long; they gave up, and wandered back to the others, some with their arms about each other's shoulders, their breath steaming.

Someone began to sing 'Silent Night' and the others took it up. Massie joined in, his voice loud and cheerful, and the two other cavalry officers followed suit, in German. *'Alles schläft, einsam wacht . .'*

Jack fingered the photograph. His throat was constricted. Something suddenly occurred to him. 'By the way—you do have another picture of your family, I hope?'

'Oh yes.' The Austrian made a dismissive gesture. 'Many others.'

'Good.' Jack waited a moment. The singing was beginning to peter out, no one could remember all the words. As they started on 'Adeste Fideles' he said: 'I'm sorry, I really can't sing.' And began to walk hurriedly back towards the wire with Massie's 'Hey, come on, sir!' ringing in his ears.

In the dug-out he read Thea's letter. It was so unusually quiet he could almost hear her voice; he half expected to find her standing next to him when he looked up. It wasn't a long letter.

'Dear Jack,' it said. *'Thank you for writing to me. I'm afraid I was rather rude at our last meeting, and I apologize. I was interested in your letter because it seemed to say everything and nothing. I now know all about your routine, but not how it feels. I suspect it must be terrible and that all of us at home are having the truth kept from us as though we were children. Please don't misunderstand me, your letter*

was fascinating, but if you have time to write again, tell me everything.

'I suppose you know that Aubrey was taken prisoner. We were worried sick for a while but two weeks ago we did have a letter from him. It was very short—I imagine they must be heavily censored, so we can't expect more—but we know now that he is in a camp in a place called Tregau, and is being reasonably well-treated. Mother is convinced we shall none of us see him again, but I feel sure he will be back when the war is over, and cursing his bad luck for having missed everything, poor Aubrey. Maurice is having a pretty horrid time, I do admire him. Sometimes I wonder where he gets his strength from, he looks as if a breeze would blow him over but perhaps he bends with it, you know what they say.

'Father had a very bright and breezy letter from Dulcie, asking for money to set herself up in some kind of business. I can't imagine it, can you? But she says she has friends who will help her and that it's to help the war effort, some kind of shop. We are all completely baffled, but it was such a cheerful letter we think she must be all right. Father, having fulminated like Jove in his wrath, sent off the money like a lamb!

'As for me, I start work in Southwark (for Father) straight after Christmas. I do look forward to it, it will be wonderful to be useful and busy after marking time at Mrs Hoskins's all through the autumn. All the same, I feel terribly restless. Everything has gone into the melting-pot since the start of the war and I suppose I want to strut on a wider stage. We shall see. I must do the job I was trained for for a few months at least, but I may take another turning after that.

'Happy Christmas, Jack. What a thing to say! I don't suppose it will be in the least happy, how could it? We shall think of you, and if you have time, think of us, too. Perhaps I should add that last Christmas seems very long ago and unimportant.

'Stay alive if you can. We want you to. Thea.'

He re-read the letter several times and then put it in his pocket to read again at night.

The following day saw a volley of enraged memoranda buzzing forth from GHQ like hornets, condemning the fraternization that had taken place on certain parts of the Western Front, and utterly forbidding the repetition of such a reprehensible exercise; it was simply not compatible with the offensive position which the Allies were trying to maintain.

Bill Massie, while obliged to admit that there was something in this, reiterated that he had found the Germans, and especially the cavalry officers, 'very decent fellows' whom one would quite happily 'invite into one's house'

Unfortunately, his flattering remarks could not be heard two hundred yards away and that afternoon he was hit by a sniper's bullet while supervising the digging of a latrine sap. He died at once. The bullet entered his head just in front of the right ear and emerged through the left cheek, wrecking the aristocratic beauty of his face, but ensuring that an habitual smile remained its most striking feature.

CHAPTER TWELVE

'. . .I should love to see my best girl,
Cuddling up again we soon shall be—
Oh! Tiddley, iddley, ighty,
Hurry me home to Blighty
Blighty is the place for me.'

Mills/Godfrey/Scott

By the time the Ministry of Munitions was set up in May 1915, Thea had been working for her father in a mainly secretarial capacity for nearly five months.

Their day together began at seven-thirty when they breakfasted rapidly and usually in total silence. They then left for the station in the Lanchester. Edgar had not been replaced, so unless conditions were very bad Thea drove in the mornings and Ralph did the evening run. He was never at his best before ten a.m. and since being forced into his company at this hour, day after day, Thea had learned that speed and silence were the best policy. She would never volunteer the first remark, nor try in any way to prise him from his shell of tacit gloom.

The first cracks in this shell would appear spontaneously on the train, when his initial perusal of the newspaper would provoke comments on the state of the war. The news was not good, and the picture it helped to paint of the nature of the conflict was not encouraging either. It appeared to have become bogged down in a harrowing and bloody stalemate. The weaponry of modern warfare was cutting a swathe through the armies of both sides, but gaining them little or no advantage. The sombre printed columns of the missing and dead grew longer each day, and the suffering of the living as described, not without occasional grim humour, by Jack in his letters was terrible.

On 10 March, for the first time in the war, the British infantry had broken the German line at Neuve Chapelle, but had hesitated, fatally, to fill the hole they had created. Instead, they waited for reinforcements. By the time they arrived, so had German reinforcements. The gap was closed

379

and the two sides went on bludgeoning each other for three days. To disguise his failure General French blamed the very lack of shells which had precluded a preliminary bombardment and enabled him to take the Germans by surprise in the first place. The flustered Goverment chose as its scapegoat drink, the curse of highly-paid munitions workers in particular, and hastily introduced legislation to restrict the opening hours of public houses.

'I tell you, Thea,' Ralph had said, his finger stabbing the air between them, 'that when we have forgotten everything else about this war these blasted licensing laws will still be with us. Fatuous!' He snorted. *'And,'* he added *con brio*, as though Thea had been about to argue with him, which she had not, 'it will simply ensure that drunkards get drunk more quickly.'

Further offensives were launched, to no effect and with appalling cost to life, at Festubert and Aubers Ridge. The Germans attacked only once, at Ypres on 22 April where they had used poison gas, thus adding a new and terrifying dimension to a war which was fast becoming a nightmare. However the news, no matter how grim, never failed to rouse Ralph from his early-morning brown study. By the time they alighted from the train the adrenalin would once again be coursing through his system.

On arrival at Southwark they would, in all but the very worst conditions, walk to the factory, because Ralph regarded it as healthier to do so, both for the body and for industrial relations. He liked to stride briskly through the slower-moving throng of his employees, through the tall iron gates, across the austere grey forecourt and up to his office, receiving and returning their greetings as he went. He believed, as Aubrey did not, in the power of proximity. If, as an employer, one were always present and always accessible, one allowed no space in which germs of discontent might flourish.

The pattern of Ralph's day, and thus of Thea's also, was this. On arrival he attended to his mail and any accumulated paperwork. He despatched both with astonishing speed, maintaining that deliberation bred vagueness and inertia. A spontaneous decision, swiftly expedited, was the hallmark of his style. After a short apprenticeship he left the drafting of letters to Thea and delegated a good deal of the less technical paperwork to her also This done, he kept whatever appointments he had, adopting the same policy of brevity and incisiveness. Thea, watching him, could only wonder at his energy. He had a knack of always appearing to be in command whether or not this were actually so. If he had an appointment at another venue he would be back by half-past one, preferring to have his midday meal either in the canteen or sent up on a tray to his office. The habit of business lunches was one he abhorred, regarding them as a waste both of time and money. Also, he had given Thea the task of overseeing the works menus with a view to maximum economy and nutritional value, and was keenly interested in the results of her efforts.

The afternoon was given over to internal business. He would first patrol the factory, 'getting the smell of things' as he put it, trying always to pick up a grievance at source in its early stages rather than allow it to fester and breed trouble.

The final hour of the day—he left at five—he gave over to internal matters, simply leaving his office open to anyone who wanted to see him no matter how apparently trivial the reason. In cases where he claimed not to be completely sure of his ground he would ask Thea to see the person first and give him her opinion. Such cases usually fell into the category of complaints about food, or the state of the washrooms, upon which he supposed, obscurely, that she was better qualified to comment.

Thea was not entirely happy with the job. Somehow, the much-vaunted independence of salaried employ seemed to have escaped her. She felt trapped, on three counts.

Firstly, though she had never expected favouritism, nothing could have prepared her for the change in her relationship with Ralph that took place the moment they passed the factory gates. For the first hour at least he was terse, cold and preoccupied. He would snap at her on the least pretext and openly criticize her slowness, and she smarted under this apparent injustice. Ralph had, after all, given her to believe that she would be an ideal assistant, and she was doing her very best, yet he was making no allowances for her lack of experience.

Secondly, she had unwillingly to admit that she found the factory depressing. She recognized in herself a certain over-fastidiousness about her environment, an involuntary shrinking from the greyness and grime of industry. Aubrey's office, which she had inherited, was a room of average size with a scrubbed wooden floor alleviated only by a small square of threadbare Persian carpet, and walls which had once been carbolic green but were now stained a topical khaki by years of tobacco smoke. One long, small-paned institutional window stared out mournfully over the smoky chimneys and sheds of the works. An oil stove created a small island of warmth in an area that was otherwise uniformly chill, even on quite fine days. Sitting there, with the stove pulled as close to her desk as she dared, her numb fingers fumbling over the typewriter keys and her cardigan huddled about her, she was tempted to see herself as a sort of female Bob Cratchit, shivering and put-upon. This in spite of the fact that Ralph's adjoining room was equally austere and draughty.

But, and this was the chief cause of her malaise, she was sure that her surroundings would seem less bleak if her job were more interesting. She felt isolated from the real business of the factory; it was because she was not a part of it that she saw it as grim and unfriendly. The envisaged torrent of female workers had not as yet materialized, there were only a few women in unskilled jobs, so the notion that she would be a sort of personnel officer had come to nothing. The times she most enjoyed were those when she went down to the factory floor either as Ralph's emissary or on one of her own largely domestic missions. She was good with people, she knew it, she could inspire confidence and liking, and yet these talents were not being properly employed. Instead she was no more than a glorified secretary, incarcerated in a dreary office at the beck and call of an unappreciative employer. Her contact with the workers was minimal, and yet there was no one of like mind whom she could look on as a friend. She was a lost soul.

As it turned out, she was wrong to suppose that Ralph was either ignorant of, or indifferent to, her discontent. The revelation came towards the end of May, a month that saw Asquith, finally defeated by criticism of his lax handling of the war effort, forming a coalition government with the Conservatives, and setting up a Ministry of Munitions, headed by Lloyd George. Both events were seen by Ralph as vindication of his gloomy prophecies in August of the previous year, and while not jubilant—the facts were depressing enough—it was satisfying to be proved so resoundingly right.

It was no secret that Ralph, anticipating the chronic

shortage of shells at the Front, had in early March begun conversion of plant near Dartford for munitions. Thea had never herself been near the place, but Ralph had made regular trips to oversee the progress of the work. It had seemed a slow and distant process, a sort of sideline of her father's, having no relevance to her own situation.

So she was not unduly excited when one evening on the train Ralph set aside his paper, an action that always presaged an important announcement and remarked: 'This new munitions outfit . . . I've been giving it some thought.'

'Oh yes?' Thea was cool. It had been a particularly trying day with Ralph pricklier than usual; she felt disinclined to draw him out, even had he needed it.

'Yes,' he went on. 'It will be controlled directly by the new ministry. Lloyd George is empowered to suspend all union practices that might bar women from working there. Since it will be mainly light stuff anyway—shell-filling, bullet-making, that kind of thing—we shall employ a lot of women.'

'Of course.' She could not keep the hateful note of sarcasm out of her voice but he did not rise to the bait. To atone, and to appear interested, she added: 'I thought you were considering turning Southwark over as well.'

'Not practicable, dear girl, nor safe. The buildings are too large, if there were to be an explosion the lot would go up. Dolton Green has a collection of long sheds, much more suitable and easier to convert. Job's almost done, as a matter of fact.'

'When will it go into production?'

'Middle of July, all being well. The Ministry johnnies will probably want to inspect it at the end of next month. I'm happy to say that as far as I know we shall be the first privately owned new factory to throw ourselves behind the war effort.'

'Good.' It was an effort, pandering to his complacent good humour, especially after his crotchety behaviour at the works.

'I'm keeping Bailey, the manager who's down there now,' he said. 'He's a good man and too old for soldiering. But I am going to need a competent female supervisor. I think it's important that the women have someone in authority who understands their special needs and problems—' he grinned hugely, 'whatever they may be.' Thea knew she was being gently goaded. 'Would you care to fulfil the role?' he asked.

As soon as the words were out she wondered why she had not seen them coming. She felt flustered at having misjudged him and this made her ungracious. 'Of course I'd like to. But I'm not even remotely qualified.'

'Very few women are, at present; this is a whole new area for them. But there are one or two training schemes. If you want the job, it's yours.'

'Thank you. Can I think about it?'

'For a few minutes.' He caught her expression and laughed out loud. 'Thea! You know you want it. You're bored to death at. Southwark.'.

'I wouldn't say that . . .' She was blushing and embarrassed.

'I would.' He leaned forward, hands on knees, staring into her face. 'I haven't been entirely fair to you, don't think I don't see that. This job you're doing for me at the moment —it's not for you. In fact it's quite taken the spring out of your step, and I blame myself. No, no, don't bother to argue about it. I have not delegated enough responsibility, I have not allowed you even to start to replace Aubrey, and the result is that you've been slowly dying of ennui and I've been foul-tempered with overwork.'

'Father, for goodness sake . . .'

'It's because you're my daughter, does that make sense?'

'I think so.'

'I've been over-protecting you!' he cried with manifest delight over such an odd conclusion. 'I must say it doesn't conform to the picture I generally have of myself, but it's the only explanation.'

She smiled, partially disarmed. How like Ralph to apologize for behaviour which in most men would have been regarded indulgently as a natural paternal instinct. 'It's been useful experience,' she said guardedly.

'Ha!' He threw back his head on the seat and stared down his nose at her. 'Invaluable, I'm sure—typing and running errands and doubtless observing what a lot of humbug I employ in the course of a working day.'

She changed the subject. 'Who will take my place?'

'I shall find a nice matronly lady who will idolize me, and who hasn't an original thought in her head.'

Thea wondered if Ralph realized how truthful he was

being. But at the same time she experienced a pang of remorse. There were, after all, good reasons for Ralph's unpredictable behaviour. He was no longer a young man but into his sixties, and though he still affected a blustering ebullience about whatever shocks life dealt out, there had been altogether too many of late and their combined force had taken its toll. He had lost the invaluable help and support of Aubrey, and added to that was the worry over Aubrey's present plight. She knew him to be anxious and guilt-stricken about Dulcie, concerned for Maurice, and in a grey depression over Venetia's gradual steady decline, which he could not understand. It was hard for him, a creature of fire and action, to be called upon for endless sympathy and patience.

The only ameliorating factor in all this was Sophie. Having been a thorn in Ralph's flesh for years her demeanour had improved dramatically of late. She was agreeable, helpful even, and her attitude towards Eddie Dilkes, whose advent she had regarded with the utmost pessimism, was nothing short of saintly. She had made it her business to teach him his various simple tasks, and he was responding well.

So relieved was Ralph by this turn of events that it never occured to him to be suspicious of it, or to equate Sophie's metamorphosis with the dispersal, and somewhat freckled fortunes, of the other members of the household. Thea did so, and was sceptical, but in Ralph's interests she kept her doubts to herself. Hers was a delicate position. *Faute de mieux*, she had stepped into the shoes of several different people in her father's life, she was the one consistent element in his fragmented world, and if he took comfort from his sister's alteration it would be churlish to cavil, especially as there was no actual proof that Sophie was not acting from the best of motives.

'We must now give our minds,' said Ralph, 'to what happens next.' He had, of course, already done so. Thea knew him better than to suppose that he had left anything to chance.

What happened next was that Thea left Southwark at the end of June to begin a four-week munitions training course. The course, run by the London Society for Women's Suffrage, was conducted at a technical college in Lambeth, not far from the Elephant and Castle, at a cost of 10/6 a week. As far as was possible in the time, it covered most aspects of

385

munitions work, from fitting and turning to shell-filing, and did so in three-hour shifts, from 9.30 to 12.30, and 1.15 to 4.15, five days a week. Thea and her co-pupils, almost all middle-class young women with little experience of physical work, came off these shifts aching in every limb, with stiff joints and sore feet. The group of them got along well enough, but they had neither the time nor the energy to spare for forming close friendships: over lunch in the canteen conversation tended to be confined to commiseration over blisters and backache, and at the end of the day they all hurried home, exhausted.

It was during this period that Andrea reappeared. Thea had not seen her since Christmas; she had been much tied up with the recruiting drive and not interested in what she saw as Thea's distinctly unadventurous job at Southwark. However, the munitions training course represented, in her view, Thea's return to the fold and she wasted no time in contacting her friend and suggesting they lunch together. There were no smart little restaurants in the area, and if there had been Thea would have felt distinctly out of place with her scraped-back hair and oil-stained fingers, so they settled for the ABC eating house on the corner opposite college. The fare was plain and the decor strictly functional, but it was a little cosier than the canteen.

'I think you made such a wise decision,' vouchsafed Andrea over the semolina with jam. 'You needed to break away.'

This was true, but Andrea was up to her old trick of appearing to have arranged everything herself. Thea bridled. 'The job at Southwark was fine, but Father needed a woman supervisor at Dolton Green.'

'And you were the obvious choice. You don't have to justify everything so frantically, Thea.' Andrea lifted a slim, pale, well-manicured hand to silence her, causing Thea to hide her own hands beneath the table. 'By the way, forgive me for being frank, but you look terrible.'

'I'm dressed for work, not socializing,' replied Thea with asperity.

Andrea was dressed in a white silk blouse and black suit. Her hat had a brim that swept down dashingly on one side and was adorned with a single long pheasant's feather.

Now her sharp features softened as she said: 'I know that, silly. I meant you look terribly tired.'

'That's because I *am* terribly tired. This is the hardest work I've ever done, and here we only do three-hour shifts. At Dolton Green it will be four hours at a time.'

'Yes, but when you're there you will be supervising. You're doing this course, presumably, simply so that you understand the job the girls will be doing.'

'I suppose so . . yes, that's true. I'm sorry if I was rude just now. It's all so new, and I'm discovering muscles I never knew I had.'

'Don't give it another thought.' The stout, tight-lipped waitress advanced to remove their dishes. 'Coffee? Two coffees, please.'

Andrea lit a cigarette as they waited for the coffee to arrive. Thea had the feeling she was planning her next conversational gambit, and she was right. But even so, when it came it was a surprise.

'Have you seen Louis lately?'

'Louis? No. Should I have?'

'Oh, I just wondered.' She glanced around the room, avoiding Thea's eye, almost as if she might spot Louis there and then. 'Because I haven't, or hardly at all.'

'I see . . . I'm sorry.'

'No need for that.' Andrea brought her wandering gaze back to the table and smiled brightly. 'He's extremely busy and so am I. We lead our own lives, I certainly don't expect to monopolize his time. I just wondered if you'd bumped into him anywhere. He likes you.'

'Does he? Heavens, I did nothing to deserve it . . .' Thea did not want to appear rude by pointing out bluntly that the feeling was not reciprocated, but at the same time she was anxious to disabuse Andrea of any notion she might have of mutual attraction. 'I wouldn't know. I certainly haven't seen him, anyway.'

'Oh well, I just thought I'd ask.' Thea noticed her friend's expression brighten perceptibly. 'I dare say he'll be at the rally.'

'Rally?'

'The Women's Right to Work Rally on the seventeenth of July, you must come. It's going to be a huge demonstration of women's solidarity, with a big march down Whitehall and a meeting in Trafalgar Square. You *will* be there?'

'I might. I'm awfully busy at the moment.'

387

'It's a Sunday.'

'I'll see.'

'Good. Honestly, Thea, I think you'll find it interesting, especially now you're one of the workers.' She gave Thea a sly grin, her humour apparently restored, and they both laughed.

But afterwards, sitting on a hard bench in a hot room and trying hard to concentrate on a cross-section of a howitzer, Thea found herself going back over the exchange. It had been, she thought, a first glimpse of a more vulnerable side to her friend, and in an area where she would least have suspected it.

Primmy sat back on her heels and surveyed the grate. Even by her exacting standards it was a good job of work. She was terribly hot and filthy, her hair stuck to her forehead and her hands were blackened, but she was pleased as punch. Not for the first time since becoming a VAD she thanked heaven for her training as a parlourmaid.

The conversion of Oak Ridge House, outside Canterbury, into a Red Cross Auxiliary Hospital, was almost complete. Beds and equipment had been installed, and the kitchen extended and brought up to date. This was the final dab of powder and paint, as it were, before it started functioning next week, but heaven knows how many girls had fallen by the wayside in the process. Acres of floor had been stained with Condy's fluid, dozens of grates black-leaded, miles of skirting board scrubbed with a small brush, windows washed, stone floors sluiced, furniture polished and carpets beaten.

It was certainly not what Flavia Atkins had in mind when she joined. As Primmy gathered up her things and stood up, she heard a faint but plaintive moan from the corridor outside. She walked briskly to the door of the six-bedded ward and looked out. Three girls were on their hands and knees polishing the patchy wood floor on either side of the worn carpet. The girl nearest the door was kneeling back, wringing her duster in long, elegant hands, tears pouring down her face.

'What's the matter?' asked Primmy, as if she didn't know.

Flavia let out a choking sob and put one hand to her face. 'I can't. I *can't*!'

'No such thing as can't,' said Primmy, squatting down

beside her and possessing herself of the duster and tin of wax polish. 'You don't want to look at the whole lot at once, just do it a little bit at a time.' She began to polish. The activity gave her immense satisfaction; the movement of her arm was like putting a well-maintained machine into use, it was no trouble, no trouble at all. Flavia sniffed and sighed.

'You're a brick, Miss Dilkes,' she said. Primmy smiled, but did not reply.

Flavia began to polish half-heartedly in her wake. 'You mustn't let the Commandant see you, she'll murder both of us.'

'No she won't.'

'I don't know how you keep cheerful. It's all so dreadful.'

'It's hard work.'

'Oh it's that all right, but it's not *nursing.*' Flavia tucked a long strand of baby-fine ash-blonde hair into her cap. 'If it was cleaners they wanted they should have said.'

'We'll get to the nursing in the end,' said Primmy, applying more polish, 'you'll see.'

'Well, I certainly hope so.'

Primmy completed another yard or so, and stood up. 'There you are. You can finish it off now.'

'Oh thank you, Miss Dilkes, what would I do without you?'

'Manage, I expect.'

As Primmy marched off down the corridor she wondered exactly how the gently reared Miss Atkins with her soft hands and delicate sensibilities would cope with the messy chores of nursing, if she couldn't face up to a simple bit of polishing. It was not in Primmy's nature to be smug, but as time went by she felt a great ground swell of confidence. At first she'd been a little taken aback by the other girls, with their smart appearance and the fine ideas which they put across so eloquently. But she knew now without a shadow of doubt that she had nothing to worry about. She could cope. She might not be half as well-educated as some of the others, but she had commonsense and energy and application, and they would see her through.

She returned her things to the broom cupboard at the head of the stairs and stood for a moment, looking round. The old place was looking very nice. Very nice and very businesslike. You had to make a place spanking clean if you were going to look after sick people in it, it stood to reason. She didn't grudge one scrap of the effort. She just hoped that Flavia Atkins, whom she liked but pitied, realized that cleaning up the human body was an infinitely more gruelling and distasteful job than wax-polishing floorboards. She had been only six when she had helped the midwife clear up after Lily had had a stillbirth, and it hadn't shocked her even then. She had mopped up blood with systematic thoroughness, and packaged up the pathetic little bundle, all neat and tidy. It was, after all, no good crying over the dead; your tears didn't do *them* any good, you'd best get on and mind the living. She'd lost count of the buckets she'd held while her father heaved up his excess beer, of the bottoms she'd wiped and the beds she'd changed. People were all the same when their stomachs played up, grand or common it all came out the same way.

'Finished, Miss Dilkes?' It was the Commandant, Miss Rowse, coming up the stairs at a brisk trot.

'I've done the grates. Do you want me to make up those beds on the top floor?'

'If you would. Have the others done in the corridor?'

'Almost.'

'Mm.' Miss Rowse strode away to see for herself and Primmy made off for the linen cupboard. Unlike the others she was not in awe of Miss Rowse. She was a good person to work for, you knew exactly where you stood with her, and she was fair. She liked a job well done, but then Primmy did too. And Miss Rowse was organized. When you came on duty at seven-thirty there was a little notebook with your name on it pinned up in the hall with all your duties for the day written down; all you had to do was get on with it.

Primmy was beginning to realize what she had previously only half suspected: that here was a field in which she could excel. She hummed as she staggered up to the top floor with a pile of clean sheets. She had never been so happy in her life.

Eddie in his turn was not so sure that he could even grasp the principle of fire-laying let alone excel at the art. He sat before the fender in Sophie's room, fumbling with kindling and newspaper. He desperately wanted to do it, for he wanted a bar of chocolate, but at the moment he was getting nowhere. His enormous hands felt like bunches of bananas, stiff and awkward; jobs inside the house always made him feel like this. He would much rather be out in the garden, but today it was pouring with rain.

Sophie had summoned Eddie to lay a fire in her room not so much because the weather merited such a thing in July, but because she wished to teach him to do it. Eddie was her pride and joy, her hope for the future. Such child-like simplicity combined with such strength! And docility too. She had never come across anything like it, especially in her brother's household where everyone was too clever by half and never so much as passed the salt without making an issue of it.

She sat in her high-backed chair watching him. 'Paper. Sticks. Coal,' she said, pointing to each item as she named it. 'First the paper. Then the sticks. Then some coal.'

'Pa-per.' Eddie furrowed his brow and licked his lips. He picked up two sheets of the *Herald.* On one of them Andrea Sutton announced 'Women Must Work!'

'That's it. Now scrumple it up.' Sophie demonstrated. He laughed, and followed suit with the other page. When all the paper was in the grate Sophie indicated the kindling. 'Now those. Stand them up over the paper.' She made a roof-shape with her hands. Eddie propped the sticks with shaky hands, breathing heavily. 'Good! Good boy. Now last of all some coal. Use the shovel.' She passed it to him. 'Just small pieces to start with, or it won't light. Little pieces.'

He found it almost impossible to marry the use of the shovel with her request for little pieces. In the end she did it for him but she seemed pleased.

'Very good.'

He sat back and gazed up at her, anticipating the chocolate.

'I know what you want, Eddie,' said Sophie, 'but I've got another treat for you today. Look!' She reached down a box of matches from the mantelpiece. 'Would you like to light the fire?' she asked.

He stared blankly at the small box. The rain spattered and dribbled on the windows. Sophie took a match out and struck it on the side of the box. She held the burning match out for him to see, like a flower, and he watched it, enchanted. When it had finally burned down almost to her fingers she tossed it into the grate and handed him the box.

'Go on, Eddie, you light the fire.'

Reverently he took the box and fumbled in the tiny drawer

for a match. At last he got hold of one, and struck it with a jerky, stabbing movement. At the second attempt it flared.

Sophie pointed to the grate. Slowly he leaned forward and applied the lighted match to the paper. 'That's the way. Now you can put the match right in.' He did so.

He had never seen anything so exciting. The dry sticks caught at once and the flames billowed and roared up the chimney, their heat unfolding like a flower to make his face glow. The things in the grate stirred and crackled and changed shape as the fire devoured them. He was mesmerised, enthralled. And he had done it! He had caused this leaping, snarling, creature of red and gold to burst into life. His creation, at his bidding!

'Eddie!' Lily Dilkes appeared in the doorway. She had knocked twice but no one had heard her. ''Scuse me, but Eddie's needed downstairs. Come on.' It was part of Lily's policy of non-subservience that she never used titles. She glared at Sophie. ''E shouldn't be up 'ere.'

'It's all right, Mrs Dilkes. I asked him to come up.'

Lily pursed her lips. 'Hm. Well, 'e's needed downstairs now.'

Sophie leaned over and placed her hand on Eddie's shoulder. He was still hypnotized by the fire. 'Run along, Eddie.'

He got up obediently, his cheeks flushed from the heat, and began to shuffle towards the door, still casting glances over his shoulder at the hearth. Sucking her teeth, Lily stepped forward and wrested from him the box of matches which he still clutched. She passed them back to Sophie.

''E shouldn't be playing with those,' she warned. ''E's not responsible.'

'Oh, he wasn't *playing* with them, Mrs Dilkes,' said Sophie, with her most ingratiating inflexion. 'He was lighting the fire with them. He's a very good boy.'

'I'm glad 'e's been no trouble,' responded Lily. But as she frogmarched her son from the room, she flung back: 'But 'e shouldn't touch matches.'

The door closed. 'What perfect nonsense,' Sophie said.

On 17 July Thea did attend the Women's Right to Work Rally in London but not, as Andrea had suggested, as one of the 'workers' or as part of one of the suffragette groups. If she came, she insisted, it would be as an independent individual.

It was a fine spectacle. It was no secret that Lloyd George had forged an effective working relationship with Mrs Pankhurst, even to the extent of giving her a £2000 grant to organize the demonstration on the largest scale possible. She had fulfilled her side of the bargain admirably. Thea managed to squeeze into the crowd about half-way up Whitehall and had a pretty good view of the proceedings, a view which improved as the afternoon wore on and the appalling weather drove many of the onlookers home. The rain teemed down mercilessly, and a gusty swirling wind played havoc with the huge banners. Many of the instruments in the brass and silver bands gave up the ghost entirely and some of the less experienced marchers appeared distinctly disheartened.

But at the head of them all was Emmeline Pankhurst. It was Thea's first sight of this redoubtable lady, and she craned and pushed to get a better look. She saw a tall, handsome woman with high cheek-bones and bright, piercing eyes which seemed to see every face in the crowd. In spite of the unseasonal weather she wore a flowered hat with a veil, and she strode through the ever-increasing puddles with utter disdain, her head held high, like a queen. Behind and above her bobbed a sodden banner bearing the legend: 'The situation is serious! Women must help to save it!' Thea, her feet rapidly becoming soaked, and her hair trailing damply over her coat collar thought that Mrs Pankhurst, like all natural leaders, probably had not the least idea of the small anxieties and inadequacies of lesser females. To her, all women carried the seeds of greatness, and she would brook no backsliding. The intelligent, energetic, ambitious Andreas of this world were her henchmen; she marshalled her forces like a general without perceiving the frail clay of which most of them were made.

In Trafalgar Square marchers and crowd assembled to hear the address by Lloyd George. Thea, fortified by a cup of tea purchased from a stall outside Charing Cross station, stood on the fringes of the crowd, the pigeons sidling and fluttering about her feet. As well as Lloyd George she thought she could see Winston Churchill, one of those who had been ejected from office in the May crisis, and, standing back in the far corner, Louis Avery. She wondered if Andrea had seen him since their last meeting.

Lloyd George's speech was full of fine, ringing phrases.

'Without women victory will tarry,' he cried, one hand held high above his head. 'And the victory which tarries means a victory whose footprints are footprints of blood!' It sent a shiver down the spine, and a long sigh of approval broke from his audience. When the meeting was over and the crowd began to disperse it was impossible not to feel stirred and invigorated. Thea forgot her cold feet and damp clothes. She was, at last, going to be part of the joint effort, what she did would count, it would have purpose and meaning.

As she was so close she decided to take a train from Charing Cross, and change if necessary. It transpired that there was a Bromley train, but not for another half-hour, and as the crush was terrible, with all the people pouring away from the rally, she bought herself a newspaper and a sandwich and found a place on a bench opposite the departures board. She had only just finished the sandwich when someone sat down beside her, a little closer than was necessary, and said: 'I saw you, Thea Tennant, and you needn't think I didn't.' It was Louis Avery. He returned her look of chilly surprise with a complacent smile.

'I didn't think about it at all,' she said. He looked dapper in a fawn mackintosh and brown felt hat. The shine on his shoes had survived even the downpour of the last few hours. He wore tan leather gloves on his small hands. They encapsulated exactly what Thea didn't like about him. His very presence seemed an insult.

He ignored her remark. 'Mind if I keep you company for a while?'

'Very well.' She did not know what she had to do to rebuff him. 'I have a train to catch soon.'

'All right, till then.' She returned to her paper; probably only near-rudeness would deter him. 'I'm in no hurry,' he added, slapping his hands down on his knees and gazing at her amiably. 'I think the rally went well, don't you?'

'Very well.'

'Pity about the weather, but you can't have everything. I think it was effective, and the old boy did his stuff. He's a fine speaker, isn't he?'

'Yes indeed.'

'He and La Pankhurst have formed an unholy alliance. What a team!' He chuckled to himself.

Thea could not go on ignoring him. 'Have you seen Andrea today?'

'No, as a matter of fact. She'd be too busy anyway.'

'She had lunch with me a couple of weeks ago. She was asking after you.'

'Was she now? Good old Andrea.'

'What does that mean?'

'It means good old Andrea, always on the scent.'

'I had the impression she wanted to see you,' said Thea coldly.

Louis twisted round on the bench, one arm along the back behind Thea's shoulders. 'Look, Thea, I don't know what you're getting at, but don't bother. There is nothing between Andrea and myself. Not any more. If she did want to see me—which I doubt—I am quite certain she had some political motive. So if you have misguidedly cast her in the role of a damsel in distress, forget it. It is just not her style.'

Thea was obliged to admit to herself that this sounded plausible. In his presence she could not recapture the feeling she had had about Andrea before. Of *course* Andrea was independent and ambitious, not a clinging vine. And if she *were* disposed to cling, she would not let anyone know about it. Thea felt a little foolish for having flown to her defence.

'So what are you doing these days?' asked Louis. 'Still working for your father?'

'Yes, but not in the same capacity. I'm doing a munitions training course at the moment.'

'Don't tell me he's going over to munitions?'

'Not entirely. Just the smaller factory at Dolton Green. I'll be going down there as a supervisor at the end of the month.'

'Well, well, well! Here we all are, exhorting the country's women to put their backs into the war effort, and you're already in there getting on with it!'

She was embarrassed. 'Not exactly. Not yet.'

'What's the name of this place?'

'I don't know yet what its exact title will be. It's at Dolton Green, near Dartford.'

'Ah yes, *I* know . . . that would be just across the river from the big Bridge Road arsenal.'

'Probably. Yes, I think so.'

'Excellent. . . .' He beamed at her. She felt only a weary dislike for his mannerisms, his flattery, his relentless interest in her. She rose.

'I must go.'

'Must you?' He glanced at the departures board. 'I suppose

so. And I must hie me hence to Hertford, I have a constituency meeting tonight. We'll meet again soon, I hope.'

'Possibly.'

'I'm sure of it. In the meantime take care of yourself and give my regards to that cousin of yours.'

'Maurice.'

'As ever is. What's he up to these days, in the New Army?'

'I'm sorry, I really must dash.' Thea began to move away. 'Nice seeing you again . . . Bye!'

At the ticket barrier she turned to see him moving away, a neat, smart figure threading a path through the crush. As she handed her ticket to the girl to be clipped she realized that she feared Louis Avery with a deep and instinctive fear.

Three weeks after her meeting with Louis Thea began work at the new Trench Warfare Filling Station, as it was now called, at Dolton Green. She herself earned four pounds a week, and the girls in her charge received thirty shillings a week, with five shillings a week for fares, and a bonus of a further five shillings for those who could fill sixty or more shells a day.

At present, with the factory still in its early stages, the male staff—mostly older skilled men or soldiers invalided home from the front—worked the gun shop, and the women were employed in the bullet-making and shell-filling sheds. The cramped cubicle which was Thea's 'office' was in the latter, separated from the factory floor by a wooden partition with a panel of frosted glass at the top. Mr Bailey, the existing works manager, paid a call on her on her first morning.

'Don't you stand any nonsense,' was his advice. 'They know who you are, they'll try on anything.'

'I'm sure we'll manage,' she replied politely. She sensed a degree of resentment in Mr Bailey. Things had been re-arranged round him more or less overnight, and new staff foisted on him. Even his standing was somewhat diminished by the arrival of this lady supervisor although Mr Tennant had assured him that she was under his jurisdiction. Mr Bailey knew that *that* was just a load of old soft soap. She was the boss's daughter and that put her in a special position.

This was one prejudice Thea was most anxious to dispel.

She knew what the work entailed, she would work *with* the girls before presuming to oversee them. It was a challenge she set herself and of which Ralph, when she told him about it, heartily approved.

The morning shift began at eight-thirty. Ralph had agreed to leave a little earlier himself in order that they might both catch the same train. She got off at Dartford, waited five minutes for a bus, and generally arrived just a couple of minutes early, a state of affairs that suited her nicely, since it was clear that none of the girls had expected her to put in an appearance till mid-morning. The factory gates were closed at eight thirty-five and late-comers were not allowed in, a state of affairs which Thea thought barbarous, but which Mr Bailey assured her had always paid off.

A special train was laid on from London Bridge to Dartford, for the benefit of the large number of girls who came down from town. The train was supposed to leave at ten to eight, but in practice the driver simply waited until it was full. Meaning to be kind, he frequently did the girls a disservice, for if they missed the bus the other end they had to walk the three-quarters of a mile or so to the factory, and stragglers would be locked out.

It wasn't until the first time Thea herself missed the bus that she discovered the trade that was being plied along the road. Her train had been held up owing to a derailment, and the bus had been just moving away as she arrived, panting, at the stop. Resignedly she set out to walk, already out of breath, and thinking how ridiculous she would look standing outside the closed gates, with her charges laughing at her on the inside. Not to mention the verbal barbs she would have to suffer at the hands of Mr Bailey who, she felt, was only waiting for her to do something wrong. She broke into a run, feeling a stitch bite into her side. Hearing footsteps behind her she turned to see a group of three other late arrivals, local girls, giggling sheepishly.

She stopped to let them catch up. 'Good morning. It looks as though we shall have to hurry.'

'Yes, miss.' More giggles.

They had gone no more than another hundred yards when a couple of open army lorries from the nearby transit camp passed them, and the second one slowed down and stopped. A clutch of helpful hands leaned out of the back.

'Come on, girls, hop up!'

Nearly hysterical now, the other three girls complied and Thea, too hot and breathless to argue, followed suit, taking her place on the end of one of the side seats surrounded by soldiers.

'This is very kind of you,' she said. This remark provoked bellows of laughter, and she smiled, wondering what she'd said that was so funny. They arrived at the factory gates with a couple of minutes to spare. The young man next to Thea held out his hand.

'That'll be twopence each,' he declared.

'What? I'm sorry . . .?'

'Twopence each. That's the fare. Isn't that right, girls?' The other three hid their faces, shoulders shaking at seeing their supervisor made to look such a fool.

But they paid up and Thea, seeing she had no choice, did so too, vowing not to be late again. As she climbed out, she asked: 'Do you do this often?'

'You bet. Regular service, innit lads?'

'I see.'

The soldier winked at her. 'Worth it though, eh?'

When she later remarked to Mr Bailey that the soldiers were running a racket between the town and the factory he quite overruled her complaint, saying that it was a racket that had saved more than one person's bacon, and that twopence wasn't much on a basic wage of a shilling a day, and would at least buy the brave lads a packet of cigarettes. Thea felt she had been churlish to mention it.

On arrival, the women had to go to the cloakroom and strip, removing all outer garments and any bits and pieces that might cause friction: watches, all jewellery and metal hairslides. The slightest spark could be the one that ignited the hundred-odd tons of TNT stored on the premises, and as a further precaution all movement between the sheds was confined to raised plank walks, to avoid contact with the stony ground. The uniform the girls donned was hideous enough, consisting of a long white oilcloth overall and species of mob-cap, both of which seemed to come in two sizes: large and enormous. But this didn't prevent some of the men from playing their favourite trick of pulling girls off the gang-planks for a kiss and a cuddle with cries of 'Give us a kiss, love, then we'll all go up together!'

The shell-shop was a long, narrow shed with small horizontal windows set high up in the walls, prison-style, so that you could only see the sky. The girls worked at benches, in groups of about half a dozen, and when each batch of shells was complete it was transported on a kind of trolley like a wine rack, out of the far end of the shed and along a covered way to the inspection room. The temperature in the room was kept low, for above a certain level the powder would melt.

The most common shell to begin with was one affectionately known as the 'toffee apple' because of a stem-like protuberance at one end. When full it weighed 56lb, but even then it was nothing compared to the aerial torpedoes, which were both heavier and up to three feet long. The only way to get these from A to B was to swing them along the floor. It seemed incredible to Thea that with all the safety regulations these huge warheads were bundled about the factory like sacks of dirty washing; and that by slips of girls and young women who would normally have been considered too feeble to lift anything heavier than a teapot.

She found that once her charges realized that she intended to work alongside them—so much for Andrea's soothing predictions—and not merely to stand by, she developed a good relationship with them. They were perfectly amenable to broad directives, and patriotic to an almost manic degree, but quite impervious to small rules, no matter how necessary. They were supposed to keep their mouths shut in the shell-shop because of the danger of powder reaching their stomachs: half a pint of milk a day per girl was provided to counteract any incidental side effects, but it was hopeless. Despite the threat of abdominal pains, severe vomiting, and even in extreme cases death; and in spite of the fact that they could see what the powder did to their clothes, they continued to talk and sing. The doctor who came down from London fortnightly to examine them, was pessimistic.

'Half of them will never have babies,' he informed Thea gloomily. 'And the rest will be sick for the rest of their lives.'

'But we've had no illness so far.' Thea realized how lame it sounded. 'And I really do my best to enforce the rules but—'

'My dear Miss Tennant,' the doctor put up a hand to silence her, 'I don't doubt that for a moment, and I certainly don't blame you. Your father has a well-run, properly equipped establishment here and I'm confident that the girls are looked after. But it's in the nature of the work, hauling around heavy weights, standing for hours at a time, and absorbing TNT through every pore in their bodies.'

'They're marvellous. They work terribly hard.'

'And they'll pay the price.' The doctor picked up his bag. 'And so may you, Miss Tennant, though I'm bound to say I find you fit at the moment.'

'Thank you.' Thea was not sure why she felt so grateful to him, as though he had the power to hand round portions of good health.

After this exchange she renewed her efforts to keep the girls quiet, but to no avail. They said 'Yes, miss' to her face and then carried on chattering and chirping like canaries the second her back was turned. And, like canaries, their skin turned yellow under the influence of the powder. Their front hair—all hair was meant to be drawn back into the cap, but fringes were invariably on show—turned orange to match and they wore these badges of honour with pride. It made them recognizable, they said; if they were late for the train the ticket collector would wave them through because he knew they were 'on war work'.

But their disobedience was always amiable, and their industry colossal. Thea couldn't help liking them. At least two-thirds of the girls in the shell-shop had come straight from domestic service. They had never in their lives had so much money, nor so much independence in which to spend it; who could blame them for being high-spirited? Their patriotism was blind and boundless. On more than one occasion when she pulled one of them up for doing things too fast, the reply came back, quick as a flash, 'But I don't mind if I die for me country, miss!' And the men in the factory who were not ex-servicemen were jeered at mercilessly.

This patriotism, allied to a very natural desire for more cash, led to high productivity. To fill sixty or more 'toffee apples' was one way of helping to put the mockers on the Boche and earn an extra five bob. But few girls were selfish. If you were a quick worker who regularly filled your sixty-odd, you went to help someone else who was slower. That way everyone got something out of it.

It wasn't until the Annie Turner affair that Thea discovered just how tough the girls could be, and it brought her up short when she was in serious danger of idealizing them.

There were at Dolton Green several 'simple simons' as they

were called—girls down from the north in search of the rich rewards of war work. Many of them were far from bright, they lacked the natural cheek and cunning of the indigenous London girls; they were innocents, teased but tolerated and not infrequently taken for a ride.

One morning one of these girls, Annie Turner, approached Thea as she made her round of the benches. Her eyes were reddened in her buttermilk face and her mouth was puffy.

'Annie! What's the matter?'

'Could I have a word with you, miss?'

'Of course. Let's go to the office.' Thea closed the door after them and leaned on the edge of the desk. She was grateful to Annie Turner for providing her with the first chance to get the weight off her feet since eight-thirty that morning. 'Now what's the problem, Annie?'

The girl stood with hunched shoulders, her clasped hands held to her face, the tears leaving grey tracks down her cheeks. 'Oh Lord—I done it this time. I've really gone and done it.'

'Done what?' Thea searched her person for a hankie, realized she was pocketless, and stood up wearily. 'Come on, you must tell me, it's what I'm here for.' She liked the sound of those words, they gave her confidence.

But the confidence receded again when Annie replied: 'Pregnant, miss. I'm pregnant. Whatever am I going to *do*?'

If anything were needed to remind Thea of the changes that had taken place in her life, this was it. She was quite simply and utterly taken aback, without the knowledge or the experience to cope with such a contingency. The enormous weight of her responsibility in the matter descended on her. This, then, was what her father had meant by the girls needing a female supervisor, this was one of the special needs with which she was supposed, by some mysterious natural means, to be able to deal.

Now, all she could think of to say was 'Oh you poor girl!' and then 'You must go home.' It was the only solution she could think of. If such a terrible thing happened to her, what would she do? She would go home, even if it were to face up to Ralph's rage and Venetia's tears, because home was safety and, ultimately, understanding. But the suggestion merely precipitated a fresh storm of sobs.

'No, miss, I can't do that! They couldn't help anyroad, they got no money, and me father'd turn me out. He never wanted me to come down here in the first place, he said this would happen . . . and he were right.'

'Did he?' Thea was nonplussed at this callous example of parental pessimism. She stared hard at Annie Turner's middle, but beneath the factory overall all but the most mountainous bulge would have been invisible. 'Umm . . .' she sought the right words, 'when is the baby due?'

'End of December, I think. Christmas. Oh miss . . .!'

'Now now, don't get yourself into a state. I wish you'd sit down.' She looked around for a chair, saw there wasn't one, and moved her own round to Annie's side of the desk. She put an arm round the girl's shoulders and pressed her gently down onto the seat. At least this difference in their relative positions made her feel in command.

'Now then. Where are you living?'

'YWCA, miss.'

Thea was relieved. 'Well *they* can't turn you out, they're a Christian association, you're all right there.'

'But not after the baby; it's for single women.'

'We'll cross that bridge when we come to it. I think I can get hold of information about hostels for girls in your position.' Thea had an idea that Andrea might be able to help on that score, and prayed she was right. 'Till then, you need money. Yes, money to buy things the baby will need, and so that you can save a bit.'

Annie stared, sniffing. 'Yes, miss.' She sounded dubious.

'I'll organize a collection,' said Thea. 'I'm sure everyone will give generously to help out a friend.' She heard her own voice, anxious and well-meaning, and it rang hollow. 'It's only common sense after all,' she added.

'But they mustn't know! You mustn't tell them!' Annie grabbed a handful of Thea's overall and almost pulled her over. 'Promise you won't tell them!'

'But, Annie,' said Thea, gently disengaging herself. 'I can hardly elicit money from them without saying what for, you must see that. I'm quite sure they'll understand. Anyway—won't they notice before long?'

'You mustn't tell them!' Annie was beginning to weep again, this time unrestrainedly; it was clear she would not listen to reason.

'All right, I won't say anything. But we'll see you right, I promise.'

She ushered the still choking and snivelling girl back to her place, and into the care of an equally lugubrious friend. Back in the office she suddenly wished she were endowed with her mother's natural tact and competence in such matters, the ability to be sympathetic yet detached, custodial but not condoning. But this was her test, she would not ask advice, she would not be beaten by it. The solutions to the problem must be severely practical. She sat down at once and wrote to Andrea.

The following day, taking a deep breath, she took advantage of the lunch break to begin her collection.

'What for, miss?' came the inevitable question.

'It's for a girl who's sick—TNT poisoning. She may need some special treatment and her family can't pay for it.' She hoped to God this sounded plausible, and begged Him to forgive her for the deception.

'Who is it?' The chief interrogator was Mabel Stack, a girl instantly recognizable as a natural ringleader. She was full of spirit and energy and talk; wherever two or three were gathered together, plotting, she was to be found at the centre. 'Who is it? Annie Turner?'

'No.' Thea frowned and sat down at the table, glancing round to make sure Annie was not present. 'And anyway I don't wish to mention names, for obvious reasons. She might be next door in the bullet shop, not here at all, for all you know.'

'But *you* know, don't you?' said Mabel.

Thea ignored her. 'I know you'll all give something, just a few pence at least. If it was you who was ill, you'd be glad of it.'

'I bet it's Annie,' Mabel went on inexorably. 'She's been throwing up all over the place, and I know why.'

'Annie may be ill,' said Thea, 'and if she is the doctor will diagnose it.'

'Nice easy job for him!' riposted Mabel.

'I wouldn't ask for a donation unless I thought it really necessary.'

'Oh of *course* not, miss,' said Mabel, with a face of round-eyed innocence. 'It's just that we wouldn't give no money to help some daft slut that got herself in the family way. That's all.'

A murmur of endorsement greeted this fighting speech. Mabel's expression of steely defiance was mirrored by the other faces round the table. Jaws rotated on the mutton stew and mash, forks quivered, poised above plates awash with greyish gravy.

Thea began to feel angry. She had not anticipated opposition of this kind. It was disappointing. The girls were being not just uncharitable but downright vindictive. She became increasingly determined to do right by Annie Turner. 'This is ridiculous!' she snapped. 'I am not going to sit here arguing with you, neither am I going to justify my actions. I have always been fair, you've no cause to mistrust me, and I had hoped that you would be willing to help a fellow-worker. Mabel, I am going to leave this tin with you. Please pass it round and return it to me this time tomorrow.'

When it was returned, it contained the princely sum of three shillings and sixpence. She read the riot act again and chastised them for their meanness, but it was no good. It was like addressing a stone wall. In desperation, and against her better judgement, she approached Ralph, who agreed to add a 'bonus' to Annie's next pay packet. But the others found out about it and succeeded in persuading her that the best way of investing it would be to get rid of the unborn child. This she did, and returned to work two days after, to suffer an acute haemorrhage. So poor naive little Annie Turner had to go back up north anyway, doubly-disgraced now, and unwell, to face her father's fury.

The incident toughened Thea. She became stricter, and kept more of a distance between herself and the girls under her. The night of Annie's departure she had cried herself to sleep, but she knew she would not do so again. One particular spark of charity had been doused. Ralph never asked her what became of the girl, and she never told him.

She had all but forgotten about Louis Avery when Ralph informed her that a bright young man from the Ministry would be visiting Dolton Green. At once, before he had told her the name, she knew who it would be.

'Why is he coming?' she asked.

'To show interest, to see round, to talk to the staff. He will come in peace, I assure you. You must make him welcome.'

Louis came down one day towards the end of September, but Thea left it to Mr Bailey to do the welcoming. This was a good move on two counts. Mr Bailey was gratified that the boss's daughter knew her place, and it absolved her from forming part of the reception committee. She was very tired and depressed. The war had been in progress for a year and there was no sign of its ending. It was weeks since she'd had a letter from Jack and she expected every day to see his name among the list of those missing and dead. Also, in his last note Aubrey had implied that he might be moved to another camp, but that had been two months ago and they had heard nothing more.

Worst of all, she wondered about Josef. Determinedly she had thrust him to the back of her mind, attacked her work with furious energy so that there would be no time to think of him during the day, and she was too exhausted at night. But her present job had pushed him forward again. With every shell she inspected, every tray of bullets counted and passed, she could not help but think of him as he might be: broken, bleeding, perhaps dead. And if that were so, she would have had a hand in his death as surely as if she had shot him. She knew from Jack's letters the kind of injuries this war inflicted, and the conditions in which the wounded had to suffer.

As if to stretch her taut nerves further, there had been a number of air-raids over the last few weeks. Mercifully the factory had not been hit and in most cases the planes had not even come into sight, but the anxiety which they engendered was an added trial. Once, one of the new girls, panic-stricken, had forgotten to turn off the oven in which the powder was drying out. Returning after the raid she had opened the oven and the resulting blast had blown her eyes out. The other girls, white-faced and cowed, had told Thea she had been courting a sailor, but that would all be over now, of course.

So Louis's arrival was merely an annoyance. She felt not the slightest desire to be agreeable to him, and he certainly did not need anyone to make him feel at home; that was something for which he had a natural aptitude.

She was quite right. Louis was a great success. He had dressed 'down' for the occasion, and wasted no time in donning overalls to see round the factory. On his tour he impressed Mr Bailey with his lively curiosity and interest in how things were done. He displayed enough knowledge to show he had done his homework, and to make his questions intelligent, but not so much as to make those he questioned appear uninformed.

He chose, cleverly, to make his speech in the canteen during the dinner hour. It contained certain recognizable elements grafted from the one Thea had heard him make at Andrea's meeting, but it was shorter and pithier, and he had judged his audience with uncanny accuracy.

'All of you here, every one of you,' he said, leaning forward on the edge of his table and gazing round at the faces turned up to him, 'are fighting this war as surely as our boys at the front, and on the ocean and in the air. It is *your* hard work, *your* loyalty, *your* dedication that supplies the vital fuel we need to drive forward for victory. Never forget that, nor think that your part is a small one in the theatre of war. Your country called. And you came.'

He sat down to rissoles, greens and carrots amid rapturous applause, and cleared his plate. Thea went back to her office and sat alone. It was nothing short of breathtaking, the way in which he had made the girls feel as if they had made a noble sacrifice by taking on their present jobs, whereas they had in fact been simply grabbing money and independence with both hands.

And how they loved him. Not for him the jeers and goadings that the other young men had to suffer; he had somehow managed to persuade them that he was a creature apart, a god-like being concerned with the Grand Scheme and not a mere frightened mortal like the rest of them. As they trickled back to their benches, Thea heard Mabel Stack say: 'He really expressed hisself lovely, didn't he? I mean he made us feel really important.'

It appeared Louis had done his job perfectly.

But if Thea had hoped to get through the day without any direct contact with Louis, her hopes were dashed when at two-thirty, just as he was about to leave, the air-raid whistle went.

Poor Mr Bailey, horrified that the Germans should dare to attack when he had a VIP on the premises, rushed about like a madman, screaming 'Out! Everybody out!' and in some cases pushing and shoving the girls from their seats.

Louis's official car and its driver were waiting just inside the main gate, but Louis showed not the slightest intention of leaving. Mr Bailey, almost in tears, implored him to go. The planes seemed horribly close, they could actually be seen downriver, and the sound of their engines throbbed in the air.

'No, I intend to stay. I'll fall in with whatever drill you normally observe, Mr Bailey. This is most interesting for me.'

'Oh my Lord   '

Thea, last out of the shell-shop—she had latterly taken it upon herself to see that the ovens were off before leaving —found Louis still standing on one of the raised walks, one hand to his eyes, gazing up at the planes that were now hovering no more than a mile away. Exasperated, she grabbed his arm.

'Don't stand there, come on! Out on the grass!'

The entire work force converged on the factory gates and spilled out like a colony of ants, across the road, through a ditch and on to the field beyond. The field sloped down to the river bank, and on the other side they could see the massive red-brick bulk of the Bridge Road Arsenal, with buses issuing from it, evacuating the workers. There was no such transport available here.

They spread out over the field, and lay down flat on their faces. The men from the gun-shop, who wore green baize aprons, removed them and laid them over their backs. All the men, suddenly gallant, distributed themselves among the women and girls. It was customary for these raids to be used as an excuse for canoodling: after all, if a bomb was going to drop on you, you might as well be enjoying yourself at the time.

Thea lay with Louis, her face pressed into the dry grass. There were some dandelion clocks inches from her nose. Overhead she could hear the buzz of the planes, there were about six, and they seemed to be hovering almost directly above them. She had never felt so vulnerable. When Louis's arm stole across her back she barely noticed. Her eyes were squeezed tight shut but she felt his breath on her face when he whispered: 'Good grief, does this often happen?'

'Keep your face down!' She was terrified. She suddenly had a vivid recollection of the eagle they had seen hovering in the sky over Wolzhof: this was how it must have felt to be that eagle's prey. 'No. This is the closest they've ever been.'

'There'll be a God-almighty bang if they hit the works.' He seemed to be expressing a detached, almost an academic, interest.

'Be quiet, for heaven's sake!'

'They can't hear me, you know.' She felt him shake, and knew he was laughing at her. Laughing! She had grudgingly to admire his sangfroid. She laid her cheek on the ground, her teeth gritted, her heart banging like a pile-driver against the earth underneath. The shuddering shadows of the planes

moved across the field like searchlights, exposing them
Louis's arm was a comfort, warm and friendly over her back,
lying between her and the hunters.

The planes veered away across the river. She relaxed, then
a new fear gripped her. The Bridge Road Arsenal. It was a
huge place, a far better target than Dolton Green, and if it
was hit the explosion would be catastrophic, they would all
be killed . . .

'Oh no! Please God don't let them,' she prayed aloud.

Louis sat up. 'It's all right,' he said. 'They're going away.'

Slowly she lifted her head. All over the field the others
were sitting up, looking up at the bland, blue sky, brushing
off their clothes, tousled and bewildered like surprised lovers
or drowsy picnickers. Downriver the planes dwindled into
the distance, the sound of their engines no more than a
shimmering ghost of sound in the warm air. Everything was
the same, the danger past. The river was idling on its way,
the Bridge Road Arsenal as massive and solid as ever.

People began to laugh with relief, to help each other up
and take advantage of the general relief for a quick kiss and a
cuddle. Louis took Thea's hand and pulled her up. But
instead of releasing it he held it fast.

'I don't see why I should be left out,' he said teasingly and
kissed her on the cheek. His lips were soft and warm. His
skin smelt of soap. Thea had a sudden nervous impulse to
cry. She had been very afraid—afraid for her life—and he
had seen her fear. She felt weak and ashamed. But his kiss
did not repel her, nor did she want to pull her hand away
from his. It was, after all, the hand of friendship.

'Go ahead and cry if you want to,' he said. He passed her a
handkerchief. It was silk, no good at all for mopping up
tears, but Thea did her best with it.

'I'm sorry,' she muttered. 'I'm not usually so hopeless. You
shouldn't have done that . . . if the girls see, they'll never let
me forget it.'

'They didn't see. Come on.' He let go her hand and stood
watching her as she regained her composure. He looked odd
and out of place standing in the field with his shiny shoes and
neat, urbane clothes. But now his appearance seemed more a
comfort than an irritant.

When she was ready they walked back together to the
factory, and she heard the girls behind them saying how good
Mr Avery had been, just like one of them.

CHAPTER THIRTEEN

'. . . But it ain't worthwhile to tell 'em
You might talk till all was blue
But you'd never make 'em compree
What a bloke out there goes through.'
George Will—'I don't get on with civvies'

Bethune, 15 October 1915.

Dearest Father and Mother, I can't say how sorry I am for being such a poor correspondent, and hope you haven't been worried to death. Thank you for all your letters and parcels, they mean such a lot. I think we'd all go stark staring mad out here if it weren't for news from home. I don't know what you've read in the newspapers—we've given up reading them, they distort things so much—but suffice to say that things have been pretty bad out here. Our division was moved up for the Loos offensive, the spirit of the men was terrific, but the affair was a dismal shambles with the usual appalling losses and nothing to show for it. We were expected to launch an infantry charge through a coal-mining area littered with slagheaps, pits and miners' cottages. Due mainly to the courage and determination of the men we broke through the German lines at one point but, when reserves were sent up, they tangled with the troops leaving the line and in the ensuing chaos we lost whatever small advantage we'd gained. I felt desperately sorry for the soldiers, many of whom had made the ultimate sacrifice, and for what? Sometimes I think the generals and staff officers are not fighting the same war as the rest of us. If I ever thought that factors such as background and upbringing determined friendships, I think so no longer. It is the man who shares your burdens who is your friend.

I remain undeservedly fit, in spite of everything. I've had recurring bouts of the stomach trouble, but then we all have, and our lot got a whiff of gas the other day. Fortunately it was mustard and arsenic, if it had been mustard alone we'd all have been done for. As it was our eyes were bad and we were pretty sick, but nothing to what I've seen some fellows suffer, it literally removes your stomach layer by layer.

Sorry, I never intended this to be a catalogue of gloom. It's almost impossible to convey the depression that settles over you out here. It's like another world. But one or two improvements have filtered through. We have fresh food in the front line trenches now, as they have at last agreed to move field kitchens closer, and in fine weather the stuff even arrives fairly hot! Also we are now issued with a gas mask of sorts, a kind of grey hood with mica eyepieces in which we resemble beings from space. They are not a hundred percent effective, but better than the ammonia pads. Some of the men reckon it was better to piss on your handkerchief, and use that!

But my main reason for writing is to tell you that I have at last got leave, very overdue, but the losses to our regiment have been so dreadful that I couldn't expect more. I should be home in a week or so. I am literally living for it, like my first term at Winchester, counting the days, that's the kind of thing we're reduced to. When I do get back I just hope I'll be able to keep my eyes open long enough to see and do all I want to, the vision of a comfortable bed with clean sheets swims before me day and night!

If you're in touch with the Tennants, would you tell them I'm coming, and would like to see them some time? I simply don't have time to write more than this one letter just now. I know Thea's working, but I hope to see her as well, she has written regularly since Christmas. Just thinking about you all cheers me up. All fondest love, Jack.'

'Come off it, Garrick, you can't monopolize the lady.'

'I'm not. She's here at my invitation, which she accepted of her own free will. It is you who are *de trop*.'

'That's typical Guards complacency. Dulcie, put him in his place.'

'Push off, Read.'

'Not unless she tells me to.'

'Push off!'

'Gentlemen!' Dulcie raised both hands in mock horror, though in fact this was precisely the kind of situation she relished. 'Stop it at once or I shall go home this minute and leave you both to wrangle to your hearts' content . . .' Hands still raised, she began to twist a ring, a heart-shaped opal surrounded by tiny diamonds. It had been a present, but not from either of these two. 'Oh I do so adore this ring,' she murmured, moving her finger so that it caught the light. 'It's quite, quite my favourite . . .'

She glanced through her fingers at Simon Garrick, on the other side of the table, and then upwards, from beneath demure lashes, at David Read. As she had anticipated, both had been reminded of their place in her life, they would no longer presume to contest the right to her time and affections.

Consolingly, she held out her hand to David and pulled him gently down onto the chair next to hers. Confidingly, to show her appreciation of his prior claim, she leaned over to Simon. 'More champagne, darling.'

'Oh yes . . . of course.'

'And then we'll all drink a toast—to friendship!' She threw her head back as she said this, and laughed, knowing very well what effect she had on them. They wouldn't like that 'friendship', either of them. Each wanted, and half expected, something more for himself, something special and exclusive, and it suited her to let them all live in hope. Her style consisted in casting an aura of romance about herself like a gauzy veil, while remaining, beneath it, utterly practical. She knew precisely what it was she offered, the issue was never blurred in her mind. If it was blurred in theirs, well, that added savour to their side of things.

Simon ordered more champagne. The waiter smiled at all three of them, and especially at Dulcie. She was often here at Le Casse-Croute. He knew perfectly well what she did for a living, but with what charm and style! Everyone regarded Dulcie's presence as an asset to the place. Like a fresh flower pinned to a plain and faded dress she enhanced the war-time restaurant; her exquisite clothes gleamed against the drab ranks of uniforms, her laughter rang out, full of optimism and *joie de vivre* when both were in short supply, her beauty was a candle in the dark. She always sat at the same table with her friends and Albert, the patron, went to some pains to make it special for her, by providing little 'extras': a rose in a glass vase, sugared almonds in a silver dish, a perfect peach from the market. He did this not because she was a good customer who in turn generated more custom, though she was certainly that. He did it because he felt, like every one of her clients, that she was 'his' as well as being everybody's, and that it was a rare woman who could be both these things and remain wholly *sympathique*. The sagacious Frenchman spoiled her because he admired her.

Now Dulcie watched as Simon poured champagne. Then she lifted her glass, gazing at them through the dancing bubbles and said again: 'To friendship!'

'To friendship.'

She took a long draught of her drink, then helped herself to a crystallized fruit. The pianist played a sentimental tune, lifted a hand in salute to her, and she waved back, humming and tapping her foot. She was enjoying her companions' slight discomfort, and had no intention of easing it just for the moment. They were wondering which of them she would take back with her. Would she reward Simon, for having bought her a superb dinner, for having earned her favour as it were? Or David, for his forthright and flattering persistence? She would let them wonder till all the champagne had gone. And then she would return with both of them!

This notion so tickled her fancy that she laughed out loud again, shaking her head at her own audacity. They smiled at her, and at each other, pleased she was happy, but uncertain of their ground.

'What's the joke?' asked Simon. He was the one she had to be careful with, for all his extra years, his poise and his impeccable pedigree. Like the oak he would break. If she ever let him down he would carry the scars for the rest of his life. He was so handsome, though, with his dark eyes, and his white skin from which the black hairs sprouted like wires, and his big hands that made her feel tiny and frail.

She brushed his cheek with her fingers. 'Nothing. I'm having a lovely time, that's all, and thank you for it.'

She transferred her gaze to David. The contrast between the two men was so startling that she felt her whole body light up in happy expectation. David was thin, and young and excitable. Everything about him had the startled, flyaway air of a highly-strung animal. His fox-coloured hair sprang from his brow in a rush, his eyebrows arched and furrowed like caterpillars, his hands were never still. When he made love to her it was like being rippled over by a busy, gurgling stream that flowed through and round her with continuous fluid energy.

'Dear David . . .' she murmured. She put out her hand to him and he caught and kissed it passionately. His lips were hot and open, he could hardly wait. Hardly, but it was possible. And he would not break, he would bend. She turned away.

'Dance with me, Simon,' she said, and walked away from them onto the tiny square of dance floor. She wore a white dress and silver shoes and a waxy hothouse gardenia in her hair. She felt like a sprite, a will-o'-the-wisp, she knew instinctively that there was magic at work. Tonight nothing was beyond her. They would not be three, but one, and there would have been nothing like it. She twirled, her skirt flying, into Simon's arms.

Thea and Louis had what he had come to call their 'usual table' at the Savoy, in one corner, overlooking the Embankment. Screening them from the rest of the room was a tall column from which ivy and ferns cascaded in tropical abundance. Louis had presented her with an orchid and she wore it pinned to the shoulder of her dress. The meal, just finishing, had been excellent. the orchestra played rag-time and the scent of the orchid wafted delightfully with her every movement.

She had learned over the past few months to accept his attentions with a good grace, even to luxuriate in them a little. She would not have done so had she seriously thought she was the only recipient, but as it was she was reasonably certain that she was one of many. They did not meet that often and besides, hadn't Maurice said before she had even met Louis that he was a ladies' man?

Also, since the air-raid at Dolton Green she had looked on him in a new light. His behaviour that day had been impeccable, he had been astonishingly cool under pressure and even the kiss had been more of a comfort that an affront, she had to admit. She was lonely these days, it would be nothing short of ill-tempered perversity to reject the hand of genuine friendship when it was so repeatedly offered. And having made the first moves it was very difficult to harden one's heart when eating delicious food in an elegant restaurant, with music in the background, and wearing on her dress an orchid that would not have disgraced the conservatory at Kew.

They finished eating, and Louis poured out the last of the Mouton Cadet. 'Enjoy that?' he asked.

'It was superb. Thank you.'

'I must say it's a pleasure to take out a woman who eats with such enthusiasm.'

'Oh heavens . . !' she laughed. 'Did I make such a pig of myself?'

'You have a healthy appetite. I was complimenting you on it. There's no satisfaction in buying an expensive meal for a woman who just picks it over. Tell me, was yours one of those families that set great store by clearing the plate?'

'Not really. I don't think we were ever made to. But then my brother and I usually did anyway. My sister was dreadfully fussy.' She stopped and stared down at her glass.

'What's the matter?'

'That's all in the past tense now.'

'Cheer up.' He sat back to allow the waiter to take the plates. 'That was delicious, Guido. They're both alive.' All three sentences were spoken in the same tone.

'Yes . . .' She didn't pursue the topic. He had made it abundantly clear that any but the most superficial discussion of her family, or other friends, bored him. He liked those who were with him to relate only to him and not bring a retinue of other associations to which he had to pay court. It was vanity, of course, but then it worked both ways. When he was with her he treated her as if she were the only woman he had ever known. It was his way, and he was consistent.

'I like your dress,' he said. 'I haven't seen it before.'

'No, I suppose you haven't. I bought it in Vienna. It's a pity about my face and hands.'

'What's the matter with them?'

'My face is yellow and my hands are dirty.'

'Unforgiveable. That's the last time I take you anywhere respectable.'

She laughed. 'It's true!'

'Why must you always be so self-deprecating? I think you look pale and interesting. And your hands bear the stigmata of honest toil. Let me see.' She brought her hands up from her lap and laid them on the table, turning them over like a child for inspection. Round the base of each nail and in every crease was a thread of black: oil, which she could not remove. 'Not too good, I agree with you,' conceded Louis, 'but a sign of the times, and an honourable one at that. Let me tell you,' he added, picking up her right hand and stroking the knuckles with his thumb, 'that I would rather have them like this than lily-white and manicured.'

'Gallantly spoken.'

'Truthfully. But you will also have noticed my skill at winning over an audience, for gaining their confidence . . .' He spoke as if quoting, but he never bothered with modesty, and the words could just as easily be his own. Two months ago Thea would have found this speech odious, but now she could laugh at him.

'Tell me something,' he went on, over coffee and liqueurs—brandy for him; crème de menthe for Thea. 'You never did say what became of Maurice.'

'Oh—he's still up at Cambridge.'

'Doing what?'

'His thesis. It's ages since I heard from him actually.'

'M-hm.' He stared at her as if waiting for her to say something more. 'Not one of these pacifist johnnies is he?'

She took a sip of her drink. 'I honestly don't know, we haven't discussed it.'

'Thea!' he reproved her. 'Of course you have, you and he are thick as thieves. You don't need to be frightened of me, you know, I don't give a damn what the fellow does.'

She looked at him squarely and realized that she had no way of knowing whether he was telling the truth or not. He had perfected the art of presenting the right face for the occasion, it was part of his job and one he was very good at. She felt again the old fear. If she thought of Maurice in connection with Louis Avery he seemed painfully vulnerable; he so glaringly lacked all Louis's savoir-faire, his manipulative mind, his gift of the gab.

'He's always been against physical violence,' she said guardedly. 'Any violence, in fact.'

'Absolutely,' said Louis, with an air of satisfied finality. 'You need say no more.'

'I didn't say anything.'

'Enough though. I can read you like a book, you are the most inept liar I ever came across, you might as well accept that and not bother.'

She coloured. 'I see.' She wished fiercely that he wouldn't patronize her, nor presume all the time to know what she was thinking. She could not help noticing how like Andrea he was in that respect. The fact that he was, on this occasion, quite correct, made it still more annoying. She remembered something Jack had said to her in a similar conversation. 'He's always been a pacifist,' she remarked. 'That doesn't mean it has to be a political stance.'

'Oh come *on.*' His tone was one of complete disbelief.

'It has nothing to do with anyone else anyway,' she muttered.

'"Oh what a tangled web we weave . . ."' warbled Louis. And then, more seriously. 'I quite realize it's none of my business except that he and I were quite friendly at one time. I knew Maurice before I knew you, remember?'

'Yes. Of course.'

'So a student friendship does entitle me to enquire about him, I think, without at once being cast in the role of the snooping villain?'

'Very well. Let's leave it there, shall we?'

He sat still for a moment, smiling at her teasingly. Then he rose. 'Would you care to dance? I like this tune.' The orchestra was playing 'If you were the only girl in the world'. Louis hummed as he led her onto the floor. She couldn't help laughing.

'What's so funny?'

'I didn't realize you were so sentimental.'

'Who me? Horribly so.' He clasped her to his chest. '"Nothing else would matter in this world today, We would go on loving in the same old way . . ."'

'For goodness sake!' She pushed him back to a more decorous distance. 'People are looking.'

'Let them.' He squeezed her again, his cheek pressed to hers, her hand clutched to his shoulder.

'Stop it!'

'All right then.'

They continued to dance in a more measured fashion with Louis humming in her ear. She was conscious of the fact that he had neatly achieved his objective, which was to defuse the potentially acrimonious situation generated by their discussion of Maurice. She was glad he had, and that the subject had been discarded, but resented his skill in doing both.

He was a good dancer when he chose to be, and she remembered, a little guiltily, how well he had stepped out with Andrea that evening in Cambridge, and how she had envied them their practised partnership.

The music ended and they went back to their table. The atmosphere, in spite of the elegance of the setting, was unaffected, friendly and informal. The room was full of uniforms, not glittering and showy as the 'emperor's coat' had been in Vienna, but plain and subdued: a uniform for a new kind of army in a new kind of war. And the hotel presided, like an august but kindly aunt, over its drab, youthful heroes.

'Do you mind if I smoke?' he enquired.

416

'You don't usually ask.'

'I don't usually think it's necessary.'

'Of course you can.'

He lit the cigarette and leaned back, one arm hooked over the back of his chair, rocking it onto its back legs. 'Cheer up,' he said, for the second time that evening, so that she could not help but feel she was boring him. She tried to articulate her feelings as clearly as he would do.

'I can't help looking round at all these uniforms and realizing that for, say, half of those men, this will be their last fling in London.'

'That's probably correct.'

'It doesn't trouble you?'

'I didn't say that. But feelings never ended a war.'

'A friend I've been writing to hasn't replied for weeks . . .' she said, almost absently. 'I'm afraid he may be dead.' She had said it. She had faced up to that short, black, grim word and made herself comprehend its finality.

'You've not heard from anyone else to that effect?'

'No.'

'Then I'd say your fears are groundless. He could be injured, or in front line action where it's impossible for him to write; you must keep an open mind about it. Perhaps there's some way I could find out for you.'

'Could you?' It was a possibility that had never occurred to her.

'I might be able to. I could contact the War Office, make out it was a kind of official enquiry—if you'd like me to.'

'I understand.' Unexpectedly he put his arm about her shoulders, turning her to face him, and kissed her forehead. He was given to such unpredictable demonstrativeness and she submitted to it, even feeling a little foolish for ever having taken it seriously. 'Let's go soon, shall we?' he asked, crushing the butt of his cigarette in the ashtray. 'It's a long drive.'

'I wish you wouldn't, it's too much for you, all the way down there and back in the night.'

'Far from it, it does me good. I'm a creature of the night, my energy increases into the small hours of the morning.'

'I wish I could say the same!' she laughed. 'It's my precious day off tomorrow, and I always mean to get up early and make the most of it, but as it is I'll probably sleep till eleven.'

'You're entitled.'

'It seems such a waste . . .'

In a few minutes they left. Outside it was cold, and very dark. London was observing a partial black-out since the zeppelin and air-raids had begun. Louis had parked his car on the far side of the Strand, in Drury Lane. He linked arms with her as they crossed the road and walked up Southampton Street, and hummed to himself. She wondered at his unruffled self-satisfaction. He had never asked who the friend was about whom she worried, he lacked curiosity about others to a quite unusual degree. He simply refused to acknowledge the existence of separate ties and affiliations in the lives of those he befriended. She wondered what he would think of her if he knew how she dreamed of a German officer and how sometimes those dreams woke her imperiously even from her deep, exhausted sleep. The more she stifled the feeling, as she knew she must, the more it flourished and grew like a plant in a hothouse. She could ask about Jack, but never about Josef, and her wild imagination supplied a host of answers she did not want to hear.

They reached the car and Louis held the door open for her. She wrapped her cape around her, and as he got in he reached a large check rug from the back seat and spread it over her knees. The cape had a wide collar and she turned it up to keep her neck warm. In the market the porters moved around in the light of small oil lamps, like acolytes in some weird religious rite. It was a quarter past eleven.

They set off, down Drury Lane, along the Strand, over Vauxhall Bridge and thence to the Elephant and Castle and down the Old Kent Road. There wasn't much traffic around, and they bowled along at a steady thirty-five miles per hour. To begin with Louis talked, but eventually, what with the dark and the cold and the throb of the engine, he fell silent. Thea began to feel irresistibly sleepy, her head began to nod heavily and her eyelids to droop until at last she gave in to it. She was dimly conscious, before drifting into total unconsciousness, of Louis tucking the rug around her with one hand, and she was grateful to him.

Dulcie let Simon come to her first, because he had earned it, and she knew form mattered to him. For him she was soft, asquiescent, abandoning herself in an ecstasy of passivity to his adoration. Of all the men she knew Simon made her feel the most exalted, the most delicately feminine. The pleasure she took from his love-making was based on a joyous, greedy narcissism. She found the sight of his large hand covering her small breast immensely exciting, and he had thick black hairs on his chest that left marks on her thin skin. She felt ravished. But she knew that to please him she must be both his goddess and his plaything: he wished both to worship and to master. She would lie spread like a lily on her satin sheets, watching his face move between her thighs, feeling the rasp of his moustache and the soft push of his tongue, allowing sensation to bloom unaided, with delectable slowness. And then he would rise above her, his elbows resting on either side of her head so that she was small in his shadow and she could feel how much he wanted her. Only then did she express her readiness; her hand would clasp and guide him. He sank down and into her and she felt herself crushed and enfolded like a flower, and like a flower her juice and her scent would flow for him. She was deliciously used and squeezed, carried by his irresistible strength, lifted, rocked, transported.

Afterwards, she curled up besides him like a kitten, licked his nipples and curled her fingers in his hair. She put her lips to his ear and whispered, with warm breath: 'Now David's coming, and we'll all be friends, and in a little, little while, you'll be ready to begin all over again!' He rolled his head and began to speak, but she put her hand over his mouth and her other fingers to her lips. 'No! My rules.'

She called David and he slipped into the bed on the other side of her. Delighted with her own cleverness, she realized she had been right in her stage-management. David, like her, was excited by an audience; they were both exhibitionists whose desire was fanned by their exhibitionism. With David it was different; the roles were uncertain, sometimes she could scarcely tell where her own body ended and his began. Where their bodies met there was a slight shock, a crackle of electricity, and like two electric eels they twined and joined and slithered together. He set her on fire, she could not be still, she shivered with excitement. They never wanted it to end so they went on and on, postponing the moment of joining till they were desperately panting and gasping. And then it was so quick and explosive that they simply collapsed and lay there, feeling the slow trickle of moisture ebb and grow cool on their hot skins.

But Dulcie had not forgotten about Simon. And as she lay, smiling, with David's damp head tucked beneath her chin, she felt him move close. And his long arm reached out to embrace not only her, but both of them. She had done it. She was enfolded by not one lover, but two, and the joy was so direct and intense that she cried out: 'I love you!'

She meant it, but did not expect them to understand how.

Thea woke about an hour later because the car had stopped and her feet were cold. Looking about her she saw they were out of London, for there were trees, and she could smell the resiny odour of pine needles. There was a full moon, pale and calm, and everything was bathed in its strange bleached light. Louis was not beside her, but she could make out his silhouette at the edge of the trees, and the small spark of his cigarette.

Stiffly she clambered out. She felt suddenly apprehensive. 'Louis?'

'Over here.'

She stumbled over to him, her cape hugged round her. Her eyes felt puffy, her mouth dry from the wine she had drunk, and her hair was in disarray. She wondered what on earth she had looked like, asleep, with her head lolling and her mouth probably open. She longed for a cup of tea. She stood next to him, stamping her feet, which were fast becoming numb. She could think of nothing but bed and rest and being warm.

'Why did you stop?'

'You were asleep, I felt like a smoke, and this is a nice place.' They were standing on the edge of the same stretch of wood that Dulcie and Jack had visited nearly two years ago. But now there was no bonfire in the valley below; the fields lay still and frost-bound in the grey moonlight.

Thea rubbed her arms. 'I'm frozen.' Her breath came out in a cloud.

'Are you?' He looked at her in apparent amazement. 'Let's walk a little, then—get the circulation going.'

'To be honest, Louis, I'd really like to get home. I'm awfully tired.'

'Are you?' he asked again. 'All right.'

'I'm sorry.'

'No problem.' He dropped the cigarette and heeled it into the pine needles. 'Come on then.'

They walked back to the car. For the first time since she'd known him Louis seemed tetchy; there was an atmosphere.

420

Thea felt guilty, but too tired to make further apologies. All she wanted now was to be at home, alone in her own comfortable bed with nothing expected of her. She wished that she had kept her distance more earlier in the evening; why did she always overdo everything?

He held the door for her and then got in himself. But he did not start the car. Instead he leaned over, without touching her, and said in a silky, half-teasing voice: 'Have you any idea how mad I am about you, Thea Tennant?'

She did not have the energy to respond in the same bantering tone. 'Oh Louis, no I haven't. And anyway, you're not.'

'Heartless girl. How would you know?'

'It wouldn't be in character,' she said simply.

'Ah! You have me marked down for a Don Juan.'

'Not quite that. But you do like the ladies, don't you?'

'Only one, at present.' His eyes rested on her face acquisitively.

'Louis. Please take me home.'

But as she spoke she felt his hand on her waist, beneath her cloak, and his face closed in on hers in the cold darkness. She sensed the difference in him. All levity had fled, he had stopped teasing and was trying to impose his will on her. There was no seduction, no persuasion; his lips bit down on hers, she could feel his tongue against her teeth, and his arm across the small of her back, pressing her to him so that she could scarcely breathe. There was something parasitic in his clinging embrace, as if his kiss drew on her strength. She felt nothing but revulsion and panic as though she'd wakened in the night to find a spider walking on her bare skin.

She managed to tear her mouth from his and twist her head violently to one side. 'Louis! Stop it, please . . !'

He kissed her neck, she could feel his voracious mouth sucking and pinching; it hurt and she was disgusted. When he spoke his voice was husky and shaken.

'Why? Why stop, you know it's what we both want. I need you, Thea, and you know it—and you need me.'

'No! I don't want this!' She was horrified. The sound of his voice had made her realize the genuine strength of his desire and with it the enormity of her mistake. His small hand fumbled for her breast, she felt her skin shrink from his clasping fingers.

'Thea, you don't know . . .' His voice was no more than a

whisper. 'You know nothing, and I can show you. I can make you want it, you'll see.' He eased over so that he was almost on top of her; one of his knees lay across her lap, his hand was inside her dress now, hot and heavy against her frozen skin; she could feel his aroused body bunched on hers, urgent, dominating. His breath was coming fast, he was beginning to push against her. He was not a big man, hardly taller than her, and yet she was fearfully aware of his greater strength. Her own lack of response frightened her; she felt stiff and dry and brittle as a dead stick, she could not yield, she would break first. What was the matter with her? She could not bear it. All she wanted was for this panting, clutching thing to leave her body. She looked down and saw his hand kneading her breast.

With a sudden galvanic movement she wrenched away and fumbled for the handle of the door. He caught her, his face was against her ear, he was muttering something she didn't want to hear. But she had found the handle and flung the door open. Kicking and scrabbling, hampered by the rug that lay on the floor and her heavy cape which was still fastened at the throat, she made her escape, stumbling and falling on to the ground. The orchid hung crushed and broken from the bodice of her dress; she could smell the stifling sweetness of its bruised petals and she ripped it off and threw it as far as she could. Then she ran a few yards and stood, her back to the car, adjusting her dress and hair, shaking uncontrollably. Her legs were weak, she wanted to sit down but dared not. She must be alert and in control. She was terrified to think what she might see when she turned round. He might be furiously angry, his pride hurt, he might want to harm her in some way . . . Even in her present state she felt she could not blame him if he did; she deserved such treatment, for she had reacted wildly, violently, childishly, and she had made an unforgivable mistake.

But when she summoned the courage to turn he was sitting up in his seat, smoothing back his hair with both hands, and straightening his tie. He looked perfectly composed. He placed his hands on the steering wheel and looked across at her, but she couldn't see his expression in the dark interior of the car.

'I'll take you home,' he said.

Still trembling she walked over. He did not get out, but gathered up the rug and handed it to her. When she was in he

leaned across and slammed the door violently, contriving not
to touch her as he did so. While she spread the rug he sat
quietly, looking the other way, tapping his fingers on the
wheel.

'Ready?' He glanced at her.

She nodded.

He started the engine. They drove for three-quarters of an
hour in complete silence. Thea felt sick: each swerve brought
her stomach lurching into her throat and her head felt heavy,
jolting this way and that on a frail stem of neck. She hoped
she wasn't going to pass out.

At Chilverton House everything was quiet. The light had
been left on in the hall for her. Louis drew up at the foot of
the steps. He still sat with his hands on the wheel, in an
attitude peculiarly insulting, impatient and dismissive.

'Goodbye, I think,' he said, staring straight in front of him,
making no move to get out or to help her in any way.

Thea was overwhelmed with regret. 'Louis, I'm sorry.
Couldn't we just—'

'No, I think not.'

'But . . . we were friends, at least.'

For the first time he turned and looked directly into her
face. She was shocked by his expression of cold dislike; she
would not have believed it possible for someone to change so
completely and so swiftly.

'You've learned nothing about me, have you?' he asked in
a thin, scornful voice. 'Nothing at all.'

'I like you.'

'She likes me! God!' He lifted his hands and dropped them
again despairingly and then shook his head slowly. 'I never
wanted anything as much as I wanted you. But now I realize
I don't want you enough to risk humiliation twice. Once was
quite sufficient. I've already put it behind me, forgotten it.
And I shall very soon forget you, too, Thea Tennant. You'd
be amazed how soon.' He leaned across, again without
touching her, and pushed the door open. 'Goodbye.'

She got out. 'Goodbye, Louis.'

'And by the way,' he added, as he started the car, 'I don't
think I shall bother to enquire about that friend of yours. I
don't have the time.' He went, the gravel churning and
spurting beneath the angry swerve of his tyres.

After he had gone she remained where she was for a
moment, letting the blessed silence settle again, washing and

lapping gently round her. A great white barn owl flapped across the lawn and came to rest on the stable arch like a bird of ill omen, its staring, secretive face pivoting and twisting through impossible angles as it looked for its prey. Rousing herself, she went up the steps, automatically pulling at her dress and tucking in the loose strands of hair on her temples. She locked the door after her, turned off the hall light, and went up the stairs. On the landing Homer limped to meet her from his place by Ralph's door, his tail swinging, head held low. He was old now, he hadn't the energy to run downstairs to welcome her, let alone to run beside a horse or a bicycle or chase a ball. He just followed Ralph ponderously, and flopped down with a sigh wherever he came to rest. But the loyal, reliable sameness of his greeting brought a lump to Thea's throat. As she patted him she asked herself what kind of pariah she was that she couldn't order her life properly, so that damage was not done.

Venetia opened her door and looked out, her pale hair hanging in a braid over one shoulder. 'Thea?'

'Hallo, Mother.'

'Did you have a pleasant evening? Did Louis bring you home?'

'Of course.'

'Mrs Duckham left out some things in the kitchen, did you find them?'

'I didn't want anything.'

'But you had a good time?'

'Yes, yes. A fine time.' Thea knew that her mother sensed the half-truth in her voice, but the time was long past when she could have gone and laid her head on Venetia's shoulder and asked for sympathy. She had to be strong for herself now, so she began to move away, before she was caught in the soft net of intuitive sympathy that lay around her.

'Good,' Venetia was saying, 'you deserve some fun, darling. By the way, I told Mrs Duckham you'd have breakfast in bed.'

'Lovely. Thank you, Mother.'

'Good night, darling.'

'Good night.'

She went to her room and began to undress. The caramel lace and moire dress was spoilt, the lace on the bodice was torn and there were marks on the hem where she had tripped and trodden on it. The desecration of her most beautiful dress

424

seemed the worst possible tragedy, but she hung it up carefully, and when she opened the cupboard door she was confronted by her reflection, staring back at her. She had lost half a stone since starting work at Dolton Green, her collar bones and pelvis were angular—like a worn-out old horse, she thought. Her sallow face looked sickly, with the eyes shadowed and deep set in the middle of it. Perhaps if I had my hair cut, she thought, I shouldn't look so awful, and it would be more practical; a bob is becoming quite fashionable these days. She leaned against the mirror and sobbed.

Whether it was the events of that night or the news received the following day that Jack would shortly be home on leave, Thea couldn't say, but for the whole of the following week she felt restless and dissatisfied. At work she was full of a nervous energy that caused her to roar through the sheds like an east wind, chivvying the girls mercilessly; arguing with Bailey about the attitude of the male employees, and writing a lengthy and carping memorandum to Ralph on the quality and cost of the canteen food. She was angry at herself and work was her whipping boy. She felt by turns darkly depressed and irrationally enraged. She could feel the undertow of resentment coursing round her, but she had what in her childhood would have been called the black dog on her shoulder, and nothing could shift it.

On the Thursday, as if something were needed to jolt her from this uncomfortable mood, a British plane nose-dived into the edge of the river no more than a few hundred yards from the factory.

It was mid-afternoon when they heard the whirr of propellers overhead. There had been no whistle, and there was only one plane so they all knew it wasn't a raid, but one of the boys from the airbase at Hythe, either on a test-flight or returning, somewhat circuitously, from a recce. Apart from vociferously wishing him well and exhorting him to do for the Boche next time he had the chance, the girls paid him no further attention. Until, that is, they heard the engine stutter and falter. It seemed to do so almost directly above the sheds, the noise whirring, then stopping, then whirring again, like a fly in a spider's web, fighting the inevitable.

It was no good trying to stop the girls. Almost anything would do as a diversion from the tedium of work this week, with Miss Tennant snapping and nagging, nothing ever right. They rose as one woman and went out to see what was going on, standing in lines on the board-walks, pointing and shouting as the plane dipped and spiralled sickeningly. When it abruptly and terrifyingly plummetted, disappearing over and beyond the shed roofs in the direction of the river, the girls ran out of the gates and down onto the grass, with Thea and some of the younger men following. Mr Bailey had gone back to his office to phone for help.

There were some cows and a couple of old skewbald horses in the field, and they scattered nervously before the horde of yelling young women. Beyond them the plane lay tail-up, like a dart, plunged into the slimy alluvial mud at the edge of the river, and Thea could see the pilot, apparently unhurt, half-crawling, half-stumbling away from it, glancing over his shoulder, tripping and picking himself up. His progress had a nightmare slowness; he was trying to run but could not get a purchase in the mud.

His fears were justified. The crowd of girls was only half-way down the field when the plane burst into flames with a shuddering bang like thunder. A blast of heat struck Thea and stopped them all in their tracks. For one second, she could see the black pin-man figure of the pilot just standing there among the great unfurling orange petals of fire before he keeled over and was engulfed. The air was full of small black fragments; she could taste the fire in her mouth and feel it searing her eyes. She heard a voice from behind yelling, and saw Bailey, ordering them back: the fire engine was coming, and the soldiers, everything would be all right if they just got back in.

They ran back to the gates, some of the girls crying and screaming hysterically. The terrified cows and horses raced back and forth at the top of the field, seeking a way out.

In the entrance to the shed Thea was almost bowled over by Mabel and her cronies, who came behind her. She saw that they were carrying something, a flat piece of metal, warped on one side.

'What on earth's that?' she asked sharply, pulling Mabel out of the way of the on-coming girls. 'You can't bring that in here, it could cause an explosion. What a ridiculous thing to do!'

'It's only a souvenir,' said Mabel sulkily.

'*Souvenir?* Off that plane?'

'Yes, it landed right at our feet when the plane went up.'

The others had gathered round, they were fascinated by the piece of metal, fingering it and discussing it and staring admiringly at Mabel. Thea snatched it away.

''Ere—miss!'

'I never heard anything so callous! That pilot died right in front of your eyes and all you could do was collect souvenirs!' She was almost inarticulate with rage, her voice didn't sound like her own. The girls, all but Mabel, stood round looking sheepish. They could hear the shouts and engines of the firemen and soldiers arriving outside, and the cows mooing.

'We didn't collect it,' said Mabel, 'it landed right at our feet like I said.'

'I don't care about that!' yelled Thea. 'It's the principle of the thing, and you brought it here to boast about it, you just don't understand anything, do you?'

Still carrying the piece of metal she went into her office and slammed the door. There was complete silence in the shed; you could hear the sounds of the firefighters down on the river bank. Thea laid the fragment on her desk and sat down unsteadily, but with a very straight back. Perhaps if she stared at it long enough and hard enough she could send some kind of message to the people who had loved the pilot, to say that she was sorry. When she finally emerged into the shed an hour later, they all behaved as though nothing had happened. And when it was time to go home, there was nothing left to see in the field, and the animals were grazing placidly once more.

The following morning Andrea arrived. She appeared in Thea's office at half-past twelve. 'I hope I'm not disturbing you,' she said, but without much feeling. 'I was down this way so I just thought I'd come.'

'Are you on an article or something?' Thea was not pleased to see her friend; she had work to do and she was in no mood to cope with Andrea.

'No . . . it's not work.' Andrea perched on the edge of the desk, pulled off one glove, a finger at a time, and stood up again. She seemed nervy, her voice sharp and hurried.

'Well,' said Thea, 'it's coming up to lunch time, do you want some?'

'Not particularly.'

Thea sighed and leaned back in her chair. 'To be honest,

I'm not even sure you should be in here. You're not properly dressed.'

'Too bad!' Andrea made an impatient gesture.

'Sorry.' Thea was puzzled. This was an Andrea she had seen only a few times before, and that usually at home with the Suttons in Fulham. There, she had often been like this: snappish, ill at ease, uncomfortable in her setting. Her frame of mind affected her appearance, and today she lacked the vital spark that normally prevented her from being painfully plain. The black suit that had looked so chic a few months ago now appeared ill-chosen, too severe for her thin figure and pale complexion.

She took her other glove off and rolled both of them into a tight ball in her long, pale fingers. 'So,' she said in a high, brittle voice, 'how's the world treating you, Thea Tennant?'

The turn of phrase was so exactly like someone else's of their mutual acquaintance that Thea saw at once how things were.

'Andrea . . .'

'You seem well settled in here. Pretty busy, is it? I bet you're awfully good at this kind of thing. Do all the girls think you're wonderful?'

'I doubt it.' Thea kept her voice low. If it was going to be like that, there was nothing to do but ride the storm. She stared at the dusty surface of her desk where a tiny red money spider toiled across the canyons and ridges towards the cliff edge.

'What about the family? All well?'

'Yes, thank you. At least, not bad. Mother's not in very good health these days.'

'Is that so? I'm sorry about that.' Andrea sounded as if she truly were sorry, but was fighting it just the same. 'And Dulcie?'

'Still in Paris.'

'Maurice?'

'Cambridge. Look, Andrea, I wish you'd say whatever it is you came to say, and if I've done something wrong, I'd like to know.'

Andrea went over to the narrow, speckled window and stood staring out. Her back in the black suit was arrow-straight, her hands out of sight in front of her, still kneading and squeezing the gloves. 'Oh, you've done nothing wrong.' Her voice was sing-song, artificial.

'Then what?'

'After all,' went on Andrea, as if Thea hadn't spoken, 'you can't help what you are. We don't blame animals for acting true to form, do we?'

'What am I, then?' Thea was pricked. She got up and went over to Andrea; she simply did not have the energy for all this double-meaning and half-truth. 'Andrea, is it Louis?'

'Louis?' Andrea spun round. Her eyes and the tip of her nose were pink, but there were no tears. 'Louis? Oh, you mean *that* Louis.'

'Yes,' Thea was puzzled, '*that* Louis. I'm afraid somehow you may have gained a quite wrong impression and I'd hate you to think—'

'But of *course* you would! You don't mean to hurt a soul, I know that.' She gave a cold little smile. 'You just can't help it.'

'That isn't fair.'

'It's a fact, though. You have so much, don't you, and you take it all for granted. I've had to make the best of the little God gave me, and work for the rest. Even feelings. Yours were carefully nurtured, allowed their freedom; mine were tidied away in a big drawer with mothballs like other messy things. The trouble was, all of a sudden I discovered a real feeling. Imagine!' Her self-parody was painful, both for her to utter and Thea to hear. Thea wanted to stop her, but couldn't. 'Oh yes, there was a regular Pandora's box of tricks waiting to be opened by someone.'

'I'm sorry. You have got it all wrong, though.'

'Sorry? Whatever for? Being yourself? Nonsense! The fortunes of war and so on.'

'I suppose you hate me now.' The weary recognition of yet another failure engulfed Thea. Andrea sidestepped the question; she seemed to have encased herself in a wall of irony that deflected all attempts to get through to her.

'Of course,' she said, 'he didn't attempt to keep it from me. He thinks me such a level-headed, independent girl, it's what he likes about me. And he's absolutely right. No secrets between us, good Lord no. So!' Abruptly she began to put the gloves back on, pulling tight and smooth the fingers of one hand with those of the other. She had come spoiling for a fight, but ultimately had refused herself the relief of having one. Feelings, along with understanding, had once more been tidied away.

Thea stood helpless, agonized, watching her go to the door. There must be something she could say. She stepped forward and caught Andrea's arm. 'Andrea, dear Andrea, please. Just one thing. I was never even remotely attracted to Louis.'

It was the worst thing she could have said. Andrea looked down at her hand and removed it as one might an unpleasant insect. Her voice, when she spoke, was icy.

'Thank you, Thea. Thank you so much.' She shut the door swiftly and quietly behind her.

The following Sunday Thea went riding. It was something she did less and less often these days, partly due to lack of energy and partly because she felt that, when at home, she should be with her parents. Whether or not her presence was of any benefit she didn't know, but she suspected that almost any distraction, especially for Venetia, was therapeutic. But on this occasion she was being deliberately selfish. It was essential that she get away from other people's needs and their problems, to lick her own wounds in peace.

She took Amira, who was too old for all but the gentlest hacking, and set off up the road, turning right after about half a mile to cut across the side of the hill, with the rusty autumn woods frowning down on her to the north, and the Ewhurst valley folded snugly in on itself below the fields to the south. The hedges were covered in berries, hips, hoars, brambles and elder, and the first few gulls sat like white sailing ships on the brown waves of ploughed furrows. She was following a ride that she and Aubrey had often taken together years ago, across the hill, down the church path as far as the wicket gate, and back up the Elm Walk. It wasn't far, a children's ride, really, and Amira knew it by heart. Thea let the reins lie on the old mare's neck and tried to recall the special feel of those long-ago rides—the shouting, and the cantering, the wheeling and turning and daring: the perfect, unalloyed, unvalued pleasure of being young and free, with nothing better to do than enjoy oneself. And after all, what was there better to do than that? She mourned the inevitable passing of that selfish joy, the easy tears and easy healing. She could feel her present solitariness hardening her, changing her, making her stronger she supposed, though even that was a kind of failure, a setting of the face against life's variety.

It was five o'clock when she reached the bottom of the Elm Walk, dusk. A stealthy autumn mist was settling over the countryside, giving the twin rows of trees a church-like presence, deadening the sound of the mare's hooves on the path. As she rode she could hear the bell of St Catherine's tolling mournfully for evensong. There wasn't a tumbling peal any more, for there weren't enough able-bodied young men left in the village to pull the heavy ropes. George Aitcheson rang the bell himself now, a lonely, dogged note calling in the wilderness. Up ahead she could make out the twin-peaked silhouette of the house, with lights on at either end—the kitchen and the library. There had been a time when this return from winter riding had been an experience akin to entering the gates of heaven, a delightful sensation of moving from dark and cold to light and warmth. They would gee-up the ponies and trot briskly up the Elm Walk; Mrs Duckham would hear them coming and toast the muffins.

But now there was no comfort at the house, and she did not hurry but let Amira dawdle, with her head hanging. Now it was she who had to comfort, encourage and listen. The balance had shifted, she could not even say precisely how and when, and the backward vista of childhood was truly cut off behind tall gates.

She rode Amira into the stable, removed and hung up her tack, filled the hay net and strapped a blanket over her. The scent of the mare's damp coat and the pungent straw had once been the very essence of happiness. Now it made her sad because the horse was old, at the end of her life, and the stable was almost empty.

Then she went out into the yard, across the drive and into the house, not noticing the car parked in the shadow on the far side of the steps.

'Jack!'

He was sitting, legs crossed, on the sofa. Sophie was in her usual upright chair with the tea trolley before her; Ralph and Venetia were on either side of the fire. Jack stood as she came in. There was a huge delighted smile on Venetia's face. The library felt warm and welcoming and complete, as it had not done in months. She would not have believed it possible to be so pleased to see anyone. She experienced an enormous sense of relief as though she had suddenly been lightened of a terrible burden.

431

'Jack, it's so good to see you!'

She went over to him and he took her shoulders and kissed her cheek as he had always done in the old days. The feeling of his being there, of the wholeness he created by his presence, was so powerful, that she hardly saw him, hardly needed to. His hands on her shoulders, his light, brotherly kiss, the meaningless words he said to her, the way he sat on the sofa: they were perfect, and she drank them in with speechless joy through every pore in her body.

'Isn't it splendid?' Venetia was saying. 'He got home only this morning. I think it's so good of Daphne and Robert to spare him.'

'Says he mustn't stay long,' added Ralph drily, looking over at them, 'so let the fellow have his tea.'

'Muffin, dear?' asked Sophie. Thea took one and promptly abandoned it to cold sogginess on her plate while she studied Jack, who was responding to some question of Venetia's about his journey. He looked thin, gaunt really, since he had never carried much weight, and there was a dullness about his eyes as if tiredness and the witnessing of too much death were a poison that had entered his very bones and sucked the goodness from them.

He turned to pass Venetia's cup to Sophie and looked at her with a quick, understanding smile.

Thea found herself saying yet again: 'It's wonderful to have you back,' and he gave her hand a little pat. 'I still can't believe it,' she said, laughing. 'We knew you were coming but we didn't know when. And somehow it's been so long, I could hardly believe it, but now you're here . . .'

'I thought I'd surprise you,' he said quietly to her, and then smiling at everyone to show he meant all of them. There was a new and special gentleness in his manner as if he had, in his absence, come to value them all as he had never done before.

Venetia said: 'Jack, it's been so long. Surely it's going to end soon?' Her voice was full of anxiety; she really believed, thought Thea, that Jack might tell her the war was almost over.

'I don't think so.' He cleared his throat. The room was very, very quiet; you could almost hear the fog pressing on the windows. 'It's a sickening business. But I do know one thing, no one who has fought in this war will ever be the same. It is a kind of death, and if any of us come through it we'll be ghosts.'

Thea thought: already he is not the same. And she asked, almost in a whisper, 'As bad as that?'

'Yes. Oh yes.' The little words were matter of fact as if he wondered she had doubted his analysis. She saw that he had brought down some kind of shutter which excluded them—all of them—from the things he kept in the back of his mind and which were now part of him. 'But anyway,' he said, 'let's not talk about that now.'

'You haven't been wounded, that's good,' said Ralph.

'No. A few small complaints, no one escapes without their share of those, but as far as the Germans are concerned I seem to have a ring round me with "Do not touch" written on it.' He spoke quickly with a nervous, facetious note. 'Sometimes,' he concluded with a funny little laugh, 'I feel ashamed. As if I'm living on other fellows' credit, you know?' He looked round, saw that they didn't, and muttered 'Anyway . . . as I say . . .'

Thea could have cried for him. He wanted so much for this to be a happy occasion, she could see that, but he was dragging a terrible burden of sad memories and exhaustion and it was beginning to sap his strength. She pictured a gaping black hole to the edge of which he clung gamely, but with increasing weakness. It was up to them to rescue him.

'I've just been on one of the old rides,' she said brightly. 'Where we used to go with Aubrey, as children. It hasn't changed.'

'Poor boy,' sighed Sophie. 'In the hands of the enemy.' Thea could have kicked her.

'Oh, the enemy's not so dreadful,' replied Jack, 'it's the bally war that's dreadful.' He laughed again, whistling in the dark. 'As a matter of fact I've got something here that might interest you.' He unbuttoned the breast pocket of his uniform tunic and brought out several pieces of paper, one of which Thea recognized as her most recent letter. He selected a dog-eared photograph and returned the rest of the things to his pocket. 'Remember Thea, I told you about the fraternization between our chaps and the Germans last Christmas?'

'Oh yes,' she nodded. 'And what a stink it caused among the generals. I thought how sad it was that someone in a position of power didn't make the most of it and cease hostilities there and then.'

'Quite.' He stared at her as she spoke, and then appeared to rouse himself back to the matter in hand. 'Well, this is a photograph that the cavalry officer gave me. I wonder a lot if he's still alive. I liked him.' He passed it to Thea. 'He's written his name on the back, but he has that kind of curly copperplate writing, it's hard to read . . .'

An eternity passed.

'. . . something von Crieff, I think,' he said.

CHAPTER FOURTEEN

'I don't want a bayonet in my belly
I don't want my buttocks shot away;
I'd rather stay in England,
In merry, merry England
And rusticate my bloomin' life away.'
Wimperis/Finch

'Thea! Dear girl, are you going to allow the rest of us a look?'

'*Is* it them, Ralph?'

'Truthfully, I wouldn't know; it's donkey's years since I clapped eyes on any of them. Though I don't know . . . that could be your sister, her face is familiar . . .'

'Let me see. Yes! Yes, that's them! Jessica looks just the same, and Thomas. He was such a fine-looking man, though I must say he's aged. And the little boy. It's certainly them. What an extraordinary thing!'

'I had no idea he was anyone you knew, it seems incredible. He was an awfully nice fellow. I said that in my letter at the time, didn't I?'

'May I see?'

'Jack, pass that to Sophie, would you?'

'Thank you. So these are the famous von Crieffs! You and your sister are not much alike, are you?'

'More alike than that picture would indicate, actually, but she's always been plumper. She's such a dear. I must say it makes me realize how long it is since I saw them, and now goodness knows . . . It's funny how things turn out. Of course we've never met the children. Isn't Josef handsome?'

'Typical Prussian. Looks good in uniform.'

'Ralph!'

'It's all right, I'm not impugning his character. Thea?'

'Darling!'

'It's all right, Mrs Tennant, let me go.'

'Jack, would you? Oh dear . . .'

Thea stood in the middle of the dark, chilly hall and took long breaths. The last thing she had wanted was to make a

435

scene on this, of all occasions, with Jack home and everyone happy. But she had had to escape. The shock-wave emanating from that photograph had abruptly shattered the newly pieced together order of her mind, and blasted the warm feeling of relief and contentment which now seemed spurious. She would go back in and make some excuse, she just needed a moment.

'Thea?'

The library door opened, emitting a wedge of soft, yellow light and the murmur of anxious voices. It closed again.

'What's up?'

'I'm sorry. It was such a shock.'

'Don't worry.' He came and stood beside her, hands in pockets. 'It's I who should be sorry.'

'You couldn't possibly have known.'

'Well, no. All the same, it must be a chance in a million, something like that. They're the people you stayed with, the summer before last?'

'That's right.'

'I should have put two and two together, dammit.' He kicked viciously at the rug. 'I'm sure your parents must have mentioned them, mentioned their name. I just never dreamed . . .'

'It doesn't matter!' Her voice rose, with a break in it, and she folded her arms tight, literally taking a grip on herself. Jack paced across the hall and then turned to face her.

'Perhaps you could write to them? They're part of your family after all.'

'Jack.'

'What is it?'

She took a deep breath that snagged and caught in her throat. 'It's Josef.'

'Oh I *see.*' His response was so immediate, so carefully unsurprised. 'Yes, I understand. Poor Thea!' He came over to her and held her by the shoulders, giving her a little shake. 'Stiff upper lip. He's probably all right. He's cavalry, as I'm sure you know, and they haven't seen much action in this war. My God!' He clapped a hand to his brow. 'If only I'd known.'

She was comforted by his directness. 'Thank you,' she said simply.

He tilted her chin gently with one hand. 'Are you ready to rejoin the company?'

'Yes.'

'Good girl. Come on then.' He took her arm and led her towards the library. 'No need to suffer alone, you know. You are among friends.'

'I know.' She smiled at him as he pushed the door open, and there was something in his face which disturbed her, but which she was too weakened to read.

The others began busily to ladle oil onto the troubled waters.

'Shall we see you tomorrow, Jack?' asked Venetia. 'I did mention it to your parents.'

He shook his head. 'You must count me out, I'm afraid. I have an unpleasant duty to perform over at Sherbrooke. My young second in command was killed last Christmas, and the least I can do is to go and visit his family. He was a first-rate officer.'

'Sherbrooke, you say?' Ralph tilted his head back and peered down his nose at Jack. 'What name?'

'Massie.'

'Yes, I remember old Massie, he and his wife came over once or twice in the old days, when the D'Acres were still here. And we met them once at that bally awful dance at Sherbrooke Hall. Just after we left London, remember Venetia?'

'I quite enjoyed it.'

'Ghastly evening.'

Thea had to smile at her father's vehemence. 'I don't remember going.'

'You and Dulcie were too young.'

'Yes,' said Jack, 'Bill mentioned the dances.'

'There were three sons, if my memory serves me,' went on Ralph. 'William would be . . .'

'Bill was the youngest,' said Jack.

Thea saw Jack again the following Sunday, after a week at the factory which seemed interminable. Depression hung over her like a heavy blanket, dragging at her legs, stifling her, inducing a terrible grey tiredness which made every movement an effort. It frightened her, she hourly half-expected to make some fatal mistake, cause an accident, or destroy forever her fragile links of understanding with the girls. They knew, and she knew that they knew. They watched her, covertly, and were unusually deferential, as though dealing with a sick person. To make matters worse there was the knowledge that as 1915 neared its end the war was no nearer its conclusion. Indeed, as far as the Allies were concerned, it had been a disastrous year of muddles, blunders, deadlock and failure. The second Christmas of the war loomed up ahead like an ominous milestone. Two of the girls at Dolton Green had contracted severe TNT poisoning, and one had died. The news sent a thread of fear buzzing through the shell-shop. Ralph came down and read the riot act about the safety regulations and after that silence, correct but gloomy, had been the order of the day.

Thea thought she was going mad. She did not understand herself. The depression, the exhaustion, the peculiar numbness that gripped her, body and soul, were things she had thought quite foreign to her. She had always felt things keenly, had gone out to meet the best and the worst that life had to offer with a kind of irrepressible relish. Now, her senses were dulled, her energy running at such a low ebb she found herself wondering just what it would take to rouse her. Like an animal going into hibernation she was sliding ever deeper into an emotional torpor—safe, protective, removed from reality.

When the Tennants arrived at Long Lake in time for Sunday luncheon, Jack remarked this change at once. Watching her as she greeted his parents and came across to him, her hair whipped across her face by the sharp autumn wind, he felt a wave of helpless tenderness for her. The comfort he could give her was so limited and he so ill-equipped, at present, to offer it. Like two poor trapped animals in neighbouring cages they met, both bewildered and unhappy, but each mourning a separate loss.

He placed a quick kiss on her cold cheek. 'I'm so glad you came.'

'Why, did you think I wouldn't?'

'It's your only day off, I'd have understood.'

'What, and stay at home all day with Aunt Sophie?' She gave him a wry smile, and he took her arm to lead her indoors, but she resisted. 'No, don't let's go in for a moment, it's such ages since I've been here, let's walk down the hill a little way.'

'All right. You're not cold?'

She shook her head, although her hand, holding her collar across her neck, was bluish, and her face tight.

'Hey!' Robert Kingsley called after them. 'Where are you two off to?'

Jack cupped his hand to his mouth. 'Just a little walk, back in a moment.'

'There's mulled wine!'

'We'll be there!'

He stepped backwards for a few paces, watching the group walk into the house. They looked old. There was something about the movement of their heads, the way they touched each other, a solicitude as if they saw the mark of time on each other and tried to lessen its impact by sharing. It was disconcerting, the way the house looked not one jot different from the way it had always looked, while the people were changed beyond recognition. The implacable four-square grey stone facade of Long Lake would still be staring down the hill when they were all dead. He ran to catch up with Thea. The wind had whipped some colour into her cheeks, she looked more herself.

'They've knocked down the folly!' she said, pointing across the lake to the opposite hillside. You could still just see the scar of bare ground on the tussocky grass.

'Yes, ages ago. It was very dangerous.'

'You never took me there, did you, you were determined to keep it a secret.' She grinned at him to show she didn't mind.

'You know,' he said, continuing down the hill, 'I found a body in there, the last time I ever went there. About two years ago, before the war.'

'A body? What sort of body?'

'An old tramp. He must have been there for ages, the smell was appalling. He'd got all the things out of my box, and used all the candles.'

'That's dreadful. And you have no idea who it was?'

'None. The police came and retrieved him but there was no hope of identification.'

'What a terrible thing. It must have been awful for you, finding him.'

Jack did not reply. He remembered all too clearly the selfishness of his response. He had wanted to escape, but someone had got there before him. He had felt resentment, disappointment, revulsion. No pity.

'I've got something of his somewhere,' he said instead.

'Oh? What?'

'I think it's a picture, but it's absolutely filthy. Actually I don't know where it is now. I don't really even know why I took it, just a magpie instinct, I suppose.'

'You are funny.' She shook her head. 'I'd have wanted to clean it right away, and find out about it.'

'I wasn't in the mood.'

They reached the water's edge, the ground felt springy and treacherous beneath their feet. Close to, the water was brownish and opaque, its surface furrowed and wrinkled by the wind, its dry border of thickly massed reeds whispering and rattling.

'Looks bleak, doesn't it,' he said. 'Let's go back.'

'I've always liked it,' she said as they started back up the hill. 'It's so open, not like Chilverton House, buried in a hole.'

'It's open all right. One of the coldest places I know.'

'Misery.' She tucked her hand through his arm and pressed up to him, as though to make him warm. It was the old Thea for a moment, but with some difference that he could not at first pinpoint. When he did so, he had to smile at the nice irony contained in it. For now, he realized, she liked him. Whatever separate metamorphoses they had undergone in the year since they'd seen each other had swept aside that barrier of awkwardness, and they were friends.

He threw back his head and laughed and she looked up at him, smiling but baffled. 'What's the joke?'

'None of your business.'

She didn't seem to mind, and they clung together, trudging and leaning against the bullying wind, all the way up the hill.

During lunch the conversation was conducted mainly amongst the older members of the group. Jack and Thea sat on their opposite sides of the table like a couple of foreigners, understanding but unable to join in on the same level. With agonizing politeness no one discussed war. Not even Aubrey's name, usually considered a 'safe', neutral topic, was mentioned.

'What have you been doing with yourself this past week, Jack?' asked Ralph over plum tart and cream. 'Good to be back?'

Jack didn't answer the second question. 'I've been enjoying myself, tinkering with the car, fixing fences, lopping branches and chopping logs.'

'Doesn't sound very restful!' They all laughed.

'A change is as good as a rest.'

'I don't know.' Daphne beamed benignly on her son. 'It's like having a March gale in the house. He's also been clearing out all the old trunks and bits and pieces from the loft.'

Robert leaned towards Venetia. 'I thought we'd never be rid of the several hundred copies of *Boy's Own*. I was seriously considering papering a room with them.'

Jack smiled at them, unembarrassed. Thea realized that they were talking about someone else, someone who no longer existed. 'One has to slough off all that junk some time,' he said. 'And now seemed like the moment. There's something immensely satisfying about throwing things away, it's a great relief.'

'Don't you feel sad about any of them?' asked Venetia. She was looking especially beautiful, Thea thought, in a silvery grey dress and a long double row of pearls. Beautiful but frail.

'Not at all,' said Jack. 'I'm ruthless.'

'But *I* am retaining one or two souvenirs, on the quiet,' put in his mother, and everyone laughed again. The atmosphere was delicate, tremulous, like fine tender skin stretched over a painful swelling. They were all frightened of hurting themselves, there weren't enough of them left that they could afford casualties.

When lunch was over Jack said to Thea: 'Do you want to help me dispose of the last boxful of juvenilia?'

'Why not? Except I'll probably slow down the throwing-away process.'

'Never mind.'

They went upstairs to the big, square landing. Long Lake was not as large as Chilverton House, but it was infinitely more stately. Thea put this down to the fact that it had always been emptier, whereas Chilverton since the time of the Tennants' occupancy had positively bulged at the seams. The first floor here was impeccably tidy and very cold. Their breath steamed. The doors, symmetrically placed around the landing, were mostly closed, except for Jack's, through which were visible a black oblong trunk, unfastened but with the lid down, and a square school tuck box, the wooden variety with black metal corners and the name 'J.R.KINGSLEY' painted on the top in shiny black capitals.

Thea went into the room and looked down at the trunk and the box. 'Where do we start?'

'The tuck box. I've been through the other, it's all expendable.'

While he leaned down and undid the box she looked around the room. She had been up here sometimes, when they had first come to visit, and it had hardly changed. It was still austere and, she thought, rather grim, with watercolours of military uniforms hanging on one wall and a massive mahogany tallboy and wardrobe lowering against the other. Jack's slippers beside the bed and his check dressing-gown hanging on the back of the door looked rather forlorn. As a child from a large family she had always looked with pity upon only children. The photographs of Jack downstairs in the drawing-room, Jack at every stage in his career, had always worried her. In all of them the face had worn an expression of dogged dignity, a little aloof, a little sad but full of determination. What a load to bear, all the love and expectation and hope of one's parents.

She looked down at him. There was something poignant in his narrow, close-cropped head bent over the tuck box, a youthfulness about the back of the neck where the hair grew in a smooth point on the white skin. She no longer felt the least tension in his presence. Perhaps it was just the simple recognition of mutual need, the spontaneous huddling-together of two animals in a corn field as the reapers close in. They had neither of them, since his return, mentioned the letters that had passed between them, not from any sense of delicacy, but just because it did not seem necessary. The written words had closed and healed the wound, gradually but perfectly. And they had helped her to see his reserve no longer as a form of arrogance, but of defence, and with improved understanding the balance had tipped. It dawned on her that the gladness and relief she had experienced on finding him back were mutual.

'Stamp album.' He sat back on his heels to examine it. 'I had rather a good collection.'

She kneeled by him and looked over his shoulder. 'It must be quite valuable.'

'I don't think so—quantity rather than quality.' He dumped it to one side. 'Now what's this?'

He thrust his arm down the side of the box, beneath a pile of curled and yellowing sheet music, and drew out a small, round blackened object. 'Well I never, here it is—what I was telling you about.' He rubbed the object on his sleeve. 'You have a look.'

Thea took it and rose, going over to the window and holding it up to the light. It was a picture in a little oval tortoise-shell frame, but the glass was covered in a peculiarly adhesive species of black dirt. She rubbed it with her thumb and it cracked and peeled off in greasy flakes, like paper. The picture, a crudely tinted studio photograph, was of a slim young woman in a checked dress with a high collar and long tight sleeves. She was not pretty but there was about her thin, long-nosed face a formidable quality of strength and indomitable determination that made it handsome. Her reddish hair was pulled back tightly, the fringe frizzed at the front, but the forbidding, haughty expression in the eyes seemed to contradict this frivolity.

'She's nice,' said Thea, showing the picture to Jack. 'She reminds me of someone.'

He studied it. 'I know, she's like old Primmy.'

'That's right! She's got just that look about her, strong-willed and independent. I wonder who she was?'

'The old boy's daughter, I imagine, she looks too young to have been his wife.'

'You know, they could have used this for identification. Shouldn't you have handed it over?'

He shrugged. 'It never occurred to me. But I don't think it would have done much good. They said he'd been on the road for years. Besides,' he tapped the picture with the back of his fingers, 'she doesn't look an awfully forgiving young lady, not the sort who'd want to be reminded her papa was a gentleman of the road. Take it if you want,' he added. 'I've got no use for it and I feel pretty bad about robbing the poor chap anyway.'

'Thank you.'

'You can clean her up nicely.' He laughed. 'She looks damn steely to me!'

They spent the rest of the afternoon peacefully going through the remaining contents of the box, to no great effect since Thea snatched back every summarily rejected item and subjected it to exhaustive examination and discussion. It was dark by the time they finished and went down to tea, and sleety rain was battering on the windows.

In the drawing-room Ralph and Robert Kingsley were comatose after two hours' post-prandial slumber, but Venetia

and Daphne had that genial, soft-eyed look that accompanies
mother-to-mother conversation of the pleasantest kind. Thea
had the odd sensation of the years having fallen away, of a
sort of conspiracy to re-create childhood. Everything about
this day had had that feel about it, a bitter-sweet unreality in
which it had been impossible not to participate because it was
so soothing. Tomorrow, with all the tough, unavoidable
challenges of a day at the factory, seemed like years away,
and the war no more than a half-heard rumble in the
distance. But when the time came to say goodbye, with
promises to meet again next week-end, Jack's last, she caught
on Jack's face again the look of detached strangeness, as if the
reverse shadow of imminent departure had fallen across him,
reminding him of the other world which was now, for him,
the real one.

The success of Dulcie's enterprise was beyond her wildest
dreams. It proved both profitable and enjoyable. Since the
sergeant she had only had to solicit a few more times. Simon
Garrick of the Grenadier Guards had been so delighted with
her that he had at once assured her of a select and generous
clientele of unimpeachable pedigree. From that moment, she
did not have to go onto the streets unless she felt like it. She
had moved to a better apartment, hired a Corsican maid and
found that it was possible to run the business as if it were
pleasure, treating each client as a guest, which suited both
sides nicely. She was amazed that it could be so easy to make
money, and the independence it brought her was an enchanting experience. She cared more about her surroundings,
spent her earnings on pictures and furnishing, and had some
cards printed so as to ban the sordid side of things forever
from her life.
The nature of the commodity in which she dealt disturbed
her not at all. She rejoiced in her talent and perfected her
skills. She discovered the ability to move easily from one man
to the next, adapting to their different requirements. In her
way, while she loved none, she loved all. She liked men: to
see their coats and caps in the hall, to hear their voices on the
stairs and to satisfy their bodies in bed. Her reaction to them
was instinctive and animal, dictated by the moment and
untainted by expectation or aftermath.
She felt calmer and happier than at any time in her life,
and this was not only due to the greater material comforts

that she could now afford. She valued herself more because of the value others put upon her. At Chilverton House she had resigned herself to being a sort of permanent ornament. Now, though she did not think of it in such precise terms, what had previously been the mere icing on the cake had become the cake itself, something of real worth both to herself and others. On a rare free evening she would buy food in the market. She taught herself to cook, something she had never had the slightest desire to do before, and found she enjoyed it. There were even times when her men visited her to do no more than talk, and have a glass of wine, and bring her little presents. Then there would be a group of them there. It would be so friendly and warm and full of affection that she was truly glad that her life had taken the funny turns it had. She had found a niche at last.

The change in Dulcie was crystallized one Sunday afternoon, the maid's day off, when she received an unexpected visit.

She was a little put out to hear the knock on the door. She normally reserved Sunday for close friends and for herself, and certainly expected no casual callers. She was sitting in the window of her little drawing-room reading a novel, another pastime she enjoyed these days.

On her way across the room to answer the door she automatically glanced at herself in the mirror. She wore a blue blouse and check skirt and her hair was loose. She looked about sixteen.

She opened the door. A small, slight young man in officer's uniform stood on the dark landing. He was by the banisters, looking down into the stairwell as though he hadn't really meant to ring her bell at all. She knew the type.

'Yes?' She stood in the doorway, smiling at him.

'Teddy said I might call.' He still stood to one side, turning his cap between his hands, a bag of nerves.

'Teddy?' she tested, but still with a smile, only sounding him out.

'Teddy Reynolds.'

'Oh yes. Well, do please come in.' She held the door open for him and he entered, rather sideways, as if squeezing between two fat ladies. Dulcie was glad for his sake that she had on her 'ingenue' rather than her 'femme fatale' face. Knowing from experience how to put him at his ease, she did not give him another glance but turned and went along the passage to the drawing room, saying over her shoulder: 'Come and have a glass of wine and we can talk.'

She went straight to the side table, leaving him to follow and look around as he wanted, and poured two glasses of white wine. When she turned back he was standing looking out of the window, his cap still held in front of him like a schoolboy. Gently, she took the cap from him and put the glass in his right hand. Then she sat down and looked at the cap badge.

'I see you're in the same regiment as Teddy.'

'That's right.' He nodded and took a quick swig of the wine, half-emptying the glass. He was like a frightened rabbit.

'How much leave do you have?'

'Only today. I go back tonight.'

'Then it's good of you to call.' She put her head a little on one side, trying to catch his eye and make him return her smile, but without success. He was nice-looking, she thought, in spite of being small and slight: he had a sensitive, well-boned face and a tremulous mouth. She put his age at about eighteen and a half and his experience at nil. She decided that she would enjoy teaching him, the feel of his soft, boy's skin, and the special pleasure of making his first time marvellous.

'Why don't you come and sit down?' she asked, laying her hand on the couch beside her. He looked at her almost furtively out of the corner of his eye. 'Come on, let's be friends.' She meant it.

As if plucking up all his courage he drained the glass and turned to face her. It took all Dulcie's newly acquired professionalism not to gasp in horror.

The left-hand side of his face, now exposed to the sunlight pouring through the window, was a glistening mass of scar tissue, the corner of the mouth pulled down, and the eye grotesquely slitted as if there were no longer enough skin and flesh to frame it properly. But worst of all, the face was misshapen; there was a hollow where the corner of the jaw should have been, and the ear, protruding from an area of newly grown stubble, was no more than a vestigial knob of purplish flesh.

There was a dead hush, and then he said: 'Would you like me to go?'

'No.' Dulcie stared down at her lap, tracing the checks on

446

her skirt with one finger, trying to take a grip on herself. All her old squeamishness, the shrinking from everything coarse and ugly, rose up in her. She had seen scars before, certainly, but this was something on its own. The whole of that side of the boy's face was scarcely recognizable as human. She was revolted.

Hearing a sound, she looked up and saw him walking towards the door. Everything about his diminutive backview spoke of dejection.

'Oh no, don't! Please stay!' she called out and rose, her hand outstretched. She was suddenly quite certain that it would be a failure on her part to let him go.

He stopped, but would not look at her, standing there hanging his head. She sensed that he was now in a kind of spasm of youthful embarrassment, too agonizing to allow him to move either forward or back. It was up to her. She went to him and slipped her hand into his from behind, pulling slightly.

'Come.' She led him back to the couch and sat down, the boy on her right. She kept hold of his hand, linking her fingers through his, on her lap.

'Poor you,' she kept saying, 'poor you.' To remind herself that it was he, and not she, who suffered.

'This is awful for you,' he muttered. 'I should never have come.'

'Yes, you should.' With a mighty effort of will she looked up. Sitting on this side all she could see was the terrible damaged side of his face, the stretched, discoloured skin, the obscene knot of ear, the mock-lugubrious clown's eye and mouth. But then, when he turned a little and she could see all of him, the scars seemed different, merely superficial, with the natural and beautiful part of him still there underneath, and the left eye, bright and pleading, looking out at her like an animal in a cage. 'I'm pleased you're here,' she said simply, finding it was true. 'Really I am.'

'You're kind,' he said, more cheerfully, touchingly ready to be consoled. 'Teddy said you were wonderful.'

'I'm not that,' she blushed. 'Certainly not.'

'I sort of wanted to . . . test myself, if you know what I mean.'

'Yes,' said Dulcie. Slowly and deliberately she leaned forward and kissed his cheek. There was nothing to it, she found. The feel of it was much like any other cheek, warm

447

and smooth, and the strange little ear no more than an ear of a different shape. Having touched once she took courage, kissed the corner of his mouth, and his eye, stroked the ugly stubble with light fingers. 'You passed,' she said.

The boy sighed. He kneeled down and laid the scarred side of his face on her lap and they stayed like that, she stroking his hair, for half an hour or more until it was time for him to go.

'And so did I,' she thought. 'And so did I.'

On the first Saturday in November, Primmy had a day off. She left Oak Ridge House at two and cycled back to her billet in the village. It was a dark, dank afternoon drowned by a heavy swirling mist that clung in droplets to her black winter coat.

She had recently been re-billeted with a nice couple, the village postmaster and his wife, in their house at the back of the post office stores. She had a pleasant enough room overlooking the high street, Mr and Mrs Pett having been kind enough to move their nine-month-old baby, Ruth, in with them, and Mrs Pett's cooking was excellent. They were friendly, easy-going uncomplicated people who liked and admired Primmy, and she sensed their natural desire to be on more intimate terms with her. But she had always been a loner, she wasn't used to confiding in people or sharing her particular allocation of space and time. So she kept her distance, remaining polite and helpful but detached, and so far there had been no awkwardness. She didn't want to hurt their feelings, but when she was off-duty she preferred to be solitary.

The fact was, she only felt really at home at the hospital. It was her natural milieu as no other place in her life had been; she slotted in as smoothly and easily as though everything that had gone before had been merely a preparation for this. Which it had been, in a way. All her experience with brothers and sisters, all her domestic expertise, now stood her in good stead. Nowhere could supersede the hospital in her affections. When she was away she itched to be back in the swim, and chafed under the frustrating sensation of being cut off from the things that mattered. She was unsentimental about the patients, but determined that they should recover and that she, in whatever way was open to her, should be instrumental in that recovery. Far from feeling tired she

448

actually drew energy from her work, and the more urgent and pressing its nature the better she liked it. It was nothing short of torture now to have to go back to the post office stores after what they had all been through last night and this morning. She knew she would worry about the Canadian until she got back on the wards tomorrow. But Miss Rowse was adamant on this: that all the girls in her charge should take their proper time off unless it were absolutely unavoidable. She said—and Primmy could see the sense of it—that they owed it to the patients to go home and rest, and catch up on chores, so that they could return to work fresh. It was just selfish to court exhaustion and possible carelessness by refusing to do so. She would find out about the Canadian's condition the second she got back, though obliquely of course, and without rushing to his bedside, for any show of favouritism was quite out of the question.

The young man's sciatic nerve had been completely severed by shrapnel. When he had arrived off the hospital train late yesterday afternoon he'd looked as good as dead: his face a greyish-blue, his eyes sunk deep in their sockets, his right leg useless. It looked like another amputation, for sure. But the surgeon, Mr Venning, one of the top men from Barts who came down weekly, had said there was a chance of saving the leg, and while that chance existed he was damned if he'd start sawing it off. Primmy had been on theatre duty so she'd been able to watch him. Mr Venning had actually located the two ends of the nerve, which had sprung apart like elastic thread and were buried in a welter of damaged tissue and blood clots. Primmy saw them, all ragged and shredded by the shrapnel. The surgeon had trimmed them and sewn them together with the neatest, tiniest stitching she'd ever seen, even more finicky than Mrs Maxwell's petit-point. Then, very carefully in that great, gaping, gory hole, he had wrapped animal fibrin round the join to strengthen it before closing the wound. It had been the most awe-inspiring and the most thorough piece of work Primmy had ever witnessed, and she set great store by thoroughness. Mr Venning had helped her dry the instruments afterwards in the sluice, because it was late, and he had talked in such a humble, businesslike way about the operation, hoping it would 'do the trick' and so on, and thanking her for her invaluable assistance. She'd told him it was only her job, but it was nice to be thanked all the same, and by someone so august.

The massage sister was under instruction to move the leg, just a little, every single day. It would be a miracle if the Canadian walked away from Oak Ridge on his own two feet. Well, no: she shook her head to herself because she didn't believe in miracles; not a miracle, but a well-earned victory.

Maurice, hanging about outside the post office stores, was just beginning to wonder if Primmy were not after all inside. On arrival he had been suddenly overwhelmed with shyness and had not gone in. He was fairly sure that she would not be back until two-thirty or so, but now he was beginning to wonder. He must look awfully foolish, not to say suspicious, loitering out here on the pavement, with the fog blurring his glasses, and Mrs Dilkes's letter growing soggier by the minute. He glanced down at it, his passport to Primmy. He was shivering, and not only from the cold. It came home to him that he really had not the least idea why he was here, or what he intended to say. It was just that there were certain ineluctable drifts and currents in one's life that could not be ignored, one had to be carried by them and see where they led. In his case, pacifism was one, and Primmy another. And somewhere in the tidied-away muddle at the back of his mind he knew the two had to be brought together, for better or worse. Before, it would have been unthinkable. But Primmy's new independence made it possible. And he had a strong sensation of time being at a premium, of the future being severely circumscribed, and opportunities running out.

As he turned to open the door of the post office he saw her, freewheeling down the hill, very upright, with her starched cap fluttering. Apart from the cap, she was mostly in black—a black coat belted tightly round her, black knitted gloves, black stockings and rather fierce-looking black laced shoes—but he could see the light blue hem of her VAD's dress just showing beneath the coat.

She took one foot off the pedal and began to slow down, using the foot as a kind of brake. She was almost next to him by the time she stopped, and was actually lifting the front wheel of the bicycle onto the pavement before she noticed him.

'Oh. Hallo.' She sounded not in the least surprised, but a little disgruntled, as though he had disturbed her. Maurice felt a flush of awkwardness, his blood swirling hotly against his cold skin.

'Hallo, Primmy.'

'What are you doing here?' she enquired tersely, not looking at him, busy manoeuvring the rest of the bike over the curb.

'I've been down at Chilverton House for a few days, I wanted to see Jack Kingsley, he's on leave you know . . . I thought I'd come and see how you were getting on. Your mother told me when your half-day was—as a matter of fact I brought this letter from her, to save her the postage, you know . . .' He thrust it towards her and she took it. This was not at all the way he had intended the delivery. He'd wanted to save it, make something of it, but now he felt like a messenger boy.

'Thank you,' she said. 'Well then.' She stood there, holding the handlebars of the bicycle before her like a shield, defensively. 'How did you get here?' she asked, as though it were clearly impossible for him to use conventional means.

'Train to Canterbury and bus. I wondered how you were getting on,' he said again.

'Very well, thank you.' For a moment he thought she was actually going to send him on his way, having taken the letter and given him the answer to his question. But her sense of propriety won through. 'Do you want to come in? I could make a cup of tea.'

'Thank you. If you're sure it's no—'

'It's no trouble,' she said curtly. He waited there while she pushed the bicycle into the narrow alley at the side of the shop and methodically padlocked it. Looking round at the village of Oak Ridge, about the same size as Ewhurst but of unimpeachable gentility, Maurice thought that the padlocking could only be a hangover from Primmy's East End upbringing. She was taking no chances.

Slipping her mother's letter into her coat pocket she came round and opened the door of the stores. A soft, two-note chime signalled their entrance and a plump little body, younger than Primmy surely, appeared behind the post office grille.

'Oh, Miss Dilkes, it's only you.' She glanced affably but curiously at Maurice with a hint of perceptible, though quite inoffensive, coyness. 'And a friend.'

'This is Mr Maxwell from where I used to work,' said Primmy, with a strongly implied denial of anything so frivolous as friendship.

'Pleased to meet you.'

'This is Mrs Pett.'

'How do you do.' Maurice extended his hand, realized they could not shake hands through a wire grille, and thrust it instead into his pocket to jingle his loose change. Names, he could see, were a problem. Mrs Pett looked a jolly soul, not the kind who would call a lodger 'Miss Dilkes' unless it had been clearly indicated that she should. Probably they had no idea what kind of employment Primmy had been in before joining the VADs and Primmy was keeping it a secret. She had so far called him nothing at all to his face, for the old 'Mr Maurice' was far too deferential to be in keeping with her new life, 'Mr Maxwell' too formal, and 'Maurice' not even to be considered. The tone of her introduction must have made it abundantly clear that he was not a follower, but had given no clue to the unfortunate Mrs Pett of the precise nature of their relationship. Well—he jingled furiously—what *was* its precise nature? He didn't know himself.

He had never expected that her quiet acceptance of his hand after the nose-punching incident would make much difference. It was probably just the naturally kind and somewhat dutiful reaction of a practical, down-to-earth girl. He'd never dream of mentioning it, it would have been hideously embarrassing for her and the last thing he wanted was to cause her any discomfort. He must do his best to wear with plausibility whichever hat it suited Primmy to put upon him.

Now she took off her gloves and unbuttoned her coat, revealing the startling brightness of the red cross on her apron.

'Could I make a cup of tea?' she asked in a tone which implied that it was an almost impossible request.

'Of course you can!' Mrs Pett was not playing the game. 'You take Mr Maxwell in the kitchen and I'll take baby in the front room.'

'That's very kind of you.' Primmy shot a barbed glance over her shoulder at Maurice to make sure he realized all the trouble he was putting people to. Mrs Pett opened a flap in the post office counter and led them through a door at the back into a narrow dark corridor, full of the delicious smell of cake-baking.

'Cake'll be ready too,' she confided in Maurice, with a nod and a pop-eyed grin that showed she had him marked down for a follower anyway. 'Do you like cherry cake?'

'I'll say.'

Primmy hung her coat on one of a row of wooden hooks on the wall, and Mrs Pett showed them into the kitchen, which was warm and fragrant and cluttered with a big table covered in cracked red oilcloth. Beside the table, in a high chair, sat the baby, banging its tray with a metal potato masher and yelling.

'You make yourselves at home,' said Mrs Pett placidly, not bothering to raise her voice in spite of the din. 'Take the cake out and help yourselves.'

'But what about you?' asked Maurice. The potato masher fell to the ground with a clang and the yells increased sharply in both volume and frequency.

'Don't worry about that, I'm going to do a spot of mending in the parlour. You carry on and I'll have something when Arthur gets in.'

'It's most kind of you,' Maurice enunciated clearly, hoping she could lip-read.

The clamour subsided as Mrs Pett wrested her daughter from the high chair and jiggled her up and down. 'What a noisy girl, then! What was all that about? Eh? What then?'

The baby understandably made no reply but fixed Maurice with a glare so baleful that he had a sudden insight into the meaning of 'the evil eye'. He was also aware of a faint but unpleasant smell underpinning that of the cake. He had no experience of babies, had never, indeed, seen one this close to before. He glanced nervously at Primmy and noticed she looked quite indulgent. But then of course she came from a big family.

'She needs changing,' she said, 'unless I'm much mistaken.'

'That's right!' Mrs Pett addressed the baby. 'Of course she does! And we'll see to it right away.' Beaming amiably, the huge baby perched on her arm, she edged her way out of the door and left them to it.

Maurice sat down at the table and watched as Primmy, with brisk efficiency, assembled plates and cups and removed the cake from the oven, pricking it with a skewer and turning it out onto the blackened wire rack on the side. He felt comforted by the snug, everyday-ness of the kitchen, and the cake and the jingle of crockery. No one could get at him here and, for the moment, no one here knew the dreadful thing about him for which they might vilify and ostracize him. In these circumstances he might even find the courage to tell Primmy about it, as he intended to. He *fully* intended to . . . only, for the moment, it was bliss not to be hampered by that great load of painful but necessary self-justification.

Primmy put the kettle on to boil and sat down opposite him, reaching down to retrieve the potato masher and laying it at right angles to her as though it were of great significance. Maurice studied her thin, red hands. They were sensitive hands with tapering fingers, but the skin had a dry, papery quality and the palms were hard with shiny callouses. In spite of their redness he was sure they were cool, always cool. In contrast to their colour her face was as peaky as ever, small and taut, with the straight brown hair pulled severely back into a bun, not a strand of it loose. Because she was looking down, busy aligning the handle of the potato masher with the apex of the cross on her apron, he permitted himself the luxury of admiring her mouth, the only overtly sensual feature she possessed and all the more disturbing because of that. She had a short upper lip with a well-marked bow, and gappy, crooked, but very white teeth— proper teeth for biting and crunching and snapping string, not just face furniture, he thought.

'How long is it since you left, Primmy?' he asked. He felt suddenly more confident. Her starchiness was after all only a form of shyness; he had appeared out of the blue and it was up to him to ease things along. 'Over a year, I suppose.'

'The beginning of the war I left Chilverton,' she acknowledged 'It doesn't seem so long, though.'

'Your mother and Eddie have settled down well,' he said, and was gratified to see her look of real interest.

'Have they? Eddie's managing, is he?'

'He's absolutely splendid, does all kinds of things—he really earns his keep. My mother seems to have taken him under her wing for some obscure reason. I mean it's not like her,' he added, not wanting to be misunderstood. And in his eagerness, said a little too much: 'I mean, I suppose I'm a bit of a disappointment, but your Eddie she can mould, if you know what I mean . . .'

'Oh Eddie can be moulded all right,' said Primmy with a dry little laugh, 'it's just what I'm afraid of.'

'You mustn't be, he's fine, honestly, so much better than when they first arrived.'

'I dare say,' was all she would add.

He tried a different tack. 'I must say you look jolly impressive in that uniform.'

'We all wear it.'

'Now tell me properly how things are going for you. You enjoy the nursing?'

'Yes. Yes, I do.'

'I bet you're frightfully good at it.' He was astonished at his own boldness, but it paid dividends in the form of a small smile.

'I wouldn't know about that.'

'What are the others like?'

'They're not bad. All sorts, you know.' The smile grew a fraction to include a trace of something like impishness. 'Some of them never did a hand's turn in their lives before they came here.'

'What a shock! Not like you.'

'I've never been afraid of work.' She recomposed her features into their earlier expression of properness, but the thawing-out, once begun, was not so easily arrested. As she got up to make the tea she added, with an odd kind of brusque bashfulness: 'I'm going to Canterbury to take the Blue Stripe examination in the new year.'

'Really, are you?' He was unsuccessful in keeping the admiration out of his voice. 'Now tell me what that means.'

'If I pass I'll be better qualified. I might train as a proper nurse after the war.'

'I think that's splendid,' he said truthfully. It was surprising, really, how simple it was to talk to her once one had plunged in. 'Do you all take this exam?'

'No. Just a few.'

'Ah! You mean the best ones!'

She did not reply to this but poured the tea, handed him a cup, and brought her own cup, and the cake, to the table. 'Cake?'

'Please.'

She cut him a slice, still warm in the centre and moistly crumbling. He felt again that disconcerting stirring and quickening as he watched her hands, and scented the crisp, hospital smell of her apron bib as she leaned forward. He was perfectly certain she was an excellent nurse, and even experienced a pang of jealousy when he thought of the patients in her care, whose every wish was her command.

'How about you?' she asked, sitting down and pulling her chair up to the table.

'Muddling along.' Now for it; no more playing for time.

'Will you go for a soldier?' He could not tell from her tone if the question were loaded or not, but he had always suspected that her reaction would be one of conventional patriotic horror. She was not the type to espouse what she would see as woolly liberalism and neither was she a compromiser. Still . .

'No, I'm not,' he said, taking a big mouthful of cake.

'What, not at all?' She sounded interested rather than accusing.

'No.'

'M-hm.'

Like a guilty child when the expected smack does not come he glanced covertly at her face and was met by a steady, examining gaze, her eyes flicking from one to the other of his. He was glad he had not insulted her with half-truths.

'Why?' she asked with a quizzical upward inflection.

'Because I don't believe in fighting. No,' he waved his hand to erase the wrong word. 'I don't believe in violence —but I am fighting for that belief, if you like.'

'Yes. I see.' She nodded. He was touched by her serious, careful effort to understand and warmed to his theme.

'Also, I don't think anyone has the right to force people to engage in an activity they find abhorrent. We'll have conscription pretty soon, and that's when the real fun will start.'

'You must be scared.' It was a plain statement.

'Scared witless.' He squeezed some crumbs together between bunched fingers and popped them in his mouth. He felt a rare, pleasurable leap of vanity.

'What will they do to you?'

'Put us in prison I suppose.'

'There are lots of people like you?'

'Enough. But even if there weren't I should feel the same, it's very personal.'

'More tea?' She stood up, taking his cup. By the teapot, with her back turned safely towards him, she added firmly, as if she had taken a deep breath to say it: 'Well I think you're very brave.'

Maurice's heart sang, his spirits soared, his blood fizzed like champagne, but he knew his subject too well to overreact. Instead, when she returned his cup to him he said quietly: 'I'm glad you don't condemn us—' 'us' sounded less personal than 'me'; 'I thought you might feel differently, seeing all the casualties from the Front as you do.'

'No. I don't think about it. My job is when they're here.'

They finished their tea, with a little general conversation about billets and time off and hospital life, and then it was dark and time for Maurice to leave. Primmy saw him out through the now-closed post office, opening the door with its soft ting-a-ling and stepping out into the chill, clammy darkness

'I'm jolly glad I came,' he said, 'and congratulations on everything.'

She smiled her small, contained smile in acknowledgement. 'You could always drop by again if you're down this way.'

He was astonished; it was an invitation. 'I will, of course, but I don't quite know how things will . . .'

'No. We'll see.' She was like a little old lady with her tags and clichés, but somehow her response was exactly right. All afternoon her tact and commonsense had not failed her, or him. He held out his hand, suddenly desolate at having to leave her.

'Goodbye, Primmy.'

She put her hand in his, dry, cool and firm, gripping his sturdily. Through it he seemed to feel the tense uprightness of her arrow-thin figure, the set of her narrow shoulders and the tilt of her head. This, only the second meeting of their hands, was almost too much. Profoundly shy though he was, he nearly spoilt everything, but the agonized caution of years prevailed and he dropped her hand as if it had given him an electric shock.

'All the best then,' she said, folding her arms because it was cold.

'Thank you, and the same to you.'

He walked away quickly, hunching his shoulders and burying his chin into his woollen scarf. He did not have to look round to know that she would stand there in the cold damp darkness until he was out of sight.

Primmy stepped back into the dark post office and stood still for a moment, trying to collect her thoughts. She could still feel Maurice's hand in hers just like that other time, and it brought it all back to her. She was all stirred up and confused. It had been nice seeing him. More than nice, a real pleasure, and she hadn't wanted him to go. She'd stood watching until he was out of sight, in spite of the cold. She hoped, in a way, that he would drop by again.

She encountered Mrs Pett in the passage, and was treated to a coy smile.

'What a pleasant young man, Miss Dilkes, really nice.'

'Yes.'

'Have you known each other long then?'

'Quite a while.' Primmy made for the stairs. Somehow Mrs Pett's attitude heightened her confusion. She felt trapped.

'You must invite him down again, you must, really. He should come for a proper meal next time.'

'Well, perhaps . . .'

'Of course!' Mrs Pett was in full flight. 'You know what they say about the way to a man's heart—'

'Mrs Pett!' Primmy shocked even herself with the loudness and angriness of her voice. 'I don't *want* to get to his heart! Goodnight!' She ran up to her room and closed the door behind her, aware of the amazed silence she left down in the hall, and only too well able to imagine Mrs Pett's aghast expression.

She had felt happy and optimistic. Now she was cross and miserable. Mrs Pett's remarks had exactly pinpointed the problem. Doing a job well was not all there was in life. There were other options, other preoccupations and Maurice was the chief of them. She had set aside Dick, but he had been of the past. Maurice was of the here and now, and so utterly different that she was surprised she even allowed him to unsettle her so. It should be simply out of the question; it *was*, and yet . . .

She sat down on the hard chair, taking care not to squash tomorrow's clean apron which hung over the back. The suddenly vivid recollection of how close she had come to kissing Maurice that evening at Chilverton brought home to her the gravity of the situation. Maurice was a threat. Here at Oak Ridge she had the beginnings of what she'd always wanted: independent status, interesting work and pride in the doing of it. She must not dwell on Maurice, with his gentle voice and skin like a baby's bottom. That kind of thing was not for her. If he came again, all well and good; but she must not encourage it, or the apple cart would be well and truly upset. She must, and would, be very, very careful.

Maurice was arrested just over two months later, in the middle of January 1916, shortly after conscription was introduced for all single men. It was no surprise: it had only ever been a matter of time and he was quite prepared for it. He and the other members of the Cambridge Branch of the No-Conscription Fellowship had devoted hours of exhaustive discussion to the problem of what their attitude should be in the event of forcible enlistment. Opinion varied. The Cambridge group had no especial religious or political basis but were what later became known as the 'aesthetics': individuals who were anti-violence and military authority, and pro the things of the mind. Most of them disliked the name because it implied exactly the kind of effete shrinking from reality and conflict which had no place in their strongly held beliefs.

But as a collection of separate and highly opinionated individuals, it was difficult to formulate any kind of collective policy. Maurice, among the least clubbable of beings, did not deem it strictly necessary but acknowledged the expediency of presenting some kind of united front to maintain credibility. He was obsessed with detail.

'What if they make us put on uniforms?' he asked. 'Do we refuse?'

'Not "if" but "when", and the answer is yes.' This was Stafford Deans, a mathematician whom Maurice privately thought odious. Perversely, Maurice couldn't help comparing him to Aubrey. He had all the latter's pig-headedness, tunnel vision almost, but somehow without Aubrey's incontrovertible sincerity. Maurice had not gone so far as to actually label him a fraud, but he was deeply suspicious of Stafford's love of display. In spite of his pacifist stand he seemed to Maurice to cleave to all the more unpleasant tenets of militarism.

Now he said, pounding one meaty fist into the opposite palm, 'We should not just refuse, but do everything in our power to prevent them putting us in uniform.'

'You mean lie on our backs and kick our legs in the air?' asked Stephen Martin facetiously. Maurice liked Stephen, who was the youngest among them, and managed to bring some humour to the otherwise relentlessly grim proceedings. Stafford glared at him; he appeared to see all levity as a form of insubordination. He was a pompous bore, thought Maurice dispassionately.

'Yes, indeed, Stephen,' he said. 'Or any course of action

that seems appropriate to you at the time.' His glance raked round the room as if to challenge anyone else to make clever-clever suggestions. They were gathered in his room, so he clearly felt he had an unofficial right to the chairmanship.

'I've no intention of kicking my heels in the air,' said Maurice. 'None.' He was perched in the windowseat, like an undernourished owl roosting in a kind of nest of books, papers and periodicals. His long thin hands were laced round his knees, his socks wrinkled round his ankles beneath an expanse of thin, white shank.

'Maurice, you have to!' Stafford's colour, high at the best of times, became apoplectic. He had grave reservations about Maurice's ability to stay the course under pressure. 'Look,' he went on, more persuasively. 'Our attitude is—correct me if I'm wrong—that we object not only to fighting, but to having our labour directed by an outside authority. No one has the right to dictate to others in that way, or to make us wear clothes we don't want to wear. It's an insult to human dignity.'

'Oh absolutely,' replied Maurice, 'and it's that dignity I'm anxious to preserve. I will not demonstrate my dislike of violence by indulging in it. If anyone wishes to put me in uniform it's up to him to do it. I won't co-operate, but neither will I fan the flames of opposition by behaving like a street urchin. Anyway,' he combed his fingers through his hair, suddenly embarrassed by this speech, 'I don't somehow think I should win.'

A number of heartfelt 'hear hear's' caused him to blush furiously. The least suggestion that he was a moulder of opinion threw him into confusion; but at the same time it was a fact that he was now crystal-clear in his own mind as to his own attitude and intended course of action. He was frightened, all right, 'scared witless' as he had told Primmy, but he no longer saw that as an obstacle to doing the right thing. The confrontation with Aubrey, which he reckoned had been infinitely more agonizing on all levels than anything he might have to face in the future, had shown him that physical pain and the fear of it were in the last analysis not as strong as his belief in pacifism. Stoical passivity, he had decided, could be a powerful weapon.

'I just think,' he concluded diffidently, almost apologetically, sitting on his hands and rocking back and forth, 'that if we don't recognize military authority we should neither defer to it nor fight it, but simply ignore it. But of course others may feel differently. . . .'

He had to concede there was ultimately no chance of a consensus, either among the aesthetics or in the NCF as a whole; too many widely divergent political, religious and philosophical groups were represented: Quakers, Salvation Army, Seventh Day Adventists, Anglicans, Roman Catholics, all shades of political opinion, and a host of individuals with their own private reasons for joining. But from the autumn of 1915 things had moved too rapidly for anyone to believe they had time to make decisions. The fight was on, even if it were to be one of refusal and negation, and Maurice steeled himself for it.

Early in the new year he made a pilgrimage into London to attend a mass meeting of the NCF addressed by its two instigators, Fenner Brockway and Clifford Allen. It had been a great support and comfort to be with so many others who held the same views, to know that there were many hundreds of men and women, from every walk of life, who were prepared to flout public opinion and risk vilification and possible imprisonment for those same views. But outside afterwards they had had to run the gauntlet of a hostile crowd only just held in check by dutiful but equally unsympathetic police. The angry shouts were mostly of 'Cowards!' but occasionally as Maurice pushed his way through, terrified his glasses would be broken, he heard a newly coined term of abuse, 'Conchie!' and consigned it to memory along with the rest of the unpleasant experience, so that he would be a little bit more prepared the next time it happened. It was only on the train on the way back to Cambridge that he had suffered a delayed wave of shock, and began to shiver uncontrollably so that he had to stumble to the lavatory for privacy, there to retch repeatedly and violently, spitting out a bitter yellow liquid, the juice of fear.

On 15 January, he received call-up papers, which he burned, watching them crumple, flare and disintegrate with rapt attention.

On 18 January he was arrested in the early afternoon as he attempted to absorb the latest erudite commentary on the Aeneid. He knew the moment he heard the firm advancing footsteps on the stairs, and when Dawson opened the door he was already standing composedly in front of his desk. The whole thing was quite polite and orderly, a relief almost. He

461

was permitted to take a change of underwear and a few essentials, which he had already packed in a small hold-all like an overdue expectant mother, and he had tidied his room. After all, it was the end of something; one didn't want to leave a mess of loose ends for others to deal with. He left the room without looking back and with head held high. At last he could say, 'This is it.'

And it wasn't so bad, to begin with. After a couple of days' custody in the local police cells there was a hearing by a local tribunal. It was not so much an ordeal as a farce. The cases were heard by men of severely limited vision and understanding and no legal qualifications, and the pacifists had no legal representation. It was quite clear that the terms in which Maurice couched his plea for total exemption were nothing short of a foreign language to the men on the bench. They stared at him, and one even nodded from time to time (though whether out of interest or somnolence Maurice wasn't sure) but it was apparent they didn't actually *hear*, because their stiff elderly brains were stuffed with fine phrases about how sweet and right it was to die for one's country. His claim was rejected and he was returned to the cells with the rest of his particular batch, which included Stephen Martin, to await the appeal tribunal at county level.

It was during this period of waiting that Thea came to visit him. He was escorted to a small drab room, sat at a table and told he might have ten minutes with his cousin, who had come all the way from Kent to see him. This last was said in a tone of utter amazement, that *anyone* should come all that way to visit such a low and despicable form of life as himself.

Unaccountably, left for a moment in the bleak room, he felt ashamed. He had left a note for Dawson to send to his mother, so that he knew the Tennants must be aware of his situation, but now to be confronted by someone from that other life was going to be painful. He couldn't help feeling he had dragged them in, marked them out for unwelcome attention that they did not deserve. Perhaps he was just being selfish. . . .

But the minute Thea walked in, he knew it was all right. She waited, smiling—no, *beaming* at him as the constable closed the door behind her and drew the shutter back so he could keep an eye on them. Then the first thing she said was: 'Well done!'

He was overwhelmed, unmanned by her loyalty and her

unstinting generosity. All the strain of the last few weeks was suddenly too much for him. His throat constricted and his mouth shook uncontrollably. He took his glasses off quickly and clumsily and laid them on the table so that he could cover his face with his hands. She came and sat down opposite him, not touching or speaking until he had composed himself. Then, when he could look her in the eye, she stretched out and gave his wrist a little squeeze.

'It's all right, Maurice. It's all *right*. We're proud of you.'

'And Mother?' He had to ask.

Thea frowned. 'You don't want to worry about that. She's not well, Maurice, you saw.'

He had indeed. It had been perfectly plain when he had last seen her that Sophie's sanity was now in the balance. She had completely disowned him, would not acknowledge his existence even, and yet she was infinitely more agreeable in her manner than he could ever remember her. All her frustrated, demanding affection was centred on Eddie Dilkes, and the rest of the family, somewhat irresponsibly, had heaved a sigh of relief.

'I suppose so,' said Maurice. 'I just hope it's not me that's done this to her, I feel so damn guilty.'

'Don't. You go ahead and fight your battle, Maurice. Tell me, are you being treated well? Is there anything you need?'

'Nobody's been malicious, if that's what you mean. And no, I don't need anything, I don't have time for anything, or energy. We just go from day to day hoping we won't let ourselves down.'

'What happens next?'

'The Appeal Court, and if I'm rejected again there, prison.'

'Oh, Maurice . . .' There was so much love and sorrow in her voice.

'It may not be so bad—I might even get some reading done.' She laughed, though her eyes were reddened. 'What about you?' he asked. 'Still at the factory?'

'For the moment.'

'You have other plans?'

'Yes. I'm going to train as an ambulance driver.' She stared at him rather defiantly.

He was flabbergasted. 'My God, Thea! Don't you ever want to lead a quiet life?'

'Do you?'

'Touché. But why, all of a sudden?'

463

'Lots of reasons.' She was evasive. 'Some of them the same as yours. I couldn't just resign myself to going on producing those bombs, no matter what Father says about speeding the war up and getting it over with. I can't have any more to do with killing, but then I'm not brave enough just to opt out and be tormented, like you. I have to be involved, so I might as well be involved in some way that helps.'

'Will you go to France?'

'I hope so, eventually. I've answered an advertisement for a job with the Metropolitan Asylums Board,' she made a face, 'but I hope to do that for just a few months and then go out. I can drive already, you see, so I am half-trained.'

'I know.' He stared at her, shaking his head in affectionate disbelief. She took her courage so much for granted.

'Any news from Aubrey?' he asked.

'At a place called Matteburg, making mental notes for a book of memoirs.'

'That sounds like him,' said Maurice without rancour.

The door opened. 'Time's up.'

They sprang to their feet like guilty lovers, suddenly panicky about all the things they hadn't said.

'Just tell everyone I'm fine, and I'll try to let them know where I am.'

'I will.'

'Time's up.'

'Coming. Good luck, Maurice.' Unabashed by the disapproving stare of the constable she enfolded him in a mighty embrace. He closed his eyes to help him memorize what it felt like to be so loved and admired. Then he disengaged himself.

'Same to you. Off you go.'

The appeal tribunal was no kinder to either Maurice or Stephen; exemption from military service was denied them and they were taken under military escort, along with the siftings of other county courts, to prison.

The institution in question was the Garfield Redoubt, a military penal institution of Dickensian grimness on the marshes outside Ely. As they bumped along the road towards it, its great black bulk looming like a battleship from the grey undulating flats, Maurice couldn't help laughing. He amazed himself at times.

'What's so funny?' asked Stephen.

'Look at it! I never thought the day would dawn when someone would consider me enough of a threat to put me in a place like that!'

They laughed till the tears ran down their faces and the guard told them to quit making such a racket.

That same evening the uniform arrived. A round-faced young officer marched into Maurice's cell and threw the neatly folded clothes down on the bed.

'Right, Maxwell, get them on.'

Maurice did not reply. He was busy twisting a loose thread round and round one of the buttons on his jacket, with studied concentration. He heard the officer sigh, and felt rather sorry for him. What a rotten job.

'Get a move on!' Maurice continued twiddling the thread. 'Maxwell,' the officer came over to him, lowering his voice almost respectfully as if he didn't quite know what he'd got on his hands, 'be a sensible chap and put the uniform on. Please.'

Maurice looked up at him. There was a distinct look of anxiety in the chap's eyes, as though he dreaded the prospect of having to dress, forcibly, a fully grown man, a gentleman at that, and one who looked as if he might topple over if you coughed.

'I'm afraid I won't,' said Maurice in his quiet, unexceptionable voice, which always made people think they hadn't heard him correctly.

'I beg your pardon?'

'I said no.'

'We shall have to make you.' Firm but rueful. Poor chap. 'That's up to you.'

'Right then.' The officer went to the door, summoning the two soldiers who stood outside waiting for just such an eventuality. They marched in; the officer out. Maurice thought they looked a good deal less sympathetic.

'Up!' commanded one of them, a tall, hard-eyed man who looked as if, had not the army claimed him first, he might have been carving out a fruitful career in petty crime. Maurice felt the increasingly familiar cold trickle of fright in his stomach at the thought of being hurt. He had to some extent lost his hypersensitivity over abuse and rough treatment. The suffering of such indignities, especially in public, was something you learned by getting outside yourself, as it

465

were, and looking on your body—your 'self'—as a mere object, the vessel of your opinions, to which it didn't much matter what happened. But this was a little different. These men were doing their job. He was a prisoner, and one that they especially despised and he was alone with them in this small, drab, empty place.

He sat still, feeling his hands and face grow icy, and his muscles tremble with tension. It took every ounce of his imagination and willpower to appear impassive, but not truculent: he would never have believed it could be so hard.

'Come on.' The private took him by the arm and hauled him to his feet, and he allowed himself to be hauled. To resist was to acknowledge their importance; he must be unresponsive and inanimate, like a doll.

'Get these things off,' said the second soldier, who had crinkly ginger hair and a white, pocked skin. Maurice stood stock-still. To prevent his face taking on any particular expression he concentrated on the wall facing him, where some past inmate had wittily inscribed:

'Believe you me, sergeant, I'd rather be out
In the mud and the whizz-bangs and fighting the Kraut,
Than stuck with you here in the Garfield Redoubt.'

'All right,' said the first soldier. 'Let's get 'em off.'

He felt their hands, rough and impatient, tugging at his clothes. He tried closing his eyes, but that was worse, he felt things more keenly, so he opened them again and went on staring at the verse. Over and over it he went as they removed jacket, tie, shirt and braces. By the time they got to the trousers they had eased up a bit, realizing he was not going to resist, but he sensed that his passivity enraged them. They were building up a great head of steam, so that if he did the least thing wrong they would be down on him like a ton of bricks. The sense of power was heady, but unnerving. When they'd got everything off, including his shoes and socks, they left him standing there for a little longer than was strictly necessary as they fetched the uniform and shook out the various items. Maurice felt, and knew all too well that he looked like a plucked chicken, pale and scrawny and goose-pimply. He was shamefully conscious of his skinny physique, his poking knees and sharp elbows, beside these paragons of manliness with their broad shoulders and scornful eyes.

The stone floor struck bitingly cold through the soles of his bare feet.

The uniform went on, bit by bit. It was exactly as he'd always imagined, utterly foreign, not only because it didn't fit properly but because all the material was harsh and stiff, grating on the skin and resistant to natural, small movements. He felt as though he were encased in cardboard.

'Proper little soldier,' one of them said, looking him up and down.

'Right, we'll take these.' The ginger one scooped up his clothes—the brown velvet jacket, the worn, wrinkled braces still warm from use, the brown check shirt, the trousers with the baggy knees—wound them into a kind of unrecognizable knot, and left. The door closed quietly, and the bolt slid across with a small click. Maurice wondered mournfully if he would ever see those friendly clothes again, the accoutrements of a happier life, shabby but comfortable garments to which he had never given a moment's thought till now but which he suddenly missed violently.

He looked down at himself and experienced an obscure satisfaction. There was no chance he'd *ever* feel at home in these clothes. The trousers and tunic seemed to stand there by themselves, stiff and hard and inflexible, with his meagre, unsoldierly form crouching within like the soft, vulnerable body of a mollusc. He looked again at the inscription on the wall. It wasn't at all bad, really, being succinct and delightfully insulting. He sat down, thought for a moment, and then said aloud:

> *Dulce et decorum est*
> *The Conchie is an awful pest.*
> *It all depends on how he's dressed—*
> *We'll strip him down to pants and vest—*
> *And God will see to all the rest.'*

'That's much better,' he said to himself.

CHAPTER FIFTEEN

'Pack up your troubles in your old kit bag
And smile, smile, smile;
While you've a lucifer to light your fag
Smile boys, that's the style.
What's the use of worrying?
It never was worthwhile,
So pack up your troubles in your old kit bag
And smile, smile, smile.'

Asaf/Powell

On 21 February 1916, a fourteen-inch shell exploded in the Bishop's Palace at Verdun. It was prophetic: the advance guard of some of the heaviest and most destructive bombardments the world had ever seen; the beginning of ten months of slaughter on a gigantic scale.

But like many such omens it passed unrecognized for what it was. The French generalissimo, Joffre, had spent most of December 1915 persuading the other Allied commanders, and Haig in particular, that the middle of the following year should see massive and simultaneous offensives on all fronts. When for a variety of reasons this turned out to be impractical in the case of both the Russians in the east and the Italians in the south, he concentrated his attention on the Western Front, and more particularly the area around the River Somme. The choice of the Somme was strangely arbitrary, for it was not a position of any great value, nor was there any prize to be gained by extending it.

Haig, newly appointed British Commander in Chief of the British forces in France, had always favoured attacking in Flanders and 'rolling up' the Germans from the north, but on Kitchener's instructions he deferred to Joffre. The raw recruits of the New Army were swelling the British contingent almost daily, and by July Joffre calculated there would be something approaching one hundred and fifty French, Belgian and British divisions under his command on the Western Front.

So enthused was he by his plans for the summer that the

attack on Verdun seemed nothing more than an irritating distraction. He sent little assistance, and ordered 'scaremongers' to be punished. Verdun was not worth bothering with. It stood at the head of a virtually useless salient and was no longer in any true sense a fortress since it had been stripped of its guns. He did not see fit to strengthen it now.

Ironically, it might have been better both for Joffre as commander and for the French nation if he had persisted in this casual attitude. The German General Falkenhayn had selected Verdun as a target not for its negligible strategic importance, but as a symbol of French pride and defiance. He was banking on the French leaping to its defence with characteristic spirit. It was his clear intention to break that spirit and bleed the French army white, leaving the British, whom he saw as the heart of resistance to Germany, exposed and alone on the Western Front.

On the evening of 24 February Joffre at last capitulated testily to mounting public opinion and gave the order that Verdun was to be defended to the last, thus signing away the lives of 315,000 Frenchmen for the sake of a symbol. They were to die before the Somme offensive, so close to his heart, had even begun.

But Aubrey awoke at 6.15 a.m. on 25 February and cursed the French. The sour smell of unwashed bodies and clothing and the accumulated odour of numerous piles of unaired bedding pervaded the room like fog. He pulled a face. He had been dimly aware of the usual charade being enacted in the watches of the night: one of the continentals had crept over to close, surreptitiously, the two tiny panes of window that had been left open; half an hour later one of the British contingent had stealthily opened them again. But this morning it was evident that the French had had the last word as usual. That which the British regarded as welcome fresh air was shunned as a near-lethal draught by the rest. The two sides pursued their objectives with tenacity. God knows what hour of the night one of them had summoned the energy to get out of bed and shut the windows, but shut them they had. He turned onto his right side with a grunt. He had the unpleasant but familiar sensation that certain bones had bored through their protective layer of flesh during the night and were busy doing the same thing to the planks beneath. He had learned by experience the knack of sleeping through, and in spite of, acute discomfort; it was so much preferable to remaining awake and brooding on one's captivity; but he could not overcome the shock of waking up in the morning. No amount of self-preparation could eradicate the daily unpleasantness of finding oneself a prisoner, with nothing to look forward to but the prospect of being imminently and rudely turfed out of bed to face another twelve hours of stupefying boredom and brutalizing triviality.

He heaved a sigh and his breath hung in a frosty cloud in the dark above his face. All around him the chill air prickled like a forest with the small slumber sounds of the twenty-seven other prisoners in this particular room. Aubrey tried not to listen. Lack of privacy was a dreadful thing.

The strident clangour of the bell in the corridor outside made him wince. He steeled himself for the moment when the door would crash open and the clanging reach its full volume. It drew nearer. He heard the voice of the under-officer who wielded it.

'Heraus! Alles heraus!'

The door swung open with a bang, the bell was clashing and ringing, splintering the rank, still air with sledgehammer blows.

'Alles heraus!'

A drowsy ripple of rebellion greeted this order. The under-officer stepped into the room and pulled back the bedding of a few unfortunates close to the door.

'Schnell!'

He stamped out. The door slammed behind him. The ripple faded as most of the room's occupants relapsed into a further stolen half-hour of slumber. Aubrey, on the other hand, braced himself to get up. He had his own preferred routine in the early morning, specially evolved to enable him to escape the awfulness of the living quarters between the hours of seven and eight. He drew a deep breath, pushed down the species of coarse, thin sleeping bag tied with tapes that took the place of bedclothes, and swung his feet out onto the chill wooden floor. Down below, in the kitchens, he could hear the orderlies going about their tasks, brewing coffee and slicing bread for breakfast. The sound kindled a sense of gratitude. Until some prefabricated outbuildings had been erected in the exercise yard shortly after Christmas there had been no accommodation for servants of any kind at Matteburg and all the menial jobs had been done by the officers themselves.

Even now there were only two orderlies to serve the needs of each dormitory of twenty-eight, but the wretched chaps went about their work with good-natured diligence.

Aubrey went over to the trestle table in the centre of the room, expertly smashed the crust of ice on the surface of the nearest pitcher, and poured about a quarter of the contents into a bowl. He sluiced his face and hands with the stinging water. He was aware, as usual, of one or two frankly hostile onlookers, peeved at being disturbed. But he was undeterred; his timetable paid dividends. He picked up his precious remaining slice of cracked green soap and scribbled it over the lower part of his face preparatory to shaving. It was one of the worst ordeals of the day, this freezing shave. It was impossible not to cut oneself when one's skin was so cold that it puckeréd like a cheese-grater. The razor-blade bumped and scraped its way across this inimical landscape to no great effect. One of Aubrey's most recurrent daydreams dwelt on shaving as it used to be, with a large soft brush, a sharp blade, steaming hot water and lather as luxurious as whipped cream. He surveyed the results of his labour in a freckled triangle of mirror. The mottled grey and blue skin of his jaw stared reproachfully back at him, flecked here and there with scarlet where the razor had nicked the top off a goose-pimple. One thing about the February temperature, it stopped you bleeding; the stuff froze the second it came into contact with the air.

Ablutions completed, he returned his shaving tackle to the suitcase beneath his bed and from the same receptacle removed his outer garments. They felt half-frozen and inhospitable and he pulled them on with a shiver. He wound a scarf about his head, placed his cap over the scarf, donned mittens, leather jerkin and greatcoat and was leaving the room just as the orderly entered to light the stove. By mid-morning the atmosphere in the living-quarters would have gone from arctic to stifling. It was a moot point, in Aubrey's view, which was the less desirable.

He nodded good morning and closed the door behind him. Out in the corridor two heavily overcoated guards bestowed an incurious look on this odd prisoner to whose baffling habits they had become quite accustomed in recent months. Aubrey walked past both of them and descended the open-runged wooden staircase at the end of the corridor to the stone-paved ground floor where the kitchens were situated.

The Matteburg laager was an old wagonhouse. The ground floor had once accommodated wagons and horses, and the upper storey tack. The vast cavern-like area had been converted into rooms by the use of plywood partitions resistant to neither cold nor sound. The kitchen was large and communal, but its amenities were divided among the different messes and the orderlies operated accordingly. No. 3 Mess, of which Aubrey was a member, had no extras for breakfast that morning, but the smell of coffee, strong, bitter and reviving, wafted out to him. As he appeared in the doorway one of the men came over to him, bearing a mug of the coffee and a chunk of rubbery, dark bread, smeared with margarine.

'Morning sir. Only basics this morning, sir.'

'Good morning, Tasker. Thank you.'

Aubrey took his breakfast and went outside. The muddy rectangle dignified by the title of exercise yard was bordered on three sides by a cloister-like covered way. This was paved with large, uneven stone flags, now covered by a thin sheet of ice. Aubrey took up his customary position in the centre of the cloister, immediately opposite the main entrance of the *Wagenhaus*. He sipped his coffee and munched the unappetizing bread, chewing vigorously. 'You can't expect your poor tummy to crunch things up for you,' Nanny Dorcas had been wont to remark. 'That's not its job, and it will complain if you send down big lumps.' Aubrey adjudged this advice to be sound in the case of the Matteburg bread. He chewed each mouthful thirty-two times.

There were four guards in the yard at this time of day. Aubrey rather enjoyed standing there in the cold, early twilight, perfectly within his rights and presenting no threat whatever to security and yet, he knew full well, annoying his overseers mightily. The morning ritual not only suited him personally but served to maintain the offensive posture so keenly advocated by the Allied leaders.

When he had finished the bread he swallowed the rest of the coffee and returned his mug to the kitchen. Then he began to walk round the yard. He had worked out that about twenty circuits filled the time necessary for the pandemonium in the living quarters to subside. To help him keep up a steady pace, and to keep boredom at bay, he had built up a repertoire of suitable tunes: the 'Battle Hymn of the Republic', 'Pack Up Your Troubles' and 'Onward Christian Soldiers' were all ideal. The monotony of the walking and the repetitious humming of the tunes freed the mind wonderfully and he was able to concentrate on his memoirs. No provision was made at Matteburg for intellectual pursuits, in terms of space or materials, so Aubrey had developed the ability to make thorough and systematic mental notes. Each morning he found his place by starting from scratch and going through these 'notes', checking off each section.

Looking back now, in the particularly inclement conditions that prevailed at Matteburg this morning, it seemed incredible that they had thought their first camp so bad. Compared to this Tregau had been luxurious. But then they had all been soft and inexperienced and reeling under the shock of having been taken prisoner at all. For the first few days after that nightmare journey most of them had slept almost continuously, rousing themselves only to eat and to attend *Appel*. It was not until they had returned to full consciousness that the direness of their situation had become apparent, and depression set in.

When he had completed no more than eight circuits, a fine, teasing sleet began to fall. He was going to be forced back indoors and he had as yet 'written' nothing. At this rate he would fall seriously behind on the project. Five minutes later he plodded back up the stairs to the living quarters cold, cross and frustrated.

The worst was over. Most men were up and breakfasted and the orderlies were in the process of cleaning the room. Nobody assisted them in this enterprise by getting out, they had to do the best they could in the spaces between persons and furniture. The air was murky with fumes from the now-lit stoves, clouds of dust rising from the floor, and smoke from the strong continental cigarettes which protruded from the lips of at least half the occupants.

Major Coddington was, as usual, on his hands and knees in the midst of all this, sorting out his bedding. The blanket tended to work its way down to the bottom of the sleeping bag during the night and stay there, unless it was regularly retrieved and straightened. Most of the prisoners waited till lights-out for a last-minute scramble: not so Coddington, who actually crawled into his sleeping bag head-first every morning after breakfast, to restore order. His disappearance was the signal for the subalterns to stumble over him 'accidentally'. Snappish but muffled rebukes issued from the writhing bag in response to their profuse apologies The faces of the onlookers were mostly amused: the Russians in particular found the high spirits of the young Englishmen most entertaining. But Aubrey felt sorry for Coddington. He recognized that his obsessive reorganization of the bedding was the same as his own early morning routine: a means of imposing a little order and dignity on a life of soul-destroying tedium.

He went to his own bed, smoothed it and sat down on the edge—a practice forbidden but still indulged in as there were only half a dozen hard upright chairs in the room—and lit his pipe. He had bought the pipe in the canteen at Tregau, it was not such a good one as his own had been, but the smoking of it, especially now that he regularly received decent tobacco from home, was one of his few pleasures.

He didn't speak to anyone. He was a loner here as he had been everywhere throughout his life. The others respected him and even admired him for his stolid independence, but something in his character precluded friendship and repelled intimacy. A lot of the younger ones laughed at him, too; he knew that. He told himself he didn't mind: he had never had a close friend in his life, and what one had never had one couldn't miss. Perhaps it was even an advantage in this place, not to lean on others too much. But there was no getting away from it. For the first time in his life Aubrey was lonely. He himself might not need to lean, but he did like others to lean on him. At home, that had been his role, the niche he filled. They might tease him good-naturedly about his 'stuffiness' but they recognized it as a necessary counter-balance, an essential ingredient in the cocktail of family life: Aubrey would see to it, Aubrey would do it, you could depend on Aubrey. There were times when that role had been almost forced on him willy-nilly, but in the end it had become wholly natural. He had regarded it as a kind of duty to the others, to behave in a certain way. Duty and loyalty were the two key impulses in his life and here he could find no outlet for those impulses. Coddington was the closest thing he had to a friend here, they had gravitated towards one another out of a sense of their similarity, but Aubrey saw their relationship for the poor, tedious thing it was: two dry sticks together. He missed the vibrancy of his family, their colour and vitality and display, their teasing and needing of him. Did they miss him? He hoped so He missed them with a ferocity he would not have believed possible, even those among them with whom he had not seen eye to eye. Maurice, for instance.

He puffed thoughtfully. By the time he'd finished this pipe it would be time for morning *Appel*.

When they did eventually assemble in the yard for this purpose the sleet had built up in intensity and nobody, the Germans included, wished to stand outside for too long. Normally roll-call (a misnomer anyway, since no names were called unless numbers were down) was used as an excuse to make announcements, deliver reprimands and clear up odds and ends of business, all of which took up an unconscionable time. So the weather in this instance was an ally. After a mere ten minutes they returned gratefully to the pungent warmth of the living quarters. Some wrote letters, some read books that they had read scores of time before, or mended garments past mending. Most talked, and talked, and talked. It was a bone of contention—carefully concealed from the Germans who were always on the alert for friction upon which to capitalize—that the continentals spoke too much and too loudly. Every exchange was conducted at full volume and often with both or all participants talking at once. This, the fresh air debate, and the Frenchmen's regrettable habit of spitting were the only sources of conflict in conditions specifically designed to reduce the inmates to a state of dog-eat-dog. The Germans had even arranged the dormitories so that the unwilling French and Belgians had beds beneath the windows while the British were as far from them as possible. But the ruse was recognized for what it was and a pact was made: no matter what battles were fought under cover of darkness or behind closed doors, there would be nothing but brotherly harmony for their captors to see.

At eleven the camp Commandant arrived. His advent was marked by a loud burst of invective at the main gate of the *Wagenhaus* as the unfortunate sentry received a drubbing over some imagined sloppiness or breach of military etiquette. The Commandant would then take a turn round the *Wagenhaus* before retiring to his office on the far side of the yard to attend to the business of the day.

Coddington came over to Aubrey at eleven-thirty and perched on the edge of the bed next to him. 'Baths this afternoon,' he said.

'God, no. How did you come by that?'

'Whatsisname. Walder, the fat one.'

'Damn. In this weather.'

'Still, maybe it'll keep the audience at home.'

'Maybe.'

Aubrey tamped the tobacco down in the bowl of his pipe with his index finger. Bathing at Matteburg was an ordeal. The boredom of the morning now seemed a peaceful prelude to the rigours of the bathing expedition. Outside the fogged window the sleet whipped and whined in a mournful, bruised darkness.

Later, they split into groups for language tuition. This was not all that successful because of the obvious difficulties of teaching several languages concurrently in the same small space, but it was a form of constructive mental exercise, and helped to cement good relations between the different nationalities.

'Good morning. How are you?' enunciated Aubrey to his group of Russians. They were immensely keen, like amiable woolly bears huddled round his bed, but their grasp of English was as yet minimal.

'How are you?' he repeated, looking round hopefully. The bearded faces smiled encouragingly back, blank. Then, incredibly, understanding dawned on one of them, a hand flew up.

'Yes?'

'It iss cold.'

Aubrey sighed.

After lunch, which consisted of a kind of stew (it was always a kind of stew) of sausage, haricot beans and onion, accompanied by the inevitable black bread, they gathered up their wash things and assembled in the yard for the trip to the bath-house. A couple of subalterns were kicking a lump of the bread about like a football in the grey, gritty mud. Unfortunately for them the Commandant chose that particular moment to emerge from his office to oversee the departure of the bathers, and spotted the soggy missile hurtling at chest height across the yard to the accompaniment of whoops of delight. One of the guards was leaping about, vainly trying to catch it, the pig in the middle, his rifle bouncing on his well-upholstered seat.

'What is this? What is this?' He came down the flight of wooden steps with measured tread. He was a handsome, choleric-looking man with luxuriant grey hair. Aubrey suspected that under any other circumstances he might have got on rather well with the Commandant.

Like Ralph, he was blunt, peremptory and extrovert.

'What are you doing?' he enquired of the two subalterns. They stood panting and red-cheeked before him, the lump of bread lying nearby, a soggy proof of misdemeanour. The other prisoners stood miserably round the edges of the yard, their wash-bundles clutched under one arm, hands in pockets, chins sunk deep into their collars in an attempt to expose as little skin as possible to the stinging sleet.

'Well?' The Commandant bounced on his heels, as though if his patience were to be tested any further he would have risen from the ground like a hot-air balloon.

'Playing football,' replied Lieutenant Bishop. Aubrey sucked his teeth; Bishop always had to make a show of it.

'Football? With rations?' The Commandant pursed his lips and narrowed his eyes threateningly. He turned to the less ebullient Maynard. 'So you have too much to eat, Lieutenant Maynard, food to spare.'

He was a shrewd judge of character. Maynard dropped his eyes and blushed. 'No.'

'Too much black bread,' interjected Bishop.

'Really?'

'It's damned indigestible.'

'Is that so? I see.' The Commandant bestowed a vulpine grin on both miscreants. 'Then your digestions will benefit, will they not, from a day in the cells on short commons.'

It was a very palpable hit; Aubrey had to concede that they'd asked for that one. He watched dispassionately as Bishop and Maynard were marched off.

'I'm sorry you have been kept waiting in this fashion, gentlemen, and in this weather.'

Dispiritedly, they formed twos and set off for the bathhouse. As soon as they were out of the gate the torment began. Any movement of prisoners outside the *Wagenhaus* was an excuse for the townsfolk to gather and make the most of their opportunity. Despite the rather half-hearted efforts of the escort they managed to hurl missiles, mostly potatoes and lumps of mud containing small stones, and to barge into the exposed flanks of the column to knock over those who appeared most vulnerable.

Experience had shown that the front or extreme back of the column were the safest place. For this very reason Aubrey

477

eschewed them. There were others far more sensitive to both taunts and physical pain than he, and he felt it his duty to stand between them and unnecessary punishment. Recent events had made him more tolerant, even compassionate. It was a rare fellow, he observed, who did not have something to offer. Dodson, who was timid, was a wit; Tasker, the rat-faced orderly, could apparently spirit streaky bacon out of the ether; one unusually obtuse subaltern was a dab hand with a needle and thread, and would do anyone's mending for them. Aubrey marked these things. Each had his place, and while he himself could not tell jokes, nor play clever tricks on the guards, nor sew a button on expertly, he could take the knocks, and was prepared to do so if it would help another.

By the time the column reached the gloomy portals of the bath-house, Aubrey's left side was caked with mud, his ears rang with the battery of imprecations which had been hurled at him over the half-hour march, and his leg would be a mass of bruises where the citizens of Matteburg had let fly with their stout winter boots.

The bath-house was situated in the basement of an old fort, a forbidding castellated building on the outskirts of the town. A vast metal door, pushed open by two soldiers, admitted the prisoners to a subterranean passage only partially lit by gas lamps. Their footsteps rang eerily on the stone floor, the occasional cough reverberated like a lion's roar. The passage, and the temperature, descended gradually but steadily until both reached a nadir at a small flight of stone steps, at the bottom of which, after a minute space large enough for one man to stand, a further door admitted them to the bathhouse.

The shower system operated in a dungeon where the echo was so marked that the noise was like that of a busy rail terminus. The water that spurted from the ceiling when the guard turned the tap was generally hot, but there were insufficient jets, so that two or three men had to share. On arrival they filed into a large cubicle, about the size of a loosebox, to undress, and herein lay the main drawback. The cubicle contained no furnishings or fixtures of any kind—no hooks, racks or lockers—and the walls streamed with moisture from condensation and leakage. It was consequently almost impossible to keep one's clothing dry. Returning cleansed and tingling from the shower one had to face the misery of donning damp garments. The most you could do was to preserve a precious set of clean underwear wrapped in a towel so that the layer next one's skin at least was dry.

Afterwards, the prisoners had to circumnavigate the bath-house, almost wading in places since the fort's archaic drainage system could not cope with the sudden influx of torrents of filthy water. Aubrey was continually amazed that he did not pick up some disgusting and painful foot infection during these shower sessions, and would sit on the edge of his bed after lights out, subjecting the soles of his feet and crevasses between his toes to exhaustive examination. But miraculously nothing appeared. In camp, as at the Front, verrucas and the common cold were virtually unknown. It appeared that one's body, having so many larger problems to tackle, simply hadn't the time to bother itself with minor nuisances.

Then it was out of the dank darkness of the fort into the biting late afternoon cold for the march home, and the accompanying harassment. When they got back, and he was seated on his bed lighting up his beloved pipe, Aubrey would see that his hands trembled violently and his whole body —lips, neck, stomach, fingers—was taut and shuddering with suppressed anger, like a barrel about to burst its hoops. When he watched the younger men fooling about, and even characters like Coddington applying their idiosyncratic therapies, he felt himself to be a pariah: was it only he who could not resign himself to captivity, who still chafed to be involved in action? All the determination and resolve he had summoned for the service of his country was still there, ready and waiting, and wasting with disuse. Eighteen months now and he still felt the frustration gnawing at him like a rat.

His thoughts returned to Maurice, and he experienced a twinge of envy. Maurice's fight would be fought, there was no way of preventing it. With innate fairness he acknowledged that there was no doubt Maurice *would* fight. The scene in the library had showed that Maurice was not a coward. The reversal of their situations was like a horrible practical joke: he, the man of battle, stuck here, dying of boredom and obsessed by such matters as rations and underwear and letters from home; while Maurice—thin, mild, intellectual Maurice—was standing up to the whole might of the State, the Army and bureaucracy at home.

Aubrey had felt very badly about punching Maurice. On

the simplest level it had been poor form; he was both bigger and fitter than his cousin and had been no mean middle-weight at Marlborough; on another and more important level, it had been unreasonable and puerile. Maurice had gone to a great deal of trouble not to be provocative either in the content of what he said or in his manner of saying it. On the contrary, he, Aubrey, had done all the provoking, as if years of silent suspicion had finally come to a head. Looking back on it he could see that Maurice's passivity had actually fuelled his outburst. God, he burned with shame just recalling the incident. The irony was, he had actually gone upstairs a little while later, with a view to proffering if not the hand of friendship at least that of apology. But he had encountered Primmy on the landing; she had clearly been playing the ministering angel, and something in her manner had thrown him into confusion. He had hesitated, fatally, and finally gone back downstairs outwardly the same as ever but churning like a raging sea inside. To this day he regretted it, and most bitterly.

By the time they returned to their rooms after evening *Appel*, not even the bacon and eggs which No.3 Mess had obtained for supper could lift Aubrey from a grey depression. He knew it to be only temporary, but here there were none of the usual antidotes to such a condition. At home, self-pity would have been sternly subjugated under the yoke of industry and soon forgotten. Here, recognition of its existence was forced upon him. A task, that was the thing, something to take his mind off himself. He cast about in his mind for such a task and it came to him with the startling clarity of a revelation. He would do it, now. He would apologize to Maurice.

He took out his writing paper and began at once, without forethought or preamble. It was as though the letter were being dictated to him. *'Dear Maurice,'* he wrote. *'This letter is long overdue, doubly so since I have little to do but write letters at present. I should like it put on record that I am aware I behaved unpardonably at our last meeting, and that you have nothing whatever to reproach yourself with in that regard. I hope you will accept my apologies, and also my sincere good wishes for your personal struggle. I am not immune to the ironies of our relative situations. Yours is a very real battle and requires courage of a particular kind. I know that now, and believe you have that courage.*

'I am not good at this kind of thing, but it is my earnest wish that, should we meet again, we should make some kind of fresh start. Recent events have proved to me that life is indeed too short to harbour grudges. This letter requires no answer. Let it stand. Good luck. Yours, Aubrey.'

He re-read the letter once. Short and succinct though it was, he was pleased with it, and with himself for writing it. Some part of him that had long since grown rusty with disuse was creaking back into life. When he had sealed the letter up, he lay back on his bed, his hands clasped beneath his head, and did something he had not done for months, which was to give himself up, utterly and willingly, to thoughts of home. He did not mark the moment when the conscious recollection slipped away to become a dream, but when he did it was to find himself riding over the hill above Chilverton House with Thea. The drum of the ponies' hooves sent shivers through him, and her shouts way ahead of him were like the calls of birds, far away and poignant. And all the time she was going, going . . . until she was out of sight.

In the end Thea did not take up an appointment with the Asylums Board. It was her firm intention to get to France, and the Red Cross were now advertising for women with driving experience to go over to the big clearing hospitals on the Channel coast. There was no longer any question of protracted apprenticeship or training: the situation was acute, and worsening. The Western Front was swallowing tens of thousands of shells a day and regurgitating wounded at about the same rate. The advance dressing posts and casualty clearing stations were desperately hard-pressed, they had their work cut out simply to patch up the wounded and send them on their way. Drivers were sorely needed to meet the hospital trains as they arrived and relieve them of their dismal burden.

Not that Thea had been idle in the few weeks that elapsed between leaving Dolton Green at the beginning of February and the acceptance of her application by the Red Cross. She spent the best part of each day, clad in a borrowed boiler suit and with her hair bundled beneath a cap, learning the mysteries of motor maintenance from Ted Bingley, who ran a small garage on the Bromley road. She was blissfully happy, and an apt pupil. The two other mechanics at the garage who had regarded her arrival with the utmost gloom and scepticism were obliged to concede that she was quick, and had a good head on her shoulders. Moreover they discovered that she was not easily shocked, and they soon stopped trying. Her time at the factory stood her in good stead. She was not daunted by machines nor by technical terms nor by her colleagues' determined attempts to make her blush. After barely a fortnight she was accorded the supreme accolade of being despatched, alone, to collect a faulty motor car from a client in the town for servicing. This duty she discharged with speed and efficiency: she had won her spurs.

But if she had expected her own efforts to be simply the grounding for further, more intensive training, she was wrong. When her application was accepted she was merely supplied with a uniform and told to 'stand by'. The uniform, when she tried it on, caused great hilarity.

'Good grief!' exclaimed Ralph, taking a turn round her to perceive the full effect. 'A veritable dog's dinner!' He called over his shoulder: 'Come and look at this, my dear.'

Venetia appeared behind him in the library doorway. Her interest was never fully awakened these days. She looked wan. The sight of Thea in the uniform did nothing to cheer her; she could not, as her husband obviously did, find it amusing.

'Oh my dear . . .'

Thea stood there in the middle of the hall, her face spread with a huge smile, her handsome figure completely disguised by the most ghastly clothes imaginable: a navy, ankle-length tubular skirt and toning, but shapeless, jacket with four buttons placed rather below the waist. Beneath the jacket was a blue shirt and tie, and crowning the whole ensemble a hideously unflattering felt hat, also in dark blue, with the brim turned up in front. The hat perched on Thea's mass of hair as if it had dropped there accidentally from a tree.

Thea pivoted, holding her arms away from her body like a mannequin. 'Like it?'

'It does nothing for you.'

'Oh I don't know . . .' Thea grinned at Ralph who stepped back, shaking his head in astonishment.

'It doesn't fit,' said Venetia.

'But uniforms never do! The thing is, do I look the part?'

'Indubitably!' averred Ralph. 'I especially care for the titfer,' he added, pushing the offending headgear forward so that it slid over her nose to the ground. At this moment Sophie came in from the garden, muffled up in her fur-collared overcoat, with a bunch of early daffodils in her gloved hand, and Eddie, as usual in tow, carrying a pair of secateurs and more daffodils in a trug. Thea picked up the hat, replaced it and turned to face her aunt.

'What do you think, Aunt Sophie?'

'What, dear?'

'My driver's uniform.'

Sophie removed the scarf tied round her hair in the stiff March wind and peered at Thea. Eddie beamed, and craned his neck, copying.

'Very nice. Very appropriate.'

'That's what I thought.' Thea would have said more but her aunt was already half-way to the stairs.

Placing her own bunch of daffodils on top of those in the trug, Sophie said to Eddie: 'Put the flowers in a bucket with plenty of water, and then come and light the fire in my room, there's a good boy.' Eddie went docilely in the direction of the back stairs and Sophie up to her room without another glance at any of them.

Thea shrugged and turned back to her mother. Venetia was staring at her with a look of complete desolation. She appeared to have shrunk of late, as some people do with age, and her appearance wrung Thea's heart.

'Oh Mother . . .' She went over and hugged her. 'Please don't be sad, don't worry. I'll take care of myself, I promise, and I'll write often. If you knew how happy I am to be doing this you wouldn't upset yourself so much.'

'I do know. But I'm still losing you.' Venetia disengaged herself and returned to her chair, sitting down carefully and arranging her skirt with slow, thin hands. 'Everything is changed and I must get used to it.'

'Don't say that.' Thea went over to her, pulling off the hat and throwing it down. She crouched on the floor by her mother's chair, trying to look into her averted face. 'You mustn't behave as if we're all against you, it isn't fair on you—or the rest of us. You must begin to live again Mother, we want you to, we love you—'

'Don't shout, Thea.' Venetia's voice was small and expressionless. 'It gives me a headache.'

Thea felt a touch on her shoulder and looked up to see Ralph standing behind her. The laughter had all gone and he looked haunted. As she stared up at him he gave the merest shake of his head and mouthed the word: 'Enough.'

Thea stood up and he put his arm about her and she laid her face against his neck. His black hair, the hair she had inherited, was grizzled. It was true. Nothing could alter the fact that she was leaving them.

Another week elapsed after the arrival of the uniform before Thea was summoned to the Red Cross headquarters at Shorncliffe, during which time they received a letter from Dulcie. It was the third that month. Each time one arrived Thea hoped against hope that it would announce Dulcie's intention of coming home, but it never did, and this one was no exception. It was cheerful, amazingly so, and full of news about a proposed new apartment. There was no mention of the business, but the tone of the letter implied it was going well. There was also no mention of Peter, nor had there been for some time. It was all clothes and decor and food and wine and new friends. Thea found the letters disturbing: you would never guess that the writer lived in the capital of a country literally torn apart by war. Ralph seemed to share her feelings, for he read the letter swiftly and passed it to his wife with a grunt. Venetia was at first elated that Dulcie was so well and happy, then cast down that yet again there was no word about returning to England.

When Thea left two days later she felt like a torturer, turning the knife in the wound. They all turned out to see her off with Meredith to the station—Ralph, Venetia, Sophie and the staff all standing together outside the porch, waving cheerfully, wishing her well. But just as the car turned out of the drive she cast a last look back and saw Venetia drop her face into her hands.

But in the manner of those who depart, her attention was necessarily focused on her destination and the future; she could not be looking over her shoulder all the time. Also, in retrospect she felt a slight and rather demeaning resentment towards her sister, that so much hope should be invested in such an unworthy object. Her mother now seemed to regard Dulcie as a symbol of happier times, and her father to be letting well alone for fear of shattering the illusion. It was unhealthy, reflected Thea, with the objectivity that distance gives, and the opinion had a fortifying effect.

At Shorncliffe she was billeted with the dozen or so other

recruits in a dormitory of an erstwhile convent school. None of them was asked for anything more than their own account of their driving skill and mechanical training and Thea had no way of knowing where her experience at Bingley's garage placed her in the hierarchy: not very high, she diffidently supposed.

Over the next few days the girls were given a short course on the most rudimentary aspects of first-aid, delivered in the form of lectures, and introduced to ambulance driving by taking turns in the three ancient Siddeley-Deasy models kept by the Red Cross for this purpose. They were not in any sense tested and it was made plain to them that they would be going to France without delay.

But delay there inevitably was. At the end of the week, by which time they were all in a state of high excitement, they were informed that in spite of their own manifest preparedness for the great task, accommodation for women had not yet been completed at Merville. Useful interim work had been found for them, packing Red Cross parcels for the prisoner-of-war camps. The next ten days were spent in a draughty drill hall doing work which, although undeniably useful, was also stupefyingly dull and, in the instance of string-tying, painful. Each girl was supplied with the contents of the parcel—bootlaces, tin of salmon, tea, butter and so on—each of which had to be packaged in a certain way and then placed in a certain position in the box, according to a displayed diagram. If the small packages were not arranged just so, like a jigsaw, they would not all fit. The box then had to be double-wrapped and tied with string, also in the regulation manner (no granny knots allowed). String-tying was by far the worst part of the process, and was undertaken by groups of girls in twenty-minute shifts; even so, the coarse string cut their hands to ribbons. An issue of special gloves was ordered and arrived too late, but all the gloves were too large so would not have been much use anyway.

One advantage of this otherwise tedious episode was that it enabled the girls to get to know each other. Most of them were from middle- and upper-class backgrounds since it was only the better-off young women who had access to motor cars, but they were nevertheless a mixed bunch. At one end of the scale was Lucy Catchpole, a vicar's daughter from Cheshire, who cried herself to sleep in the bed next to

Thea on their first night in the convent dormitory, her small frame wracked by snuffles and sobs of a childlike intensity. She had never been away from home before, she confided in Thea, nor had she worked, but this was something she could contribute.

'I could drive when I was fourteen,' she said, without a trace of vanity. 'It's the only thing I can do. I just wish I didn't feel so terribly homesick.'

'You'll get over it, we all will.'

'I'm sorry I cry at night.' She looked at Thea beseechingly.

'Don't be silly.' Thea squeezed her hand. In truth, she admired Lucy's grit. Despite the nocturnal weeping she worked like a trojan during the day, red-eyed, peaky but composed, and her skill as a driver was undeniable as she perched like an undernourished sparrow behind the wheel of the cumbersome Siddeley.

At the other end of the spectrum Rosemary Sutcliffe towered like a colossus: huge, confident and competent, always ready with helpful suggestions and intelligent questions, a self-appointed leader of women. When Rosemary was around there was little initiative left over for anyone else to take; she hogged it all. You couldn't dislike her, she was so manifestly well-intentioned, but on the other hand you couldn't make a friend of her: she was too preoccupied with larger issues.

In between these two were the rest, all seeming more confident than Catchpole (surnames were the order of the day) but still not half as confident as they seemed. There was Dellahay, who had been the most sought-after debutante of the season two years ago; and Townshend who had a passion for sweets and whose father had been Master of Fox Hounds with the Beaulieu; and Lockie who was a great games-player and kept telling them all they should play hockey twice a week when they got to France; and a whole host of others, equally mixed. And then there was Tennant, whom the others secretly regarded as a challenger to Sutcliffe's position as leader, but who didn't seem to have any aspiration in that direction.

The day after the arrival of the useless gloves they were told that they would be leaving by troopship from Folkestone the following afternoon, embarkation at three o'clock. All they needed to take with them was a change of clothing and washing things. No supplies would be necessary, they were told sternly, as their rations at Merville would be quite sufficient.

The girls travelled to Folkestone by train at midday the following day. The jubilation which the prospect of departure had engendered faded somewhat as they drew nearer to the coast. They stared out of the windows in silence, each wrapped up in her own thoughts, her own private goodbye to England.

They were the only females on the troopship, sitting in a circle in the corner of the packed lounge trying not to appear prim and nervous, but failing. The packet was bulging at the seams with raw recruits, the harvest of Kitchener and conscription, mostly painfully young and filled with an unjustifiable optimism. They ate chocolate, and sang, and glanced curiously at the women drivers. The truth was that a high proportion of them had never been away from home before in their lives, and the singing and joking was no more than a smokescreen of bravado. They suspected that these young ladies were more seasoned travellers than they: it was a disconcerting sensation, one which did not help to promote the illusion that they were the saviours of the mother country.

The Channel was ruffled by a tetchy wind. By the time they reached Boulogne the sky, which had been blue over Kent, was full of racing black clouds, the sea in the harbour was turbulent and the temperature noticeably lower. Even the hardiest of the party felt the pangs of anxiety and homesickness as they stood on the windswept quay waiting to be recognized, and Catchpole, who had suffered from appalling *mal de mer*, was ashen.

The troops, for all their youth and inexperience, were better off at this juncture, for there was the whole mighty machine of the militia to see that they were not forgotten. The little band of drivers, conspicuous in their brand new uniforms, their suitcases at their knees, huddled together and gazed about them hopefully. It was a full half an hour, during which time rain set in, before they were approached by an orderly with a red cross on his sleeve.

'Detachment of ambulance drivers from Shorncliffe?' he enquired tersely, eyeing them up and down.

'That's right,' said Sutcliffe, stepping forward. 'For Merville.'

'Follow me.' The orderly led the way to an ambulance in

487

which he then drove them the four miles along the high cliff road to Merville.

The girls were silent, sitting in the back in two rows, staring towards, but not at, each other, glassy-eyed, rather in the manner of waxwork dummies. They were tired, and a little disorientated. The day had lost its newness; it was that late afternoon hour when one's thoughts turned naturally to hearth and home. Outside the rain spattered and hammered and the wind moaned. Catchpole's eyes grew large and staring. Only Thea had the energy left to observe that the ambulance in which they travelled was a Wolseley, a superior model with good springs and solid bodywork, including a windscreen; she had also noticed that it was self-starting. She could hardly believe that they were all to be put in charge of such exalted vehicles. Her spirits rose, cautiously.

Their first sight of the drivers' accommodation did nothing to assist their rise. From what had been said to them at Shorncliffe they had assumed that quarters of above average comfort and privacy were being prepared for them. But clearly it had been a case of obtaining more beds and erecting, as speedily as possible, a superstructure to house them. The latter turned out to be a flimsy-looking wooden edifice on the flat roof of a large garage. The garage itself belonged to what had once been an extremely smart modern golf hotel, the Quatre Pins, now in use as a rest home for convalescent cases and for walking wounded not sick enough to be sent home. Then, the garage had housed the expensive automobiles of the hotel's patrons; now it contained about ten ambulances. A further twenty were parked in two rows, stretching away on either side of the garage along the smooth white gravel drive of the Quatre Pins. Opposite the hotel's wide, glass-porched front doorway an expanse of well-manicured lawn stretched to where a low stone wall, with seats carved in it, afforded a magnificent view of the sea. The eponymous four pines stood in the centre of the lawn and a circular wooden bench had been erected around their trunks, a pleasant shady seat in summer.

The orderly, who introduced himself as Corporal Mackintosh, parked the Wolseley at the end of the row nearest the main gate, and showed the girls to their quarters. They reached the upper storey by means of an outside staircase which was slippery with rain and creaked ominously in the high wind.

The sleeping quarters were freezing. If Thea had only known, she was housed in much the same manner as her brother at Matteburg laager, with the *'Wagenhaus'* below and thinly partitioned cubicles for the inmates above, two to a cubicle. The wind moaned through the chinks in the walls and an icy draught bustled about the floor. At the far end of the building a slightly sturdier full-length partition divided the sleeping area from the wash-room and a small sitting-room, equipped with half a dozen chairs, a table and the building's only form of heating, a squat solid-fuel stove. It took no more than three minutes to see round the entire place.

'Right,' said Mackintosh, 'I'll leave you to settle in. Supper at six-thirty.'

Settling in consisted of finding oneself a vacant cubicle—all the best ones had already been occupied by the group of drivers who had arrived a week or two earlier—and stowing one's case beneath the bed. The promised lockers, the other girls told them, not without that air of glee that accompanies being the first to know, had not yet arrived. Thea, sharing with Catchpole, was not quick enough to obtain one of the few remaining desirable cubicles, in the centre of a row and on the landward side, and was left with possibly the worst in the building: at the end of a row, facing the sea, and immediately next to the wash-room. Catchpole plumped down on the bed. She seemed to get smaller and paler with each new shock to her system.

'Cheer up,' said Thea.

'I can't help it. I seem to be a rotten traveller.'

'You'll feel better in the morning. And I'll tell you another thing. This is going to be a lovely spot in the summer.'

'I suppose so . . .'

'Think—we'll be able to go swimming.'

'I can't swim.'

'You can paddle, then. Anyway, things'll look much rosier when we've had a good night's sleep.'

As one, they both glanced doubtfully at the beds. They were the folding variety, stained green canvas on a metal frame, with a thin, bumpy palliasse and pillow and three whiskery brown blankets folded on top. It was to be a full year before they were issued with sheets and a good few days before they hit on the idea of using quantities of newspaper for insulation. They caught a whiff of engine oil and looking down Thea could actually see, through a chink in the floorboards, a mechanic tinkering with one of the ambulances in the garage below.

'Living over the shop,' she said, to cheer herself as much as Catchpole.

To her relief Sutcliffe appeared in the doorway, her broad shoulders and imposing bust seeming to fill the aperture.

'I say you two, supper in ten minutes. Over in the main building.'

'Good, I'm famished.' Thea realized that she was. None of them had eaten since a snack on the train at midday.

'The Commandant came over,' added Sutcliffe airily. 'She said she'd speak to us here after we'd eaten.'

'Thank you.' Thea smiled at her.

'You two all right?'

'Yes, thank you.'

Sutcliffe nodded in a businesslike way. 'Right you are then. Supper it is.' Having reinforced her position as the person most intimate with the authorities Sutcliffe marched away, making the partitions shudder with her purposeful strides.

The drivers ate in a kind of annexe to the hospital kitchen, an area which had been the still-room in the palmy days of the Hôtel Quatre Pins. The food was quite the most disgusting Thea had ever tasted. Illogically, this depressed her as no other aspect of their arrival had succeeded in doing. It was peculiarly insulting to be served such revolting food. Later, it became tolerable by virtue of its sameness: the unvarying ghastliness of both content and cooking deadened the palate so that one no longer noticed taste and texture, but simply refuelled. On this occasion the meal consisted of bullybeef encased in a leathery envelope of batter made from dried egg, and accompanied by damp and rubbery carrots. This was followed by figs drowned in thin but lumpy custard. The drivers were to realize, in retrospect, that the batter represented a special effort in honour of their arrival. The only variations were the occasional replacement of the figs by plums, and of the carrots (in warmer weather) by lettuce and tomato. On high days and holidays horsemeat was served instead of bullybeef. It had a distinctive sweet flavour and the English girls, coming as they did from a nation of renowned hippophiles, could not stomach it, no matter how often they were assured that it was everyday fare on the continent. The cooking for the drivers was undertaken by a

VAD who felt she had been slighted; she had joined up to do her bit for our lads at the Front and instead found herself preparing meals for a bunch of lah-de-dah young ladies by whom she was not appreciated. Her name was Rene (pronounced 'Reen') and her response to those brave enough to complain was always the same: 'If you don't like it, don't eat it.' And that was that.

After supper they returned to the living quarters and drew the chairs in the sitting-room into a semicircle for the Commandant's address. Miss Courtney was a tall, handsome woman, every plane and angle of whose upright form bespoke discipline and self-sacrifice. Thea put her age at about fifty, but she had the kind of aquiline features which change little, and her pepper and salt hair, uncompromisingly cropped beneath the felt hat, had probably always looked the same. Only a humorous expression in the eyes prevented her from being a rather forbidding personage.

'Now I don't yet know your individual strengths and weaknesses,' she said, looking down at them over the long perspective of her tie. 'And the only way I shall find out is through experience. For the moment I have divided you quite arbitrarily between "A" and "B" sections and in the morning your section leaders will show you the vehicles you will be driving. There's unfortunately no time for detailed preparation. Tonight, and tonight only, you are exempt, but from the moment you wake tomorrow morning you are ambulance drivers doing vitally necessary work. Convoys usually arrive at night, you will rarely have more than half an hour's notice of their arrival. You will find your first run tiring and probably distressing, but I assure you it will become easier in time. The section leaders and orderlies are always ready to assist you, you are not alone.' She gave them a kindly smile. 'I'm so glad to see you. We badly need your help. Now, are there any questions?'

Thea's head teemed with so many it would have been invidious to select one. Practical matters—bathing, washing, shopping, laundry, mail, time off: how was life conducted when not taken up with vitally necessary work? But suddenly she was tired. She caught Miss Courtney's eye and shook her head: no questions.

Sutcliffe made some pertinent and well-worded enquiry about hours of duty.

'There is a roster. But I should point out that if an

especially large convoy comes in you will all be expected to meet it. I also rely on you to familiarize yourselves as soon as possible with the workings of your machines so that you are not completely at a loss if anything should go wrong in the course of a run Corporal Mackintosh is there to answer your questions.'

That night not all the exigencies of a new and uncomfortable environment could prevent Thea falling into a deep sleep. But when her eyes snapped open just before dawn she realized she had been wakened by the distant, uneven pulse of the guns.

As if out of consideration for the new arrivals there was no convoy for another two days and in this short hiatus a pattern of life soon emerged.

For one thing it became clear that Miss Courtney's admonitions about motor maintenance were scarcely necessary: it was one of the very few leisure occupations open to the girls, and the best part of every morning was spent in the yard peering under the bonnets of the vehicles, with varying degrees of comprehension, under the dour supervision of Corporal Mackintosh. There was no NAAFI, no library, no petrol to spare for what one might term social motoring, and even if one had the energy to walk the three miles to the small town of Merville, down in the fold of the cliffs, the amenities it provided were far beyond the allowance given to the girls to cover their laundry and other necessary expenses. So the engines were stripped down, itemized, reassembled and cleaned endlessly.

About one thing Thea had been wrong: the Wolseleys, of which there were only two, were reserved for the section leaders. The rank and file drivers had to be content with Buicks, bulky, poorly-sprung machines, with only three gears and no windscreen. The rear of the Buick, beneath a lashed-down canvas cover, was capable of carrying four stretchers, two a side, one on top of another, or eight sitting cases. Three blankets were provided for each stretcher, but not even the most rudimentary medical kit. A sliding shutter separated the driver from the passengers. In view of the lack of cover in the ambulances, and the persistent sharp off-sea winds, Thea providently wrote home for a supply of jumpers and cardigans to wear beneath her uniform jacket. They had all been issued with a 'good' top coat, but it was heavy and

492

cumbersome; besides, one did not wish to run the risk of ruining such a valuable garment with oil or petrol. She also borrowed needles and remnants of wool and began to knit herself a gigantic scarf to shield her face from the wind. The knitting was therapeutic in itself—that, and cards and conversation. They were in the middle of pleasant rolling, chalky downland, similar to Sussex, and Thea promised herself some long walks at a later stage, but for the moment it did nothing but pour with rain.

After only thirty-six hours Thea felt dirty. She had not realized the extent of her dependence on plentiful soap, hot water and clean clothes. Here, the supply of hot water varied according to the good will and energy of a grudging and— since most of the orderlies were men invalided back from the Front—frequently infirm orderly, whose task it was to stoke up the boiler down below. Sufficient stoking would provide a sullen trickle of water, enough to splash your face and neck and leave for the next person as quickly as possible, for it lost heat rapidly in the cold washroom. There was no bath except an old-fashioned tin tub, and it was obvious that to obtain sufficient hot water for this purpose they would have to form fatigues for coke-haulage, stoking and water-carrying on a grand scale. No one had the energy, so the question of baths was postponed indefinitely. All the girls had long hair, but Thea could see only too well why Miss Courtney had chosen to crop hers. Washing waist-length hair was going to be difficult, and drying it still more of a problem. She cursed her own superabundance of springy black tresses. Fortunately it was not fine and did not therefore become greasy, but it was coarse and thick, and without regular washing it took on the texture of wire wool. She determined to ignore it as far as possible, twisting it into a tight knot and skewering it with a veritable army of clips and pins.

The new arrivals had missed the laundry women's visit for that week, but were told that any washing would be collected the following Tuesday and returned on the Thursday afternoon. Most of them used up their self-assigned quota of clean underclothes far too early and realized the folly of such improvidence. Even small items like pants presented a problem, with tepid water and no drying facilities; such anti-social practices as draping them on top of the sitting-room stove were unanimously decried.

Another small but intimately dreadful problem was that

493

of sanitary towels. Poor Catchpole had the misfortune to begin her period within twenty-four hours of arrival, and using the customary thick linen towels soon discovered that these disgusting reminders of female frailty had to be bestowed somewhere both private and hygienic until—and this was the worst of it—they could be passed on to the tight-lipped, black-shawled washerwomen.

Appalled at the distress and discomfort this was causing her room-mate, Thea approached their section leader, Mayhew, to enquire if any of the new disposable variety might be available from the hospital. The response was sympathetic, but negative.

'Sorry. It's awful I know.'

'But surely one of the nurses . . . ?'

'Oh you can get them all right, though they're fearfully expensive. But the last time someone used them when we were in transit at Boulogne, the idiot put them down the lavatory and they blocked the drains up for days. Miss Courtney nearly had a fit and the smell was awful. So now they're not allowed.'

'But what do you do?'

Mayhew shrugged and spread her hands. 'Perform a holding operation and give them to the washerwomen on Tuesday. It seems awful, but they don't appear to care, I suppose they've seen much worse. It's surprising how soon you stop feeling bad about it.'

Thea doubted that Catchpole would ever stop feeling bad about it and tried to turn a blind eye and a deaf ear to her miserable rustlings. But all these day-to-day matters were put abruptly into perspective when they were called to the station on their fourth night.

A severe late frost had bitten the night before and details of drivers had had to go down to the yard regularly all through the hours of darkness to hand-start the rows of ambulances. The only alternative to this miserable procedure was to drain the radiators, which would have caused too much delay should the whistle have sounded. There was nothing for it but to keep the engines warm. The system was for two drivers to begin at opposite ends of the line, starting each machine, and then on meeting in the middle to return to the first ambulance and turn it off. In this way each engine was left running for three or four minutes. The whole exercise was then repeated an hour later. The result of this was that none of the drivers got a full night's sleep, and most were aching in every limb the next day. That evening the dormitory was quiet by nine o'clock, and the occupants either sound asleep or in a pleasant, rapidly declining state of semi-consciousness. Then at about nine-thirty, the whistle went. Stott, 'B' Section leader, appeared in the doorway with her cheeks bulging, and the shrill, imperative screech of the whistle cut across sleep.

'Convoy up the line! Convoy! Everybody out!'

Thea was never again to hear a whistle on a station or sportsfield without her hair rising and her whole body fizzing with an almost unbearable anticipation, somewhere between excitement and dread. She could hardly believe that at last she was to do what she had come here for, tonight of all nights when her arms ached and her eyes swam with tiredness. She scrambled out of bed, her skin shrinking into goose-pimples as her bare feet struck the cold floor. She was already in her underwear and she pulled on the rest of her uniform dazedly. She glanced at Catchpole, but she seemed composed.

'Good luck!'

'Good luck!'

Already some of the others were clattering down the outside steps, quicker than her and more practised. She ran out into the corridor and along to the door to join them; Stott was standing there holding the door open impatiently. As she went down the steps Thea was still buttoning her jacket, her fingers clumsy with cold.

Outside the cough and rattle of engines starting up filled the night air, she could see Mackintosh's stooped form moving up the line, swing and jerk, swing and jerk. Beyond the smooth lawn the Quatre Pins, with a light burning in the hallway, looked tranquil and civilized.

She raced along the line—one, two, three, four, five, six! She jumped in. Damn, no, it wasn't started, Mackintosh had begun at the far end. Cursing, she got out again and attached the handle. The engine spluttered and sparked at the fourth attempt, by which time ambulances were already beginning to move out of the drive and along the cliff road. She felt panic filling her throat. She had forgotten her gloves and her hands were numb from the cold metal of the crankshaft. Brave and calm! Trying to stifle her anxiety she joined the queue of vehicles; she wasn't last, there were two behind her.

She followed the ambulance in front, turning right out of the white gates of Quatre Pins onto the Merville road.

There was a two-thirds moon and a clear sky and she could see the slaty, white-ridged sea racing towards the cliffs. Way below she could make out the blacker patch that was Merville, one or two brave small lights twinkling in the darkness. The wind whipped at the Buick's canvas cover, smacking it like the sails of a ship, making steering difficult, and buffeting her exposed face. She reminded herself to complete the scarf at the first possible opportunity.

As the road began to wind down into the fold of the cliffs, towards the town, they were more sheltered; she could hear the engines of the other ambulances and felt less alone. The grey night-time countryside rolled away on either side, austere and treeless. There was no other sign of life but them. Only one ambulance in three was permitted to use head-lights.

They were met at the station by the Railway Transport Officer, emerging like a London nightwatchman from his little hut, who told them the hospital train had been held up about twelve miles up the line but should arrive in half an hour. Suddenly at a loose end, they milled about. Merville station was hardly more than a halt, with one small shelter and a couple of platforms through which hardy weeds sprouted tenaciously. The ambulances, lined up in the road, their backs towards the platform, steamed like warhorses in the cold air. Thea turned to the girl next to her.

'Now what?'

The girl grinned. She had white, gappy teeth. 'We wait.'

'Where?' Thea looked round. 'Back in the ambulances?'

The girl shook her head. 'Better not, you might fall asleep. I'll show you the best place.' She led Thea round to the front of her own vehicle and perched on the mudguard. 'Wind's in the right direction tonight,' she explained. 'Sometimes there's nothing to do but freeze. Would you like a cigarette?'

'I don't smoke. Should you . . . ?'

'What the eye doesn't see.' The girl lit a cigarette, and by its small glow Thea saw that she had a long-jawed, humorous face and fly-away eyebrows that gave her an amused expression.

'My name's Thea Tennant.'

'How do you do, Tennant.' She held out her hand. 'I'm Collins, "A" Section.'

'I think everyone's here tonight, aren't they?'

Collins nodded. 'Must be a big one.'

Thea felt a pang of foreboding. 'Have you been here long?'

'Only about ten days. Don't be taken in by the air of authority. I think I know how you feel. Nervous?'

'Terrified.'

'Don't be. You'll find something happens when the train comes in.'

'What sort of thing?'

'Well . . . you'll suddenly realize the job is straightforward: common sense. There's no mystery, you can't go wrong if you follow your humanitarian instincts, and once you're loaded up you just get them there. We take them to General 16, the other side of the town, but it only takes about ten minutes. Just follow Mayhew or Stott. Or me, if you like.'

'I see.'

'What are you assigned to?'

'Medical.'

'So am I, for the moment. I believe they put you on to trickier cases later on, if they think you're up to it. Medical are ill, not wounded, you see. Mostly trench fever and dysentery.'

Thea stared at her. 'Collins—is it awful?'

Collins exhaled a smokescreen. 'Yes, it's awful. But not as awful as all that, because you're busy doing something about it. And remember, nobody's watching you, nobody's interested in you, you're just a pair of hands. Don't drop anyone, and go easy on the clutch and you'll be fine.'

Thea liked Collins and appreciated her breezy encouragement, but she knew instinctively that this was one of those things you only knew about when you had actually done it for yourself, and nothing anyone said could prepare you for it. They sat together, their chins buried in their jacket collars like a pair of roosting sparrows, until they heard the faint clacketty-clack of the train up the line, still far away but drawing inexorably closer.

'Come on,' said Collins, screwing her cigarette into the road. 'Here it comes.' They ran up the bank onto the platform. 'The smell's the worst thing,' she added, almost to herself.

The train drew in like any other train, a dragon roaring out of the peaceful darkness, black and important, huffing and snorting, dwarfing them with its majestic size and power, emitting jets of white steam that swirled about them. But as soon as the doors opened the character of the train altered and Thea had her first taste of the war.

The smell was indeed the worst thing. It streamed out like sewage as two harassed-looking orderlies jumped down from the coach marked 'Medical I', and Thea clapped her hand to her face to shut it out. All the special odours of the trench, so often remarked and analysed by Jack Kingsley, were here overlaid by the sickening stench of soiled clothing, for at least half the men on the train had dysentery and there had been neither the means nor the time to change them en route. Peering into the semi-darkness, Thea saw what seemed to be literally hundreds of men piled on top of one another like some painting by Hieronymus Bosch. The air seethed with moans and coughs and retching and breathing, and a whole tapestry of small rustling, creaking, gurgling sounds as sick and suffering humanity tried to ease its pain.

But, as Collins had predicted, there was little time for reflection. The train was full and the drivers had to lend a hand carrying the stretchers down the bank to the waiting ambulances. The men were heavy and the bank was steep; there were terrible shouts as stretchers were unintentionally jolted. The sheer size of the operation overwhelmed Thea. There could be no more than two hundred men on this train, and yet the papers at home spoke of thousands—wounded, dead, gone without trace—every week. And they were not individuals any more, with their unshaven faces and dirty dressings, but simply cases, the excreta of war to be cleaned and tidied away, quickly, quickly.

By the time her ambulance was full Thea was bathed in sweat. She was to deal with far worse cases in the future, but she always looked back with special horror and pity on those 'medicals' of her first run. Psychologically, the sick men were the worst off; they were neither elated at having copped a 'blighty' one, nor in a comatose state of shock like the most severely wounded. Lacking the concentrating power of extreme pain they could still feel shame, and their consternation on being handled by these well-bred lady drivers was plain to see. Filthy, demoralized and desperately weak, some of them still apologized for their condition. Thea hated herself for the nausea that heaved in her throat as she touched uniforms sticky with vomit and excrement and damp with blood, when every movement sent the smell

498

rushing up at her so that her mouth filled with a rancid taste.

She tried, helplessly, not to stare at the orange lice that went methodically about their business over skins mapped by runnels of ingrained dirt. But looking away she saw other things, terrible things; ends of bone glinting whitely through rent flesh, and bodies that were no longer the right shape, but bulged and sagged, and mountainous wads of material packed vainly round re-opened wounds, soaking steadily scarlet there before her eyes. Her head span, her cheeks felt cold, and her stomach bitter and hot. Oh God, I mustn't faint, I'm not the fainting type, don't let it happen to me now.

She had four in the ambulance. An orderly looked in as she fussed with blankets.

'On your way love. Nothing the matter with that lot that a rest between clean sheets won't cure. Be back soon, we're not finished.'

Back! She must be quick. She glanced down distractedly at the man nearest her and smoothed the blanket under his chin. His eyes were open, and their fixed stare held her for a moment.

'Excuse me,' he said. She was astonished by his voice, soft and well-spoken. There was a person down there. She leaned over.

'Yes?'

'I wonder, do you have such a thing as a cigarette?'

'No, I'm so sorry.'

'It's all right.' The eyes closed resignedly, the face lost its brief identity.

Thea got out and ran round to the driver's seat. They had got the engines started before the train came in. But she had forgotten to put the back up, and got down again to do so. Returning to the wheel she forgot in her haste to let the clutch out gently; the machine lept forward and she heard, with her nerve-ends, a long snagging exhalation of breath from one of the men in the back. This was awful, awful. Who did she think she was to take on this job?

She was too late and too flustered to have picked out Section Leader Mayhew, so she simply followed the vehicle in front and hoped it was not a case of the blind leading the blind.

But the trip went smoothly. After no more than twelve minutes there was the relief of arrival, with light and efficient, expert hands relieving her of her burden No one spared her a glance, her job was done, the ambulance ready for another load. She had not failed: it would be all right.

She made two more runs that night, each time with medical cases. By the third run she was beginning to feel tired, and with tiredness came a welcome dulling of the senses so that she was less flustered. She borrowed a handful of cigarettes from Collins and offered them to her passengers before moving off, lighting them up herself and placing them gently between the lips that opened to receive them, like baby birds asking for food. One man, a Scot with suppurating boils over his back and groin, even managed a small, flirtatious joke.

'We must stop meeting like this,' he said, round the cigarette. 'People will start to talk.'

For some reason she had to scurry back to the driving seat to avoid displaying a most unprofessional excess of emotion. And when she regained control she thought how strange that someone with an unquenchable sense of the absurd should almost bring on the tears she had not shed all night.

When they got back to the dormitory it was past midnight. She and Catchpole undressed in punchdrunk silence. As they climbed into bed, Thea asked: 'How was it?'

'Worse and better, if you know what I mean.'

'Yes.' They could not have said more even had there been more to say. Both were fast asleep.

The morning after meeting a convoy the drivers had to be up early to spring-clean the ambulances. All vehicles had to be thoroughly washed, the interiors scrubbed with disinfectant and the blankets fumigated. The girls themselves had been issued with a special lotion which, they were told, if used correctly would deter even the hardiest louse from taking up residence on them. As they went about their chores Thea sensed that they looked at each other with a new respect and affection after their baptism by fire. Not all the horrors of the previous night could prevent her feeling happy.

It was only a matter of days before Mackintosh, a shrewd judge of both character and ability, felt able to recommend one or two girls, Tennant among them, for more onerous duties His judgement was based on an evaluation of their skill as mechanics and an instinctive—usually correct—assessment of temperament. Driving experience, while important, was fairly evenly distributed through the unit; but expertise under the bonnet and a quick, decisive nature were rarer. If a vehicle carrying badly wounded men suffered a minor breakdown en route from the station, the ability to set things right, however temporarily, could mean the difference between life and death. Tennant was quick and clever, and had a sound grasp of how an engine worked. Also, she was good with her hands and not afraid to dirty them. He had no hesitation in putting her name forward.

So Thea became a Class One driver, assigned to severely wounded and fracture cases. Gratifying though it was to be publicly labelled proficient, this elevation was a mixed blessing. The driving of acute cases entailed mental agony of the most wearing kind. She was constantly torn between a natural desire to get the passengers to hospital as quickly as possible, and the certain knowledge that to travel at more than ten miles an hour was to cause unspeakable pain and further damage. The least jolt or bump could cause a jagged broken bone to pierce a lung or kidney, start a massive haemorrhage or displace the splint on a multiple fracture, so it was essential that both clutch and gear box be in A1 condition. The clutch of the Buick was of the ball and cup variety, the ball covered with a leather-like substance which, if it became worn, would prevent the clutch engaging smoothly. Thea became fanatical about vehicle maintenance; hers was the cleanest and best-kept ambulance in the unit. There was so little one could do to ease the patients' pain, she had neither the training nor the equipment. Her job was to provide transport, and her responsibility to render that transport as safe, speedy and comfortable as possible. She would concentrate on this as she crawled back up the cliff road in the dark, with a bad case yelling and screaming in the back. Better to press on, to drive as well as you knew how, than to give way to misplaced pity and stop.

The badly wounded tended to fall into two categories: those who were deep in shock, silent and grey-faced, mustering all their waning strength to stop themselves from crying; and the others, some terribly young, who had long since blundered blindly through the barrier of self-control, and who screamed and wept incessantly. The young ones tended to be the most reduced. Many of them cried all the time for their mothers, they had accumulated no other resources in their pitifully short lives to fall back on. Thea never overcame her feeling of inadequacy. But she did learn certain tricks to minimize the men's discomfort and her own anxiety. One of these was her obsessive care for her machine. Another was to stand at the far end of the ambulance as the stretchers were loaded, head first. The train orderlies were exhausted and dangerously near the end of their tethers at this stage; they were understandably a little less careful than they might have been and you could hear men yell in agony as their stretcher jarred against the partition. She now hoarded cigarettes jealously and offered one to all those well enough to smoke: it was months before it occurred to her that there was no means of extinguishing a fire if someone should set themselves alight. She also provided extra insulation for the stretcher by placing one blanket, folded in three lengthways, beneath it. Once she had set herself these tasks she never neglected them.

The only circumstances in which medical assistance was provided on the journey were tourniquet cases. If a tourniquet remained too tight for too long it could prevent all circulation in the area beneath it, and the lack of circulation could in its turn cause gangrene. It was therefore necessary for an orderly to travel in the ambulance with the patient to loosen the tourniquet when and if required, and allow the blood to flow for a minute or two. The sense of relief occasioned by the presence of the orderly was immense It was like a holiday.

The first time Thea was actually obliged to stop on a run to the hospital was one wet night towards the middle of May The weather had become much milder of late, and the rain was gentle. Only 'A' Section were on duty that night. The four men Thea was carrying were bad, but quiet. They were all slightly older men, and she had noticed a tendency in the older ones to be more stoical, or perhaps just wearier They were never so jubilant about going home, but they were never so vocal in their distress, either. She had begun to climb out of the valley and to ascend the steep, winding road towards General 16 when there was a muffled tapping on the partition. So small and irregular was the sound that she took it at first to be simply the rain dripping from the roof, until it was backed up by a voice, urgent with anxiety.

'Lady! Oy!'

Thea put up a hand and slipped back the partition without taking her eyes off the road. 'What is it?'

'Better come and have a look.'

Something solid and authoritative in the man's voice made her pull in at the side of the road and stop. It was her second and last trip of the night. The rest of the Section were scattered over the route. If one had to stop the procedure was to signal to the next ambulance passing in the same direction so that they could bring a nurse or orderly down from the hospital on their return run. She switched off the engine and alighted, the rain falling in a soft, pattering curtain all around. It was ominously quiet. She looked down the hill: nothing; the road was calm and gleaming wet and empty. She tried to remember whether there had been others after her at the station—what if she were the last? Perhaps she should never have stopped, but it was too late to dither now. She had made her decision, she must follow it up.

She walked round to the rear of the ambulance, hooked up the flap and leaned in. It was dark as a bag but she could see the pale disc of a face above the bottom right-hand stretcher—the man who had called her—and the eye sockets dark and staring. It was quiet but for the patter of the rain on the canvas . . . something else: a faint, unidentifiable undercurrent of sound in the muffled closeness.

'What's the matter?'

'It's him, he's choking I reckon.'

'Which one?' She climbed in, rasping her knee on the tail board, cursing her clumsy blindness.

'Up there.' He pointed to the top left.

'Are you sure?' She glanced at the other two. The man above the one who had called her was lying still, in a coma; the code on the ticket attached to the foot of his stretcher indicated a shrapnel wound in the abdomen. The man on the bottom at the other side was staring at her, she could make out the glint of his wide open eyes. Delicacy, a ludicrous sensation under the circumstances, prevented her from studying his ticket while he watched her.

'Take a look,' urged the first man, leaning up on his elbow. He had a chest wound, she observed; next to sitting cases chest wounds were usually the most buoyant. She went to the head of the man on the top left. He was heavily bandaged: only the right-hand lower corner of his face was visible, and his mouth There was a sharp, new, instantly recognizable smell: the man had vomited. But where? Then she caught sight of a streak of moisture like a snail's trail issuing from the corner of his mouth, and that faint sound, a kind of crackle, a seepage.

'You're right,' she said, 'he's been sick.'

'He could drown,' said her mentor, not without a trace of pride. 'I've seen it happen before.'

The man suddenly emitted another dreadful noise, explosive yet stifled, and a fresh stream of fluid slid down his cheek: she could see his mouth brimming with it. She supposed she should turn him, but he had a bad head wound; should she . . . ? Panic seized her.

Bottom Right heaved himself into a sitting position. 'You want to lift his head a bit,' he offered.

'Yes, but I should get help . . .' She glanced distractedly out of the back at the still-empty road.

Bottom Right stood up with a lurch. 'Go on then.'

She turned on him, worry making her shrill. 'You *must* lie down!' She saw the stripes on his arm, he was a huge barrel-chested man with a curly moustache. 'Sergeant, lie down. This is my responsibility.'

'You get on with it then. I'll hold his head for a mo.'

There was no denying the sense of this suggestion. 'Very well.'

'Attagirl.' With a big person's cautious delicacy he slipped a large paw beneath the man's head and tilted it slightly forward and to the side. She glanced anxiously back at him. 'Go on.'

She got out and stepped into the middle of the road, looking up and down, her heart galloping. Thank heavens! The blacker moving form of an ambulance was approaching from the direction of the station. She waved her arms wildly like a windmill in a gale.

'Stop! Stop!'

The vehicle slowed down and Collins's welcome, quizzical face came into view over the steering wheel. 'Tennant? What's up?'

'Oh God, I'm so pleased to see you, I thought I must be last.'

'I had to wait. My lot are all goners.'

'Look, I've got a crisis on my hands, a man's choking in here.'

'Vomited?'

'Yes, and he has a head wound. Someone else is with him but he's bad too and I shouldn't leave them. Can you bring a nurse, I'm—' She was going to say 'terrified he'll die' but bit off the words. 'I'm doing the best I can,' she substituted.

Collins nodded. 'No sooner said than done.' And she was gone, with a roar and a hiss of tyres on the wet road.

Thea went back inside the ambulance. The sergeant was still standing there huge and stooped in the cramped space. 'Let me,' she said, and took his place. The man's head felt unnaturally heavy. The sergeant sat down with a great creak, his shoulders hunched beneath the stretcher above. 'Are you all right?' she asked. 'Thank you so much.'

'My pleasure.' He blew gustily through his moustache like a carthorse, as if he'd run a long way. Thea transferred her attention to Top Left. His head, like a grubby football, stared blankly at the side of the ambulance; the distant subterranean gargling projected a now-moving trickle onto the under blanket. With her free hand she sought out her handkerchief and wiped his jaw. The resulting stain was suspiciously dark, even in the gloom.

'There's blood in this,' she said.

'There would be.' The sergeant sounded immeasurably weary. Of course, she must seem pretty silly to him, he had seen such a lot of death and suffering.

It occurred to her that the man might be conscious. She bent over him. The area round his just-visible nostrils was white, his upper lip had a strange bruised appearance. 'Are you comfortable?' she asked, clearly and loudly. There was no response. But as she straightened up she felt a small, mouselike movement near her hand where it rested on the side of the stretcher. She would not have noticed it but for the man's otherwise complete stillness. It was made by his fingers, feebly groping for hers. She slipped her hand beneath the blanket and felt it held, or rather let it lie there, for there was no strength in the grasp. She stood motionless, terrified of breaking the spell.

The rain had stopped but the silence was punctuated by other small, ominous sounds. The man above the sergeant was still unconscious, his breathing shallow but audible. The sergeant himself had lain down once more with another great puffing sigh. By Thea's knees the fourth man had stopped watching her so brightly and accusingly; he had wandered off

505

into his own private nightmare world and was muttering and scratching.

It was only about ten minutes until Collins returned, but it seemed much longer. The time passed mostly in silence. Thea's skin crawled with apprehension . . . Only once did someone speak, and it was the sergeant whom Thea had thought asleep.

'It hasn't been all bad,' he volunteered. She looked over her shoulder at him. His eyes were shut, but as she looked he opened them. 'You know what they say, it's an ill wind.' She nodded. He went on: 'It'll be good to be home for a while. I been out since the start of this show, you know, one of the Old Contemptibles, me.'

'And this is . . . ?'

'The first time I copped one, that's right. Amazing when you think of it. But as I say, it's not been all bad, I've had some good pals . . . and I went to Paris. Always wanted to go to Paris . . .' He was beginning to wander a bit, not really talking to her but to himself. Quite unexpectedly he gave a little laugh. 'I'm fond of my old lady, and I reckon I been a good husband, but in Paris a chap'd have to be a saint . . . ! Went with one girl there, she was a good class sort of girl, a really lovely girl, must of been driven to it by the war—but she was a peach. Shan't forget her in a hurry, lumme no . . .'

His voice trailed away and Thea glanced down at him. He had fallen asleep, smiling. Thea experienced a fleeting admiration for the Parisienne, the mere memory of whom could so cheer a man *in extremis*.

Shortly after that Collins arrived with a nurse, and all four men were delivered to General 16. A couple of days later she took the unprecedented move of asking Miss Courtney if she might drive over to the big hospital to visit; after such an ordeal that they had all shared, it was the least she could do.

Permission was given and she drove over in the afternoon. General 16 was a purpose-built hospital, rather large and gloomy with narrow, small-paned windows. But inside there was an air of calm. Thea was struck by the way in which the men regained identity when they were clean and cared for and propped up in a well-laundered bed; they did not seem like members of the same species that she and the other drivers ferried from the station.

She approached the nurse in reception and stated her

business. 'The Commandant said I might just come and see,' she explained. 'The circumstances were rather exceptional.'

'Yes, now let's have a look . . .' The nurse, who was plump and pretty and freckled, with a West Country accent, took the particulars and rustled off down the passage. She was back very soon, smiling. 'Captain Wright, the one with the head injury, is going to be all right. You can't see him, I'm afraid, but he's doing fine. No more war for him.'

'That's splendid.' Thea and the nurse beamed at each other over this triumph. 'May I see Sergeant Watkins for a moment? It was partly due to him, you see, that—'

The nurse was shaking her head. 'Sergeant Watkins was dead on arrival.'

That shocked Thea. She felt it as a reproach, a personal defeat. She was haunted by the notion that the sergeant had died at that very moment, as he finished speaking about Paris, and she had been more concerned with other matters . . . But there was no way of knowing and speculation was fruitless.

The fact of death itself was commonplace. Many men died on the train and these 'stiffs', as they were termed by their fellow-travellers, were kept back till last to be transported on their own. Not that the men would have minded travelling with a stiff; they'd put up with that any day in preference to sharing an ambulance with an 'SIW' case: self-inflicted wounds were the lowest form of life. But it streamlined the transport operation if the corpses could be taken straight to the doctor for certification and then on to the mortuary.

The carrying of the dead, both from train to mortuary and from mortuary to cemetery, was part of the drivers' everyday work. Corpses were numbered and labelled as part of a rationalization of burial: first dead, first buried. During a big 'push' there would be a shortage of wood for coffins and the dead would be unceremoniously parcelled up in blankets tied with string. The cemetery, spreading like an unwholesome rash on the grassy downland slope above Merville, was a mere five-minute run from General 16, and if she were quick Thea sometimes made time to stand there for a moment, along with the priest and the few convalescent officers and men who had made the effort. She had the idea— probably quite fanciful and erroneous, she realized that—

that she, as a woman, might serve as a kind of symbol for all those mothers and daughters and sweethearts who couldn't be present.

For some reason, though, the beauty and stoicism of the funeral service enraged her. Its fatalism seemed an admission of defeat. And she would drive furiously back to the mortuary for the next batch of dead, her teeth gritted, the elegant cadences ringing mockingly in her head.

'He cometh up, and is cut down like a flower . . .' Indeed.

Jack Kingsley arrived to see Thea the very day she cut her hair off. She had been building up to doing so for some time, as what with its habitual dirtiness and the frightful tangles caused by bundling it up under a cap in the middle of the night, it had become a downright nuisance. She wasn't proud of her hair, there had always been too much of it and it seemed to have a will of its own. She just took a pair of scissors first thing in the morning, hacked it off, and put the cuttings in the stove. In her fine frenzy of decisiveness she made no attempt to shape it, so it was lucky for her that it was thick and sprang naturally into close curls. The other girls were amazed at her bravery.

'How could you?' asked Catchpole. 'You've got such marvellous hair!'

'I hate it,' said Thea. 'I'm glad to be rid of it. I might start a new fashion.' They stared at her, admiring but not envious.

However, when Miss Courtney told her she had a visitor and she saw Jack Kingsley standing in the drive, she felt an unwelcome stab of regret and embarrassment. She who had never given much thought to her appearance, and certainly never wished to impress Jack Kingsley with it, longed for her hair back, washed and brushed and shining. She pulled her hat on tight as she came down the steps to meet him. He looked up at her and she felt again, as she had in the library that autumn afternoon, a sense of grateful relief. He didn't comment on her hair, but smiled and kissed her cheek and gazed at her in that way he had, as though he watched her through a window.

'We're in rest camp for a few days and I knew you were here, so I took a thirty-six-hour pass. I hope you don't think it a liberty.'

'It's lovely to see you. I thought you were way up north.'

'We were. But there's to be a big push in a few weeks and we're all being lined up ready.'

She heard the irony in his voice and forebore to ask more. 'I'm afraid there's nothing to do here,' she said. 'But I do have the afternoon free till about four.'

'I only came to see you,' he replied affably. 'Let's go for a walk, it's a beautiful day.' It was certainly that, a perfect end-of-May afternoon with that shiny fresh sunshine of early summer and the sky a great twittering, breathing vault of blue. The neatly spaced white crosses on the hillside looked like daisies, and the sea was drowsy and voluptuous at the foot of the cliffs. They crossed the road and walked over the springy, chalky turf towards the cliff path. Glittering gulls scythed the air below them, round the ledges where they had their nests.

They walked in amicable silence. He linked arms with her and, unlike a notable previous occasion, she found it quite natural and easy. Their strides matched and there was no strain in their quietness now. She glanced at his straight, somewhat ascetic profile, made more austere by the moustache, and thought that although he had no right to he looked better than when she had last seen him at the station, going back after leave.

It had been awful, trying to find something appropriate to say in the parrot-house din of Victoria, he withdrawing all the time, seeming to get thinner and whiter and more tense before her eyes, his whole being pressed and reduced by the strain of departure. All around them others had been making their farewells more how farewells should be, with tears and clinging, but they had not been able to. Instead they had stood in miserable silence amidst the surrounding clamour, buffeted by other people, utterly at a loss. She could not even summon the courage to make a clean break, and go, leaving him to it. That might have been better for him, but not for her. She believed in giving occasions their correct value; it would have been like cutting off a hand to walk away from him without the proper observances. So she had stalwartly and wretchedly remained at his side, holding his arm fiercely, bearing him the company she was not sure he wanted, while he stared ahead stiffly and, once, cleared his throat as though he were about to say something. And then the whistle had gone and all around them there had been a kind of frantic coming together, and then a parting, a sigh and an audible

509

tugging as hundreds of people wrenched themselves apart. The surge of movement was affecting. She had put her arms round his neck and pressed her cheek to his gaunt, cold one.

'Take care of yourself,' she said helplessly, and he had boarded the train and pushed down the window to look out at her through the first shreds of smoke, heartbreakingly smart and spare and soldierly in his newly cleaned uniform. She had put her hand on his arm and began to walk alongside as the train moved off, parting sometimes as other people got in the way, but coming back to him, beginning to run, just to be with him till the last possible moment. It no longer mattered whether he wanted her there or not; she would *make* him see that he was loved and missed.

The train had outstripped her long before the end of the platform, but she managed to focus on his pale face, among all the others that bloomed like snowdrops from the dark carriages in the grimy winter air, until the train had snaked round the long bend and was gone.

Now he seemed not only to sense her eyes on his face but to read her thoughts also, for he said, without looking at her: 'It was terrible at the station.'

'Yes. How funny, I was thinking about that.'

He seemed to take this for granted. 'I hope you've forgiven me for being so boorish.'

'You were no such thing. You were . . . what I'd have expected.'

'And that is?'

She paused. 'Wrapped up in what you were going back to.'

He glanced at her respectfully. 'You're absolutely right.'

When they'd walked for about a mile the cliff path began to descend and curve inland a little and they found a sheltered hollow, a rabbit warren, where they sat down, looking out over the valley. Thea sat with her arms clasped round her knees; Jack lay back, ankles crossed, propped on one elbow. He picked a long stem of grass and put it between his lips. From behind her his voice came, light and casual, as it invariably was when he paid her a compliment.

'You look marvellous, Thea. I like the hair.'

'Do you . . . ?' She ran a hand over it. 'I don't know. It was just so impractical, I got sick of it.'

'I think it suits you. Especially as you are now.'

She laughed. 'Whatever does that mean—"as I am now"?'

'So busy and independent.'

'Oh *that*.'

'That.'

'I'm no different really.'

'But you're glad you went in for this driving?'

'Yes I am. I do at least feel that I'm helping in some way, and that I understand—just a bit—what you all have to go through.'

He didn't respond to this remark, but just gazed steadily at her, moving the grass stem up and down between his lips. 'What news of your family?' he asked 'Are they well?'

'Mother's not at all well. I'm not sure she ever will be again, and of course that depresses Father. There have been too many sudden changes, for both of them, and they're not so young any more. They feel like a couple of dinosaurs left over in the new world.'

'Your parents could never be dinosaurs!' He laughed and sat forward so that his shoulder touched hers.

'They are getting old. You know—' she rested her chin on her knees and plucked at the grass by her feet, 'that Christmas . . . that was the last time I felt properly young, and that they were my parents, who knew more than me and provided safety and certainty. Isn't that awful?'

'Not really.' He spat out the stem. 'I suspect that may have had something to do with me.'

'No. *Everything* changed, it's odd how quickly it happened. I suppose it would have been gradual but for Dulcie and me going away, and the war . . . When we left, the change was just beginning, and when we got back it was complete. It's like an amputation; I still feel the bit that isn't there any more, I'm not quite resigned to it yet.'

'My parents must be dinosaurs too,' he suggested.

'No.' She shook her head. 'It's not quite so bad for them because they've always been more peaceful, more entrenched. But Father's always liked to see himself as an innovator, a stylist, and now suddenly he's left behind. He's had to face the fact that Mother can't sustain life without her children about her, and his feelings are hurt. It's sad.'

There was a cluster of square grey farm buildings down in the valley and as they watched two women in black came out of the farmhouse and began to peg out washing, the little squares of colour flapping like bunting in the bright sunshine.

'Also,' she went on, her train of thought unbroken, 'I think he's a bit hurt by my giving up the job at the factory and

511

doing this. He was very good about it, but I know he sees it as a criticism of all he's done. And it's not so.' She turned to look at Jack, asking for his reassurance. 'I don't blame him or criticize him for a thing. I understand him and his reasons, and he's *not* a war profiteer.'

'I know.'

She returned to plucking the short grass. 'I wish Dulcie would go home,' she muttered.

'Do you hear from her?'

'Yes, she's written a lot lately.'

'How is she?'

'Oh, full of herself. Bright and breezy. Saying all the time that business is good and the new apartment's wonderful, and that she might come back when the war's over.'

'You don't believe any of it?'

'It's not that I think she's lying exactly. It's just a feeling I have that she's feeding us all this good news just to keep us at arm's length.'

'You think the lady doth protest too much.'

'In a way.'

'Try not to worry.' He put his arm across her hunched shoulders and bent to look into her face. 'You can't worry for everyone.'

'I suppose not. Anyway, perhaps I might get to Paris while I'm over here, and see her, you never know.'

They continued absent-mindedly to watch the two women outside the farm. One of them went back into the house but the other stood facing towards them and after a few seconds raised an arm, with the black fringe of a shawl hanging from it.

Thea nudged Jack. 'Wave back, it's the uniform.'

He did so. 'Shall we walk down there?' he asked. 'Say hallo?'

'All right.'

They set off, half-running, half-walking down the tussocky hill. When they were almost at the bottom the woman went into one of the outbuildings and emerged to meet them carrying four brown eggs in a cardboard box.

'*Pour vous,*' she said, holding them out.

She probably wasn't very old, not much older than Venetia, but she was desiccated and lined and bent like a hawthorn twig and her black clothes accentuated the under-nourished pallor of her skin. She invited them in, and made tea. The other woman, a girl in her twenties, was peeling potatoes at the table: she looked at them and nodded but didn't speak. The only other occupant of the kitchen was an old man sitting in a wooden high-backed chair by the stove, and he didn't spare them a glance. The whole place had a forlorn, run-down air about it, yet it was the typical French farm of wartime, worked by the old and the women at a grim subsistence level. Thea knew the French women thought the English girls odd and daring to wear uniforms and drive ambulances, but they grudgingly admired them too: hence the eggs and the invitation.

They drank their tea at the table, Thea and the old woman carrying on a halting conversation while the girl scraped the potatoes viciously and dropped them with a splosh into a two-handled pan full of water. She was dark-browed and sullenly beautiful, like an imprisoned panther in this place of old age and hopelessness.

When they were outside again Thea asked: *'C'est votre fille là dedans?'*

'Belle-fille. Mon fils est mort à Verdun.' She stared at them, her crow's eyes bright and defiant in her creased old face as if daring them to be consoling.

'Merci, madame.' Jack picked up her bent hand from where it lay on her apron and clasped it in both his. *'Merci pour votre gentillesse.'*

She stepped forward, putting her other hand on his neck and drew his face down to hers, kissing him fiercely on both cheeks without a trace of self-consciousness.

Then she pushed him away. *'Assez. Allez-vous en, tous les deux.'*

They trudged back up the hill and when they reached the false crest, the warren where they had sat and talked, they looked back and she was still standing there; a little lumpy black figure like a child's wooden toy.

When they got back to Quatre Pins, Thea said: 'I can't very well ask you in. What do you want to do?'

'That's all right. I ought to get back to the station anyway.'

'So much travelling, just for two hours.'

'It was worth it, I promise you.' He grinned at her, with something of the old, foxy, disconcerting Jack. He took her by the shoulders and kissed her forehead. Although he was neat and clean she could smell the smell on him. It seemed more pronounced now than on his arrival, as though it crept back to reclaim him. 'By the way,' he asked, still, holding her shoulders as if fixing her attention. 'Did you ever write to the von Crieffs?'

'No. There didn't seem much point.'

He didn't reply but released her and gave the peak of his cap a tug. '*Au revoir* then. Keep your pecker up.'

'I'll come to the gate.'

'No.' He paused, gazing at her. 'Very well, then. But don't let's say goodbye again. I'll just carry on walking when we get there. Is it a bargain?'

'Done.'

They began walking, extremely slowly, back towards the gate. 'What about this big push?' she asked tentatively. 'What will that be?'

'The biggest Allied offensive of the war, we are reliably informed, around the river Somme. Beginning of July. Should keep you busy.'

She was shocked at the bitterness of his voice. It was the last thing he said to her. He reached the gate and simply walked away along the cliff road in the sunshine, not looking back.

CHAPTER SIXTEEN

'If you want the old battalion
We know where they are,
We know where they are,
We know where they are,
If you want the old battalion
We know where they are:
They're hanging on the old barbed wire.'

Anon.

'Dips! Come and get it! All lovely and 'ot—!'

George Rowles was first there: he'd been hanging about waiting for this moment. He plunged his chunk of bread into the swimming hot bacon fat, pulled it out, dripping and steaming, and dropped the saturated end into his mouth. It scalded him, and he rolled it frantically from one cheek to the other with his tongue. But the bliss Smashing, tastiest thing he'd eaten in weeks. He closed his eyes as the others jostled for their dips, and a trickle of grease ran down over his chin for he was unable fully to contain such an enormous mouthful. Greedily he stretched out his arm and dunked the rest of the bread.

'Leave it out, Georgie! Eff off and give another fella a look-in.'

'Sorry . . .' He still couldn't speak properly for bread.

'Piss off out of it, then!'

This exchange was entirely without rancour. George rose and pissed off out of it, passing the rest of his loot, still boiling hot, from hand to hand. Outside, the mellow evening sunshine struck warm on his face. He strolled over to the low white picket fence at the end of the garden and leaned his knees against it, staring out over the fields as he munched.

Odd thing, the way the little fence had survived, while most of the rest of the hamlet of Verigny had suffered war damage of one kind or another. Even the villa in which they were billeted had the whole of one corner stove in, and the row of cottages next door was wrecked. The damage wasn't

515

that recent; the great leap of vegetation that takes place in June had asserted itself over snapped timbers and collapsed walls, and swallows had made nests. What's more there was a nectarine vine growing up the garden wall of the villa, and it had been covered in fruit when they arrived, the first they'd seen in months. He grinned to himself and wiped his greasy mouth on the back of his sleeve—it wasn't covered in fruit now! They'd swarmed over it like locusts and scoffed the lot, what a treat. The thing was, they'd only been expecting to have one night at Verigny, or they might have rationed the nectarines a bit more. As it was, due to some cock-up at Brigade HQ they'd had a whole extra day here, and most of them with very loose stomachs what with all that unaccustomed fruit.

He sighed happily. They'd earned the rest, mind. Thirty miles they'd marched, yesterday and the day before, not all in the same direction either. George's feet bore witness to that, they were a tender puffy mass of blisters, but he bore his commanders no ill-will. On the contrary, he was content; he looked no further than the end of today. Tomorrow they set off for the town of Albert, four miles away, en route for their appointed position in the Big Push, and a mighty victory; it was all a bit blurred in George's mind but there was a feeling of optimism abroad in the air to which he was not immune.

Before him the soft, grey-green countryside of the Somme valley rippled in a tickling breeze. As with the buildings, so with the fields; the good weather had ensured that ugly holes and scars were now covered in grass, poppies, cornflowers and convolvulus. He looked down; nice little dwarf azalea they'd got here, still going strong, and some young rambling roses badly in need of pruning. George shook his head; they should've pruned in March, cut them right back to two or three strong stems, then they wouldn't have gone so straggly. And there was a good deal of fly. He cupped one of the yellow and orange roses in his palm, the stem between his two middle fingers. He had a gardener's touch, firm and confident but gentle, like a vet or a good mother. It was the only thing he missed, really, the garden, or at least the only thing he was entitled to miss. The war had done a lot for him. No one here seemed to think him especially simple, he had pals, and a sense of belonging and the good moments, like these, were among the best he'd known.

He thrust his hands in his pockets and began to suck his teeth noisily, closing his eyes as an aid to concentration.

'Georgie!' He turned. Bob and another two men were standing in the doorway, Bob holding aloft some playing cards, spread in a fan. 'Fancy a game?'

'Yeh . . . coming.'

That was what he liked, being one of the lads. It didn't matter that he always lost, they played for cigarettes and he wasn't bothered. They included him, that was the main thing.

He relieved himself first, carefully and pointlessly projecting the jet over and not onto the fence, and then went back to the villa. Throughout the ground floor there was an air of well-being, a haze of smoke and the smell of bacon. Someone was playing on a comb and one or two lazy voices sang along:

> *'There once was a gay Cavallero,*
> *Who dwelt on the banks of Navero,*
> *Flashing about with his wonderful,*
> *Wonderful, to-ra-la, to-ra-li-ay . . .'*

George hummed as he threaded his way over to where Bob and the other two were sitting. They were in the corner of what had been the front parlour, George guessed, you could still see the ghosts of pictures on the walls and the tidemark where the carpet had ended. He wondered what had become of the well-to-do people who'd lived here.

Apart from Bob and Tiny there was another chap whom George had seen before, but didn't know, one of the Londoners grafted onto the regiment after their last show. A bit of a lad, he was, regaling the others with a lurid account of a *'maison de tolérance'* he had visited in Le Havre. George picked up his cards and sat down, trying not to listen. He knew what the *'maisons'* were, but had only the haziest idea what they might be like. Some of the talk he heard shocked and frightened him, and although most of the brothels were regularly inspected and infected women turned out, he had known plenty of chaps catch something nasty and have their pay docked for every day they spent in hospital. Whatever it was, it couldn't be worth incurring such displeasure.

'I promise you, there must've been thirty of us in the queue,' the raconteur was saying, pushing the air with his spread hand to emphasize his point. 'And when I got in, there's this great big woman, built like a zeppelin, legs hangin' over the tops of her stockings, moustache like a sergeant—'

'Get away.' Bob was smilingly impressed, but sceptical.

'No, honest. And when I come in, all she says is: "Like usual? Like usual?" I wondered what to say.' He paused, with a nice sense of timing and tension. His audience watched him expectantly, except for George who blushed fiercely.

'Well?'

'Nah—' he waved a hand at them, 'I'm a shy little thing at heart. "Usual," I said, and usual I got.'

'All right was it?' Bob raised his eyebrows in a way that implied a wealth of experience with which to compare the incident, but the storyteller sidestepped this question neatly.

'Quick,' he said. 'Very quick. You can imagine, with a coupla dozen more waiting outside.'

After this they played cards for an hour or so with a vague sense of disappointment, tinged with satisfaction, for the man's experience had evidently been no great shakes. The leisurely midsummer sun dawdled down over the horizon and in the distance there was the boom and crump of the front, but it didn't bother them. If you weren't there, just for the moment, you made the best of it.

On 29 June the 1st Kents took a short break on their way through the town of Albert. The weather was perfect, but not for marching, and the men were dusty and footsore. With some time to spare there was no point in pressing on through the worst heat of the day. Most of 'B' Company were strung out sitting on their packs in front of what had been a row of shops. Their faces gleamed, red and sweaty, but cheerful. They watched, amused, as two of their number engaged in energetic bargaining with the proprietor of the last remaining shop, a baker's, but most of them weren't hungry: it was too hot to eat.

Jack, sitting on a low wall that had once bordered a neat front garden but now stood forlornly before a pile of rubble, stared up at the tall church tower on the far side of the square. He squinted, the glare of the noonday sun making his eyes water. It glinted off the gilded back of the Leaning Virgin, but her calm face was in shadow as she hung out a full 95 degrees from vertical; she had been hit once, early on in the war, but it was the French who'd bent her over to her present position, to prevent the enemy gunners using her as a 'fix'. People liked to say that when she finally collapsed the war would end. But she'd been like that for over a year now, the metal struts at her base sticking up haywire like the roots of a felled tree, her body pointing accusingly over countryside that had once been tranquil and cultivated, roads and cart-tracks which had seen nothing faster than horse-drawn farm vehicles, and buildings which had housed busy people leading humdrum lives. Now the new traffic of wartime flowed through the streets of Albert in a flood tide.

Jack brought his gaze down to street level, rubbing his eyes to rid them of the sunspots that danced in front of them. The square teemed with soldiers, horses and army vehicles swarming like ants under the lofty blue sky. On the far side of the square, on a patch of waste ground that still bore the vestigial walls of a house, the band of some Highland regiment were playing a Scots tune, wistful but catchy. A strathspey, Jack thought, and tapped his foot as the music threaded its way, swelling and fading, through the general hubbub.

He felt ridiculously cheerful. It was, he knew, a kind of abdication of responsibility to let oneself be swept along on this great wave of movement and foolhardy optimism when as little as a week ago he had been gloomy, sceptical, at the end of his tether. Now, for no good reason, he was almost prepared to believe that this *might* be the beginning of the end of the war. It just might. He regretted having been so brusque and pessimistic with Thea. God knows, she was the very last person he'd want to upset. But at the time he had meant to be cruel to be kind, to prepare her for the very worst that might happen. Now he felt he had only been cruel.

The sun was hot on his face. There was a smell of bread. The music of the pipes lilted jauntily over the clatter of hooves, and wheels, and boots and voices. With eyes closed and a very small effort of imagination he might have been in a fairground.

The march to the front was not long, and they were in high spirits. Once they had left the crowded streets of Albert the men began to sing, but as the platoons marched at fifty-yard intervals they soon fell out of time with each other and Jack, near the head of the column, could hear the men at the back following on, like an echo.

> *'Bonsoir old thing!*
> *Cheerio, chin chin,*
> *Napoo, Toodle-oo, Goodbyee*

They passed along a sunken cart-track with high grassy banks on either side. There was plenty of evidence of front-line activity. There had been no question of the British troops *in situ* keeping a low profile before the start of the great offensive. On the contrary, they had been kept on their toes with patrols, raids, recce parties and continual light bombardment of the enemy position. The element of surprise was not one to which the British commanders attached much importance. Lying doggo was tantamount to cowardice. To be aggressive and purposeful, and to be seen to be both, that was the thing.

But they were used to seeing dead men; it didn't shock them when they came to a part of the bank that had been a gun emplacement, and found the gunners, dead for some days, with their heads and trunks buried in scratch-holes like so many ostriches, the legs stiff and bloated and seething with flies. Nor were they horrified when they rounded a bend and discovered the best part of a platoon blown literally to bits by shell-fire. They'd been a carrying party, most likely, for there was the wreckage of a wagon, and two mokes with their legs jutting out ridiculously from their puffed-up bodies.

Once, by a farm gateway, they passed a small canopied crucifix of carved wood, about three feet high. But there was something defeated in the tilt of the lolling head, the closed eyes and sunken cheeks and the limp, elongated body. It affected them in a way that the corpses had not, and a spot of silence ran down the side of the column as they marched by.

They were very close to the front now, they could smell it and feel it and hear it, and they stopped singing. The weight of their packs became oppressive. They'd all been issued with steel helmets, which they were later to bless, but which now seemed nothing but a tiresome addition to an already intolerable load of equipment.

They reached their position soon after 1500 hours, with things pretty quiet. The trench itself was a miserable shallow ditch so fatigues were set to deepen and reinforce it. Jack acquainted himself with their exact position. The 1st Kents were near the top end of a horseshoe-shaped valley, with a wood immediately to their left, and a Warwickshire battalion flanking them on the right. The wood was quite large, and followed the high curve of the horseshoe almost round to the other side. There were British Vickers guns strategically placed at the near edge of the wood but then, as far as Jack could ascertain, an area of uncharted territory before the British line resumed on the far side. He sent a messenger back to Battalion HQ, which had been set up in a barn about half a mile behind the line, to enquire about the wood. It worried him.

His anxiety was not alleviated when he trained his binoculars on the enemy line. He had known, of course, how they were placed, but reading was one thing and seeing another. Their line followed the ridge on the far side of the horseshoe and was higher than their own position at every point. Allied to this distinct natural advantage their barbed-wire entanglements were of colossal size and density, a black impenetrable mass like a thicket snaking along the brow of the hill. The enemy up until now had neglected their defences in the Somme area, knowing it to contain little value for the British and French, but they had clearly been alerted by the ceaseless activity of the opposition over the past few weeks, and prudently strengthened them. What was more, Jack knew that the visible wire was simply the first barrier, shielding the German guns in the sunken road at the top of the hill; there would be more wire beyond them, probably even thicker, in front of the actual front line trench which was about a hundred and fifty yards further on. He only hoped that the massive bombardment scheduled for early next morning, and the work of the sappers tonight, would do something to break down the wire, for as things stood at present he could not for the life of him imagine how any man, even if he reached the wire in one piece, could possibly hack his way through it. He felt a cold, curling worm of fear in his stomach, but it was too late now, too late. His system was preparing itself automatically for the ordeal ahead, the adrenalin was flowing, memories and associations were falling away, expectation ended with the moment when they would go over the top. Nothing he said or did would make any difference now, they had to go through with it even if every shred of evidence shouted 'Don't!' And then he felt

Massie's ghost at his shoulder like the voice of conscience —confident, courageous, uncomplicated—and he remembered the bright blue eyes staring up at him over that great scarlet gash of a smile, and was ashamed of his doubts.

Harman came up to him, carrying a mug of tea and a tin plate on which reposed a slice of bread, spread liberally with red jam.

'Thank you, Harman.' He peered at the jam. 'Plum and apple?'

'No, sir.' There was a note of quiet pride in Harman's voice. Jack took a bite.

'It's never strawberry!'

'Sir.'

'How in the world did you come by that?'

'Bit of bargaining in Albert, sir, all quite above board.' Harman was nonchalant.

'You're a marvel. Thank you very much, I shall enjoy this. And Harman—'

'Sir?'

'Spread it about a bit, won't you?'

The word from Battalion HQ was that the Division on the far side of the wood were as certain as they could be that they held it, at least as far as the apex of the curve, and that their patrols had not discovered an enemy strong point. Jack supposed he would have to be content with this, but determined nonetheless to take a party into the wood after dusk to see for himself. He could at least do this one small thing to minimize the risks of tomorrow's attack.

Jack, Peter Hallett and a dozen men entered the wood at 21.30 hours. It was a pretty wood. The path they followed wound between widely spaced, slim-trunked larches, the ground was thick with bilberries, and about twenty yards to their left, where the trees thinned out to meet the open country behind the lines, was a hazy carpet of blue.

'Astonishing bluebells,' observed Hallett. 'Late, surely?'

Jack agreed that they were a bit late. Their presence was soon to appear doubly astonishing, for the character of the wood changed completely once they reached the top of the crest along which it ran. Here, most of the trees were decapitated and stripped, and the branches lay criss-crossed and piled so thickly that there was no hope of following the path, and they had to hack their way through. All around, the dead were sprawled among the leaves and twigs like picnickers; occasionally Jack trod on a man's face or hand where it lay half submerged. The men on the Vickers gun said there had been some enemy movement at the far end of the wood a couple of days back, but they reckoned they'd blasted them out. Still Jack wasn't satisfied. It seemed incredible that such a well organized force as the Germans at this point undoubtedly were should pass up the chance of a choice position, commanding a view of the whole valley, and of the exposed flank of the attackers as they advanced. It was getting dark now, and they were all a little jumpy. It was unpleasant to be up to your eyes in vegetation, all of which crashed horribly every time you moved, and to be exposed to full moonlight by the bare trunks above. Everything was dead quiet now, waiting for the big day tomorrow.

'I think we're wasting our time, sir,' ventured Hallett. And the moment he'd said it they all but fell into an enemy dugout.

It was an old one of course, no one there. Jack wondered hopefully if it might have been the centre of the enemy activity described by the gunners. It was impossible to tell, since it was deep and well constructed enough to have escaped damage. Compared to this the British lived in mere furrows. Here was a dugout built to keep people safe, to afford shelter while the storm raged outside. They could stand comfortably upright in it, and it was spacious enough for all fourteen of them to enter without a crush. The walls and floor were solid and timbered, it had been wired for electric light, and a collection of empty wine bottles stood in one corner. Against one wall substantial wooden bunks had been constructed. As they stood gazing about them Jack thought, and knew the others did too, of that ridge opposite, the black tangle of wire, and a confident, well-protected enemy who sat beneath the ground carousing in warmth and comfort, awaiting their chance. He shivered.

As they left he noticed an empty cigarette packet on the floor and picked it up. Woodbines, and it was quite new. So other British soldiers had been here recently, and this was not the strong point. Chastened and uneasy they returned to the others, to sit out the short midsummer night with their uncomfortable thoughts.

When the weather is set fair at the beginning of July, and the sun filters bright and early between the curtains, it's hard to stay asleep. Venetia, indeed, had hardly been able to sleep at all. The night had been very warm and she'd passed the hours of darkness fitfully, disturbed by nagging pain and unhappy thoughts. Ralph had taken up more than his fair share of the bed, and had snored like a grampus. By half-past six she could stay in bed no longer. God knows, she felt no eagerness or anticipation about the day ahead, and couldn't recall when she last had. She felt stale, unrefreshed, with no appetite for anything; but at least one more night was gone, and the sun was shining. She went to the window and held back the curtain. To her amazement there was a fox on the lawn, spruce and businesslike, his handsome brush held out behind him, his pointed face like an arrow It was early, the garden was still his domain, and she the outsider, watching him. Genuinely delighted she was about to turn and call Ralph to come and look, but something arrested her, a strange sound. The fox, too, heard it, and paused for a moment with one forefoot raised before trotting away to the cover of the long grass.

She listened intently, opening the window a little to catch it more clearly. It was still there, a sort of vibration in the air, rising and falling like the sound of the sea in a shell. She was baffled. It didn't feel like thunder

She turned. The light from the window fell across Ralph's large, hunched, noisily breathing form which she suddenly wanted to be near. Letting the curtain drop she slipped into bed, threading her arm beneath his and around his chest.

'Ralph,' she whispered against his wide, warm back

'Mmm .?'

'What's that noise?'

Primmy, coming off night duty, recognized the sound at once. Being near the Channel coast she heard it quite often on still days, and she understood its implications all too well. As her bicycle wheels fizzed down the gravel drive she didn't slow down, but reminded herself, in her severely practical way, that she had better get a good day's rest

At the gate she stopped and looked back at the big house, as she always did, because it gave her great pleasure to think that she belonged there As she looked, a light went on in the bathroom on the second floor. Now a dark silhouette, shoulders hunched, appeared in the window, and one hand went up to pull the top pane down an inch or two. Primmy sucked her teeth. Somebody smoking, and she was as certain as she could be that it was McClusker the Canadian, whom she had had to address on the subject on more than one previous occasion. She was in two minds whether to storm back up there and give him a piece of her mind, but professionalism stopped her. It was someone else's job at the moment, not hers, and she should hurry back and get some sleep; time enough to haul McClusker over the coals tomorrow.

Two of her colleagues zoomed by, one of them waved and she caught the words 'D'you hear them?'

They veered round the gatepost into the road, coats flapping. More sedately, Primmy scooted a couple of yards to get up some speed, and then hoisted herself onto the saddle where she sat, erect and motionless, as she freewheeled down the hill to the town. Her knuckles were white on the handlebars, for she felt that the noise, like an avalanche, was chasing her down the hill.

In the overgrown graveyard of St Delfine the horses cropped placidly among the half-submerged graves and the men of the 1st Kaiser Franz Cavalry Regiment sat about in the church itself, roofless now, but still with a few pews left standing. They played cards and talked and polished tack. On the far side of the church, in the lee of the north wall, the farrier was attending to one of the animals that had picked up a stone, the hoof bent upwards between his clasped knees.

It was a peaceful scene. The cavalry had found themselves largely redundant in this war. Indeed, for much of it they'd had to play the part of infantrymen, in the trenches with the rest, and many of the valuable horses had been put to work pulling guns, ammunition and provisions; only about half the original regiment was left. Now they were reassembled and standing by, about a mile behind the lines, for it was thought that today might be a turning point in the war, with a massive French and British offensive along eighteen miles of the Front. Among a host of imponderables it was just possible that the cavalry might serve a purpose, spring a surprise, in the unlikely event of the enemy actually breaking through.

Josef sat on the bumpy, moss-covered stone wall on the south side of the graveyard, where the ground sloped gently away. At the bottom of the slope crawled a sluggish, rush-impeded river and he could see a moorhen with her chicks sculling along busily. It was a beautiful morning, and going to be a perfect day. He recalled very vividly another such morning when he had been out in the garden early, watching the sun swim up over the rooftops of Vienna, but then he had been full of anticipation. Now he was saddened. This war had become a travesty; there was no honour in fighting it, nor would there be dignity in dying: men buried in underground labyrinths, or crouching in ditches of stinking mud, being slaughtered as soon as they emerged, or simply battered to death by shells and bombs as they lay there like beleaguered rabbits. The killing of men, by whatever means could be devised, was the prime objective of both sides, and one they pursued with relentless fixity of purpose.

Ghitti, his grey mare, was tethered near him, munching some michaelmas daisies that sprouted at the base of a plot. At the other end, staring down with disdainful virtue on Ghitti's chomping, whiskery lips, a stone angel with a chipped nose stood with folded hands. Josef leaned forward and slapped the mare's taut, barrel-shaped flank and she puffed through her moustache in acknowledgement of this attention. She was a dove grey about the head and neck, fading to the colour of a snowy sky over the body and darkening again down the legs. Her mane and tail, and the lashes that fringed large, melting, seal-like eyes, were almost black. She was beaubiful, and Josef admired her.

She was also unintelligent, like the rest of her tribe. Grass, daisies and the rest now filled her small brain; her horizon was no further than the next damp, inviting clump. The rope from her halter slithered between her front legs as she grazed, like a snake. When the noise burst upon them, punctual and expected but still shocking, she turned her head almost phlegmatically in its direction, jaws still munching, eyes vacant. Only her ears, like lily of the valley leaves, were pricked tremulously over her fanned forelock. There must have been some unseen, past damage to the stone angel, for the vibration of the sound caused it to slide, lean, and finally topple over with a crash, its plinth in the air and its snooty, chipped face buried in the grass.

'To Berlin!'
Jack heard some lunatic shout it, in a high-pitched, crazy

voice as they went over the top, and then realized it was him. They were in the second wave, you couldn't see the ridge any more, or the wood, or any damn thing to remind you that you were on earth and not in Hades. Smoke and noise filled the air, and the dead and dying littered the ground making it difficult to run, though you knew you must. He heard himself screeching away like a banshee, he was still going, still alive, his feet still thumping down one in front of the other, but all around him men were falling, and he could hear the rapid, efficient blast of the machine guns. On the left. In that bloody wood, just as he'd known they would be, raking up and down their flank, eating them up disdainfully for the trusting idiots they were.

Mad with rage he yelled, 'Come on! Come on! *Come on!* Don't let them have it!' He wasn't entirely sure what 'it' was—the satisfaction? the victory? the day?—but he did know he'd never felt so vicious in his life. He felt the ground beginning to slope upward and realized he'd reached the foot of the ridge. Now you buggers, now I'm not so easy to pick off, I'll crawl up here like a snake and bite you right where it hurts. Grinning, he looked over his shoulder; perhaps a dozen men were still stumbling towards him. They'd been issued with revolvers, and discarded cumbersome rifles in favour of short sticks, with their bayonets attached to the end. They looked bloodthirsty and primitive and he loved them. By the time they reached him, two had fallen, one of them Hallett, whose face bore a laughable expression of round-eyed amazement as he sank down.

'Now we'll go for them!' Jack yelled. 'Now we'll get them!'

Somebody asked him if he was all right and he realized he had a shallow bullet wound somewhere in his hair above his left ear. The awareness of having missed death by a fraction of an inch raised his spirits still further. He was bloody indestructible!

'Where are the others?' he bellowed. 'Where *are* they? We're damn nearly there!'

He and the rest of the little group spent all day on the slope, and advanced twelve yards. Even that cost them the lives of another two of their number. The German gunners in the wood kept up continuous, withering fire from the left and the attack from their own side appeared to have lost all impetus. There was no one in front and no one behind and at dusk they retreated. Only five of them got back and for some reason which no one could fathom there were congratulations from Battalion HQ on their sterling work and magnificent performance.

Dawn revealed the full extent of the battalion's casualties. They were strewn over no man's land like debris tossed up by the tide. Because they had not been dead long, and some of them were still not dead, their attitudes were full of mobility. In some cases you half expected to see a man rise to his feet, dust himself off, and continue running on his hopeless mission. Jack could see one or two writhing and humping along the ground like caterpillars in search of the nearest shell-hole.

Beyond them, on the crest of the ridge, the wire was still there. The heroic work of the sappers the previous night, in planting torpedoes, had done nothing but blast a hollow in the ground into which the wire had flopped back, intact. And yesterday's bombardment had only lifted it with the result that it had come down more densely tangled than before. Now there hung in it several hundred of the 1st Kents who had gone over in the first wave, stranded like fish in a trawl. Some had been struck while running at full tilt with God knows what desperate measures in mind, and were spreadeagled, face first, arms outstretched as if trying to sweep the prickly embracing tentacles aside with their bare hands. Others had been hurled by shell-fire onto the top of the wire, landing in weird acrobatic attitudes. Every so often, as Jack gazed through his binoculars, he would see the barbs release their hold on some part of a man so that he slipped, his skin tearing heedlessly, into a new position. He let the binoculars fall and leaned his head on the side of the trench. He was filthy and exhausted, and he could feel the grime on his face combed by blood. But when he put his hand up to wipe it away he found tears, too, trickling wearily from him like the last ounce of sap from a withered tree.

At the outset of the great offensive the battalion had numbered over a thousand. When casualty returns had been completed at the end of the first day it was estimated that there now remained three hundred and fifty. In a few hours three-quarters of the battalion had gone. No ground had been gained.

By the latter half of the morning it became apparent that any further attempts at an organized rescue operation were out of the question. Only two of the regular stretcher-bearers remained and they, with a bunch of volunteers, had made superhuman efforts to clear up the mess, under constant fire.

The MO, Hargreaves, had set up an advance dressing post in the front line trench, working with manic, blinkered concentration, cursing and snapping and cutting and stitching for nearly twenty-four hours now, without sleep. The dug-out in which he operated was no more than a recess scooped out of the parados with some planks laid overhead, weighted down with assorted debris. The noise was absolutely deafening and Hargreaves swore continually, and apparently without realizing that he did so.

The Germans, having caught accurately the mood of the moment, were responding to yesterday's bombardment with spirit, hurling everything they'd got in the direction of their shaken and exhausted enemy. Once, a coalbox had overshot the mark, landing a few yards beyond the MO's dug-out, and hurling the improvised roof and a large amount of earth over on top of Hargreaves so that he was bent double, his chin about six inches from his knees. Jack and a couple of others began frantically to dig him out with their bare hands, hurling the debris out behind them like dogs, with Hargreaves damning their eyes and blasting their hides the while.

When they'd got off about half of it Jack leaned over and yelled: 'Can you crawl out now?'

'No, dammit, I'm attached to someone else!'

When they were eventually able to free him he was found to have the fingers of his right hand closed like pincers on the severed artery of a still-breathing corporal.

It was stiflingly hot. The walking wounded, blundering along the trench, careened off the sides like drunks, faint and nauseous but still, most of them, jubilant.

One private grabbed Jack by the shoulder and shouted at him with obvious elation: 'Take a look at that, will you? I'm going home!'

Jack looked. A bullet had entered the boy's hand between the middle and forefingers and travelled up the forearm, bisecting it longitudinally like a bridge roll before bursting out just above the elbow. The arm hung in two pieces tenuously connected by a sticky web of skin and sinew. Above this horror the young man's face was grinning and exalted, because most of him would be going home.

George Rowles had managed to get into a shell-hole. He had followed Major Kingsley the very best he could, but just as the former had reached the foot of the hill, and yelled at him to get a bloody move on he had felt a tremendous blow, like a body-punch in his ribs. There'd been no pain but he had been lifted clean off his feet and thrown to one side. As he lay there with his bent arms shielding his ears, a great many men had leapt over his recumbent form, their legs parting like scissors, their faces unrecognizably the same with yelling mouths and screwed up eyes. When there was a gap in the smoke and the people running over him he spotted the sun, shining away calmly.

Eventually there seemed to be a spacing-out and a slight diminishing in the din and he remembered instructions about finding cover and using the field-aid kit. When he did set out for the nearest crater it seemed a lot further than he'd thought, nearer twenty yards than eight or ten. He was about half-way there when someone fell heavily across his legs so that he couldn't move and he had had to kick and thresh about wildly to free himself. He glanced over his shoulder and saw that the man was dead, the eyes rolled up and the black hair spattered with gouts of brain tissue. You could see the fillings in his teeth. George gave him a final shove and he rolled off, the hole in his forehead making a sound and spewing out more brain like an extra mouth.

George reached the shell-hole and slithered down into it, thankful and perspiring. He found two others there already, a Tommy and a dead German, the latter an occupant of some duration judging by the state of him. Both stared at George like people in a railway carriage. He lay back, panting; he was soaked. When he looked down at himself he noticed that it was not all sweat, but a good deal of blood. The left half of his body was black with it, and through a huge hole in his tunic he could see pink, shiny bubbles oozing and subsiding, their movement corresponding with his own regular intakes of breath. He watched the bubbles, fascinated and not a little horrified by this evidence of damage to his person, but still not feeling any pain.

He did, however, feel terribly tired. Folding his arms across his chest to cover the hole, he let his head fall back and closed his eyes.

He had a weird dream. It started off all right, with a bit out of a Charlie Chaplin film they'd seen in rest camp a few months back, where the little fella was a waiter, trying to find a chair big enough for a fat lady . . . but then the fat lady suddenly stopped being funny and became threatening, with a black moustache and glaring eyes, chasing after George with her big wobbly thighs snapping like hungry jaws ready to engulf him.

He woke again in the late afternoon, feeling light-headed and distinctly unwell. Flies hummed and hovered gluttonously over the dead German: he had deteriorated even in the few hours while George had dozed and now looked less like a human being and more like an assortment of offal, lights and bones contained in a grubby covering of skin and cloth. The other Tommy, who George now observed was in an awful mess down south, was also severely shell-shocked. He no longer lay with a fixed stare but was blubbering and whimpering, pawing all the time at his face and lips as though they didn't belong to him but to a suffocating rubber mask which he wished to remove. This behaviour was even less companionable than the fishy stare, thought George.

Everything was ominously quiet. There seemed to be no gunfire in this section, though he could hear the familiar sound in the distance. Perversely he missed it; the silence unnerved him and he wondered wildly if everyone was dead, everyone except himself and the twittering loony opposite. He craned his neck a little, but could see nothing over the edge of the crater except the shell-blighted tops of some trees and the sole of a booted foot. He thought he should eat or drink something, he felt so rum and swimmy, but when he put up his hand to his pack which was wedged behind his left shoulder he was arrested by a shocking and violent pain in his chest; on looking down he observed that a fresh river of blood had burst from him. Shaken to the core, he subsided, and now there was real panic, like a bird trapped in a small room, flapping and beating with increasing wildness against his sides. He shut his eyes tight and clasped his arms about his chest once more to hide the hole, and the bubbles and the blood, all of which added to his terror. But when he closed his eyes there was nothing to distract him from the pain, which was getting inexorably worse, so he opened them again and stared at the Fritz, for there was nowhere else to look. Crikey, was he going to have to sit here till he rotted, as that bloke had, and watch that body going mouldy right under his nose, just a few stages ahead of his own?

Suddenly, to his utter horror, the German moved. His head jerked as if he were waking and would sit up and stretch at any moment. The flaccid skin of his face dragged sluggishly, a little behind the movement, and then bulged as if the man were blowing a bugle. The lips pushed forward and then parted, revealing two rows of shiny, even, yellowish teeth, and an object which George took to be the man's tongue, churning about inside.

Then the teeth popped out with a click and fell onto the German's chest, grinning inanely, and George saw the eyes of the rat peeping out at him. It slithered forth and hopped leisurely onto the slope by the German's head, where it began to wash its dank whiskers and coat with squirrelish movements. George could hear the small rasp of its paws. Its sides bulged, it was replete, and occasionally it darted a calculating, rapacious glance at George, who passed out.

When he came round it was to semi-darkness and the whine and thunder of guns on both sides. Instinctively he took a peep at the German and saw that the rat had gorged itself on the last of the available delicacies, leaving the eye-sockets empty; the remains no longer looked like a man at all. George wondered miserably where the rat had entered the corpse, and his imaginings led him to clamp his knees together until they shook. The shell-shocked man had calmed down a bit, and was making little repetitive hooting sounds.

George was terribly thirsty. He recalled with masochistic clarity the nectarine vine at Verigny and every cool, clear glass of water he'd ever drunk. The lofty summer night sky was criss-crossed with trails of smoke and fire, like fireworks. Isolated and framed like this, by George's view from the crater, it was quite pretty.

Suddenly, out of the enveloping wall of noise came the rapid thud of feet, and a louder thump as someone lay down. A scrabbling and rattle of grit followed, and a fourth man came into the hole. It was Harman, clutching a large knapsack. George stared at him, wondering if he was wounded; he appeared like a creature from another planet. Now he squatted down, took a water bottle out of the knapsack and waddled over to George still crouching, like a pavement artist George had once seen in Bromley who had no legs and walked about on stumps.

'What's the matter with you?' Harman's puggish face, with its short nose and joined eyebrows, was thrust into his.

'I've got a hole here,' George said, opening his arms for a moment. He couldn't bear to look down, the sight really bothered him.

'You have, 'n' all.' Harman didn't look very hard either. 'Still, doesn't seem to be bleeding too badly at the moment.'

'Just when I move.'

'How d'you feel?'

'Thirsty.'

Harman held the water bottle for him. 'We're running a bit short,' he said, as if to explain the taste, which was brackish and oily. George had heard a joke about the gunners using the water from the Vickers gun's cooling jacket to brew tea, and wondered if this was it. But it slipped down all right, and Harman's stubby, black-etched hands with their broken nails and corny fingers seemed like those of the most genteel ministering angel.

When he'd had his drink, Harman presented George with a wad of cotton bandage out of the knapsack, putting it over the hole and replacing his arms round it, to hold it in position.

'Just stay put for the moment,' he advised, unnecessarily. 'We'll try and get a stretcher over later. Want something to eat?'

'Wouldn't say no to an orange,' replied George, realizing as he said it that he must be slightly off his head to request such a thing. His remark was met by a pitying silence.

Instead, Harman eased his pack out from behind him, got out the iron rations and passed him a piece of biscuit, closing the tin and placing the pack in a more accessible position afterwards. He then went over to the other man, pouring some water into his mouth and examining his condition, muttering something about it being a waste of bleeding time.

'Cheerie-pip, then,' he said to George. 'Chin up, we'll try and get to you soon.'

'Yes,' said George.

Harman slithered out over the lip of the crater and George saw his humped back pause for a moment at what must have been the head-end of the owner of the boot before he ran off, bent double. A shell fell somewhere beyond him and a great sunburst of soil and debris rose like a grey cloud, marking his exit.

Poor Harman: Jack had seen him running back, his squat,

bandy-legged form instantly recognizable as it separated itself from the black and noisy chaos all around. The shell must have fallen right on him, for when the debris subsided he simply wasn't there.

Even as he frantically tried to get his footing on the sliding parapet to reinstate the Lewis gun that had been dislodged by the blast, Jack told himself that Harman must be recommended for a posthumous honour. The man had spent the last five or six hours of his life scuttling about no man's land like a demented spider, with the enemy swatting and swiping at him. He had dragged wounded to cover, and gone from one hole to another with a water bottle and a supply of bandages: all this on his own initiative and with no thought for his own safety. The painstaking tenacity which had enabled him to light fires and brew tea and sniff out strawberry jam, all in the most adverse conditions, had on this occasion undoubtedly saved lives, and cost him his own.

Partly because there was no one else to do it, but mostly because he was determined not to let Harman down, Jack took out a volunteer stretcher party at 0100 hours. He discovered how singularly nasty it was to be engaged on a task which required concentration, a sharp eye and a steady hand, but which precluded your defending yourself. His skin flinched and jumped shamingly, and he streamed with sweat.

They went back and forth with their wretched burdens until 4 a.m. when the grey early light was making them doubly vulnerable and they were too physically spent to do more. Jack was so tired now he felt that his skin had turned to a burning, hypersensitive jelly against which his uniform rasped and dragged agonizingly. Suddenly, his head had begun to hurt fiercely and insistently, and he had spots before his eyes. And the noise, always the noise, like a great crushing solid weight, mercilessly bearing down, grinding your body and your nerves to bits. He thought all the time now: *I wish I might die.* But at dawn the Kents received reinforcements in the shape of a battalion of Devons, along with instructions to launch another assault, after a short battery, at dusk. All was not gloom, apparently; some prisoners had been taken, and a platoon of the Warwicks had won, and held for some hours, a hundred-yard section of enemy trench: not Berlin, exactly, but an avantage well worth following up. Bully for them, thought Jack.

George expected the stretcher party hourly. He didn't doubt Harman's word for a moment, and he had nothing but respect and admiration for his commanding officers. But by dawn he felt very bad, and the other Tommy had sunk into deep unconsciousness, his face pale and speckled and damp like a fish and his mouth hanging loosely open.

He remembered he was near the edge of the wood and seriously wondered if he might be able to crawl there, but when he pulled himself forward he realized it was going to be hopeless. Better just wait here, as Harman had instructed, until help arrived.

At about five-thirty, it did. He became aware of someone walking about near the edge of the crater, a cautious, deliberate tread on the rough ground. With visions of being back with Bob and the rest by breakfast time he twisted his head this way and that to catch a glimpse of his rescuer, who eventually appeared up behind his right shoulder. By arching his neck he could just see him.

'There's two of us in here,' explained George. 'But I reckon that one's a goner.' He was proud of himself for being so lucid and helpful.

His saviour went round to the other side and jumped down beside the Tommy, saying something monosyllabic which George didn't quite catch. Excitement and colossal relief sapped him of his last, tiny reserve of energy. He just lay there, waiting to be taken away.

The man came over to him. As he did so, various small fragments of information floated into George's befuddled brain, too late and quite in vain. The uniform, the cap, the voice, even the smell, were foreign, and one side of the bayonet as it flashed down towards him was serrated like a breadknife. He'd heard about that—

When the 1st Kents were withdrawn to bivouac behind the lines on 6 July they numbered two hundred men and four officers. The Colonel made a point of telling them how splendidly they'd done, and a great many individual acts of bravery and self-sacrifice were duly noted, among them MO Hargreaves and Corporal Harman for their selfless work with the wounded, and Major Jack Kingsley, officer commanding 'B' Company for his inspiring leadership in repeatedly trying to storm the ridge with a handful of men, without regard for his own safety. Sadly, many hundreds were missing without trace, including Private George Rowles of Ewhurst in Kent.

Thea, Catchpole, Sutcliffe, Collins and a couple of others had been moved up to the field hospital north of Albert. There had been no warning and no time to write home beforehand, they had simply packed their few belongings and been bundled onto the train. They were tired before they even started, for the great offensive had, as Jack had predicted, kept them busy and they were desperately short of sleep. On top of this they were all shaken by the death of Caroline Lockie who had thrown herself over the cliff only two days earlier. If Lockie, with her rosy cheeks and her passion for games and her gaggle of younger brothers, could be driven to do such a terrible thing, was it then only a matter of time for the rest of them?

But at the field hospital there was no understanding female commandant, only a bunch of tired, hard-pressed medical orderlies, nurses and army surgeons to whom the new arrivals were no more than extensions of their vehicles. The drivers were to link the field hospital with the advance dressing post and the railhead at Dorremont. They were assigned once more to Buicks, though in considerably worse condition than those at Merville, and began work the same night they arrived. There was no roster here; you drove out whenever you were told, and grabbed sleep, fully-clothed, when you could. If Thea had thought herself dirty at Merville, here she forgot what it was to be clean. They went so long without washing or a change of clothes that their underwear had to be peeled off, removing a layer of skin with it. The collection of khaki tents that made up the field hospital afforded no privacy and little comfort. All sense of home, and a past, were finally buried. She wrote to her parents to tell them of the move, but these days when she pictured them it was as shadowy figures, standing on the far side of a vast, pure-white, crisply turned-back bed, smelling of lavender. She kept half-expecting to come across Jack, while realizing that the chances of such a meeting were remote to say the least. The red crosses of the hospital tents, turned skywards like daisies to deter enemy bombers, were a small fixed point in an area that seethed like an ant's nest: troops, going up and returning; horses, mules, wagons, lorries, guns clogging the lanes and cart-tracks; the air shuddering and moaning day and night with the noise of the Front.

Here, she quickly learned to identify different types of wound. The Germans had a serrated entrenching tool affixed to their bayonets, and this inflicted an appalling jagged rent, ripping flesh and intestines literally to ribbons. Shrapnel tended to tear off sections of the body—feet, hands or whole limbs—and Thea saw more than one man with half his face missing, but still alive. Beside both of these a bullet was clean and wholesome, it either killed you honestly or sent you back to England in fairly good shape. In many cases a phenomenon known as gas gangrene would set in after a wound had been sutured; the sewn edges would puff monstrously and take on a gelatinous, mummified appearance. Unless this could be prevented by continual and painful saline irrigation, amputation could be the only answer. The phenomenon was caused by bacilli, normally present in horses' faeces, which flourished in the rich agricultural soil and became active when carried, with other debris, into a warm human body.

'Shell-shock' she observed to be a blanket term, embracing two sorts of casualty. There were those men in whom the cerebrum had been physically displaced by shell-blast, causing an air bubble to form; and those who had at long last, and often after heroic service, succumbed to the horrors they were exposed to day after day. Neither received much sympathy, and the latter almost none, but Thea's heart bled for them. She remembered Jack, in the library at home, saying, *'It is a kind of death, and if any of us come through it we'll all be ghosts.'*

She saw them, the ghosts. She saw the shuffling lines of blinded men, victims of lachrymatory shells, being herded onto the grass beyond the tents and left to sit there and wait, because they weren't all that bad. Left to wait like bewildered animals, their sightless blindfolded heads turning despondently this way and that, not talking because they couldn't see and the loss of one sense had affected the others.

And the ghosts who were unquiet. Victims of chlorine gas, dying a slow death by asphyxiation, often lasted for days, conscious and fighting for breath to within minutes of the end, their lips mauve and their eyes terrified and incredulous.

And men caught by mustard gas—of which, she remembered with horror, Jack's mother had cheerfully reported that he'd 'caught a whiff'—mustard gas with its sweet smell, that took twelve hours to come into effect and then initiated an appalling death that could take up to five weeks. Thea had had to help strap down men who were in such extremes of agony that they were uncontrollable. The gas burned and blistered the whole body inside and out, stripping away the mucous membranes from the bronchial tubes and causing intolerable pain. The skin erupted into huge suppurating blisters; the eyes closed, swollen and gummed up with the same revolting discharge; the excruciating effects on the stomach caused repeated vomiting.

Ghosts, all ghosts, who had started out as men with some notion of patriotism, however paltry and misguided, but had now crossed to the other side where there wasn't a single thing for a fellow to hang on to.

But as they entered the second week of July the weather remained fine and Thea was reminded daily of the resilience of all of them at the field hospital. Perhaps it was just a natural, inborn safety mechanism, you had to bend or you might snap, but it was possible to be cheerful. She was still encouraged when the day dawned sunny, and the food was marginally less foul than usual. And there was an almost tame starling that hopped in and out of their tent and ate off the edges of their plates. They also had some hilarious games of mixed football with the orderlies, quite often with funerals going on on one side, and amputations on the other, and with shells blasting away not a mile up the road. The offensive had not cut a swathe through the enemy lines but, you told yourself, at least we were giving them what for, and tried not to count the numbers who came back.

On the evening of the eighth, Sutcliffe and Tennant were sent to collect a group of wounded enemy prisoners about two miles up the road. They were to spend the night at the field hospital and then on to the train at Dorremont the next morning. It wasn't quite dark when they set out, which was a mercy, as they were not allowed to use lights here at all. The pavé roads were pitted and cracked and as often as not had deep irrigation ditches on either side, so that in swerving to avoid one hole you fell into another, deeper one. A small sliver of red sun showed on the horizon and the last soft buttery beams filtered between the poplars which lined one side of the road. Once or twice shells which had overshot the front line fell no more than a hundred yards away and a spray of grit landed on the ambulance's canvas roof.

Thea was very tired, more so than usual, but the job was a relatively straightforward one. She'd carried German soldiers many times before, at Merville, and they were rarely any trouble apart from making a lot of noise because they were frightened. She told herself, almost happily, that she would be back in less than an hour, and would get some sleep right away; the others could take the next call unless there were a great many to be picked up. By the time they reached the prisoners, accompanied by a platoon of the Black Watch, it was dusk. There were twelve of them, all sitting cases but for three. The Scots helped them load up, six in each vehicle, with four seated on one side, and stretcher cases on the other side. They were mostly pitifully young, cowed and miserable. When Thea offered them cigarettes they shrank back as if it were arsenic. They were only boys, and here they were being delivered up, defeated and in pain, into the hands of an enemy endowed by propaganda with a fearsome reputation.

Seeing herself marked down for a callous virago, Thea gave up on the cigarettes, closed the ambulance and set off back to the hospital, anxious to get there before real darkness set in. On the way back the Germans moaned and wailed and she began to feel irritable. On top of this, when she did arrive, she found the other drivers out and small chance of any rest. The place hummed with activity and she and Sutcliffe with their loads of prisoners were clearly regarded as the last straw.

Sutcliffe had arrived before her and was drawn up at the edge of the field. As Thea got out an orderly ran over to her.

'More prisoners?' He was fed up.

'I'm afraid so, but none of them particularly bad. Four sitting and two stretchers.'

'In that case, go over there and relieve your friend.' It was always 'your friend' if the friend were proving a nuisance. 'She's hanging onto a haemorrhage and going green. Some-one'll be there in a minute.'

'But what about—'

'Don't fuss about them, we'll get them over in a tick.'

More than a little incensed by the orderly's tone—she had not 'fussed'—Thea went over to Sutcliffe's ambulance. It had been emptied except for one stretcher case on the right. 'Let me,' she said. 'They sent me over.'

'Oh lord,' moaned Sutcliffe, 'I'm going to be sick.'

'Go on then.' Thea scrambled in. 'What do I do?'

'It's his lung,' said Sutcliffe through scarcely open lips. 'You hold this thing tight, and press this wodge of stuff, hard as you can. Hang on like grim death till Thingy gets back.'

They performed the changeover. Thea felt Sutcliffe's slippery hands, the sodden strips of bandage and the 'wodge'. 'I've got it.' She could actually feel the awesome pressure of the bounding, captive arterial blood, the life force seeking its escape.

Outside on the grass Sutcliffe was retching and spitting, then her large form reappeared. 'Sorry about that, not like me at all. Feel as if I'm going to get the squits as well.'

'Poor you,' said Thea.

'Are you managing?'

'Yes. But go and hurry them up, could you?'

'Will do.' Sutcliffe shook her head importantly. 'I think it's hopeless though.'

'Yes,' agreed Thea, feeling a fresh squirt of blood trickle over her clenched fingers. 'So do I.'

She sat there. Outside the darkness was full of bustle and noise; in here it was still and hot and all sensation seemed centred on her two gripping hands. She wished Sutcliffe and the orderly would get a move on, she was keeling over with tiredness. How weird that she, who had always felt things so keenly, could be almost asleep when she held life, literally, in her hands. All she wanted to do was hand over to someone else and get some rest.

At last, two figures separated themselves from the rest and ran over. The first man jumped up, making the vehicle bounce slightly. To her horror, tiredness had made her relax her grip and with the jolt her hands sprang apart. A warm rush of fluid soaked her skirt.

'Oh God! God, I'm sorry.'

'Grab a hold of him again, quick.' The orderly's voice was rough and impatient, he was tired too. She fumbled hopelessly, the blood pumping over her clumsy hands in the darkness.

'I can't!'

'Christ. Let's get him out of here. Out of the way.'

They picked up the stretcher, barging her to one side, and lowered it to the grass outside. One of them squatted down, then lowered his head, listening and feeling. Made pettish by weariness, wishing they'd leave her alone, she scrambled out, barking her ankle as she did so. For the first time she thought, shamelessly, 'It's only a German, we're killing thousands of them every day, why make a thing of it?'

'Too late,' said the orderly. 'We'll leave him here a tick and deal with him in a moment.'

She flopped down on her knees beside the stretcher. 'I'm so sorry.'

'You did your best. He didn't stand much chance.' Their voices were kinder now, they were relieved the crisis had resolved itself.

They hurried off and Sutcliffe came over, touching her on the shoulder and saying something to which she automatically replied: 'I'm coming.'

It was the morning after a particularly heavy and exhausting night that Thea saw the tie-pin. She and Sutcliffe had been detailed to sort through a mass of small articles belonging to the recently deceased, and to put them in neat piles ready for despatching home. They had pulled the long table out onto the grass as it was a fine day and the sun shone brightly on photographs, cigarettes, pay books, letters, buttons, badges, playing cards, dice, sweets: all the pathetic ephemera with which men reminded themselves of their own identity when there was little else to hang onto. Some of it was British, some of it Canadian, a small proportion German, the property of prisoners who had died at the field hospital. Thea saw the pin at once, glinting at her from beneath a webbing belt, like a winking eye. Her hand darted to it and she picked it out, holding it in her cupped palm. It was well polished, and caught the sunlight.

'What's that you've got there?' enquired Sutcliffe, craning over.

'A tie-pin.' Thea stared at it. Fear swelled up in her throat like a bubble, threatening to choke her. She did not trust herself to say any more.

'Mm . . .' Sutcliffe pushed it with her finger. 'It's rather nice.' She went back to her job for a moment, then looked up again. 'What's up?'

'I know who it belongs to.'

'Oh God.' Sutcliffe clapped a hand to her mouth; then waved both hands dismissively in the air. 'Come on, there must be hundreds like that. It's not specially unusual. Surely.'

'I don't know.'

Sutcliffe gained confidence. 'I shouldn't get in a tiz if I were you.'

'All the same . . .' Thea backed from the table, still gazing down at the pin. 'I think I'll go and . . .' She suddenly began to run, urgently, in the direction of the nearest hospital tent.

It was stiflingly hot inside, humid under the heavy canvas. A nursing sister blocked her way, polite but firm. There was some feeling between the nurses and the drivers; demarcation lines were clearly laid down and observed.

'Can I help you?' asked the sister.

Thea held out the pin. 'I found this among the dead men's things. I think I know whose it is.'

'I see.' The nurse surveyed her with dry sympathy.

'Where are they?' persisted Thea. 'Where are the dead?'

'Buried already, or should be, in this weather.' Thea knew she was not being harsh, simply factual. 'You could try over there.'

'Over there' was the mortuary tent. Thea ran over, the pin digging into her hand. In the greenish, underwater light two orderlies were tidying up half a dozen corpses. Three were already packaged, ready for interment.

'Excuse me . . .' She hesitated on the threshold. One of the orderlies answered without looking up.

'Yes? What is it?'

'I think I may know one of these men. Could I . . .? Would it be all right if—'

'All Fritzes, love, every last one.'

'But I'm sure I know who this belongs to.' She persisted, and opened her fist, showing him the tie-pin. Her hand shook. The orderly sighed, patient but harassed, and came over to look at the pin.

'Doesn't look out of the way to me,' he commented, in a clumsy attempt at reassurance. 'Shouldn't be surprised if the Fritzes had those too.'

Perhaps. She felt hope flutter in her like a butterfly, bright but fragile. She looked past the orderly at the body on the table, looking for, dreading to see, Jack.

She stared, ashen-faced, and whispered, 'Josef . . .?'

His face was calm, the lips set together quietly, the eyelids round and smooth. The skin was unmarked and had a bleached, near-transparent pallor, so that the little white streak of scar tissue on his lip was camouflaged, and did not show at all. There was a horse blanket thrown over him, but one of his arms hung down at the side of the table, the fingers of the hand softly curled like a child's. On one of them she could see the slight indentation where he had worn his grandfather's signet ring.

She went closer. Death, like sleep, had removed the hint of severity from his features and left them mild and serene. He looked as though, had he opened his eyes, it would have been with a smile. His hair appeared darker, though, because it was dirty. She touched it and it felt gritty.

The orderly, losing patience with this weird female, had busied himself with another corpse. Thea stood by Josef, leaning forward like a mother watching a sleeping child, fascinated, possessive. She bent and lifted his hand which did not feel as it had looked; it was cold, stiff, heavy. She buried her nose and mouth in the dank palm and began to weep. The sound of her weeping was terrible, long, rasping moans, sucked out of her by utter despair. No tears oiled and eased her grief; it was a dry and bitter agony. All her tender, hopeful memories and fledgling desires, all the feelings she had cherished but kept hidden, they were all for nothing, blasted away and brutally murdered. She spread her arms over him, shielding him but also wanting to feel him this last, last time, when it was too late.

When they came for the body they were kind, flicking the blanket over it expertly, helping her to her feet and telling her to grab some kip because she looked terrible.

She took their advice, going to the tent and curling up on the camp bed. They must have said she wasn't well, for no one came near her. Alone, she indulged in an orgy of selfish animal grief, loathing herself for still being here when he was gone, dragging at her hair and picking her cheeks with her nails until the blood ran. Far from sleeping, she lay all night awake, shivering in the heat and staring into the past.

CHAPTER SEVENTEEN

'Mademoiselle from gay Paree,
Parlez vous?
Mademoiselle from gay Paree,
Parlez vous?
She was true to me, she was true to you,
She was true to the whole damned army too,
Hinky dinky parlez vous.'

Carlton/Tunbridge

Maurice thought to himself: 'It's getting worse. Much more of this and I'll be a liability.' What he said was: 'This is becoming monotonous.'

'You're so right,' replied Stephen Martin. 'But do we honestly want them to devise any variations?'

The face of the man on guard duty appeared in the barred aperture in the door. 'Quiet you two, or you get another day of it.'

The guard had proved himself a man of his word on several previous occasions. Maurice and Stephen stopped talking, but not before Maurice had added: 'Emphatically not.' Just to show that they were completing the exchange rather than obeying orders.

Along with six others, they were standing roped back-to-back in a wooden cell ten feet by nine feet at the Field Punishment Barracks outside Le Havre. They had been transported thither two days before, from the popularly named Soot Street camp a couple of miles up the road: it was not their first visit to the FPB nor, they were perfectly certain, would it be their last. They were tied together at the ankles and wrists in an attitude known to the *cognoscenti* as the 'Crucifixion'. Each was obliged to stand fairly straight to avoid putting undue strain on the other, and herein lay the Crucifixion's special aptness as a punishment for Conchies. Apart from the fact that it was uncomfortable, it also ensured that the victims stood to attention for the two hours of its duration.

The pattern of Maurice's life since arriving in France in

March had been an oft-repeated cycle of 'crime' and punishment, tedious in its inevitability. It was a source of wonder to him that the military authorities could continue to issue orders that they knew for certain would be not simply disobeyed, but totally disregarded. They were sent to FPB from Soot Street (so called because of its black cinder paths and parade ground) about once a fortnight, for refusing to take part in drill, and other displays of unmilitary behaviour. In a military environment it was impossible for the pacifists not to repeat continually those crimes for which they had been imprisoned in the first place. Every morning they were herded out onto the square with the resident troops, mostly non-combatant and labour battalions, and yelled at to fall in, ten-shun, right turn, forward march, left wheel . . . On and on it went, the NCO's voice becoming more hysterical by the second as the eight of them stood there with the rest marching past and round them. It had become so embarrassing latterly that Maurice had taking to writing his name on the cinders with his toe, just to avoid the NCO's incredulously boggling eye.

Maurice was not by nature a rebel, but a conservative, who liked tranquillity and order. He would normally have shunned attention, especially of such an unwelcome kind. But in a world turned upside down it had to be thus. So he stood there, doing his best—unlike millions of his compatriots—to appear as inoffensive as possible, and to show that he was unconcerned with, rather than hostile to, the authority invested in the apoplectic NCO.

Unfortunately it was these peccadilloes, rather than their basic refusal to fight, that enraged the top brass at Soot Street. In fact, Maurice had come to realize that many of the 'old sweats' were sympathetic towards them, once they appreciated that Conchies were not simply in a funk but fighting for their beliefs. Unquestioning patriotism had been killed along with hundreds of thousands of men on the Somme. In the late autumn of 1916 a grey mood of doubt, depression and cynicism pervaded the British forces in France. Back in Westminster the debate raged, but the anti-pacifist lobby was no longer so sure of its ground. Maurice, Stephen and the others were beginning to feel that if they could stick it out a little longer they might be offered a course of action that they could take with pride and a clear conscience.

It had been a long haul so far, reflected Maurice, flexing his shoulder muscles to restore circulation. They had been moved from the Garfield Redoubt long before completing their fifty-day sentence, but since they refused to recognize martial law in the first place they could hardly object to its miscarriage. From the Redoubt they'd been taken to Mill Hill Barracks in North London for a week and thence by train all round the outskirts of the city in a shuttered compartment, down to Southampton and over by troop ship to Le Havre. Their treatment en route had been reasonable, and Maurice had sensed that the occasional pushing and shouting had been for the benefit of onlookers rather than evidence of real malice towards themselves. Their worst misgivings had been not about the handling of the move, but its motive. 'You're free men now,' they had been told by the CO on leaving Mill Hill Barracks. 'Your fate is of your own choosing.' *Free* men! It was a trap and they knew it. The thinking behind their transportation to France was simply this: that if the Conchies could be placed in a military camp close to the actual fighting it was only a matter of time before they could be court-martialled for refusal to obey orders. At Mill Hill they were forced on three occasions to listen to the details of the death sentence handed out to such-and-such a pacifist, the veracity of which they had no way of checking. It was all bluff and threat, but the message was plain: the ground was being prepared for far sterner measures when they arrived in France. Once in Soot Street the punishments had begun, at first nothing worse than a couple of days on bread and water, but soon the nastier refinements of the FPB.

Maurice found the war of attrition waged on his person very trying. He had never been tough physically, and no matter how much he stiffened his spiritual sinews the flesh and blood part of him suffered horribly. It hadn't actually let him down yet, to the extent of weakening his resolve, but he feared that some day it would. He hadn't been feeling well recently, he had an uncomfortable feverish cold and it had gone on his chest. The icy winds that swept the parade ground, the draughty dormitory and inadequate bedding, the poor food and now yet another dose of the Crucifixion—all were placing an almost intolerable strain on his system and consequently on his morale.

Aubrey's letter—which had eventually caught up with him at Mill Hill, thanks to the good offices of a sympathetic old sweat—was creased and faded almost past legibility from the number of times he had perused and pored over it. He had been deeply touched by it, and prized it highly. The mere fact that Aubrey, who had seemed to epitomize those forces which he opposed, could display such humility was in itself encouraging. If Aubrey could find it in himself to behave in this way, then so might the powers that be. He longed to return the generous impulse, to make the 'some kind of fresh start' to which the letter referred, promised himself time and again that he would do so, when all this business was over.

'How are you doing?' asked Stephen. They made a point of breaking the silence rule every few minutes or so.

'Quiet in there!'

'Not so bad,' said Maurice.

'Did you hear me, Maxwell?'

'My arms have gone to sleep,' he concluded in his soft voice.

The guard began unbolting the cell-door with much sucking of teeth. He entered. There was barely room for him, the prisoners were so tightly packed. When he pushed his face into Maurice's the latter thought, not for the first time, how ironic it was that they were forced by a universally unpopular war to play such inimical roles. The guard was in all probability not a bad chap, but there was no hope whatever of simply looking him in the eye and saying: 'Hang on a minute, let's talk this over.'

On the contrary: 'Maxwell, do you want another day of this? Is that it?'

'I haven't thought about it.'

'Well think about it now.'

Maurice's nose was beginning to run. He already had a painful and unsightly herpes sore on his upper lip, but it was possible to turn such indignities to one's own advantage. 'Could I have a handkerchief?'

'Could I have a handkerchief, *sir*,' said the guard wearily, producing one from his trouser pocket. He offered it, realized Maurice could not take it, and dabbed Maurice's nose.

'Thank you.'

'Now shut up, will you.' He went out and slammed the door.

Maurice sniffed. He wondered if Primmy knew of his plight. As they had made their circuitous journey round London he had managed to throw a couple of notes from the train's lavatory window straws in the wind, but he hoped someone had found one of them and passed on the information. He told himself that it was important that people should know of their whereabouts but in his heart 'people' became simply Primmy. Primmy, who might then think of him from time to time in her front room over the post office, and perhaps even worry a little.

As it turned out, Primmy did know. One of Maurice's notes blew onto the platform at Clapham Junction and was picked up by a girl cleaner. Though she had not been able to make head nor tail of it herself she had sense enough to realize that it was a form of communication, and had handed it to the station master, who had in his turn passed it on to the area organizer of the NCF. The families of all the men listed in the note had subsequently been informed. One or two unguarded remarks of Mrs Maxwell's had ensured that the staff at Chilverton House understood the situation, and when Primmy had gone to visit her mother and Eddie Mrs Duckham had mentioned it.

'I always liked Mr Maurice,' she said. 'He had a really nice nature.'

'Where have they gone to in France?' Primmy had asked. 'Does anyone know?'

But the topic had only limited interest for everyone else in the servants' hall and was abandoned.

In fact, Maurice would have been gratified to know how much Primmy did worry about him. She told herself it was just normal concern for his welfare: he was so skinny and useless, how on earth would he survive in a military prison, or if anyone knocked him about? But the fact was she had a job keeping him out of her thoughts. The only way she could do it was by work, work, work, busy all day and almost too tired to think or even dream when she got back at night. The minute she stopped she would begin thinking of him, the way he'd looked with that great swollen nose, which had seemed so out of keeping with the rest of him, a kind of violation. But the more she worried about Maurice at night the harder she worked the next day, trying to exorcise that wispy, ever-present ghost of feeling that she knew she mustn't acknowledge.

On the morning of Monday 24 November, the day after she had heard of Maurice's removal to France, she arrived as always punctually at seven a.m. Ever since she had heard the guns they had been fearfully busy, but it was essential to keep oneself on an even keel, and never to appear panicked or flustered even when the convoys came thick and fast. An atmosphere of crisis would be most detrimental both to the condition of the patients and the running of the hospital.

She left her bicycle in the shed and entered by the main door into the hall, depositing her coat and scarf in the corner cupboard. It was no longer necessary to consult a tag on the noticeboard for her duties, but she did pause before the large mirror to check over her appearance. No matter what, she paid attention to a neat, clean turn-out. Now she tweaked the bib of her apron so that it was perfectly straight and central, and made some minute adjustment to her handkerchief cap. The cap and the starched Peter Pan collar that went with it had recently superseded the goffered Sister Dora headdress and high collar, and many of the girls at Oak Ridge regretted the change, thinking the old accessories more flattering and feminine. Primmy, however, was perfectly content. The new things were simpler and more practical which was surely all that mattered.

For just a second she touched, with pride, the blue ribbon pinned to her lapel. She had passed, not with honours, but quite creditably. The ribbon made not one jot of difference to her work—she had been doing a senior's job for some time anyway—but she gleaned enormous satisfaction from the achievement.

She skimmed upstairs and encountered Flavia on the landing, outside the dispensary. Much to Primmy's surprise Flavia had stuck it out, and now that their duties included 'proper' nursing she was quite good at them. She was popular with the patients too, she had a pretty smile and a nice manner and these qualifications, though Primmy lacked them herself, she knew to be useful.

'Good morning,' she said.

'Hallo, Primrose,' replied Flavia, their relationship having progressed thus far. 'Did you hear the planes last night?'

Primmy shook her head. 'I was asleep.'

'They came right over,' went on Flavia, 'but I suppose they must have been coming back from London, there weren't any guns.'

'I expect that was it.' Primmy glanced at the clock on the

549

wall. She didn't like chit-chat, she was anxious to start work.
'You in the dispensary this morning?'

Flavia pulled a face. 'Yes, worse luck.'

Primmy was sympathetic; she didn't care for dispensary
duty either. In fact, she felt it was her weakest area. The
phalanxes of bottles and jars with their almost illegible labels
made her nervous, and she became slow and clumsy. After
surgery there was Eusol to be mixed—vast two-gallon drums
of the chlorine-based disinfectant lotion which had to be
shaken for twenty minutes by hand—but she preferred even
that to the barely-suppressed panic she experienced when
dishing out medication.

'See you later,' she said to Flavia, and went to fetch the
dressing trolley.

As for the planes, they rarely woke her these days. After
all, there wasn't a thing you could do about it: if they bombed
you, they bombed you. She'd only had one really nasty
moment, one night when she'd been cycling back from
Canterbury at dusk. Quite suddenly a German plane had
swooped down on a gun emplacement not a quarter of a mile
from the lane; she had actually seen the tracer bullets buzzing
through the air like hornets. That had given her a fright, and
no mistake; she'd never pedalled so fast in her life, and when
she did get back to the post office she was shaking and bathed
in sweat.

Very occasionally there were daylight raids over the
Downs, and they'd cluster at the windows to watch the
planes swooping and darting in the sky, and the puff-ball
clouds of shrapnel shells bursting in the air. After one of these
raids a girl had found an unexploded pompom shell in the
garden, and taken it up to show a couple of her friends in the
sluice. She'd only been a young thing, one of the housework
VADs from the village, but Primmy hadn't half put the fear
of God into her when she found her giggling over that bomb
by the sink. Even now it made her shake her head to think of
the girl's lack of common sense. They'd put the pompom
back in the garden and called the Canadian air base to come
and deal with it. She collected her trolley and set off on her
round of the second floor. The first room she entered was a
three-bedder, and the man nearest the door was Binns, a
recent arrival with a shattered femur.

'Morning, General,' he said. He was a Brummy with
a smooth, flirtatious manner, and he always called her

'General' for some reason. She wondered how he had the energy, the state his leg was in, but then most of the patients were surprisingly jolly, considering.

'Good morning,' she said. 'Right then.'

Binns put down the regimental badge he was embroidering, and cast her a speaking look. 'Be gentle with me, General.'

'Come along.'

It was a bit of a problem with a fractured femur, because the area surrounding the wound had to be exposed without disturbing the splint. With the old Lister model it had been a terrible business, for the leg had been strapped rigid to a length of board reaching from armpit to ankle. Now they used the Thomas splint, a metal frame ending at the groin, down the centre of which the limb was slung, rather than strapped. It was much more comfortable for the patient, and easier for the nurses to handle, but all the same you had to be careful. She got Binns on to his side and set to work.

'Tell me,' said Binns, who always liked to chat. 'How do you keep that slim figure of yours?'

'Hard work,' replied Primmy briskly. She removed the soiled dressing, and the pus-filled drainage tube from the wound and placed both in a container on the second shelf of the trolley. The tube would have to be washed out by hand and boiled, and the cleanest part of the dressing salvaged for re-use later in the morning.

'Besides,' she added, as she syringed out the wound with a peroxide solution, 'we don't get good army rations like some I could mention.' She knew the peroxide must hurt ferociously, and made herself talk to take Binns's mind off it.

'*You're* complaining?' queried Binns, with heavy humour.

'It's good sustaining food, and well cooked,' she reproved, syringing again, this time with Eusol. 'There's shortages for the rest of us.'

'I'm willing to bet you've never been fat,' went on Binns, his voice a little strained. 'Not the type, are you?'

'I wouldn't know.'

'That's right. Some people like well-covered women, but not me. I prefer 'em slim, trim and sprightly.'

'Do you now. Good . . .' said Primmy absently. The wound seemed fairly wholesome now. She inserted a clean drainage tube, and opened the big metal Thermos bin on the top of the trolley to take out a scalding fomentation of pink boracic lint.

'I'm going to put the fomentation on now,' she said, and did so. She heard Binns hiss between his teeth. 'There we are.'

She covered the fomentation quickly with a square of jaconet, and then a folded pad of wool for insulation, before bandaging it once more and checking the splint. Then she helped Binns onto his back again, plumped his pillows and stood back. 'Comfortable?' she asked.

'Never better.'

'Same again in four hours,' she added, giving the covers a final stroke and a pat with brisk competent hands, and handing Binns his sewing.

'Thanks, General. Toodle-oo.'

She pushed her trolley to the next bed. Unlike Binns, the face on the pillow was wan, and one pyjama sleeve pinned, neatly pressed and empty, to the lapel.

She did dressings for most of the morning. Then came the messy bit in the sluice, washing and boiling the tubes, and snipping and saving on bandages and fomentations to make do for another time. There was a truly shocking short-age of materials for dressings, particularly lint, but Primmy appreciated the need for thrift, and you used the remnants only as outer dressings and not right next to the wound.

Dina Shipping entered as Primmy stood at the sink. 'Do we have any more meths?'

'Very little, and I have to clean the theatre this afternoon, you'd better ask Sister.'

'That chap in Number Three has bedsores already,' moaned Dina. 'Why do we keep running out?'

'We *don't* keep running out,' retorted Primmy snappishly. 'We have to be careful with it because it costs thirty-seven and sixpence a gallon.' She had no patience with these girls who could not see the need for economy. They expected to be ministering angels with everything plentiful and to hand, they hated to say a cross word to a patient or do anything that might spoil their popularity.

Primmy was a little late for lunch, which they took in shifts at the Commandant's house in the lodge. There was a man on her floor with shell-shock—he'd been buried alive in no man's land, apparently—and he chose the time allotted for Primmy's dinner-break to relive his experience. He set up a blood-curdling racket, screaming and yelling, and began tearing off his pyjamas, his dressing and his bedclothes under the mistaken impression that they were a mountain of soil. Primmy and the day sister did their best, but they'd never have coped without the assistance of one or two other men in the ward who were fit enough to come to their rescue. By the time he'd quietened down enough for Primmy to come away she was already late and had to run to the lodge, arriving red-faced and breathless. She could have happily done without lunch altogether, but they were supposed to eat it, to keep their strength up, and she could see the sense of that.

Many of the girls had to come to the lodge for their breakfast as well, but Primmy was lucky with her billet. What with Mr Petts away, and having to be up early for the baby, Mrs Petts was only too glad to make porridge at a quarter past six in the morning. There was no sugar of course, but they clubbed together to buy a tin of syrup when they had a real craving for something sweet.

Now she pulled up a chair in the dining-room and addressed herself to a plate of mince with rice—potato was now a rare luxury—and a bit of swede.

Dina was there before her. 'Mince again,' she said, pushing it around.

'It's all right,' said Primmy, getting on with hers. 'No lumps.'

'I suppose we should be grateful for small mercies,' sighed Dina, laying down her fork.

'You're never leaving that?' said Primmy. 'It's an awful waste.'

'I'm not hungry.'

'But you ought to—'

'Keep my strength up, I know.' Dina pushed her chair in. 'But that's too high a price to pay.'

Primmy finished her own, darting shocked glances at the abandoned food. She remembered the dog eating scrag ends in the back yard at Deptford, and felt a stab of sympathy for her mother.

After lunch she ran back up to the house. The surgeon was due to come at three o'clock and it was her special task to keep the theatre spotless and sterile. The risk of sepsis was ever-present, for the theatre doubled as a surgery where the walking and convalescent cases came each morning to have their dressings changed. Primmy went over every part of it with a one-in-twenty solution of carbolic and methylated spirits. It took her over an hour and by the time she finished she could hear the surgeon down in the hall, talking to Matron. She scrubbed up in one of the row of basins, put on her enveloping white overall, lit the tiny sterilizer and popped the instruments in to boil. Keeping the sterilizer going was like tending the Olympic flame; the gas jet was ancient and temperamental and would go out in the slightest draught, or sometimes for no reason at all. Besides which, if anyone dropped an instrument they couldn't use it again till it had been boiled for the proper length of time, and added delay might prove fatal.

She assisted in the theatre from three until six. Most of that time was given to two secondary amputations, the removal of damaged or septic material from limbs that had been hastily truncated at the advance dressing post. Then there was a tidying-up operation on an abdominal wound. And finally the surgeon dealt with a man who had terrible mustard-gas burns, and was in such agony that he needed a general anaesthetic to have his dressings changed. Throughout all this Primmy was enthralled. She was never squeamish, and didn't feel tired until afterwards, when the surgeon had gone and there was the theatre to clean all over again. With help from the other two theatre nurses that took until seven, and just as she was ready to go the night sister bustled up to say Dina Shipping had gone down with a stomach bug and could Primmy just, very kindly . . .?

So she made a further two rounds of the top floor, once with a tray of night-lights in china mugs, which had to be set down in all the corners to make up for the ban on lights; and again with a torch, peering under the bedclothes of the men who'd had operations that afternoon, to see they weren't haemorrhaging. That was a job she disliked, ever since she'd discovered a haemorrhage her very first week on night duty. The man had been in a bed right at the top of the house, and there was a monkey puzzle tree outside the window. Its angular arms and stubby crooked fingers had thrown menacing shadows on the curtains as she'd lifted the sheet to reveal the wet, black, spreading stain. . . . She still didn't like that particular room, though the patients did, because it was high up and they could see the sea in the distance. That man had died, she recalled, as she took the torch back to Matron's room, but he was an exception; the mortality rate was surprisingly low.

Tonight there were no unpleasant surprises. Quite a few of

the better patients were wide awake and made little comments as she went by.

'Goodnight, Sister, sleep tight!' A lot of them called her 'Sister' because they were used to army nurses and didn't know the difference.

'Goodnight Sleep well,' she replied.

'See you in the morning, Sister.'

'Toodle-oo, General. If you can't be good be careful!'

Binns's implication that she led a riotous social life made her smile to herself. Her greatest dissipation was to take the bus to Canterbury for a bun and a cup of tea in a café, or to Folkestone to walk alongside the barbed wire on the prom and watch the waves come in. The patients didn't know it, and wouldn't believe it, but her greatest pleasure was to be found here, working hard and watching them get better.

When she finally fetched her bike from the shed, she ached in every limb. Fortunately there was a clear sky and a good moon so she mounted and rode down to the village: on dark nights it was better to push, for you couldn't use a lamp. She was back at the post office in ten minutes. She had a cup of cocoa with Mrs Petts and then went to her room. She took off her cap without untying it and set it neatly on the bed post; discarded her apron and stockings and set out fresh ones for the next morning; hung up her dress and laid her underwear neatly over the back of the chair. Then she washed, brushed out her hair and slipped into her cold bed, where she thought of Maurice for a few minutes before falling asleep.

As they emerged from the hut door Maurice hunched his shoulders and clenched his fists against the lashing attack of the wind. At that moment coping with the cold seemed more important than the sentence about to be passed on them. He had suddenly realized over the past week, as the court martial galumphed on its elephantine way, just how near the end of his tether he was physically. His cold was no better, and his whole body complained bitterly over every demand made on it. When he coughed, which was often, his chest rasped painfully, and he was feverish all the time.

Because his bed was nearest the door he found himself at the head of the line. He would, on this occasion, actually have preferred to march briskly as he was being ordered to do, but habit prevailed and he strolled along as slowly as he could.

Soot Street was the bleakest place Maurice had ever come across, utterly without grace or intimacy; beside it, the Garfield Redoubt seemed cosy. Here there were no trees, and no grass. The dark brown wooden huts stood in uniform and equidistant rows around the edge of the black cinder parade ground, each hut separated from its neighbours by a border of gravel and a narrow black path. There were no hedges, walls, fences or flowers. Today the only spot of colour was a Union Jack, snapping in the stiff late November wind above a dais on the far side of the square.

A huge concourse of troops stood three deep, at attention, round the edge of the square. They were completely silent. There was an atmosphere of expectancy and foreboding. Maurice's group was led to a position facing the dais, and rather in front of the troops. Automatically they broke their line and formed an untidy group. Maurice began to cough, a harsh barking sound, wrapping his arms about his chest and bending double. His eyes streamed, he felt wretched: had anyone honestly supposed they could make a soldier out of him? He knew for a fact that following a medical at Mill Hill he had been passed as fit only for service in Great Britain, so what in God's name was he doing here coughing his stomach up on a draughty French cliff? Stephen was holding his arm and patting him on the back, while several hundred of His Majesty's officers and men stood round looking on in po-faced and strangely sheepish silence.

By the time he'd recovered himself, straightening up and running both hands through his wind-tangled hair, the CO had taken up his position on the dais. Poor devil, thought Maurice; he'd been up and down from his office like a yo-yo giving evidence at the court martial, and now here he was being dragged into the mire yet again. He was a very decent, well-brought up man, torn between a natural sense of fair-play and blinkered loyalty. Now he began to speak, but two words in every three were snatched away by the wind. He kept looking down at a sheet of paper in his hand, and then looking up again and intoning something, like a schoolboy learning lines for a play. Maurice stared at him with detachment.

The sound of his own name, torn to tatters by the wind, floated to him, but he had long since trained himself not to react to it. He coughed again, intentionally this time, covering his mouth with his hand and closing his eyes to cover the inevitable moment of embarrassment when they repeated the summons.

Two men came over and took him by the arms, not roughly. 'Step into the centre,' said one of them, his voice ominously quiet and considerate.

When they saw he was not going to resist they released their hold and simply escorted him to the middle of the square. Maurice was swept by a sickening wave of stage fright. He tried to put faces to one or two of the hundreds of rigid, staring figures, that surrounded him, but found he couldn't; it suddenly seemed that they were all ranged against him, blank, dutiful and uncaring.

'. . . refusal to obey a lawful command . . . continued and wilful disregard of army regulations . . .' The words drifted raggedly to Maurice, half-drowned by the shuddering wind. He wondered how they could persist in such blind and stubborn folly. He began shivering again; the glands in his neck felt tender and swollen, his eyes were sore and his joints ached. The CO droned on and on and there were a few drops of cold rain falling now, big drops that fell with a splash like crocodile tears.

'. . . sentence of the court, therefore—' the Colonel's voice had taken on a stiff and lofty tone suitable to the portentous nature of his words; 'that the defendant . . .' Maurice fixed his gaze on the straining flag. The sky was racing, full of storm and threat. He felt that he looked down on himself, standing ant-like in the middle of this great black square, the unworthy recipient of so much high-powered attention.

'. . . death by firing squad.'

The rain was stepping up, a handful of it spattered on his face and he put his hand up to rub it away. For some reason he badly wanted to swallow, but couldn't because his inflamed tonsils seemed to fill his throat.

'. . . sentence confirmed by the Commander in Chief . . .'

Wasn't it someone else's turn? And were they really going to wade through all this verbiage with every one of them? God, he'd have to wait for hours in this wind, he couldn't stand it, they might as well shoot him now to put him out of his misery, like a horse with a broken leg.

'. . . subsequently commuted to ten years' penal servitude.'

At last he felt the hands on his arms. They took him back. He caught a glimpse of Stephen's face, white and startled, staring at him. But suddenly he felt really bad, his head throbbed, his legs shook and his eyes seemed to grate in their sockets like corks in sandpaper.

'I have to go and lie down,' he said to whoever was nearest. 'I have to. Sorry.' He started walking, rather unsteadily, back to the hut, blundering and barging through the ranks of soldiers, aiming for his narrow, hard bed. A chill fog of pity parted before him as he stumbled along, the Colonel's voice rose, fell, and finally faded.

He pushed open the door of the hut. He was shuddering so badly now that his teeth were chattering and he had difficulty keeping his head still. Someone followed him, and held the door open, and a voice said: 'You lie down mate, I don't blame you.'

Maurice fell across his bed, his face buried in the hard mattress. He felt too rotten even to hoist his feet up, and lay draped over the bed like a corpse. He didn't sleep but lay there dozing and shivering until the others came back and Stephen put his legs up and covered him with a blanket.

Bereavement, Sutcliffe told Thea, was best regarded as a sort of journey. She spoke as one who knew, for she had lost two relations in the war, her brother in the very first week and more recently a favourite uncle. She explained that the initial shock was generally followed by a period of disbelief, an inability to accept the truth, and then numbness. Not for some months, said Sutcliffe, would she be able to grieve properly, and when she did so it would be a good sign, an indication that she was coming to terms with her loss.

Thea listened to all this and wished fervently that she had told Sutcliffe nothing. But she had needed to give some explanation for her behaviour, and had opted for the truth but not the whole truth. The man had been her cousin, she explained, whom she had stayed with just before the outbreak of the war and of whom she was fond: a reminder of happier times, now gone. They nodded, they understood, they inveighed against the war and its unfairness, they advised Thea to take leave; she had every reason, they said. But they didn't understand—how could they?—and she wished she'd never mentioned it. By not understanding, through no fault of their own, they rubbed salt in the wound. Their well-meant kindness and advice insulted her desolation.

There was some truth in her explanation to them. It was

indeed not only Josef she had lost but the memory of Josef and the fragile shoot of hope concerning him that she had nurtured almost without knowing she did so. The fact that she suspected both memory and hope had played her false was no comfort to her now, rather the reverse. A little longer and they might have faded, gently and naturally: instead of which they had been brutally hacked off before their time.

And, she realized, there was that part of herself that had died with Josef and could never return, the part that had been optimistic and truly young. While he had lived a spark of that part survived. Now it was quenched. But her body still jangled with remembered desires, and gave her no peace.

Desperate to share her misery she wrote to her uncle and aunt in Vienna, a long rambling letter, part condolence, part confession.

The Baron, sitting in his garden utterly alone, glanced at her signature and tore the letter up without reading it. Annelise had married, and Dieter was staying with her. In her curtained bedroom his foolish wife cried all day long. He was alone, a tall rock against which the feeble waves beat ineffectually. All he wanted was his solitude.

Thea did not know that her letter had not been read, and when no reply came she assumed that yet again she had done the wrong thing. She sank still lower in her own esteem.

In the middle of November they were recalled to Merville. Some of the girls they'd left behind had gone, and others had taken their place. Thea could not believe she had once found this place so strange and challenging, when now it seemed a haven of comfort and order. She worked like an automaton, efficient, reliable and dispirited, aware of the Commandant's eye upon her but oddly indifferent now to her opinion. If she had only known it she was in a state of clinical shock, and it took her father's letter, which arrived at the end of the month, to restore her to reality with the salutary harshness of a slap in the face.

'Dear girl,' wrote Ralph. 'Can you come home? Your mother is far from well now. I called in Bruce Egerton a few days ago and he tells me she has a growth in the stomach. There is no point, apparently, in her going into hospital even if she wanted to. She is going to die. It is not as hard for me to write that as I expected, partly because she has been in good spirits in spite of her pain. She is extraordinarily calm and

sensible—more so, I should say, than for some time—and her
behaviour carries me with it. I look at her and I can't believe
it, but that, I suppose, is the way of these things.

'*I need not say what a difference your presence would*
make, both to your mother and myself. If you could bring
your sister with you, so much the better. I'm afraid I am a
cantankerous and inadequate companion even now, when she
needs me most.' Here Thea could almost see her father's
frown of angry anxiety and hear the stertorous clearing of his
throat. *I look forward to hearing from you, and to seeing you*
as soon as may be. Your loving and anxious Father.'

The effect of this letter was to restore Thea's numbed spirit
to a state of agonizing sensitivity. For the best part of two
days she could hardly stop weeping, the tears poured out of
her in a healing flood. The familiar longing to go home,
compelling and undeniable, rose strong in her. Leave was
granted, though she knew she would have gone anyway.

On 6 December, she arrived in Paris. Both this visit and
her previous one had been made with the same purpose, and
en route to England, but there the resemblance ended. Paris
had settled into her wartime existence. It was no longer hectic
and turbulent but exuded a kindly gaiety, offering with
dignity the pleasures of peacetime as an antidote to the poison
of war.

There was a poignancy, too, for Thea in this pilgrimage,
for now she returned to the city as one of those who had seen
the worst, who shared the terrible secret with the laughing
uniformed men in the bars and cafés. In spite of everything,
she felt a new spring of confidence inside herself. Part of her
had gone; she was not so profligate of herself and her
emotions. But there was growth too, and a maturing. She
would survive.

Dulcie's new apartment turned out to be no more than a
few hundred yards from the Place d'Agnette, in a secluded
cul-de-sac of pretty terraced houses with tiled roofs and
coloured front doors. There was a little oblong garden
running down the centre of the cul-de-sac, and the long keen
snout of an anti-aircraft gun pointed skywards from the
damp winter shrubs. Number Two was yellow brick, with
cream-painted door and windowsills, each enlivened with
a window box in a cream wrought-iron holder. Thea
was impressed by its solid smartness. It looked a bourgeois residence of the best kind. She realized that she was

looking forward to seeing Dulcie, to making up and being friends once more as they surely must after two years when so much had happened. She hoped Peter would not be there.

It was four o'clock in the afternoon, just beginning to be dusk. She had sent a wire to Dulcie, and hoped that she was expected.

Her ring was answered by an elderly concierge, whose appearance confirmed the impression that Dulcie's circumstances had improved radically. She was spotlessly dressed, with a starched broderie *fichu* round her shoulders, and a crisp white apron covering the front of her blue skirt.

'Bonjour,' said Thea. '*Je suis venu visiter ma soeur—*'

'Yes, yes . . . ' the old woman beamed and ushered her in, closing the door after her. 'Mam'selle Tennant ees on zee first floor.'

'Oh. Thank you.' Thea was a little taken aback by such ready and affable co-operation. She also wondered that Dulcie, cohabiting openly with Peter, had been able to keep her single name in what was clearly a respectable neighbourhood. But perhaps that was wartime . . .

'Is she expecting me then?' she asked.

'She said you would be coming.' The concierge nodded. 'I recognized you.'

'May I go straight up then?'

'*Certainement.*'

Thea started up the stairs. On the half-landing she turned to see the old lady still standing in the hall, smiling benignly up at her. She nodded again, as if to encourage Thea, and then bustled back into her room on the left of the front door. The first floor landing had a fluffy rug on the polished floor and on one side an elegant long-legged table on which reposed a wicker jardiniere containing a glossy rubber plant. The door was painted pale blue and had a small brass knocker in the shape of what Thea took at first to be Prince of Wales feathers but then realized was a fleur-de-lis.

She knocked, and the door was opened almost at once by a plump, dark, olive-skinned girl in maid's dress. Behind her in the tiny hallway stood a young man, obviously just about to leave, in the uniform of the Royal Army Flying Corps.

The little maid lifted her eyebrows interrogatively. 'Yes?' It was strange that they all spoke English.

'I'm Mam'selle Tennant's sister,' she explained. 'I sent a wire.'

'Oh yes! But of course!' All smiles, the maid admitted her. 'Excuse me one moment.'

She passed the young man his cap from a peg. He seemed slightly ill at ease and Thea smiled at him awkwardly. Dulcie had not yet appeared and there had been no introduction.

The second the door closed behind him, Dulcie made her entrance. The unavoidable impression was that she had been waiting for him to go.

'Thea! Darling, I'm so glad to see you!'

If there was one thing Thea had not expected it was an entirely warm welcome, and this one was positively ecstatic. Her coat and case were whisked away by the beaming maid, her cheeks kissed repeatedly, and she was led by the arm into a small but exquisitely furnished drawing room.

'Sit down, sit down, you must be *exhausted!* Tea?'

'Thank you, that would be lovely.'

'Céline!' The maid appeared in the doorway. 'Could we have some more tea, please, and toast.'

'At once.' Céline bustled into the room and removed the pink and white tea pot which with the rest of a tea service stood on a lacquered table near the fire. There remained a little cakestand with plates of petits-fours, florentines and tiny eclairs.

'I bring another cup,' added Céline for good measure.

'I hope your guest didn't leave because of me,' said Thea, indicating the cakestand.

'Guest?' Dulcie looked as though she didn't know the meaning of the word. 'Goodness no! Now let me look at you . . .' She perched forward on her chair and scanned Thea's face.

Thea felt ill at ease. Somehow the encounter had been taken out of her hands, it was Dulcie who was orchestrating their meeting, and not her. She had intended to march in, state her reasons and march out again, preferably with Dulcie in attendance. It was plainly not going to be as simple as that. Also, she was taken aback by Dulcie's appearance, which was nothing short of breathtaking. Like Thea, she had cut her hair, and its golden tendrils curled on her cheeks most becomingly: at the back it was cropped almost like a boy's, revealing the delicate and gamine nape of her neck. She was a little plumper, but it suited her, and though she did not appear to be wearing make-up her skin, eyes and lips had a sheen and a brightness that Thea could not believe were due to nature alone. She wore a low-waisted dress of shot silk in dove-grey that gleamed violet when she moved. Having Venetia's colouring she could wear to advantage all those pale, almost neutral shades which would have made Thea look drab. The skirt of the dress reached mid-calf and revealed the lower part of her legs in flesh-coloured silk stockings and grey kid shoes with a tapering high heel. About the deep V-neck, the cuffs, and the upward swathe of the skirt were clouds of soft violet frills. It was a tea-gown, Thea recognized, an exquisite, delicate garment appropriate to only one hour in the entire day. She felt the coarse material and heavy lines of her uniform in unflattering contrast to Dulcie's filigree elegance.

'You look so *tired*,' Dulcie was saying, her fingers clasped on her knees, her face full of what might or might not have been genuine admiration. 'I think you're wonderful for doing what you do.'

'I chose it. I wanted to.' Thea didn't mean to be brusque, it was just the way it came out.

Dulcie changed her tack, became sparkling and elated. 'I can't tell you how marvellous it is to see you, it's been far too long, you know that.'

'You could have come home,' Thea pointed out. 'We wanted you to.'

Dulcie did not appear to have heard this. 'Ah, Céline, put it here, will you?'

'Is there anything else?'

'No, that's perfect, thank you, Céline.'

Dulcie poured each of them a cup of tea, and handed Thea a plate of wafer-thin slices of hot buttered toast. The china was almost translucent. Everything was so nice. Thea took the tea and toast stiffly and perched them awkwardly on her knee. She was disconcerted. Surely somewhere in all this there must be the key to their old relationship which, with all its faults, had at least been real.

'Where's Peter?' she asked.

'Back in Hungary, I imagine.' Dulcie sipped her tea.

Thea put her cup down with a clunk. 'You mean he's gone?'

'M-hm.' Dulcie smiled at her, not avoiding her gaze. 'He and I went our separate ways a long time ago.'

'And all that talk of marriage—'

'Just talk. You were sensible enough to see that at the time, and I soon realized it. *Alors.*' She gave a little shrug. Thea wanted to take her by her prettily lifted shoulders and shake her so that the mask fell off.

'You mean to tell me you're entirely self-supporting?'

'Entirely. And don't look so flabbergasted, I'm not a complete idiot you know.' Ah, a glimpse of the old, easily ruffled Dulcie. Thea smiled.

'I just can't imagine how you've survived all this time with the war on and everything. Well done.'

'But the war has been my ally!' exclaimed Dulcie coyly, taking a tiny biscuit and popping it whole into her mouth.

'Tell me about the business, then.'

'There isn't much to tell. I manage very nicely, as you see.'

'Obviously.' Thea glanced about her. 'But what is it exactly? I mean, this lovely flat, and all these beautiful things, and your clothes—you look marvellous, Dulcie.'

'Thank you.'

'You must be rich!'

'Not rich, but I have lots of kind friends who have my welfare at heart.' She stood up.

'Would you like to see the rest?'

'Yes I would,' said Thea truthfully.

Proudly, Dulcie showed her round. The apartment was small, but well-appointed. There was a room at the front for Céline, a tiny kitchen, a bathroom with pink onyx taps, and Dulcie's own bedroom. She seemed particularly pleased with this, wandering about it as Thea looked, adjusting the glass bottles and ivory brushes on the dressing-table, and smoothing the blue satin nightdress-case that lay on the frilled pillow. The bedspread was turned down, and the corner of the sheet folded back. The room had a self-conscious, inviting charm, like a stage set. Something about it bothered Thea, especially when Dulcie flopped down on the bed, leaning her chin on her hand, and said: 'Pretty isn't it? I've always wanted a room like it.'

'It's very nice.' Thea stood gazing down at her sister. She looked like the pearl in some carefully constructed oyster, lying there surrounded by ice-blue satin. She walked out into the hall, asking over her shoulder: 'Who was that I saw leaving?'

'That was Mark Bingham, he's in the Flying Corps, you know.'

'Yes I saw. Do you see much of him? It must be difficult to keep friends when they're never in Paris for more than a few days at a time.'

'Oh, they come back all right.' Dulcie closed the drawing-room door after them and went back to her chair, curling her feet up on the seat next to her. 'Real friends do.'

'You haven't mentioned the business,' said Thea. 'Can I see it?'

'Oh, Thea . . .' Dulcie shook her head and smiled fondly at her sister. 'Dear Thea, do I have to spell it out?'

'I'm sorry . . .?'

'You couldn't just take the hints, could you, darling, not you! You have to be all innocent and straightforward and enquiring, sitting there in your uniform just waiting to be shocked.'

'I've no idea what you mean,' said Thea. But somewhere, like a train approaching through a tunnel, realization was bearing down on her.

'I mean,' said Dulcie, taking a cigarette from a box on the lacquered table, and lighting it, 'that my friends give me money. My men friends, that is.'

Thea leaned her head back and closed her eyes. Dulcie watched her, she could feel it. She wasn't all that shocked, for a course of action that is entirely in character is no surprise in the end. It was all perfectly logical, but she had to come to terms with it and the enormity of its implications.

'. . . not the end of the world,' Dulcie was saying, as Thea opened her eyes. She had put her cigarette into a little jade holder which she now held at a jaunty angle. 'I'm very *recherchée,* the people who come here really *are* my friends. But they understand that I have to live. I may not be very brave or very clever, but I hope I know how to capitalize on those talents I have.'

Thea had the impression that it was not the first time Dulcie had made that particular speech. It was a little too pat, moved a shade too trippingly on the tongue. She stared at her sister, trying to re-focus her in this new light and finding it remarkably easy. In the end the only course of action open to her was to come straight to the point.

'You got my wire?' she asked.

'You said you were coming,' Dulcie nodded.

'But not why.'

'Fire away.'

'Mother is dying. I'm going home to see her and Father would like you to come too.'

'I see.' Dulcie crossed her legs, with their neat ankles and shapely calves. 'I'm sorry but I can't.' There was a tiny break in her voice.

'No one's asking you to stay there,' went on Thea. 'It would probably be only for a few days. Mother misses you terribly, you know.'

'No she doesn't. None of you do, you're glad I'm out of the way.'

'That's ridiculous! And besides, just for the moment I don't wish to discuss you, but Mother. She is going to die very soon, and it would make her happy to see you again. There's no trap about it. Do you *understand*?'

'Yes . . .' Dulcie stubbed out the partially smoked cigarette and sat hunched forward, picking at her skirt as though there were crumbs on it. She looked very young suddenly, and uncertain. 'Is she—really?' she asked softly.

'Yes, Dulcie, yes. She has a growth in her stomach, there isn't a thing anyone can do. Except to go and be with her. Father says she's being very brave.'

'I couldn't bear it!' Abruptly Dulcie's hand flew to her mouth to cover its trembling, her eyes filled with tears. Thea rushed to her, kneeling and putting her arm round her shoulders.

'I know. I can't either.'

'She was so beautiful . . . I only wanted to be like her . . .' Dulcie spoke from behind her hand. Her other hand still plucked at her skirt, and Thea caught it and held it tight in both of hers.

'Please, Dulcie. Please come.'

'I can't!' There was a shrill note of childish panic in Dulcie's voice.

'You *can*. There's nothing to it, and no one will be anything but overjoyed to see you.'

Dulcie stood up jerkily, brushing at her tears with her frilly cuff. Thea, looking up at her, could tell just from the set of her shoulders that the momentary lapse in composure was at an end. She stumbled to her feet, and caught sight of herself in the gilt mirror over the mantelpiece. She looked extraordinary, all black clothes and hair and pale skin, and too big for the dainty room.

'No,' said Dulcie.

'But why not?' asked Thea wearily. 'It seems so natural—'

'Natural?' Dulcie turned to her. 'Natural? For the prodigal daughter to go back in powder and paint to take part in the great deathbed scene?'

'I don't see it like that.'

'Well I do. It's grotesque. You just want me to fit in with your bizarre Mother Earth ideas about family, and blood ties and rituals! I'm terribly sorry about Mother, but if I went back I should just be the black sheep, everyone would stare and whisper . . .'

'Everyone?'

'It's all nonsense, and it has nothing to do with real life,' concluded Dulcie incomprehensibly.

'It has to do with mine.'

'Oh well, you're a paragon of virtue as we all know!'

'Dulcie!' Thea grabbed her sister's elbow and swung her round. Carried by the impetus of her movement she lifted her other hand and delivered a ringing slap on Dulcie's cheek. Dulcie's head jolted to one side, and when she faced front again the cheek was reddening fiercely.

Thea was not sorry. On the contrary she felt calm and triumphant, as if the smack she had aimed at Dulcie two Christmases ago in her bedroom at Chilverton House had finally found its mark. To her astonishment, Dulcie laughed.

'I deserved that.'

'Yes, you did.'

'But you didn't do it because you hate me?'

'No, just the opposite.'

'I know.' Dulcie sighed, and reached down for another cigarette with a shaky hand. 'Don't I know it. You have to stop trying to reform me, Thea. Just let me *be*.'

'I only want you to come home. For a few days.'

'Well I won't. For no other reason than that I can't face it. There.'

'Very well.' Thea turned away. 'I'll go then.'

'Stay the night at least.'

'Dulcie—Mother may be dead when I get back.' That was cruel, and she knew it.

'Couldn't you just sit down for one moment and *listen*?' asked Dulcie. Thea looked back at her. She stood before the mirror, back to back with herself, small and straight and defiant, her scarlet cheek in sharp contrast to the jade cigarette holder and grey silk tea gown. At that moment, sophistication and bloody-mindedness were mixed in Dulcie in about equal parts, and Thea could not resist her.

She went back, but did not sit. 'Go on then.'

'I only want to say I'm not ashamed of what I do,' said Dulcie. 'I said before, it's my talent and I have to use it.'

'Then you should make a gift of it,' said Thea firmly.

'But I need the money. I am on my own.'

'You didn't have to be.'

'Oh yes I did, but I don't expect you to understand why. At any rate, I've made my bed, so to speak.' She gave a little laugh. 'The fact is, I was calculating when I started, but I'm not now. I enjoy what I do, I manage it as gracefully as possible and I think the men go away from here happier. They must do, because they come back, and not always to take me to bed. I really think I'm doing some good, making life a bit nicer for them.'

Thea remembered the sergeant and the smile on his face in the dark and smelly ambulance. She was too honest to deny the memory. 'Yes, I see that.'

'Do you really?'

'Yes.'

'Good. I may come home one day, but long after you've stopped asking me.' She smiled.

'Now you're just being perverse.'

'Ah well, that's me all over, isn't it?'

Thea shook her head. She was tired and she felt empty and pale, without identity. She would have liked to tell Dulcie about Josef but saw now that it would be quite inappropriate. As usual Dulcie had created an atmosphere in which attention centred naturally upon herself. 'I think I will go, then,' she said. 'If I leave now I might catch a night train to Dieppe.'

'Just tonight?'

'No. I must get back soon.'

They said goodbye in the little hall. As Thea kissed her goodbye Dulcie whispered: 'What will you say to Mother?'

'Don't worry,' said Thea, brushing Dulcie's red cheek with her hand. 'I'll make it all right. Promise.'

But as the door closed behind her she heard Dulcie's quick steps running back to the drawing-room to cry, alone.

'Dulcie's fine,' said Thea, a little too loudly, as though talking to a deaf person. 'She couldn't come with me right away, but she'll be here soon.'

There it was. She had lied in her teeth, and all on the assumption that her mother would die, but die in hope, not to know that Dulcie had no intention of returning. Miserably, inevitably, she compounded the felony by adding: 'She wanted to come at once, of course, but she has her own life now, one or two things to clear up . . .' She tailed off, realizing how hopelessly inadequate it sounded. 'I'm sorry,' she muttered.

But Venetia seemed not to have heard or, if she had, not to have cared. 'You're here anyway, darling,' she said.

Thea was sitting on the edge of Venetia's bed. It was late afternoon, the day after she had seen Dulcie, and she had only been back in the house an hour. She was still in her uniform, and the bedside lamp was lit. On the other side of the room Ralph fidgeted about, unsure of the part he must play.

Thea smiled at her mother. There seemed so little left of Venetia now, both in body and spirit. The wax had all but melted away, and the precious flame wavered and guttered. The serene, silvery beauty of her mother's face was wasted to near-transparency, the hand she held was bird-like, tiny fragile bones in the thinnest covering of flesh, and the beautiful ash-blonde hair looked dead and dry. Thea could remember, as a child at Ranelagh Road, kneeling on her parents' big bed in her nightie, watching her mother pile up her hair for a dinner party, or an evening out, and thinking her the cleverest and most beautiful being in the world to make the waterfall flow up hill, like that.

Now Venetia said: 'I'm so glad she's coming back for a while. And you, darling, thank you for coming.'

Thea squeezed her hand. 'It was high time I had some leave.'

'And I gave you an excuse.'

'That's right.' Thea was torn apart.

'Are you managing over there, darling? I can't tell you how worried I've been.'

'I manage perfectly. It sounds dreadful to say I enjoy it, but I do. If you allowed the bad things to get you down you wouldn't last two minutes. I love the work, and I have friends, and I'm happy. But tired.'

'Of course you are . . .' Venetia stroked her forehead. 'And you cut off your lovely hair.'

'Oh, Mother, I had to, really. I practically never wash it, you see, and you know very well I've never been any good with it.'

'It becomes you,' said Ralph, coming over and sitting down heavily on the opposite side of the bed. Even now at this eleventh hour he was no use in a sick room; his restlessness plucked at the peace of the room. Now he slapped his knees with stiff hands. 'Definitely,' he added, for good measure.

'Most gallant of you,' Thea responded.

He glared at her in the way he had that was part admiration and part reprimand. Between them Venetia lay, a fragile and threadbare link.

'How are the Kingsleys?' enquired Thea.

'They're well,' replied Venetia. 'You know Jack is expected home on leave?'

'No! No, I didn't.' Thea felt a sudden wild upsurge of anxiety at the thought of meeting Jack. She could not attribute this turbulence to anything in particular; their more recent meetings had been nothing but a source of pleasure and peace to her, but now she felt that to speak to him would involve distress and treachery.

Ralph was watching her. 'We heard from the von Crieffs,' he said.

'Oh.' That wasn't worthy of him. He said it now, here, so that she must stifle her reaction.

'Yes,' said Venetia, 'what a terrible thing, and after Jack meeting him like that.'

Thea sat still as a statue, hoping someone would change the subject, but the silence was absolute.

At last she laid down Venetia's hand and rose. 'I think I'll go and change, if that's all right.'

'Oh do,' said Venetia, 'go and put on some proper clothes.'

As she went to the door Ralph got up too, slapping his pockets, clearing his throat, looking about him as if he'd mislaid something.

'I must telephone the works.' he announced. 'Lord knows what's going on.'

Thea opened the door and waited there for him. But when he was half-way across the room Venetia said: 'Ralph.'

He turned. Venetia had one arm outstretched towards him. 'What is it old thing?'

'Don't go, Ralph.' She moved the fingers a little, beckoning.

'I only want to—'

'Don't go.'

Slowly he went back to her, his huge hand enfolding her wasted one. Thea's last sight of them as she closed the door was together, in a typical attitude, her silvery head tucked beneath his chin, her expression quiet and content, his fierce, perfectly opposite and complementary in the lamplight.

Thea went to her room and changed. She felt oddly lighthearted. She sought out a blouse, skirt and cardigan and was astonished to find that they hung loosely on her. She had to put a belt round the waist of the skirt and leave the cardigan unbuttoned to look even remotely respectable.

As she brushed her hair fiercely in front of the wardrobe mirror she decided that her loss of weight had done nothing for her looks. Being big-boned with decided features she needed the softening properties of a little more flesh. Her shoulders were now too square, she thought, her jaw and cheek-bones too angular, her nose too prominent; even her finger joints looked knobbly. Looking at herself in this harshly critical light she could not imagine that she would ever again wear a pretty dress and a shady hat, and elicit extravagant compliments such as Josef had paid her in the sunny gardens of Vienna.

She turned off the light and walked along the dark corridor to the stairs. Down in the hall she could make out a tall figure hanging about in the corner by the door to the back stairs.

'Hallo, Eddie,' she said, as she reached the bottom. 'How are you?'

'Very well.' He stood there uneasily, twisting his big fingers in front of him.

'And your mother?'

'She's all right. Thank you.'

Thea walked over to him, her hands in the pockets of her cardigan. She was not to know how formidable she appeared to Eddie, who was a little frightened of everyone. She spoke differently from any of the other women he knew, her whole manner had a freedom and implied familiarity that quite unnerved him. And what with that and her short hair and peculiar clothes, he positively quaked as she advanced upon him.

571

'Is Mrs Maxwell keeping you busy?' she asked, in a frank and friendly way that reduced him to jelly. He nodded energetically and suddenly dived one hand into his trouser pocket to clasp the box of matches he had purloined from the kitchen cupboard. He suspected she might be able to see right through cloth.

'And you're both quite happy here?' she pressed on, just standing there, with her head a bit on one side.

'Yes, yes,' he assured her, beginning to sidle towards the back stairs. She laughed in a jolly, joking sort of way: *could* she see the matches?

'I'm very glad to hear it. Goodnight, Eddie, see you tomorrow.'

'Goodnight.' He fled.

As she crossed the hall, someone was coming down the stairs with slow, heavy steps. It was dark, and the lamps were not yet lit down here.

'Father?'

He stood still, not needing to answer, nor able to. Homer came from his blanket in the stairwell, whining. She didn't have to ask any more, but went up to Ralph and into his arms, glad of the dark that hid the tears on his handsome face and of the silence that they did not need to break.

That was on the Wednesday. On Friday they buried Venetia at St Catherine's Ewhurst, at three o'clock in the afternoon.

The funeral did not upset Thea as those funerals in France had done. It was simply a formal closing, a solemn farewell, and the elegiac cadences of the service seemed right and proper. She could not forget that at the very end her parents had been together again, that Venetia had wanted only Ralph with her when she stared death in the face, thus making everything graceful and healed and whole once more. This one fact was more important somehow than her death, and more enduring, cancelling out the loss and completing the picture that she had thought spoiled for ever.

And as they stood round the muddy hole into which was lowered the narrow box containing Venetia Tennant's mortal remains, she sensed that Ralph knew it too. If he was lonely, which he surely would be for the rest of his life, he would know that finally nothing and no one had usurped him in his wife's affections, and that she was less lost to him now than she had been for the whole year preceding her death.

It was a soft, mild, rainy afternoon. The trees still wore tatters of soggy brown leaves, brims of hats dripped and dark coats were beaded with drops of moisture. Only Thea, Ralph and George Aitcheson were there. Eddie and Meredith had acted as pall-bearers and carried the small coffin down the Elm Walk, their footsteps soft on the carpet of wet leaves. Sophie wasn't well, and had watched them go from an upstairs window, her handkerchief to her face. Ralph had wanted no one else, he dreaded the prospect of a funeral tea, small sandwiches passed around in an atmosphere of formal and obligatory gloom. Besides, death had taken on a different perspective since the war. There was too much of it to indulge in unnecessary ceremony. Those nearest and dearest must make their farewells in whatever manner they saw fit, and get on with the business of living.

They shook hands with George Aitcheson and set off back to the house. Ralph walked fast, with long strides; Thea had almost to run to keep up with him.

'Slow down.' She tucked her arm through his and made him match his stride to hers.

'I don't know why I'm in such an infernal hurry,' he said gruffly. 'That damned great empty house is the last place I want to be.'

'I shall be there,' she told him.

'Dear girl.' His face was damp with the soft rain.

They opened the wicket gate at the bottom of the Elm Walk, and as they did so a narrow, dark figure came down the path towards them from the house, solitary and aloof between the rows of trees like the cat that walks by itself.

'It's Jack,' said Thea, not because she could see that it was, but because she knew.

They walked towards each other, and when they came face to face all he said was: 'I'm so sad about this.'

He shook Ralph's hand, and looked at Thea. His hands were thrust deep in the pockets of his black overcoat, his face pale and set against the turned-up collar. He had said the right thing, not offering sympathy but identifying himself with their sorrow. Nothing else was needed. He turned and walked back to the house with them, adding: 'I knew you didn't want anybody.' It was an explanation, not an apology. Ralph shook his head: that hadn't meant him.

Back at the house they had a cup of tea in the library, brought to them by a wan and red-eyed Mrs Duckham, and then Jack said he should go. Thea went out with him to the porch. His car stood on the gravel in the pattering rain.

She suddenly thought there was something she must say to him, and she blurted it out quickly while he tied his scarf.

'Josef von Crieff was killed.'

He looked at her sharply. 'I'm sorry. My poor Thea.'

'I'm recovered now,' she said cautiously, wondering if it was going to be all right to say that and finding that it was. 'I've come to terms with it.'

'I see.' He walked down the steps ahead of her. When he reached the bottom he turned and said: 'I wonder if I might tell you something.'

'Do you have to ask?' She joined him. The gentle rain breathed around them, the tall trees and rhododendrons creaked and trickled with damp.

He answered her: 'Because it is the worst possible moment, but the only one I may have before we both go back.'

'I understand.'

'I'm certain you do.' He grinned at her. 'It's one of the reasons I love you.'

'And I you.' She smiled back, arms folded, not bothered with the rain.

Shocked and embarrassed, he lifted one hand awkwardly in a kind of stiff wave, got into the car and slammed the door with a crash. The moment had come, and gone, and she had misunderstood him utterly.

CHAPTER EIGHTEEN

*'We're here because
We're here because
We're here because
We're here . . .'*

Anon.

As Eddie turned the handle of the study door he heard Homer plodding across the hall towards him. The old dog was too stiff these days to get up the stairs to his former post outside Ralph's bedroom. As time went by he spent most of the day watching the world go by from the stair well, only lifting his head and thumping his tail when he heard Ralph's voice.

Eddie stopped with the door half open and waited as Homer came to him. He bent and patted the dog's iron-grey head. He liked all animals, and especially Homer, who seemed to have singled him out for favour second only to Mr Tennant.

'Good dog,' said Eddie, patting vigorously. 'Good, good dog.'

He pushed the door wide and went in. It was six o'clock in the morning and in the cold, grey December half-light the contours of the room were blurred beneath piles of accumulated debris like a ruin overgrown with lichen and ivy. Homer, following Eddie, crossed to where Ralph's old jacket lay on the floor beneath the window, and flopped down on it with a groan, laying his head on his paws. Eddie closed the door, shutting them both in.

He knew exactly what he was going to do. He was going to tidy the place up. All through his life he had only absorbed snatches of what other people said, so his understanding of the world and its way was scanty and fractured. But he had taken in the fact that Mr Tennant's study was a disgrace; his mother and Mrs Duckham said so, often, and Mrs Maxwell had reinforced the point in a confidential way that had made him feel it had a special importance for him. The place was filthy, they all said that; Mr Tennant had never allowed it to be tidied or aired, even though he'd scarcely used it since his wife had been ill, and probably never would now she was dead.

Eddie felt sorry for Mr Tennant. He himself had helped carry Mrs Tennant's coffin down to the churchyard in the rain, and it had felt very light, like a child's. He sensed his employer's growing isolation, and that the women were more uppitty and ready to criticize. The day of the funeral had been one of those rare occasions when he had seen everything quite clearly, but he hadn't the words to convey his sympathy to Mr Tennant, even had it been proper to do so. And as usual that one day of clarity had been followed by seemingly endless ones of gloom and confusion, when he could scarcely keep track of what was going on. Mrs Duckham had cried all the time, his mother had been especially snappish and free with her hands, and Mrs Maxwell had been ill, lying on the couch in her room and murmuring faintly that Mr Tennant would now go 'utterly to pieces', whatever that meant. The atmosphere had been cold and uncertain and unhappy and Eddie was frightened by it, wanting to curl up in a corner and sleep, like an animal, until things got better.

But today he had woken early, full of decision and purpose. He had dressed himself with a minimum of difficulty and crept out of the bedroom and down the back stairs, perfectly confident of his mission, its needfulness and its success. 'Someone should put a match to the lot,' his mother had said. And that was precisely what he was going to do.

He had been waiting for weeks to find a use for his precious box of matches. Now, he struck one and stood admiring it until it scorched his fingers and he dropped the charred end on the floor. He was about to strike another when it occurred to him that when Mr Rowles made a bonfire in the garden he raked everything together in a big conical pile before lighting it. He would do the same. He put the matches back in his pocket and began gathering up the rubbish to form a heap in the middle of the threadbare rug. Magazines, books, papers, folders, pencils, there was no end to it. Beginning to enjoy himself, he started on the shelves, sweeping off whole rows of volumes with his long arms and dropping them into the ever-growing pile. Finally, he emptied out the waste-paper basket, but left the tattered old jacket to Homer. The air was full of dust as he stood back to survey his handiwork. He could hardly believe that he, Eddie, had wrought such a striking change; for a full minute he gazed about him, enchanted.

Then, the great moment. Quaking with excitement he crouched down and struck a match, which he held carefully to the edge of the heap at one or two points.

At first the pale new flames licked and flickered sinuously like snakes, but as they took a hold they began to rush and roar like hungry lions. It became very hot very quickly, and Eddie's eyes smarted and stung. Homer stood up on the jacket, his tail swinging placatingly.

The fire was between Eddie and the door, so he went to the window and opened it. It was a bit stiff at first, not having been opened for months, but eventually it yielded and flew up with a bang. A stream of dark smoke, spotted with dancing black flakes, poured out into the dark garden. Eddie felt the first stirrings of anxiety about what he had done. It was all somehow noisier, smellier, more extravagant than he had planned. The heat was flaying his back and the smoke made him cough. This was nothing like the fires he had lit in the grate in Mrs Maxwell's room, nor even those with which he had assisted Mr Rowles in the garden. He could not sit and watch this, enjoying the flittering patterns of heat on his skin. It had rapidly and completely outgrown his power to control it. This fire beat and snarled at the walls like a captive dragon, there was no longer room for both it and its creator, who prudently conceded defeat and climbed out of the window, slamming it down behind him. He was gasping for breath and his face, neck and hands were scorched and scarlet.

On the terrace he turned and stood looking back at the rampaging jungle of smoke and fire that he had begun, with a mixture of pride and apprehension. As the latter gradually gained the ascendancy, so the old, familiar darkness seeped into his head, quenching the small spark of coherent thought and blotting the light.

Ralph was the first to be made aware of the fire, because the fumes from beneath the study door wafted up the main staircase. Awakened by the smell, he observed that the air outside his window—he no longer drew the curtains at night—was full of swirling black snowflakes. He lay there for some seconds without reacting, reflecting that William must have lit a bonfire somewhere . . . but in December? And at—he picked up his fob watch from the beside table—six-fifteen in the morning? Galvanized by appalling misgivings he leapt out of bed, pulled on his dressing-gown and ran along the corridor to the head of the stairs. As he stared wildly down into the hall Mrs Duckham appeared from the direction of the kitchen, with Mrs Dilkes in close attendance, both fully dressed.

'What the devil's going on?' He raced down the stairs, catching sight as he did so of Sophie coming along the corridor from the direction of her room, swathed in dark brown flannelette and with her iron-grey hair loose on her shoulders. He jumped down the last three stairs.

'Fire! Fire!' shrieked Mrs Duckham unnecessarily.

'I know there's a perishing fire, woman!' roared Ralph. 'But where?' He pushed her aside.

'I only got down a minute ago and I knew at once but I couldn't for the life of me make out what—I mean, you don't expect . . .' Mrs Duckham babbled hysterically as Ralph stared at the smoke pouring from beneath the study door. The door itself shuddered and groaned as though an angry crowd were on the other side, intent on forcing their way out.

'Don't go near that door—don't in God's name open it! Do you understand?' he bellowed at the two women. Mrs Duckham began to cry, her face crumpling as if it, too, were being devoured by flames. Blasted women! 'Go and find Meredith!' he ordered, giving her a not particularly gentle push. 'Tell him to round up some help while I ring the fire station. Quick!'

With a distracted moan she departed, and Mrs Dilkes, suddenly sure of where her duty lay, went in search of her son.

She found him, beaten back by the heat now that the window had blown out, standing in the middle of the lawn, looming through the crepuscular swirling smoke like a totem pole. She could tell by the tilt of his head and the set of his shoulders that he had completely 'gone'. She ran over to him, coughing and spluttering, took his limp arm and shook it like a terrier. His face was vacant, the unfocused deep-set eyes like tunnels under the lowering bumpy brow. Lily hated him with a pure, untarnished hatred. Hated him for his lumpen ugliness, his uselessness, the continuing dead-weight of his presence in her life. She drew back her arm, rose on tip-toe and whipped the back of her hand across his face. He didn't move, but his eyes glanced down at her without shock or surprise. Enraged, she hit him again, this time with her fist on his shoulder, so that he rocked a little.

'I hope you're satisfied!' she screamed. It was quite a luxury to stand there, hidden in the smoke, knowing she could be heard by no one but Eddie, and let it all come out. 'I hope you're pleased with yourself, Eddie Dilkes, burning the bleeding house down! Just had to go and spoil everything, didn't you? You stupid, great—' Words failed her and she contented herself with pummelling him until her strength wore out, while he gazed imperviously over her head.

Inside the house, Ralph had telephoned the fire service, and had organized a human chain from the scullery sink, out of the kitchen door and round to the study window. He was afraid that if he opened the door into the hall the fire would take a grip on the rest of the house, which it would anyway if help did not arrive soon. The kettles, saucepans and bowls of water came along the chain with agonizing slowness to begin with, since with the exception of Meredith the firefighters were all elderly and mostly female. But by the time the fire engine arrived the number and quality of the helpers had been swelled by the few remaining able-bodied men from the village. They had attached a hose to the stableyard pump so that the fire, which had now burst through into the hall, could be attacked from both sides. All their efforts were centred on preventing it reaching the staircase, for if it took a hold there, at the spine of the house, there would be no checking it at all.

In the middle of the drive at the front of the house stood Sophie, still in her dressing gown, each of her hands tucked into the opposite cuff, like a mandarin. Ralph, running to the pump, experienced a moment of truth: his life-long impatience with his sister turned in that instant to hatred. His wife was dead, his children gone, his house burning, and yet there she stood, clinging to life and to him like some tenacious black parasite.

By ten o'clock, the fire had subsided, but for a few sullen flames in what remained of the drawing-room. Mercifully it had not reached the stairs, but the study, part of the hall, and the drawing-room with all its priceless contents, were wrecked. Their labours had been assisted by the absolute stillness of the morning, and a soaking valley mist which had rolled in and prevented the blaze tearing away at too great a rate.

Dejectedly Ralph inspected the damage. The place was like a battlefield, the air still full of smoke, the blackened rooms hissing and smouldering, strange people running here and there, shouting through the murk, bumping him occasionally as he stood there in his filthy dressing-gown. It was such a terrible mess, a gaping infected wound in the side of the house. He reflected gloomily that it would almost have been better if the place had been razed to the ground. That at least would have been clear-cut and complete, the end of everything. As it was, how the hell would he cope with this? He gazed about him, appalled. What would he do? Where would he begin?

He found Homer's body in the study, trapped by a pile of wreckage where part of the ceiling had collapsed. The corpse looked singularly horrible, charred and twisted and emaciated, more like a rabbit than a large dog. Ralph remembered when he had first brought the puppy home, ten years ago. He and the children had raced up and down the Elm Walk with it, laughing and shouting and throwing sticks, delighted with its big feet and scything tail, and the great eager bat-ears, slightly bent in those early months. They had quickly become accustomed to the reliably ecstatic greetings, the ready soaking-up of praise and abuse; they had stopped noticing, as people do with dogs. But it hurt Ralph now, to think of Homer, old and stiff and not understanding, lying on the jacket he regarded as sacred while the flames advanced to consume him. He had met a terrifying and painful death in the very place he had thought safest.

Now, thought Ralph. Now I am alone. No one is on my side now. The completeness of his separation hit him with stunning force. If one spent one's life not caring what others thought there had to be one, at least, who understood. That had been Venetia's role; he knew it now if he had never done so before. Her beauty, her sweetness, her serenity had all been secondary to this: that she watched over him as he indulged his whims and caprices and, when he came back to her at night, called out the best in him so that he should not hate himself. Thea? Ah, but Thea was different. She was like him, of him, a joy but not necessarily a comfort.

He craved Venetia's otherness, the wonder of knowing that someone so different, and so wholly admirable, could love him.

George Aitcheson came up to him. He looked odd, in a cassock topped by a riding mac and tweed cap, his feet encased in rubber boots. He touched Ralph's shoulder. 'There's some coffee made, old chap,' he said. 'Come and have a cup, and something to eat. It could have been worse.'

Ralph pointed at the dead dog. 'Look.'

'Oh God.' George leaned over, peering, shaking his head in distress. 'That poor, wretched animal. I'm so sorry, Ralph.'

'Only a dog,' muttered Ralph, feeling a Judas for saying it, but a little ashamed of himself for minding so much.

'Yes, I know, but what a way to go.' They stood there, side by side, staring down at the corpse as if paying homage, and then George took Ralph's arm. 'Come on.' He led him across the hall. 'I know it's hard for you to appreciate it now,' he was saying, 'but you were unbelievably lucky. Things could have been so much worse.'

'Mm.'

'Frankly, with more wind the house would have burned down.'

'And I'm supposed to be comforted by that?'

'I'm sorry. It's just a way of looking at it.'

They entered the library. Everyone was standing about there—the firemen, the men from the village, the staff, Sophie. Someone put a mug of coffee in his hand. On the desk stood a large oval meat dish piled with bread and butter, and next to it a jar of marmalade with a soup spoon protruding from the top. Funny the way your life could be in ruins but you still took refreshment. Bread, the staff of life. He took a gulp of coffee, sensing everyone's sympathetic gaze on him and hating it. He wanted to shrug off their sympathy and cast it aside like a hated piece of uncomfortable clothing.

'Not too bad, sir,' said the fire chief gamely, obviously feeling it his duty to make some helpful remark. 'Could have been a lot worse if the door and window had been open.'

'And with more wind,' said Ralph, flatly. Versicles and responses. Everyone nodded and murmured and reacted like a bunch of well-drilled bit-part actors, glad to see he was taking a positive line. Why did they have to keep telling him how fortunate he was when their faces were full of nervous pity?

Mrs Dilkes stepped forward, claiming his attention, her mouth like a rat-trap, eyes defiant.

Ralph looked at her wearily. 'What it is Mrs Dilkes?'

'I thought I should say—it was him.' She jerked an elbow. 'What?'

'It was Eddie done it. Started the fire. And—' with a superhuman effort she swallowed her pride, 'after you've been so kind as to give us employment.'

Ralph looked over her shoulder at Eddie who stood motionless, staring at his boots, his great hands hanging like paddles at his sides, his hair falling in his eyes. Poor old Eddie. 'That's perfectly all right Mrs Dilkes,' he said.

'Pardon?' She was taken aback.

'I knew it must have been Eddie. It doesn't matter. He's not responsible, is he?'

'He had some matches in his pocket, I found them, he must have stolen them.' She turned to her son. 'Eddie! Give those matches to Mr Tennant. I told him he was to give them back to you in person . . . Eddie! Do as you're told!' She took his sleeve and shook it, and then grabbed his hand and thrust it in the direction of his pocket, but it simply fell back again, a dead weight.

Seeing her become frantic, Ralph said: 'Please don't, Mrs Dilkes. Just pass them back yourself, if you would, and take Eddie to his room.'

'Oh. Yes—right you are.' She felt for the matches, and handed them over.

'Thank you.'

She took Eddie's sleeve again and pulled until he stumbled after her.

Ralph was utterly exhausted, but he looked up and caught Sophie's eye as she followed the Dilkeses from the room. 'Sophie . . . we should have a talk.'

'As you wish.'

He sank down in the nearest chair. 'Do you mind all going?' he asked. They began to drift compliantly from the room, hushed and respectful. George Aitcheson said something about taking it easy, and calling in again this afternoon, and out in the hall he heard him organizing Meredith and one or two of the other men to do some clearing up, being practical, restoring order like the good friend he was. Imagine, they would say in Ewhurst for some time to come, imagine, so much bad luck in such a short time . . . never rains but it pours . . . of course he should never have taken in that mental lad, that was asking for trouble . . . and no family to help him over it—if she'd been still alive it might have been different . . . but I promise you, he looked a broken man. . . .

Just before Christmas Thea received an odd, restrained letter from her father, saying that he was considering moving from Chilverton House. He cited as his reason his present solitariness, and the reminders of Venetia that were all about him. It was not until the final paragraph that he wrote, apparently as an afterthought: *'. . . Besides, young Dilkes took it into his head to burn some of my papers the other day, and unintentionally started quite a blaze. I am told by everyone that it could have been worse, but it has caused enough damage to convince me I can no longer afford to go on living here. The house is insured, I shall set the repairs in hand and start looking for somewhere more suited to my needs, probably in the Bromley area, or even in town near the works. I have never been a country squire, after all, so why go on pretending when there is only myself left to impress? I shall of course let you know what I decide.*

'I shall be spending Christmas Day and Boxing Day at Long Lake, where we shall doubtless commiserate with each other over our respective offspring in foreign parts. Have a happy Christmas, dearest girl. Father.'

Thea re-read the letter several times. What on earth did he mean by 'quite a blaze'? Her anxious imagination ran riot. It was unlike Ralph to understate, but the whole tone of the letter was untypical: he sounded defeated, that was it. The fire, whatever its size, constituted the kind of practical challenge on which he normally thrived, and yet he was allowing himself to be driven out by it. She cursed the distance that separated them and prevented her from pulling aside the curtain of evasion and lassitude.

She worried about him all over Christmas, though she was glad he would be with the Kingsleys. She had not heard from Jack since they had met after Venetia's funeral and though she half-hoped he might appear at some time over the festive season, he did not.

In spite of this, she enjoyed Christmas. The drivers were kept busy, the war did not stop for religious feasts, there was no time to dwell on how they might have been spending their days at home. There was chicken and spotted dick for lunch, and in the afternoon they had got up a concert party for the convalescents at Quatre Pins. Thea participated in sketches and musical numbers got up, because of her height, in striped blazer, boater and handlebar moustache, and had been told by more than one member of the appreciative audience that should she change her mind about driving, a career awaited her in the theatre.

Only that night did she suffer a stab of homesickness. It was during her last trip up the hill from Merville Station to General 16. She had three men in the back, all surgical cases: two with bullet wounds and one whose arm had been whipped off at the elbow by shrapnel. In spite of the fact that the condition of all three was poor, they were in high spirits as the severely wounded often were at this stage. It was Christmas night and they were on their way home, and no amount of pain and discomfort could tarnish their optimism.

Thea had caught their mood, laughing and chatting as she settled them in the ambulance and lit cigarettes. She fished her handlebar moustache out of her jacket pocket and stuck it on and this had caused further hilarity.

'Bet you wouldn't wear it when you get out at the hospital,' one of them said.

'Bet I would.'

'Go on then.'

'You're on!' She clambered back into the driver's seat still wearing the moustache and they began to climb the long hill. It was a perfect night with a thin sickle moon, and stars scattered like dragées on the smooth sky. The landscape had a crystalline sharpness as though it had been rinsed and purified, then quickly sealed by the frost to preserve its sparkling beauty. Thea began to hum:

> *'It came upon the midnight clear*
> *That glorious song of old,*
> *From angels bending near the earth*
> *To touch their harps of gold . . .'*

It was her favourite carol, one that had made her scalp tingle and her eyes prick since she was a little girl.

> *'Still through the cloven skies they come*
> *With peaceful wings unfurled . . .'*

584

She could see those angels so clearly, with their wise faces and their huge, throbbing wings, she even fancied she could hear their distant, trilling voices.

> *'But man at war with man hears not*
> *The love song that they sing . . .'*

She stopped. Her voice was stifled by a huge lump that rose in her throat. She felt foolish but she was overcome. Suddenly a voice from the back picked up where she had left off.

> *'Oh hush the noise, ye men of strife,*
> *And hear the angels sing!'*

The man sang in a fine tenor, with an extraordinary declamatory resonance. Confidently he went into the final verse and the others, not knowing the words but recognizing the tune, joined in, one gruff and slightly flat, the other harmonizing quite competently.

Thea drove, seeing the white road through a shimmer of unshed tears, no longer able to sing.

> *'When peace shall over all the earth*
> *Its ancient splendours fling,*
> *And the whole world give back the song*
> *That now the angels sing.'*

Some angels. And yet the very fact that these tired, dirty, battered men could lift their voices and sing those words of Victorian certainty did have something angelic about it. She was completely overwhelmed by the strong, emotional charge of Christmas. For that one moment she would have given anything, everything, to go back in time to Christmas at Chilverton House, the rustle of paper, the crackle of fires, the distant joyous pealing of the church bells, the thrilling resiny scent of the tall tree in the hall. Whatever splendours eventual peace might bring, they would not, it seemed, include another such Christmas. The tears rushed down over her cheeks.

In the back, encouraged by their success, they started on 'Silent Night.'

When they reached the hospital she went round to the back and helped the orderlies unload the stretchers. As the last man was brought out, she said: 'Thank you for singing. It was lovely.'

The man looked up at her, the one that had lost an arm. He was in his forties, little and balding, with a pinched face and boot-button eyes. 'It's a good tune, that,' he replied, in the accent of the Royal Welch Fusiliers. 'One of the better ones. I was in chapel choir, see, so I know a thing or two about singing.'

'Yes.'

They began to carry him up the steps to where the night sister stood at the entrance to the lighted hall. As he went, he called back to her, 'See you won the bet, then!'

And Sister O'Neill, fresh from London and new to General 16, glanced over her shoulder as she closed the door, and wondered how normal it was for the women drivers to wear moustaches on duty.

Jack sensed something portentous in his return to the Ypres salient in the high summer of 1917. It was where the war, for him, had begun, and he had come full circle.

Two years of total stalemate in the sector had been broken by the blowing up of the ridge at Messines in early June. A million pounds of explosives had been buried beneath the 150-foot high ridge, which ran to the south of Ypres, and had all been set off at once in the pre-dawn darkness of 7 June. The German defences had been shattered, and the British occupied the ridge with virtually no losses to themselves. Success was, for a change, quick, clean and complete. No one was cynical enough to point out that the enterprise had taken two years to prepare and had advanced the British a mere two miles. On the contrary, it was taken to be a foretaste of the ultimate victory to come. The great lesson of Messines—that of the value of surprise—went once more unlearned.

Haig, elated and impatient, decided to capitalize on the Messines triumph by following it with a mass offensive in the Ypres salient. At long last he saw an opportunity to put into practice his long-cherished plan of attacking in the north. In support of the plan he cited the necessity of taking the Belgian ports of Ostend and Zeebrugge, to check the predations of German submarines on British supply vessels. In fact, the submarines operated almost exclusively from home waters, and their effectiveness had been greatly reduced by the recent introduction of convoys. He also implied that Marshall Petain had pleaded with him to launch a British offensive in the north to divert the Germans from the ragged and mutinous French army further south.

Both Lloyd George and Admiral Foch were against Ypres as a setting for a big offensive, the latter pointing out on more than one occasion that one could not fight *'Boches et boue'*—Germans and mud—but the British War Cabinet had many of the vital facts kept from them and lacked the necessary ammunition with which to withstand Haig's *idée fixe*. To the north of the salient the dykes had been broken and the sea allowed to flood a large area, so one German flank was secure. Besides which, the Germans had been fortifying their line around Ypres for years past. They had an excellent position; the city of Ypres was situated in the centre of a saucer of land, with the ground rising in a series of shallow undulations on three sides, and the low ground to the rear reaching back to a point where on clear days the English Channel might be seen gleaming a mere mocking thirty miles away. Whatever activity took place in the bottom of the saucer, the Germans had a grandstand view of it from the ridges above the broken towers of the city. The soil in the salient was heavy, non-porous clay from which the habitual heavy rainfall never fully drained, and which was churned by bombardment into a glutinous sea of mud, many feet deep.

Haig did not take these factors into account. He did not even inspect the front line for himself. The British forces would assemble in the natural amphitheatre behind Ypres and, on 31 July, would launch a fan-shaped offensive up over the ridges, sweeping the Germans before them and reaching Ostend and Zeebrugge within a week. It was left to those of his men, like Jack, who knew the salient, to entertain the gravest misgivings.

The opposition of the War Cabinet, who were anyway much occupied with other matters, was gradually eroded to the point where they told Haig to go ahead and prepare for the offensive while they gave it further thought and reached a final decision. It was all the leeway Haig needed to take the matter completely out of their hands. On the night of 16 July, he gave orders to begin the preliminary bombardment. On 25 July he announced that he was ready, and the Cabinet had little alternative but to give him their blessing and pledge their whole-hearted support for the plan about which they had such serious doubts.

The preparations for battle, conducted on the usual grand scale, had ensured that the Germans were fully forewarned. By the end of July both sides had crammed nearly a million men into the Ypres salient. The flat land behind the city positively teemed with troops. Every village became a garrison, every field a parade-ground, every barn and outhouse a billet. The roads rumbled and rattled with lorries and wagons. And behind the massed infantry the cavalry divisions drew up in readiness for the moment when they could thunder up the gentle slopes in a long-awaited hour of glory.

Because of the excellence of the weather it was hard even for Jack to recall quite how bad it was here when the inevitable rain set in. A holiday atmosphere prevailed. The Kents were billeted in Loubevin, a small village to the south-west of Ypres where they enjoyed the experience of being treated like heroes. Loubevin's one café pulsated nightly to the sound of English songs accompanied on an ancient piano by the establishment's resident musician. The wine was cheap and plentiful and the maidens of Loubevin, Anglophiles to a woman, seemed to think heaven consisted of sitting on the knee of a Tommy, replenishing his glass and shrieking with laughter at his incomprehensible jokes. Drunkenness was common, and generally overlooked except when it occurred on duty, when punishments were harsh. It was usual to find at least one private soldier tied to a wagon wheel in the main square of Loubevin, or doubling wretchedly round a field at midday in full kit. The battalion had changed. It consisted now of a small proportion of veterans and a great many youthful raw recruits. Discipline had to be right and harsh if such unpromising material was to be battle-fit by the beginning of August.

Jack himself was calm. A mood of not-unpleasant melancholy had descended over him during the past weeks, he experienced no turmoil of either anxiety or excitement as he had before the Somme. He was tired, physically and spiritually. Massie had gone, and Hallett and Harman and hundreds of others. He himself had survived thus far very much against the odds and the knowledge made him feel solitary and rock-like. He knew the men in his company and got on well with most of them, but he no longer made close friends among them. It was no fault of theirs. He was undergoing the queer metamorphosis from soldier of the King to war veteran. For three years he had breathed in death, along with the smoke and the smell, and scepticism had entered his very bones.

He felt no surprise on the evening of 31 July, at the end of the first day of the third battle of Ypres, when it became known that the greatest advance had been only half a mile. The German line had not been reached at any point, it had rained stair-rods all day long, and the hillside on which he and about twenty of 'B' Company now sat was a quagmire. Since it was clear they were going to have to spend the night in the open they set about pitching bell-tents on the quivering porridge of mud. There was still continuous fire from the enemy line three-quarters of a mile further up, and the rain sizzled furiously all around, but Jack was conscious of the dogged atmosphere of silence in which they worked. It was an unbelievably awkward and laborious task to get the tents up. In trying to brace your feet against the slope you drove yourself knee-deep into the mire, and the effort required to pull one foot out sent the other further in.

It took them an hour to erect three tents and it was then necessary to dig eighteen-inch trenches inside the tents in which they could lie, to protect themselves from flying shrapnel and other debris. The digging took a further hour, for the mud kept avalanching into the holes and filling them up again. Being midsummer it was not quite dark when they finished, but the sky lowered and the sheeting rain blotted out what residual light there was. They were all exhausted. Jack sensed the feeling amid his younger and less experienced fellows that things were bad, that failure loomed, that the glorious advance had fallen on its face. How could he explain to them that this was all perfectly normal and predictable, that it was nothing to get cast down about, not yet anyway? He decided it would take too long; they would have to find out for themselves, as he had done.

They crawled into the tents. Jack could not remember when he had last been so wet. Every item of clothing and piece of equipment he wore was completely saturated and weighed about twice its normal weight. From the hips down he was encased in a sucking, clinging skin of liquid mud. He did not feel cold for his energy had been running at full throttle since they had gone over the top that morning. He had waded and struggled up a few hundred yards of sodden clay with no thought whatever for his own safety. Not that he, or many others, had ever given much thought to the matter, but there had once been a reverencing of life and a natural healthy fear of death. Today he had blundered along at the head of his men with no sense of occasion whatever.

Automatically, he closed his eyes. All his waning energy went into the effort of concentrating on sleep. He imagined that his eyelids were getting thicker and thicker so that he simply could not open them: this often worked well. The rest of his soaked and filthy body and its accoutrements became dead, forgotten matter, not to be bothered with. That also helped, it stopped you fussing about yourself.

He was almost asleep when some well-tuned warning signal inside his head sounded the alarm. His eyes snapped open, the forgotten area of his lower legs came back to life. Water was lapping about his calves, cold and deep and rising steadily. He looked down. The hole it had taken them so long to dig was filling like a paddling pool with water draining from the slope above. Opposite Jack, the hem of Second Lieutenant Jamieson's cape floated serenely on the scummy surface.

Jack leaned across and gave Jamieson a shove. 'Come on—time to bail out.'

They dragged themselves out of the hole, backing out of the tent's aperture, their feet slithering and sliding on the wet clay.

'We'll move the tent up a few feet, but not bother with the trench,' shouted Jack. The others emerged from their tents, intent on the same operation. They squelched around, as ponderous as dinosaurs, while the retaliatory fire from above flew about their ears and blasted fresh craters in the mud to right and left.

In the end they were forced to give up the idea of using the tents and retired to a nearby crater, where they huddled in their capes against the sides, so that the water flowing from higher up the hill would pass between rather than over them.

They spent a week on the slope, shifting from place to place, occasionally moving forward a few yards only to fall back, beaten by the enemy fire and the mud. There was no line, no wire or trench, nor any of what now seemed the comforting familiar boundaries of war. They lost their field telephone in the slough, and the conditions made it impossible for relief to get up to the men of the first wave, so they were bogged down in limbo, unable to move either forward or back. They could not even make contact with other members of the battalion if, indeed, there were any left. They could only huddle together in holes and pray fervently that some act of God would deliver them from this hopeless stalemate.

By the end of a fortnight, by a process of osmosis rather than decisive action, a new front line of sorts had been established on the crest of the first rise, but it was now depressingly apparent that such German positions as had been taken were mere outposts in front of the main line of defence. In the folds of the land ahead lay a veritable forest of concrete pillboxes, each manned by two or three crack marksmen. The British, weary and soaked in their makeshift trenches and dug-outs, saw failure staring them in the face. Some relief troops had made it through the swamp, but the chief problem now was supplies. The terrain made transport by lorry quite impossible, so the supplies were loaded into panniers and brought up by mules, along painstakingly-laid duckboard tracks. This was assuming they reached their destination at all, for the sound of the supply trucks on the pavé roads down below was the signal for every German gunner for miles around to open fire and blast them to kingdom come.

If, on its agonizing journey, the mule slipped off the track it was almost certainly a goner, since the weight of its burden caused it to sink inexorably. Some men of a more determined nature would stand braced on the slithering boards and put every ounce of strength and bloody-mindedness into the effort of dragging some wretched animal out of the mire, but it was invariably hopeless. The more the creature pawed and struggled, its head lifted, its eyes rolling frantically, the more deeply it became embedded in the mud. At the eleventh hour the panniers would be removed and the mule abandoned to its fate.

Jack found the daily sacrifice of animals acutely distressing. The fact that an animal's life was arguably less valuable than a human's did not seem relevant. It was the mules' stupid innocence which made their demise so painful. They did not remember, or anticipate, or calculate the risk. They were driven on to do their meagre best, and left to die without comfort. Their deaths seemed to mirror the futile slaughter that had characterized this war for the last three years and which showed no signs of ending.

Once he had been so incensed by the sight of a mule half-in, half-out of the mud that he had run back to help the bewildered private in charge. It was teeming with rain as usual, and the boards were slimy and treacherous, but they had eventually succeeded in heaving the animal to safety by main force. They had grinned at each other over its back, only to discover that it had almost severed one of its hind legs on a piece of corrugated metal submerged in the mud. So Jack had had to shoot it anyway, when they'd unstrapped the supplies, and they'd watched it sink back, with a kind of slow and fatalistic grace, into the glooping hole from which they had rescued it.

Communications generally continued to be a problem. Field telephones sank in the swamp, carrier pigeons starved and messengers lost their way as they ploughed through a countryside devoid of landmarks. It did, however, become known during the next weekend that the objectives of the Third Battle of Ypres had subtly altered. It was no longer necessary to reach Ostend and Zeebrugge, but simply to dislodge the Germans from their position, killing as many as possible in so doing. In this they were led to believe they had so far done pretty well.

When Jack and his much diminished party eventually possessed themselves of a pillbox, it was on 20 August, with the weather worsening daily. They had had to fight for every yard gained, and had suffered half a dozen casualties. Four of these had been killed outright, the remaining two had been strapped to salvaged German duckboards and were carried by the others. They had no MO, and had not succeeded in locating an aid post, so the injured men received only the most rudimentary care. There was not room in the captured pillbox for the whole party. They put up a couple of bell tents in the lee of the back wall, but the stretchers had to be left out in the open under layers of tarpaulin and waterproof capes. Here they sank slowly and had to be regularly fished out and moved to another position. Occasionally they were forgotten and the water would be starting to run into their mouths by the time someone got to them. The wounded were sodden, starving and in agony, yet they groaned and gargled on, refusing to die with near-ludicrous tenacity. Jack felt no particular pity for them. Frankly, they were an encumbrance he could have done without, just one more thing that had to be lugged about, cared for with the same degree of efficiency as the rest of one's kit and no more. There was no question of abandoning them like the mules, but at the same time it was folly to pretend there was much one could do. Like the burden of Christian in *Pilgrim's Progress,* the wounded seemed to grow heavier with every tottering, slithering step.

They remained in the pillbox for a couple of days, and then received orders to press on. It continued to rain. The further forward they went the more dead there were, both German and English, forming a kind of spongy superstratum. The smell was sickening. Jack thought it even worse than that of the trenches, because of its implications: they were in the open here, in open country, and yet still the air reeked of putrefaction. It wasn't so bad when the dead were just saturated, shapeless mounds, like sandbags, but every so often your foot would slip and disturb something, and as you clambered back onto the track you would see a face looking up at you, eyeless and rotten, ghoulishly amused at your feeble efforts to remain alive and sane.

On 25 August it filtered through to them that the end, for them, was at hand. They were to be relieved, and there would be a respite for the first fortnight of September while preparations were made for another great push. The idea was to get across the Menin Road, and thence along the ridge to the ruined village of Passchendaele, which had taken on a kind of mystic significance in the scheme of things. Passchendaele! The very name had a sacrificial ring to it. The road that led to it had already been the scene of unbelievable casualties, the narrow strip of land that lay between it and the village of St Julien was thick with the dead. As Jack and his men grew closer to it, the smell became stronger, there was a fog of death that sickened the stomach and oppressed the soul. The finger of land, no more than two fields wide, had become the valley of the shadow. Tanks, which had yet to prove their usefulness, had been sent in near St Julien in mid-August only to become totally bogged down in terrain which could not support a man, let alone several tons of machinery. Following this fiasco Haig had been asked yet again to call off the whole venture, but he now felt there was no alternative but to go forward. Passchendaele was the key to it all. If they took Passchendaele they stood a chance of sweeping round to the coast and taking the ports before the high autumn tides and the onset of winter made it impossible. The offensive would continue, with fresh men and new impetus.

In the interim Jack and the others availed themselves of a ruined enemy dug-out. It was in poor shape, but it was large, and they managed to clear most of the rubble and build it up into a kind of rampart on the eastern side. They dug a sap at an oblique angle from this *ad hoc* wall to use as a look-out post, and settled down to sit it out. No more than a few hundred yards in front were the clusters of bare and broken tree-stumps still held by the enemy, the remains of the spinneys which had caused such havoc on attempts to reach the road. There was no colour in the landscape. The sky was grey, the tree-stumps brown or blackened, the ground a monotonous khaki.

The conditions were the most appalling Jack could remember. Here one did not even have the false sense of homeliness and continuity of the trenches. They felt desolate and abandoned. One of the casualties had died, and the other they had dumped at an aid post shortly after leaving the pill-box. But strangely they missed them. It was as if the presence of men in extremis had prevented them noticing their own afflictions. Without the stretcher cases, morale sank, feet became sore, hunger bit fiercely, lice seemed to proliferate. The stomach cramps which plagued Jack from time to time returned, so that at least he experienced no hardship from the acute shortage of rations.

Only the smallest trickle of supplies was getting through, and there was no question of parcels from home being brought up, so they lived on biscuit, and tea. The water to make the tea they took from any handy rain-filled hole. These pools were often a repository for the dead, or bits of the dead, and had usually doubled as a latrine at some time or another, but they were long past worrying about that. One might just as well combat the misery with a cup of tea and not agonize about where it came from.

At least, Jack had thought he was past worrying. It was a shock, therefore, on the morning of 28 August when he trudged out to the nearest puddle with the dixie-can, to find he was not completely immune to disgust. As he squatted down to break the rain-freckled surface of the water he saw a corpse of quite recent origin staring up at him. The German uniform was still grey, the buttons and buckles bright and intact. Strands of intestines and gut, emerging from a hole just below the belt, waved and floated like exotic waterweed. He only looked at it for a second before his stomach exploded into his mouth. There was nothing much in him to come up, but he retched and hawked until his abdominal muscles ached, spitting out a thin, sour fluid, as if his system was trying to rid itself of the poison of war.

He staggered back to the dug-out on shaky legs and slumped down against the side.

'What's up, sir?' enquired Jamieson. He was nineteen, and beside him Jack felt like Methuselah. All of them were so young, still whole and pristine under their layer of mud, still capable of observation and surprise. It was witness to his customary emotional numbness that they saw at once something untoward had happened. He stared back at them, trying to marshal his thoughts.

'I'm all right. Spot of tummy trouble, that's all.'

A random shell landed disturbingly close to the dug-out, sending up a spray of mud and rubbish which rattled down on the tarpaulin roof. It was a whizz bang: they heard the crash of its landing first, then the howl of the shell's flight, the boom of the gun that fired it last. They sat accustomedly, looking at each other, waiting for the noise to subside. When it did, a dollop of mud dislodged by the blast slid down one wall and onto the legs of the boy underneath. Private Lumm let out a shriek of anxiety and struggled while a couple of others helped to free him. Jack glanced at him with distaste: Lumm was a liability. His raw nerves would affect the others sooner or later, one could only hope they would be taken out of the front line before he went over the edge completely.

'I'm afraid I didn't get the water,' he added, like Rip Van Winkle. 'Sorry about that.'

'I'll get it sir.' Jamieson took the dixie can and scrambled out.

A couple of the other subalterns were placing a piece of candle in an empty tin. This would generate enough heat to provide a warm, if not boiling, cup of tea. Jack stared at their filthy hands, fumbling with matches, painstakingly extricating the tiny stub of wick from the grubby lump of reconstituted wax, lighting it, dropping a few gobs of the wax into the bottom of the rusty tin to hold the candle in place, then lowering it with infinite delicacy, shielding it from the rivulets that leaked through the roof, crouching over it with Red Indian-like concentration. Their faces, beneath the dirt, were round and wholesome as apples: faces from the common room and the games field and the chapel choirstalls, still sure enough of themselves to take all that trouble over a candle in an old tin can. Not that they were very good at it: he shook his head; Harman would have made a little palace of this place.

He felt dreadful, faint and sick. The accumulated cold and wet of the last few weeks had finally caught up with him. His teeth chattered embarrassingly and he wrapped his arms about his chest to stifle the shivering that now took him by storm.

Jamieson returned with the dixie-can and they placed it on top of the makeshift burner. Lumm came over and sat down with the others. He had only been in France since June; Jack could find it in his heart to feel pity for him. Looking at him now Jack could easily picture the kind of letter Lumm sent home. Censoring was one of the most unattractive of an officer's tasks, the most that could be said of it was that it provided an insight into the contrariness of human nature. For they all of them widened the gulf between here and home, perhaps without even intending to. Lumm might be a shameless bag of nerves, but his letters home would be totally phlegmatic.

'Dear Mum and Dad and Elsie' (or whoever), *'Hope this finds you as it leaves me in the pink. As you see I am still doing alright. Thank you for the parcel, socks tea etcetera which will come in very handy, and for your letter. Sorry to hear about Uncle Ted, give my best to Auntie. Last week we were in rest, but not much time what with drill, inspection, games etcetera. We had a film with Clara Bow. This week we are back in the line but we have not seen much of the Hun. It is still raining but the food is not bad. Well, must close as they keep us busy. Kind regards to all, not forgetting Chipper and Polly. Your ever loving son—'* That was the basic letter, thought Jack, with one or two minor variables. It would be written with much pencil-chewing and brain-racking, but it always came out the same: stilted and evasive and relying heavily on the word 'etcetera'. Further up the social scale the letter would be longer and more articulate, containing more news but scarcely more truth. All had as their basis a kind of fastidiousness about expressing the true misery of life at the

Front. Though Jack shared the reserve, he could not fully explain it. After all, they continually vilified the British press for painting a misleading picture of the conduct of the war, all agreed that nobody at home understood what it was like, yet none was prepared to set the record straight. Like members of an exclusive club, they did not wish to include outsiders. Was it that they felt 'home' might be contaminated if the people there knew too much? Or that the odd but enduring friendships conceived and maintained under these highly specialized conditions must be kept sacred? Only to Thea had Jack attempted to convey the whole truth. For the rest, he was jealous with his sufferings and selfish with his feelings.

Jamieson passed him a mug of tea. It felt pleasantly warm in his hands but he doubted whether he could face drinking it. He watched the others, two officers and half a dozen men, sip their tea and chat as if they had been in the snuggest tearoom in provincial England.

That night, Private Lumm cracked up while he and Jack stood sentry duty. It was about eleven-thirty, and the enemy had begun a creeping bombardment, the shells following at intervals in a wide arc and then, on reaching the end of the arc, sweeping back in the opposite direction, but a few yards further on. In this way a good gunner could sniff out an enemy position like a bloodhound gradually closing on a fugitive. The wear and tear on the nerves was terrible, for you were a sitting duck; all you could do was keep your head down and pray. It was a moot point which was worse—the unbroken din of a protracted heavy barrage, or the intermittent, searing whine and crash of these searching shells, with the ominous bubbling silences between.

The gunner reached a point to the left of them and began to swing back. Along the line they could hear the comforting retaliatory fire of a Vickers gun, much good might it do them. The German was now dead in line with their dug-out. He'd either land one right on them or leapfrog from one side to the other, it would just be a question of luck. As the explosions grew closer Jack slid down and pressed his face against the slippery wall of the sap. He hoped his tin helmet was not a dud. A favourite game of the men in rest camp was to wallop stray helmets with a rifle butt: most kept their shape but every so often one stove in like papier mâché. No point in finding out which yours was at this stage, one might as well have blind faith in the product.

The mud by his face had a sweet, unhealthy smell. At home he used to like picking up a handful of soil from one of the fields, rubbing it between his hands, sniffing it: clean and wholesome like bread. This was not the same; he shuddered to think what it must be like to drown in this huge charnel pit. There was a nasty taste in his mouth, he felt bad. Inside the encasing shell of his mud-caked uniform and tack his body was quivering feverishly. He had dysentery, over which it was increasingly difficult to keep control, or even to care whether he did or not. Then Lumm started up.

'Mother! Mother! Mum, I don't want to—'

His whimpering was cut short by the thunderous explosion of a shell only yards from the dug-out. In the whizzing aftermath of the flying debris it continued: 'Oh Mum, I can't, I can't, I—'

'Private, *quiet!* Stop that!'

'I don't want to, don't let them kill me Mum . . .'

'Shut up, damn you!' Jack felt his nerves snapping thread by thread like a tearing rope.

'I can't! I don't want to! I want to go home . . .'

Christ, the boy sounded like some character in a second-rate melodrama; any moment now he was going to say that he was too young to die, a theory which had been disproved many times over in recent years.

Crash! This time the gunner was dead on line, but he had overshot a little. Lumm let out a howl and began climbing out over the edge.

'Soldier—where the *hell* do you think you're going?'

'Home!'

In a sudden access of fury Jack caught the boy's ankle and yanked him back in. He was crying like a child now, sobbing and sniffling, and Jack took some pleasure in dragging him down the side of the sap, his face ploughing snottily through the mud.

'Be quiet! Shut up or I'll—' He didn't know what he would do, and the well-trained though weakening officer in him stopped him from completing the threat.

Private Sydney Lumm, raising his head for an instant, thought the shell must have got him after all and that he had passed into Hell. He had felt himself sliding down and down, his legs tugged by hard, demonic hands, harsh voices ringing in his ears. Now, looking up, his impression was confirmed by the terrible face that hung over him, thin and white as a death's head, smeared with black, the hair plastered in elfin strands to the sunken cheeks and temples, the eyes unnaturally bright, the mouth snarling. That was it—he was in Hell! Death had not hurt as much as he'd feared, but the Devil had got him now, for being a coward, and now there would be no peace, not ever. He heard his own voice rising in a shrill and gibbering scream: why, he even sounded like a soul in torment, his voice going on and on in a crazy spiral that required no effort from him. Then there was an explosion in his head and he drifted slowly, weightlessly, backwards.

Jack peered at Lumm. Had he hit him too hard? He had struck him in anger, not merely as an antidote to hysteria, and his hand had met the side of the boy's head with satisfying force. It had been a release, but now that he'd done it the adrenalin drained away and left him cold and weak. Lumm lay on his back at the bottom of the sap, his face resting against the side, eyes closed, his chest palpitating with shallow ragged breaths. Looking down at him Jack felt remorseful. He covered him with his own cape, and settled down by him to sit out the watch. The shells were moving away to the right, they'd been lucky this time.

He was relieved at 0100 hours, and told them not to disturb Lumm. 'I think he'll be all right,' he said to them. 'With a bit of luck we'll get out of here tomorrow.'

'Poor little blighter,' said one of them. They were tolerant and generous, considering.

Jack went back into the main dug-out, but couldn't sleep. When he did doze it was to be tormented by a dream in which he was trapped, but invisible, while people he knew passed by and went about their lives unable to see his tortured face looking out at them, or to hear his stifled screams. He awoke at six with a splitting headache and feeling rather short of breath. The enemy appeared refreshed by their night's rest and were laying down a brisk and businesslike box barrage around the position of the Vickers gun, further up. When he relieved himself it was plain that his stomach had ample cause for complaint.

It had, however, stopped raining. There were no shells in their immediate area, a watery sunlight made the landscape glisten, and they could hear a bird singing.

Jamieson confessed himself a bit of an ornithologist and assured them it was a thrush. Mistle, probably. They made tea, and some porridge with oatmeal and biscuit. When they put the porridge pan down, the thrush appeared and perched on the rim, jauntily pecking at the remains and watching them with strangely knowing eyes. They all felt more optimistic.

It was the man that Jack had handed over to the previous night who remembered Lumm and went to wake him. He came back looking haunted.

'Sir—I think you'd better go and look at him.'

'Oh?' Jack got up. His uniform weighed a ton, and his head swam sickeningly for a moment.

'He's dead, sir. At least I'm pretty sure he's dead.'

'Good grief.' Jack stumbled into the look-out sap. As soon as he saw Lumm he knew the man was right. The mound under the gleaming wet cape looked just that: a mound. Full of dread he went over and pulled back the neck of the cape. Back in the dug-out the others laughed about something, as who should blame them? They were cheered because of the break in the rain, and the thrush, and the fact that the Boche had missed them last night.

He saw at once how Lumm had died, but all he could feel was relief. It was not his fault. Water running off the side of the sap had trickled into his open mouth and the boy had drowned.

'He's dead all right,' he said tersely, pulling the cape up over Lumm's face. 'Swallowed too much water.'

Leadenly, he went about the business of retrieving Lumm's pay book and other personal possessions. His turn now to write a stilted letter to Mum and Dad. They constructed a cross of sodden planks and buried him in watery sunlight at the back of the dug-out. During the frequent pauses in Jack's cobbled-together funeral service they could hear the thrush tap-tapping on the porridge pan.

The sense of time running out that had been with Jack since the beginning of the battle was stronger than ever. When they'd mumbled amen he stood there for a second, just too tired to move. To take one step would have been to upset his equilibrium and he would fall, never to rise again. His morale, his health, his spirits were at rock bottom. He prayed fervently that no more would be asked of him, for he could do no more. He had nothing left to say to anyone, nowhere to go. He would just have to stop here and hope someone would be kind enough to scrape him up.

When the sniper's bullet struck him it was the answer to his prayer. Such a clean, quick sound, and a sharp blow on the back of the right shoulder, pitching him face-first onto Lumm's makeshift grave.

He felt a profound sense of gratitude. So there was mercy after all. He lay there spreadeagled as Jamieson kneeled down beside him, making encouraging noises like a dorm prefect. His eyes closed. He felt the mud ooze between his outstretched fingers, and the grave yield like a cushion beneath his cheek. The mud no longer disgusted him. He embraced it, wanted nothing more than to sink down into its friendly depths and be covered up for ever. But as he moved eagerly toward unconsciousness he remembered Thea, for whom it would be worth surviving. And it was her face he saw, with torturing clarity, smiling with love and laughter as the dark curtain sank down to divide them.

CHAPTER NINETEEN

'My mind's made up,
I'm going to marry him!
He'll have to come to church,
If he won't, I'll carry him . . .'
Dan Leno—'I'll Marry Him'

Primmy could not have been more astonished to see her mother in Oak Ridge than if the Kaiser himself had called in for a chat. Mrs Dilkes was not one of those who moved about. She was the still point in the turning universe. Primmy had long been resigned to the fact that if she wanted to see her mother, she must go to her; it was a law of nature.

'Come in,' she said. It was a cold Sunday afternoon in late November and the post office was closed. Mrs Pett had taken the baby to a neighbour's for tea. 'You're lucky to find me here, it's the first Sunday I've had in weeks,' she added, with feeling. Yesterday had been non-stop with top brass down from the War Office for a medal ceremony, she had been on her feet for thirteen hours solid, and on duty again this morning from eight until dinner-time. She had been really looking forward to this afternoon off, and it wasn't often she could honestly say that.

'I'd've seen you anyway,' declared Mrs Dilkes, stepping over the threshold with a martial air. 'I'd've come to the hospital.'

'I'm not available when I'm on duty, Ma,' said Primmy firmly, leading her mother through into the back passage and opening the kitchen door. 'Would you like some tea?'

Mrs Dilkes hung back, stiff and severe in her rusty black coat, topped incongruously by the rose-trimmed hat that she had worn to the variety on Primmy's last trip to London. If Primmy had needed any further evidence of the importance of her mother's visit, the hat provided it.

'Don't you have a room of your own then?' she asked accusingly.

'Of course I do, but I thought—'

'And you're not going to invite me into it?'

'If that's what you want.'

'It's best.'

Primmy led the way upstairs. Mrs Dilkes came tramp, tramp, behind her. Primmy was a little put out that her mother had demanded to be taken to her room. At Oak Ridge she had enjoyed real privacy for the first time in her life and had acquired a taste for it, keeping her room as neat and austere as a hermit's cell. She even kept Mrs Pett at arm's length. On the other hand she knew exactly what had prompted Mrs Dilkes. She did not want to be found sitting in someone else's kitchen, drinking their tea, even if she did have a perfect right to be there. Such weighty matters as she clearly had to discuss were best brought out on the safest possible ground.

Primmy went in first. Seeing it now through someone else's eyes she realized it was not very homely, even though it was the way she liked it. The bedspread was so smooth it might have been hewn from marble, and the evidence of her habitation was scarce; hairbrush, dressing gown, slippers, wash things, a clean cap and apron hanging on the side of the wardrobe. There was a ladder-back chair next the chest of drawers and an ancient upholstered one by the fireplace. In front of the wrought-iron fender lay a wool rug made by Mr Pett's sister and given to them as a wedding present, patterned from perimeter to centre with ever-decreasing circles, each a different colour. Aside from these basic furnishings Mrs Pett had put in one or two things before Primmy's arrival to make things a bit nicer and more welcoming: a bowl of dried lavender on the window-sill; a photograph of the Oak Ridge cricket team, with Mr Pett in the front row; and a painting of a sheepdog. All of these touches Mrs Pett had fondly imagined would make 'all the difference' to a lonely London girl, and she would have been cast down to know that Primmy actually disliked them. The lavender was in danger of being knocked off every time she opened the window and of the two pictures she did not know which got on her nerves most, Mr Pett with his beefy forearms, or the dog with its expression of mawkish trustiness.

'Sit down,' she said, almost sharply, indicating the upholstered chair. 'Now shall I make you some tea?' She knew she sounded surly and impatient, but she was acutely unsettled by her mother's presence.

'No thank you.' Mrs Dilkes lowered herself gingerly on to

the lumpy horsehair cushion. Primmy brought over the ladder-back chair and placed it on the other side of the rug.

'Well then. What brings you all this way?' she asked.

'I'm going back to London,' replied Mrs Dilkes. 'When he moves I'm going back to town.'

'But Mr Tennant is moving to London, isn't he?'

'Lewisham.' Mrs Dilkes sniffed. 'I'm not going with him.'

'I see.'

There was a pause. Having made the opening sally Mrs Dilkes obviously wished to have her tidings wrung from her.

'So what are you going to do then, Ma?' Primmy enquired dutifully. 'What about Eddie?'

'He'll be all right,' responded Mrs Dilkes cryptically. 'I've always done right by him, haven't I?'

'Yes you have. But where are you going?'

'Lisbeth and Jim are opening a new business in Clapham. They want someone to mind the old shop.'

'You?'

'Well, there'll be a manager of course, but there'll be plenty for me to do, and rooms over the shop.'

'For you and Eddie?'

'Eddie'll be all right,' repeated Mrs Dilkes.

Primmy didn't like the sound of it. Lisbeth and Jim? Why, Mrs Dilkes had never got on with her younger daughter and couldn't abide Jim, how could she even entertain the idea of working for them? At this distance, it was all crystal clear to Primmy. Lisbeth saw her mother at a relatively low ebb, chastened by the events of last Christmas, guilty and unsettled. An ideal opportunity to kill two birds with one stone; to get the old battleaxe firmly under their thumb and obtain cheap labour at the same time. A perfect, well-organized, and apparently charitable revenge.

'I don't think you should do that, Ma,' she said.

'My mind's made up. Service never suited me and I haven't felt right about it since . . . I just haven't been easy with myself. It's all settled. He moves beginning of January, and I'll go then.'

Primmy saw it was useless to object but at the same time her heart sank at the thought of what her mother was letting herself in for. And it was all on account of her stupid, pig-headed pride which made her feel she was under some obligation to quit Mr Tennant's household because of what Eddie had done. Primmy could not believe that Mr Tennant would have held such a thing against a simpleton, no matter how great the damage, and he certainly wouldn't blame Mrs Dilkes. Himself, more likely. Primmy was perfectly certain that her mother and Eddie would be safer, freer, happier, throwing in their combined lot with Mr Tennant than with the odious Jim Saunders.

She would have protested once more, but Mrs Dilkes's lips were set so thinly and tightly together that the protest sank back again, unspoken.

After an uneasy hiatus Mrs Dilkes picked up her large, battered black handbag which she had placed on the rug at her feet. Primmy, taking this to be the signal for her mother's departure, half-rose, but the handbag only travelled as far as Mrs Dilkes's narrow lap.

'I've got something for you.'

'Oh?' Not a Christmas present, surely? In the Dilkes family Christmas presents had only been given to children up to the age of ten, and then only when funds permitted.

'I found it—with all the packing up and clearing out.'

'Oh yes?'

Mrs Dilkes's cracked, purplish fingers clasped the top of the bag tightly. Suddenly, taking the bull by the horns, she opened the bag, dived in her hand and brought out a small object in a brown paper bag. This she handed, straight-armed, to Primmy while she herself continued to peer into the depths of the bag as if looking for something of far greater importance.

'Is this it?' Primmy removed the object from the bag. 'Well I never!' It was truly the last thing she had expected to see.

'You can have it.'

'I've always wanted it, did you know that? I looked for it that last time I came up to Grove Road.'

'It's yours now.' Sniff. 'I don't want the thing.'

Primmy gazed down at the picture of Lily: her mother as she used to be. Dad had told her to remember how pretty Lily was and she would be able to, now. 'Thanks, Ma.' She was touched.

'You don't have to thank me.'

'However did you come by it? Have you had it all along?'

'Certainly not.' Mrs Dilkes was appalled at the suggestion. 'It was in Miss Tennant's room.'

'But how did it get there?' Primmy shook her head in disbelief, still gazing down at the photograph.

'I asked him if it was all right to give it to you.'

'Well? Did Mr Tennant know where it came from?'

'Yes. As it happens.' Mrs Dilkes's mouth hardly moved as she spoke, she was in the grip of embarrassment.

'Go on then.'

'Mr Kingsley found it on a dead tramp over on his land.'

'A dead tramp?' Primmy's mind raced. 'What—Dad?'

'How should I know?' Lily's voice rose shrilly, her shoulders twitched. 'I only know what I've been told, that Mr Kingsley found it on this dead tramp and kept it, and Miss Tennant brought it back to clean it up for him.'

'But it must have been Dad! Who else would have it?' Of course it had been him. It was horrible that, dying alone and homeless and uncomforted, but still carrying the picture as a kind of talisman. Primmy felt they were all very much to blame, but most of all herself and her mother because they had known there was good in Dad but they had still put him out of their minds, shut him out of their lives, behaved as if he were dead from the moment he left the house in Grove Road. Good riddance, they'd said, and taken it as further evidence of a shiftless nature. But now she couldn't help wondering if he might not have had some grand scheme, some idea of going off and seeking his fortune and coming back rich and successful. That would have been more like him. But they would never know, because of course (and also typically) the scheme had failed and he had finished up on the road and sleeping rough, drinking when he could earn the cash and dreaming of better things.

'Poor Dad,' said Primmy.

'I don't know about *that,*' retorted Mrs Dilkes. 'What good did he ever do us?'

'He was kind.'

'He was no good.' Mrs Dilkes leaned forward and stabbed the air with her forefinger. 'No good!'

'You can't have thought that always, or you wouldn't have married him. He told me once you had lots of beaux, you could have chosen any of them.'

Mrs Dilkes stood up. This kind of bold, emotional talk was not for her. 'In that case,' she announced, 'I'll be going.' The 'I know when I'm not welcome' was strongly implied.

'Oh *Ma . . .*' Primmy stood too, trying to regain some of the initiative. 'Don't be like that. I just think we might as well think the best of Dad now he's dead.'

'I know what I think,' said Mrs Dilkes darkly, and headed smartly for the door. She would not even allow Primmy to accompany her to the bus stop, so anxious was she to get away. Primmy returned to her room with a depressing sense of failure. Her mother's visit had ruined the precious afternoon off and neither of them had come through it with much dignity.

She sat on the edge of the bed, staring at the picture of Lily and thinking of her father. The past loomed over her like the shadow of a pursuing ogre, dark and ugly and powerful, impossible to escape. Only the thought of going back on duty next morning helped her to keep it at bay. *That* was where she belonged now, that was her new, real world, and she must cleave to it with all her strength until the ogre finally gave up and went away.

Jack laid down his book and stared out of the window. His bed was at the end of the ward; he had a good view of the nursing home's extensive garden, now brown and sodden in the late English autumn. The muddy lawn was spattered with damp, yellow leaves, the sky cushiony with rain-filled clouds, the grey paths gleaming with puddles. Two boys walked haltingly down one of the paths, arm in arm and heads bowed like old men.

A nurse rustled along the ward, giving out letters. None for him, today, she remarked, with a cheer-up look on her face. But he wasn't bothered. He wanted as few disturbances as possible to the even tenor of his life. His wound had healed, but the circulation in his arm was poor, and giving cause for concern. He still had a good deal of pain, but he welcomed it. The pain, the well-defined physical problem, was a diversion, it prevented him from feeling too keenly other and worse kinds of pain. It was simply his duty to get better; his future was neatly circumscribed by this one necessity.

He had not been able to bring himself to repeat to Thea what he had tried to tell her after Venetia's funeral. He knew it was cowardice. Her misunderstanding of him probably meant that she could not conceive of him in that light, and would probably laugh in his face. No, she wouldn't do that; she would be all concern and understanding, which would be worse. Christ. He rolled onto his side, hurt his arm, cursed, and rolled the other way, pulling the bedclothes tight around him.

He had just let their correspondence peter out, using the big push at Passchendaele as an excuse. He had not even written to tell her of his return to England, horrified that it might look plaintive, attention-seeking. But at the same time he half-hoped that she would hear, perhaps from his parents or Ralph. He wanted her to know, he wanted her to care. But he *didn't* want her bloody sympathy!

He sat up and picked up his book again. There was no earthly good agonizing over it. He must put her out of his mind, concentrate on getting better and plan his now uncertain future.

The man in the next bed leaned over, grinning.

'Hey—Kingsley!'

'Mm?' Jack glanced at him discouragingly.

'Who's this Thea, then?'

'I beg your pardon?' Was the fellow a mind-reader?

'Thea—who is she? Own up, man!'

'I do know somebody called Thea . . .'

'You bet!' The man winked. 'The woman of mystery . . .'

'I'm sorry,' said Jack coldly, 'but I'm at a loss to know how you could have heard of her.'

'Simple, old man. You talk about her in your sleep every blasted night!'

It was not so much that Thea took a violent dislike to 5 Mapleton Road when she came back on leave in January 1918. Her strong streak of practicality told her the house in Lewisham was far better suited to her father's needs and present circumstances, and she told him this repeatedly in encouraging tones, aware that he knew already, and that it was herself she encouraged.

As a house, it was interchangeable with thousands of others built in and around the big cities about twenty years earlier: semi-detached, red-brick, on four floors, with a large basement and a long walled garden at the back dominated by a giant lombardy poplar at the far end. A mews, now converted into garages, ran along the backs of the gardens and served both Mapleton Road and the street that ran parallel to it, Cholmeley Avenue. The house was sound, conveniently situated and well appointed, and not without a certain honest bourgeois charm. All this Thea readily conceded. And yet she could not resign herself to the loss of Chilverton House. Like bereavement, it did not at this early stage seem real. Was she really never again to run up and down the wide stairs, or sit by the library fire, or look out of her bedroom windows in the early morning and see the rabbits nibbling warily at the edge of the Elm Walk? She could not believe it.

She wondered at the apparent ease with which Ralph had divested himself of his old life. But of course, the place had not been his home in the way it had been hers. He had never been a country squire, as he had said in his letter, and with Venetia gone there had been no particular reason to stay. The fire had given him the push he needed. He had sold the house to a charitable trust as a nursing home, disposed of the horses, the second car and a great deal of the furniture, and fled, taking only Mrs Duckham with him. When Thea enquired about Sophie he rolled his eyes to the heavens.

'I did my best, dear girl, you would have been proud of me. I exhibited patience above and beyond the call of duty.'

'In doing what?' Thea could not help smiling.

'In attempting to persuade her to come with me. God knows it was the last thing I wanted, but I tried.'

'And she refused?'

'Mercifully, yes. She was adamant. Even had the gall to suggest I was forcibly uprooting her from her home. *Her* home—'

'So where is she?'

'Sulking in a very pleasant cottage in Ewhurst, more than comfortably off with the money I've settled on her, and doubtless spreading scurrilous rumours about my character.'

They were unpacking books in the room Ralph had designated the drawing-room. Most of his favourites had been destroyed in the fire, and these were the rows of morocco-bound classics from the library in Chilverton House. Thea had a scarf knotted round her head, and an old shirt of Aubrey's over her dress, both of which lent her a faintly piratical appearance; Ralph was in his shirtsleeves, threadbare old pinstripe trousers and carpet slippers. He had put on some weight in recent months and his paunch made his red braces bulge outwards like brackets. A tray with their tea things on it stood on a stray table in the middle of the room and a neglected fire glowed in the grate.

Thea sat down in front of the fire with a sigh, and poked

the embers absently. She had detected a change in her father. Or perhaps it was just that he was now more himself than he had ever been. Severed from all those, and especially Venetia, who had influenced and modified his behaviour, his eccentricities had free rein. She surveyed him now, as he glared accusingly at the spines of innocent books, with a certain wariness. He was in a mood to let everyone, including himself, go hang.

'Do you think she put Eddie up to it?' she asked musingly, still stirring the coals with the tip of the poker.

'What's that? Do you suppose anyone's ever actually read this bilge?'

'I said, did Sophie put Eddie Dilkes up to it—the fire?'

He shrugged. 'I blame myself. She took the lad over, and they were both happy. Venetia was ill . . . The lad was simple, she taught him various jobs. It happened.'

'Poor Eddie.' Thea got up and went over to the tray to pour another cup of tea. 'Still, I suppose he'll like being in the shop with Mrs Dilkes.'

'Yes.' Ralph clumped an armful of volumes onto a shelf and dusted his palms on his trousers. 'As a matter of fact he's not going there.'

'Where then?'

'He's been committed.'

'I don't believe you.' She meant it.

'You'll have to. He's in the asylum in Southwark, near the works. Very well cared for, it's by far the best thing.'

Thea sat down with a bump on the step ladder. 'But how *could* you?'

'It wasn't my decision, dear girl. His mother felt it was the best thing to do, for his sake and hers. She exercised her prerogative in the matter, but I'm obliged to say I agreed with her.' He riffled the pages of *Ivanhoe,* raising a small cloud of dust. 'It was Mrs Dilkes's decision,' he said again.

'Yes, but what does she know?' Thea was impatient. 'She's a completely uneducated woman.'

'His mother, nevertheless.'

Thea brought her hands down with a thump on her knees in a gesture of frustration exactly like her father's. 'But you took him on, you accepted responsibility for him—what about that?'

'Correction. I was asked if I would take him in, and I did so.'

'Don't split hairs, it's the same thing. And now you've shuffled him off.'

'I have done no such thing!' Ralph slapped *Ivanhoe* down on the table, making the tea things jump and jingle. 'I have *not* "shuffled him off" Mrs Dilkes may have done, but then the wretched woman is entitled to some freedom after all these years. If I have to feel guilty about something it is for taking the boy in in the first place and subsequently failing to take a proper interest in him. He was uprooted from familiar surroundings and carted down to Kent where he instantly came under Sophie's influence—'

'But he was so much better, you all said so!'

'Indeed, indeed he was, and likewise we were all delighted to see the improvement from a distance It cost us nothing, and it kept my sister happy as well, what could be nicer? The fact was that after the fire he was a great deal worse. A *great* deal worse.'

'So when he deteriorated you gave up?'

Ralph came and stood over her. 'Are you trying to infuriate me?' The bottom button of his shirt was hanging by a thread. She snapped it off and handed it to him. He dropped it in the hearth.

'It's not like you to give up on someone,' she said more quietly. 'Did you tell Primmy?'

'I assume her mother has done so.'

'I bet she hasn't. I bet she feels as guilty as sin about it, and so she should.'

'God Almighty!' Ralph clapped his hands to his head and took a turn across the room. 'The boy is in the best possible hands! Go and see for yourself instead of trying to put me in a hair shirt!'

'I will!'

She went the next day. In retrospect she was not entirely certain why she had been so angry with Ralph. His course of action had been understandable under the circumstances, he had enough to deal with at present. She decided that a combination of factors had sparked off her attack on him: her own mental and physical tiredness, her inability to accept the new house as wholeheartedly as she should, the feeling of an old and treasured world gone for ever.

However, there was still enough righteous indignation left to prompt a visit She went up on the train after lunch, feeling frumpish and dowdy in her old-fashioned civilian clothes. A girl clippie gave her her bus ticket and there were girl porters in the stations at both ends. She refrained from buying a paper to read on the short journey, knowing that its bland half-truths would enrage her, but did purchase a quarter of coconut ice from the shop in the station arcade at Southwark.

It was bitterly cold and a north-east wind lashed her coat round her knees as she battled up Asylum Road at about half-past two. In a side street a Salvation Army band thumped and warbled optimistically. As she approached the asylum gates the coconut ice seemed to burn a hole in her pocket. How would that look? As if she were visiting a zoo? But he did like sweets, and it would serve as a clear and tangible evidence of good faith if words proved inadequate.

The asylum was a long, low, semi-circular building with a quite pleasing classical air. The wall between garden and street was not so high as to be forbidding and the garden itself was laid out with immaculate symmetry, gravel paths radiating out from a central round flowerbed, with further wedge-shaped beds in the interstices between the paths. The patchy winter grass was shaved almost to ground level, and the neatly raked beds set out with wallflower plants, each precisely equidistant from its neighbours.

She gave the porter her name and waited while he produced a book which she signed, and finally opened the gate and admitted her. She walked up the centre path somewhat self-consciously, feeling the many long, narrow windows watching her like eyes, but before she reached the main entrance she saw two nurses coming along the top path.

'Excuse me.' She approached them. 'I'm Thea Tennant. I was hoping to see Eddie Dilkes.'

One of the nurses smiled broadly. 'Miss Tennant? Mr Ralph Tennant's daughter?'

Thea was taken aback. 'That's right.'

'Eddie's in his shed, I'll show you.'

The nurse led the way along the left-hand branch of the top path, while her companion peeled off and disappeared through the main door. Their footsteps sounded brisk and solitary on the gravel, the wind snapped at their faces. Once, Thea caught sight of a pale, narrow face gazing from one of the upper windows, big sad staring eyes and an almost comically turned down mouth.

They continued round the side of the building, past what was clearly the kitchen entrance, marked by several over-flowing dustbins, loud voices behind a steamy window and a cat that streaked away at their approach. They emerged from the alley into a kitchen garden, about a quarter of an acre square, the far end of which was divided up into allotments. Jutting from the main building into the back garden was some sort of red brick annexe, a bathhouse possibly, with transom windows set high round the wall. In the angle between this annexe and the asylum proper was a large timber lean-to. The nurse went over to it and knocked.

'Eddie?'

There was no reply, but she smiled over her shoulder at Thea and went in. Thea followed. Eddie was standing at a workbench on the far side of the shed. He held a garden fork in his hand which he was clearly in the process of mending with a ball of twine, though not very successfully. The two halves of the fork joined at an uneasy angle and the twine was hopelessly knotted and tangled.

'Someone to see you, Eddie,' said the nurse loudly. 'Miss Tennant.'

'Hallo, Eddie.' Thea smiled encouragingly at him. He stared back without the smallest flicker of interest.

The nurse made to leave. 'When you want to go just come round to the main entrance and tell the nurse on duty, would you?'

'Yes, of course.'

The nurse went. Eddie stood there, still facing Thea, but transferring his attention back to the broken fork, breathing heavily. His nose ran a little. It was freezing cold in the shed.

'Well . . .' Thea looked about her. 'This is a good shed, I must say.'

Eddie sniffed richly, his mouth open in concentration. His tongue came out and partially cleared his upper lip. In spite of the apparent aggravation of his mucous membranes he looked well. He wore a charcoal-grey serge suit and a grey and red muffler, hand-knitted.

'I brought you something,' said Thea, diving her hand into her coat pocket and producing the coconut ice. 'There you are.'

He looked up as she held it out and stared at the gift for a moment before taking it and peering into the bag. He put in his finger and thumb and brought out a bright pink lump which he scrutinized minutely, holding it no more than four inches from his nose and squinting horribly, before popping it into his mouth.

'I hope you like that,' said Thea, watching his expression anxiously. For the very first time she felt a little nervous. The shed was claustrophobic, Eddie was so large, and so taciturn. What if he took violent exception to her visit? He was well over six foot and still clutching the garden fork in his right hand.

'Do you spend a lot of time in here?' she asked. 'Is it your shed, or do lots of you use it?'

'Work,' said Eddie, looking directly at her for the first time. 'Work here.' He put the bag of sweets on the table—he had no pockets in the suit, she noticed—and began fiddling once more with the recalcitrant twine. Thea wondered why she had come.

There was nowhere to sit in the shed, so she went to the far end of the table and leaned back on her hands against it. This was a bad move, for it was a trestle and tipped violently, sending the coconut ice and assorted seed trays and plant pots hurtling to the ground. Eddie took not the slightest notice.

'Heavens, I'm so sorry, what a clumsy thing I am . . .' Frantically she began picking up the things that had fallen, replacing the grubby coconut ice in the bag, re-stacking the plant pots, and gathering up handfuls of loose soil. When she finally got up again she was thoroughly hot and bothered but Eddie hadn't so much as glanced at her.

'How are you?' she asked, when she had regained sufficient composure. 'You look well.'

'Well.' It was more repetition than answer.

'That's good. Do you have a room of your own to sleep in?'

'Dormitory.'

'And nice food? What sort of things do you have to eat?'

'Treacle sponge.'

'What else?' She seemed to be gaining ground.

'Treacle sponge.' So much for that.

'What do you do all the time?'

'Work.'

'What, *all* the time?'

He nodded energetically, seemed to forget himself, and went on nodding for thirty seconds or so like a clockwork mandarin.

Thea stuck it out for another five minutes and then left. 'Goodbye, Eddie. I'm glad you're so well.'

He did not acknowledge her farewell in any way. Thea retraced her steps back up the kitchen alley and round to the main entrance. In the lobby she encountered the nurse who had taken her to Eddie, deep in conversation with another, in a grubby white overall. They stopped at her arrival and the nurse came over to her, grinning. She was a huge young woman, with square shoulders and big muscular arms.

'How was Eddie then?'

'He seemed fine.' She shrugged and smiled, baffled. 'He doesn't say much.'

'No, he's a doer, not a talker, our Eddie. Likes to be busy.'

'Does he have plenty of visits?'

'Oh yes, his mother comes about once a fortnight, and of course Mr Tennant comes every week.'

'My father? Does he really?' Thea was suitably impressed.

'Every Friday, early afternoon, round about dinner time.'

'I can't imagine what they find to say to each other.'

'Bless you, they don't talk!' The nurse laughed heartily at the suggestion. 'They work together, either in the shed or out in the garden. Happy as Larry. It was Mr Tennant suggested we give Eddie some gardening, you know.'

'No, I didn't know.'

'He's very concerned about Eddie, more so than the mother, I'd say.'

'I see.'

A bell clanged long and loud in some inner corridor. 'That's their tea time.'

'I must go then.'

Thea walked back down the path knowing that she owed Ralph an apology.

She gave it to him that evening as they sat eating cold beef and pickled beetroot off a gate-legged table in the drawing-room window.

'I'm sorry I lost my temper yesterday,' she said.

'You found Eddie well, I take it?' Ralph speared another slice of beef and addressed himself to it with gusto.

'Very well. He was working in his shed, mending a garden fork.'

615

'He's been mending that fork for weeks. There's not much to do out of doors at this time of year, you see.'

'No.' Thea studied him, not sure whether he intended his visits to the asylum to be secret or not. 'Anyway the main thing is that he has something constructive to do.'

'Exactly. He'll be all right.' Ralph placed his knife and fork together and sat back, slapping the generous expanse of shirt between his braces. 'Excellent beef.'

They didn't discuss Eddie again. Apparently Ralph had organized his small private penance to his own satisfaction.

They settled down over the next two weeks, working hard around the house and gradually establishing a new balance in their relationship. Ralph had given himself time off, and made only occasional visits to the works one of which, Thea noticed, was during Friday afternoon. He made one trip to Dolton Green, and she accompanied him, but it was a chastening experience. Aside from Mr Bailey there was scarcely a face she recognized. Many of the girls who had been there with her had been scared off munitions work by the terrible Silvertown explosion, and others, hardier and more ambitious, had gone in search of better things at Woolwich Arsenal where labour was getting organized. Thea could not wait to get away. Dolton Green was one of the very few areas of her past that she wanted utterly to forget. Its associations were uniformly unpleasant—exhaustion, depression, failure, conflict.

After the initial skirmish with Ralph she found herself enjoying their new, and more equal, friendship. She no longer had the slightest compunction over criticizing him, and he accepted her criticism quite affably. They laughed, and argued and conferred and conversed, gently easing their way into their new partnership. They liked doing things together, going shopping, playing draughts, putting pictures up only to take them down again and put them up somewhere else. They ate gluttonous scratch meals amid the crates and dust sheets, with dirty hands and aching legs, making an effort every third night or so for Mrs Duckham's sake, changing for dinner and eating three courses at the dining-room table. Thea knew that such goings-on would have been unthinkable in her mother's household, but salved her conscience by telling herself that she and Ralph had to establish a *modus vivendi* which suited them, if they were to order the future Also—but this was a notion she only admitted to herself last thing at night before going to sleep—she kept busy to prevent herself wondering why Jack Kingsley had not written for months.

It was Maurice, quiet, peace-loving Maurice, who unintentionally, and not for the first time, put the cat among the pigeons. Afterwards, he was to reflect gloomily that he seemed doomed always to stir up trouble from the very best of motives.

He turned up, unannounced and unexpected, one evening when Thea and Ralph had finished their supper and were sitting rather sleepily by the drawing-room fire. The house parlourmaid had gone off duty, and Thea answered the door.

At first she quite literally could not believe her eyes.

'Maurice?'

'Hallo, Thea.'

'Is that really *Maurice*?' She stepped back, open-mouthed and watched as he edged somewhat apologetically into the hall, pulling his nose with his finger and thumb as if wishing to extend its length by a couple of inches.

She closed the door and leaned back against it. 'It *is* you, isn't it?'

'I think so.'

'Maurice!' She could not think of anybody, except one, whom she would have been more pleased to see, and 'even that one would have brought with him elements of tension and anxiety. This was pure childish pleasure, a piece of the past restored. She flung her arms round him and rocked to and fro in a kind of dance. When she released him, his spectacles had slid halfway down his nose.

She took his hand and led him into the drawing-room. 'Father! Look what I've got!'

Ralph turned. 'Well, I'll be damned! Maurice!'

'Uncle . . .'

They sat him down on the sofa and took up positions on either side of him, fascinated and delighted, scarcely able to take their eyes off him. Thea in particular kept her hand on his arm as if to remind herself that he was real.

'You make me feel like someone back from the dead.'

'Well, you are in a way, aren't you?' She laughed delightedly. 'Nobody's heard anything since you were moved to Winchester. What have you been doing? How are you? Where are you living? How dare you keep us all in the dark for so long?' She laughed again to show she meant nothing.

'My dear fellow, have a whisky.'

'I won't, thank you, Uncle.'

'Brandy then? Warm you up on such a filthy night.'

'No thank you, honestly.'

'Mind if I do?'

'Please, do.'

Ralph got up to pour himself a whisky and Thea peered into Maurice's face. He looked much the same, thin, gentle, studious, and yet there was a difference. He appeared a little harder, there were lines around his mouth that had not been there before, and this hardness was accentuated by a severely short prison haircut.

'We've been worried to death, you know,' she said.

'I was myself at one stage.' He smiled a little ruefully.

'Was Dartmoor frightful?'

He shook his head. 'Not bad at all really. Nothing like so bad as the military camp in France.' He turned to Ralph, who had sat down again on the other side of him, glass in hand. 'You see, we were able to stop repeating the crimes we'd been imprisoned for, it was such a relief. At Le Havre we were just continually in the punishment barracks, it was ludicrous.'

'I can hardly believe you've been through all this,' said Thea softly.

'Neither can I, sometimes. But there was nothing brave about it, I couldn't have done anything else.'

'I'm afraid you chaps have been shockingly maligned and ill-treated.' Ralph frowned. 'But you've stuck to your guns wonderfully.'

'It wasn't so difficult. Most of the time we were in a group, and that made it easier. At one stage they split us up, but it didn't work so they put us back together again. And of course once we were back in the civil prisons in England we knew the debate was hotting up. It was only a matter of time before we were offered some course of action we could take with dignity, all we had to do was stick it out.'

'The Home Office scheme?'

'That's right. I'm on the War Victims' Relief Committee now. Perfectly respectable,' he added, with gentle irony.

'And how did you track us down?'

'I went to Kent to see Mother. Er . . .' He paused, drawing his brows together. 'She wouldn't speak to me. But since I was down that way I took a cab over to see the Kingsleys and they put me in the picture.'

'Blasted woman,' muttered Ralph, referring to Sophie.

'She can't help it, she doesn't understand.'

'Where are you living?' asked Thea. 'Can't you come here?' It struck her suddenly that Maurice and her father might make a successful team. They were different enough not to aggravate one another, but liked each other sufficiently well to rub along.

Maurice smiled bashfully. 'I don't think so . . .'

'You can if you like,' said Ralph, guardedly.

'No. That is to say, it's extremely kind of you, but I do have rooms in Malet Street with a friend. It suits me better to be fairly central.'

'Of course, of course.' Ralph nodded enthusiastically. 'But now you're back in the world, so to speak, you will come and see us—me—from time to time?'

'Certainly I shall.'

'Maurice . . .' Thea picked up a battered velvet cushion and began playing with the braid that edged it. 'Did you go to Chilverton House?'

'Well yes, I did, because you see I didn't know you'd moved and—'

'What was it like?'

'Oh—just the same.'

'Who was there?'

'I didn't go in. I met old William in the garden, grumbling like mad, obviously well. I didn't hang about.'

'It wasn't all full of nurses, and so on?'

'It didn't seem to be. I imagine it takes some time to convert a place like that.'

'Yes, I imagine it does.'

Ralph got up to pour himself another whisky. 'She's determined to make herself miserable. Talk about something else would you, Maurice, there's a good chap.'

Maurice glanced at Thea, but she seemed wholly absorbed in demolishing the braid, thread by thread. He cleared his throat, and then said in a conversational tone: 'Have you been to see Jack Kingsley then, Thea?'

'Jack Kingsley . . . no. How do you mean?' She didn't understand him. Her cheeks were rather red.

'I just wondered if you'd seen him since he got back, down at this place in Sussex.'

'What place?' Thea looked at him sharply, and across at Ralph who seemed to be having a terrible time introducing the whisky into the glass.

The sensation began to dawn upon Maurice that he had unsuspectingly blundered into a minefield. As always, the small measure of self-confidence acquired through his recent trials disappeared when confronted with a problem on a more social and domestic scale. 'I'm awfully sorry—' he blurted. 'I assumed that you knew . . . Have I said something—'

'Knew what?' Thea had picked up the scent and was closing fast.

'Knew that he was wounded back at the end of the summer, Passchendaele. He's in this convalescent home outside Chichester, you *must* have known.' He heard his voice clattering on in confusion. No, clearly Thea did not know. Ralph was standing over by the window staring intently at the pattern on the closed curtains.

'I didn't know.'

'Oh. Well, that's it. He's up and about, apparently, but not A1 yet; there's some risk of infection or something, I don't understand these things.'

'I see.' Thea transferred her gaze to Ralph's backview. 'Father, did you know this about Jack?'

Ralph turned round, coughing mightily, slapping his chest. 'Yes.'

Maurice sat wretchedly between them. Everything spoilt, and by him, as usual. But Thea, bless her, slipped her hand into his, guessing how he felt.

'Thank you for telling me,' she said. 'I shall go and see him.'

'Sorry. Didn't realize . . .' Maurice was nearly speechless with mortification.

'Of course you didn't. Now you must tell us properly all about what you've been doing.'

He looked her in the eye. 'Actually, I must go.'

'But you've only been here five minutes!' She held fast to his hand.

'Nevertheless. It's late and I've a long way to go. I'll come again.'

'Promise?'

'Promise' He stood up.

'And next time you'll stay, and tell us all about everything.'

'I'll stay—I don't know about the other . . .' He began to shuffle crabwise in the direction of the door. 'I don't terribly like talking about myself, as you know.'

'We know, we know.' Ralph came over to him, hand extended. 'I can only say how jolly nice it is to have you back in the fold, so to speak. Don't disappear again if you can possibly help it.'

'I won't.' Maurice shook the hand. 'Goodnight, Uncle.'

Thea came with him to the front door. In the dark hall he turned to her, his face contorted with anxiety.

'Thea, I'm—'

She put up her hand. 'It's perfectly all right. I'm very glad to know.' She managed a wry little laugh. 'You are a funny soul to let such a thing upset you after all you've been through.'

'It's the kind of thing that does upset me . . . always has done.'

'You're a love. Don't ever change.' She knotted his scarf round his throat and tucked the ends into his jacket. 'Don't you have a proper coat?'

'I suppose so, somewhere, I forgot to bring it.'

'I think we have a trunk full of your things in the basement. Next time you come we—well, we must have a rummage. If I'm here, that is.'

'Yes.' He took a cap out of his pocket and put it on his head.

She felt it with her hand. 'That's wet.'

'Is it?'

'Idiot.' She opened the door. 'Go along as quick as you can, and put those damp things to dry when you get back.'

'I will.'

She watched from the doorway as he walked up the road, skipping and sidestepping puddles. He looked like a schoolboy, frail and slight, hands in pockets, his cap rather too large on his narrow, close-cropped head. As she closed the door she heard him cough as he rounded the corner. Her affection and admiration for him were boundless.

But when she re-entered the drawing-room her face was bleak. 'Well?'

Ralph stood legs astraddle before the fire, clasping his third whisky.

'Why didn't you tell me about Jack?'

'I was putting it off.'

'But I go back to France the day after tomorrow, how long were you putting it off *for?*'

'I don't know.' He drained the remains of his drink and set the glass down on the mantelpiece.

Thea sat down on the sofa facing him, legs crossed, arms folded. 'You'd better tell me now then.'

'I don't know all that much   he got crocked in this Ypres fiasco—'

'Crocked?' It was unlike Ralph to use jargon terms, she recognized it as a measure of his unease. 'What do you mean, crocked?'

'Caught one in the back, apparently.'

'In the back?' She was confused. 'But—in the back?'

'Honour intact, dear girl, it was a sniper. Six inches to the left and that would have been that, Robert tells me.'

'How bad was it?'

'I'm not clear on that point. I mean he's up and about, I gather, but still not A1, and as Maurice says they're keeping him there because of this circulatory problem. He wasn't at all well when he first came back, bad case of dysentery.'

Thea remembered the 'medicals', their shame and discomfort, their terrible depression. Poor Jack. 'Where is he?'

'Sussex, outside Chichester. It's called . . Burleigh Park, something like that.'

Thea got up and went over to him, confronting him, with her arms still folded. 'It was unpardonable of you to keep it from me.'

'I was going to tell you.'

'When it was too late!' she shouted. She was furious, without altogether knowing why; it wasn't that serious a crime Why was she so touchy?

'. . . lucky it wasn't fatal,' Ralph was muttering a bit sheepishly. 'As it is he'll be as right as rain—'

'It's not that! Oh God, you don't understand . . .' She pressed her hands over her eyes. Her emotions had raced away with her and she was not quite able to keep pace with them. She felt Ralph's arm round her shoulders and turned a little towards him, acknowledging her unreasonableness.

'As a matter of fact, I do,' he said quietly.

She looked up.

'I do understand, dear girl All too well, and better than

you yourself I shouldn't be surprised. And being a notoriously selfish fellow I thought I'd monopolize you for as long as I could.'

She couldn't bring herself to answer him. She hated his honesty almost more than his evasion, for it carried with it a direct demand on her affections which she could not unreservedly meet. That, at least she now knew.

The next day she got up early, breakfasted alone and was heading out of town in the Lanchester by half-past eight. She had telephoned the Kingsleys late the previous evening, and they had been remarkably pleasant considering she had clearly got them out of bed, and said of course she must go and see Jack, it would do him more good than anything, and they were going to enjoy having him at home for a while. Did she, they enquired earnestly, coming as she did fresh from the theatre of war, know whether it would all end soon?

Fond as she was of Daphne and Robert she had experienced a rising impatience with their ageing fussiness and told them quite crisply that she was no more privy to the decisions of the War Cabinet than they, and that most of her time in the theatre of war was divided between driving up and down a monotonous stretch of road in a draughty ambulance, and playing *vingt-et-un* with her room-mate.

It was 20 January and the icy rain of last night had given way to sparkling winter sunshine. The dour brown fields and tangled black hedges seemed to breathe more easily beneath its unseasonal caress, and the road gleamed before her as she sped along. The activity of driving caused her spirits to rise, she was full of energy and purpose, free to do as she wished, to sweep aside muddle and restraint and liberate the truth.

But as she approached Bury Park her confidence deserted her. As the car slowed down so her exuberance flickered and died. She had not considered what she would do or say, she had acted on instinct and had not the least idea how she would be received. What if he quite simply did not want to see her? Or was not well enough? Or not available? And if she did see him, then what? She could be about to make the most dreadful mistake.

She sat in the car for about five minutes wrestling with her anxieties. More than anything she felt foolish. First Eddie, now this; why must she always blunder in, take things into her own hands, not allow others their secrets and their reservations?

But in the end she got out and began walking slowly to the front door. She saw it like this: the worst periods in her life had been those when she had acted in contradiction to her natural promptings. Others might hang back, but what was to be gained by her doing the same? You could only be yourself, it was all you had, even if it did mean risking humiliation and defeat.

She kept on telling herself these things as she pushed open the door and entered the hall. It was cool and dark and smelt of polish. On a big round table in the centre of the hall stood piles of magazines, a visitors' book with a pencil on a string, and a white china bowl with mauve hyacinths in full bloom. It was a little like Chilverton House and she took courage from the fact. Through a glass door opposite she had an impression of a long, sunny room and a garden beyond.

A nurse came rustling briskly from a corridor on the left, smiling interrogatively.

'Yes? Can I help you?'

'Look, I'm afraid I didn't ring or anything, I feel rather . . .'

'Who did you want to see?' The nurse was patient, practised.

'Major Kingsley, Major Jack Kingsley. Would that be all right? My name is Thea Tennant, I'm an old friend.'

'Let me see . . .' The nurse consulted a notebook. 'Ah yes, Major Kingsley, Churchill Ward. Would you wait there for a moment, Miss Tennant, and I'll see what the situation is. Sign the book, please.'

She rustled away. Thea signed. The scribble of the pencil, a clock ticking, the small sounds were sharp in the silence. All this ordered tranquillity, and she was breaking it.

The nurse returned with another, older woman in the darker blue dress of Matron. 'Perhaps you could have a word with Matron, Miss Tennant.'

'I'm sorry for turning up like this, Matron, but I have to go back to France tomorrow and I didn't know until yesterday that Major Kingsley was here. Do you think I might see him for a little while?'

'Certainly.' Matron looked somewhat baffled by Thea's stream of self-excuse. 'He's in the reading room. It might have been different if he'd still been in bed, we do have proper visiting hours you know. Come this way, would you?' Before Thea could unleash another torrent of apologies she led the way down the corridor. Thea's heavier shoes clumped loudly on the linoleum.

They turned into a big, sunny room set out and furnished rather like the lounge of a country hotel, with chintz-covered armchairs, flowered curtains, a fire burning in a brick fireplace and a couple of desks with writing paper and blotters. On the far side of the room was a kind of glassed in loggia, with about half a dozen wicker chairs and a number of potted plants on a wooden table. Beyond the loggia an expanse of impeccable green lawn stretched away to a clipped laurel hedge.

There were four men in the room. Three of them, including one in a wheelchair, sat round the fire, talking quietly. They looked up as Matron opened the door; Thea thought they were probably disappointed to see it was her, and not somebody for them. She smiled, and they smiled back.

The fourth man sat in the loggia, with his back to them.

'There's Major Kingsley.'

'Thank you.'

'Shall I leave you to it?'

'Please. I think it's best.'

Matron bestowed a kindly look on her. 'Not too long. An hour or so.'

'Yes, of course.'

Matron went out and closed the door.

Jack sat leaning forward with his elbows on his knees, reading a newspaper. He wore the blue hospital shirt and trousers familiar to Thea from Quatre Pins, and a sleeveless cricket sweater, his own. The shirt and trousers looked rather too large and he had rolled the sleeves of the former back as far as the elbow. A fat marmalade cat appeared from beneath the plant table and jumped up on the arm of the chair, rubbing its cheek on his shoulder and pressing its flank passionately against him. At Thea's approach the cat jumped down rather huffily and stalked away, its tail waving airily above its short, bloomered legs. Jack turned the page of the paper—yesterday's, she noticed—and gave it a little shake to straighten it.

She had been watching him so closely that when he looked

up she started guiltily as if surprised in some shameful indulgence.

'Hallo, Jack,' she said. 'I came to see you.'

Jack read the war news with weary detachment. It was hot in the reading-room, with the winter sun pouring through the glass, and he could scarcely keep his eyes open. The Matron's marmalade tom jumped up soundlessly onto his chair and began to flirt and fawn, emitting a droning purr like a giant bumblebee. It was a fat cat, a scrounger, and Jack ignored its blandishments. In the end it jumped down, piqued, and marched away with its nose in the air. Jack gave the paper a shake. Good riddance. When a shadow fell across the corner of the page he looked up quickly, startled.

'Hallo, Jack, I came to see you.'

She looked so exactly as he had last pictured her that it took his breath away, it was almost as if he had conjured her up through sheer longing.

'Hallo, Thea.' He stood up, dropping the paper on the chair as he did so. He couldn't think of a damn thing to say to her. His life in recent months had been so utterly tranquil that his emotional as well as his physical energies, had become wasted with disuse. He felt weak and slow, unable to respond as he would like.

'How are you?' she asked. 'I mean, really?'

'Not bad. Really. A bit shaky, you know. . . .'

The marmalade cat jumped up into another chair and settled there, tucking its paws beneath its fluffy chest and surveying them with drowsy disdain. Thea went over and scratched it beneath the chin with her finger.

'Whose cat?'

'Matron's. An accomplished freeloader.'

Thea laughed. 'Cats are. It seems to have claimed that chair. Shall we sit where we can see the garden?'

'Wherever you like.'

On the far side of the plant-table was an ancient and battered leather-covered chesterfield which afforded a good view of the grass, and the box hedge and two men playing catch with a tennis ball. They sat down there and he felt her eyes on him like hands that sought, and missed nothing. He had been so insulated in the cocoon of routine and safe dullness that his skin flinched under the directness of her look.

'Where were you hit?' she asked.

'Here.' He put up his left hand and clasped the fingers over his right shoulder. 'Just at the back, above the shoulder blade.'

'Actually that one does look rather angular,' she commented, scrutinizing it.

'Yes, it's wasted. It looks even more peculiar undressed, I can tell you—comes to a kind of sharp point.'

'I wouldn't have noticed if you hadn't told me,' she reassured him. 'Does it still hurt much?'

'It complains from time to time. But the main problem is the circulation.' He stretched his arm out in front of him and flexed the fingers. 'It hasn't come back as it should, and I don't have much grip in this hand. I shan't be going back.'

'That's good news—' She looked at him questioningly, not quite sure if he saw it that way too.

'Yes, it is. I'd reached the end of my tether.'

'Then I'm glad for you.'

He looked at her. He was overwhelmed by her untutored, uncompromising beauty that managed not only to transcend her ill-fitting pre-war clothes but actually to be enhanced by them. Her curly hair had grown again almost to shoulder-length and she had attempted to put it up in a chignon, but it had wilfully escaped and gone its own way. As he looked she put up a hand and did something quite ineffectual with one or two loose ends that hung just behind her ear, glancing at him as she did so with an apologetic grin.

'Same old·problem. I must have it cut again.'

He wanted to tell her how utterly beautiful she was, exactly at that moment, that there was no need to do a thing to make herself smarter, or more pleasing, that he wanted to put his face against her untidy hair and breathe it in, and feel her skin with his mouth and her body with his hands. But he stayed silent, eaten up with jealousy of all the men who had seen her since he had last seen her, even those she drove in her ambulance, and those by the fire in this very room who had watched her come in. And he felt himself a cold, closed unlovable being next to her, the sort of creature she could never care for.

The two men on the lawn finished their game of catch, one of them pocketing the tennis ball, and began to walk in their direction. Thea realized they were going to come in by the garden door. They did so, bringing with them a rush of cold air and the sudden nearness of their red cheeks and muddy shoes. They were talking loudly and cheerfully.

'Hallo, Jack,' one of them said and glanced amiably at Thea, awaiting an introduction. But Jack just nodded curtly and they went off through the reading room, rebuffed.

'You know them?'

'Oh I know everyone.' He was sarcastic.

'You weren't very polite,' she reproved.

'Well,' he turned a hard stare on her, 'did *you* want to talk to them?'

'No—if I'm honest.'

'Right then.'

She felt his sudden black mood claiming him, taking him away from her. She had to pull him back.

'Jack . . .' He turned that hard look on her again and she had to struggle to find the words. 'I didn't just come out of politeness.'

'I never supposed you had,' he said, still brusquely, but with affection too. 'That wouldn't be at all your style.'

'No, but . . .' She didn't want to have her speech deflected by humour, either. She possessed herself of his hand and held it in both hers, staring down at it as though it could help her say and do the right thing. 'I came because of something you said to me, ages ago, after Mother's funeral.'

'Oh, that.' He looked at his imprisoned right hand as if it didn't belong to him. 'Forget it.'

'No, I won't. I was too stupid to see what you meant.'

'I meant nothing. Not a thing.'

'Don't say that!' Her voice rose and she lowered it again hastily. 'I came all this way to say I know what you were telling me, and to give you my answer.'

'Thea, I wish you wouldn't . . .' He turned his head away and tried to free his hand but she wouldn't let him. She must be herself, that was it, not play the game by his rules, but by her own. She had come thus far, she must continue.

She stretched out her right hand and turned his averted face to hers. 'I love you, Jack,' she said. She had not realized until the moment she said it just how much she meant it.

'I love you,' she said again, just for the joy of it.

She leaned forward and with a delicate, almost sacramental concentration, placed her lips to his. The feel of his mouth and of his cheek beneath her hand contained the special wonder of objects familiar, but never so much appreciated as when they are thought lost, and then regained. She knew the look of him so well, he had been there in her life for so long, and yet to touch him in this new and deliberate way was wholly strange and sweet. Times without number their cheeks had bumped in friendly, casual kisses, their hands had joined and their arms linked, and yet she knew she had never touched him before.

She drew back, her hand still against his face. She was shaking. 'I love you,' she said for the third time. They seemed to be the only words her brain could formulate or her lips could speak. She would go on saying them until he believed her.

He stared into her eyes, glancing from one to the other as if suspecting treachery. 'You have to mean it, Thea.'

'I mean it.'

She slipped her arm around his neck and he drew her towards him with a little sigh. Thea had the sense of coming home, of reaching a blissful and longed-for haven after a journey of unimaginable hardship. There was no more to say. They could do nothing but press together like some weird two-headed, four-legged animal, while the marmalade cat wreathed their ankles with sensuous figures-of-eight.

They scarcely spoke until it was time for her to go. They could neither of them believe their luck, nor the awfulness of having to part. The genteel, chintzy hush of the reading-room imbued their embraces with a forbiddenness which made them shake with laughter, so that Jack had to stifle Thea's face against his shoulder. They were awed by this new right granted to them: the right to each other. Overawed, for words utterly deserted them, and they could do no more than hold each other close and promise themselves more and better things another time.

But when? Panic overcame them when Thea had to go. Laggardly they trailed across the now-empty room, stopping, kissing, stretching time by agonizing inches.

'Do you have to go?' he asked desperately. 'You could stay for lunch, people do.'

'I can't. I have to be on the boat train at eight tomorrow and I haven't even packed. No, that's not it. I couldn't bear to share you with all those strangers.'

'I know.'

They stopped again in the corridor. 'We are going to get married, aren't we?'

'Yes.' She nodded vigorously. 'I love you.' The words were a mnemonic, reminding her it was true. The corridor grew shorter in front of them. 'Where will you go—after here?' She was terrified of losing him.

'Long Lake for a while. But, Thea, there are things I want to do, I've done a lot of thinking. If I went abroad when the war's over . . . would you come?'

'Of course I'd come, what do you think?'

'It would be a long way.'

'Anywhere.'

They reached the hall. The little nurse who had welcomed Thea was sitting at the desk, writing something, self-effacing and discreet.

They held hands, tightly.

'I'll come back,' she said, 'as soon as I can.'

'How long will it take?'

'I don't know, but I'll be as quick as I can. Will you speak to Father?'

'Yes.'

'He knows anyway.'

The luncheon gong boomed tremulously in some distant corridor and a faint whiff of fish wafted through the hall.

'I'd better go . . .' The nurse, the soul of tact, rose and rustled away. 'Goodbye.' She kissed him, in tears now. 'I can't bear this, I can't bear it!'

He held her so close she could feel every bone in his body, he kissed her wet cheeks and smoothed back the hair from her face. 'Don't cry. There's nothing to cry about.' He was unconvinced.

'No, I know . . .' He foraged for a hankie and passed it to her.

'Think of next time,' he said. The thought of it made him kiss her again, on her neck where he had always wanted to kiss her.

She pushed him away, pressing the crumpled hankie into his hands. 'Go on, let's go at the same time. I don't want to feel I'm leaving you.'

'All right.'

They walked away from each other. But they both cheated, and looked back at the last minute. He saw her in the doorway, tender, tear-stained, dishevelled, gripping his heart like a vice. And she saw him with his hands thrust in his pockets—fists clenched, she knew—watching her go with a passionate intensity while the gong boomed imperiously a second time.

CHAPTER TWENTY

'We all go the same way home—
All the collection in the same direction,
All go the same way home,
So there's no need to part at all.
We all go the same way home—
Let's be gay and hearty, don't break up the party,
We'll cling together like the ivy on the old garden wall.
        The Great Macdermott- 'Sweethearts and Wives'

As soon as Thea obtained her discharge she wrote to Jack.
For three months she had fretted and fumed, unable to
concentrate properly on her work and hating herself because
of it. Her impatient, disjointed letters had streamed across
the Channel in volleys, sometimes two in one day, imperiously demanding to know how he spent his time, remorse-
fully chastising herself for a jealous, possessive female,
beseeching his forgiveness, asking again if he thought of her.
And his returned like homing pigeons to soothe her, and tell
her over and over again that he loved her, and was waiting
for her.

To make matters worse the spreading stain of the Luden-
dorff offensive was creeping inexorably over the long-fixed
boundaries of the Western Front, creating salients that
stretched like grasping fingers into Allied territory and
clawed at Paris. In the course of the offensive the German
army had made the greatest advances of the entire war but
ironically, in so doing, they also restored the war of
movement and revitalized the opposition. Allied reserves
could be sent up more speedily by train than the German
infantry could advance on foot. Tempted by success, Luden-
dorff pushed his army too hard. Exhausted by their own
offensives they were further dispirited by the spectacle of
seemingly endless reserve troops and plentiful supplies being
poured into the Allied defence. There was a feeling abroad
that the war could not be won, that it must end as indeed it
already had done on the Eastern Front where the former
combatants were now wrestling just as fiercely with the

intricacies of peace-making. There was mutiny, too, in the air. If the Somme had killed the bright bird of patriotism the mud of Passchendaele had drowned the faithful old dog, duty. There were instances of whole battalions refusing orders, of drunkenness on a massive scale, of an unhealthy tendency for men to behave like men and not soldiers. Thea noticed it in those she took in her ambulance. An innocence, which she only recognized now it had gone, was replaced by truculence and the delight at going home had an edge to it—glee over having in some way beaten the system.

The mood was catching, and in Thea's case aggravated by her all-consuming longing to get back to Jack. The war seemed a tiresome nuisance, dragging her back when she wanted to be free, to be with him—and then she'd see the 'tumbril', jam-packed with makeshift coffins on its way to the cemetery and she would wonder what had happened to her that she'd become so callous and selfish.

It was in such a mood that she wrote her succinct letter to Jack, at the beginning of May. *'My love—on 1 June I'll be free! But all of a sudden I can't wait till then, I want to see you soon and convince myself it's all real. When I'm with you I know all my feelings are right and I know where I belong, and I need that knowledge now. If I get a twenty-four hour pass could we meet in, say, romantic Dover? I shall probably just gaze and gaze, and you will have to put up with it. It's terribly important to me. Thea.'*

He replied with a wire: *'Just say when. Gaze away. Jack.'*

She got the pass, from an understanding but faintly reproving Miss Courtney, and went over to Dover on the leave ship on 10 May. She stood on deck the whole way, straining her eyes for the first glimpse of the white cliffs, elated by the rough sea, and the wind that whipped her hair back from her face, and the jubilant mood of the men who crowded the rail with her. She spotted him right away, standing on the crowded quay but looking characteristically aloof in spite of the crush all round him. He looked elegant and countrified in a tweed suit, his right hand in his pocket, his left holding his cap which he tapped against the side of his leg as he scanned the boat, looking for her.

She waved frantically, her arm just one stalk among the forest of arms, and called his name; miraculously he saw her, and from that moment it was as if they threaded their way towards each other hand over hand along some invisible rope that joined them, weaving and sqeezing through the crowd until they were in each other's arms. In contrast to the serene hush of the reading-room at Bury Park which had so stifled and inhibited their last meeting, here they had the anonymity afforded by the crowd, the perfect privacy of a jostling, uninterested throng.

When they could bear to release each other he took her to his car. As he got in beside her he said: 'I take it you have no objection to being Mrs Kingsley? I mean, for today?'

'None.'

'Good.' He smiled to himself as he pulled on his cap and started the car.

He was staying at a small hotel right on the prom, below the castle. They had lunch in the hotel dining-room, at a table in the window. They could watch the grey sea racing in the harbour and the stalk-legged gulls perching on the barbed wire along the sea wall.

'It's a funny feeling, Dover,' she said. 'Almost half in France.'

'I know what you mean.'

They hardly talked, except that once, as he lit a cigarette over coffee, he remarked, 'I see you're catching up on the gazing!' And grinned at her.

'I told you I would.'

He laid his right hand down, palm uppermost, on the white cloth, waiting for hers, and when she placed hers in it he said something odd.

'I can't hold you tight with that hand,' he said, folding the fingers as far as they would go. 'You will just have to stay of your own accord.'

She let her hand lie in his until he had finished his cigarette and her coffee had gone cold.

Then he stood up. 'Coming?'

She nodded. They left the dining-room, Jack asking for lunch to be put on his bill, Room 15. At the desk he asked for the key with complete composure. The receptionist didn't spare them a second glance as they walked up the stairs, being inured to the necessarily concentrated meetings of married couples with only a short time to spend together.

Room 15 was a double. Small, neat, characterless. A black Bible on the bedside table, a white lace runner beneath the glass top of the chest of drawers, a ferociously laundered but somewhat frayed white handtowel with 'Hotel Esplanade' embossed in one corner. The room was at the back of the hotel and from the window they could see the backyard, with dustbins, and a small park where children were playing and shrieking.

He locked the door and laid the key down on the chest of drawers. He came over to her and stood facing her, very close but not touching. 'Thea . . .? This is right, isn't it?'

In reply she put her arms round him. 'Absolutely right.' She wanted him so much it was almost a pain, but some remembered anxiety warned caution, so she stayed still, put herself in his hands.

He began to undo her blouse, clumsily with his still unpractised left hand, and as he did so she stood quietly, watching his face. His expression was intent. The first time she had ever met him he had looked just so as he wiped her cheek with his handkerchief. That look of intense concentration was typical of him. But now there was also a glint of honest relish in his eyes which excited her. She was suddenly sure that shame had no place here. It was truly her that he loved and wanted, Thea Tennant as she was, body and soul, her instinct had been right.

Quickened by desire she began to undo his tie but their fiddlings and fumblings and especially his one-handed slowness got in the way and they began to undress themselves, still close together and bumping each other, with increasing speed and urgency until their garments were scattered about the floor like so many sloughed skins.

They stood facing one another, utterly enchanted by discovery. So this was how it was . . . and this . . . and this. Like children they touched each other to begin with, with wondering curiosity and a delicious holding back. She had not expected his body to be so beautiful—spare and white but for that strange orchid-like growth sprouting from its tuffet of dark hair. She touched it gently with her fingers, and stopped his sigh of pleasure with her lips. And then she kissed his funny pointed right shoulder with its tunnel-like hole, and his hand which was stiff and slightly discoloured and could not hold hers properly.

He put his hand beneath her breast and felt its smooth weight cradled in his palm, and saw her nipple darken and move where his thumb caressed it. He lowered his head and fastened his mouth upon it, feeling the silken cushion of flesh yield to his pressure and her hand on the back of his neck, holding him there, wanting him.

They lay down on the neat, plain bed, still not too close for they were in a mood to luxuriate and enquire. He ran his hand down over her stomach, combing his fingers through the hair at its base and between the smooth, secret, joining warmth of her thighs which parted slightly at his touch so that he could feel the welcoming moisture. He was overwhelmed. He moved his face over her, breathing in her scent, feeling her skin with his lips and cheeks, tasting it with his tongue, in a journey of exquisite animal sensuality, and all the time he felt her move beneath him for his delight. He knew that he had never been so much wanted and desired. She made a gift of herself, completely. Her beauty, her strength, her joy, her generosity lay spread before him like a feast. Her eyes were warm and bright, and through her long-fingered hands he felt her growing confidence, demanding as well as giving. He had been anxious, frightened of hurting her, wary of his own longing, but he saw now that his fears were groundless as he should have known they would be.

It was she who asked for him, pulling him down, lifting and parting her legs so that he slipped into her as sweetly as wine into a glass. Only for a second did she falter, her head rolling to one side, her arms tightening round him, and then she moved with him and for him, not just for his pleasure but for her own, her thighs guiding him, her lips parted against his face telling of her love. He felt her hands, urgent on his loins and placed his own beneath her in response, lifting her onto him and then her whole body, as he knew he could go no longer, began to ripple with his, to flicker like a flame, to move with an independent and complementary life until it seemed to clench and release, dragging his own spurt of love from him so that he called out her name as he had done so many times before, but silently.

Thea lay, blissful, in the damp and luxurious lassitude of after-love. She realized he was crying. She folded her arms about his head. 'My darling, what is it? What is it . . .?'

Child-like he shook his head a little, without raising it, a bit ashamed, not wanting to be pressed. She continued to hold him, stroking his hair, wrapping her legs round him, simply wanting to envelope him with the comfort of her love. They remained like that for some minutes and then he rolled onto his back, his arm across his eyes, the other still beneath her. She could see the tears on his cheeks, the mouth a little uncertain beneath the clipped moustache. In a passion of anxiety she kissed and stroked him, pressing her face into his neck, trying to feel what the matter was.

'Please tell me—you're not unhappy? Jack?'

'I'm sorry.' Abruptly he let fall his shielding arm and looked down at her. She saw that his face was not sad. 'I'm sorry,' he said again. 'It's just that I've wanted you so much, for so long, and now it's almost too much for me.'

'So long?' She did not know what he meant by it. Then, she could not resist: 'How long?'

'Ah—!' He laughed now, and that made her laugh too. 'You'd like to know that, wouldn't you?'

'Yes.' She gazed up at him, quite happy for that moment to be characterized as a jealous woman.

'For as long as I can remember.'

'Since . . .' She hesitated, but only for a second. 'Since before Dulcie?'

'Oh since long before Dulcie.' There was a weariness in his voice as if he'd gone over this exchange in his mind many times before.

'Then why did you, that time?'

He turned onto his side and lay staring into her face, very serious. 'I wanted you, and she came in between, if that makes any sense.'

'Yes.'

'I like Dulcie. Love her in a way.'

'I know.'

'But I've regretted that business almost every waking minute since the day it happened.' He kissed her and then added, 'You were unforgiving.'

'Because I minded so *terribly*!' It was agony to her, that he might not understand how it was. '*Terribly*—without realizing why.'

'You're so honest, aren't you?' He put his arm across her and pulled her close. 'How can you bear to be so honest?'

He felt her shrug, and knew he wanted her again.

He told her, later, as they sat on a seat on the prom, of his plans to go abroad.

'I can't live here any more. I have to start somewhere afresh.' He lit a cigarette and squinted through the smoke, out to sea, organizing his thoughts so as to make them clear to her. She could not help staring at him, she was completely fascinated by her new and proprietary view of him. He looked so crisp and dapper in his English country tweeds, the perfect gentleman. It was titillating to reflect on their activities of an hour before. What an odd couple they must make, what did passers-by think of them? She was thrilled by the notion of their secret, their new intimacy which the rest of the world did not know.

'. . . may seem perverse,' he was saying, 'but having fought for this country for all that time I now find the thought of living here quite intolerable. Are you listening to me or am I casting my pearls before swine?'

'Swine, I'm afraid.' She kissed him. 'Sorry, go on.'

'Thank you. England seems stale and lifeless, it makes *me* feel stale and lifeless. I'm not like you, Thea, I've always conformed and held back and chafed privately against the traces.'

'A sort of closet rebel?' She laughed, she was almost incapable of taking anything seriously.

'How charmingly you put it!' He had to laugh too. 'Still, it doesn't deserve nicer words, it's not a very edifying thing to be. But now, you see, I've made a start. I have you. And perhaps I can go from strength to strength, with you.'

'Where will you go?'

'Kenya, I think. I've made a few enquiries. The colonial office are keen for people to go, and the land is plentiful and cheap. Think of it, starting with a clean slate.'

'Yes . . .' She felt a little curl of anxiety. 'What about Long Lake?'

'I've talked endlessly to the parents about it and they've been marvellous. Sad, but not reproachful. In any event, I have to do it.' He dropped his cigarette end and heeled it hard into the ground. 'I'm convinced that I'd make a terrible mistake in staying.' He looked at her. 'But I'm going on *ad nauseam* about myself. It's you I worry about.'

'Me?' She felt guilty.

'Yes. It would be asking you to give up all the things I know you love—your family, your ambitions, England. Ralph will hate it.'

'Have you mentioned it to him?'

'Yes. He'll hate it.'

'Oh well . . .' She felt he was testing her, challenging her to come down on his side. 'He'll get along. The war will end, Aubrey will come back . . . Anyway, you say I shall be giving up all the things I love and you forget one thing.'

'What's that?'

'That I've gained what I love most of all. What I want is where you are.' It was no more than the simple truth.

He felt for her hand. 'Thank you,' he said. 'Promise you'll always be on my side?'

'Promise.'

'I'm a solitary devil, will you be able to stand it?'

'You know me,' she grinned. 'I like something to get my teeth into.'

It began to rain and a woman walking past began to run, impatiently dragging her grizzling child by the hand. But they couldn't bring themselves to move, and sat there laughing helplessly and getting wet.

When Aubrey received Ralph's letter, posted in mid-May and announcing Thea's intention of marrying Jack Kingsley, he was astonished. He even went so far as to mention it to Coddington during exercise period. It was a warm afternoon and the sanitary squad were engaged in some specially malodorous operation with the main drain, rendering the air in the quadrangle noisome. As supplies in Germany had dwindled the diet at Matteburg had become even more monotonous, consisting almost entirely of a species of haricot bean stewed in gravies of shades varying from beige to dark brown, and occasionally punctuated by lumps of grey and gristly sausage. It was the sausage, lovingly preserved and eked out in the mild summer weather, which was the most likely cause of the current drainage problem.

'Do you know—' blurted out Aubrey explosively as if the words had burst from him despite his efforts to restrain them. 'My sister's getting married!'

'Really?' Coddington was polite. 'I say, that pong really is appalling, why can't we stay indoors while they do that?'

'Yes,' continued Aubrey, who had not heard Coddington's second remark. 'I heard from my father today.'

'Well, that is good news.'

'I suppose so . . . the thing is, she used to hate the fellow.'

'That's women for you,' said Coddington gloomily.

'Mm.' Aubrey, not given to personal remarks, nonetheless

felt he could not allow this generalization to pass without comment. 'Thea is different, actually.'

'Oh?' Coddington was sceptical. 'In what way?'

'She's very straight, has very decided views. Also—' Aubrey hesitated, wondering if this might be going too far.

'Also what? God, honestly . .!' Coddington put his hand to his face as they passed the offending corner.

Aubrey decided the information was germane. 'This chap, the one she wants to marry, had an affair with my other sister.'

'Good grief!' At last Coddington's interest was properly aroused. 'I see what you mean.'

'She seems to have done a complete *volte-face*.'

'And him.'

'Yes! Extraordinary.'

'You know this fellow I suppose?'

'Kingsley? Oh yes.'

'What do you make of him, yourself?'

'I rather like him as a matter of fact. Quite approve of her choice.'

'But this business with your other sister . . .?'

'Ages ago. Before the war. Anyway, she asked for it.'

'I see.'

Actually, Coddington did not see at all. This brief exchange had entirely altered his perspective on a brother officer whom he had always taken to be pretty much like himself: sensible, orderly, self-possessed, conservative. But now, in the space of a few minutes, Tennant had revealed an area of his life hitherto unhinted at, and certainly not to be dreamed of from his conduct at Matteburg. It appeared that this solid English oak had sprung from a steamy jungle of passion and intrigue in which hot-headed sisters vied for the love of the same man, where venomous female jealousy (of which Coddington had a healthy, inexperienced terror) could turn to love—and Tennant actually seemed to condone these goings on, and to approve of the Lothario Kingsley, whoever he might be!

Such was Coddington's perturbation that it actually took his mind off the smell for the rest of the exercise period.

Thea and Jack were married three days after her return from Merville, at the church of St Jude's, Lewisham. At one time, long ago, she used to picture her wedding—to whoever it might be—and indulge herself with plans for flowers, music, the reception. It had been a sort of game she played that appealed to the theatrical in her. It had seemed to her then that a so-called 'quiet' wedding must be a poor affair, something mean and clandestine. People lucky enough to be getting married should proclaim it to the world, celebrate and mark the occasion with proper rites and observances.

Now, those things meant nothing to her. She found the austerity of her wedding utterly satisfying. Its quietness echoed the feeling she had of reaching a haven, safe waters after a troubled journey. She was already Jack's, and the short ceremony in the great barn-like Victorian church simply set the seal on their union and bestowed on it a blessing which she was happy to have, but which made little difference.

There were only four guests—Ralph, Maurice, and Robert and Daphne Kingsley. Sophie claimed it was too far to come and refused a lift when offered it, and Dulcie sent an exquisite Limoges tea set which arrived miraculously unbroken. With the tea set was a note—violet ink on thick white paper—saying how '*desolée*' she was not to be attending but that things were 'rather uncertain' her end . . . This last was clearly a delicate euphemism, since it was known that the Germans were now menacing Paris from as little as fifty miles away. All through May they had moved south with astonishing secrecy, utterly baffling Allied Intelligence, and finally attacking on the Aisne which was held by a mere five exhausted British divisions sent there to rest after the fighting in Flanders. At the end of the month fourteen German divisions had broken through the line and swept on to the Marne, refreshing terrible memories among Parisians of 1914.

Worry about Dulcie was the only cloud on Thea's day. The sun shone, and long shafts of dusty yellow light filtered through the stained glass on to the ranks of empty pews. A few people, some of them children, came into the back of the church off the street to watch, but that was all. Afterwards they went back to Mapleton Road for champagne and a majestic cake, groaning with expensive wartime fruit, created by Mrs Duckham. She thought the wedding a pretty paltry affair, but the cake at least had given her a long overdue chance to practise her culinary skills. She was sick to death of rationing and shortages and the economies of war, not to mention Mr Tennant's plebeian—common, she called it—taste in food now that he lived on his own. He actually liked sprats, and brawn, and trotters, and had even on one or two occasions had the nerve to purchase these items of his own accord and present her with them, for immediate preparation and consumption. She suspected that the cockney parlourmaid, Pet, did not believe her tales of pre-war dinners at Ranelagh Road, and the cake had provided her with an opportunity to show off. She had stinted nothing—brandy, fruit, butter, sugar, dozens of eggs, not to mention icing of an ornateness that would not have disgraced a baroque cathedral.

Disappointingly Mr Tennant, usually the most appreciative consumer of her cakes, was rather unwell on the day of the wedding, but as he was keeping the whole of the bottom tier she consoled herself that he would be able to enjoy it for weeks to come.

In fact Ralph was going down with a dose of the three-day fever that was rife. The epidemic had already swept the troops in France, causing havoc, and was having a field day in the big cities in England. It had become popularly and rather unfairly known as 'Spanish' influenza after its supposed country of origin, but the plain fact was no one knew where it had started or what caused it. But the virulence of its symptoms were such that by his second glass of champagne Ralph was pale, perspiring and weak at the knees and had to be escorted to bed by Thea, only feebly protesting, where he instantly fell into a shivering sleep.

Maurice left, and then the Kingsleys. Thea and Jack went into the road to see them off. They had aged; Robert's exuberance was almost gone, Daphne had become stout. Thea sensed their sadness which, unlike Ralph, they were too kind and reserved to show.

'So you're fixed on this Kenya thing?' Robert asked, rhetorically but a little wistfully, as they walked to the car Jack had at last persuaded them to buy.

'Absolutely fixed.'

'And you, Thea?' Daphne slipped her arm through Thea's. 'You're happy about it?'

'I want to be with Jack.'

'Of course, of course . . .'

'He's damned lucky to have you,' said Robert, with a flash of his old ebullience. 'You're one in a million, I've always said so.'

They stood by the car, making their farewells From now

on, Thea knew, each parting would be a little more final, they would ease their way towards the last separation with gentle British tact, avoiding suddenness and pain. She could only guess at what it cost this nice, affectionate elderly couple to lose their only son, their pride and joy. She remembered the photographs in the drawing-room at Long Lake, and Robert saying 'We could paper the walls with those old copies of *Boy's Own Paper* . . .' Suddenly she loved them very much, for themselves and what they were giving so generously to her. She hugged and kissed them and sensed their slight embarrassment, but she could not help herself.

Back at Mapleton Road she looked in on Ralph, who was still asleep, and gave instructions to Mrs Duckham to see that he took plenty of fluids and remained in bed till the temperature was down. The doctors were too hard-pressed to come out to yet one more case of Spanish 'flu; there was nothing to do but sweat it out. She put a note by his bed: *'Behave yourself, drink plenty and stay in bed. I'll come and see you tomorrow. Thea.'*

She and Jack returned to town. They had rented a suite of rooms in the Buchanan Hotel off Green Park while Jack conducted his enquiries about Kenya and Thea ordered furnishings for the future home she could not even begin to visualize. It had been agreed between them that they preferred independence to moving in with either family, and that to take a house, however small, might fatally persuade Thea in particular to put down roots. The Buchanan was comfortable, convenient, and provided a kind of peaceful neutral ground in which they could draw closer and become used to the idea of the separate and foreign future.

But that night, after they had made love, Thea remained awake long after Jack had fallen asleep and all night, until she dozed off exhausted just before dawn, she listened to his dreams and knew there was a world, inside him, which she had not yet begun to enter.

Maurice encountered Primmy in Trafalgar Square at the end of July. It was extremely hot, and he was on his way from visiting at the Charing Cross Hospital. It was part of his job on the WVRC to inspect and evaluate the most needy cases, and report back. He did not terribly care for this aspect of his work, since it smacked of playing God, but it had to be done. He found the hospital visiting harrowing and exhausting, and the sight of the fountains playing in the sunshine was seductive. He crossed the road by St Martin's in the Fields and went to sit down on the wall where he could watch the water. Pigeons rustled and pecked round his legs.

He had felt much better of late. He had had a dose of the influenza, probably contracted from Ralph at Thea's wedding, and though it had lasted for about a week, as opposed to his uncle's two days, it had not turned into anything bronchial, and the recent excellent weather had done wonders for his chest. He lived a fairly solitary, but not a friendless, existence, glad of Stephen Martin's company in the rooms at Malet Street but perfectly happy to spend much of his days alone. He paid regular visits to Mapleton Road, finding that he was able to enjoy Ralph's company more and more. The relationship had almost been jeopardized by Ralph's pressing an embarrassingly large sum of money on him, but had even managed to transcend this stumbling block and was now on an excellent footing. Maurice had eventually accepted the money, partly because it was clear that refusal would not be brooked and partly because he divined his uncle's need to give it to him. Now that he had it, he felt the use of it to be an awesome responsibility. It never crossed his mind to spend it on himself, he would not have known where to begin. He relied on the probability of some likely cause presenting itself sooner or later.

It was while he sat in the sunshine reflecting upon this that someone sat down a couple of yards further along the wall. He glanced up incuriously and saw that it was Primmy.

At first he was not sure whether to address her or not. All his beastly social ineptitude and strangulating lack of confidence rose up in him and turned him into a pillar of salt. He was still sitting there, staring in stupid silence, when she got up again, and was about to walk on.

'Primmy!' Then, of course, he shouted too loud, sounded urgent and ridiculous, blushed to the roots of his hair.

She turned. She was out of uniform, dressed in a faded print dress and a straw hat. Her arms, pale and thin, protruded stick-like from the floppy sleeves of the dress and her narrow ankles, for which Maurice had always had great admiration, disappeared into unseasonally heavy regulation shoes with criss-cross laces ending in huge double bows.

'Hallo,' she said, in that way of hers that implied they'd

only seen each other a few days instead of years ago, and had anothing left to say.

'Where are you going?' he asked.

'I've got a train to catch in half an hour,' she explained, stiffly. But her stiffness forced the initiative upon him and gave him confidence.

'What, from Charing Cross?'

'That's right.'

'Shall we have a cold drink or something?'

'Very well.' She sounded as if she were making a big concession, as if he had left her no option, but he was readjusting rapidly to her terse manner and even found it rather comforting. It was more restful not to be overpowered. Everything had to be dragged from Primmy, and it quite suited him to do so.

He indicated a small café on the corner of the Strand and they set off in that direction, she walking parallel with him but some way off, looking about her as if not wanting to be associated with him. He knew what it was, he had surprised her and she was a creature who liked to be prepared.

They went in and sat down at a table near the window, ordering lemonade. On the other side of the road a man in a mask was walking backwards down the steps at the entrance to the underground public lavatory, energetically pushing the lever of a spray can.

Seeing her watching, Maurice appealed to her medical knowledge. 'I wonder how much good that does?'

She pulled her mouth down. 'Helps a bit, I should think. But the germs just breed in big cities.'

'I suppose so. Have you had this 'flu thing?'

'Not me.' She sounded positively offended, then conceded. 'Our Eddie has, I've been to see him this afternoon. He's over it now, but they've all had it in that place.' She spoke the last two words with clear distaste.

'So that's why you're in town, is it?' asked Maurice. 'Seeing Eddie?'

'Yes. That and visiting my mother.'

'Where is she now, refresh my memory.'

'Working in my brother-in-law's shop in Deptford.' Primmy sat very straight, holding her tall glass between both hands. Her pale arms were freckled by the sun. As always, Maurice found her toughness touching.

'And she likes that?'

'I don't know I'm sure.'

Maurice almost asked her why, since both her relations resided south of the river, she had come up to the West End. But since her reasons were obviously what she would think of as frivolous he decided against eliciting them.

He tried a different tack. 'How's the nursing?'

'Fine, thank you,' she responded. 'I'm moving to another place soon.'

'Really? Where's that?'

A suspicion of colour crept into her cheeks. 'Chilverton House as a matter of fact.'

'Never!'

'Yes. It's a nursing home now, you know.'

'I did know, but what a coincidence you going there. I shall have to tell Mr Tennant, he'll be tickled to death.'

'Do you think so?' She smiled a taut little smile, but then cancelled it with: 'But I shan't be going on nursing after the war.'

He was shocked. 'Primmy, you must!'

'No must about it. The VADs'll be disbanded and I haven't the money to do a proper training. Can't be helped.'

Her dour defeatism infuriated him, especially because it was not like her. 'That's no way to talk, Primmy, and you know it.'

'It's got to be faced. I'm lucky to have got where I have. I've gone as far as I can, so that's that.'

'If it's money that's the only problem, I'll give you some.' He said it almost before he thought it, but once said it seemed the most obvious thing in the world, even in the searchlight glare of her starchy amazement.

'Money's for using,' he asserted, forcing home his point before she had time to assemble her defence. 'I'm not interested in having the stuff sitting about in my account and I want very little for myself. I've actually been trying to think of what to do with it. In fact,' he warmed to this theme, 'I'd regard financing you for nursing training as an investment. If training nurses doesn't constitute relief for war victims I don't know what does!' Pleased with this last point, and quite out of breath, he leaned back, draining his lemonade with a flourish.

'I couldn't possibly,' she said emphatically, but there was just enough doubt implied in her answer—she hadn't, after all, said 'no'—that he pressed on.

'Yes you could! Look, Primmy, what do you want from your life? Some sort of purpose, doing what you're good at, helping other people, or just messing about with a lot of second-rate, second-best jobs because you were too proud to take a bit of money that I've got no earthly use for?'

He coughed for a moment or two, fishing for his handkerchief, aware of her watchful gaze on him, her readiness to dart for the smallest escape route.

'What's that cough?' she asked tartly. 'What are you coughing for in this weather?'

'Something caught in my throat, a tickle—what does it matter?' He was quite cross with her evasive tactics. 'I've had the 'flu and got over it, so don't start jumping to conclusions. Now what about my offer?'

'It's out of the question.' He saw her resolve hardening before his eyes. The issue had suddenly become vitally important to him.

She glanced up at the clock on the wall. 'Time I was off.'

'What time is your train?'

'Four-thirty.'

'Then you've got twenty minutes and only a hundred yards to walk. I forbid you to go until you've properly considered what I'm saying instead of running away.'

'No. It wouldn't be right.'

'On the contrary, it would be absolutely right! You can't imagine the pleasure it would give me to do it.'

'No . . .' Her voice was slightly querulous, he saw that he had flustered her a little, got through to her, and that was something.

'There is another alternative.'

'What's that?'

'You could marry me, and have the money that way.'

Time stood still. Had he really said that? He didn't mean it of course, he'd blurted it out as a kind of challenge, to show her how sensible the other course of action was. The waitress, perspiring in her dusty black dress, came and removed their glasses and Maurice fumbled in his pocket and handed her the fourpence for the lemonade without taking his eyes off Primmy's face. They were still sitting there in silence when she came back to wipe the table top. They watched her damp red hand going round and round between them, as if hypnotized, using its intervention as an excuse. When she moved away, Primmy got up, smoothing her limp print frock and holding her bag tight. 'Thank you for the drink. I must dash.'

'Wait, I'm coming.'

She marched off at a great rate with Maurice stumbling after her, bumping people and knocking tables and chairs and finally catching up with her on the kerb outside. They crossed the busy road together. He knew there was nothing else he could add, she was not susceptible to persuasion, so he'd gone as far as he could. He could almost hear her brain whirring and clicking as she walked along. It struck him that she had not, during the entire conversation, expressed the slightest curiosity about his activities either past or present.

He stood by her in the queue for tickets, and walked with her to the train, all in complete silence. She walked briskly to the very front of the train and then stopped by the carriage door.

'All right then,' she said.

For a second, Maurice was taken in. His brain reeled.

'I'll take the money, and thank you.'

Only after she'd said that, and boarded the train, closing the door behind her, did he realize how badly he'd wanted her to take his proposal seriously.

Primmy sat tight in her seat next to the corridor, her hands clenched round the handle of her bag, her teeth gritted behind firmly closed lips. Her legs were pressed together so hard that her knee and ankle bones hurt. Her eyes stared out at the grey outskirts of London sliding past the window, but she didn't see them.

But after a moment, and partly because there was a big fat man opposite who would keep gawping at her, she got up and went into the corridor. She held onto the rail that ran along the inside of the window and stood there swaying. All she could see was Maurice's face bobbing before her eyes with the rhythm of the train, with that expression it had worn just before she climbed aboard. What had she said? 'I'll take the money.' It had been as though she'd hit him with a sledgehammer. Why had she said it in that way, so rough and blunt? She hadn't meant to hurt, only to be practical. She thought of herself as someone who was in control, and yet there was a whole area of her character which she scarcely recognized, let alone controlled.

Of course there was nothing else she could have said or done, the other idea was ridiculous, unthinkable, he'd only suggested it to make her do the sensible thing, she supposed . . . She closed her eyes, squeezing them tight to get rid of Maurice's face and the squeezing caused a tear to ooze onto her cheek. She felt the bump of someone's shoulder against hers, and started. It was the staring fat man from the compartment.

'I say, are you all right? You look a bit rum if I may say so ' He only meant to be kind, but his manner was ingratiating. He was red and bulging and shiny and coarse-grained, the very opposite of Maurice. She glared at him and drew herself up with a sniff, looking very like her mother.

'I'm perfectly well, thank you,' she said tartly, and edged past him. She went along the corridor to the toilet. She locked herself in and sat down on the seat, leaning her forehead on the edge of the basin and feeling it bruised as the train clattered and jolted over the points. She was not perfectly well: something was very much the matter with her, she was afflicted with Maurice. But she had a terrible feeling that she had just rejected the cure, and finally.

She began to cry, at first in a small way, then noisily and violently, not bothering to wipe her nose or eyes nor to respond when someone hammered impatiently on the door. Make the most of it, girl, she thought. Cry now and never again.

On 18 September Thea sat waiting for Jack on a seat in Green Park. She quite often came out here at the end of the day because she missed the country and this was the nearest she could get to it. She had with her the volume of Manley Hopkins poems that Maurice had given her for Christmas 1913, but she read only intermittently for the sun was hot, and she could not help wondering how the auction had gone. She had kept busy all day long, choosing curtain fabrics at Liberty's, and lunching with Andrea Sutton, who had smoothly reappeared in her life since she and Jack had been living in London. Thea had not been in the least surprised to learn that Andrea was now married to Louis. He was an under-secretary at the Ministry, she was women's editor on the *Herald*, and they ran a smart household in Knightsbridge, just off Exhibition Road. In bringing Thea up to date on her own doings Andrea had never once mentioned the scene at Dolton Green; it was as if she regarded it as some shameful lapse, whereas Thea firmly believed it to have been a glimpse of reality under the carefully maintained veneer. She could not dislike Andrea, but she was puzzled that a confrontation which had caused both of them distress should now be swept so thoroughly beneath the carpet.

To her horror, Andrea had invited them to dinner, but it had not been as dreadful as she anticipated. For one thing there had been a great many people present, so close contact with the host and hostess could easily be avoided, and for another it had been a genuinely entertaining evening, the food, wine and company excellent and the conversation absorbing. It was only afterwards that both she and Jack had realized how expertly staged it had been. Andrea was in her element, the perfect politician's wife, and their presence had been no more than grist to her social mill.

It was then that she'd told Jack, somewhat diffidently, about Louis.

'What, that chap?'

'Yes.'

He had burst out laughing. 'I can't think of anything more incongruous . . .'

She smiled. 'Well, neither could I, that was the trouble. I felt terrible, though, because he'd been so kind to me when I was low.'

'Kind? My darling love, his type doesn't know the meaning of the word. I've got nothing against him, I quite liked him and he's obviously very good at his job, but I am perfectly certain you have nothing to reproach yourself with in that quarter. He quite probably found you attractive—'

'Thank you.'

'—not at all, and he also envisaged you as a charming and useful accessory to his public life. You did absolutely right not to be flattered into a horrible mistake.'

She began to giggle. 'I should have been simply useless at that kind of entertaining . . .'

'And she's very good at it. She lives for advancement, that one.'

'That's not entirely true.'

'It is, however, my opinion. Come here.'

Thus had the ghost of Louis Avery been laid to rest, and Thea and Andrea continued their friendship, though never so close as they once had been, content now to run along their parallel but separate courses and agree to differ. Still, Andrea could not resist voicing her opinion.

'*Kenya?* But my dear, what on earth will you do? Till the good earth with a couple of cattle and a hand plough?'

'I'll do whatever has to be done. Work, whatever. I shall enjoy it.' Thea always wished on these occasions that her own small doubts would go away and leave her in peace.

'But it's such a waste, you've been so busy with your war work.'

'I wish you wouldn't call it that, Andrea. It wasn't "my war work", it wasn't a cause, it was just a job I wanted to do.'

'Oh well, that's always been your line of course, it's so middle class to be categorized, isn't it?'

'I—'

'But, anyway, I can see you are sublimely happy with Jack and I suppose that's all that matters. He is quite heavenly to look at, I will say that. So tantalizingly unapproachable. I just hope he makes it up to you for dragging you away to the Styx . . .'

'He's not "dragging me away" anywhere,' Thea would protest. And yet she always came away from these meetings with butterflies in her stomach. She would spend days calming her fears and in an instant Andrea would have stirred them up again.

Some soldiers, newly back on leave, had sat down in a circle on the grass beyond the path, in the shade of one of the big trees. They were in high spirits, singing and laughing in loud voices, passing a bottle round. They had the strangeness of beings from another planet. She hoped they would be gone by the time Jack arrived: such direct reminders of the Front upset him profoundly; he would quite likely go into a brown study from which it would be almost impossible to shake him, and then at night there would be the dreams . . . .

The sun struck warm on her face, and she lowered the book, open but face-down, onto her lap, and closed her eyes. She gave herself up to the heat, gazing into the red of her eyelids and picturing herself elsewhere.

The red darkened suddenly as someone stood between her and the sun, and she opened her eyes. 'Jack!'

'Hallo, you.' She stood up, straight into his arms, but when he had kissed her, he pushed her back down. 'No, sit down.'

She did so, and he sat beside her, one arm along the back of the seat, feeling with his free hand in his breast pocket, from which he took a manila envelope. His face was alight with excitement, he had not even noticed the soldiers on the grass, and she felt her heart sink. This was it, what she had been waiting for and she knew she was dreading it.

'I did it,' he said. 'I did it!'

'What?' she asked stupidly, as if she didn't know.

'You see before you, my darling, the new owner of four thousand acres of prime farmland in the Kenyan rift valley. All ours.'

She stared at him, trying to absorb the force of it, trying to arrange her features into a pattern of ecstatic enthusiasm. 'That's marvellous,' she said mechanically. 'It really is.'

Normally sensitive to her moods, his own elation prevented him from instantly detecting her unhappiness. 'Look—she gave me a photograph.'

'She?'

'Mrs Aitken, the present owner. Correction, the *previous* owner. She was most insistent I show it to you.'

Thea took the photograph. It showed the corner of a bungalow with a wooden verandah encircling it. Leaning on the verandah rail, clearly posed, stood a tall, thin, nice-looking woman with a labrador lying at her feet. The woman was gazing out over a vista which even the small black and white photograph showed to be spectacular and apparently infinite.

'. . . awfully nice, you'd have liked her,' Jack was saying. 'She and her husband built that house and she says she can hardly bear to think of never looking out at that view again.'

'Then why's she selling up?' asked Thea, handing the photograph back.

'It's a sad story. Both her sons were killed in the war, and her husband died at the beginning of this year. She can't go on living in a place like that on her own, much as she might like to. There was nothing for her to do but sell up. But I think she liked me—I said she must come and stay when we're established.'

'Yes, of course.' Thea stared ahead, blinded by tears. The sun was now low and striking full on their faces so she hoped that might account for the tears if Jack saw them. But his attention was now drawn to the soldiers who struck up with a favourite song.

> *'When this bloody war is over,*
> *No more soldiering for me . . .'*

652

'Damn row,' he said. She could feel that cold, closed mood coming over him.

'Let's go in,' she said. The singing was loud and intrusive. She got up but he caught her hand.

'What's up?'

'Nothing—or not very much, honestly. But it would be nice to be quiet, and alone.'

'Yes, you're right.'

He got up at once and took her arm, but as they started down the path in the direction of the Buchanan the soldiers also began to move off, and two of them advanced on Thea and Jack, blocking their way. They were red-faced, tipsy, hot and elated, somehow threatening though they didn't mean to be. They were singing the closing lines of the song with a sort of studied impudence, wanting, if not to hurt these smart civilian people, at least to shock them a little.

> '. . . No more asking for a pass:
> You can tell the sergeant major
> To stuff his passes up his arse!'

They stood there, their arms about one another's shoulders, beaming and swaying. Thea felt Jack stiffen and knew just how his face would look, tight and drawn and clouded.

'Out of our way please,' he said, in a tone that she knew would confirm the two soldiers in their prejudices. 'Stand aside.'

'Have a nice leave,' she added softly.

The men fell back amiably enough and watched as they walked past.

In the hotel Jack went straight upstairs to their room, opening the window and going out onto the tiny balcony, breathing deeply as if he had been on the point of suffocation. His face was absolutely white. She went over to him and put her arms round him, leaning her cheek against his back. He was completely rigid.

'What is it? What's the matter? Are you cross with me?'

'You?' He turned round and stared at her in total incomprehension. 'Why you?'

'Oh, I don't know . . .' She didn't have the courage now to tell him of her earlier selfish anxiety. 'Then what?'

'It's so hard to explain . . .' He put his hands to his face, rubbing his eyes and temples as if to dissipate the problem, make it easier to tell. He went into the bedroom and lay down on his back on the bed, with one hand behind his head, staring up at the ceiling. The other hand he held out to her. 'Stay close.'

She went and lay down next to him, laying her head over his heart. She could feel it skipping and racing. 'Please try to tell me,' she said. 'Don't shut me out.'

'I miss it,' he said in a peculiar tight voice as though the words were being wrung from him under torture. 'I ruddy well miss it.'

'What? The army?'

'Not just that. The front, the trenches—the bloody war.'

'But you said . . . you told me so often how you hated it.'

'It was true. I meant it. I'd had enough. I was sickened by it, I loathed being responsible for men's lives—it was all true. But now I'm out of it I find I feel—left out.' He rolled his head from side to side. 'God, it's so childish, but they're the only words I can think of. When you've put all your energy into something for so long you're like an addict, and when it's taken away you can't cope. I feel wasted, redundant. And I actually resent those men—like those two in the park—who are still part of it. I *envy* them!'

'I do understand,' she said, meaning it absolutely, so glad he had told her.

'I behaved abominably.' His voice shook.

'They were drunk. You were curt. It was all right.'

'No it wasn't, and you know it. They were treating me as an outsider, rubbing my nose in it, I wanted to grab them and shout at them 'I've *been* there! I *know* what it's like!'

Suddenly he rolled onto his side and into her arms, clasping her shoulders and pressing his face into her breasts. In a muffled voice, he said: 'Do you see now why I can't live here?'

'Yes.' She held him close, stroking his head and neck. 'Yes, I do . . . .'

In a little while he fell asleep and she gently disengaged herself from his embrace. Leaning up on her elbow she took the photograph from his jacket pocket and studied it.

Kenya. She would learn to love it.

At 5a.m. on 11 November 1918 a group of elderly gentlemen, heavily wrapped up against the autumn chill, assembled in a railway carriage in a clearing in the forest of

Compiègne to sign a document which would end the war. Long hours of exhaustive discussion in the converted restaurant car had made them stiff and tetchy and all of them were sombre. An outsider would have been quite unable to distinguish victor from vanquished, and might even have been forgiven for assuming, from their demeanour, that all had somehow lost. However, it might have been noted that one of the delegations was obliged to cross from their train to the armistice carriage by means of duckboards through the mud, and were thus marked out as the losers.

Inside, they moved around cumbersomely, for there wasn't much room between the central table and the desks that stood along the sides. Anxious aides and interpreters got in the way and murmured apologies, someone had a thick cigar-cough which was beginning to get on all their nerves. It took almost three hours for every page of the text to be signed and at the end of it all some of the men were in tears. The representative of the vanquished nation read out a protestatior which concluded, on a clarion note: 'A people of seventy million men are suffering, but they are not dead.'

'Très bien,' responded the victor, and walked away without shaking hands.

So the war that had been sparked off by a hot-blooded youth in the sunshine of Sarajevo, and had greedily consumed the flower of half a dozen nations, was finally and inconclusively brought to a close by proud and unforgiving old men in freezing pre-dawn darkness. The nominally vanquished but still unbroken might of the German army stood everywhere on foreign soil. The British were back precisely where they'd started.

When Maurice set out from Malet Street to attend armistice celebrations with the Kingsleys and Ralph at the Buchanan, it was his intention to take a cab. Stephen warned him against even attempting the journey.

'You're potty if you go out tonight,' he observed cheerfully, making toast at the gas fire.

'But I want to go.'

'No you don't, you're just being polite. I don't even think you should go, what's the war to you?'

'I'd like to see them.'

Stephen turned his toast, wincing as he burnt his fingers. 'On your own head be it.'

655

Maurice left. He did not, as a matter of fact, feel too jolly, but he put it down to his usual reaction to the onset of winter. The change in the weather, the cold, the damp, the fog and the short, dark days, none of them suited his system, and he knew he would have an almost permanent cold and cough until next April. His indisposition was certainly not sufficient to put him off going to the Buchanan. Though, as Stephen had said, the winning of the war meant nothing to him, he nonetheless liked to see Thea and Jack and Ralph and felt that the warmth of their affection would more than make up for any inconvenience en route.

By the time he got to Leicester Square he was not so sure. The streets were filled with a raging torrent of humanity, like a swollen river, rushing and dangerous. They swarmed over the roads as well as the pavements and it was abundantly obvious that his chances of finding a cab were nil. He was buffeted, pushed and jostled and the noise was deafening.

He cut through to Cambridge Circus, knowing it was out of his way but hoping to hop on a bus in the Charing Cross Road, but the only bus he saw was piled high with tier upon tier of young men, filling the interior and clinging to the outside. Some were in uniform, others in civvies, some in a mixture of the two. Their arms waved and fluttered from the sides of the bus so that it resembled a gigantic moving sea anemone with a thousand fronds.

He utterly abandoned the idea of any form of transport and resigned himself, rather fearfully, to reaching the Buchanan on foot. He was irrevocably committed to the journey now and the knowledge made him panicky. The exuberant crowd seemed a howling, predatory mob, he mistrusted them. The atmosphere abroad in the streets resembled nothing so much as that which had so sickened him at the outbreak of war. These normally sane people, the survivors of the war and inheritors of the peace, who for four bitter years had been so courageous and full of sense and fortitude, had now gone mad. They were not celebrating peace, but war and the winning of it, demonstrating with lunatic vivacity that it had all been worth it. They were conquerors!

In Trafalgar Square it was worse than ever. The place where he had sat with Primmy, both water and wall, was covered by a crowd so dense it resembled a field of corn, the surface riffled by the swaying of heads as they sang. The concourse was made up of several different factions, each singing its own song at full blast, oblivious of competition. The resulting dissonant roar reminded Maurice of the sound of the guns, heard far-off from the Soot Street camp. At the foot of Nelson's Column some Canadians had lit a gigantic bonfire. Its shivering coppery light illuminated the aloof faces of the stone lions, and sparks flew up into the dark sky like scarlet stars.

On the steps of St Martin's in the Fields an elderly woman leaned up against the wall. At first he thought she was drunk, but on closer inspection it was plain she had the 'flu. She was clammy and feverish and her face had a darkened appearance, symptom of the pulmonary complications which had made this second outbreak so lethal. Thousands had died, it was like the final kick in the side of an already fallen man. Maurice shouted in her ear, but she was too far gone to hear. He considered taking her to the Charing Cross, but she would have been far too heavy to carry and the street was packed. She looked ominously close to death.

After that, he felt markedly worse. His own mild chesty cold seemed to take on a new dimension. Not that he seriously thought he would get the 'flu, he imagined that his bout in the summer had afforded him some kind of immunization, but nonetheless . . . He buttoned the top of his jacket and pushed his hands deep into his pockets. Thea had found his coat, and given it to him, but he was hopelessly forgetful, and always walked out in whatever he had on.

Tortuously, he circumnavigated Trafalgar Square. All the grinning faces, the noise, the sparks, the buffeting, began to induce a kind of delirium in Maurice. He was miserable and frankly terrified. The old feeling of his physical vulnerability overcame him. Why, they could literally trample him under foot and never notice! Worried that his spectacles would be broken he took them off and put them in his jacket pocket, holding them there in his hand. The yelling grimacing faces receded, became amorphous, reeling blobs of colour. Using the comforting bulk of the National Gallery on his right as a lode star, he staggered along in the direction of Lower Regent Street.

A row of men, arms linked, doing the Lambeth Walk, advanced along the pavement towards him. He shrank to the side, out of their way, and they didn't even see him, but as they passed the one on the end lurched and Maurice felt the glasses crumble in his hand like a dry biscuit. He pulled out what was left of them. They had cut his hand, which was wet with blood. One lens was irretrievably smashed, the other crazed in a dense cobweb of cracks. He tried to put them on, so that at least he could see a little through the cracked lens, but one of the arms had snapped off too, so that was no good, and he had only succeeded in getting blood on his face. He could have wept for fear and frustration.

As he stood there, holding the smashed spectacles, his heart racing in panic, he felt a touch on his arm, a different kind of touch, sly and deliberate.

'Hallo, duck. Need a hand?'

He smelt her sour breath and cheap scent, and saw the creased powdery skin of her face as she grinned invitingly at him. Stained teeth, and orange beads and a stubby hand on his arm. . . .

'No!' He wrenched away from her and barged on, hearing the sharp sound of the insults she threw after him, cutting through the general din.

In Piccadilly a man was standing on a suitcase in the middle of the road, waving a Union Jack and shouting in some personal and drunken patriotic ritual. He paused, as Maurice passed, to be sick, but straightened up and continued almost at once, the mess all down his front and on the flag, too.

When Maurice at last turned into Buchanan Place he was trembling like a leaf and his breath was labouring painfully. His lungs seemed to be seized by a kind of cramp so that it took an enormous physical effort to inflate them. Sweat was running into his eyes and making them sting, though he didn't feel hot, but cold.

He paused, leaning on some area railings to catch his breath. In the house above the area, there were lights on and the rooms were full of people, laughter and talking, civilized celebration. In a minute he would be with them, and it would be all right.

Staring blankly down into the dark of the area he spotted a movement which he took at first to be a cat. But as his breathing calmed and his eyes focused he saw that it was a man and a woman copulating, right there on the dirty concrete of the half-way landing. The woman's skirt was bunched round her middle, her fat white knees stuck up comically as the man puffed and humped between them like a hedgehog.

Dismayed, Maurice turned away. He stopped again at the foot of the steps leading to the Buchanan's main entrance. Above him the glass doors leading to the warm yellow light and the carpeted hall beyond were like the gates of heaven. He took a deep breath and stumbled up the steps. It took all his strength, but at the top the door opened before him, held by a puce-coated commissionaire, not easily surprised on this particular night, but a little taken aback by this wild-eyed, bloodstained young man on the point of collapse.

He made some remark to Maurice—polite, concerned, could he help? But Maurice only wanted the people he knew. The hall was full of people, they fell away before him. The carpet was soft beneath his feet, the chandeliers sparkling and benign above.

He blundered through into the lounge, and then he saw them, on the far side, standing by the fireplace. Ralph had his arm round Thea and Jack, was pouring champagne into their glasses. They were laughing. When he was with them, he would be all right, understood, loved and cared for, and these people would stop looking at him like this.

He tried to call to them, but he had no voice left, to wave but couldn't lift his arm, to walk, but his legs were like lead. More than at any other time, Maurice experienced a crushing sense of defeat. They had won the war, but the war had won.

As Thea saw him, started towards him with a look of concern, the victory became complete. The light went out and he keeled over flat on his face among the hastily sidestepping feet.

CHAPTER TWENTY-ONE

'And for all this, nature is never spent;
There lives the dearest freshness deep down things;
And though the last lights off the black West went
Oh, morning at the brown brink eastward springs . . .
        Gerard Manley Hopkins—'God's Grandeur'

The funeral was on 21 December, the shortest day. Brief, dark, cold, a day to be scurried through with your collar turned up. They wouldn't have set it for this day if there had been any alternative, but unfortunately death resists organization. From the moment he had collapsed in the lounge of the Buchanan on the evening of 11 November, it had borne down on Maurice as irreversibly as pack ice. They had taken him to Mapleton Road and called in Bruce Egerton, although he was retired, because it was well-nigh impossible to get a doctor in with the epidemic raging. Nervous exhaustion, he said: nervous exhaustion and a touch of bronchitis, needs to be watched. Rest, and warmth and good food should do the trick. It had, for a while. By the end of the month he was much recovered and in early December insisted on returning to his rooms in Malet Street, and to work. For a couple of weeks all had been well but then one night Stephen had returned to find him collapsed, with a high temperature. He had contracted the 'flu, against which his always-frail and much-battered body stood no chance. He died at Mapleton Road on 17 December, with his face turned to the wall. He had not spoken for four days.

It had been the day Aubrey got back, Thea remembered. Maurice had stopped breathing at 4 a.m.—the sick-room had turned instantly into a tomb without that terrible whistling sound—and Aubrey had arrived at eight-thirty as they stood about in the dining-room, drinking tea and in a state of shock.

He had been wonderful: practical, quiet, unselfish, taking over as naturally as if he'd never been away. That, at least, had been good, that he had come back at a time when he was much needed and relied upon, slipping back into his old role but with a new gentleness, Thea noticed, as if the long years away had given him time to think and reach some private conclusions concerning the rest of them. She was immensely glad that he was there, now, with Ralph, for she and Jack were due to sail on the twenty-third and with every day her father had evinced more of a kind of fierce and clumsy dread of their departure. One moment he would be congratulating them, encouraging them in their independence, saying how envious he was of their future; the next he would suddenly clutch her and tell her not to go, it wasn't fair, how did she expect him to . . . ? All this half-laughing, but Thea knew how much he meant it and it was as if the fabric of her heart, always a sensitive organ, were being stretched to breaking point.

Dulcie had come, too, arriving at Mapleton Road the night before from Paris, very brittle and polite and withdrawn and utterly unexpected. So they were all there, in the front pew at St Catherine's Ewhurst, with the Kingsleys and Bruce Egerton in the row behind. And at the back, two more: Primmy, who had simply walked down with her coat over her uniform, from Chilverton House, and Sophie. They had been sitting, waiting in the church for half an hour before she turned up, accompanied by George Aitcheson. Ralph was unable to imagine what George had said to induce her to come, since all his own (limited) powers of persuasion had failed to do so earlier in the afternoon when he'd called in. She looked old, wasted and pinched and slightly bent, for she now had an arthritic back.

'For man walketh in a vain shadow, and disquieteth himself in vain . . .' said George, and Thea reflected that it had not been true of Maurice, though he himself had thought so at the end. His disquiet had affected them all, and so had not been entirely in vain.

They sang 'He who would valiant be', and then Robert, Jack, Aubrey and Ralph carried the coffin—why did coffins never look big enough?—out into the churchyard. Outside it was bitterly cold. A dead and deadening chill, the very epicentre of winter. Black ice on the path made Ralph slip once and Dulcie's small black-gloved hand flew to the veil before her face. The hole dug the previous night to receive Maurice was black and deep, but the mounds of soil at the side had frozen over like miniature mountains covered with a grey rime of ice. On the face of the field beyond the lychgate was a great black circle, the scar left by the armistice bonfire, and a scattering of scrap metal, the non-flammable parts of the junk that had fed the pyre.

They stood round the hole, together once more, but each very separate. Only Thea allowed tears. Beside her Jack stood very straight and gaunt, his hands folded in front of him, his head bent, but staring grimly at the grave. Ralph—awkward, never easy in distress—clearing his throat and rising slightly on his toes. Aubrey dignified, appropriate, standing dutifully by Sophie who looked blank, watching something in her mind's eye. And Dulcie. Thea looked across at her. Her small heart-shaped face white behind the crisp web of black veiling, her black kid shoes edged with graveyard mud, her scent occasionally wafting to Thea when she inclined her head. There was something almost foolhardy in her attendance. Thea wanted to hug her as she used to do when Dulcie did something brave but silly as a little girl. To come now, for Maurice, whom she had so mercilessly teased and terrorized: it seemed the oddest and yet the most heroic thing to do, a penance and a show of humility. And she looked so beautiful.

A horse and cart clopped by in the road, the cart carrying a fir tree. The driver, hunched on his seat, his face pinched with cold between cap and collar, glanced incuriously over the wall from his moving vantage point at the small group in the churchyard. The horse's breath made shunting clouds of steam before its nodding, blinkered face.

Primmy stood a little way off from the others. It had not been easy for her to come, though she had known she must. She had shed all her tears—awesome how many there had been—that afternoon on the train, and this formal expression of grief seemed dry and empty. She knew, with a kind of calm fatalism, that with Maurice's death a door had closed. There would not be another chance, she did not even want another chance, he had been too special. She felt a spring of pride that she had been singled out by him. And in final tribute to him, and to defeat the demon of stubbornness and blindness, she whispered: 'I love you, Maurice.'

Just to have said it was a release. At that moment she knew that if she could go on saying those words from time to time during the rest of her life, she would hang on for always to what he had given her.

'We therefore commit his body to the ground . . .' The handfuls of frozen soil rattled on the lid as if the coffin were empty, and not full of Maurice at all.

After the blessing, with 'ever more' hanging like a threat in the bitter air, they moved away from the graveside, instinctively in the direction of the lychgate because that was the way they had always gone. Once there they hovered, realized they had made a mistake, spoke in flat, quiet voices, separated and re-joined. All that united them at that moment was Maurice, and he was dead. It was darkening rapidly.

'I can't go up there,' said Ralph. 'I'm parked in the road.'

'Will you come and have some tea?' Daphne enquired. 'Please do, don't rush back.'

Ralph coughed explosively, and Aubrey answered: 'Why not? That would be nice.'

'Yes, thank you,' echoed Dulcie with a quick, bright smile. She was just like spun glass, thought Thea, exquisite and terribly breakable. And yet they had all grown up now, they were so politely incurious, so careful, they would be too civilized to insist on the answers they wanted.

'We'll go on then,' said Robert. 'See you people at Long Lake.' He held out his hand to Jack. '*Au revoir*, old chap. You are coming in on the way to Southampton, aren't you?'

'That's right. See you then.'

The last postponement. Thea kissed him and squeezed his hand; hugged Daphne. She saw Sophie, walking alone to the main gate, and ran over to her. She had a sudden conviction of exactly what she should say.

'Aunt Sophie!'

Sophie turned. She looked frightened and hostile. She had been handsome once, like Ralph, but that had gone.

'Aunt Sophie—we all admired Maurice so much. He was the bravest of us all. I had to tell you.'

Sophie pulled her mouth down, staring at Thea as if trying to remember who she was. Her eyes were rheumy. For one dreadful moment Thea thought she was going to be ignored. Then her aunt reached out her hand and gave her wrist a little squeeze. 'You know,' she said, in a quirky, grudging voice, 'I think you're right.'

Thea went back to the others.

'Right,' said Ralph. 'We'd better go if I'm going round by my sister's first.'

'Don't be too brusque with her.' said Thea. 'She came, at least. She's unhappy.'

'Dear girl.' Ralph took her in his arms, slapping her back, stifling her. More quietly, he added: 'So am I, you know. Where's your sympathy for me, eh?'

'Go on.' She gave him a push. 'We'll see you tomorrow.'

'I've decided to stay over Christmas,' said Dulcie. 'I think I might enjoy that.' She didn't manage it very gracefully, but Thea recognized it for what it was: a small attempt to make up for her and Jack's absence.

'We'll bring the presents tomorrow,' she said, smiling at Dulcie, but terribly near tears, 'we'll be with you in time for lunch.'

Ralph began to move away, walking backwards. 'Come on, you two, it'll be pitch dark in a moment.'

'Coming. See you tomorrow then.' Dulcie lifted her hand and ran after her father. Thea watched them walk side by side, Dulcie taking almost two strides to his one, only a tiny crescent of golden hair showing between her black hat and her black fur collar.

Aubrey hung back for a moment. 'Good luck. You're doing the right thing.'

'I think so.' This was Jack. He had been very silent, watching, as he always was when they were all together, not unsure of his claim on her but not wanting to flaunt it before her family.

Thea put her arm through his, taking his side, but said: 'Oh, Aubrey, I do so hope you're right. Father—'

'He'll be fine.' Aubrey suddenly and uncharacteristically laid a hand on each of their shoulders. 'Go on and be happy. I'm back. I'll take care of him.' He gave them a little push, sending them on their way.

'See you tomorrow.' She looked back at him, standing there, his overcoat a little baggy on him for he had lost weight and not yet bought more clothes. She felt the dependable strength of his presence like a firm handshake. She waved, and he lifted his fist and gave it a little flourish, as if bracing them.

'Where's Primmy disappeared to?' asked Jack, as they circumnavigated the bonfire patch. 'I take it you did want to come this way?'

'Yes. We might as well say goodbye.'

He stopped her for a moment. 'Don't if it's going to upset you.'

'There are times when I want to be upset. I'm a wallower.'

'I love you.'

'And I you.'

They continued up the field, across the footpath and through the wicket gate into the Elm Walk. The long grass had been mown, everything looked tidy, clipped, conscientiously cared for. The house was a mass of lights.

They caught up with Primmy in the front drive, where she appeared to be standing waiting for something. It was almost dark. Here too the garden had a neat, cut-back appearance. Three ambulances and a couple of cars stood in the stable yard, and an *ad hoc* cycle shed had been erected against the outside wall. There was some kind of bustle in the hall, and someone came out of the kitchen door, laughing, shouting back, then went in again and slammed the door. It was friendly, workaday. Thea found it easier to accept her own not belonging than she could have imagined.

'Primmy—' She walked round in front of her, for Primmy was standing staring expectantly at the gate. 'Primmy, we just wanted to say goodbye. We're off the day after tomorrow.' She extended her hand and felt Primmy's thin, hard one, in a woollen glove, grasp it firmly. Easy and natural now, it would have been unthinkable four years ago.

'What will you be doing, Primmy?' asked Jack.

'Carrying on with my nursing. I'm going to do a proper training at St George's when the VADs are disbanded.'

'That's splendid. We do wish you well.'

'I expect we shall see you again,' said Thea.

Primmy nodded. 'The world's a funny place.'

'Thea—darling, we ought to go. We have to walk back to the car and it's dark already.'

'Yes. Goodbye then, Primmy.'

'Goodbye, miss.' The old term slipped out. It was her only sign of sadness.

As Thea and Jack walked towards the gate a horse and cart trundled out of the darkness, turning in from the lane, the same cart that had passed the church earlier. The horse was steaming and puffing, the man craning over his shoulder to see that the overhanging trunk of the fir tree was getting through the gate all right, giving incomprehensible nasal orders to the horse, slapping the reins on its broad, patient back.

'What are they doing?' asked Jack, when they'd stood back to let him pass.

'Taking in the Christmas tree,' said Thea.

The door of the house was opened and a group of people came down the steps, pointing, talking, laughing, a couple of girls in uniform like Primmy's and three men, one using a walking stick. Primmy was standing at the bottom, talking to the driver, assuming responsibilities.

'It's their Christmas tree,' said Thea again. 'A lovely one.' She turned away and walked out into the lane. The surface had been properly made up now and she walked quickly between the concealing comfort of the towering dark hedges. Whatever happened he mustn't see this foolish eleventh-hour weakening.

She did not realize he was not just behind her until he ran to catch up with her, and pulled her almost roughly round to face him.

'Hey—!'

'Sorry, I didn't know . . .'

'Got you something. Here.'

'What is it?' She smiled at him in the dark, his nearness a joy to her, and a comfort.

He felt for her hand, and pressed into it a little sprig of something rough and prickly and full of life. 'There you are,' he said, walking on, pushing his hands into his pockets. 'A piece of the Christmas tree for you.'

As she lifted it to inspect it more closely, she could smell its special evocative fragrance. How she loved him. She put the sprig in her button hole, clumsy with her gloves on. 'Thank you,' she said.

*　　　*　　　*

ACKNOWLEDGEMENTS

The author and publishers are grateful to the following for allowing them to quote song lyrics and poetry:

George Allen & Unwin (Publishers) Limited: 'I don't get on with civvies' by George Will, from *Any Soldier to his Son*.

EMI Music Publishing Limited: 'All in a day' by Hargreaves and Harrington, 'Dear old Blighty' by Mills/Godfrey/Scott, 'When this bloody war is over' by Biem-NCB, 'Parlez-vous' by Carlton/Tunbridge (published by B. Feldman & Co. Ltd); 'Goodbyee' by Weston/Leigh, 'Pack up your troubles' by Asaf/Powell, 'I don't want to be a soldier' by Wimperis/Finch, 'The coster girl in Paris' by Powell/Leigh, 'Poor John' by Pether/Leigh, 'For old times' sake' by Osborne (published by Francis Day & Hunter Limited); 'Sweethearts and wives' by Ellis (published by Reynolds); 'I'll marry him' (published by Sheard).

Oxford University Press: 'God's Grandeur' by Gerard Manley Hopkins from *The Poems of Gerard Manley Hopkins* (fourth edition, 1967) edited by W. H. Gardner and N. H. MacKenzie, published by Oxford University Press for the Society of Jesus.

Punch

A FLOWER THAT'S FREE

Sarah Harrison

Kate Kingsley – an exotic flower from the harsh soil of Kenya, blooming in London, in sun-drenched Malta, in decadent Berlin. Amid the turbulence of World War II she confronts personal danger, faces conflicting loyalties, loves two different men, aches over the heart-breaking choice and finds a kind of freedom at last. Beautiful, restless, impulsive, Kate is an unforgettable heroine to capture every heart.

'A compelling and intriguing book, the work of a fine storyteller'
Catherine Cookson

'Full of unforgettable people, places and passions'
Woman's World

'You'll love it'
Woman's Own

FICTION

HOT BREATH

Sarah Harrison

Thirty-five, fit and solvent with children at school and the sweet scent of freedom in my nostrils, I was ripe for it . . .

What has transformed Harriet Blair, contented mother and bestselling author of torrid hot historicals into a rampant vamp?

Could it be the arrival in sleepy Basset Parva of Constantine Ghikas, blond Greek god and latest addition to the local medical practice?

With husband George safely marooned in the Middle East, Harriet feels the Fates have conspired to throw a real-life romantic hero in her path. But her carefully-staged seduction scenes are thwarted by the unwitting sabotage of family and friends. Not to mention the demands of her publishers, panting for the new masterpiece . . .

Hell-bent on indulging her dishonourable intentions, Harriet lurches from crisis to hilarious crisis, delighting and entertaining everyone who has ever cast a greedy eye over forbidden fruit.

FICTION

Other bestselling Warner titles available by mail:

☐ Half Hidden	Emma Blair	£5.99
☐ Flower of Scotland	Emma Blair	£5.99
☐ The Conquest	Elizabeth Chadwick	£5.99
☐ The Champion	Elizabeth Chadwick	£5.99
☐ The Italian House	Teresa Crane	£5.99
☐ Siena Summer	Teresa Crane	£5.99
☐ The Dancing Stone	Evelyn Hood	£5.99
☐ All That She Wants	Maeve Haran	£5.99
☐ Soft Touch	Maeve Haran	£5.99

The prices shown above are correct at time of going to press. However, the publishers reserve the right to increase prices on covers from those previously advertised without prior notice.

Ⓦ

WARNER BOOKS   WARNER BOOKS

Cash Sales Department, P.O. Box 11, Falmouth, Cornwall, TR10 9EN
Tel: +44 (0) 1326 569777, Fax: +44 (0) 1326 569555
Email: books@barni.avel.co.uk

POST AND PACKING:
Payments can be made as follows: cheque, postal order (payable to Warner Books) or by credit cards. Do not send cash or currency.

All U.K. Orders	**FREE OF CHARGE**
E.E.C. & Overseas	25% of order value

Name (Block Letters) _____

Address_____

_____

Post/zip code:_____

☐ Please keep me in touch with future Warner publications

☐ I enclose my remittance £_____

☐ I wish to pay by Visa/Access/Mastercard/Eurocard

Card Expiry Date

_____